WORD OF TRUTH

A *Buried Goddess Saga* NOVEL

VI

RHETT C. BRUNO

JAIME CASTLE

WORD OF TRUTH

©2020 RHETT C. BRUNO & JAIME CASTLE

Print and eBook formatting, and cover design by Steve Beaulieu. Artwork provided by Fabian Saravia. Cartography by Bret Duley.

Published by Aethon Books LLC.

All characters in this book are fictitious. Any resemblance to actual persons, living or dead, is purely coincidental. All Pantego/The Buried Goddess Saga characters, character names, and the distinctive likenesses thereof are property Aethon Books.

JOIN THE KING'S SHIELD

Sign up to the *free* and exclusive King's Shield Newsletter to receive early looks and new novels, peeks at conceptual art that breathes life into Pantego as well as exclusive access to short stories called "Legends of Pantego." Learn more about the characters and the world you love.

Did you know we have a Facebook group too? All the same perks as the email readers group plus instant interaction with Rhett and Jaime! The Official King's Shield Fan Club.

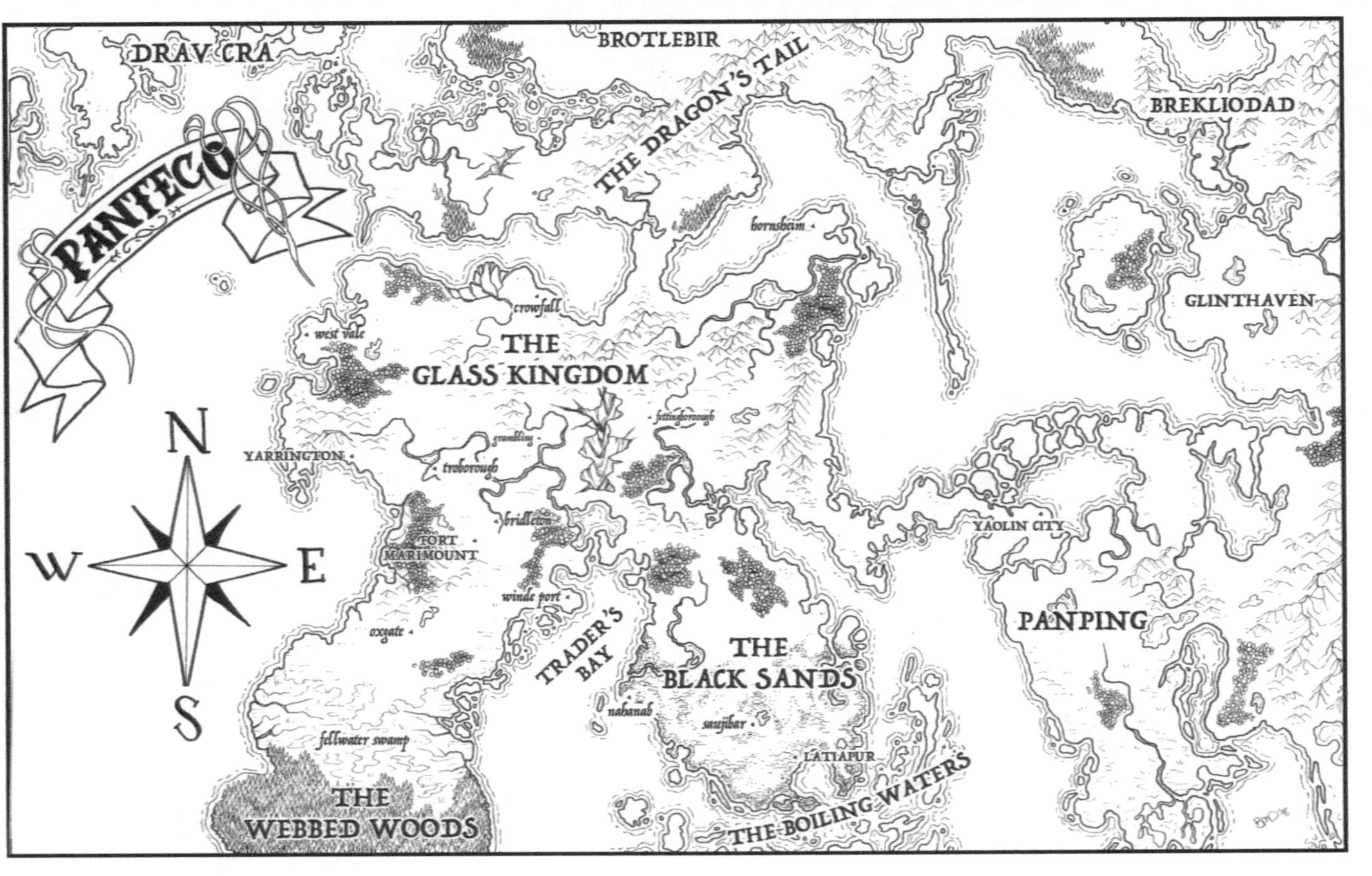

PANTEGO
DRAV CRA
BROTLEBIR
THE DRAGON'S TAIL
BREKLIODAD
bornsheim
crowfall
GLINTHAVEN
west vale
THE
GLASS KINGDOM
fettisborough
grandling
YARRINGTON
troborough
N
W
E
S
bridleton
YAOLIN CITY
FORT
MARIMOUNT
winde port
PANPING
oxgate
TRADER'S
BAY
THE
BLACK SANDS
nahanab
saujibar
fellwater swamp
L'ATIAPUR
THE
WEBBED WOODS
THE BOILING WATERS

PROLOGUE

Freydis couldn't help but admire the ingenuity of dwarves. Their subterranean cities were absolute marvels, and Balonhearth, the Heart of the North, home of Lord Cragrock, King of the Three Kingdoms, was no exception. Though she had to admit, she preferred seeing these places crumbling and filled with dead dwarves.

They were cowards, the lot of them. Humans drove them away, and instead of fighting back, they hid from the elements in their caverns, hoarding gold. Her people could have dug into the Drav Cra and escaped the bitter cold, but they didn't. They braved it, let it harden them.

The dwarves, on the other hand, grew soft and fat. They barely posed a threat as Freydis snuck through their city, right to the door of King Cragrock himself. She'd only needed to strangle a few guards, though she'd prepared to slaughter anyone in her way.

So, this is why they cower in their holes during our raids, she realized.

She stopped at the door. Ashes from a clanbreaker guard filled the hall after she'd incinerated him. A gust of magic wind and they spread to appear only like dust. A bandage wrapped her hand where she'd drawn the blood to cast him down, so she didn't leave a trail.

Those were Nesilia's instructions. She would not disobey them. She wasn't like the charlatan Redstar, or even Bliss, who questioned Nesilia's every motive. She loved the goddess, and the goddess loved her, and every day she breathed as Arch Warlock would be a tribute to that love.

It took no effort to undo the lock and enter the Iron Bank's antechamber. Gold towers shadowed her. Gold and jewel-encrusted dishware, a helmet, and armor that surely didn't fit the king's bulbous form any longer. She poked a chalice, expecting it to be heavier, and the thing wobbled. She didn't even bother to stop it. It toppled off its display table and clanked along the stone floor.

Nobody shouted for her head.

And dwarves claim to have legendary hearing, she scoffed to herself.

Riches beyond measure could have been hers, but she pressed on.

Freydis cracked her neck, then lifted her freshly bandaged hand to the lock on King Cragrock's quarters. Ever since Nesilia breached Elsewhere, magic had come easier to Freydis. She no longer called to Elsewhere with her sacrifice, it reached out to her.

As she'd done at the iron bars, a tingle ran up her back as a vine extended from her palm, slithering its way into the lock and then growing to break it open. It barely made a sound.

Slinking in, she rooted the vine in the rock floor to jam the door. Then she looked around. The King slept on his back in an oversized bed, snoring as loud as a dire wolf with too many layers of fur blankets. The winged crown sat upon his head, drooping forward over his eyes.

Men and their crowns. They can't even sleep without them.

The room was simple, unlike the chamber outside with untold treasures. Useless trinkets. Toys. In the Drav Cra, these things meant nothing, but that was why dwarves hid. Their greed was outdone only by the Kingdom of Glass, whose time was swiftly coming to an end.

Freydis strolled around the edge of the room, running her finger over the smooth walls.

"King Cragrock the Fat," she said, not even looking his way.

The King startled awake, and before he could shout for guards, Freydis extended her arm and vines grew around his wrists, ankles, and mouth. Her hold on them was weak, but with her other hand, she used a knife to deepen her cuts and strengthen her bond with Elsewhere.

Freydis said. "I've been longing to meet you. We don't get to deal with you rich southern dwarves much."

He yelled into the vine, voice muffled. His eyes were wide with terror.

"What was that?" she asked. "I can't hear you?"

The vine fell from his mouth, but she shot forward as he again tried to scream and seized his throat with her bloody hand. His windpipe closed in her crushing grip.

"Now, I'm going to release you so we can have a little chat," Freydis said. "But if you call for help, the next vines will fill your throat. Nod if you understand me."

He didn't move. She leaned over and stared right into his eyes.

"Nod!" she hissed.

This time, he listened.

She grinned and released his neck, leaving him gasping for air. He hacked and coughed, unable to cover his disgusting mouth with his limbs bound.

"W… w… who?" he stammered, sounding anything but kingly.

"So eloquent," she said. "I am the Arch Warlock of the Drav Cra, Freydis," she said. "But who I am, is unimportant. I serve the will of Nesilia, once the Buried Goddess. Now she has returned to free this world."

"Returned? That be impossible."

"I assure you, it is not. Ask your son. He had the privilege of meeting her at the White Bridge."

"Bah, my son spent too much time with humans," he said, voice gaining strength again. "He returned tellin their fibs of goddesses and evil beins. But they only want to use us for war. Gold or soldiers, it's all the Glass Kingdom ever asks for."

"He saw the truth. She is here, King. And she will wipe the children of Iam from the face of Pantego once and for all. But she is a generous Goddess. She has no quarrel with the dwarves or any of the children of Muengor."

Cragrock yanked at the vines, then cleared his throat. "Then what's yer business here?"

"To make you an offer." She turned away and continued skirting the room. "My Goddess is willing to forgive your people's intrusion at White Bridge. She will not touch the head of another dwarf so long as your people remain locked within their holes during the war to come.

It's quite simple. Stay out of her affairs, and soon the dwarves will deal with wicked men no longer."

She whipped around, pointing her bloody dagger at the King.

"But if so much as a single one of your banners fights beside them. Whether it be your son or some vagrant dwarves who think men deserve your help, Nesilia will send her armies here after Yarrington falls, and she will bury the dwarves in their mountains." She slit her hand, and another vine grew, extending over his neck. "You will all suffocate in darkness, as she did for so very long."

The lump in the dwarf's throat bobbed under his gray, wiry beard as he eyed the vine.

"So, King Cragrock," Freydis said, clenching her fist and urging the vine to tighten. "You tell me. What do you desire?"

I

THE TRAITOR

Rand and Sigrid sat together on the docks along Autla's Inlet, on the grimy end of Dockside if there could be a distinction. Spring was in full swing, and with the thawing waters, came the familiar stench of mercantilism. Rand loved all the blending of smells. Fresh fish, saltwater, and spices carried on trading vessels from regions all over Pantego. Languages and dialects ebbed and flowed, chaotic, but so beautiful, too.

He liked to try to decipher the words. If not the words themselves, at least the accents, and then guess where each person was from.

Their feet danged from the docks, not yet long enough to reach the water lapping up at the old, gray wood, cracked and soggy-looking. Their father had lent them his fishing rod. Rand knew it was just to keep them busy while he worked his loading job down the harbor. Mother would be at home prepping supper, with or without their success. But it felt good to be out and about. Maybe they'd even catch something they could eat.

But Rand was never any good at it. Two years older than his sister, and she was the one teaching him. Even turned away, he could feel her watching his hands with hawkish focus.

"Rand, ye hooked one!" Sigrid said.

He was so concerned with all the ships, coming and going, he didn't move until she shook him by the shoulders. She was strong for her diminutive stature. Her hair, like a red mop, plopped down over her head, making her face seem small and squat.

"Rand!"

He snapped to attention, but by the time he did, the fish was gone.

"Iam's gold-coated shog!" Sigrid swore as she threw her hands up in frustration.

"Sigrid!" Rand scolded.

"What? Daddy says it all the time."

"A lady shouldn't... Not if ye ever wanna get out of this rotten place."

She grinned. "I ain't no lady." Then her attention returned to the fishing line. "And ye clearly ain't no man. Ye couldn't feed a stray cat, let alone all of us."

"Oh yeah? Ye try it." Rand reeled in the line and shoved the fishing rod against her arm.

She gladly took it, lacing it with another worm they'd dug up behind old man Gunter's mussel shack. Rand had nearly retched when he put the last one on, but she didn't even flinch. His brave, fearless sister.

"Don't ye worry big brother, I'll keep ye fed when we grow up," she said as she cast the line.

"It's just so boring. Maybe out there, sailin round on a big ship, it'd be more fun."

"We have everything we need right here," Sigrid said, taking in a deep breath.

"Maybe ye do."

"Ye and yer big plans," she groaned.

Rand rolled his eyes. Shouts drew his attention as a ship from all the way in the Black Sands arrived. He knew by the gray-skinned crew zipping around, working the sharply angled sail and the ropes as if it were second nature. He guessed they were from Latiapur, the Black Sands capital city. He'd heard about their giant gold palace and frothing waves.

And they were only half as impressive as the proud Shieldsman who rode up to greet them. Sir Clorus the Courageous, Rand recognized. He knew all of the Shieldsmen who frequented Dockside; all of the peerless warriors who traveled Pantego, fighting wars and keeping peace.

The man's armor gleamed like a pearl. His steed was white as freshly-fallen snow, tufts of fur billowing around its massive hooves. Standing beside the dockhands, the beast's back stood as tall as any of them.

Now, there was a dream Rand could get behind. A Shieldsman of the Glass Kingdom; the best of the best in the army led by Sir Uriah Davies and the great King Liam.

Sigrid shrieked. Rand instinctually grabbed her by the arm, fearing she was going to fall in. Instead, he noticed that something was pulling on the line and the fishing rod bent.

"It's gonna break!" he shouted.

"No, it ain't," Sigrid spat. "Watch."

She rocketed to her feet, nearly barreling into a merchant holding a crate over his head. The man cursed something fierce as he strolled on, but she wasn't fazed. Rand couldn't even help if he'd thought she'd needed it. His little sister, small as she was, battled that fish with all of her adolescent might, and before Rand knew it, she had it out of the water, squirming from the hook's end.

"Ha, I beat ye!" she exclaimed. Without even a hint of hesitation, she pulled the fish free and tossed it into their basket. The first one of the day.

It was nothing impressive, about the length of her forearm. Still, she kneeled over it and marveled at the catch, eyes glinting like that of a conquering hero returning home. Rand imagined she looked about as proud as Liam after he'd defeated the wicked mystics of Panping once and for all.

"See, I told ye I'd keep us fed," she said.

Rand forced a grin, desperate not to let his wounded pride show. "What, on this tiny thing?" Rand lifted the fish by its tail. "Even mother can't make a meal out of this."

"Yer just jealous."

"Gimme that." He snagged the fishing rod. "I'll show ye how it's really done."

"Oh, do ye need help hookin another worm—or just a bucket for when ye puke?" She chuckled and gave him a nudge.

"Very funny." He got to work preparing. "But ye see, little sister, I'm just lettin ye win so ye'll feel better."

"Oh, then ye won't care when I tell Dad I beat'chya?"

Rand gritted his teeth, glancing over to see her wearing that mischievous grin she always donned when up to no good.

"Ye won't." He cast the line and this time, forced himself to focus. He'd only ever been good at fighting. Nothing else. Fighting to protect her, or himself, or just because. Sigrid, on the other hand, seemed to be good at everything, ever since she'd learned to walk at half the age Rand had been when he had. His darling, impetuous, perfect little sister.

A part of him always knew that when they were older, she'd look out for both of them. But he'd be damned by Iam if he didn't find a way to look out for her, too.

***

The memory of that day came rushing to Rand as he stood before Lake Yaolin, watching the soft ripples about the still water. It looked like a sheet of iron beneath the dark gray clouds. And just like that day when he hadn't caught another fish and Sigrid went bragging to their parents, he spotted nothing living within the waters. Not even weeds.

"Why have you come here, Rand Langley?" a ghostly voice addressed him. He looked up and saw a mystic floating over the water. Her body was ethereal, phasing in and out of his vision as she moved, flowing robes swelling beneath her.

He sighed and looked around. From a distance, Yaolin City was in fine shape. The field of sweeping roofs—pinks and oranges and reds— extended in every direction, most of their tiles undamaged. Some portions were covered in ash from buildings suffering fires, but all in all, the city remained pristine. It was nothing like how Dockside had been after Nesilia's cultists had their way with it.

But her streets were a different story. Bodies littered them haphazardly, left to rot, and breed disease, and nobody seemed to care. Grimaurs, filthy, humanoid birds pecked at the remains while others filled the sky, looking for territory to claim. Rand had lived a long time, and he'd never even seen these foul beasts said to inhabit mountain caves. Now, they were everywhere.

Those that weren't dead—Panpingese men and women, cultists in robes so red, Rand couldn't even tell that they were soaked in blood, visitors from the rest of the Glass Kingdom—all roamed aimlessly. Some stopped to watch him from a distance but never got closer.

"I want to see my sister," he said.

"Good for you," the mystic said. "And now you can leave knowing that she doesn't want the same."

"I don't believe that."

The ghostly mystic swooped down before him. He turned his cheek against a cold, like death itself, that seemed to radiate off of her.

"Leave. Now," she whispered, her voice piercing his soul. It felt like icicles formed along his spine.

He swallowed hard, then shook his head. "No."

"Do you know who I am, mortal?" the mystic asked. "I could make you wish… beg for death. A mere snap of my fingers and I could make you squirm. I don't care that your sister shares a body with my own."

As she spoke, a great beast emerged from the water. First, Rand saw the thick tentacles, long as two dozen horses nose to tail. They slapped around the coast and in the water, sending waves coursing every which way. Then, two large, black eyes followed and a maw filled with enough sharp teeth to render Rand unrecognizable.

He stood proud, defiant until the monster roared, sending him shrinking back. His breath stuttered, but he didn't run. He closed his eyes, drew a deep breath, and shakily stood his ground.

"Now, now, Bliss, there's no need to be so rude to our guest."

Rand looked up and spotted his sister standing atop the sea creature's head. Or, at least, this version of her. White hair whipped in the wind like a phantom. The tenor of her voice carried on the wind, familiar, and yet so different. It sounded like a refined version of the Sigrid he knew, with no Dockside accent. Her eyes were dark and menacing. Rand had seen them like that only one other time before White Bridge —when she fired an arrow through a Drav Cra warrior trying to have his way with her.

"You're back?" the mystic called Bliss said.

"Still as observant as ever," Sigrid said.

"Watch it, dear Sister. I buried you once before."

Sigrid hopped down from the monster. The fall was far, but she landed as if it were only a step. No buckle in her knees, no strain.

"It won't be so easy to stab me in the back this time," Sigrid whispered. "Besides, we both want the same thing. We know now who the true enemy is."

"That we do," Bliss said, staring up to the sky, where dark clouds swirled over the Red Tower at the lake's center. It looked like one of the hurricanes which sometimes tore through Dockside, only there was no wind or lightning. And the still, gentle silence of it was unnerving. "And He can't see us now."

"No, He can't—"

"Sigrid!" Rand barked to get her attention.

He stomped forward, bracing himself in the face of the glare she shot his way. There was none of the sister he'd once known in it, but as soon as her expression softened, he saw her again. Every memory of their lives rushed through him in a flash. For so long, he'd dreamed of leaving Dockside, of being something great, like a Shieldsman. In the end, only Sigrid really mattered to him, and it took too long for him to realize it.

"Watch your tone," Bliss said, winding her spectral form around him. Her fingers grazed the back of his neck like steel left outside during the last days before Freefrost.

"That's all right," Sigrid said. "He's just confused. Iam taught these poor mortals so little. They can't be blamed for their ignorance."

"Buried, but not dead," Rand said. "You said that when I was last with you. I know what it means; I was a Shieldsman. You're more than just an upyr now, aren't you?"

Sigrid smiled, her one cheek dimpling how it always had. The sight of it made Rand's heart skip a beat. "You know who I am."

"I heard Sir Unger and the others speak it on the battlefield. But I cannot believe…"

"Say it, Rand," Sigrid teased. "I want to hear it from your lips."

"Why are you doing this, Siggy?"

"That's not my name. Say it!"

"You… you're the… you're Nesilia. The Buried Goddess."

"Yessss," she moaned. Her eyelids flickered, jaw trembling as if she'd just taken a hit of manaroot.

Rand stepped toward her for a closer look. His muscles seized. He wanted to shrink away and cower, but he fought the urge.

"Are you even in there, Siggy?" he asked softly.

"Of course, she is," his sister's tongue answered. "Sigrid has been a wonderful host. She understands what this world needs."

"And what is that?"

"Freedom," she said.

"I watched what you did at White Bridge," Rand said. "I see what you've done here... I..." He cleared his throat. "The Sigrid I know wouldn't do all this. She wouldn't kill all of these people."

"Do you really know her, now?" Nesilia asked. "After all, you did leave her alone to die in Yarrington."

"I was trying to save her!" Rand shouted, verging on tears that had become all too familiar. "I thought I was helping."

"That's the problem," Bliss said. "Men... they always think we need their *help*."

"I know what you are," Rand said. "I've seen what your followers do. Sigrid has seen it. There's no way she would help you. You're the darkness that everyone in the Glass Kingdom fears at night— man or woman. You're the absence of Iam's light."

"Iam," Nesilia scoffed. Bliss joined in somewhere behind him but he dared not look. "Is that what the priests teach you while He plunges this world into war and greed? While He watches from high above as you slaughter each other? Sigrid has seen what my followers are capable of, and she realizes that there is no madness in their pursuit of freedom. There are only those strong enough to live free with them. And, now, she is amongst them."

"I don't want to talk to *you*," Rand said, finally. "I want to talk with my sister."

Nesilia was close now, pacing. She eyed him in the way a wolf does a lone, injured doe. He'd always been taller than his baby sister, but now he felt small, minuscule even.

"Your sister wishes for me not to harm you," Nesilia said. "And so, I will not. You are lucky; her will is too strong for me to defy her wishes."

"You should have taken a body like mine," Bliss said. "The mystic's spirit is barely a whisper in my ear. Pathetic, yet oh, so powerful." She extended a palm, and lightning crackled around her fingers.

"Sigrid understands what she must," Nesilia replied. "This world has fallen to greed and false idols. They've lost their way like a ship out to sea, surrounded by fog. Together, we will change that."

"By killing everybody?" Rand protested.

"Purification. Think of it like a forest fire—by erasing generations of lies whispered by the gods who'd cast me aside. They crave your prayers as they watch the wars among men."

"And you don't? Your cultists burned down our home! Sigrid, have you forgotten that? How they danced and murdered and raped?"

His sister's lips twitched, but only slightly, smoothing over just as quickly. "Do you mean how they managed to infiltrate Yarrington without a soul realizing, while all your lords could think of was the gold in their pockets?"

"Sigrid can't believe that. You say you want to free the world, but what about her? Let her out! Let her free, and she'll speak the truth. I know she will."

"She is freer than ever before." Nesilia extended her arms. The great water beast at her back—which Rand had somehow forgotten about under the caustic gaze of the goddess—extended its tentacles with her, causing the very ground to quake.

"Let her out!" he roared.

He stomped toward his possessed sister, clutching her by her high collar. In an instant, the one called Bliss sent a potent gust of wind into his back that sent him flying forward into the wall of a waterside home. Vines then grew forth from the stone itself, manipulating his movements, and constricting his arms and legs.

He faced them both now, and as he struggled to catch the breath that was knocked out of him, he saw others approaching him from all sides. He couldn't turn his head to get a better look, but they were clustered and moving as a singular unit, better even than the Shieldsmen were capable of. Surely, Nesilia was controlling them, too.

"You promised not to kill him, but what a host he might make," Bliss said, moving in front of him and stealing his attention.

"No," Nesilia said. "He will do what's right. The poor soul has just spent a lifetime being lied to." She sauntered toward him in a way his sister never would've. She was beautiful, but never one to flaunt it unless that bastard, Gideon Trapp, the owner of the Maiden's Mugs, had forced her to. And she never walked like a proper lady of the court hoping to marry a noble, but like a scrappy Docksider. No longer. Her hips swayed in a way that might mesmerize any man who didn't call her "sister."

"Liam Notthelm, Uriah Davies, even Torsten Unger—they all lied to you, Rand Langley. They told you Iam was loving and kind and cared about you. But what kind of god allows such death? Have you forgotten the wench, Tessa? That poor girl. Iam let her die, at your hands nonetheless."

The mention of Tessa gripped Rand's heart like a giant's fist.

"You have seen what evils the Glass Kingdom is guilty of," she said as she moved in front of Bliss. The tentacles of the water beast slithered up behind her. "It took a woman of the North—my free North— Oleander and made her a monster. Countless wars. People living in the filth of Dockside and with nowhere to climb. Weaklings breeding and killing and leeching the life out of Pantego. Now, they follow her child —a boy so weak, even the slightest hint of me freeing him from Iam's grasp caused him to throw himself from a window."

"You drove him mad," Rand said.

"He drove himself mad. Imagine, half the known world being ruled by a child because 'Iam said he's worthy.' He rewards weakness with favor. You're smart, Rand Langley. I know that because I know your sister's every memory and the happiest ones are with you. I can see you both now, running through the streets, laughing, living freely until the claws of life in Iam's kingdom dug into you both and stole your liberty."

Rand's eyes went wide. "How can you see that?"

"I see everything. The question you must ask yourself, Rand, isn't who I really am. No. It's whether you've been lied to your entire life. Iam is no holy being to admire, and certainly not one to worship. He's just one of the few gods who survived after letting the rest of us slaughter each other."

"If I recall, He had your help," Bliss chimed in.

"Because He lied to me, too!" Nesilia hissed at her, baring fangs sharp as the sea monster behind her. Then she turned back to Rand, her expression turning sickly sweet. "I understand exactly what you've been through. But you saw the truth, didn't you? You fled Iam's Kingdom."

"To save you," Rand said. His gaze fell to the ground, though his head still didn't move. "To save Sigrid."

"From a man like Valin Tehr, who fed on the corruption of Iam's followers like a leach. I promise you, everything that we do—that we *will* do—is done with your sister's blessing."

Tears welled in the corners of his eyes. He lifted his head as far as the restraints would allow and stared straight into Sigrid's unfamiliar eyes. "Then let me talk to her."

"She doesn't want to talk," Nesilia said with venom. "You failed her before, and while she may love you enough to want me to preserve who you are, she doesn't forgive you. How could you expect her to?"

"I... I..." Rand stammered. His throat went dry. He frantically swiped at a tear running down his cheek. Everything the Church of Iam had taught him about the Buried Goddess, how she betrayed Iam to spark the God Feud and take over, how she sought only to drive men into entropy and chaos, just like the nature she lorded over, he never expected her to be so right.

"It's okay," Nesilia whispered. She reached out and cupped the sides of his face in her hands. Like Bliss, her skin was cold, but in his heart, it was warm. Comforting. Reminded him of home. "You have a chance to redeem yourself now. A chance to make things right. And if you do, I promise, you will speak with your sister again. When Pantego is free, I won't need the power her body possesses any longer."

"She'll be herself again?" he asked, barely able to raise his voice above a whisper.

"She'll be the best version of herself you've ever known. Just as Pantego will be the best version of itself. Help us, Rand Langley, and neither of you will have to scrape by any longer. The strong will be as kings and queens in the new world, and you both are so very strong."

"Help us?" Bliss asked, appearing over Nesilia's shoulder. "What could we possibly need this pathetic sack of flesh for?"

"I have some ideas." Nesilia released him, rose to her full height, and stepped back.

The vine withered away, releasing Rand's limbs. An instant later, he felt hands all over, helping him to his feet. He hadn't noticed how close the inhabitants of Panping had grown until just then. They were all around him, hundreds of them, gathering in the streets—maybe thousands—all their eyes black as midnight.

II

THE MYSTIC

Warm gusts of wind gently caressed Sora's face, uncharacteristic for the season. There was something special about the Glintish capital of Myen Elnoir. Something that not only warded away the harshness of the land surrounding it but also, seemingly, defended against Nesilia's demonic army as well.

For days, they'd been seeing thick plumes of smoke pouring into the sky from the south—Panping. They swirled up and joined an ever-growing mass of lingering dark clouds. Rumors had spread quickly that a white-haired devil was terrorizing the region, but no one had called her by name. It didn't matter, Sora knew it was Nesilia. She could almost feel her.

Along with Whitney, Tum Tum, and the Glintish woman called Lucindur, Sora had spent her last weeks on the Covenstan Depths, running from grimaurs as they soared above, often daring to swoop down upon the *Reba*. Aboard his ship, Sora had to continually remind herself that Gold Grin had been under the influence of Nesilia when they were together, just as she had been. That he'd done what any old man would have if a young lady threw herself at him. The memories still made her skin crawl.

Each night, as the sun went down and the moons rose, so too did her fear of the night. As someone with an affinity for fire magic, darkness never once scared her. Not until Nesilia dragged her into the place called Nowhere—a place where night seemed to swallow her whole.

Now, she sat alone in the crow's nest. They were docked just outside Myen Elnoir, overlooking the breathtaking city. Here, there was not a flying grimaur in sight, just a city like nothing she'd ever dreamed possible.

No walls were encircling it, no watchtowers with archers like there'd been throughout Yaolin City. From there, high above, she had a clear view of the streets, sprawled like the spokes of a giant wagon wheel. Lining each one, on both sides, was building after building, all pristine and so clean they almost glowed. Every single one was the purest white.

If someone had told Sora about that part, she'd have thought it sounded boring… but this was anything but. It was gorgeous, immaculate, and magical—a tiny paradise nestled in the mountains between landscapes of war and death. Even the Glass army's presence was minimal like they never expected trouble here.

Golden arches cast shadows upon golden roads, bridging rooftop to rooftop, smaller versions of the towering one at the western entry that garnered so much fame. Joyful sounds echoed throughout the entirety of the city—music, dancing, playing. It was as if no one worked around here, and if they did, they treated the job like it was their greatest dream to fulfill.

However, Sora couldn't enjoy it. None of it.

None of it mattered.

Instead, her mind was drawn to the Drav Cra warlock, Freydis. Sora hadn't been able to forget a single moment of her imprisonment deep within her own mind. Even the times with Nesilia in complete control, Sora remained aware of the things she was doing. Even if the memories were faint, they were there.

The murder. The sex. The manipulation.

She'd fought—with every ounce of her considerable strength, she'd fought, but all of it was in vain. Nesilia may have been cast out of Sora's body, but the Buried Goddess remained at large. And now, with hints of Nesilia in Panping and talk of cultists and worse ravaging the city her ancestors had called home—it was too much to bear.

Every time she closed her eyes, Sora felt taunted, like Nesilia was right there, just beyond her mental grasp, prepared to strike again.

At that moment, high above the pristine streets, Sora felt like Freydis. Not the vicious Freydis she'd left in the Citadel at Brekliodad, but the one she'd met in the alley on the dirty streets of Dockside. The tongueless, hopeless Freydis… that was how she felt. Despite all her rehearsed words, explanations, complaints, and petitions for help or forgiveness or whatever else, Sora had barely been able to utter a single word since the initial shock of her freedom had worn off.

Weeks spent plowing through ice-dotted waters, and Sora hadn't so much as said, "thank you."

And poor Whitney…

After all he'd already been through, he'd had to endure her reticence, too. And endure it, he had—with unexpected grace. He talked, sure, spun his exaggerated tales, tried to get her to open up in all his silver-tongued ways, but he never pushed.

Nesilia had forced her into silence, and Sora didn't even know how much time she'd lost. Whitney claimed he'd been deprived of years in Elsewhere—torn from this world, buried beneath earth and water, bound to a world not his own. The whole time, Sora had searched for him, desperate to hold him, to speak to him, to tell him how much he meant to her.

Now, even the thought of speaking had her terrified.

What if she said the wrong thing and Nesilia burst out of Nowhere like it was all an act, driving Sora back into those depths? Maybe the Buried Goddess hadn't been stored within the bar guai at all. Maybe she hadn't been cast into that awful upyr's body. Maybe she was waiting. Biding her time.

The gray clouds looming to the south told a different story. Sora could make believe it was a storm on the horizon, but no dream could be so sweet. Even looking at it made her heart sink.

For so long, a genuine fear that Nesilia's presence would forever remain with Sora ravaged her mind—a soul tie, she'd heard it called. One of Madam Jaya's many lessons about possession spoke of the lingering effects—a piece of the soul left within the body. The thought was terrifying. But she had been equally frightened that the Buried Goddess would leave and occupy another, like Freydis—powerful *and* willing.

Possession remained a very mysterious thing, but every text in Wetzel's shack and every word spoken by her teachers at the Red

Tower agreed that the key to a demon fully taking control of any being on Pantego was willingness and weakness of will. Sora's will had nearly been broken battling Nesilia before Whitney arrived, and Nesilia was far more than some mere demon.

Freydis had been willing, but Nesilia said she wasn't strong enough. The upyr Sigrid, on the other hand, had been powerful... very powerful... and what should stop her from being willing? She was already a pawn of darkness. What higher service than playing host to the vilest of all deities?

Yet here we sit while Panping burns, scared like children abandoned in the streets of Winde Port, she thought.

As a young girl, Sora had spent many long nights in fear, lying awake in the small room below Wetzel's shack, surrounded by dust-covered books and scrolls, wishing she could be someone else... anyone else. Never did she think her wish would be granted in such a gruesome manner.

She'd shared a body with a goddess, and she couldn't lie—there'd been times when the power felt good. She'd been tempted to give in, to give Nesilia full control and let the world that had been so cruel burn.

But she couldn't...

Her own life had its value—but the lives of everyone in Pantego were worth so much more. If Nesilia had indeed found a willing host as powerful as Sigrid seemed to be, everyone was at risk.

The wind blew shining black locks of hair over Sora's face. She brushed them back, letting her fingers linger a moment. With thumb and forefinger, she traced the point of her ear, recalling every crude word ever spoken to her about her heritage. All the ways she'd been treated, used, abused, hurt, shamed, broken, lied to, forgotten...

"Who cares about you, Sora?" Nesilia had repeated time and time again while she occupied Sora's body. She would laugh and say, *"A thief? You think he'll come and steal you away from here? No one is coming. We are the same. You are forgotten, like me."*

It was a tool Nesilia had tried to use against her. Useless at first, but after time in Nowhere, Sora slowly started to believe it until finally... Whitney had done the impossible. Now there could be no doubt. A man capable of breaking into the mind of a powerful mystic possessed by a goddess, and retrieving his prize—that was the World's Greatest Thief.

But she could never let him know that. His head was big enough already.

She laughed a tiny little laugh before her gaze flitted to the southern cloud, and her mouth went straight as an arrow. She thought of all those who were, no doubt, suffering in Yaolin City at Nesilia's hands, just as she had. Her mind traveled back to Winde Port and the Panpingese District, where Tayvada Bokeo had lived and died.

The world was doomed.

Sora had felt Nesilia's immeasurable power. No one could stop her.

"This vessel is powerful." Sora remembered Nesilia's words after she overtook Sigrid.

Sora cleared her throat, feeling a new sense of resolve. She glared south and said, "I am the daughter of the most powerful mystic to ever walk Pantego and its greatest King." She was almost shocked by the fervor in her own voice after so long in silence, trapped in her own thoughts, but defiance rose up within and with it, so did she.

"That's right," Sora said, Elsewhere's magic bubbling up inside her, siphoning the energy of her blood like a true mystic. Fire and embers danced around her clenched fist. She was in control. "I'm not some tongueless dog, Nesilia. I am Sora…"

Something prickled against her hand, which now rested upon the smooth wooden rail. Opening her eyes, she found Aquira's head nuzzling there, little yellow orbs looking up at her, blinking both sets of eyelids over and over. A soft purr escaped the wyvern's scaly lips.

Sora's eyes watered, and she leaned in.

"Oh, Aquira," she said, so soft it was barely audible. But the wyvern heard her and chirped.

Sora wrapped both arms around her reptilian friend and pulled her in close. The spot on her chest where the bar guai had been remained tender. Still, her healing power had made its former presence nearly imperceptible—physically, at least.

"I'm so sorry for leaving you, Girl. I'm so—" Her words cut off as she let out the emotions she'd been bottling up for so long.

Aquira blew a small puff of steam from her nostrils and settled in, still purring.

"I'll never leave you again," she said. "I promise. We are together forever."

Just then, a dark, foreboding sensation choked her. Visions of Nesilia, larger than life, brooding and hovering over Yaolin City assaulted her mind.

Forever, she thought.

That word held such little meaning now. What did "forever" look like when a crazed goddess was on the loose, bent on destroying all life? Because as much as Nesilia proclaimed her desire to purge the world of weakness and let the strong rule, Sora had seen her true heart. No one would be worthy in the end, not in her eyes. Nothing would fill the void that Iam had left inside of her. So, she'd fill it with the suffering she'd known for countless years until there was nothing left to suffer.

"I can't keep going like this, Aquira," Sora said.

The little wyvern, who, admittedly, wasn't very little anymore, drew back her long neck. Her frills folded, and her rough tongue flicked outward as she stared right into Sora's eyes. Aquira's horns had begun growing in, Sora noticed, and new tears formed in response to all the things she'd missed.

After her shoulders stopped bobbing, she sucked in a deep breath and said, "I've got to talk to Whitney—to everyone. No one understands just how awful what she has planned is. I've seen what she can do, and I was fighting it. I can't imagine what will happen if Sigrid wants it too. Panping will just be the start. I can't believe I've been so stupid."

She took a deep breath and turned away from the black cloud above Yaolin.

"I never should have let us waste time in coming here," she went on. "What was I thinking? We have to stop Nesilia, no matter what. I've been… selfish."

"No, you haven't," said a voice from behind her.

It startled her, but only for a second. She'd recognized Whitney's voice every time, whether in Elsewhere or Nowhere and now, even on Pantego. There was no mistaking it. It kept her sane for Iam-knows-how-long.

"Whit," she said, turning and running toward him. He didn't even budge as the full weight of her slammed against him. "I'm so sorry." The words came out muffled, mouth pressed against his shoulder. His arms felt so good around her. It may not have been cold here in Myen Elnoir, but the frigid feeling of Nesilia's presence had yet to leave her, even after so many weeks, and he warmed her.

"Sora," he said, pushing her back, but only enough that he could see her eyes. "You have no reason to apologize."

"But—"

"None!" The word was abrupt but not harsh. "Listen, what you did… what happened to you… it wasn't your fault."

"I went looking for them, for *mystics*, without you, because of what my powers did to you. It was a mistake. Iam and all the gods, I don't know what I was thinking."

"You were being you, Sora," Whitney said. "You never were one to sit back and let others have all the fun. When we were kids, and you heard I was breaking into Galleo Donavan's dad's bakery—what did you do?"

Sora's gaze fixated on the silver clasp of his cloak, anything to avoid his eyes. Then she felt his finger lift her chin. Her eyes remained downward. He brushed her cheek, the wet of a tear smearing across it.

Whitney leaned down, forcing himself into her line of sight.

"What did you do?" he asked again. When she didn't answer, he said, "You broke in first. You ate all the sweet cakes, so I didn't get any."

She laughed, barely.

"Then, the next day, you told Mr. Donavan it was me," he went on. "That night, when I returned, he was waiting with his rolling pin. That hurt, Sora!" He rubbed at his head, playfully.

Sora remembered how mad Whitney had been that day, but now, he laughed, and she couldn't help but join in.

Whitney never knew how much it had upset her that he'd been breaking into Mr. Donavan's place without her. That was the moment she realized Whitney had a whole world of adventure that she hadn't been invited to take part in. She hadn't even eaten all the sweet cakes, she'd just tossed them to the pigs in Mrs. Dodson's farm. And she cried that night, too, though she'd never have let Whitney know. She'd done everything to mask those tears from him.

But that was the day things changed, and he hadn't the slightest clue. Standing here now, she'd give anything to go back in time and just tell him everything. How he was all she had in Troborough. That Wetzel, for all his guidance, was nothing more than a crotchety old man who'd never so much as hugged Sora, much less played the role as a father after her real father, King Liam Nothhelm, left her with him, so she'd never be discovered.

That the only time she'd felt accepted was when she was with Whitney. That knowing he'd been hiding things from her killed her inside. That the day he'd left her younger self standing in the woods while he trudged off to explore Pantego was the day her heart shattered into a million pieces.

She wanted to tell him that when she'd followed him and Torsten to those dwarven ruins, it was to drive a blade through his heart so that he'd feel half the pain she'd felt for so long, but she hadn't been able to. And it was that fact which proved she was nothing like Nesilia, no matter what the goddess had said. Sora had chosen forgiveness.

She loved Whitney as a child, she loved him in those ruins, and she loved him now, more than ever. She'd often used anger as a means of escaping this very emotion, but no longer. Her lips formed a small, involuntary smile.

"That's my girl," Whitney said, wearing that same crooked grin he would affect before getting up to no good. "Now, it's time you stop beating yourself up and join us. We need—"

"I can't, Whit," she said. "Not yet."

"You can."

"Just let me talk. I just—I *knew* you weren't dead, but I went to Panping anyway. I... I abandoned you." With that, her head pressed against him once more.

"Abandoned?" Whitney scoffed. "Are you mad? You were *searching* for me, same as I was you. Only the mystics could have helped you."

"I went for myself too... I was so selfish."

"I'm always selfish, and I promise, you weren't. And no, you didn't *know* I wasn't dead, but c'mon? What were you supposed to think? I disappear into thin air, and the next time you see me, I'm in Elsewhere, being chased by demon hounds. If our roles had been reversed, I'd have thought you were dead."

"It was my fault you were there to begin with!" Sora said. She wasn't even sure her words carried beyond the nook of Whitney's armpit. She just stayed there, releasing emotions she'd forgotten she had. Screaming in Nowhere had grown so tiresome with nobody listening, she'd given up on it.

"Sora… you didn't do that," he said. "That wasn't you."

Pulling back, Sora wiped her nose with the sleeve of her kimono. She couldn't speak, but she looked up at him in a way she hoped encouraged further explanation. As always, Whitney knew exactly what she was asking.

"It was the Sanguine Lords. They banished…" Whitney stopped for just a fraction of a second before saying, "… Kazimir and he was holding me. That's it. Bad timing."

"What?" It was all Sora could manage. The knowledge, whether true or not, that she hadn't been responsible for sending Whitney to that awful place brought a small sense of relief to her overburdened heart.

"Yeah," he said. "Kazimir disobeyed his gods, or masters, or whatever they are—were. They exiled him to Elsewhere to atone for his sins or rebellion. It wasn't the first time, but it was the longest. I don't even know how he got out… it might have been better if…" His breath caught in his throat.

Sora knew it must have been trying for him to talk about the vicious upyr that he'd apparently befriended—the upyr who'd tortured her. Although she'd barely spoken on the trip back from Brekliodad, Whitney had. It was one of the many things about him that simultaneously made her love him and infuriated her—Whitney never knew when to shut up. He'd told her all about Elsewhere, and living with Kazimir for six years, and Fake Troborough, the whole thing, even when she'd made believe she was sleeping.

"Come here, sit down," Whitney said.

He dragged her down a couple steps to a bench bolted to the deck, and she was snapped back to the present. Aquira landed beside them, and Sora suddenly found herself grateful that the main deck was empty. Whitney took the seat next to her and reached out to scratch Aquira on the top of the head.

"Aquira missed you," Whitney said.

"I'm so sorry, Whit," Sora whispered. She rubbed the top of his hand. "I really am."

"You never have to be sorry with me. You did what you thought you needed to."

Sora pulled her hand back and stared down at both of hers. She saw blood there even though she knew they were clean. There was always blood on them now.

"You cared about the upyr, didn't you?" Sora asked.

Whitney was quiet, something he rarely ever was. He shut his eyes, cleared his throat, and said, "I know it doesn't make sense. When you knew him, he was a monster. But then—"

"He saved my life," Sora interjected. "You were going to say it might have been better if he'd stayed in Elsewhere, but that's not true. If he hadn't escaped with you, I might still be trapped with her. She... she might have used me to destroy the world already."

His hand moved from Aquira's head and clasped Sora's. He smiled —not the same as earlier, though. This time, it was distant, diffident, and she quickly realized why. Whitney Fierstown, as caring and thoughtful as he might be, loved receiving credit. Even more so when he *actually* deserved it. This time, it wasn't some tall tale.

"You saved my life too," she said. "I'd still be stuck in that awful place if not for the both of you and the others."

Whitney perked up noticeably and chuckled. "Kazimir may have been a blood-sucking pile of undead shog, but he was *my* blood-sucking pile of undead shog. And now, because of me, his apprentice is..." He exhaled, grew serious, and said. "Six years, I was there with him, Sora. That's a long time. It's a long time to forget past... indiscretions."

Sora wondered if he was referring to his actions when they were younger, and he left her. He'd told her he was sorry about a million times on that trip back from Brekliodad, and every time, she'd just stared at him.

Sora shook her head solemnly, thinking about her own time buried deep in her mind and couldn't imagine doing it for six years. Then, she looked up. The sun was nearly tucked behind the Pikeback Mountains to the north, and Pantego's moons could already be seen hanging in the sky. Then she looked south again, fighting back the irrational fear of night that she'd been feeling ever since Nowhere.

"What was it like?" she asked softly, trying to picture a world where the sun and moons didn't exist. She'd been there with Whitney, but not for long, and most of that time was spent trying not to die from monsters and giant squids.

Whitney's face scrunched up, and he followed Sora's gaze to the horizon. "It wasn't all bad," he said.

His answer surprised her, and it must have shown on her face because he leaned in closer as if to comfort her.

"You were there," he said. "Well, not you-you, but old-you. Not *old* you. Younger-you."

"Me?" Sora asked, incredulous.

"And younger me, and my parents and, well, everyone. All I can say is it was the weirdest experience of my life," Whitney said with another chuckle. "I relived so many things there. It was like being an outsider to my own life."

Relived? Sora thought, wondering if that was why Whitney had brought up the bakery and had apologized so much. Had he seen her crying? Had he recognized how much he'd hurt her so many times? What about the time he'd left for good?

"You keep apologizing to me. I owe *you* an apology," he said.

"You've offered plenty of those on the trip here," Sora said.

"I wasn't sure you'd heard me."

"I was sad, not deaf." Now it was Sora's turn for a slight snigger, mirthless as it was.

"Well, all I know is that Little Whitney was a shog-headed triss," Whitney said.

"And big Whitney isn't?" Sora added. This time she chuckled. A real one.

"Point taken. But either way, it was me who abandoned you. I was an idiot. I never should've left. If I hadn't—"

"You probably would have died right beside your parents in the plague," Sora cut in. "Besides—and I can't believe I'm saying this—Iam or the *Pinyun tsu chahn ji duo*, or whatever other gods there might be controlling things... they had a bigger purpose for you, Whitney Fierstown. World's Greatest Thief or not... you helped saved Pantego more than once."

"No one is controlling my destiny," Whitney said, puffing out his chest. "Nor yours. And you know what? We *did* save the world once already. Together… and Torsten, I guess."

"Iam's shog—"

"Sora! Language!"

"Where… how is Torsten?" Sora asked.

"He's in Yarrington, last I heard. Blind as a priest."

"Blind? What? How?"

"Redstar. The same night you and I were together in Elsewhere… burned out his eyes. Tssssss, pop!" Whitney placed his fists over his eyes and spread his palms like they were bursting.

"That's an awful thing to joke about," she scolded.

"He's fiiiiine."

Sora had heard Freydis and Nesilia discussing Redstar's death during the Earthmoot, which established Freydis as the new Arch Warlock. Though she wasn't there when it had happened, when Sora tried to put her mind on Redstar's death, she could see fragments of the very moment he'd died—the instant Nesilia left King Pi's body and entered into hers.

"But Torsten killed him," she said, low. "Drove a sword right through his chest after the Drav Cra killed Wren the Holy."

"How did you know all that?" Whitney scratched his chin. "I don't remember talking about that oversized knight on the sea."

Sora's chin dropped to her chest. "Because Nesilia knew."

Whitney's eyes went wide. "Do you know everything she knew?"

She shrugged. "I shared every memory with her… sometimes I think she's still…" She couldn't finish the sentence.

"Still what?" Whitney's brow furrowed.

"Nothing… never mind. I think I need sleep," she said. "I just want this to be over." She went to stand, but Whitney slid in front of her and kneeled so she couldn't.

"Still what?" he asked. "You still feel her, don't you?"

Sora went quiet, stroking Aquira's tail. She was exhausted just from having the conversation in the first place. She'd grown used to Nesilia merely talking at her. Telling Whitney that she believed Nesilia might still be in her mind somewhere, lurking… it was too much.

"It's nothing," she lied.

"It's not nothing," Whitney said. "I know you, Sora... *Nothhelm*... I know all there is to know."

"Nothhelm... I—you—what?" Sora stammered. Her hand slipped off Aquira and banged against the bench as she went slack, stunned. Aquira flapped away to the crow's nest. "How did you..."

"I have my secrets, too." Again, he put on that mischievous smile Sora had practically been begging to see one last time, until now that she was a victim of it.

"Whitney..." she said, breathless. "I don't know how you know that, but you shouldn't."

"I shouldn't?" Whitney said, standing. "Are you kidding? Sora this is the greatest thing to happen to either of us. Do you know what this means?"

Sora tilted her head in question.

"You're not just a princess—"

"No. Stop it now."

"You should be Queen," Whitney continued as if she hadn't spoken at all.

"Queen? Are you mad?" Sora asked.

"You're older than Pi. Smarter too. *Definitely* prettier. Plus... think of the gold!"

"Bastard princesses don't get the throne," she muttered. "Besides..."

"Well, at least a castle." He extended his palm like a potion salesman. "Sora, Lady of New Winde Port."

"Stop," she said, stern. She looked back toward Yaolin City. "I don't want to be a lady of anything. Whitney, you have to promise me you won't tell anyone else. No one, do you understand?"

He blew out a raspberry. "You're madder than the real Queen was."

"I mean it. No one else knows, right?"

Whitney's head rolled back. "I can't believe you won't even consider this."

"Not even a little bit. Now, I'm serious. No one knows, right?"

Whitney put on a puzzled face, finger to his chin. "I don't think Kazimir will be talking."

"It was only him?"

He let out an exasperated sigh, leaned in, and said, "You could be something grand, Sora. Have the influence to do… well… something grand."

"Promise me," Sora said.

"Promise you what?"

"You won't tell anyone."

"If Torsten knew—"

"Especially not Torsten! Iam's shog, Whitney. You aren't thinking straight. If Torsten knew, he'd probably have me killed just to make sure no one found out his precious King was a whoremonger."

"Or he might think you're the better option over a sickly child," Whitney offered.

"I mean it, Whit. No one."

He sighed. "I promise not to tell anyone that you are the rightful queen of the whole yigging world. Happy?"

She crossed her arms.

The wind whistled as it passed through the many ropes hanging from posts and netting throughout the ship. Out there, on the Covenstan Depths, things had been quiet and peaceful beside the occasional grimaur attack. Even here in Glinthaven, it was like paradise. But it was just the calm before the inevitable storm, and Sora knew it.

"You don't get it, do you?" she said.

"What don't I get?" he replied.

"Queen of what? What's going to be left? You've heard the rumors, same as I have, haven't you? All throughout the docks. You can see what's happening in Panping." She pointed to the smoke and storm just barely visible now in the darkening sky. "You don't believe that's just her cultists. You can't. Not after what we saw in the Citadel. We are out of time, Whit. First Yaolin City, then Yarrington, then the whole world. There's no time to make people further doubt the King of the only Kingdom strong enough to stand against her."

Still kneeling before her, Whitney held out his hand as if offering for her to take it. After a few seconds and a pleading look in his eyes, she did. "Yes, I've heard the rumors," he said. "White hair, black eyes, pretty but terrifying, rides a sea-monster? Yeah, that's obviously her."

"So, what do we do?"

"I've got a plan."

"Oh, do you?" Sora asked, skeptical.

"While you've been… recovering, we've been scheming. We're going after her."

"Just like that? There's nothing to steal this time, thief." She tried to be playful with the term, though she wasn't sure it came off that way.

"Well, good thing I'm retired, then. I'm in the 'saving damsels' business now."

Sora rolled her eyes.

Whitney's features darkened. "She hurt you, Sora. You may not admit it, but I can see it in your eyes. And she hurt Kazimir, Gold Grin, Torsten—she'll pay for all of it. So, before we worry about you taking your rightful place as Queen of the World, and me by your side—your dashing King—or even what's happened while you were with her, and I was in Elsewhere, if you even *think* you might still have a connection to Nesilia, we need to talk with Lucindur right away."

She stared at him, unblinking. She couldn't stop herself. Whitney Fierstown, thief and braggart. Always out for himself, now willing to throw himself at Nesilia even though he'd already accomplished his mission, saving Sora—all for her and others. And as she watched him, hanging on with a dumb look smeared across his face, eager for her response, she knew. She could finally forgive him for leaving her behind all those years ago. Really, truly forgive him.

"Did you just propose marriage?" she asked.

Whitney waved her off. "Sora, stop messing around—"

His protest was cut short as she threw himself at him. His back hit the deck, and she landed on top of him.

Pinned beneath her, he said, "Sora, what are you…"

It was so long in the waiting—months, years, a decade even. She didn't want to waste another second when any second could be their last. Her mouth found his, and for once in his life, he quit talking.

She pawed at his britches, unlacing them quickly with one hand as the other shoved back on his tunic.

"Ow," he squealed.

She noticed the magical embers building around her hand as she lost control. "Get used to it," she replied, pushing him harder. He stared into her eyes, then his hand tangled her hair, and he pulled her toward him, kissing her again.

III

THE KNIGHT

"**S**ir Unger, I'm sorry," Sir Lucas Danvels said.

The young Shieldsman rode beside Torsten, heading east on the Glass Road. Their journey so far from White Bridge had been mostly silent. After Nesilia's arrival and on the battlefield, Lucas seemed particularly shaken. These were the first words he'd spoken.

"For what?" Torsten asked.

"For bringing her—the Buried Goddess—there. The blood pact Rand made… it was against me."

"You did nothing wrong, Lucas. The fault rests squarely upon my shoulders—as usual." Torsten went silent, watching creatures flying in the distance, too big to be gallers. *Grimaurs.*

"I kept Rand among us when he was clearly more damaged than any of us knew," Torsten said.

"For a Shieldsman—even a former one—to unleash such wrath… It's inconceivable."

"If he knew what she would do, I have to believe he wouldn't have done it. Not if anything of the Rand I knew is left in that frail form."

"Maybe, but I should've stopped them. Him, at least."

"Nesilia killed Muskigo Ayerabi like it was a game," Torsten said. "Like he was a mouse caught in the grain bin. She would have killed us all if not for Dellbar the Holy—Iam."

Torsten paused again. It seemed a dream that old, drunken Father-Morningweg-turned-Dellbar-the-Holy had carried the manifest presence of his God. Iam had been there, on that battlefield, protecting his chosen children.

Torsten cleared his throat. "There was nothing you could've done."

Lucas exhaled. "And now, Rand Langley is in the wind again."

"No, he's not."

"You know where he is?" Lucas asked, hopeful like a hungry child at the smell of bread.

"No, but I know him. He'll be heading east, just like us. He'll never stop believing his sister is still inside of whatever twisted thing Sigrid has become. He'll go to her—"

"And she'll kill him," Lucas finished.

"Or he'll serve her like a mindless beast."

"Like he did with the Mad Queen," Lucas offered.

"Don't call her that."

"Sorry, Sir Unger. I didn't intend to speak ill of the dead. But it is true, right? The things she made Langley do will be nothing compared to the goddess' desires."

"In that, you may be correct."

"I spoke with her, Sir Unger." His voice was shaky, as if reliving a horrific memory. "There was nothing human about her. Sh... sh... she looked right through me. It was as if I weren't more than cattle."

"The Buried Goddess and an upyr as one," Torsten said. "I can think of nothing more wicked."

Thick clouds blotted out the sun, casting an eerie, gray blanket over the Wildlands. It felt like months since Torsten had seen the sun, a precise mirroring of his soul.

"You know, it's funny, Sir Unger."

Torsten glared at Lucas.

"Poor choice of words. It's just that I didn't even believe there was such a thing as upyr until recently. Like everyone else, I figured they were just stories meant to scare children from sneaking away at night. But now, every horrid nightmare has become a reality. It seems lately, nothing makes sense. What happened?"

Torsten knew precisely what had happened. "King Liam died."

It seemed too simple a response, but often the truth was just that, simple.

"How do we stop her?" Lucas asked. His words no longer came out merely shakily. Now, he quaked, and the horror there was unmistakable.

Torsten felt it, too. That oppressive feeling of hopelessness latching onto every and all parts of him. He'd witnessed a miracle when Iam possessed Dellbar the Holy's body, and still, he felt it.

"I have no idea," he admitted. "But we have to try."

Torsten had to see the truth for himself. After what happened outside White Bridge, he thought they'd have more time. That Iam himself had provided a chance to collect themselves for what was sure to be the second God Feud, Torsten thought it to be a sign of ultimate victory.

Then, the rumors started flooding west. From Glinthaven and the Wildlands, the eastern dwarven kingdoms and even Brekliodad—Yaolin City had fallen, and darkness spread across all Panping like a plague. Torsten had sent messages east by galler and even horseback in efforts to confirm these tales with Governor Nantby and the garrison commander at Fort Wuxia.

They didn't answer. Nobody answered. And none of the messengers had returned.

And so, Torsten and Lucas rode east, garbed in nothing but the rags of devout priests of Iam. It wasn't long ago that Torsten had berated that dastardly Whitney Fierstown for posing as a priest—but Torsten had little choice. With the blindfold he already wore over his eyes, blessed to allow him sight despite his burns, the disguise fit.

Besides, they couldn't very well wear glaruium Shieldsman armor. Torsten knew now that the enchanted metal mined in the heart of Mount Lister, from the place where Nesilia had been buried bent to her will. He carried only *Salvation*, tucked beneath his robes. Even the gorgeous, gilded, dragon-shaped hilt and the Eye of Iam pommel were shrouded by the folds of his hood.

Their horses whinnied and reared back as they crossed the boundary into the Panping Region as if somehow sensing the new dangers the land presented.

"Whoa!" Lucas exclaimed, struggling to calm his tawny mare. He'd grown up in Dockside, where horses weren't a necessity, so he still had a lot to learn. Torsten trotted his sideways, the same chestnut he'd ridden for months. She was a faithful girl, and he swore to her many times over that he'd retire her as soon as they'd returned to Yarrington.

"You control him, not the other way around," Torsten said. He grasped the mane of the young Shieldsman's mount.

Lucas nodded, then leaned over to stroke his horse's neck.

Then, together, they looked up. Panping's border was unassuming. No wall or moat, just a gentle shift from the rolling plains of the Wildlands to Panping's white rocks and lush jungles. The temperature was usually balmy, especially in these summer months, but not now. Clouds swarmed above, and it wasn't fully snowing, but flakes drifted on the wind like ash.

Maybe it is ash.

Torsten caught one on the tip of his finger, feeling the nip of an icy breeze as his arm stretched behind the folds of his sleeve. He touched it to his tongue.

"Snow," he said to Lucas, who was busy staring up at them as well.

Torsten wasn't sure which was worse. At least ash was explainable. Nesilia's followers did so like to burn things—Torsten's own eyes could attest to that. Snow, however, made no natural sense in the heart of summer, not this far south. Panping was no stranger to magic and mysticism, causing the world to reject the nature Iam had designed for Pantego. Mystics would summon rainstorms over farms, strike enemies with bolts of lightning, erase winter entirely.

This felt different.

"That storm looks bad," Lucas said, pointing east over a ridge.

"I don't think it's a storm," Torsten replied. "At least, no storm like you and I would be familiar with."

Toward the horizon, the clouds turned darker and darker still, until they were black as a crow, and swirling like a murder of them toward a converging point.

A vortex centered around Nesilia's new seat of power, Torsten thought.

Yaolin City was still many leagues to the east. Still, the weather anomaly was spreading, slowly gobbling up the world Torsten knew. The grass was browning. Cherry trees amongst stark white stones, usually full and bright this time of year, had wilting flowers and leaves flaking away. Beyond that, the jungles looked starved. No animals roamed. Apart from what Torsten was now convinced were grimaurs, no birds soared. No people—Panpingese or otherwise—traveled roads that were typically rife with sojourners.

And the smell…

In blindness, Torsten's other senses had grown more acute, and that was the strangest part. Smell was almost wholly absent.

"Should we check that inn?" Lucas asked. "Maybe they saw something."

"If anyone is still alive to see," Torsten said, then nodded. He gave his horse a kick, and they trotted farther into the bleakness to a quaint old cottage house set just a short walk from the Glass Road.

Their horses clopped toward a garden just west of it. "I know this place," Torsten said. He couldn't mask the pride in his voice, and he was sure his face showed it as well. "Sir Uriah and I stayed here on a trip east to meet with Governor Nantby. That was when King Liam installed the man into his position."

"Was it always this quiet?" Lucas asked.

Torsten shook his head. "I've never cared much for fancy food, but the owner made a rabbit stew fit for any King."

"Not better than my mum's. Trust me."

Torsten shot his ward a sidelong glare, wiping the smirk right off his face. He appreciated Lucas' uncanny ability to stay chipper, but there was a time and place. Here, in a countryside cursed by darkness and silence, was neither.

As Torsten neared the inn, he recalled the aromatic outdoor garden set around a babbling, trickling waterfall stemming from a stream zigzagging through the stones. Spices he'd never even heard of had grown there in plenty. Now, his horse's hooves cracked stale, frozen dirt. What was left of the plants were dead, and centered amongst them was an arrangement of corpses.

"By Iam," Lucas said, covering his mouth.

Torsten brought the neck of his robes up over his nose. The stale air grew rank with the stink of death, radiating toward him in waves. These were not fresh bodies. They'd been laid in a circle, with more forming the shape of a triangle between them—the cultist symbol of the Buried Goddess.

There was no telling how long they'd been left to rot in the open air, but they were so decomposed, it was unclear how they'd died either. He could see straight to the bone, flies buzzing around them, worms feeding on their insides. He'd seen the horror of battles and not been so overwhelmed. Both the stench and the sight had tears welling in his eyes.

"Who could do this?" Lucas muttered.

A clatter from within the inn stole Torsten's attention. A red-robed figure swept by a window. Unlike the trampled, rotting garden, the building itself appeared to be untouched. Nothing was destroyed; none of the paper walls torn. It merely seemed quiet.

"I think I saw someone," Lucas said.

"Me too." Torsten hitched his horse to the front porch and climbed down. Lucas followed him. As they edged closer to the entry, a blur of red moved again.

"Stay here and watch the horses," Torsten ordered.

"What if there's more than one of them?" Lucas asked.

"Come running. At times like this, Nesilia's followers aren't the only ones we have to worry about. Two western mares would make quite a prize for bandits and leave us stranded a good way from the city."

Torsten stopped just outside and fished behind his back, hands coming to rest on the grip of his claymore. "In the name of Iam and the Glass Kingdom, show yourself!" he hollered. His voice carried far, the only sound for miles in any direction. Nobody answered.

"I won't ask again!" Torsten shouted.

Again, nothing. True to his word, Torsten kicked through the sliding entry door, drawing *Salvation* at the same time. When no attack came, he quickly scanned the room and found that the many undisturbed tables still had tankards of ale sitting on them. Tankards were lined up on the bar, half of them still full, and the rest clean and empty, like the bartender had vanished in mid-preparation of an order. Some seats even had bowls of stew set before them, only they were covered by flies and edged with mold.

All of it coalesced to form an odor worse than the desiccated remains outside. Torsten tried to fight it, but it overwhelmed his senses worse than any dungeon. He staggered toward a table, needing the sword to stab down into the wood floor to stay upright.

He gagged, somehow managing to keep the contents of his stomach down.

"Sir Unger, is everything all right?" Lucas asked, now at the door with his longsword drawn.

"I said watch the horses," Torsten ordered, then continued onward.

A cackle from the kitchen behind the bar made him spin. It was followed by a small voice—a child's voice.

Torsten held his breath and rushed for the swinging doorway. He couldn't talk without the taste of the room lingering on his tongue, so instead, he gripped his sword tight and held it before him. Once inside, he spotted a red-robed Buried Goddess cultist beside a little Panpingese girl.

The man's white mask was cracked in half, and on the exposed side, Torsten saw skin as white as the paper walls of the inn. Dark veins bulged around his eyes, which were entirely black, no whites to them at all, just dark and shiny like onyx from lid to lid.

"Step away from the girl!" Torsten demanded. He'd seen what these cultists were capable of and now, emboldened by Nesilia's return, he could imagine no depth of evil to which they wouldn't sink.

The man stirred a bubbling cauldron, laughing and whistling as he did. The young girl stood behind him, facing the wall. Her shoulders heaved as if she was crying and couldn't bear to watch.

Torsten discovered why, fast. The body of a plump, middle-aged woman hung above the bubbling pot, strings holding her limbs at different, unnatural heights like a marionette. Blood dripped from her sliced throat into whatever they were cooking. All Torsten knew was that it was dark red, and it didn't smell like rabbit.

"What unholiness is this?" Torsten demanded.

He pointed his blade at the cultist, keeping his feet spry and ready to pounce. The man's hands wrapped a ladle, but he could have had a dagger hidden anywhere on his person, ready to practice the blood magic his perverse cult was known for.

"We're preparing a gift for our Lady," the man said. His voice was low, but resonant. The worst part was that he didn't carry the Drav Crava accent—this man was of the Glass through-and-through. It sent a chill right up Torsten's spine that wouldn't relent. "When she arrives, she'll be hungry."

He laughed maniacally, then ladled up a bit of the contents of the pot and let it spill back in. There were chunks amidst the deep red, and Torsten spotted what looked like a carrot, and though he knew its true identity was far more obscene, he couldn't even bear to think it.

"Nesilia is coming here?" Torsten asked.

A nightmare grin appeared beneath the broken mask. "Everywhere. Nowhere." He started to laugh even harder, unable to control himself. He released the ladle, covering his mouth with both hands, and backing up across the kitchen.

"Don't you dare go near her!" Torsten said. He slowly sidestepped toward the girl, keeping his blade aimed at the man.

"Open your eyes, holy man," the cultist spoke, as if purposefully trying to insult Torsten for his handicap.

"She'll free you all from Iam," the girl then said. Like the man, her voice seemed to carry with it an ethereal quality. Every word filled Torsten's ears, echoing from all directions, and also from within.

She turned slowly, holding a bloody knife in both hands, and he realized that she wasn't crying at all. Like the cultist, she laughed so hysterically that tears ran down her cheeks. And like him, her eyes were entirely black, veins spreading out across the skin surrounding them like spokes of a wheel.

Startled, Torsten stumbled back. His hip bumped the cauldron, and it wobbled once before the boiling liquid and chunks of meat sloshed across the floor, running against their feet. Neither the cultist nor the girl reacted to the heat, even as it ate through the skin of their feet and ankles. They merely looked down, then to each other, and started laughing harder.

"No more gift for her," the cultist said, shrugging.

"You'll pay for that, holy man," the girl added.

She stepped toward him, raised her knife. Only the cultist's eyes moved, watching with his head tilted to the side. More curious, it seemed, than anything.

"Don't come any closer, demon," Torsten growled, gripping *Salvation* tighter. However, he couldn't bring himself to point it at the girl. He'd seen demonic possession before when mystics trifled with powers they shouldn't have in the Third War of Panping. He knew, just as

Sigrid was possessed by the goddess, this girl was inhabited by another being of Elsewhere.

"Won't you kill me, Sir?" the little girl asked, affecting a pouty voice. "Won't you free me from Her?"

"I said no closer!"

Of course, she didn't listen. One small step after the other, she neared. Sweat poured down Torsten's nape. His heart pounded, and he could almost feel it against his bones. Blood pumped like a water well behind his eyes, but he remained frozen, squeezing *Salvation* so tight his knuckles whitened.

"Please," the girl whimpered. "Save me. Save me!" She threw her head back and raised her knife to her own throat. Torsten sprang to action, reflex taking over. He swatted with his blade. Blood spurted from the girl's finger as he knocked the weapon away from her. The knife skidded across the floor, landing right by the cultist's now seared feet.

The girl stared at her hand, quietly studying it. Then she laughed again and aimed the spray toward Torsten.

"You're sick," Torsten said. "The both of you."

The cultist bent at the waist to pick up the knife.

"You can't stop us," the cultist said. "The Well of Wisdom is open. Elsewhere is empty."

"We do as we want to here," the girl added. "She promised. It's our realm now."

Torsten skirted slowly along the wall until his back was at the kitchen's entry.

It was why they were there, he and Lucas. He wanted—needed—to see it for himself. The rumors spoke of it, but Torsten needed to know by his own injured eyes that the gates of Elsewhere had truly been battered down and its most rotten inhabitants unleashed upon their world, able to easily overtake the bodies and minds of the weak-willed.

Now he knew. Nesilia had done the unthinkable.

The possessed duo didn't come after him, just turned only their heads, spines perfectly straight, watching him. He stepped back through the opening, and someone powerful wrapped an arm around his waist. He blocked a second arm by the wrist with the flat edge of his sword.

The attacker wielded a fork and came a hair's length from jabbing it into Torsten's throat.

Torsten head-butted back, knocking the assailant away from him. Then, whipping around, he gutted the man with his sword. The Panpingese man's all-black eyes expressed nothing as he dropped to his knees, cradling his innards. He didn't scream. He didn't feel.

The others in the kitchen still only watched. Torsten scrambled around the body, then felt a chill all over as the dying man's neck wrenched back, and a nebulous form screeched out through his mouth. It swirled around Torsten once, its raving laughter piercing his very soul.

Torsten held his breath and plunged through, silently praying to Iam for protection over his body, his soul. He was strong. He knew he could resist. But as the demon spirit flowed around him, Torsten felt something he never had before. A pull, like he wasn't in command of his own body.

He froze.

His heart stopped beating, or at least it felt that way.

He could feel Nesilia, her gaze on him like white-hot fire.

"Why resist?" she asked, her voice sultry and seductive like a whore in Valin's Vineyard, each word hanging like the hiss of a slithering snake. Her confidence was undeniable. Her newfound comfort in their world, unmistakable.

Hope started to fade, replaced with doubt that clawed at the edge of his consciousness.

"The end is so near," Nesilia went on. "The seat of Glass will shatter. Iam's light will go out. Give in, Torsten…"

"You'll have to kill me first," he said through clenched teeth.

"Not even death will save you from me."

"Sir Unger!" someone yelled, distant, but within reach.

It stung everywhere as a hand closed around Torsten's wrist and yanked his body free. His fingernails felt like they were going to tear out, knuckles break; his lungs like they might shred from the inside. Torsten collapsed forward, leaving the demonic entity behind, knocking Lucas over and splitting a table. His knees hit the floorboards so hard the wood cracked. *Salvation* clanked nearby, but he'd never even felt it leave his fingertips.

Flipping over, pawing for his weapon as he backed away, Torsten watched the demon spirit rush across the room, spilling everything on the bar before bursting through a window. The others in the kitchen stopped watching and slowly approached Torsten.

Lucas returned to his feet and moved to shield Torsten. "Stay back!" He was young, but he'd seen enough battle for his age. It didn't matter. His hands were trembling, and Torsten couldn't blame him after what he'd just seen.

"Lucas." Torsten coughed. "Lucas, we need to get out of here."

"Listen to Her," the cultist said.

"Why resist?" the young girl said.

Torsten found *Salvation's* grip. As his fingers embraced it, he thought about charging the poor, possessed souls. He wanted to tear them limb from limb, but he'd learned this last year that sometimes fighting wasn't the answer.

His people needed him, and he had no idea how to banish the demons. Dead bodies would only lead to them jumping to new bodies, an endless foe until all life on Pantego was expended. He needed to return to Dellbar and the priests. They'd know how to stop them—stop her—and if not, he prayed someone out there might.

"Go!" Torsten said, grabbing Lucas by the shoulder and shoving him back toward the inn's exit. "We'll send you all back to Elsewhere where you belong!" He hoped Nesilia could hear him. "Iam's light will shine ever brighter."

"Sir Unger, what are they?" Lucas asked. He gathered his balance and turned back for a fight.

"I said, go!" Torsten spun him on his way by, dragging him toward the exit.

"Run along, holy man," the little girl yelled, unbridled mirth to her every word. The cultist guffawed right beside her.

Torsten burst back outside, pushing Lucas down the step ahead of him. As the young Shieldsman staggered, an empty wagon dragged by frenzied horses raced by and would have plowed right over him had Torsten not reacted quickly and pulled him back. Its rider was headless and slumped over.

Lucas was left breathless, gawking. Torsten turned left. Their own horses tugged at their hitches, and Torsten could hear the wood threatening to break. They screeched, fearful like he'd never heard before.

"T… T… Torsten," Lucas stammered. Torsten looked to him. He no longer watched the wagon, but instead, stared south at the crest of a hill.

A cluster of Panpingese farmers stood atop it. They were far, but Torsten's blessed vision allowed him to see the contrast in light and darkness, and their eyes were dark as midnight north of the Dragon's Tail. They wielded anything they could find as weapons—sickles, shovels, rakes, hoes—anything, like they didn't care or know what a proper weapon was.

And their mouths stay shut as if sealed. They simply stood and watched, wicked grins smeared across dirty faces. A woman wearing an elegant flowered kimono pushed through the throng toward the front of the horde. Blood stained the front of her clothes and all the way up her wrists and forearms. In one hand, she gripped a decapitated head by knotted hair. She tossed it and let it roll down the hill.

"Lucas, we've seen enough," Torsten said, stroking his horse to calm her.

The young Shieldsman remained petrified.

"Lucas, let's go!"

That got his attention. Lucas ran to his horse, and they both mounted. Torsten didn't even take the time to untie either rope, just slashed them with his claymore. He smacked Lucas's on the hindquarters, knowing the young man was too stunned to do it himself. He even grabbed the reins to help lead as they sped off.

"See you soon!" the little girl called out after them, now standing in the entrance of the inn. The cultist stood behind her, his hands resting upon her shoulders like a loving father.

Torsten couldn't bear the sight of it. He couldn't even pray, though he doubted that in this tainted place, Iam could hear him anyway. His light certainly had stopped shining here.

All Torsten could hope to do was hurry to Latiapur, and finish securing the alliance that might give them a fighting chance against Nesilia. All living things needed to stand together if they had any hope, but he'd start with the newly appointed Caleef Mahraveh, and the Black Sands.

IV

THE CALEEF

Caleef Mahraveh stood alone on the northern shores of Latiapur, just beyond the bluffs of the Tal'du Dromesh. It felt fitting that her father should pass on into the Eternal Current here, in the place he'd made a name for himself.

Muskigo "The Scythe" Ayerabi.

Even with the clumps of black sand covering his eyes, her father looked merely asleep on a pad of driftwood tied together by strands of seaweed. His arms were crossed over his chest, that sickle-blade, almost as famous as the man himself, resting firmly in his hands. He'd lived by the proverbial sword, and now he would die with it.

The last of the Ayerabi Afhemate. The last blood-connection Mahi had in the entire world.

She wished she could cry as she watched the rising tide's gentle hands spread across the beach, slowing reaching out to grasp and usher him into rest. However, ever since the God of Sand and Sea spat her back out, she'd been unable to manage tears.

Foam swirled in the dark grains of sand at her feet, creating a tapestry of white and black that once reminded Mahi of clouds in the night sky. But now, she was too old for such imaginings. Too many centuries of her peoples' violent history bounced around her brain. All the lives of past Caleefs pounded like the sea against her consciousness. They offered both answers and doubts, but one thing was certain—none knew what to do about this.

Mahi's father hadn't been killed in a conflict with rival afhemates. There were no afhemates, not anymore. He hadn't been killed by a war with another people or the Kingdom of Glass, even. No. He'd been murdered by a darkness no one could understand, because they hadn't felt it like she had. He'd been killed by a goddess, and the sting went bone-deep, for within Mahi dwelled the goddess' brother, her god, whose true name was Caliphar.

"They say he gave his life defending Sir Torsten Unger," Bit'rudam said from behind.

In her previous life, his sudden appearance would have startled her, but now, Mahi simply glanced back.

The golden Serpent Guard armor fit him well. Bit'rudam had become a hero of her people, winning the tournament meant as a distraction from the horrors. As his final opponent had him on his back, ready to claim victory, Mahi felt the flitting of her heart. It was a fleeting sensation, but it reminded her of days before her god made her carry so much weight.

And Bit'rudam didn't disappoint. He was equally smart as he was skilled with a blade and his baiting of the larger opponent had worked. She should have seen it coming, but for him, there was genuine concern. He rose as the blunt end of the opponent's spear drove downward—this wasn't a tournament like the rest. Sure, blood could be drawn, but there would be no death. As the weapon spewed up sand, Bit'rudam kicked, buckling the opponent's knee, then he brought the pommel of his own sword out, and sent the man into unconsciousness.

And so, unlike the rest of the Order he now led, she didn't allow him to cover his face or cut out his tongue. She wanted to hear him, to see him, to be reminded of who she'd been before all of this, before so many years were jumbled around in her mind, and people from every background bowed to her—if they could even bear to look at her.

"Then I look forward to asking Sir Unger about his end when he arrives," Mahi said.

"My Caleef, Tingur was there as well," Bit'rudam said. "He spoke of how brave Muskigo was in the face of power he'd never before witnessed."

"And I trust Tingur. However, the rivalry between Sir Unger and my father is legendary. If he truly gave his life protecting the former Wearer of White, I must know everything."

Bit'rudam bit his lip. "I should have been there."

Mahi reached out and laid her hand upon his shoulder. She hated the way instinct made him shrink back from her, like he was scared or awestruck, or both. But at least he didn't fall to his knees and kowtow.

"I needed you here," she said.

"I know. And it is my honor to serve you, my Caleef." She noticed his knee shift. Then his foot. But before he could fall into a bow, she tugged on his arm and led him toward her father. The tide had him now, slowly dragging his raft across the sand into the sea's loving embrace. It was a beautiful custom, but painful to watch.

A Shesaitju should never place their dead directly into the water. The water itself had to accept the soul, and she knew her father would be accepted. Nobody had better-exemplified their old ways.

"If you were there, you, too, would be dead," Mahi said. "As the God of Sand and Sea said, we need everyone to stand against her."

"Well, she made one mistake."

"And what is that?" Mahi asked.

"She made it personal for you. I may not know you as well as some, but it seems that when you want something, you do not give up until you have it."

"It's more than personal, Bit'rudam," she said, stern. "She threatens everything." She knew he was only trying to be playful, but she couldn't even feign a smile.

"I know. I didn't—"

"Why are you here?" she interrupted. "I asked to be alone."

He straightened his back. "Right, I… Afhem—I mean former Afhem Nasser and nearly a hundred warriors have fled east. They don't believe that what happened outside White Bridge is the truth. They believe the Glass is coming to bury us again."

"Our own people have said the same. A woman of pure darkness stood against both armies all on her own. She killed the greatest warrior in all of Pantego without breaking a sweat." She pointed down to her father's body, rocking as the wood clung to the last few bits of sand before it was completely free. "Is that not proof enough?"

"I do not doubt you, my Caleef," Bit'rudam said. "But the Glass

King coming here for a marriage… That is quite different from a military alliance. There are many, like Nasser, who believe this is all a ploy by the Glass to end the fighting, that Babrak was right and that you weren't…"

He paused. She trusted him, but she could read the lines of struggle written all over his face.

"Say it," she said.

He swallowed the lump forming in his throat, then whispered, "Chosen."

"And what do *you* think about me marrying King Pi?" Mahi asked.

The struggle on his face transformed into something akin to pain. "I appreciate the strategy of it," he remarked.

"Then that is why I needed you at my side. I will never love King Pi. I will never love any of them. But I will do anything for our people."

"And that is why I know you were chosen," Bit'rudam said. His gaze fell toward the sand. "As much as I hate that it has to be you."

Mahi nodded. She understood. In fact, she loved that a part of him could still be honest with her. He reminded her so much of Jumaat. Sometimes, she had to remind herself it wasn't him, while at the same time, her mind told her that maybe the Eternal Current had carried him back to her in a new form.

"If I marry him," Mahi said, "can you still serve me?"

"I gave my oath," he answered, still unable to look her in the eye.

"Even though he's a Glassman?"

"Whoever he is."

Now, he looked up, eyes dark but glinting like sunlight over the waves of the far ocean. Also like Jumaat's, they were beautiful. Mahi wished she could fall deeper into them, but she knew she couldn't for fear of getting lost there. The things she wanted were nothing now. She was only the Caleef.

"Good," she said, turning away.

He pulled her back. "Just promise me you won't forget your people. Traveling with my father, trading goods… I've seen the temptations of their way of life—the riches of Yarrington. They often tempted him. And… me."

"Never forget that marrying him was my idea, not theirs," Mahi scolded, glaring down at his hand. He immediately let her go, and she immediately regretted it. It was another force driving her. That's what all the past Caleefs would have done if they'd been touched without permission. It was what they *had* done. She could see every occasion playing on repeat in her mind's eye.

"Of course, my Caleef," he muttered.

A bell rang, then another, followed by a zhulong-tusk horn signaling a friendly ship approaching the main Latiapurian docks.

"Right on time," Bit'rudam said. "Let's head back. You should be there to greet them."

"Wait," Mahi said, turning her attention back to her father. The sea nearly had him.

"I don't mean for them. Our people should see you there, or I'm not sure how they'll respond."

"I said, wait," she snapped.

"Yes, my Caleef."

She stood for minutes longer until the water grew brave, and a powerful wave reached in. The planks holding Muskigo scraped off the sand and floated out into the sea. Just like that, her father was free of all the fighting that had dominated his life. Mahi knew he would sail at the top of the Current, where only the worthiest belonged, shaping the very world of those left behind.

Muskigo 'the Scythe' Ayerabi, one of the greatest warriors Pantego had ever known, was gone. Again, she wished she could cry as she had when her mother died, or Shavi, or Jumaat. She wished she could feel that clench of her heart as sorrow took hold and squeezed with all its awful might.

She didn't. Nor did she feel the unbridled rage she should have at the one who'd killed him. She simply remained steadfast, watching the waves carry him farther, one swell at a time. But she didn't need to feel the anger to know that she wanted to make Nesilia pay. She didn't want to drown her or bury her like Iam had. She wanted to break her apart piece by bleeding piece.

Bit'rudam was right. Nesilia had made it personal, and Mahi would do whatever it took to destroy her, even if that meant marrying the boy-King of the Glass Kingdom. Even if that meant destroying any hope of a new, independent Shesaitju like her father had dreamed of.

Nesilia would pay.

Protestors cluttered the streets of Latiapur. Mahi's army had to patrol regularly to maintain order. She still had a significant fraction of the former afhems on her side, along with their afhemates. Especially all those who'd marched north and witnessed the wrath of Nesilia herself.

But not all.

Whispers of Babrak's accursed name still lurked around every corner. Rumors flittered, telling of the new kingdom he'd declared from his seat in Abo'Fasaniyah—a kingdom faithful to the God of Sand and Sea and not Mahraveh, 'the usurper daughter of the traitor Muskigo.' Or so he claimed. Spies said that even now, he doused himself in the blood of the nigh'jels like a Caleef.

Mahi's tournament to help choose a commander for the Serpent Guards built some trust amongst the people. However, after her father's death, and the news that she intended to marry King Pi Nothhelm in an effort to unify their two kingdoms, much of that trust was lost. Warriors trickled out. Afhems vanished.

Babrak had lured enough to his side that, in a legitimate war, Mahi wasn't sure which side would win to claim the Black Sands. However, with the entirety of the Glass army supporting her, all that would change. She'd command the most formidable army Pantego had ever seen, and *she would* command it.

From all she'd heard, Pi was a frightful, young boy who'd suffered greatly in his short life. A boy who'd been led around by his crazed mother like a leashed dog when he wasn't possessed by blood magic. Barely a man. When they were wedded, she'd own him, and through him, an empire. The Black Sands could become the greatest power in Pantego without shedding another drop of blood.

All she had to do was stomach consummating the marriage with a Glassman barely of age.

"My Caleef," Tingur pronounced as Mahi approached the Boiling Keep. He dropped to one knee, the other leg shaking. He lowered his head, revealing the patch of mutilated skin where his mark of afhemdom had been carved off. Since he was off in Nahanab when

Mahi erased that part of Shesaitju history, his was fresher than the others.

"What is it?" Mahi asked. She nodded toward Bit'rudam, and he understood her intent, rushing ahead to help Tingur back up. She could tell the overweight man wasn't happy about it, but he didn't resist. The injuries he'd sustained fighting Nesilia had left him battered and broken. He could help Mahi command armies, but he'd be useless in a fight.

"We caught two men wearing the markings of the Trisps'I Afhemate in the markets, sowing discontent," Tingur said.

"Where are they now?" Bit'rudam asked.

"In the palace dungeons. But they're getting overcrowded these days."

"It will only get worse," Mahi said, matter-of-factly. "Keep at it. I want patrols on every street. Pull men from the navy; we're safe on the waterfront. Anyone who speaks against this union, or even utters Babrak's name must be locked up."

Tingur's lip twisted. "My Caleef, I mean no disrespect, but that will only make the people angrier. These showings of forces—it's like tightening the reins on a zhulong in heat. It only makes them buck harder."

"This, I know, but my father and Yuri Darkings taught me much about the Glassmen. To them, perception is everything. If they feel welcome, and see our control, then they'll believe it. We can worry about our peoples' feelings when the pink men are gone."

"When *you're* gone, you mean," Tingur muttered.

"What?"

"You can't expect they'll allow you to stay here after you're declared Queen of the Glass? Oleander Nothhelm was foreign as well, and she spent the rest of her life on display like a porcelain doll in the Glass Castle."

Mahi stalked forward, towering over Tingur. It wasn't difficult now that the once-great-warrior couldn't stand without leaning on his hammer-staff. "Do I look like a doll?" she asked, which earned her a slow shake of Tingur's head. "I will stay wherever this fight requires me to. Now, you will do as you're commanded."

He bowed his head. "Of course, my Caleef."

"And Bit'rudam," she added. "Offer him the full support of the

Serpent Guards until the ceremony. I want them visible. Like Tingur said… on display."

"I'm not sure that is wise," Bit'rudam replied. "The Glassmen could be using this as a ploy to get close to you. I would rather them be nearby, keeping you protected."

"The Glassmen won't lay a finger on me."

Mahi didn't give him a chance to reply, sweeping past him and Tingur, and starting the climb up the grand stairs leading up to her palace. Shesaitju warriors were arrayed along the edges in perfect intervals. Each of them had been a member of the Ayerabi or al'Tariq afhemates—her most loyal followers. She couldn't afford any mishaps.

The castrated palace sages flocked to her, whispering about all the rumors they'd heard, desperate for her favor. Nobody seemed to believe that now wasn't the time for posturing and politics. This peace needed to be secured. In the face of Nesilia, the great unified army required the leadership of someone knowledgable in fighting.

From every corner of the world, travelers spoke of an army of monsters and demons. They said Panping had already fallen beneath the goddess' might. Torsten Unger, the only remaining Glassman with the military influence to compete with her, was off investigating what they should prepare for. A part of her hoped he wouldn't return to complicate her ambitions.

She stopped at the landing where the stairs branched off down a ravine to the docks. Beautiful, markless servants wearing little more than strands of seaweed awaited her, fit men and women meant to appeal to Glassmen sensibilities. They fanned her with great palm leaves to keep her cool against the summer heat even though the nigh'jel blood coating Mahi's every inch prevented her from feeling much of anything.

"I hope you know what you are doing," a former afhem—one whose name she didn't care enough to know—said to her from behind.

"Those who have remained with me will not regret it," she replied.

"A storm nears," spoke another, pointing east over the ridge of the palace. Dark clouds rolled over the Boiling Waters far away. Mahi hadn't noticed them down by the shore, but the wall of black was nearly impossible to miss now.

"The God of Sand and Sea weeps for my father," Mahi said. "He will be avenged."

"Right. Vengeance on a reincarnated northern goddess," the first afhem said. His tone said everything. No disrespect was intended, but Mahi could sense the doubt. She couldn't blame him or the others for it. A goddess they'd barely ever heard about, whose people hailed from farther north than they ever cared about, wanting to kill them?

She wouldn't have believed it either if she hadn't felt Nesilia's terrible presence herself, or heard Tingur's first-hand account of White Bridge.

"I swear on all our ancestors, the Current is behind me," Mahi affirmed. "Trust in me a little longer."

"I trust in the Caleef, as our people always have," the first former afhem said. "That is all."

"Then, that will have to do."

As the last words left Mahi's lips, Shesaitju musicians started pounding the stretched zhulong leather of their drums. Pulley lifts rose from the ravine docks, cranking along with the beat. Sages split open nigh'jels and dripped strings of black blood along the path.

Mahi watched like a hawk, each *clank* of the lift feeling longer than the last. Dellbar the Holy, high steward of the Church of Iam, was supposed to be here to greet his King. After White Bridge, he'd arrived with Tingur alongside a contingent of Glass Soldiers sent by Sir Unger, and they stayed as guests in the former afhem quarter of the city. Mahi hadn't had a chance to speak with Dellbar yet, as he remained locked up in his own special room within the keep.

Finally, the lift halted. A row of young-seeming Shieldsmen garbed in shining armor showed first, then parted in the middle. They revealed an older man with one arm wearing an exquisite tunic embroidered with gold.

Beside him stood a boy wearing a Glass Crown. King Pi Nothhelm, the last of their illustrious line, same as Mahi.

There was a time she would have wanted to kill him right then and there and do just that, end the dynasty, but she'd learned—from Babrak no less—the type of awful people who would be left to seize control. Pi's name had earned him respect. His history as having been revived by their god, Iam, or so they told their people, earn him even more respect. But all men were easily manipulated.

Still, he appeared older than she'd expected. Not yet her height, but it was the look in his cobalt blue eyes. It didn't speak of the naivety of a boy, but of a warrior ready to draw his last breath. They were tired. He even nicely filled out his tunic far more resplendent than the man beside him.

One of the Shieldsmen stepped forward to lead him off the lift. His hand rested securely on the handle of his sheathed sword, but he seemed calm. This one boasted a few scars, at least, even though he, too, was surprisingly young. Mahi had thought the Shieldsmen Order to be their most veteran soldiers.

Shesaitju warriors on both sides of the path fell to a knee and bowed their heads, as per Mahi's instructions. That was why she'd needed her most loyal warriors arranged. Bowing to the King of Glass may have been a push too far for many of her people.

The lead Shieldsman's gaze danced from side to side, taking in the strange new sights. The others too. From up the palace ridge, all of Latiapur was visible. Even a straight line down the coast to the imposing arena they'd likely heard legends of.

Unlike the rest, Pi gazed forward. Straight at Mahi. He never wavered even the slightest, and his posture was tall and proud; practiced. To his credit, his jawline was strong, and she dared to think, even distinguished. Though he remained far from being able to grow a beard, she could tell he would grow to be strong.

He really didn't seem near as frail or small as Yuri Darkings' whispers had said. Then again, the traitor who'd pushed Mahi through the Sea Door had been away from Yarrington for a long time. And in that time, Mahi went from a daughter desperate to save her father, who'd never fought a real fight to a champion of the Tal'du Dromesh to an afhem commanding a fleet, and now, the rightful Caleef. How much could the Glass King have changed as well?

Pi stepped right up in front of her and stopped. The last of her warriors on the route bowed, and the drumming ceased. Silence pervaded. Not a soul dared speak as Caleef Mahraveh, and the King of Glass stood face to face. Mahi wasn't sure what he wanted. Maybe for her to be the first to bow? The Black Sands had been a loyal vassal of Pi's kingdom until her father's rebellion, after all.

She, too, refused to budge.

"Caleef Mahraveh of the Black Sands, it is our great honor to meet you," the one-armed older man accompanying the King spoke, his voice like a thunder strike amid the oppressive silence. He stepped up to Pi's side and dropped his head ever-so-slightly. "I am Lord Kaviel Jolly, Master of Ships, and chief advisor to the King."

"Do you speak for him, or can he speak for himself?" Mahi asked, not letting her stare waver from Pi for even an instant.

"I can," Pi said.

V

THE MYSTIC

"It was fully dark by the time they were both satisfied. Whitney and Sora lay cradled in each others' arms, staring up at Celeste and Loutis. It was a perfect moment amid untold chaos, and Sora didn't want it to end. Celeste was particularly beautiful tonight, her light gleaming off the snowcapped mountains.

"I'd have said 'yes,' you know," Sora whispered.

"To which question?" Whitney answered.

"If you had actually been asking me to marry you. I'd have said 'yes.'"

"Truth is," Whitney said, leaning up on his elbow and brushing a lock of hair behind Sora's ear, "I've always figured I'd marry a virgin." He smirked.

Sora punched his arm and dragged him back in for a kiss. Then, he fell back against the deck, returning to gazing at the stars.

"You weren't my first, you know," Sora said.

"Is that right?"

"Yup." She let her fingers entwine his.

"Well, you'll be my last."

Her face flushed, and she was glad for the darkness. She closed her eyes and rolled her head the other way like she was drifting off.

"Sora?" Whitney asked, a short while later. His voice sounded garbled, like it was a thousand miles away. "Sora? are you all right?"

She hadn't felt it until then, but she was shaking. Not just shivering from the cold, either. Her whole body spasmed. She heard him calling to her, but it was like a dream.

For a moment, she wondered if she was back in Nowhere. Then, hard truth hit her like a warhammer. She'd never left at all, had she? It was too good to be true—she and Whitney back again, like this.

Sora couldn't process the myriad thoughts assaulting her brain. She thought she felt Whitney's hand squeeze her arm, but she didn't know what was real anymore.

Her head swam. The sky blurred and distorted.

Silence engulfed Sora, threatening to bury her.

Her heart throbbed in her chest, her temples. She swallowed hard, and it felt like daggers scraping against her dry throat. Darkness surrounded her. She forced her eyes open, fearing what she might see. Things were fuzzy, and she felt something warm against her.

"Aquira?" she asked.

But no response came.

It soon became apparent that it wasn't something warm against her, but she was against something warm. The ground. Air, thick with humidity, weighed her down, and her head rested in something wet.

Her face, her eyes were coated in something…

Blood? she thought, mortified. But no, it wasn't blood. It was mud. Just mud.

She pushed herself into a seated position and dragged her hand across her hair, caked in the stuff. Groaning, she stood and stumbled a bit.

"Hello?" she asked no one in particular. When no response came again, she raked at her eyes, finally clearing them for good.

The sky was like wine, and it cast a dour picture before her. Smoke rose from chimney stacks in a small farming town. But again, her eyes had momentarily deceived her. Those were not pillars rising from chimneys, but great swaths of the dark gray stuff from burned remains just like she expected to be rising from Yaolin City. But it wasn't Panping.

"Troborough?" she said aloud, standing.

A feeling of dread battered against her heart. She'd seen this place before, though it wasn't the Troborough of her youth, nor even the one she'd left when the Black Sandsmen attacked. The last time she was here, she'd been on the run with Whitney. She could almost smell the

death. She felt the hot breath of those demons at her heels, biting, clawing, growling.

She sucked in a steadying breath, but no sense of calm even flirted
with her.

"It's not real," she said, over and over.

Presently, her feet sloshed at the edge of the Shellnak River as she
took a few tentative steps forward. To her right, just ahead, should have
been Wetzel's shack, her childhood home, but instead, there was only a
charred hole in the ground and scraps of crisp wood.

"Wetzel!" Sora screamed. Her voice didn't echo.

She pushed forward, getting as close to the hole as she dared. There
was no bottom, at least, not one she could see.

"What happened here?" Sora whispered.

The forest loomed behind the shack, so familiar, yet completely
different. She'd never really been afraid of those woods. They'd always
held something of a comfort to her. She believed she could still navigate her way to the treehouse she and Whitney had built—although
'built' was a generous term.

But now, with scarlet-tinted fog hovering at its base, the thicket
terrified her.

She shook herself out, willing her mind to settle, her body to find
peace.

Continuing north, past all the farmhouses and barns, she took it all
in until she stood in the middle of the town square, staring at what used
to be the Twilight Manor. It, too, was nothing but dirt and detritus. She
thought she could see the slight rise of the wood floor where the stage
used to be, but the inn was wrecked.

She thought of Hamm and Alless, and her nights there watching
and listening from her hiding place as the bards performed. She knew
this wasn't truly Troborough, but it seemed a fair evaluation of things
to come at the hands of the Buried Goddess.

So sad, considering what they'd already been through with the
Black Sandsmen.

Turning, she looked beyond the blacksmith's shop to a pile of
stones. At one time, in the real world, it had been the town's Church of
Iam where Father Hullquist would have delivered about a million

sermons. It was also where, in Elsewhere, she and Whitney hid from the wianu, and where she'd first told Whitney she loved him.

Cautiously, Sora approached the building. She looked everywhere for the bronze Eye of Iam, but it was nowhere to be found. Parchment was strewn about like a windstorm tore through, but Sora knew it had been more than mere wind.

"Can I help you, young lady?" said a gruff voice behind her. It sounded like wagon wheels on gravel, and it startled her, but it wasn't the first time she'd heard it, either.

"Torsten?" she said before she'd even spun toward him.

"Father Drimmond," the man who looked and sounded just like Torsten Unger, Wearer of White of the Glass Kingdom corrected.

She tried to hide her shock but barely managed. "I—uh… okay." Her eyes drank in a man with skin the color of tree bark, eyes missing, wearing a stained and yellowing robe. Just as Whitney said Torsten was, this man was blind, dirty cloth covering his, no doubt, burned-out eyes.

"Can I help you," he repeated.

"No… thanks. I was just… I was seeking the safety of Iam," she lied.

"There is no Iam in this place," Father Drimmond snapped. "Who are you?"

"No one important. Just a passer—"

"It doesn't matter," Father Drimmond said softly. "It's not safe here for someone like you."

"What's that supposed to mean?" Sora said, absentmindedly touching her ears. It was silly to think even a blind priest would know of her heritage and hate her for it.

Father Drimmond leaned in and whispered, "Alive." Then, without another word, he turned and walked away.

Alive? she thought. *What does that mean?*

Had she died right there in Whitney's arms?

She thought about calling out to him, but instead, turned back to the place where she and Whitney had huddled together in Elsewhere, watching the real Torsten battle all kinds of evil.

This time, there was no Whitney charging across the town, nor a pale-skinned upyr. There were no flying beasts or raging infernos. It was just… empty. Now, not even the priest could be seen.

She stood alone.

Away from the river, the hot, stagnant air was even worse. Sora felt like she was swimming in it. She gasped for breath and realized the smell of shog that was so common in all farm towns was absent.

Sora tried to call upon her magic, determined to be prepared if anything unforeseen sprang up from the dirt, but only a dark puff of smoke swelled from her open palm. Cracking her knuckles, she tried again, but still, there was nothing.

With a sigh, she continued down the familiar path leading to the daub and wattle farmhouse Whitney and his parents had lived in. Unlike the rest of the town, it was still standing. So many of her days had been spent there. She'd never felt welcome, but that was true of anywhere in Troborough. Despite having lived there her whole life, she'd never been a Troboroughite, not really. She'd always been the Panpingese orphan who lived with crazy, batty, old Wetzel on the outskirts of town. She wasn't dumb, and she wasn't deaf. She'd heard the whispers, the rumors that Wetzel abused her, mistreated her.

But none of those were true.

As kooky as Wetzel had been, he'd never laid a hand on her outside of her training. In light of what she'd learned in the Red Tower—that Wetzel had been exiled for abusing magic before being tasked with watching over her—she sort of felt sorry for him.

Taking another step toward the Fierstown residence, Sora didn't know what she expected—Mrs. Fierstown to come rushing out, blueberry and ginger pie in hand? Or maybe mean, rotten Rocco, face purple from yelling at Whitney to "stop playing with that stupid knife-ear."

Her finger traced the grain of the rotting wooden fence, finding a deep chasm where she and Whitney had placed their initials. Back then, it had nothing to do with romance. They were just friends. But seeing it now…

"Whitney!" she cried out, wondering if he'd burst through the front door, or tear through the barley fields, sickle in hand.

Instead, she found silence.

The gate hung askew, only one hinge still attached. She pushed it, careful not to tear it off completely.

Then something caught her attention out of the corner of her eye. When she looked, she saw nothing. It troubled her, but she gathered her wits and took a step. She felt something against her foot and looked down. A bright red apple. It was odd enough to be so far from the apple orchard on the other side of town, but stranger still in such a dead and barren place. The thought of picking it up entered her mind, but she decided she wasn't hungry and gave it a gentle kick. It rolled, revealing gray, paste-like flesh mottled with black spots and squirming little maggots.

Something stirred again, behind her this time, and she turned. Still, there was nothing.

Then, she yelped as long, pale fingers draped over her shoulder, and a hand closed over her mouth. It was like the Drav Cra tundra, it was so cold. A shiver bounded through her, drawing out goosebumps.

"Do not cry out," the voice said with a guttural Breklian accent.

Sora attempted to agree, but it passed through as a muffled mutter.

The hand slipped off, and Sora turned to see Kazimir.

The memory of being shackled to a bell tower high above Winde Port slammed into her like a zhulong. She could almost *feel* the color leave her face.

"What are you doing in this place?" he asked. His eyes were cold and dark as lifeless coals.

"You're not real," she said. "I watched you… I saw you. You died."

"And where do you believe dead things go?" he asked.

"But you were eaten. The Wianu…"

His hand slid over to her throat, his fingers closing around her neck. She felt the warmth as his fingernails drew blood.

"Stop this," she said, trying to pull away.

"But we've both waited for so long."

The look in his eye was feral, reminding her of a galler circling above a battlefield.

"This isn't real!"

"Was Nowhere real?" he asked.

That was all she needed to hear to break the illusion. She'd never called that place 'Nowhere' in front of Kazimir. She'd barely even spoken before Gold Grin killed the upyr.

With the blood dribbling down her neck, she closed her eyes and focused. Flames seemed to burst out of her very pores, exploding outward. When she opened her eyes, the vision of Kazimir turned to ash.

A crackling beneath her feet drew her attention down to the frost forming in the dirt. Snow flurries stirred along with the ash, and a light wind picked up, bringing with it an unbearable cold. Ice-covered tendrils shot out from the soil, frozen vines. They grasped Sora's ankles, rooting her into place.

She tugged, but the vines were too strong. She bent, grabbing hold of them with both hands, pulling and tearing, but still, nothing happened.

Then, the roof exploded in a shower of dust, sending her backward onto her rear. From the wreckage of Whitney's old home, rose a figure covered in moss and flora. Her long hair fell to the middle of her back, framing that perfect face.

"Nesilia!" Sora shouted. She thought that if she ever saw the Buried Goddess again, it would be accompanied by sheer terror, but instead, anger rose up within her like a sword.

"Sora, darling," the Buried Goddess spoke. It was a teasing, manipulative sound.

Sora's skin crawled like maggots. Where there had been one festering apple, there were now hundreds of them, larvae dancing upon each other in a macabre feast. She slapped and kicked, but her feet were solidly frozen in the ice, and soon her hands were, too.

"Don't look at me like that, child," Nesilia said. "What did you think—you'd leave me, and I'd just shrug?"

"You're not real, either."

"I am more real than the breath in your lungs," Nesilia said. Her voice was like thunder rolling across the farmlands. She took a step. "I'm more real than the skin on your bones. You let your guard down, Sora, and let me peek in. You and your little friends are in way over your heads."

"You're scared. You're scared because you thought you had me forever. But you learned that you're just as weak as the day Iam buried you beneath that mountain."

"How dare you speak to me like that!" Nesilia snapped. "And to think, I let you live. I could have snuffed you out and used your body—"

"You're a liar. A child, fearful of being alone." Sora was the one to advance this time. "You couldn't control me. Not when I know what I really am. With my blood, I'm more powerful—"

"You are nothing without me," Nesilia interrupted, voice making the earth quake. "You had your chance at greatness. It's sad—a pity, really. Now, you'll just die like all the rest."

"And you had your chance at atonement!" Sora's hands became balls of burning flame, and the ice melted away in an instant. She stood. "In case you forgot, I killed your ugly sister. Now, I'm going to kill you."

A smirk played at the corners of Nesilia's mouth. As she spoke, she strode toward Sora.

Sora didn't back down. Not one bit.

"Oh, you haven't heard, then?" Nesilia said.

"Heard what?" Sora said. "More of your lies?"

"You didn't kill her…"

The door of Whitney's old house remained one of the last standing pieces. It split open, and another woman came forth, floating like a specter.

"Madam Aihara?" Sora said, unable to hide the astonishment.

A ghostly laugh echoed. The old mystic's eyes were vibrant and purple. They carried a threat that needed no words.

"I am not that weak woman you called Ancient One," the mystic replied. "She's no more Ancient than the Webbed Woods—which we created." The being looked to Nesilia, who was now only an arm span from Sora, and the already cold air became like death.

"You remember my sister Bliss, don't you, Sora?" Nesilia said. "We've reconciled; come to a new understanding now that she's felt my pain, thanks to you. She now sees the true enemy."

"You lie!" Sora thrust her hand forward, and her fire was snuffed out before it had the chance.

"Hardly," Nesilia said. "Iam was always the one to twist words. I believe in honesty, sharp as a blade."

"It's this place.," Sora said, looking around. "It's Elsewhere. None of you live. You're all dead, and damned to this place forever."

"Then what does that make you?" Nesilia taunted.

The body of Aihara Na reached out her arm, and her fingertips grazed Sora's cheek. Sora shrank back, slapping at the hand.

"So many people, all claiming to have killed me," it said. "It's... hurtful." She affected a frown but it didnt' reach her smiling eyes.

"You're not real," Sora reiterated.

"Perhaps you know this form?" The image of Aihara Na shifted into a beautiful woman with skin the color of rich chocolate, like Torsten or Lucindur. "No... of course not, no one knows my true form, just the hideous beast."

The visage faded away, and in its place stood the horrifyingly hideous Queen Bliss in all her arachnid splendor.

"I killed you..." Sora whispered.

"When you swat at a spider, but you do not kill it, you only succeed in earning its scorn. Now, your world will burn."

"This isn't real," Sora whispered again. "I don't believe you."

"Why don't you come to see for yourself?" Nesilia taunted.

"Where?" Sora screamed. She tried again to conjure up a ball of flames but couldn't. "No!"

The ground rumbled again, sending Sora stumbling. She grabbed onto the fence post, but it broke off under her grip. Everything shook with such violent force, Sora felt like she was going to vibrate right out of her skin.

She stood there, looking down at the post with hers and Whitney's initials barely visible through years of dirt. She dropped the wood and buried her face in her hands as the world rattled around her. Falling to her knees, she shouted, "Go where!"

Her eyes shot open, and she found herself standing high above Yaolin City, looking down upon the place like a goddess upon her throne.

The streets were a mess, piles of dead strewn haphazardly, buildings burning, blood staining the waters of Lake Yaolin. The death wails of thousands rose up all around her like a blanket. Above, smoke and ash mixed with dark storm clouds. They swirled all around her, like the eye of a hurricane.

Sora tried to turn, but couldn't. She had to strain to see with her peripherals that she was surrounded by red stone parapets. The top of the Red Tower.

She took solace in the fact that this felt nothing like it had when she'd been possessed. She was seeing through Nesilia's eyes—that she was sure of—but she had no fear of Nowhere. However, she didn't know the why of it all. Was this what it meant to have a soul tie? And why now?

Nesilia's gaze tracked toward a mass of Panpingese and Glass soldiers, civilians, marching west down Xiahou Boulevard. Grimaurs lined the rooftops along their paths. Goblins wrestled over spilled supplies, unable to contain their excitement as they scavenged.

Then, all in unison, the thousands of humans glanced back at the top of the tower, grinning, their eyes black as pitch. It sent a bolt of lightning up Sora's spine.

"Governor Nantby is dead," Nesilia said. "Panping will fall within days."

Considering nobody was up there, Sora had to imagine she was addressing her. Was she letting her in?

"Sora," Nesilia said.

Hearing her own name startled her, but she didn't respond.

"Come now. Watch," Nesilia added.

Nesilia turned to look across the lake toward the wide cavern, which allowed entry from the ocean. In it, dark shadows swam. Massive things moving just below the surface, filled with tendrils. Wianu.

"Don't blink," Nesilia teased, as if Sora had any control over that.

"Where are they going?" Sora asked shakily.

"That doesn't concern you."

"Nesilia, it's not too late to stop this," Sora said. "I know what you felt. Alone. Betrayed. I've felt it, too. But you created this world as much as Iam did. Face him for leaving you, and leave the rest out of it."

Nesilia cackled. "I saw so much potential in you, but you really are pathetic. Soon, you will know what happens when you cross me," Nesilia warned.

Sora's chest felt like it was rent in two. One second, she was inside of Sigrid, the next, she was facing the upyr, cold hands around her throat.

"Your thieving friend will pay for all his transgressions," Nesilia said through Sigrid's lips. "I hope your night with him was memorable."

With that, Nesilia tossed Sora off the very tower her mother had once ruled from and where she had been born. Sora's stomach flipped and turned. She tried to scream but couldn't…

VI

THE THIEF

Whitney had always considered himself lucky. His whole life had been a game, and most times, he figured himself a winner. But lately, he just couldn't believe his rotten luck.

It wasn't just all the imprisonments, either—though that was embarrassing enough. Whitney Fierstown, World's Greatest Thief, caught and dungeoned by everyone from the former Wearer of White— which might at least be considered excusable—to Barty Darkings. That one could not be forgiven. Barty was a dastardly slob and a privileged, stuck-up bastard who made a fresh barrel of shog look enticing.

Apart from all of those, not excluding being trapped in Elsewhere itself by angry old gods, Whitney had very few people he could call friends. A dwarf was numbered amongst them. One was an actually-dead upyr. One, a blind, holy knight that could hardly tolerate him. Another was a musician who used a very dangerous and outlawed form of magic. A Glintish kid who wouldn't even talk to him. And lastly, the most important of them all… Sora.

He'd expected her to be in rough shape after suffering abuse at the hands of the Buried Goddess. But to see her now, lying on a bed in their ship, docked outside of Glinthaven, pouring sweat, and unconscious, Aquira curled up next to her… it was just too much. Her skin was like hot coals, hair matted down like she'd taken a swim in the Shellnak River.

A clump of it stuck to her moist neck, and Whitney pushed it away. Aquira shifted, but ultimately held her position of protection beside her true master and friend.

That poor wyvern had been through so much, too. But it seemed now, all her many injuries had healed. And there, beside Sora, Aquira felt at home. It made Whitney more than a little sad at the thought of how Gentry would respond to his friend returning to her former master.

He also feared how Gentry would respond to the fact that Whitney and Aquira, the two people—and yes, Aquira qualified as such—on Pantego he felt he could trust had abandoned him. Gentry had just begun talking to Whitney after he'd been left behind in Panping. Now, it happened again. The kid had begged to go with them to fight Nesilia, and Whitney lied straight to his face. And Aquira helped.

Whitney didn't expect to be forgiven, but sadness overwhelmed him at the thought of Aquira's potential rejection. She didn't know what she was doing. She just obeyed Whitney's commands like the good little murderous dragon-kin she was.

Or did she? Maybe she knew *exactly* what she was doing.

Whitney had long suspected the wyvern was smarter than anyone believed. She'd all but proven she understood and could communicate with him and Gentry back in Fettingborough after the Drav Cra raiders had shackled her. She led them right to the blacksmith, where Whitney was able to free her.

However, none of that mattered as much as Sora waking and finally being present with him. Had he been a lesser man, he'd be wondering if she was so disappointed in his love-making that it sent her into shock.

Or perhaps I was that good.

Gold Grin's former quarters, now belonging to Sora, were as immaculate as any Whitney had broken into across all of Pantego. Wood walls marked only by circular windows the size of one's head surrounded them, staring out into the Covenstan Depths. The floor was carpeted in luxurious silver furs as if a hundred foxes from Brotlebir had been laid down upon it. In fact, they probably were.

"Would you sit down, you're making me nervous," Lucindur said, seated in a plush chair situated diagonally from the bed.

Whitney hadn't stopped pacing since he'd carried Sora down from the main deck. How could he?

"I second that." Tum Tum sat cross-legged on the floor beside Lucindur, looking terribly uncomfortable.

"I've been waiting for her for six years," Whitney said, a harsh edge creeping into his tone. "Six years, Lucy! Then I find her, and she can't even say two words to me for weeks! Finally, she opens up, and we…" He stopped before revealing too much of their previous evening. And this… this happens. I don't know how much more of this my fragile heart can handle."

Tum Tum let out a haughty laugh that reverberated through an otherwise silent room.

"What is so funny?" Whitney demanded.

"Whitney Fierstown, nothing about you is fragile but your ego," Lucindur said. Whitney wasn't looking, but he could picture the smile on her face. Any other time, it would have been a welcomed sight.

"Why won't she wake up? What happened?" Whitney sat down on the bed, and Aquira shifted to rest her head on his thigh. "We were sleeping, and then she started shaking violently. Then, nothing."

"I don't know," Lucindur said softly. It did nothing to ease his mind.

"Ye remember in the north when Lucy was in straits just as dire?" Tum Tum asked. "Ye were actin crazy and babblin like this. Look at her now, would ye? She's fine as a fairy and twice as strong for it."

Whitney stared at Tum Tum for a minute before ignoring him and saying, "We were together… really together for the first time…" He looked around and added, "talking for the first time since… I don't know, Winde Port!" Whitney eyed Tum Tum, who returned a pitiful look.

A long breath passed before Whitney looked up at his companions, sadness evident on his face. "You don't think—"

Sora's words bounced around in his head, the worry that Nesilia might still be present in her mind somehow. *I'm going to destroy that vengeful, no-good, witch of a goddess.*

"No," Lucindur said.

"Think what?" Tum Tum asked head bouncing between the two of them. "What are ye thinkin?"

Lucindur stood and said, "What I think, no… what I *know*… is that what we did worked. The sacrifice made by Kazimir, and Teryngal, and all the others… it worked, and the Buried Goddess is long gone from Sora."

The Lightmancer always seemed to know what Whitney was thinking. It was unnerving and comforting all at once.

"But what if she isn't?" Whitney asked.

"Wait, wait," Tum Tum said. "Ye think she ain't gone? Oi, Fierstown, that's some madness right there. We all seen it—seen that witch explode into that fair-haired demon."

"Sure, we saw what happened with Sigrid," Whitney said. "But Nesilia's not *gone*. She just switched modes of transportation, so to speak. And then Sigrid disappeared. Just *poof.* And we don't know where she went, or even that Nesilia went with her. For all we know, Nesilia jumped right back into Sora and has just been waiting for one of us to turn our back long enough for her to drive a dagger through it."

"Poppycock," Tum Tum said with a dismissive wave. "If old Nessy were waitin for a chance at us, she had plenty while we traveled. She's a goddess for Meungor's sake."

"Then what!" Whitney shouted. "What is it?"

"What you have to understand—" Lucindur started, but a knock on the cabin's door saved Whitney from hearing another of her cryptic reasonings.

"What!" Whitney barked, but Lucindur beat him to the door.

"I'm so sorry," she said as she opened it. Whitney couldn't see who it was, but he didn't care either. "Oh, wonderful," Lucindur continued. "Thank you. Thank you very much."

Lucindur reached into a pouch on her side, and the sound of autlas jingled into an open palm. Then, there was the distinct sound of them being handed back.

"Are you sure?" Lucindur asked.

A deep voice said something Whitney couldn't understand, and then, "Good luck." The door shut, and when she turned around, a broad smile filled her face all the way to the eyes.

"Who was that?" Tum Tum asked.

"Better have been the gods-damned warden himself, knocking at such an hour," Whitney said. "And who is he to board my ship?"

"Yer ship?" Tum Tum scoffed.

"Goodness, Whitney, you are in rare form, aren't you?" Lucindur said. "*That* was Mr. Onepp. I told him to see me whether the sun or moon reigned. I knew there'd be very little sleep happening, anyhow."

Mr. Onepp was the purveyor of an inn just beyond the Gilded Bridge, though Whitney couldn't remember its name. Something in Glintish that didn't translate. He and Lucindur seemed to know each other well—which was one way of putting it.

From the moment they'd docked, and Mr. Onepp had met them with a bowl of warm stew and a pint of ale, all Whitney could think of was Torsten. Mr. Onepp was large—very large—and was more suited to be a warrior than an innkeeper. In Glinthaven, however, there really was no need for soldiers. Artists made the city as beautiful as it was boring for adventurers like Whitney.

"And what, pray tell, did *Mr. Onepp* want?" Whitney asked, frustrated.

"I'd asked him to have men scour the city for Talwyn and the others."

It'd been days since the party had returned to Glinthaven from the far, bitter North. With Sora keeping to herself in her cabin, with only Aquira for company, Whitney and Lucindur had resolved to track down what remained of the Pompare Troupe. Lucindur had refused to use her gift to locate them for fear that it might reopen the door and allow Nesilia or her horde of monsters to find them. Whitney knew she was right, but it was hard to think of poor Gentry out there like the orphan boy he'd once been, living under the Gilded Bridge.

"Turns out, Mr. Onepp is a very respected man in the community now," Lucindur said. "Very respected, indeed. He's had a veritable army out looking, and he believes he's found them."

"And you know him, how?" Whitney prodded. "How can we know he's trustworthy and not one of Nesilia's pawns."

"For starters, there aren't many evil men here in Glinthaven."

"Anywhere there's men breathing, there's evil," Whitney said.

"Secondly, he's Talwyn's father."

All air escaped the room, and there was a deafening silence.

Whitney thought about what a man his size might do if he found about that night in Fettingborough. The Glintish folk were weird when it came to their sexuality. He didn't know if he should be more frightened that he'd seen his daughter naked, or that he turned her down.

Finally, Tum Tum cleared his throat, and Lucindur started gathering her things.

"What are you doing?" Whitney asked.

She stopped only long enough to toss an incredulous glare Whitney's direction. "I'm going to see my daughter, and I think you should come, too. There's nothing more you can do until Sora wakes up, and regardless of what happened with Gentry, I believe you should be there when we find him."

"Come? No way. I'm not leaving. When Sora wakes up, I'll be standing right here." He jabbed a finger at the floor. "First thing she sees."

"Whit—" Lucindur started.

"I said, no!" Whitney immediately felt terrible for snapping, but this was Sora. There was no way he would ever leave her side again. He couldn't risk it.

"Ye don't think Elsewhere's gonna open neath her and gobble her up, do ye?" Tum Tum laughed before apparently realizing this wasn't the time for jokes. "It's just—I mean…"

Whitney lifted a hand. "I'm not leaving her."

"Suit yourself," Lucindur said, returning to her things.

Whitney stopped wearing lines in the carpet to stare down at Sora. She seemed peaceful. He remembered that version of her in Elsewhere before he added himself to the list of people to abandon her. So pure, innocent, and pretty.

"Why won't you wake up?" he whispered.

He felt Tum Tum edge up beside him. The dwarf didn't speak for a moment, but Whitney could tell he was trying to.

Tum Tum cleared his throat.

"Don't," Whitney said.

"Don't what?" the dwarf asked.

"Don't try to comfort me. It won't work."

"Whitney, I known ye longer than I care to admit. I seen ye at yer stupidest. I seen ye and she together, and apart. One thing I do know is yer better together. Another thing I know? Ye ain't givin up on her. And ye know what?"

A bout of silence passed as Whitney watched Sora breathe. Then he said, "What?"

"She'll know it, too. She's gonna be fine. Her brain's been mottled up with all this yig and shog about goddesses. She ain't slept anythin but fitful naps since the day that evil witch left her body. She's prolly just catchin up. Can't blame her none."

"I can't leave her again," Whitney said, voice cracking.

"I'll stay right here. Won't even sleep till ye get back. Ye have my word. But ye owe it to Gentry, and to yerself. Go with Lucy and see the lad. Make things right."

Whitney took a deep breath. He looked at Lucindur and let it out. She was just about to head for the door. He let his gaze shift back to Sora, then, finally, to Tum Tum. "All right, where's your bucket?"

"Bucket?" Tum Tum replied.

"You said you won't be leaving her side," Whitney said. "That means if you've got to piss or shog, you'll need a bucket."

Tum Tum let out a sharp laugh, slapped Whitney's arm, and said, "Go find the kid and don't ye worry about Sora. I care about her, too, ye know."

"Last chance," Lucindur said. She slung a brown, leather satchel over her shoulder, her other hand already on the doorknob.

"Don't leave the room," Whitney told Tum Tum. Then he rubbed Aquira's frills. "You either, eh, Girl?"

Aquira puffed her nostrils twice and nodded.

"Wait up!" Whitney called to Lucindur as he followed.

"Good decision," she said, smiling.

There was something intimidating about walking on roads paved with actual gold. There was also something insulting about it. To think of all the years Whitney had spent chasing the stuff, and here, the ancient swinlars decided it was so worthless, they'd just walk on it.

"Kind of pompous, don't you think?" Whitney said to Lucindur.

"What?" she asked.

"The gold. It's just gold, gold, gold, everywhere you look. It's like someone is trying to compensate for something."

"Oh, you mean like that massive spire sticking up from the Glass Castle in Yarrington?" Lucindur asked.

"Touché," Whitney said.

"Everybody here is exactly as wealthy as they need to be, and pursuing their passions. So why waste the gold on anything but looking at how pretty it is? It's all just metal, after all."

"That's a way to look at it. So, where are we going exactly?"

"According to Mr. Onepp's directions, it's not much farther."

Talwyn's father had tried to insist upon accompanying them. "It's dark, and I wouldn't want you getting lost," he'd said from his perch at the front desk at his dock-side inn, all the while, unable to peel his eyes from Lucindur's face.

Thankfully, Lucindur politely told him they'd be fine. Whitney thought it was more for his benefit and was okay with that.

"Does she know him?" Whitney asked.

"No," Lucindur answered very matter-of-factly. "It's common here in Glint. The physical act of making love is not frowned upon in the same ways it is in more… prudish lands. Sometimes, as is nature, children are conceived through the act, and we consider it a wonderful thing."

"Wasn't it difficult raising her without her father?"

"Children are reared by us all here. The burden, if it can be called that, is shared. Even those without children of their own find themselves playing the role of parent to others on regular occasion."

"Sounds awful," Whitney said under his breath.

"Plus, I had the Troupe."

"And you're sure it's them Mr. Onepp spotted?" Whitney asked.

"I gave him a pretty clear description," Lucindur said.

"Brown skin, dark hair? Dressed in bright colors?" Whitney said, observing all the happy locals roaming the streets as if the world wasn't going to shog beyond their pleasant little valley. "I'm sure that would be difficult to mistake around here."

Whitney could almost feel Lucindur's eyes roll. That made him smirk, albeit not for long.

Despite the haughtiness of the place, Myen Elnoir was beautiful, like no other city in the known world. The brilliantly-colored clothing of each passerby was like a thousand rainbows. They all wore jewelry, hanging from ears, noses, lips, eyebrows, cheeks, and more. The Glintish were expressive people, artistic people, proud people. Whitney wondered how someone so bland as Torsten could have shared anything in common with the inhabitants of this flamboyant city.

Music rose from behind so many doors it blended into one song. The incredible thing was just how harmonious it all sounded together. Had this been South Corner, Yarrington, all the various bards would have resulted in a hodgepodge, and sloppy arrangement of individual songs that—when merged—would have made him feel seasick. This… it felt orchestrated.

Even above them, posted on the archways that led from one side of the street to the other, men and women sat fiddling with all manner of musical instrument, each of them playing for no one in particular. Whitney even saw a child that could have been no older than five or six playing a woodwind of some sort. When Whitney was his age, he could barely remember his prayers.

Bright white globe lanterns hung from the bottoms of the arches, illuminating the whole city. Whitney eyed one as he crossed under it. He remembered them from his previous visit, but it hadn't occurred to him then that there were no flames inside. There was no flicker, no coruscating waves—just pure light.

It was well past dusk, but that didn't stop the artists from painting, or the dancers from dancing. Glinthaven felt like one big party, but without all the booze and debauchery. They did it because they loved it, not to find an escape from the cruelness of reality.

"Not much of a party," Whitney muttered to himself.

"What was that?" Lucindur asked, tearing his attention from the artists.

He glanced over. He'd nearly forgotten she was there. A smile was full upon her face as she traipsed through streets he guessed she'd been on plenty of times before. It'd been a long time since he'd seen Lucindur so happy. Come to think of it, he wasn't sure he ever had.

"You seem pleased," Whitney said.

"Oh, I'm sorry, Whitney," she said. "I know you're upset."

"No, no. Look," he said, placing a hand on her forearm, "I don't expect the world to shut down because Whitney Fierstown is a wee bit sad. So, what is it—happy to be home? Or are you smitten?"

"Smitten!" Lucindur gasped.

"I saw that smile on your face after Mr. Onepp left the room.

Besides, you clearly have history."

Lucindur turned away. "He's a wonderful man. So kind, and caring."

A melancholy smile passed over Whitney's own face. He was happy Lucindur had seemingly found someone to connect with—or reconnect as fate would have it. Before today, he'd never heard a thing about Talwyn's father. However, as pleased as he was for Lucindur, the thought only furthered his resolve that he never should have left Sora's side.

"I've made a mistake," Whitney said.

"Oh?" Lucindur said, her smile downturning slightly.

"I need to go back to Sora."

"Don't be silly. Mr. Onepp said the Troupe is just beyond that portal." She pointed to a wide archway in the center of the street. Stairs climbed to a flattened, golden courtyard, and through the opening, Whitney noted the Pikeback Mountains in the distance.

"They're outside the city?" Whitney asked.

"Of course, they are," Lucindur said, slapping a palm to her forehead. "How foolish could we be? They are following the Pompare way. 'Never sleep within the city in which you're performing.'"

The Pompares taught the Troupe to arrive like magic, seemingly out of nowhere, to dazzle and captivate before disappearing once again into the night. However, here in Myen Elnoir, where everyone was a musician, artist, dancer, actor, or some other such entertainer, Whitney didn't see the point.

"No better way to honor the dead, I guess," Whitney said as they began their ascent to the courtyard.

At the top, he stopped in the middle of the portal and spun a slow circle. Not many things had the power to awe someone as worldly as Whitney, but this did it. From so high up, he could see the whole of Myen Elnoir. He'd been to the Glintish capital before, but he'd never seen it like this. The portal was far from anywhere he'd frequented in the past, never straying much farther than the Western arches. Why would he? It was the one place in Pantego he never could manage to steal a yigging thing.

However, he'd always noted how the city border was utterly unguarded. No walls were built up, nor watchtowers dotting the fringes.

Even within, despite the presence of Glass soldiers at scattered outposts, the feeling of always being watched that existed everywhere else in the Kingdom was absent.

They passed by benches sat upon by men and women deep in passionate kisses, though, it wasn't obscene or vulgar. There was a quality these people had—purity. He even recalled one of the first times he'd really met Talwyn, garbed in a soaking wet, see-through dress. She was gorgeous, tempting even... but there was nothing untoward about her.

"Tal," Lucindur said softly.

Whitney blushed, worried that Lucindur might have seen his thoughts. But then, he followed her line of sight down into the rocky landscape. At least they hadn't fully obeyed the Pompare method, having set up camp only just beyond the city on a low mesa. He saw her too, and Benon, and the others. Squinting, he suspected the small one beside the actors was Gentry. He and Benon jested back and forth as they ate around a campfire.

They weren't far off the road, where a merchant caravan was just arriving for the evening. Three carts, all pulled by Panpingese Long-hairs, giant hoofs clomping in the mud.

"Oh, Franny's food," Whitney groaned, eying the fire. "I wonder what she's cooking."

"Let's go find out, shall we?" Lucindur said, starting off toward the ramp, which led back down on the other side.

Whitney, however, stayed rooted to the spot. His mind brought him back to the battle inside the Citadel and all those powerful upyr who'd died facing Nesilia. Then to the dark cloud south of them, which somehow seemed not to be spreading here.

"Maybe we should leave them," he said.

Lucindur stopped and whipped around, eyeing Whitney quizzically. "Leave them?"

"You remember what you told me that night while we sipped Breklian brandy after talking with Modera?"

Her expression let him know she didn't.

"You said the reason Modera Pompare wanted me to take care of Gentry was that before I came around, he wouldn't even talk to anyone. Right?"

"Well, sure, but—"

"Look at him out there," Whitney interrupted. "Clearly, he's happy. Doing what he loves and what he's best at. He doesn't need me, or you, or anyone. Why would I want to disturb that?"

"You made a promise," Lucindur argued.

"Look at them, Luce. They are happy. Even Talwyn. And they're safe. If we go out there, Gentry will be furious with us for having left him here. Even if he forgives us, he'll want to join us in whatever comes next. He can't. I can't let him."

"And what does come next?" she asked. "I only agreed to help you save Sora, and we did. That Troupe, that's my family. That's where I belong."

"Oh, stop it. I know you want to go after Nesilia for all she's done. All my life, I wanted to travel and perform… then, it finally happens, and I end up in a Troupe with the last Lightmancer anybody knows about at the precise time when the only way I'd find Sora is with magic. You figured out how to separate Nesilia from her hosts. So, we need you."

Lucindur's lips parted like she wanted to speak, but nothing came out. Instead, she glanced back over her shoulder at the camp."

"This place… it's like nothing evil has touched it since… well, ever," Whitney went on. "How can we take them away from here? Maybe Nesilia won't even care about this place, it's no threat."

Lucindur continued to watch them as he spoke.

"And you," Whitney continued. "If you go down there, and you see Talwyn face to face, you won't be able to leave. Especially not after we came so close to dying up north. And if you do leave, you're not going to be yourself. You'll be distracted. We can't have you distracted if we have any hope of finding and stopping Nesilia."

Lucindur closed her eyes, then let her head hang. Whitney took a few steps until he was standing side by side with her, the beautiful snow-capped mountains stretched out before them.

"We saw them, right?" Whitney said, lightly elbowing Lucindur. "They are happy. Healthy. Alive. Let's keep it that way. If we win and defeat Nesilia, you can come back here."

"And if we fail?" Lucindur asked.

"At least they'll be here with smiles on their faces, instead of horrorstricken like we'll likely be. It's what I like to call a 'win-win.'"

"One of those sounds less like winning to me," Lucindur grumbled.

"Oh, Elsewhere isn't that bad."

"When did you start caring about others, Whitney Fierstown?" she asked.

"It was a cold night in Troborough. She'd been in labor for hours, and my mother was pushing—"

"Okay, enough of that," Lucindur said, scowling. "I don't like it."

"Like it or not, it seems only right."

Lucindur's response was cut off by a voice calling out in Panpingese.

"Wei!"

The merchants and their wagons were ascending the incline and causing a ruckus. People moved aside while the cart fought to find traction on the slick, golden streets.

"Keep it down!" Whitney shouted, glaring at the driver. A hood cast a shadow over his face.

Lucindur pulled Whitney aside, giving the merchants a wide berth.

"They'll be safe here, Lucy," Whitney said.

"There's nowhere they'll be safe," Lucindur said. "Not with Nesilia out there and ready to destroy everyone. We can protect them."

"Like we did Kazimir and the others?"

Behind them, the wagon came to an abrupt halt. The horses whinnied, and metal clanged.

Whitney shifted his gaze to the driver again. Something was wrong... The man's eyes... He wore leather armor dotted by bronze rivets—the mark of one capable of defending the goods beneath the wagon's tarpaulin.

Hopping down from his bench, he stared at Lucindur and said, "How dare you speak the Lady's name." His voice was like gurgling water, and before Whitney could respond, another—this one dressed in plain clothes—leaped out from behind a satin curtain and snatched Lucindur around the neck, pulling her back toward the wagon.

Whitney reached for his weapons, but a knife to Lucindur's throat and a threat from the driver made him pause.

"Touch that, and she bleeds out, feeding the earth and strengthening our Lady," the driver said.

Whitney began to tell him there was gold beneath their feet and not dirt, but thought better of it.

"What do you want?" Whitney said.

He looked around, hoping someone would see what was happening and come to their aid, but no one seemed to notice. They were all too busy with their art and music and kissing and peace.

"You think you've stayed hidden, but she knows where you are now," the driver went on, "She always knows. No one is safe when you are around, Whitney Fierstown."

Beneath the hood, eyes, black as night and thrice as frightening, bore pinprick holes in Whitney's own. The veins around the man's temples and forehead pulsated, skin pallid, and cold-looking.

Whitney knew what he was looking at without really knowing—a man possessed. Two men possessed. How had she found them? There was no time to wonder.

"Nesilia wants me?" he said. "Then why don't you let my friend go, and you can have me instead?"

"Our Lady desires your life by her own hands," the possessed merchant said. "You owe her for stealing her prized host."

"So, throw me in your little wagon and take me to her."

"We know of your prowess, thief," the demon said. "There's no prison that can hold you."

It was a ridiculous moment for pride, but Whitney couldn't help it. He sneered. "Perhaps she's forgotten that I've already killed one goddess. I'd love to do it again."

The merchants laughed. "You may be a master thief, but you killed nothing. "

"Plenty of corpses would argue that. I thought Nesilia wanted me for herself? You demons really should get your stories straight." He hoped the quavering in his voice didn't betray the fear he felt in spite of his bravado. "Just let my friend go, and I'll come quietly."

Just then, a drum pounded and, with a loud shout, a performer began dancing. The sound put the merchants' horses into a light frenzy. It was enough for Lucindur and Whitney to react.

Lucindur stomped down on her captive's foot while Whitney lunged at the driver. He hoped Lucy had freed herself, and the sounds of battle beside him gave him assurance. She was fighting back.

Whitney threw a punch that caught the driver in the ribs, but the driver was barely affected. He responded with a punch of his own, doubling Whitney over. Whitney swore, but there was no breath in his lungs. They were tangled up, Whitney bent, and the driver beating against his back. Whitney rushed in and caught the driver with his shoulder, shoving him hard into the side of the wagon.

The horses bucked and neighed, pulling the cart forward a bit. Whitney rose, still gasping for air, but he managed to seize hold of the driver's hood and slam his head into the wagon wheel. The Panpingese man took it like a kiss and returned with an elbow to Whitney's jaw. The taste of blood filled his mouth, and he could feel it dribbling down his chin.

Now, those who hadn't been paying attention were beginning to take notice, calling for guards.

Whitney reached again for his daggers but received a kick to his shin, followed by an uppercut that made him stagger backward.

"You! Stop, now!" A Glass guard called from still some distance. There may not have been many of them around the city, but these came quickly, with the sounds of swords slipping from sheaths.

"They attacked us! They're trying to steal our goods!" the driver shouted, feigning terror with the acting prowess of any member of the Pompare Troupe.

Whitney tried to argue, but blood forced itself down his throat. Upon looking up, he saw that the man's eyes had returned to normal, and he was, indeed, beating up an innocent merchant.

"It's not like that!" Whitney tried to say, but it sounded like nonsense.

"We've gotta go," Lucindur called out, pulling herself free from the other merchant's grip.

It looked like she'd held her own, using her salfio to defend herself until now they fought over it. He, too, pretended to be but a simple trader, and she ripped the instrument away from him.

Or maybe, they really were no longer possessed? The guards wouldn't care either way.

Lucindur took Whitney by the hand and bolted.

"What in Elsewhere was that?" Whitney asked.

"They were possessed by demons," Lucindur replied.

"I figured that much!"

Guards rushed at them from the front now, and Whitney took control and turned them pushing through a band of musicians.

"Follow me," he said. "Running from guards is my speci-al-ity."

"Clearly, the rumors of Panping's fate are true," Lucindur said, ignoring him. "The feeling in my heart after we left the Citadel didn't lie. Elsewhere is broken."

"Great. And we're her number one targets." Whitney led them down the stairs and into an alley. He'd zig-zag and confuse the untested guards. In other places, he'd take the sewers, but he didn't know this city's infrastructure well.

He went to drag Lucindur around a corner, but she resisted. Her feet slid.

"Lucy!" He glanced back and saw her standing, solemn, clutching her salfio against her chest.

"You're right. It's clear now," she said. "We have to leave them. They won't be safe with us."

"Good." He extended his hand toward her and listened for the guards. If Nesilia already had people around here in her possession, they'd be live bait locked up in a cell.

"C'mon," he said. "I won't even say I told you so, but we have to get back to the *Reba*."

Lucindur closed her eyes. "I promised you a beautiful world, my daughter," she said. "I promised you a future of light. Even if I don't want to go, even if I don't want to fight the fight the first Lightmancers said we would so long ago, that is how I know that I must. I won't fail you."

"You'll be back here soon," Whitney said, his feet twitching to run. "I promise."

"Even if I'm not, Talwyn will know I wished to be." She strummed a chord on her salfio with her fingernails. Even in all the chaos, the sound was spectacular, vibrating right down to Whitney's core. "She'll feel my sound."

"She sure will," Whitney said, unsure if he believed it. "Now, let's go. We have a goddess to kill."

He took her hand just as the steel armor of a Glass soldier appeared at the mouth of the alley. Then, he did what he did best. Escaped.

VII

THE MYSTIC

Sora heard her name like she had so many times before. Always it was Whitney, beckoning her from the depths. "Sora!"

But where was he?

She could still hear Nesilia's mad cackle as hands seized her. Sora slapped at them, desperate to be free. Feeling the call of Elsewhere, she tried again and felt the warmth of flames wreathing her hands, but it didn't matter.

"Sora, stop!"

She clenched her eyes shut. When he shouted again, they snapped open, and she saw Whitney standing next to her, hands firmly on her shoulders. He cowered back, his face aglow with orange light from the blaze burning in her own hands.

"Whit?," she said, letting the fire die away.

"It's okay, you're here now. You're better. I've got you." Whitney brushed the hair away from her face. "I've got you."

She sat forward, taking in her surroundings. She was still on the *Reba*, and it swayed as if they were back sailing on the Covenstan Depths.

"What the yig happened?" Whitney asked, still swiping at her hair, and running his hand over her face and neck.

It felt good, him touching her, like all the horrors of the world were cast off, even if only for a moment. Then they all came rushing back like a torrent.

"I don't know. I don't know at all." Her bed was soaked, and so was she. Sweat beaded under her eyes, on her palms. It was so cold despite the perspiration, or perhaps because of it.

She wore only a thin undergarment. Though it wasn't lewd, she felt it sticking to her and pushed herself off the bed. She accidentally shoved Whitney aside, then strode across the room. "Nesilia..."

"Oh, no. Not again," Whitney said.

"I'm gettin fed up with that witch," Tum Tum said, Aquira resting on his broad shoulders. Sora whipped around and realized that he'd been there the whole time. She grabbed her kimono from the plush chair and tossed it on.

"What now?" Whitney asked, taking her by the hand and leading her to sit.

As they walked, the ship lurched.

"Where are we? Are we moving?" Sora asked.

"It's a long story, but Nesilia knows where we are," Whitney said.

"What? She... This is my fault..."

"Did you see her? Do you know where she is?" Whitney asked.

"Where are we going?" Sora asked.

"We just had to get away from the city. We had... trouble."

Aquira leaped down from her perch and curled up on Sora's lap.

"What do ye know, Girly?" Tum Tum asked.

"I saw Nesilia and..." Her throat was parched. She smacked her lips, licked them, but still couldn't get the words out.

"And what? What did she do to you?" Whitney asked. He must have noticed her struggle because he retrieved a mug from the cartographer's table and filled it from another container in the corner.

Sora drank deeply, and almost spat the liquid out when she tasted the bitterness of the Glintish ale. She coughed a few times, then said, "She wasn't alone."

"Her army? More grimaurs? Goblins?"

"Thousands of Panpingese people, possessed by demons of Elsewhere. Slaves to her. And wianu, many of them. Broken free from their prison in the Citadel." She knew she was talking fast, and she felt out of breath, but the images still overwhelmed her.

"Aye, that be great," Tum Tum groaned. "Those slimy monsters."

"Is that it?" Whitney said. "We already beat all that—well, minus the possessed. That's new everywhere, apparently. But, I'd rather deal with scrawny Panpingese than Drav Cra beserkers."

"That's not all." Sora pulled her kimono tightly around her, then stroked Aquira's back. "Queen Bliss," she said softly.

"What?" Whitney questioned, eyes going wide.

"Queen Bliss," Sora repeated.

What followed was silence, thick as blood.

"Sure…" Whitney said, voice lilting, skeptical. "But we saw her in Nowhere, too, remember? She chased us—I thought we were dead… but it was just Nesilia playing games with our minds."

"No," Sora said, terse. "This was different. They're working together now. I felt it… and Whitney—"

She thought about telling him about Kazimir, but she knew that part wasn't real. It would only hurt him. It was clear that Troborough was a vision of Elsewhere—she'd seen it plenty of times in her mind and even once with Whitney. But Panping, that was as real as the ground beneath her.

She knew now that Nesilia wasn't inside of her—but the soul tie had to be real. She was tethered to the goddess like a dog on a leash, and she couldn't escape the worry that she, herself, was the dog.

"It was Troborough," she said. "But not Troborough-Troborough, and they were both there. Torsten was there."

"Father Drimmond," Whitney whispered. "Fake Torsten. Shog in a barrel, Sora. You were in Elsewhere. *My* Elsewhere."

"I think so, too. It was just as real as it had been—but there were no monsters this time, except…" She again thought of mentioning Kazimir, but after a long hesitation, she said, "Bliss was in Aihara Na's body. The mystic Ancient One. I know it was really her, too. I just know. I can't explain how, but I do."

"Could've been a trick of the mind," Tum Tum offered. "Them mystics be sneaky."

Sora shot him a gelid glare.

"Present company excluded, course."

"Okay, I want you to tell us everything—but wait…" Whitney pointed to the door. "Tum Tum, can you go wake Lucindur?"

"I'll get her. Need to check on the sails, anyway."

After Tum Tum disappeared, Whitney took Sora by the hand. "Listen, Sora, we're going to stop her," he said. "For what she did to you and what she's planning. We have to. Lucindur and I agreed. We're going to find her again and finish her this time."

Sora nodded. "I'm scared."

"Yigging right, you are. We all are. But when has a little fear stopped us?" He squeezed her hand. "We killed Bliss once. We *exorcised* Nesilia. We've won, over and over again. You know who should be scared? Yeah, that's right, the Buried-yigging-Goddess should be terrified. Shaking in Sigrid's skin."

Sora offered a hollow grin.

"Just promise me something," Whitney said.

"Anything," she said.

"Promise you forgive me?" Whitney said.

"Whit—"

"I just need to hear you say it."

Sora looked down for a moment.

"I know I shouldn't have left Troborough," he said. "I shouldn't have abandoned you. You should hate me."

Sora realized that Whitney misunderstood her movement.

"I thought last night said all I needed to. Do you even remember?" she said. "Wait… last night really happened, right?"

"I thought it was pretty memorable," Whitney said, smirking.

"Well, then you know me. Would I do… that… with someone I hate? Of course, I forgive you," she said, wiping a tear. "And I love you. More than anything." She stood and threw her arms around him just as Tum Tum re-entered the room with Lucindur in tow.

"Sora," Lucindur said, bowing her head. "Good to see you up."

"Good to see you as well," Sora said.

"Oh, and she speaks!" Lucindur joked. "How are you feeling?"

"Better," she said.

Realizing she was still hugging Whitney, she let him go and dropped to the flats of her feet. No other words came to mind. Sora and Lucindur barely knew each other. They'd spent less than a month together sailing back from Brekliodad, and Sora had said less than a sentence, cumulatively, during that time. All Sora knew was that she was a practitioner of Lightmancery, old magic that the tomes in Wetzel's cabin and the Red Tower all said was extinct.

They said the Buried Goddess was gone as well, Sora thought. *And the mystics...*

"Aye, well. We're runnin out of time for pleasantries," Tum Tum said. "Let's get killin gods. Tell us what ye know."

Sora couldn't take her eyes off Lucindur, wondering how much she could be trusted. Sure, she'd been there when Whitney had saved her from Nesilia in the Citadel, and she'd played her part, but so had Kazimir, and if he'd still been alive, Sora wouldn't trust him.

The Lightmancer spoke up as if reading Sora's mind.

"I know we don't know each other well, dear," she said, "but I know how wonderful Whitney thinks you are, and how wonderful we think Whitney is, despite his mouth."

"Hey!" Whitney protested.

Lucindur ignored him and went on. "I hope his trust goes both ways?"

"My home..." Sora said.

"Troborough?" Lucindur asked.

It was then that Sora realized she wasn't talking about Troborough but Panping.

"The darkness on the horizon speaks of the condition of Yaolin City," Sora said.

"I thought as much."

"It's worse than you can imagine," Sora continued. "Nesilia's following is growing. It's not just fire—there's death everywhere. *Everywhere.* And the demons. How do you beat an army who possesses bodies they hold in no regard?"

"More possessed?" Lucindur said. She crossed the room, shaking her head. "We encountered some in Myen Elnoir when we..." A deep pain rippled across her features. "All I know is she wants us dead."

"She said as much when she spoke to me," Sora said. "Whitney, especially."

"Wait, what?" Whitney asked.

"She blames you for taking my body from her. For taking *me* from her. She thought she almost had me on her side."

"Well then, she clearly doesn't know you."

Sora looked to him, biting her lip. "That's the thing, Whit, she almost did. She's so powerful now. So dominating. I don't know who'd be able to resist her…" Sora's jaw clenched, and her fists balled involuntarily.

Whitney grasped her hand. "You did. We will." He released her and strode into the center of the room. "She has another thing coming if she thinks she can hunt me down. Many have tried."

"Aye!" Tum Tum attested.

"Now's not the time for senseless bravado," Lucindur remarked. That pain returned to her eyes, more profound this time. Then, low but loud enough for Sora to overhear, she said, "We know what's at stake…"

"It wasn't senseless," Whitney said under his breath. "So, we know where she is now, but how do we stop her and make sure she can never hurt Sora again."

"She's in Panping, aye?" Tum Tum said. "How bout another one of them trinkets we used to trap her the first time? We sneak into Yaolin—"

"Sneak passed thousands of demons?" Sora said.

"An easy task when you've already encountered the Whispering Wizards," Whitney boasted, "Only, there are no more bar guais. That one we used in the Citadel… that was the last one, or at least, that's what Kai said."

"Kai?" Sora asked. A sudden twinge of guilt flooded her as she thought about the boy. Then it struck her—that must have been how Whitney found out who her true parents were.

"You saw Kai?" she asked. "Where is he? Is he okay?"

Whitney's head lowered, and Sora's heart sank. She knew what he was going to say before it came out. "Dead."

Sora listened in the relative silence as waves slapped the sides of the ship. Then, unable to look Whitney in the eye, she asked, "Did… did you and Kazimir kill—"

"Whoa! Sora, no. Wasn't us. It was Gold Grin."

The mere mention of the pirate king sent a chill through Sora that had nothing to do with perspiration. Her gaze flitted toward the bed, where in this very cabin, Nesilia had taken control of her, made her do things. She could still see it all clearly. Feel it… she shuddered.

"Then another person deserves our revenge on Nesilia," she growled, hoping nobody had noticed her reaction.

Whitney cleared his throat. He eyed her with gentle suspicion but didn't push. "And we'll get it," he said.

Tum Tum stepped forward. "So, it won't be the bar guai. How we gonna stop her?"

"I don't know," Sora admitted. "You saw how powerful she was in me. Now, she has an immortal upyr as a host."

"I've been thinking about this since the Citadel," Lucindur said.

"Oh yeah?" Whitney asked. "I knew you weren't going to abandon this heroic quest."

Lucindur stared blankly at him, and the smile left his face. Sora made a mental note to learn that trick.

"As I understand it," the Lightmancer said, "Nesilia is subject to the weaknesses of her host. That is what I felt when I entered her mind. Yes, Sora?"

"I... I don't know for sure with Sigrid," Sora said. "But I think so. Yeah. She definitely had my strengths."

"What about sunlight?" Lucindur offered.

"That won't kill her," Whitney said. "It'll kill Sigrid, but Nesilia can just pop into another body. We need to *contain* her in something as powerful as a bar guai."

"Would any of them treasures ye've hidden round Pantego help?" Tum Tum asked.

Whitney scratched his chin. "There is the splintered staff..." he said, hanging on the last word.

"It has to be as powerful as the life force of countless ancient mystics," Sora said. "Able to tap directly into the magic of Elsewhere. Whitney, now is the time to be honest. If you have anything like that hidden, you'd know it."

He opened his mouth, stopped himself. Then he did it again. The third time, he was left standing silently, still scratching his chin.

"The bar guai can't be the only magical artifact in the world powerful enough to store a soul like hers," Lucindur said. "We have to trust Kazimir knew that was the best way."

"Trust *him*," Sora remarked.

"Yeah him," Whitney said. "Whatever he was, he was the oldest of us by... Iam-knows-how-many-centuries. He probably watched the God Feud. He knew. The Well of Wisdom told us so."

"He entered the Well of Wisdom?" Sora asked, incredulous. The thought of an upyr communing with such a sacred source made her uneasy. It was there, in those waters, where she learned who she truly was. And it was there she learned what she really cared about. The insufferable, handsome, annoying, charming man standing across from her defending an upyr. "I don't believe it."

"So, did I," Whitney said, and that gave Sora pause. "I don't know why the mystics called it that. I didn't learn anything in there."

"Then you weren't paying attention," Sora snapped, unintentionally.

"Enough, you two," Lucindur said. "We have to stay focused. I know of nothing in this region. Even the instruments of the eldest Lightmancers were destroyed long ago."

"Hmmmmm," Tum Tum said, finally breaking his silence. He stroked his scraggly black beard, then walked toward the outer wall of the cabin and stared through one of the low, circular windows.

They all looked to him.

"What is it?" Sora asked.

"Might be nothin."

"Might be everything," Whitney said. "Spit it out."

"Well, my people have a legend—might be just that. Tale tells of a stone held by the King of the Three Kingdoms. They call it the Brike Stone, after one of me own. Supposed to be, miner named Brike Sledgeborne made a deal with a dragon. If it helped him dig a new home far from the grasp of humans, it could have all their riches. But he tricked the beast, and it tricked him. Brike didn't get to live in his new home, and the Dragon got no riches. Instead, they were both damned to see what they wanted for all eternity and never get it, their souls bound to the dragon's heart. I don't know, sounds made up, now that I'm sayin it. It's prolly just a big ol ruby."

"No," Lucindur said. "That's good. I've heard the tale, too."

"The Brike Stone?" Whitney asked. "Sounds like hogwash. I think if such a thing existed, I'd have tried to steal it."

"I'm sure you haven't heard of *every* treasure in Pantego," Sora said.

Whitney appeared wounded just by the very thought. "I guess that's possible. Dwarves do tend to talk and sing about nonsense and get me zoning out." He glanced at Tum Tum. "No offense."

"None taken. That be very true."

Lucindur ignored them and lifted her salfio off her back. She started to play and to sing. It wasn't magical, or at least, didn't seem to be. But her pretty voice and the pure sound of her strings had Sora instantly absorbed.

Strike, strike, went the pickaxe O' Brike
    Gold, and iron, and silver alike
    Piles and piles like never before
    Fell at the feet of the youngest Sledgeborne
    It was cold, he was tired, but he'd never abate
    Beneath miles of stone lay the call of his fate
    T'was none of the goodies that he'd mined before
    Which fell at the feet of the youngest Sledgeborne

She slowed down and closed her eyes as if deep in thought.

"Aye, that be a classic!" A huge smile appeared on Tum Tum's lips as he took the lead, bobbing his head and singing the words way out of tune. Lucindur smiled as she went along with him.

Strike, strike, went the pickaxe O' Brike
    Gold, and iron, and silver alike
    Grumble, grumble, the mountain did rumble
    As a monster bore down, Balonhearth crumbled

Outside, far above, where the beasts of air fly
    Brike found the source of a terrible cry
    The dragon did land; there was no time to warn
    So he took up his pickaxe, the youngest Sledgeborne

. . .

"I heard your beckon, I heard your call
   I'll give you your home, in exchange for your gold"
   The dragon did taunt, and the dragon did spur
   He'd never expected what was to occur

Strike, strike, went the pickaxe O'Brike
   A home was made, but the home wasn't right
   "I'll take the home, too," the dragon did say
   "And I'll keep the gold," said Brike clear as day

Strike, strike, went the pickaxe O'Brike
   The dragon's heart on the end of a spike
   But there was a price; Brike did pay a toll
   The cost was steep; the cost was his soul

"That was beautiful," Sora said.

"Oh, yeah. Splendid. More singing," Whitney groaned. Then he turned to Tum Tum and asked, "Do you know where it is—this Brike Stone? Or do you just know a dusty old tune?"

"So moody," Tum Tum said.

"The world's about to end, and you two are singing songs. I thought at least the salfio would do its little twinkly lights thing."

"You're insufferable," Lucindur said.

"Isn't he?" Sora added, stifling a snicker.

"It's why you love me," Whitney said. "Now, the stone?"

"Well, I never seen it with me own eyes, but I hear King Lorgit Cragrock has it in the Iron Bank—one of his many, but most-prized treasures. Like I said, probably just a big ruby, but it's heavily guarded by the craziest and fiercest of dwarves. The clanbreakers. Spiky armor, shog-shucking crazy."

"Sounds scary," Whitney said. "Nothing more frightening than half-pint men spinning with axes."

"Watch yer yiggin mouth," Tum Tum warned.

"Focus. Both of you," Sora said. "Tum Tum, do you know the way?"

"Wait a second," Whitney interjected. "We are just going to go off into Dwarfland because of some song? How do we know this stone really exists, and if it does, that it'll even do anything? I know what you all think of my old profession, and yes, I said *profession*, but I feel like I'd have heard of this."

"Or, maybe no thief was dumb enough to go after the Iron Bank," Tum Tum argued. "It's never been robbed. Never even been attempted."

"There's nothing I'm not dumb enough to do," Whitney said, probably not realizing it.

"You have a better idea?" Sora asked.

Whitney's lip twisted. "Well, no—"

"Then this is all we have. We can sit here and do nothing, waiting for Nesilia to send more demons after us, or we can go find something relatively close by that might... *might* have a chance at stopping her. And if not, we'll find something else. I won't stop..." She took a deep, shaky breath. "*We* can't stop until she's gone."

"Close by?" Whitney scoffed. "It's halfway across the yigging world.

"Closer than Yarrington," Sora said. "Closer than a lot of places, at that. Besides, Whitney, we have no other choice. By sea, it won't be that bad, we'll be to Yevet Cove sooner than later, and from there, it's a short walk."

Whitney stared, incredulous, then ran a hand through his hair. It had grown long since the last time they'd been together. Sora thought she liked it.

"Well, if you were trying to tempt me by saying all that stuff about dumb thieves, it worked. You can get us there?"

"As Sora said, it's a few days sail across the Covenstan Depths, then a short climb. But the entry ain't too far away."

"But, you can get us there?"

"Aye."

Whitney clapped his hands. "Then, what are we waiting for?

VIII

THE KNIGHT

In recent times, Torsten hadn't imagined approaching the gates of Latiapur except at the lead of an army. It wouldn't be like last time, serving under King Liam, when the Black Sands were conquered and their former Caleef bent the knee. They hadn't stayed long then. Not even to watch the tournament hosted in honor of King Liam, where Muskigo's rise to fame had begun. There'd been too many other, more pressing matters at hand.

Deep down, however, he did always hate the kinship he'd felt with the Shesaitju. How disciplined and strict they were. How dedicated to the art of fighting—and for them, it truly was an art. He hated how he felt more in common with them than most of the nobles in Old Yarrington. More in common with heathens who worshipped the sea than the people he'd grown up around.

When he'd first battled Muskigo, Torsten saw how, if it hadn't been for Uriah Davies' guidance, he would have easily become like the afhem—bent on vengeance, without boundaries, and willing to kill innocents in the name of victory. And as he approached the city of their new Caleef, he wondered if those feelings had been what pushed him to despise the man so viciously.

Now, the fate of his entire world hinged on Muskigo's daughter. A stranger. And the only thing Torsten knew about her was how soundly she'd routed Sir Nikserof's army before supposedly rising from the dead, chosen by her people's God of Sand and Sea.

She'd be another foreign Queen to enter the hallowed halls of the Glass Castle. Only, unlike Oleander, Mahraveh wasn't merely hard and forceful—she was a warrior. A commander. Liam had the heart to stand up to his betrothed, but Torsten knew Pi well enough to know that he wouldn't. Couldn't.

Mahraveh was all the things Oleander was, and older than him.

To have any hope of defeating Nesilia, they would be handing over the Glass Kingdom itself.

"Are you okay, Sir Unger?" Lucas asked.

"Huh?" Torsten glanced up. They were atop a black dune looking down over Latiapur and a field of stacked clay buildings. Along the back, sharp cliffs rose, topped by a grand, domed palace exceeded only by the Glass Castle in pure magnitude of human engineering.

"You stopped."

"Oh." Torsten breathed in a mouthful of the hot, musty air. The desert was unforgiving, and he was a much younger man when last he was there. "Just thinking."

"About what we saw?" Lucas asked. "It's all I've been thinking about. Their eyes. I've never witnessed such evil."

"Weirdly enough, no. I've seen evil. Plenty of it. That was awful, but possession isn't surprising. It's so much worse when a man grows impure all on his own.."

"Those people could have been strong enough, faithful enough to resist possession. Like you'd been."

Torsten chuckled. "I'm beginning to think it's just stubbornness. But I've seen what happens when the boundaries of Elsewhere tear. The mystics often pushed too far in their war against us, and some fell to demons. Even Wren the Holy couldn't save some of them."

Lucas seemed to shudder at the thought. He turned his attention back to the impressive Shesaitju capital, with a marketplace so bustling and colorful, it was hard to believe.

"Then what is it, Sir?" Lucas asked. "I've known you long enough to know when you're troubled."

"A desire to turn around," Torsten admitted.

"What?"

"I understand the wisdom of this marriage. Uniting our people in a way that binds blood and fates together. Muskigo wouldn't have offered it if it wasn't the right strategic move. He would have hated selling his daughter too much."

"I'm not sure what you're trying to say, Sir."

"Once they are lawfully joined under the Light of Iam, the Glass Kingdom we know dies," Torsten said. "Muskigo will get his victory."

"That's not the way I see it."

"Because you're young, and the only woman you've yet loved is your mother. If everything about this Mahraveh is true, and she's anything like her father, she'll roll right over King Pi like an avalanche in the Dragon's Tail."

"No." Lucas shook his head emphatically. "You forget who *his* father was. And his mother for that matter. And you, his chief adviser."

"Lord Jolly is his chief advisor. I am but a relic."

"You know that isn't true, Sir Unger. You are the Master of Warfare and—"

"A title created by a child to make an old, blind man feel needed."

"That's enough, Sir," Sir Danvels said. "I know you outrank me, and you've lived longer, but you're the most respected man alive. Iam's breath, to most of us, *you* should be King."

"Bite your tongue," Torsten said.

"We need you, Sir Unger." Lucas trotted his mount closer, lowering his voice as if not wanting to dare Nesilia to overhear him. "You saw what's coming. If we don't stand together, she'll destroy us all…" He swallowed hard and looked toward the ground. "She might either way."

Torsten lifted his chin. "She won't. You're right, Lucas. The time to worry about the Glass Kingdom's future is after we win. And if it is meant to end in defense of all the world Iam built, then so be it."

Torsten gave his mare a kick, and it shot down the dune toward the city gates. He couldn't let pride impede him. Nor his love for a fallen King and Queen. The kingdom of Iam needed him, and that had to mean more than a castle or a crown. Didn't it?

Latiapur neared, and the first thing Torsten noticed wasn't the host of golden-clad Serpent Guards lining the gates' entry. It was the hundred or so Shesaitju warriors leaving. Men armed to the teeth marched and rode zhulong out, turning to head north.

None appeared happy. One in the lead even watched Torsten on approach, seeming to sour the nearer he got. And when Torsten pulled up in the shadow of the gate, the leader spat in his direction. He was bald, and like any afhem, tattooed from head to toe, except right along the back and side of his skull, where the mark of his afhemate had been scraped off to leave a scar just like Muskigo bore.

"They're leaving?" Lucas asked. "Nobody is supposed to leave. We need them."

"To face off against a goddess they don't believe in," Torsten remarked.

"Don't believe in? Their own people saw her!"

"War tore the Black Sands apart. Not all their people will approve of this union, just as half the nobles of Yarrington will likely protest. It's inevitable."

"Torst… Master Unger, you saw what Nesilia has behind her. We'll need everyone."

"Everyone we can get," Torsten agreed. "Lord Brouben is already hard at work convincing his father to speak with the dwarven kingdoms and summon as large an army as they can muster. King Pi sent a dozen gallers to Brekliodad before departing Yarrington, begging their dukes to put aside any differences and aid. We will have whatever we can get, and many won't be eager to die for a world beyond their borders."

"Until she comes for them," Lucas spat.

"And then it'll be too late. But I met Nesilia, and I felt her heart. She'll aim for the Glass first. With everything she has. She'll come to snuff out Iam's light, and if we fall, everyone will fall."

"Then everyone who doesn't fight with us is a fool," Lucas said.

"Welcome to Pantego."

Torsten feigned a grin, then trotted forward into the city. Only weeks ago, the Shesaitju guards might have torn Glassmen like them to pieces for coming so near. Sir Marcos had been on the wrong end of such an interaction—killed for being a messenger.

"Sir Unger, you are finally here!" a gravelly voice exclaimed. A chunky Shesaitju man pushed through the guards, then waddled over, using his hammer-staff as a crutch. It was Tingur Jalurahbak, the former afhem who'd battled Nesilia alongside Torsten and the others at White Bridge. Presently, he had a red-stained bandage over his afhemate markings and a wrap-around both his gut and bad leg courtesy of the Buried Goddess.

"Lord Tingur," Torsten acknowledged, bowing his head from atop his horse.

"I'm no lord," he replied.

Tingur promptly shouted at some of his men in Saitjuese, and their equivalent of stable boys hurried out to help with the horses. They assisted Torsten, even doing so much as to cup their hands so he could use them as a step. They buckled under the weight of him, then did the same for Lucas. It was unnecessary, but Torsten felt some of the tension slip from his shoulders at the warm welcome.

Tingur approached him, then slapped his shoulder. Torsten had forgotten how short and stocky the gray man was, and his curling mustache seemed even thicker, but there was no mistaking his expression. He truly was pleased for Torsten to be there. It wasn't a show.

"Your injuries—" Torsten began before Tingur cut him off.

"Won't stop me from fighting that pis'truda. That lot you just saw leave might not believe what's coming for them, but I know what we saw."

"Good." Torsten gestured to Lucas and invited him over. "As my ward here has said a thousand times since we left Panping, we'll need everyone we can get."

"Smart kid."

"Our Shieldsmen always are."

"King Pi arrived with more than a handful more," Tingur said. "They're a little younger than I expected."

Torsten bit his lip. He couldn't believe it was so obvious how green the warriors of the Glass Kingdom's highest echelon now were. He wondered if, perhaps, they should consider covering their faces like the Serpent Guards. Cutting out their tongues, so they had no voices of their own, was a stretch, but something to maintain the mystique of Liam the Conqueror's elite.

"How is the King?" Torsten asked.

"Preparing for a feast," Tingur replied. "Come. I'll take you."

Torsten nodded, and two of the Serpent Guards broke off to escort them through the crowded, zigzagging streets of Latiapur. There was barely space to breathe. Markless men and women—those Shesaitju who had never committed to one of their warrior clans and instead inhabited Latiapur—cluttered around like ants, transporting supplies, selling supplies. The Yarrington markets were half the size of theirs, and infinitely less colorful.

Warriors marched on patrols. Not just single guards or even pairs, but full squads in full armor. Serpent Guards monitored every major avenue and structure. Torsten had never seen Latiapur like this before.

A show of force from our new Queen, he realized. He knew that because it was precisely what Muskigo would've done. Like hanging bodies off a wall to scare the enemy away from battle.

"So, what is Nesilia planning?" Tingur asked. "How many men will we need?"

"All of them. In the whole world. If we can get them," Torsten said.

"That doesn't sound good."

"It's worse than not good," Lucas chimed in.

"It seems that Nesilia has done what even the worst mystics in the last age have only attempted," Torsten said. "She's torn Elsewhere wide open."

"The Currentless Realm?" Tingur asked, his eyes going wide.

"Its name is irrelevant. But the demons of the damned who dwell there are not. They have infested the poor souls of Panping. Who knows how many…"

"Ah, those skinny Easterners?" Tingur scoffed. "This'll be easier than I thought."

"They are still people!" Lucas snapped.

Torsten scowled at him. But upon realizing how agitated Lucas was, his features softened. He couldn't expect a man so young and idealistic to maintain composure in such a situation. Another reason to give all Shieldsmen masks.

"I think what Sir Danvels is trying to say is that if we can save them, we have to try," Torsten said.

"That will not be up to me," Tingur replied. Then he pointed toward the Boiling Keep and said, "That's up to her."

He stopped at the base of stairs at the end of the city's main avenue. Gilded statues of zhulong stood proud on either side of it, their tusks encrusted with bands of flawless gems. It sliced up through a series of escarpments, leading into the colonnade of the domed Palace. Detailed murals were painted on the riser of every step, detailing the history of their people, faded from centuries out in the hot southern sun.

"What is she like?" Torsten asked.

Tingur chortled. "Oh, Sir Unger, you are about to find out. In the short time I've known her, she's managed to surprise me more than any one of my wives, living or dead. If only I'd been here to watch her scrape the history off the heads of so many afhems." He leaned in and whispered. "Don't repeat this, but we damn well had it coming."

"I'm not surprised. Muskigo was a brilliant tactician, coming up with that. He took away what made you all special, and with it the pride that ravaged these lands. I'm amazed Liam never thought of it."

"Muskigo?" Tingur patted Torsten on the back. "No, my new friend. In this matter, Muskigo was a victim, same as the rest of us. That idea was all our new Caleef's."

Tingur used his weapon to push off and start up the stairs. Torsten regarded Lucas, and both their brows furrowed with concern. When Torsten had learned about the erasure of the afhemates, the act had Muskigo written all over it. Now, as he took the first step, his anxiety returned in full vigor.

He'd never climbed to the Boiling Keep; only guarded the bottom of the steps while Sidar Rakun officialized his surrender to Liam. Even he had to admit—the views from the upper bluff were incredible. The low dusk sunlight splintered across an endless field of foaming waves stretching out toward an ever-shifting horizon.

The salty vapor on the air was welcome. It reminded him of being back home in Dockside. It felt like ages since he'd been there, ready to set off and defeat Mak and end a war, only now to find himself prepared to fight a bigger one.

Serpent Guards permitted them into a square courtyard beyond the outer gates. Tall blackwood trees tickled the sky, casting thin shadows. The inner doors were closed, and a crowd of confused and angry people stood just outside. Important looking people.—former afhems, Shieldsmen, Lord Jolly, and even Dellbar the Holy himself.

"What is everyone doing out here?" Tingur asked, rubbing his belly. "I'm starved."

"Lord Unger, you've returned," Lord Jolly exclaimed. He strode over, then struck his chest with his one remaining hand.

Sir Mulliner did the same, muttering, "Sir Unger."

Neither looked pleased to see him. And Dellbar remained leaning against a far column, his lips moving slightly like he was muttering to himself. He didn't even notice their arrival.

"Bit'rudam, what is this?" Tingur asked a younger Shesaitju. He was dressed in full Serpent Guard armor, but without the helmet or mask like the others, and apparently, he still retained his tongue as well.

"The King and future Queen have locked themselves in there. Alone." There was no mistaking the revulsion in his tone.

And Torsten couldn't help but feel that same way. The last thing he'd hoped for was this Caleef Mahraveh getting a chance to manipulate Pi on her own.

IX

THE CALEEF

"Blessed be this feast and the One who brings forth bread from the earth, in the name Iam, Light of our world," Dellbar the Holy said, spreading his arms over the banquet that had been laid out in the palatial throne room.

Mahi watched him. Heavy bags hung from his blinded eyes above an unkempt beard that grew wiry on gaunt cheeks. This priest looked drained and utterly exhausted. Even his voice was hoarse and barely projected.

Tingur told her what had happened to him. That, apparently, his god, Iam, had possessed his body to drive Nesilia away.

"May His Vigilant Eye watch over us," Dellbar went on. He then traced those dark circles with his fingers and bowed his head. King Pi and all the Shieldsmen seated at the smaller tables behind him did the same.

Then, Dellbar lifted his cane, and the blind High Priest shuffled back to a seat alone in the corner of the room. Mahi watched him plop down hard, then slide his plate away before leaning back.

He ate nothing. Drank nothing. Said nothing.

At the same time, the palace sages prayed to the God of Sand and Sea in Saitjuese. A nigh'jel was sacrificed, its black blood dripping down through the open Sea Door.

"*Eternal Current guide us,*" they finished. The trusted Shesaitju warriors and former afhems seated behind Mahi repeated the same. She didn't. She kept her eye on the young King of Glass and, seated directly across from her, he did the same to her.

A private, circular table had been arranged over the Sea Door of her throne room, open in the center so as never to cover the spray and whistling wind. Palace servants carried in all manner of Shesaitju delicacies, platters resting on their heads.

Their first course was a delectable rock crab curry—the very meal she shared with Jumaat on the day he was taken from her. Though it saddened her, no tears came. It was followed by broiled root mash and thick-cut zhulong ribs slathered in spices found only in the Black Sands. She didn't think the young man would be able to handle the heat, but he did so with ease. He tried a bit of it all, yet never gorged himself. Even though he had to eat with his hands like a proper Black Sandsman, his movements were refined, noble in the way Glassmen thought they were.

Mahi didn't bother with such pleasantries. She ate how she'd learned to among her father's warriors. Bones and plates clattered against the blackwood table. After every bite, she glanced up at her future husband, only to find him still silently eating as well.

"Your Grace, how are you enjoying it?" Lord Jolly asked Pi, rising from his table to come to the King's side.

"It is a welcomed change," Pi replied. "I believe I've had all the roast pheasant I can stomach."

His voice was soft but stern. Deeper than expected, too. Mahi studied him in detail. When he spoke, he maintained constant eye contact with his conversation partner, no matter who it might be. That alone spoke volumes of the man. He wasn't like Babrak or any of the other snakes with shifty eyes. She noted the way his lips rose at the corners as he momentarily allowed his gaze to freeze on her. It seemed genuine. Though, she imagined Liam smiled before he bent Sidar Rakun's knee as well.

"A little too spicy for my blood," Jolly whispered, not realizing how the wind from the Sea Door and the domed ceiling made his words carry.

"Northern pis'trudas," Bit'rudam murmured from his seat behind her, clearly having heard as well.

"What was that, my Lord?" Lord Jolly asked.

"Nothing." He then grumbled in Saitjuese with the others at his table, and they all laughed. None of it was pleasant.

"Well, we are honored to be here, breaking bread together after all this fighting," Lord Jolly said.

"There is nothing so soft as bread here," a former afhem said.

Lord Jolly grinned and nodded. "An expression."

"Bread would make this tolerable," the scarred Shieldsman called Sir Mulliner said under his breath, again not used to the acoustics of the room, designed so the Caleef could never mistake any words of his advisors, nor they, the Caleef's. The voice of the God of Sand and Sea would not go unheard.

"*So, would cutting out your tongue,*" Bit'rudam said in Saitjuese before biting a chunk out of a bellot fruit.

Mulliner glared. Though he clearly couldn't understand the language, the tone was unmistakable.

"My Lady Caleef, we agreed to all speak in one language here," Lord Jolly said, folding his one arm behind his back. The other empty sleeve flapped in the gentle breeze.

"And why don't you know ours?" another afhem at Mahi's back spoke up.

"*I do,*" Pi said in Saitjuese. "*And you are correct. Without a tongue, he would taste nothing.*"

Mahi's finger slipped and crunched through the shell of the mollusk she was preparing to eat. The young King spoke with an awful accent, but his pronunciation was near perfect. He didn't bother looking up this time either. Just continued eating, as if nobody should be surprised.

"Your Grace, your studies have proven fruitful," Lord Jolly said, lighting up like a proud father watching his baby walk for the first time.

"Lord Jolly, our hosts have provided a feast in our honor," Pi said. "You should go and enjoy it."

"No," Mahi said.

Lord Jolly took one step and stopped. His face scrunched.

"Everybody out except King Pi," Mahi said.

"My Lady Caleef, I meant no disrespect," Jolly said.

"Out!" she bellowed, pounding down on the table. A bit of boiling hot tea splashed onto her arm. It should have scalded her. Instead, she felt nothing.

The Shesaitju group at her back stood immediately. Most began marching out of the room, whispering questions, but Bit'rudam stopped at her side and lay his hand upon her shoulder momentarily, before reeling it back.

"My Caleef, is something wrong?" he asked.

"Nothing is wrong," she said. "I simply gave an order."

Bit'rudam stuttered over a response, but she glanced back at him and offered an assuring nod. He straightened his back, exhaled, then ordered the Serpent Guards arranged around the circumference of the room to leave.

"You heard her. Out," Pi said, as his people continued to loiter around in confusion. Lord Jolly bowed, and Sir Mulliner stirred the rest up. His scowl never left Mahi until he stood in the outer courtyard.

"You too, Your Eminence," Pi addressed Dellbar.

By then, the High Priest was flat on his back on the lowest level of the stands wrapping the circular room. He groaned as he stood, cracked his back, then shuffled toward the exit as if the world wasn't in danger of being swallowed by an angry goddess. He stopped in the doorway and turned to them. His eyes didn't work, but Mahi felt like he could see them. Judge them.

"Everything we know rests on your shoulders," he said. Then, he turned his face toward the ceiling. "I hope You know what You're doing."

At that, he backed out of the room. The last thing Mahi saw outside before the great doors slammed shut was Bit'rudam staring at her. His shoulders sank, eyes bulged, and he chewed his lower lip.

Fully alone now, Pi cleared his throat, pulled a folded handkerchief from his pocket, and flapped it until it unfurled. After a quaint smile, he dabbed at the corners of his mouth.

Just like Glassmen. Always prepared to get fat, Mahi thought.

Out loud, she said, "Is eating always such a fanciful affair with you?"

"Growing up in a castle, you get used to doing things a certain way," he replied. Then, refolding the cloth once, he paused and, instead, let it fall onto the table in a clump. Mahi watched closely, unable to tell if it was an act of genuine rebellion against his upbringing, or if he was merely trying to please her.

"This is the furthest you've ever been from home, yes?" she said in common.

"It is," he admitted, showing no sense of shame in it. Then in Saitjuese, he said, "*The books don't compare. The way the light catches the black dunes, shimmering on the rare white grains. It's beautiful.*"

"You speak well."

"I've had too many teachers in the years I can remember."

Mahi grunted in acknowledgement. She understood that. Farhan, Impili, her father—they were all dead now. Shavi too.

She scoured the food arrangement for the perfect bite, then ran a finger through the bowl of root mash and brought it to her lips.

"They said you were worthless," she said, sucking the last bits off her fingertip.

Pi's brow furrowed. She expected to see anger. That word would elicit ire in most men. They'd explain how that's what she was, a woman desperate to be a warrior. To be everything she wasn't meant to be.

He remained unequivocally calm as he said, "Excuse me?"

Mahi leaned over the table on her elbows. "The rumors from our spies in the west. Yuri Darkings. My father. They said you were short, scrawny, worthless, and a pale reflection of your legendary father. You're certainly one of those things, but not all."

A few seconds went by in silence, and then Pi grinned. "Worthless?"

Mahi cracked a smile as well without intending to. He'd caught her off guard, something she knew a good warrior should never be. But all the things she'd heard about him… about how he'd been a mad child scribbling on walls, or that he was quiet and damaged. He didn't seem any of it.

"Scrawny," she clarified. "Though, I expected you to look younger."

"And I thought you'd be older," he retorted. "The way the soldiers you defeated speak of you, perhaps with fangs, too. But rumors were my mother's obsession. I've learned to trust only what I can see."

"I appreciate that." Mahi shifted in her seat. "I suppose I should've known better than to trust Yuri Darkings." She leaned forward more, where the wind and rumble of waves through the Sea Door were unmistakable. "He pushed me through that opening, did you know that?"

Pi shook his head.

"No warning at all," she continued.

"'Once a traitor, always a traitor,'" Pi said, inflecting like the words weren't his own. Impressed upon him by some great Lord or one of his countless advisors, perhaps even his father, Mahi imagined. And he didn't seem to believe them, which only made her sit up straighter. That someone his age might seek to form his own opinions, she had to admit, it was impressive.

"Did you know Yuri?" she asked.

"Barely. I wasn't allowed in Royal Council meetings until Father died and by then… I wasn't myself for a long time."

"You were sick, weren't you?"

"There is no need to be coy. I was possessed by Nesilia and servant to Redstar's blood magic. It's all unclear after…"

"You died," she finished for him, deciding to take his advice and not be coy.

Pi swallowed audibly and sank back in his chair as he nodded, eyes shut, and a palpable wave of discomfort crossing his features. It was the first time she'd seen him display any sort of weakness. She thought she'd revel in it; in an opening that would allow her to twist and flex her control.

Possessed, she thought instead. *Forced into something he'd never asked for or wanted.* She understood that better than most.

"What was it like?" Mahi asked.

Again, she'd expected him to object to her intrusion or at least display the slightest hesitation. But instead, he answered softly. "Quiet. Dark. Empty."

"And your god brought you back?"

"So, they say."

"As did mine." She pointed back toward the Sea Door. "After Yuri pushed me, I fell, hit the water, met my God, and the one trying to kill us all. Then, I woke up on a beach looking like this." She gestured to her body, skin black as pitch unlike shades of gray like the rest of her people.

"I'm… sorry," Pi said.

"For what? Yuri came to us and we took in a traitor. And yet, here you and I sit—a King, resurrected by his god. A Queen brought back by hers. Each of us, the last of our respective bloodlines."

That seemed to get the young King to perk up. "All our parents' fighting over whose god is the true god," he said. "How can we say now? They're either both powerful enough to bring us back from the dead or the same god by a different name."

"Your High Priest would choke if he heard you say that."

"He wouldn't," Pi said. "He's… different. But Sir Unger might."

"Yet you believe it?"

"I'm no warrior yet, and they don't let me leave the castle much, but I've read many stories of history across Pantego. So many seem impossible, and yet, I see no reason why truth cannot be in all of them."

"Many of my own people think me a liar. They think my father fabricated all of this to make me Caleef."

"People like to doubt."

"Does this look fake?" Mahi lifted a knife from the table beside a bowl of fresh, yellow bellots. Without taking her eyes off Pi, she dragged it along her arm in a way that would scrape off paint or normal dried blood. She knew she shouldn't show a potential enemy that she, the one chosen by the God of Sand and Sea to bear His power, could bleed. She did it anyway.

Pi sat up, watching intently. He didn't squirm at the sight of her fresh blood being drawn from her completely black skin. He only focused, like she did, on how, within the cut, there was no pink as there should've been. The dark coloration spread down through the layers of flesh. Part of her.

"No, it does not," he said.

"At least you can remove a crown," Mahi grumbled.

At that, Pi lifted the Glass Crown off his head. He held it in front of his eyes, rotating it, so all the jewels cast light like a rainbow on the floor. Then, he dropped it unceremoniously onto the table.

"Maybe it would be better if you couldn't," he said. "My father wore a different crown, not this one. The day he died, slumped over in his chair in the middle of a dinner quite like this, it rolled off his head. They say it was stolen. A story very few people know."

He was smart. Matching Mahi's admission of weakness with one of his own.

"Well, King Pi, as far as I'm concerned, it's just jewelry," she said. "A King, like an afhem, is only as worthy as the things he does. My father—"

"Won many battles," he interrupted. "Yet killed many innocents."

"As did your many commanders. The Wearer of White—the one chosen to represent the whole of your army… he burned down the very town where I grew up. Slaughtered everyone there to send a message to my father. I suppose he didn't consider that my father was four days' travel away, and there was not a single warrior present. I barely escaped with my life."

Pi frowned. "I'm glad you did, Caleef Mahraveh."

Mahi smiled at the use of her title. Another mark for the young Glass King. The arrogance of his predecessors would have kept them from putting themselves on equal ground, but apparently, not this one.

"Mistakes are made in every war," he continued, "on every side. My father made many while believing all people should think like him. I'm here because I want *all* fighting to stop, so we can work together."

"Two miracle children of legendary leaders joined as one."

"Exactly."

Mahi stood to her full, impressive height. Her midriff was exposed by her lacy gold dress with black shells strung along the trim. Her obsidian skin glowed a soft green from the nigh'jel lanterns hanging around the room. She skirted around the table, letting her fingers drag along its surface.

"And so, we must marry," she said, stopping right beside Pi. "I'll be honest, I thought you'd be a rambling fool I could rollover. I thought this would be simple."

Pi stood as well. He rose only to the base of her chin, but he was younger by a few years and would likely pass her in height. And up close, she could see the slight muscles of his chest through the loose collar of his tunic. Maybe he wouldn't be Liam the Conqueror, but he would be strong.

"*I thought many things, all of them wrong,*" Pi said in near-perfect Saitjuese.

Mahi took one step closer. "If I do this, and we defeat Nesilia, can I trust you not to betray my people? Not to force Iam upon them, or your people's indulgent ways that have no place in our unforgiving desert."

"I'm not my father," he said, not backing down. "Can I trust you not to rebel and burn villages? To know when talking might be more beneficial than the sword?"

"I'm not mine," she replied.

"Then I would be honored to have you as Queen of the Glass. You need not love me or force yourself to try to. We need only work together."

"Then tomorrow, beneath the light of your god's domain, and on the shores of mine, we will be made one."

Pi smiled as he took her hand. She thought he might try and kiss it, but he only held it for a moment, staring down before releasing it and sitting again. "Then we should eat."

"We should," Mahi agreed. She stared into his eyes for a moment, only then realizing how blue they were—like the Boiling Waters on a clear day, all the many hues and shades of playing over and under each other.

She started toward her seat. "And King Pi," she said as she walked, not looking back. "If you keep your word, I do not believe love for you will be hard to muster." She fell back into her seat, catching his slight smirk before it faded. Then, she clapped twice loudly.

As if reading her mind, Serpent Guards promptly reopened the entry. Again, the face awaiting her was Bit'rudam's, as if he hadn't even moved. Sweeping in, his features lit up, which he hid by checking the room for any wrongdoing.

Then came a man she'd never seen, but immediately recognized. The massive, Glintish Shieldsman who wore a blindfold, yet could see. The legendary warrior her father had faced off against and defeated, and yet, one of the few men to be there when Muskigo died.

Pi's calm composure slipped away when he, too, realized Torsten Unger had arrived.

"Master Unger!" he exclaimed, pushing off the table so hard a goblet fell. Torsten placed a fist against his chest and bowed, and Pi embraced him, barely able to wrap his hands around the man's broad torso.

"Your Grace," Torsten spoke, tracing his eyes in prayer to Iam. Then, he returned Pi's embrace. While he did, his head lifted and the enchanted blindfold Tingur had warned Mahi about aimed straight at her. Immediately, she knew. Winning over the King was important, but winning over Torsten Unger was the key to the Glass Kingdom's army.

X

THE OUTCAST

Balonhearth.

It had been far too long since Dwotratum "Tum Tum" Goodbrew laid eyes upon the majestic mountain. Far too long since he'd breathed in the frigid air of Brotlebir and the Dragon's Tail.

It was home. He was home.

So why didn't he feel like it?

Perhaps, it was that for longer than any of his companions had been alive, Tum Tum had called Winde Port home, and he'd liked it. No, that wasn't true, he'd loved it. Every second spent serving up ales and jesting with the locals at the Winder's Dwarf—he was still proud of that name—had been pure joy. His heart had been heavy since that awful, fateful day when the fires of Elsewhere charred its walls, and the winds tore the place asunder. That's not even mentioning the dastardly Black Sandsmen.

But this... Balonhearth, the home of King Lorgit Cragrock, the ruler of Three Kingdoms, the seat of dwarven power in all the realm—this was where Tum Tum had popped out of his mum, beard already touching the floor, hand outstretched in search of an ale and a pickaxe.

Then, when he was of age, his father did what all dwarven fathers had done, sending his son out on his Commute—a day all dwarves longed for and feared. It was rare that one of his kind left the halls of the Dragon's Tail and didn't return. Why would they? Within the stone of the mountains, they had all they'd ever need. Food, ale, gold, warmth, and the camaraderie of fellows.

Secretly, Tum Tum figured they'd all covered their britches in shog when the day of their Commute arrived.

The Commute… one year under the open Pantego skies. Each one had their own path to carve, their own destiny to fulfill. The goal was simple: learn what he may from the vast, wide world. Most couldn't wait to get back to the safety of Balonhearth or any of the other peaks, but Tum Tum fell in love.

Not with some lady or wench, but with the wood of Winder's Wharf and the salt of Trader's Bay, the hustle and bustle of a city alive. No, Tum Tum didn't like adventuring, but he loved hearing the tales.

He supposed that's why he and Whitney Fierstown had become such quick friends. Sure, the kid was full of shog and spit, but he spun quite the yarn.

Tum Tum's Commute had been spent sweeping floors and polishing mugs for a cranky old man whose name wasn't significant enough to be remembered. However, the same day that old bugger'd kicked the bucket, Tum Tum used every autla he'd earned—and some of his father's—swiped up the deed, and made the bar his own.

Until this moment, he hadn't a single regret. But now, looking up at Balonhearth, the King of the Dragon's Tail Mountains, he longed to be back amid the rock, gold and silver veins, and iron mines with a goblet the size of his head filled with the most potent dwarven draught—the stuff those flower-pickers in the south couldn't handle.

It was gorgeous.

It was magnificent.

It was the place of dreams and legends.

"That's it?" Whitney said.

Shog-shuckin, thief, Tum Tum thought to himself, balling his fists.

"How could you know?" Whitney went on. "They all look the same." He pointed. "Oh, look, that mountain has a little nib at the top, too. Sure, but this one slopes a bit to the east while that one dips to the west."

Sora elbowed Whitney and offered an apologetic smile to Tum Tum.

Since the first they'd met when Tum Tum saw her walk into The

Winder's Dwarf, side by side with Whitney, he liked her. He also knew he'd seen a spark between the two of them. He couldn't imagine what anyone saw in that feather of a man.

"It's home," Tum Tum said softly.

"And a beautiful one at that," Lucindur said.

"Ooookaaay," Whitney said, dragging out the word.

"Whit, cut it out," Sora scolded.

Aquira made a little burping sound and sped off ahead, zipping under an arch formed by a fallen boulder caught between two rocky walls.

They continued to argue, but Tum Tum barely took notice. As they walked, he let his hand scoop up snow that reached his waist in some places. Closing his fist and reopening it, he watched it clump and melt.

"Up this way," Tum Tum said, then started off, not bothering to see if anyone would follow.

From there, they could see the faint outline of King Andur Cragrock, the first King of the Three Kingdoms, jutting out of the mountain, pointing the way to his city, the place Tum Tum had worked so hard to stay away from, yet couldn't wait to return to.

He only hoped they welcomed him back.

"Is it safe?" Lucindur asked.

"If ye wanted safety," Tum Tum answered, "ye should've stayed behind yer golden arches. Besides, if Kazimir—rest whatever soul the demon had—was right, and Nesilia only brought her weakest, first wave with her to the Citadel, we've got no time to be wastin."

"Hear, hear!" Whitney said. Then, he turned to Lucindur and said softer, "But it wasn't a dumb question. Looks like the whole mountain's going to turn into a landslide any moment."

Tum Tum ignored him again. "Won't be long now," he said.

The next hour was spent climbing rock, waiting for the flower-pickers to catch up, and trying to bury the feeling of dread he had at the thought of standing before King Lorgit and asking for his most prized possession. Legends spoke of a time when dragons soared the skies in great numbers, but none had been seen in many lifetimes. They'd all vanished and never returned, save for the one whose heart lay in a vault, offered for Brike Sledgeborne's life in exchange for a home for dwarves. Its power helped carve out their kingdom long ago.

Tum Tum knew this, as any dwarf of Balonhearth did.

His father had once been in the presence of the stone—so he'd said. Dwarves were known for telling tales. Though Tum Tum couldn't be sure if his father had spoken truth, he'd said that too much time within the glow of it made him feel faint—exhausted like he carried the pain of the entire extinct species. Though even with all that power, it had become no more than a trinket for the King. The last non-skeletal remnant of a dragon on Pantego.

For the first dozen minutes of their trek up the mountainside, Whitney and Sora had been hand-in-hand. But now, Whitney was huffing, and Sora was doing her best to help him along.

Strong one, that Sora, Tum Tum thought.

"Okay, come on," Whitney said, out of breath once they reached the entrance. "This it?"

A giant statue of a dwarf was sculpted into a ridge and pointed toward a flat area of rock across from it. The wide stone door carved into the mountain was nearly invisible to the eye. Tum Tum dragged his hand across the inscription, feeling the bumps and lines of an old form of his language, covered in frost.

"What's it say?" Sora asked.

"'Balonhearth, The Great Mountain. King Lorgit Cragrock, Master of the Three Kingdoms.'" Tum Tum read the symbols, but he didn't need to. He'd remember those words for a thousand years to come. This was home.

"That's nice, but it's freezing," Whitney said. Then, shoving everyone aside, he raised his hand to knock on the door.

"Oi! Do that if ye want to die a death most terrible." The voice came from up the path a ways.

Whitney's hand froze, and Tum Tum scooted around him to see the speaker. The dwarf wore fine armor, plated and blocky, but with dwarven geometric patterns set in gold that no human blacksmith had hands steady enough to inscribe. His barbute helm was equally impressive, rising to three flattened points over his forehead. Behind him marched a contingent of dwarven clanbreakers, each decked out in black mail covered in spikes.

"Meungor's frozen beard," Tum Tum said.

"Who the yig are you?" Whitney shouted at the same time.

"That ain't a question needing answerin," the armored dwarf said. "It'd best to be turned around on ye."

Whitney looked around, confused, then elbowed Tum Tum. "What did he just say?"

"Name's Tum Tum—Dwotratum Goodbrew—and these are me compan—"

"Mountain's sealed shut. No one in. No one out," the armored dwarf said.

"Sealed? By whose order?" Tum Tum asked.

A clanbreaker on each side of the speaker stepped forward.

"Whoa, whoa!" Tum Tum said. "I mean no harm. Just come a long way, we have. This be home to me."

"Anyone who calls Balonhearth home for true would know of the King's decree. No one in. No one out," the dwarf repeated.

"But why?" Tum Tum asked.

The armored dwarf strode forward. Two quick steps and the nose bridge of his helm was tickling Tum Tum's mustache.

"Think I don't remember ye, outcast?" he asked.

Those words hit Tum Tum harder than any blow could have. So many years had passed since Tum Tum had left on his Commute. That Tum Tum's name was remembered spoke to just how rare it was that someone would not return. Or maybe, it merely spoke to the famed memories of his kin.

The armored dwarf made a show of removing his helmet.

Underneath, hair as golden as the summer sun unfolded down to the middle of his back. His beard was braided, but not hanging as most dwarves wore them. His were tight against the skin of his face in sharp zig-zag patterns designed to keep the hair beneath his helm.

Tum Tum recognized him, as anyone from Balonhearth would. Gargamane the Gold had been the leader of King Cragrock's royal guard for as long as Lorgit had been king. If the commander of those elite forces was out here instead of inside guarding the throne room, something had to be wrong.

"Got lost on me way home from Commute," Tum Tum said.

"Got lost, my arse," Gargamane said. "Got used to bein warm and livin under the sun. Ye've forgotten yer people, and we *forget* just as quick."

"If ye've forgotten, then all is well."

"Ye think this a joke?" Gargamane spat. "Ye ain't welcome here no more. Ye can't just not return from a Commute. And bringing them? Flower-pickers and worse? What were ye thinking?"

"Had no choice, brother—"

"That's just it. We ain't brothers." Gargamane stepped forward. "I hope the south was worth it. Now, go."

The commander jabbed a finger, then turned, and as he did, Tum Tum said, "Ye don't think I'd just waltz back for no reason do ye? We're all in dire straits, my commander."

"Don't ye, 'my commander' me," Gargamane said, spinning back so fast his hair slapped the clanbreaker beside him. "We all know ye call Pi Nothhelm king these days. I heard what happened in Winde Port. Yer desperate. Destitute. Yer home's gone, but ye made yer choice when ye overstayed yer year."

"And it was a choice I'd have just as soon held on to!" Tum Tum said, terse. Then he exhaled through his teeth. "Look, I ain't here because me home burnt. I'm here because all our homes are about to be burnt. Includin yer own. No one's safe. Ain't ye heard what happened to the Strongirons up north? Surely, if I heard, ye have too."

Gargamane approached Tum Tum again. "Drav Cra bastards got em, what I heard. What about it?"

"It wasn't just any Drav Cra," Sora said, stepping forward.

The look on Gargamane's face as he peered over Tum Tum's shoulder could have dried up Trader's Bay.

"And what do ye know?" Gargamane said.

Tum Tum turned and expected to see Sora backing down, but she didn't at all. Instead, she took another step.

She's got a bigger set on her than all the flower-pickers combined, he thought.

"I was there," she proclaimed.

Gargamane shoved his way past Tum Tum to stand before Sora. His hand rested on the handle of a thick bastard sword. "Ye'd best explain how ye were there when me kin died and yet stand here now, tellin the tale."

Whitney now stepped up beside Sora, puffing out his chest. "I think you need to learn some manners, wee-bit."

Gargamane advanced on Whitney now. "Who ye callin wee-bit, twigs-for-legs?"

Things were quickly spiraling out of control. Tum Tum knew he had to do something, but before he could, Lucindur stepped between them. She was slight, but her presence carried a certain matronly aura with it. If it intimidated Gargamane in the least, he didn't show it. Instead, he responded in kind, stepping forward again.

Whitney mumbled something under his breath and turned away.

"Well, this is a strange party ye've brought with ye, Dwotratum," Gargamane said, eyes fixated on the Lightmancer. "Yer father would be ashamed."

"It's just Tum Tum now," he replied.

"Changed yer name, too. Aye, makes sense. Ye've abandoned everything else—why not drive the pickaxe in as deep as it can go?"

"That ain't fair—"

"Well, what is it I'm missing?" he said, cutting off Tum Tum's response. "Because all I see is a homeless dwarf."

"Commander Gargamane," Tum Tum said. "Sora… this is Sora… she suffered some horrors at the hand of…"

Tum Tum couldn't finish his sentence. He'd been there in the Citadel and still found it difficult to believe what he'd seen. Gods and goddesses in Pantego again? It seemed ridiculous.

"Nesilia, the Buried Goddess," Sora finished.

Tum Tum expected him to laugh, but Gargamane's face contorted into something between anger and fear. "What do ye know of the witch?" Gargamane asked, his voice low and brimming with urgency. Fearful muttering broke out amongst his clanbreakers as well.

"She's returned—"

"Keep yer voice down!" Gargamane hissed. "Heard rumors about this… heard some folks saw her in the south. Either way. Been strange happenins with all these beastie attacks."

Tum Tum's stomach dropped. "Ye've seen them? The grimaurs?"

"And goblins too," Gargamane said.

"Goblins be the norm here, though," Tum Tum said.

"Not like we've seen. They've gotten brave. Daring, even."

"Sora's seen her in the flesh," Tum Tum said.

"This knife-ear?" Gargamane laughed.

With a screech, Aquira swooped down directly in front of Gargamane and screeched. The dwarf fell to his backside, snow puffing up around him. A few of his clanbreakers drew their weapons and ran to him, helping him to his feet.

Aquira then landed on Sora's shoulder. Tum Tum couldn't figure out how such a slight woman bore the weight of the now full-grown beast, but Sora was no weakling.

At once, the clanbreakers all tensed.

"Aye, that looks about right," Tum Tum said, his turn to laugh this time.

"I thought all these creatures be extinct," Gargamane said, eyes ablaze with wonder.

"Nearly," Tum Tum said. "But ye should see her blow flame."

"She can't…" Gargamane said, barely a whisper. Then, as if realizing he'd lost the upper hand, he cleared his throat and raised his sword. "I asked ye a question that's gone unanswered. Balonhearth is a long way from wherever ye've been. Ye brought with ye a mystic, a Glintish bard, this… whatever-he's-good-for over there. What are ye doin here? What else ye hidin?"

"We ain't hiding nothin. Just lookin to stop the witch from destroyin life as we know it," Tum Tum said. "The King needs to know."

"Aye, so ye should be in Yarrington, tellin yer King all about it," Gargamane said. "Little tyke'd probably fancy a good bedtime story."

At that, the clanbreakers broke rank and joined Gargamane in laughter. A few bumped into each other, slapping their knees.

"This ain't a joke," Tum Tum said.

Collecting himself, Gargamane replied, "I'll be the judge of what *my* King does and don't need to know. Ye know who I be, and ye know what I'll do to uphold the King's decree."

"Oh, he rhymes," Whitney scoffed.

Gargamane eyed him a moment before continuing. "Now, regardless of what story ye got to tell, I said it before. No one in. No one out."

Brandishing his sword, this time as a threat, Gargamane lowered his gaze, and the clanbreakers returned to formation.

Tum Tum backpedaled until he bumped into Lucindur.

"We should go," he said.

"Go?" Whitney complained. "We just got here, and I was looking forward to a pint of the yig that passes for ale up here."

Tum Tum turned to him and said, "Look, that's that. These clanbreakers won't negotiate. They won't argue. Those spikes? They'll impale ye faster than ye can say 'ow.'"

"Tum Tum, we can't just turn back," Sora argued.

"Ain't got much of a choice. We'll find somethin else to use on the witch."

Just then, in a show of uncharacteristic bravery and fully-characteristic stupidity, Whitney pushed past them all. "Now, you listen to me, you pint-sized, always-got-something-to-prove, rock-eating—"

His words were cut short when Gargamane hooked his foot around Whitney's ankle and slammed a gauntleted forearm across his chest. Whitney was as fine a fighter as Tum Tum had seen, but he was no match for an expert Clanbreaker commander—a job Tum Tum was destined for but never wanted. Without so much as a warning, Whitney toppled over and fell over the ledge of the canyon.

Sora screamed, and so did Whitney. Tum Tum couldn't tell which one sounded more feminine. At the same time, Gargamane bent and grasped Whitney's boot.

Dwarves were small, but they were strong—they had to be for all their work in the mines—and Gargamane had clamps for hands. He crushed Whitney by the ankle with one of them.

Whitney hung, flailing. Heat touched the back of Tum Tum's neck as fire rose from Sora's outstretched hand.

"Keep calm," Tum Tum said under his breath.

The clanbreakers shifted. It was clear they hadn't expected such a display, but they wouldn't show fear.

"What are ye thinkin to do with that, witch?" Gargamane asked, not even stuttering at the sight of magic.

"I'll fry you alive," Sora said, stepping forward. "And your men, too. That armor will make a fine kiln."

"Doubt I'll be able to keep him from fallin if I'm burnin in me armor," Gargamane said, then turned to Whitney. "Stop squirmin, or yer gonna fall out of yer boot."

Sora's flame rose higher.

Tum Tum held her back and whispered, "Don't do it, Girly." He looked down at her hands, poised to strike.

"Give me one good reason," Sora demanded.

"Oi! Use yer eyeballs!" Tum Tum squealed. "Yer boyfriend carromin to his death ain't enough?"

"Listen to him, Sora!" Whitney shouted. "Pull me up! Pull me up, and we'll leave!"

"I don't think ye learned yer lesson," Gargamane said.

Sora pressed forward, and the clanbreakers made a wall between the two parties.

"Only one here needs to learn a lesson," Sora said.

It all happened so fast that Tum Tum didn't even have a chance to prepare for it. Sora swung her arm wide, and flame shot from her hand. The fire missed the clanbreakers and Gargamane, but it slammed into the mountain with force. A slow rumble began, and snow and ice came down in a heap. The clanbreakers barely had time to look up before they were crushed beneath it.

Gargamane, however, just shook his head. He knew as well as Tum Tum did that the clanbreakers would be fine in their armor as long as they didn't suffocate. Tum Tum hoped Sora knew the same. Otherwise, she'd just murdered half a dozen of his kin. When he turned, though, he wasn't so sure. The look in her eyes was hotter than the flame.

"Pull him up," Sora said, slowly.

"Yer shog-shuckin mad!" Gargamane cried. He lifted Whitney just a bit but didn't drag him back to solid ground.

"I said pull him up."

"I'm makin the rules round here," Gargamane said. "Ye and yer companions are gonna—"

"Sora, don't!" Lucindur screamed, but it was too late.

Sora yelled and unleashed a focused stream of fire directly at the dwarf. The flame hit Gargamane square in the wrist, giving him no choice but to drop Whitney as he shook out his arm.

Tum Tum and Lucindur shouted, reaching outward, but Sora didn't seem fazed.

"Ye killed him!" Gargamane cried.

Two things happened at the same time. Sora lowered her hand to the earth, and the ground beneath them shook. More snow and ice created a massive avalanche. Fire erupted in a line along the rock wall, melting the snow as it did so. They fought against the stream of water gushing toward them. Much of it turned to steam, the heat of which was intense. Everyone stumbled, but Sora. Whitney's cry could be heard above it all, but instead of becoming fainter, it grew louder and closer. From below, a snow-covered finger of rock rose. Gargamane leaped back.

Safely nestled within the blanket of powder was Whitney, eyes clenched tight, mouth wide open. He stopped screaming as the shifting chunk of the mountain came to a halt.

"I—what—huh?" Whitney stammered.

Everyone stared at Sora, mouth as open as Whitney's had just been. She was on one knee now, cheeks without color, panting like she'd just run from Balonhearth to Westvale and back.

"Meungor's foamy beard. What the yig was that?" Gargamane asked. He and his clanbreakers—now revealed due to the melting snow —backed up.

On his hands and knees, Whitney crawled across the small gap between the magically-raised portion of the mountain and the pass they all stood upon. When he was safe on solid ground, he threw up.

"Shog in a barrel," Whitney groaned as Lucindur helped him to his feet. Tum Tum would have, but he remained frozen in stunned silence.

"We don't even need the stone," Whitney went on. "You could bury Nesilia better than Iam did!"

"Leave now," Gargamane said. "Please. Ye've done enough. We won't pursue ye, but don't ye try to return neither. Ain't nothin here for ye, outcast. Balonhearth and the Three Kingdoms are closed to all foreigners—including those who forsook their homes."

"I don't think you're in any place to be making threats!" Whitney said, voice and arms shaky.

"Oh, be quiet," Lucindur told Whitney.

Sora rose to her full height. Her hands trembled, and she seemed a tad woozy, but she didn't back down. "You're going to open that door and take us to see the king," she demanded.

"Please, I can't," Gargamane replied. "Even if I wanted to, I can't open it. Not from the outside."

"Then how will you get back in?" she asked, voice laced with skepticism.

"Guard changes twice a day. Dawn and dusk. But before ye get any ideas… ye might be able to do wonders—whatever that was—but not even ye can fight all me men. That's no threat, just the truth. I can see how much that took out of ye."

"She'll still barbecue you in a second," Whitney spat.

Gargamane held up his palms. "I'm askin again, we're just doin what our king demanded. No one in. No one out. He's done involvin himself in the troubles of flower-pi… southerners."

Tum Tum had never expected to see a dwarf of such high-standing and military renown looking so defeated.

Turning to the others, Tum Tum said, "Let's go."

"Let's go?" Whitney and Lucindur both said. Sora was still shooting arrows with her eyeballs.

"We haven't gotten what we came for," Whitney said.

"Aye, and we won't be doin it like this," Tum Tum said, voice low. "That door ain't budgin for no man or dwarf. And he's right, we ain't equipped to take on all of Balonhearth unless Sora plans to take the whole yiggin mountain down."

"He's right," Lucindur agreed.

"You too?" Whitney said.

"We'll figure something out," Lucindur said. "We always do. Come on."

"You mean *I* always do," Whitney grumbled.

It took some coaxing, but they finally managed to get Sora to move.

"What was that!" Whitney asked once they were a safe distance away.

Sora looked down at her hands. "I… I don't know. It's like…"

"It's like you still have god powers is what it's like," Whitney finished for her.

Whitney's words seemed to trouble Sora, and Tum Tum couldn't blame her. That was raw power. He'd never found himself frightened of her until then. Such abilities were the things of legend and lore, and goddesses.

"I mean it, you could probably kill Nesilia all on your own!" Whitney said.

"Stop it, Whit," she argued. "I don't know what came over me. It's like… she unlocked something in me."

"Pff, don't give her any credit. You're just a true mystic now, plain and simple. You got it from your mo—"

Sora's hand flew over Whitney's mouth before he could finish. Lucindur then spoke up and reminded them all why they were deep in the snowy mountains.

"Okay, we need a plan," she said.

There was so much going on. All of Pantego was at risk, but there was only one thing Tum Tum could think of. "I'll never be welcome there again," he said louder than he'd intended.

"Here? Who cares?" Whitney said, sliding down the embankment to walk beside him. "You know how dark and dreary that place is?"

"Ain't time for jokes," Tum Tum said. "That was me home."

Whitney placed a hand on Tum Tum's shoulder, forcing him to stop. "You know who you're going to be next time you return there?"

When Tum Tum didn't respond, Whitney said, "The dwarf who saved the whole Iam-forsaken world. Not only will they welcome you back, but you could be the yigging king if you want to be." Then, in a lower voice, he added while glancing up at Sora, "Not that anyone *would* want to be, right?."

Tum Tum smiled. "Yer all right, Whitney Fierstown. Yer all right."

"You're not so bad yourself," Sora said, coming up from behind. They started walking again. "That speech sounded awfully familiar."

Tum Tum turned to see Whitney shrugging.

"Now, really, what do we do?" Whitney asked

"We get into the mountain and get that stone," Tum Tum said. "Ye don't think I've given up, do ye?"

"Mischievous…" Lucindur said, joining him with a grin. "What do you have planned?"

Tum Tum turned to Whitney and said, "Ready for one last heist?"

XI

THE KNIGHT

"**P**ossessed you say?" Lord Jolly asked.

He, Torsten, Dellbar the Holy, and King Pi sat in a war room located beneath the Caleef's throne room. The Shesaitju had afforded them and their people this lower wing of the keep.

"Yes," Torsten said. "It's worse than we feared. One demon tried to take me, and through it, I caught a glimpse of what Nesilia is planning. She has split the barrier of Elsewhere and corrupted all the weakest minds of Panping. They serve her now."

"Possessed…" Pi whispered.

He sat at the far end of the table, quiet and pensive as he'd been since the feast ended. Torsten couldn't believe how much he'd grown since last he'd seen him. A growth spurt had him in that awkward phase between adolescence and adulthood. Torsten had worried that the boy would always be small and frail, but he was beginning to see a clearer picture.

Perhaps his own bout with possession and being corrupted by Redstar's blood magic had stunted him, but now, he was very clearly the spawn of Liam the Conqueror and his impressive Drav Cra wife. Even the tone of voice had lowered.

The Miracle King would be formidable, just like his father.

"Yes, Your Grace," Torsten said. "Sir Danvels and I saw them with our own eyes. Or, his, rather."

"Those unfortunate souls," Pi said, staring out over the sea, eyes glazed over. Torsten could only imagine how he felt, all things considered. Nobody in the world would better know their suffering.

"If there are any of their former selves left inside," Lord Jolly said.

"There is…"

Torsten laid his hand over the King's. He knew Liam would've thought ill of such uninvited familiarity, but Pi wasn't his father.

"We'll do whatever we can to save them," Torsten said.

"I'm supposed to protect them," Pi replied, voice shaking. "That is my only duty as King. Protect the people."

"You can't be expected to face a vengeful goddess," Lord Jolly said.

"Father would have."

"And you are certainly not him." Dellbar voiced his opinion for the first time. He leaned against the wall in the corner, his blind eyes making it impossible to tell where his attentions were. Though, Torsten had noticed one peculiarity. Neither at the feast, nor this morning had he taken a single swig of alcohol. In addition, he looked like he hadn't slept in days.

"Perhaps it's time for a nap, Dellbar," Lord Jolly remarked.

"If only I could." He strode toward the table, patting for the back of one of the sandstone seats. When he found it, he leaned over it on his elbows. "I meant no offense. It's purely a statement of fact."

"Not a necessary one," Torsten said.

"But it is. King Pi may not be Liam, but he *was* possessed by Nesilia. When Iam worked through me, I felt His fear. He gave so much of Himself to drive Nesilia's new form away. Like me, our Miracle King may know Nesilia's fears."

"I don't," Pi said, without a moment's hesitation. "I don't remember anything with clarity. It's like it was her but wasn't at the same time— an echo of her, funneled through Redstar… I don't know."

"Or perhaps you'd just rather not think about it?" Dellbar moved around the chair, leaning right beside the King. "Because you miss what she gave you."

"Mind yourself, Your Holiness," Torsten warned.

"I don't miss it," Pi said, his gaze drooping toward the floor.

"I understand, Your Grace. All I can think about is Iam's power coursing through me again. How it felt. Our mortal bodies aren't meant for what they are." He stepped closer, and Torsten noticed Pi's foot tapping under the table. "Think, Your Grace. Put yourself back into those moments and see her."

"I can't!" Pi shouted, slamming his small fist on the table.

"Enough, Dellbar," Torsten ordered. "I was there, atop Mount Lister, when Nesilia was driven back the first time. Whatever she was then, she wasn't yet complete. She was weak. This is different."

Dellbar sighed and returned to his spot against the wall. "Now isn't the time for coddling."

"No, it is a time for celebration," Lord Jolly said. "For at the high sun, our King will be wed, and the two greatest armies in Pantego will join. Possession, magic—we defeated it once in the hands of the mystics. Then, we needed no tricks. The same will do again. Right, Your Grace?"

All looked to King Pi, and for a few seconds, his stare lingered on the floor before he composed himself. "We must prepare," he said, standing. And without waiting for a response, he headed for the exit, Lord Jolly struggling to keep up.

"I'll join you soon, Your Grace," Torsten said as Pi breezed by, receiving no answer. He and Lord Jolly exchanged a nervous look. The confident, growing young man Torsten had witnessed the night before had vanished the moment talk of his dark past arose.

Torsten watched until Pi left. Then he turned to Dellbar.

"He can't remember anything," Torsten said as he approached the High Priest.

"So he says," Dellbar replied.

"Either way… now is not the time to fill his head with doubts."

"You were there, Torsten. You witnessed her return, just as I did."

"I witnessed many things I cannot explain," Torsten said. Then he moved up beside Dellbar and glanced down. Up close, he observed trembling hands. "You're not drinking anymore."

"I hadn't noticed," Dellbar replied, words dripping with sarcasm.

"That's good."

The High Priest turned to face Torsten. He didn't need eyes to exhibit the heartbreak wracking his very soul. His shoulder's slumped. His cheeks were gaunt. His features all darkened like the storm lingering out over the Boiling Waters, ready to wreak havoc.

"Last night, at the feast..." Dellbar said. "All that spiced wine and... nothing. No urge."

"Well, we need your mind clear."

"It's not. I can't sleep. Can't eat. Can't yigging drink. Feeling His power flowing through me again—it's everything, all I crave. I can't think about anything else."

"He chose you for a reason, Dellbar," Torsten said. "Even if you can't see it. Your faith was strong enough to summon his power and save us all to fight another day."

"That's just it. He gave you sight when all your hope was lost. He gave me purpose when I stopped caring. He chose us, and we were right there to stop Nesilia. Right where we were meant to be. And even with Iam's aid, she somehow survived. That was the moment when I felt his fear. Not when He fought her, but when she didn't die. It's when I realized that perhaps there really is no stopping her now."

Torsten sighed. "Of all people to lose faith."

"We study demonic possession in Hornsheim, Torsten. You must know that. I'm sure the Shieldsmen do as well, ever since the First Panping War. Even if it became so rare it seemed like myth. Destroying the host doesn't destroy them. They can seek refuge in another body."

"But there's a way to banish them, isn't there? I fought the mystics, and our priests weren't only healers in the war against their magic. They called on Iam's light itself to shield us."

"That's different."

"Is it?" Torsten said. "Their magic comes from Elsewhere. So do these cursed spirits."

"I've never dealt with possession myself, but there are tomes and stories from the elders. They say Iam's light can drive them back to the shadow realm He created for those unworthy."

"Then we can stop them."

"One problem," Dellbar said. "Elsewhere has been split wide open."

"Open?" Torsten said, voice empty of life.

"How else would she command such forces?" Dellbar said.

"There must be a way. Iam's light will protect us again and provide a means of facing them."

Dellbar shook his head. "When the mystics were destroyed, such defensive arts were no longer needed, buried in texts in the Chamber of Light below Hornsheim. There was only a battered world left to heal, and together, Liam and Wren ordained that the Church of Iam should focus only on rebuilding efforts."

"Then perhaps it's time you visit Hornsheim and change that. Right now, we must gather the priests of Iam and have them join this fight."

"Those were different times," Dellbar argued. "Iam had the Order prepared to fight the mystics. Time is not on our side."

"There will be nothing to heal if we're all dead."

"Besides, Wren the Holy was far more knowledgeable than I. His faith, far more unbroken."

Torsten took Dellbar by the shoulders. "Yet Iam never deemed him worthy of working through his body, Father Morningweg," Torsten said. He purposely used the man's former name and title—a reminder of how he'd once been known.

"Only the truest followers of the Light will be able to banish Nesilia's new servants. But they won't all be eager to listen to me and march off to their deaths. You've never been to Hornsheim. It's politics more than faith, and they chose me only because they knew I had no power myself. I've been High Priest for barely a fortnight."

"And been party to two miracles." Torsten used his blessed sight to stare directly at the man. "You don't need Iam controlling you to serve Him, my friend. He's always been with you. Perhaps, this is why."

Dellbar exhaled slowly, then nodded. "I hope you're right."

"I know I am. We're still here, aren't we?"

"The parts of us that matter, I suppose. Fine, Sir Unger. At the request of the Master of Warfare, I will travel to Hornsheim and gather the priests after we're done here. But know that it still may not matter. The cursed spirits the mystics released in the wars were freed by accident. They were exposed. Solitary."

"I'll take anything that helps buy us time to figure out a way to stop Nesilia. Once she falls, they all will."

"So, we hope. But Iam was afraid for a reason, and it is because as this darkness floods our world and people lose their faith in Him, His light wanes. That is the truth I'm now unfortunate enough to know. We can call on His power all we want, and there might not be any left to help us."

"There will be."

"You don't know that."

Torsten gave Dellbar's arm a light, reassuring squeeze. Then, he pounded his own chest. "There's enough faith right here. Enough left in me alone to give." Then he turned his hand to Dellbar and laid a flat palm against the man's chest. "And combined with yours? Iam might as well have the faith of all Pantego."

Dellbar offered a small smile and bobbed his head, then shuffled to straighten out, leaning on his cane.

Torsten returned the smile, then turned to leave. He was in the doorway when Dellbar stopped him.

"Oh, Master Unger, the rest of the Royal Council convened, and we all agreed," Dellbar said, face turned away. "We see no reason why the Master of Warfare cannot also serve as Wearer of White, head of the King's Shield. The King must've been too distracted to bring the white helm here—it was his idea—but you're finally you again."

Torsten thought for a beat. He recalled that day when the white helm was stripped from him by Redstar... no, his own carelessness. He imagined earning it back would feel better than anything in his entire life. Yet, all he could picture was it on Sir Nikserof's head as he bled out from the throat. Or Uriah, having his skin worn by a vile warlock.

"I am honored," Torsten said. "And perhaps someone will wear the helm again one day. But it won't be me."

He lingered a few seconds longer in disbelief over what he'd just said. Then he tapped the stone wall twice and continued out of the room. Of all Redstar's myriad curses, none was so obvious as that placed upon the Wearer of White.

Torsten would say this about the Shesaitju, their Boiling Keep was nowhere near as complicated as the Glass Castle. All paths and hallways led toward the throne room. Even the lower chambers lacked the labyrinthian feel of his home's tunnels and crypts. But then, they had always been a simpler people. Focused. Strength meant everything to them, and for those who couldn't be strong, loyalty to their afhems was their most celebrated export. Now, all in Latiapur were loyal to the Caleef.

As Torsten traversed the city on his own, he began to see how frightening an aspect that was. The Shesaitju were skilled, ruthless warriors. It was in their blood, bred from centuries spent in the harsh Black Sands desert filled with rival armies and deadly beasts.

Liam had been able to conquer the Black Sands because of all the infighting. He knew how to exploit weaknesses and drive wedges, how to get an afhem to remove his support from another without ever having to lift a sword.

But Torsten knew what a threat the Shesaitju under a single banner would pose, all while his own Kingdom would grow soft and accustomed to victory. His only solace was that despite Mahraveh displaying her grand army throughout the streets, the vast and wild city markets told a different story.

Most wouldn't notice it, but Torsten had spent years watching the feasts in the Glass Castle, keeping an eye out for *any* signs of unrest. And they were here. Beyond colorful sarongs and intricately weaved baskets, a name Torsten recognized was whispered here and there. His hearing, enhanced by the loss of true sight, allowed him to perceive it. *Babrak.* The afhem whom Torsten had previously attempted to align with against Muskigo.

His name was like background noise, always present, but never more than a rustle on the wind. And occasionally, Torsten saw Serpent Guards grab locals, warriors and markless alike, and drag them away. They always covered their mouths to keep them from shouting.

Queen Oleander had done the same when Yarrington's people spoke out against her. Only, those people were slung by the throats over the castle walls. Torsten could only hope that Mahraveh wasn't her father.

Already, Caleef Mahraveh's attempt to unite her people, altruistic as it might have been, wasn't working. At least, not in the way she'd expected.

Afhems, even without the title, still carried the respect of their former afhemates. Torsten noted the warlords, scalped and scabbed, trouncing around the city with dozens of warriors in tow. Perhaps, in time, without inter-afhemate wars, these loyalties might dissipate completely.

He did, however, have to learn to appreciate that these people weren't his own. They were different, beyond only how they looked. King Liam had no greater fault than that. Trying to make all Pantego a reflection of himself.

In Yarrington, for Oleander to do what she'd done was monstrous. It was unforgivable in the eyes of Iam, even if Torsten had found a way to forgive and love her. But here? Death was as common as the shifting of the dunes. If Pi ever hoped to change the Shesaitju's harsh ways, Torsten knew they'd have to understand them first.

Nothing exemplified this more than the arena known as the Tal'du Dromesh. Torsten knew all the tales. How their finest warriors battled to the death on its hallowed sands in order to earn their titles. He'd heard of how Muskigo slaughtered his opponents to claim the Ayerabi Afhemate while King Liam watched.

Torsten could never understand why a culture would purposely allow dozens of their best soldiers to die on ceremony alone. To sacrifice their lives for what—entertainment?

Now, he stood before that great arena, its stone arcades rising high. The zhulong statues set along its crest clashed with their gilded tusks, home to many a bird searching for their next meal in the sea below. Giant spheres filled with nigh'jels hung in intervals, creating a soft, cool glow against the black sandstone columns. Serpent Guards stood in every opening of the entry colonnade, and they allowed Torsten passage to the place where young Pi was to be married.

What better place for the grandest performance the Kingdom has ever known?

When he reached the inside, that truth became even more apparent. Yarrington was home to theaters that could fit hundreds to be entertained by acting troupes and musicians. Torsten had helped secure countless plays put on in Liam's honor after every victory they'd achieved.

Those were nothing compared to this.

The walls were high as any castle, with dozens of layers of stands rising up them. They all circulated a walled pit of black sand, stopping only at a dam of rocks on the seaside, which kept the Boiling Waters out.

Later that day, at the highest sun, when Iam's eye was most watchful, thousands upon thousands would pack those stands to witness the union of Pi and Mahraveh. It was Torsten's job to help secure it, a task that seemed impossible. If Mahraveh's people decided to swarm the arena, they would swallow them whole.

Servants from the palace carried shell garlands, nigh'jel lanterns, flower petals, palm fronds, and more, decorating every flat surface for the event. Torsten glanced right. Sir Mulliner spoke with the head of the Serpent Guards—the only one of them with a tongue—pointing out weak spots in the arena. As if it would matter. They were placing their trust in a people who'd been in open rebellion only weeks earlier.

Shieldsmen probed with them, learning the layout. Their white plated armor stuck out against the black-colored stone. Once they were done here, putting on a show, Torsten would have them all get rid of it. They couldn't face Nesilia in armor infused with the glaruium she could manipulate.

Torsten was on his way to meet with Sir Mulliner when he noticed that the battlegrounds weren't empty. Winding his way back through the innards of the arena and emerging into the sands, Torsten heard them, silently fighting. Three Serpent Guards sparred with Caleef Mahraveh in the center. Her skin was a shade darker than the sand. The Serpent Guards couldn't talk due to their lack of tongues, but neither did she grunt or yell, no matter how much force she put behind an attack.

Her long spear parried and thrust, sparking along the sickle blades of her opponents. She ducked and weaved, and while they didn't strike her, they weren't holding back in the slightest. It was like a choreographed dance.

The muscles of her long, lean body stretched and tightened. She was slight but impossibly agile, bending backward and springing clear of strikes like a limber snake. She landed on the balls of her feet, ready to pounce, then her dark eyes fixed upon Torsten.

"Stop," she said.

The Serpent Guards pulled back mid-attacks, sheathing their weapons and falling to attention with speed and discipline Torsten could only dream of. Even Sir Davies' best Shieldsmen—of which Torsten had been one—were never so in sync.

Mahraveh crouched and wiped her hands in the sand. Then she stabbed her spear down and sauntered toward him. Torsten averted his gaze by nature. It had been hard to tell while she was fighting, but now it was clear—she wore absolutely nothing. Only long braids entwined with shells and trinkets bounced off her, clattering as she walked.

"You must be Sir Unger?" she said, stopping a short distance from him.

"I… uh… yes, my Lady," he stammered. "I am."

"You'll have to speak louder here. The winds of our God converge in this place, making it quite loud. Especially when storms brew off the coast."

"I am Sir Unger, my Lady," Torsten pronounced. "We didn't have a chance to speak at the feast."

"I know your relationship with my father. You can look at me."

"It's not that, my Lady. You're… uh…" He glanced up. The Black Sands was a hot place, and it's people dressed in a way far less conservative than his own, but he didn't expect her to be nude. And the sun barely seemed to even play against her skin, like she absorbed all the light around her.

"Oh…" She looked down at her body. "I apologize, Sir Unger. Sometimes, I don't realize."

She strolled over to the arena's stone wall. Then, grabbing a gold-and-shell-laced dress hanging from a spike meant to keep combatants from daring to climb out, she let it drape over her. While it would have been out of place anywhere in Yarrington apart from a brothel, here, it fit.

"I cannot believe you are here," Mahraveh said, returning. The arena held many large rocks that the contestants would use for cover. She found one such boulder planted and raised herself upon it. Then, she snapped her fingers toward one of the Serpent Guards, and he fetched her spear.

"Is something else the matter, Sir Unger?" she asked. "Am I still not decent enough for your sensibilities?"

Torsten drew a long breath before starting off toward her. "No, it's not that. I'm just… not used to the heat of this place." It wasn't exactly a lie. As he moved from the shadow of the entry tunnel, the hot southern sun beat down on his bald pate. Even wearing only a thin brown tunic, sweat beaded on every part of him.

He stopped across from her and bowed his head. "It's an honor to meet you."

She nodded but said nothing. Instead, one of the guards handed her a whetstone, and she started sharpening the blade of her spear. Torsten gave her a few seconds more to answer, but still, nothing came. As she slid the stone, sparks flying out, all he could picture was Muskigo. She had his eyes and nose.

"I have concerns over the security of this location," Torsten said.

"What was he like at the end?" Mahraveh asked, neither looking up nor responding to his statement.

"Excuse me?"

"Muskigo. There were others there, but I don't know if they can be honest with me, even if they want to. You don't care about our god, so *you* be honest with me."

"I see." Torsten straightened his blindfold, cleared his throat. "He was… Brave—"

"Another word for outmatched," she interjected.

"We all were. Truthfully, I have never seen anything like it, and I have fought many things. Mystics, giants, dwarves—your father stood above them all as a warrior."

"He defeated you in Winde Port," she said bluntly.

"I'd say we both lost, considering we were both going to drown before he was pulled out of the canals."

"I never heard that part of the story."

Torsten chuckled. "I'm sure you haven't. A lot of blunders were made in that battle by both of us. If that damn blood mage hadn't burned down the entire city and drove his army out, we may have all slaughtered each other."

Her whetstone slid out as she missed her next stroke. Her finger caught on the edge of the blade. Even if it drew blood, she was quick to drop her hand to her side.

If you can help it, Torsten thought, *never let the enemy see you bleed.*

One of many lessons Sir Uriah Davies had taught them, and one that had served him well over the years.

"My father razed the city to cover his retreat," Mahraveh stated.

"Perhaps he lit the fuse, but the fire came by Sora's command," Torsten said. "Your father and I were too busy focused on killing each other to strategize. Our people are the only reason either of us was pulled out alive."

She returned to sharpening her blade. "It's interesting."

"What is?"

"How history forms when there is a winner," she said. "I used to picture my father's face when word reached us that he had conquered Winde Port, stolen it right from under the nose of the great Shieldsman, Torsten Unger. I'd imagine his smile and your anger."

"Your father didn't smile. He was many things, but he was not one to celebrate until the job was done."

"And now he is dead," she said. There wasn't a hint of emotion in the words.

"He is."

"I wonder what history will say if Nesilia wipes all of us out. Will it even remember him, or you, or me? Will it even matter that we ever existed?"

"Of course, it will," Torsten said. "Even if not a soul remembers, we will know what we did. That we came together to fight the darkness. That means something."

"And yet, Muskigo is still dead," Mahraveh said.

"Not in vain. My Lady, he showed us that even the greatest warrior in Pantego cannot stand against Nesilia alone. It will take all of us."

"The greatest?" she asked. "You claimed your battle ended in a tie."

"I said we both lost, but truthfully, I would have died first." Torsten gestured to the stands of the great arena, bustling with men and woman preparing for the ceremony. "I suppose that sort of thing matters in a place like this."

"Only victory matters." Mahraveh finished sharpening and held the blade up to her face. The tip glinted in the morning sunlight as she turned it over to examine both sides, blowing away the metal shavings. Then, she extended it toward Torsten so he could see.

"Well done," he said.

"I had it reforged after White Bridge," Mahraveh said.

"These weapons will be of no use," Torsten said. "Nesilia's somehow taken control of the body of an upyr. A young woman who I knew. You remind me of her, actually, back when she was amongst the living."

"Is that a good thing?" Mahraveh asked.

"As long as you don't also plan on destroying the world."

"Only if that's what it takes to save it."

Torsten tripped over his response, then nodded. That was the Shesaitju in her. Victory at all costs, at least until their past Caleef had surrendered to Liam and broken their spirits.

They could never understand that Sidar Rakun surrendered because he knew, otherwise, the afhems would keep fighting until the Shesaitju went extinct. Just as Torsten knew that even if Sora hadn't sparked that fire in Winde Port, Muskigo *would* have razed the city just to label it a victory.

"It won't come to that," Torsten said with as much vim as he could muster. All the wars in his lifetime, he usually had the knowledge to understand what the future would hold, whether they won or lost. Not this time.

Mahraveh reeled back the spear and stood. She spun it a few times, then thrust at the air, metal humming. "You can learn almost everything you need to about a man by fighting him," she said.

"On that, we agree," Torsten replied.

"My father hated you," she went on, "but he did respect you."

"Something else we agree on."

"When I proposed this idea of marriage, my father knew that if he brought it to you, you'd understand. Not Sir Nikserof, not your King, or anyone else on his Council—only you."

"Sometimes logic dictates the only move. Our gods clearly want us to face Nesilia together."

"My God is dead," Mahraveh said, this too without emotion.

Torsten's brow furrowed. "What?"

"It is my belief that both our gods gave every ounce of power they had left to bring us all here, alive."

"That's not true," Torsten said.

"It doesn't matter either way. I have to believe that, like them, my father died protecting you for a reason."

"He was protecting everyone."

Mahraveh grunted, then sat back down. "King Pi thinks very highly of you, Sir Unger," she said. "He's not what I expected, but he ran to you like a son to a father. I don't why, nor do I care, but it's clear to me that though he is the door, the key to the Glass Kingdom is through you."

"Pi will be a strong and just King, my Lady. Of that, I no longer have any doubt. For a long time, I did, but Nesilia put him through an Exile worse than any of us, and here he is still, ready to do what it takes to face her."

"And because you believe in him, so do I. So, I ask of *you*, Sir Unger, champion of your King. Warrior to warrior. If we defeat Nesilia, and we all get a chance to keep writing history, don't let my people be erased from it."

"Be true to our King, and I promise you, I will not." Torsten took a deep breath before deciding to sit beside her. He noticed the Serpent Guards tense, closing in without being obvious about it. But his movement was purposeful. If what she wanted was ever to come to pass, the respect would have to go two ways. She wasn't his Queen yet.

"Fighting may be all I'm good at, my Lady," Torsten said softly. "But I'm so tired of it. When we defeat Nesilia, it will be the last war I ever wage."

"'*When* we defeat her,'" she repeated. "I like that."

Mahraveh looked straight at Torsten's face. For the briefest moment, the hard edge of a young woman who had to act like a goddess vanished, and Torsten saw the person beneath.

In that moment, Torsten wondered if, perhaps, Nesilia's return wasn't all awful. Perhaps, Iam let it come to pass in order to bring the people of Pantego together for once after the God Feud ripped everyone apart millennia ago.

He hoped, though, he knew deep down, it wasn't true.

XII

THE CALEEF

"**Y**ou look positively radiant, my Caleef," one of the palace sages said, smearing a bit of gold-colored makeup across Mahi's eyelids.

Mahi let them pamper her, though she didn't like it. The old eunuchs didn't bear names, none they dared to speak, at least. They were her servants, and far too many packed the tiny room in which she prepared for the wedding. She'd ensured it was the very same room—deep in Tal'du Dromesh's undercroft—where she was kept before competing in the al' Tariq tournament.

Shallow water washed over her bare feet. She couldn't feel the temperature, but she knew it had to be warm this time of year. She did, however, feel the mass of nigh'jels flocking around her. The entire cavern glowed a soft, pulsing green.

Another servant finished adjusting the hem of her dress. It draped around her feet, gold-threaded netting with shells or gems at each intersection. The dress solidified around her knees, transitioning to extravagant gold cloth with delicate ornamental embroidery, then back to a pattern of transparent netting over her midriff reminiscent of waves. Her breasts, too, were covered by the gold cloth. Around her neck, she wore an elaborate crystal necklace given to her by the Glassmen.

Mahi had never cared much about clothing, but she had to admit, the dress was stunning. Especially considering it had been crafted only in weeks. And the necklace… she'd never seen anything like it. There was a gentle beauty to the unity between Kingdoms being so captured by a single outfit. For what was glass if not sand, blown and refined?

Not only had there never been a female Caleef, there had never been a Caleef to get married. There was no reason for it. The position wasn't dynastic. For any Shesaitju woman to have ever been willing to marry a Caleef would mean they saw themselves also as a vessel of the God of Sand and Sea. No Shesaitju woman would've ever dared think that.

This was unprecedented. Mahi knew that. And so, she let these loyal servants of her position and their god do as they pleased. She even allowed them to cover her head with a veil, beads over her eyes. She let them build up the sharp points at the shoulders of her dress, and stretch the tight sleeves down her arms, which, at least—thankfully—faded to netting around her wrists.

She played along, though she hated restricting her body in such a way to be no good in a fight.

The fight comes after, she reminded herself. *For now, I need the support.*

She knew that beyond doing something no Caleef had ever done, as the first female Caleef, those were secondary concerns. She was marrying a Glassman. A King, chosen by his own god or not, that's all they'd see.

They wouldn't see the smart, capable young man she hadn't expected to meet, with loyal, worthy advisors at his side. They'd see pink-skin, a diminutive figure, and the memories of their fathers being destroyed by his.

And so, Mahi had to look the part. Beautiful, strong, unflinching, and unquestionably Shesaitju.

She manipulated the clasp of the necklace. "Take it off," she said.

"Excuse me, my Caleef?" one of the sages remarked.

"Take it off. My people, they will only see this as representation that we are again being collared. This is a union, not captivity."

"I… uh—"

"Now!" Mahi snapped, and her servants obeyed.

She lamented losing it for the sheer beauty of the thing, and truly, she didn't want her future husband to be insulted—but her people came first.

"And... finished," one of the other sages said, perfecting her makeup. Mahi wasn't sure she'd ever seen anyone look so pleased with themselves, except maybe Babrak after he'd killed Farhan and seized favor with the other afhems.

A servant woman held up a mirror, and Mahi finally had a chance to see the fruits of their efforts. Tapered lines of glittering gold circled her eyes, stretching toward her temples like wings. The way it contrasted against her pure-black skin made it feel bright as sunlight. The same color lined her thin lips.

She reached up and ran her thumb along them. Whether it be her shell of hardened nigh'jel blood or the gold makeup, she missed how she used to look. Who she used to be. She missed the chance to care about people and not *all* the people.

Mahi pulled her hand back.

"I hope this necklace will better suit you, my Caleef," one of the sages said. It took her a bit to find the speaker, there were so many, all with soft, impassive voices. He presented a necklace made of onyx pearls, found only at the bottom of the deep Boiling Waters.

"This will be fine," she said. "I can handle it. This is enough. Leave me." She snatched it from his hands, her glower sending him and all the others filing out of the room. She spun to face the rocky wall, the bottom of her dress twisting beneath the shallow water.

She stared down at the pearls. It was said that in complete darkness, a purplish glow emanated from their centers. The nigh'jels made the room too bright to tell, so she closed them in her palms and peered through the crack between her fingers.

"I can help with that, my Caleef."

The necklace slipped and splashed in the water. Mahi immediately crouched, reaching in to fish it out, but the nigh'jels crowded her arms, brushing against it with all their innumerable tentacles.

She knew the work that went into retrieving pearls like these. Her people had to dive to the seafloor, in rough waters filled with killer creatures. Some may have died in the effort to rush the production of this necklace so she could look more regal than her future Glassman husband.

"I'm sorry, I didn't mean to startle you," Bit'rudam said. He rushed in to help, but Mahi barred him with one outstretched arm.

With her other, she dug around under the water until her finger looped something, and she pulled it free. One of the nigh'jels hung from her arm as it emerged. She grunted and flung it aside, then found herself squeezing the necklace, drawing deep, ragged breaths.

"My Caleef, is everything all right?" Bit'rudam asked, not daring touch her.

"You're too smart to ask that question, Bit'rudam," she replied, exhaling slowly through her teeth.

"I just mean—"

He got tongue-tied when she turned to face him. His eyes told the whole story. They studied her from head to toe, while his cheeks went a darker shade.

"You look—"

"Is the arena secure?" Mahi interrupted him again.

"It is," Bit'rudam said. "Sir Unger and I both checked everything. Both the Shieldsmen and Serpent Guard will circle the arena around you. Two warships are moored beyond the dam. If the Glassmen try to make a move on you, they'd be killing their own King."

"I'm not worried about that."

"You should be. This Sir Unger... I do not trust any man whose eyes I cannot read."

"He has no eyes, Bit'rudam."

"So, the pink-skinned tricksters say," he said.

"Just do your job and keep the arena safe," Mahi said, a harsh edge entering her tone.

What was this all for? If her own most loyal servants refused to trust their soon-to-be allies, what good was it?

"Always, my Caleef... it's just..." He turned toward the water. Mahi waited for him to glance up before she nodded him along. "Are you still sure you want to do this?" he asked.

"Do you know how tired I am of that question?" she answered.

"I know. You're right."

"I'm trying to be a Caleef who *actually* helps our people, one who uses this power, or whatever it is I was chosen for, to change things, not sit on a throne and watch like a spectator of the Tal'du Dromesh."

"I know."

"Do I want to marry a stranger? No, Bit'rudam, I do not. But—"

Without warning, Bit'rudam lunged and kissed her. His strong arms wrapped her back and pulled her close so she could feel his chest heaving. His lips pressed tight, and her eyes closed as she found herself instinctually kissing him in return.

And then, she remembered her last first kiss in this very room—with Jumaat, right before their ignoring of the laws caused him to forfeit his life to the Siren. Her best friend ever. Her *only* friend ever.

"No!" Mahi shrieked, pushing Bit'rudam away so hard, he fell back into the water. Before she knew it, she was on top of him, stretching the pearl necklace across his throat with both hands and pushing.

His yellow-flecked eyes went wide as he gurgled. His mouth and nose were barely above water, but he didn't defend himself. Never even kicked. He simply reached out to stroke her cheek.

She rolled off, though remained crouching in the water and ready to pounce. Bit'rudam gasped, then coughed as he crawled back to lean against the cavern wall.

"My Caleef," he rasped. "I—"

"What were you thinking!" she barked.

Bit'rudam pushed off with one arm to sit up straight, still wheezing. "I thought… I needed you to know."

Mahi glared at him, fuming, unable to speak. She could hardly breathe.

"Mahraveh," he went on. "Caleef or not, I have never met a woman like you. From the moment I laid eyes upon you, I knew that the Current brought us together for a reason, and so I ask you now, as a man who loves you, do not do this."

"You would damn the entire world just for me?" she whispered.

"Is it really that simple for you?"

Mahi relaxed her stance. "Nothing about it is simple. It's just what's necessary."

Bit'rudam frowned. Tears welled up in a look not befitting a man of his status as her primary protector.

"Well, I lied," he said. "I thought I could serve you through all of this, despite my feelings, but I cannot. I will resign my duties after the ceremony."

"Stand up, Bit'rudam," she said sternly. He looked perplexed. "I said stand up. Good." She approached him, then patted his gold pauldrons, and ensured his armor was straight. "That is the last I'll hear of that. You say you love me, then prove it. Protect me."

"But Mahraveh, I—"

She placed her fingers over his lips. "I said that's the last of this. Clean yourself off, and we'll greet the future together." She stared into his eyes for a moment longer, then dragged her thumb across his lips and to his cheek before walking to the open door.

"And Bit'rudam."

He looked to her, hope in his eyes.

"Kiss me again without my permission, and you'll lose your tongue like the others."

She couldn't describe what sort of sound he made behind her, but it dripped with embarrassment before he stammered, "Yes, my Caleef."

Mahi set off through the undercroft without another word. She waited until she was out of sight to feel her chest, realizing that her heart beat like it hadn't since becoming Caleef. Then, she noted how she'd been careful to add 'without her permission.' She hadn't even thought about it, but the opening for her and Bit'rudam remained.

She didn't mind.

It was nice to have someone around who reminded her that no matter who she was, she was still alive. She'd survived the temptation of a simpler life with a man of her own race who she knew she could love—perhaps already did. Now, she knew she was ready.

"My Caleef, there you are!" Tingur said, hurrying down the tunnel on his bum leg, accompanied by guards. He froze upon the sight of her, offering a very different expression than the one Bit'rudam had displayed, though flattering, nonetheless.

"The Current flows with you today," he said, bowing his head. "In all its splendor."

Mahi stopped, straightened her dress, and took a deep breath to compose herself. "What is it, Tingur?"

"I've been advised to have you hurry. The Glassmen insist their ceremonial rites be read at the high sun, but we mustn't be a moment later. That storm will set upon us soon, and the sages predict it will be strong."

"Storms seem to follow me," Mahi said.

Tingur chuckled. "Indeed."

"What do you think this one foretells?"

"On the islands, sea storms bring ruin, but also new beginnings. A changing of the tide, so to speak. I believe it to be a good omen, my Caleef."

"Tingur, she's ready," Bit'rudam said from down the tunnel.

"I can see that," Tingur replied.

Mahi glanced back and saw Bit'rudam strolling toward them, mustering his most confident stride. His expression betrayed no sign of their latest interaction, and of that, she was glad. Sir Unger would sniff out an illicit affair in a second if Bit'rudam couldn't control his emotions. Even Tingur didn't notice, promptly turning to lead them.

Maybe it's what he needed, Mahi thought. *Or what I needed...*

XIII

THE OUTCAST

After a long trek down the mountain, Tum Tum and the others stood in a place he knew well.

"Grew up in these fields," he said. "Wouldn't know it by all the snow, but there're tracks under there. Wind all the way through that pass, and beyond."

He couldn't remember a time when the minecarts traveled on those tracks, but he knew them. At one time, they'd have been shoveled and cleared, but for as long as Tum Tum had been alive—save the few weeks a year where the plains in this southern part of Brotlebir would thaw—the tracks were a tripping hazard beneath heaps of snow.

"It's... uh... beautiful, Tum Tum," Whitney said, staring out over the stark white landscape. "I bet you had... you must have had a great childhood."

Tum Tum turned to see Whitney whispering something to Sora.

"Aye, ye dolt," he said. "But that ain't why we're here."

"So, why are we here?" Lucindur asked, her hands tucked underneath both her arms to stay warm.

"Follow me," Tum Tum said. Then under his breath, he added, "Damn flower-pickers have no appreciation for showmanship."

He led them through the clearing, trudging through snow that easily passed his belly—a belly that had, since all this mess began, shrunk quite a bit.

Yer lookin trim, ye devil, Tum Tum told himself. *Best throw back a few ales next chance ye get.*

He pointed out spots where he recalled, with dwarven precision, the exact location of iron rails. Sora and Lucindur both expressed how impressed they were, while Whitney grumbled that it "wasn't like he killed a god or anything."

Tum Tum had known Whitney long enough to know this was as close to praise as the ungrateful runt would ever give. Though, Tum Tum couldn't help but give credit where credit was due. Somehow, a two-bit, over-exaggerative thief had become a hero. It was difficult to admit, but if they'd made it through, the bards would be writing tales about Whitney for the rest of time. They'd call him precisely what he continually reminds everyone he is: a godkiller.

Tum Tum's bones ached. He'd been sore before—growing up in the mines would do that to anyone—but this was different. Worse than that, his heart ached. It had taken him the whole journey to stop shaking after their run-in with Gargamane. Ever since Tum Tum was a wee boy, he'd looked up to the commander of the clanbreakers. Sure, all the clanbreakers could wallop the snot out of anyone, alive or dead, but the commander of them all… Gargamane the Gold was a legend.

And Gargamane the Gold just told him how unwanted he was in his own home.

So much for bein over it, Tum Tum mused.

"We almost there?" Whitney complained, pulling Tum Tum from his despair.

"There," he said, stopping as if on cue. "Dwarves be a little too trustin and a lot too proud."

They soon stood before a boarded-up old iron mine. It had been that way since Tum Tum was Aquira's size. He'd always wondered how the king could be so lax with an entrance to his kingdom left unattended.

"Good as our minds are, there ain't too many with memory of this place," Tum Tum said.

He brushed aside some freshly-fallen powder. "Hole's a bit smaller than I remember."

"You fit in *there*?" Whitney asked.

"Me and me kin. Used to play down here all day, then sneak inside. Tunnel leads to the southern mead hall—suren it's no longer in use, but we'd steal us a drink or seven from the barrels, and none were the wiser."

"You... steal?" Whitney said, with mock-offense. "And to think, I've known you all these years and you never told me."

Tum Tum laughed, one big exhale. "Wasn't like any of yer grand adventures. Truth was, we didn't even need to. Anyone's of age to drink in Balonhearth, and the barrels ran free for me friend Brouben—son of the King he is."

"Son of the King—your friend? Why didn't you tell Gargamane you were friends with the Prince?" Lucindur asked.

"I *was* friends with the son of the King. Ain't seen him in many moons. Besides, ye heard him clear as I. This outcast ain't welcome here no more. Wouldn't have done no good to drag poor Brouben into things now, would it?"

Whitney unleashed an exaggerated sigh. "If by 'do any good' you mean us being inside and sipping on a pint instead of freezing off our baby-makers—ouch!"

Sora punched Whitney in the arm.

It was good to see the lass with some strength again. After that feat she accomplished on the pass, Tum Tum expected her to be out for days. But she bounced back, looking only a little worse for the wear.

"We can still get in there," Sora said while Whitney rubbed the wound to his delicate ego, stepping forward and clearly trying to put on an air of positivity.

There was positive, and then there was delusional. Tum Tum could have—maybe—fit his arm through the gap between boards... and even then, only up to the elbow.

"I remember it being bigger," Tum Tum admitted.

"That's what she said," Whitney whispered to Lucindur, who stood by his side.

Whitney dodged another hit from Sora, then approached the boards, squeezing between Tum Tum and the rocks. He ran his hand over the aged wood.

"Sora, can't you just—woosh!" He motioned his hand like a flame.

"You'll have to forgive me," she said, "but rescuing you from death kind of took a lot of out of me."

"I think that just makes us even, right?" Whitney smiled. "Fine.

Then, how about Aquira. You can blow a hole right through there, can't you, Girl?"

Whitney turned, head swiveling side to side.

"Where the yig did Aquira go?" Whitney asked.

"Where've you been?" Sora asked. "Aquira went off hours ago to search for something to eat. The poor thing hasn't had a decent meal in —what, a week?"

"Well, excuse me," Whitney said with a hand pressed against his heart. "I just nearly died. I guess I'm not overly concerned with the whereabouts of our scaled friend. She can take care of herself!"

Lucindur stepped forward, and before she could speak, Whitney said, "Okay…" He rubbed his hands together. "How do we get in there?" He grabbed one of the planks and pulled, but it didn't budge. Not an inch.

"Those're foot-long dwarven spikes holding them planks in there," Tum Tum said. "Ye'd have more luck shouldering yer way through the wood than prying them out.

Tum Tum knew dwarven forging. All dwarves did. They were all required to understand how to forge simple objects—nails, spears, forks, knives—and if the dwarf showed promise, they'd be taught to make things like battle axes and hammers. Tum Tum wasn't very adept with the anvil, so he'd flunked out at knives. Still, he'd learned to make a dwarven nail, and he knew these were staying where they were. But now, he had no dwarven weapons. He'd left his hammer behind, buried into Gold Grin's chest.

"Then what do you suggest, Tum Tum?" Lucindur asked. There was annoyance in her voice like Tum Tum hadn't heard before. She was always the definition of kind, lovely, and wise. Always had the right quip or question, but now, she stared at him with icepicks for eyes. Cold so bitter had that effect on humans.

"I dunno," he said. "That wood's gonna be solid as stone. It'll likely dull an axe before it breaks through."

There was a chorus of exasperated sighs, hands thrown in the air, and a general feeling of hopelessness.

"Now, wait a second," he said. "Just cus we have no plan doesn't mean we can't make one! This isn't the hardest thing we've faced. Not by a long shot. We can just wait for Aquira."

"He's right," Sora said. "We've come all this way, and we're going to let a bit of wood stop us?"

Sora stepped forward and flexed her hands. Then, she rolled her neck and stretched out her hand. A small wisp of fire appeared. A second later, it was snuffed out in a puff of smoke. She staggered, and Whitney caught her.

"Easy, now," he said. "Save your strength. We're going to need it."

"Damn!" Tum Tum swore. He'd expected this to be an easy way in that would give them access to some of the old mines which he knew very well. "I might not be a clanbreaker, but I gotta have some strength left in these bones."

He backed up, motioned for everyone to move, and charged forward, roaring. However, he couldn't get any momentum, with the snow being so high. His shoulder cracked against the boards, and he bounced off, not even leaving a mark where he'd connected.

Whitney laughed.

"Well, that didn't work," Lucindur said, helping him to his feet, brushing off snow.

"I'd like to see ye try," Tum Tum said to Whitney.

"Alright, everyone back," Whitney said, cracking his knuckles. He strode over to the entrance. "Guess we're going through."

Tum Tum grumbled, but Lucindur placed a hand on his shoulder and said, "He's right, you know."

Whitney gripped one of the planks, having a distinct recollection of doing just such a thing in the bottom level of Tum Tum's bar. A moment later, after there wasn't even a hair's movement, he said, "I think we should wait for Aquira." Then, he walked away, muttering, "That no-good flying lizard…"

Tum Tum stepped up to the blockade once more. He backed up and slammed into it with his shoulder.

"Oi! This be some aged, old wood." He struck it again and again. Eventually, he did indeed call Whitney back for a turn.

They'd been at it for hours before they started to see some progress. Sora somehow managed to fall asleep. At some point toward night, Aquira finally returned, gnawing on a goblin that used to be alive.

It was difficult to see Aquira as the predator she was. The wyvern was as well-mannered as they came, but seeing her with blood coating her face, and a shred of reptilian skin hanging from her lips brought it all into perspective. Tum Tum suddenly found himself grateful she was on their side.

"There you are!" Whitney groaned. "Do you know how long we've been waiting for you?"

Aquira flicked her head back and forth, sending the innards of the poor creature flying, then licked her lips. She stood, stretching her back and wings as if intentionally ignoring the urgency in Whitney's voice, then ambled over. She wasn't a child anymore. A real, troublesome teenager.

"Hey, Girl," Sora said softly, rousing enough to stroke the frills around Aquira's neck. The wyvern leaned into her touch, a clicking sound emanating from deep in her gullet.

"Aquira, will you listen to me?" Whitney said.

Before he could say another word, she took a deep breath, then blew out a pillar of fire. It hit the barrier and sprayed in all directions.

Whitney dove. Tum Tum jumped back. Even still, he felt his skin reddening as if he were smelting ore.

Tongues of fire licked out, melting the snow around them for a good twenty yards. When it abated, there was nothing left of the wooden blockade but ash, which caught the wind.

Dust billowed out. The shaft clearly hadn't been used in years, if not tens of years, and only the faintest of light could be seen due to the still-glowing embers. That wasn't a problem for Tum Tum, though. His kin saw in the dark as well as humans saw at high noon.

"You've got to be kidding!" Whitney shouted, looking down at his hands. He raised them flat against the air so everyone could see. They were raw and bloody.

Tum Tum laughed. "Guess ye had the right idea from the start!"

"Was your meal good, Aquira?" Whitney asked. "I sure yigging hope so."

"You leave her alone," Sora said. She stood and moved to scratch Aquira's head. "You did great."

"We've wasted more than enough time," Lucindur said, already walking toward the mouth of the tunnel. "Let's go."

Without a further word, the whole party followed her in.

Everything was just as Tum Tum remembered it. Dwarven craftsmanship was meant to last a thousand lifetimes. The stone walls were so smooth they looked like marble. Though their footprints left in dust was a clear indication that the tunnels hadn't been used in decades.

"I can't see anything," Whitney said.

"Stop complaining," Sora reprimanded.

"I'm just tired of crawling through dark tunnels and dungeons. I'd think you of all people could understand."

"Reminds you of Bliss's lair?"

"No," Whitney said, with the utterly embarrassed tone of someone who was indeed reminded of someplace they never wanted to remember.

"Liar." Sora raised her hand, and a few small embers danced around her fingers, providing a hint of light. Tum Tum grabbed her wrist and pulled it down.

"No need to tire yerself at all," Tum Tum said, taking some joy in how frightened Whitney seemed. "I can see fine."

Silence carried them through the next series of turns and twists until finally, they saw torchlight up ahead. But there shouldn't have been torchlight—not in tunnels that had fallen into disuse.

"Somethin odd happenin up there," Tum Tum warned. "Stay close."

"Odd? Maybe we should discuss this," Lucindur spoke up from the back of the line.

Aquira screeched low, and Sora quieted her.

"Live a little," Whitney said as he rushed to catch up to Tum Tum. It appeared some of his confidence had returned now that there was a bit of light to see by.

"What do you think it is?" Sora asked.

"Not what—who," Tum Tum answered. "That be the southern mead hall. I'd know it anywhere, no matter how long I been gone. If these tunnels be any indication, no one should be here. No one should *want* to be here."

Tum Tum moved forward, putting one hand back to tell the others to wait behind. After the way Gargamane had treated him, he wasn't exactly sure what to expect. Would the guards be on command to dispatch any and all intruders, dwarf or not? There was no way to know, so Tum Tum thought, *better safe than dead.*

He put his back to the wall near the entrance. He knew what he'd see when he peered around. Three tables, taller than most in Balon-hearth, with high stools surrounding each. Against the wall, in each of the far corners, would be stacks of barrels. They'd all be empty, or at least that's how it had always been. Just for looks.

Hanging from the ceiling would be various weapons that, along with their owners, the older warriors would attribute great heroics to. They'd said after battle, the commanders would lead their men through these very tunnels, stopping at each mead hall along the way, drinking until they'd forgotten the horrors of war.

Tum Tum believed every word of it. The dwarves of the Three Kingdoms were fearsome and fierce, and absolutely honest when it came to their exploits—unless you count the times they told tales while drinking. And they were always drinking.

"Let me go first," Tum Tum said.

Whitney gestured extravagantly with one hand as if to say, "Go ahead, no one's stopping you."

Tum Tum took a deep breath, letting the dusty air fill his lungs and bring clarity to his mind. Then, he swung one leg around, placing him dead center in the doorway.

"Arrrrrrrgggghhhh!" Tum Tum shouted.

"Bwah!" came the response. A thrown tankard of mead followed, splattering the whole room in the bitter, sticky stuff.

The dwarf inside fell backward off his stool, landed with a loud *clunk*.

"Show yerself!" Tum Tum demanded.

He felt movement behind him and knew that his companions had his back if things were to go south, but they didn't. With a groan, a familiar face peeked up over the stool.

"Ye made me spill me drink," Brouben Cragrock, son of Lorgit Cragrock, Ruler of the Three Kingdoms said. Three quick hiccups followed, then his arm slipped, and he disappeared behind the table again.

"Brouben?" Tum Tum said, incredulous.

"Aye, what's it to ye?"

Tum Tum made his way up toward the fallen dwarf at a quick clip and the two clasped arms. Tum Tum dragged his old friend to his feet and engulfed him in a hard embrace.

Brouben shoved Tum Tum back and, with a smile, said, "In here, burying me sorrows, and who do I run into but ye?" He swayed a bit, then sat down. "Where the yig ye been? I feel like I haven't seen ye in half a century."

"It's been many years, friend," Tum Tum said. Then he turned and waved the others inside. "Come, come. It's safe."

Out of the corner of his eye, Tum Tum watched his friends cautiously enter the room. They fanned out, and he could clearly see Sora's hands ready. Aquira brought up the rear, slithering along the ceiling like a snake. Her throat rumbled.

"What's goin on here?" Tum Tum asked Brouben.

Brouben stumbled over to a dark wooden barrel that was set upon one of the tables as if he'd brought it there himself. The sound of the sudsy liquid filling up an earthenware mug brought a pang of home-sickness to Tum Tum's heart.

"Oh, where are me manners?" Brouben said. "Ye want one?"

"Well, I'll—" Whitney started, but Tum Tum waved him off.

"We be fine. Got pressing business here in the heart." That's how the dwarves who called the Three Kingdom's home referred to Balon-hearth. It was, indeed, the heart of the southernmost dwarven king-doms. The seat of power.

"Ye ain't gonna be welcome here, Dwotratum," Brouben said. "Not anymore."

"That, I know," Tum Tum agreed. "That's why fate brought us to ye."

"Fate?" Brouben asked. He made his way back to his stool and plopped down. "Who be the flower-pickers?"

"You know, I'm tired of being called names," Sora said, stepping forward.

"No—" Brouben hiccuped. "No offense meant, miss."

Tum Tum raised his hand, palm out and said, "Sora, I'm sorry for me peoples' manners. It's okay though, Brouben's one of the good uns."

He turned back to Brouben and said, "These are me friends. Whit-ney, Sora, Lucindur, and that not-so-little wyvern is Aquira." Brouben's hand went to his heart, and he nearly felt back, as if noticing her glowing yellow eyes for the first time.

"Everyone, meet Brouben Cragrock, Prince of this kingdom," Tum Tum said.

"Wait—*this* is the Brouben you told us about?" Whitney said.

"Pleased to know me own fame precedes me," Brouben muttered.

"You need to help us," Sora said, stepping forward and wasting no time. "We need to speak with the King—your father. We have news. Grave news."

"Everyone, slow down," Tum Tum said. "Sorry, humans don't know how to have a conversation anymore."

Brouben lifted his pint to his mouth but stopped at his lips. "Ain't no news ye have graver than me own, and I can tell ye this much, no one's listenin to news round here." He finished the motion and drained his mug. Then, placing the ale down, he wiped his mouth with the back of his hand and burped.

"Sounds like this little chat won't be any more beneficial than the one with that other lump of shog," Whitney remarked.

Tum Tum had been given plenty of reason not to like the commander of the clanbreakers, but he had been raised to respect him.

"Gargamane the Gold was doin his job," Tum Tum stated. "Nothin more."

"Ye saw Gargamane?" Brouben asked, suddenly perking up.

"We did," Tum Tum confirmed. "He told us to get gone. No one in. No one out."

"Aye. That's what me father decreed."

"Well, I think it's a coward's move," Lucindur said. "Where I'm from, we don't even have walls, much less doors that seal themselves shut against guests."

"Well, it must be nice to know such peace," Brouben said. Then he rose again, filled his mug, and reseated himself.

Tum Tum took the stool beside his friend. "Brouben, this news… it's unlike any ye've heard."

Brouben laughed. "Try me."

Tum Tum looked to his companions. Sora nodded, then looked at Lucindur, who nodded as well. Whitney just stood with his arms crossed, Aquira hovering directly beside him now, also looking cross. And they rarely agreed on anything.

"There was a battle," Tum Tum started. "Fought things like ye wouldn't believe. Goblins, grimaurs, warlocks, upyr, and…"

Brouben sat, staring into his mug, then looked up with only his eyes when Tum Tum paused.

"And?" he said.

"And the Buried Goddess herself," Sora said.

Brouben spilled his drink, then absentmindedly swiped the mead away. "Ye saw *what?*"

"Nesilia, the Buried Goddess," Sora repeated.

"Were ye at White Bridge, too?" Brouben asked.

"White Bridge? No, we were in Brekliodad," Sora said.

Brouben's attention was rapt. "When?"

Tum Tum stroked his beard. "Seventh day of Burntwood."

"That don't add up," Brouben said. "I saw her—"

"Ye saw her!" Tum Tum shouted. Whitney, Sora, and Lucindur echoed a similar response. Even Aquira squeaked out a query.

"I saw her then, too," Brouben continued. "Same shog-shuckin day."

"That's impossible," Whitney said. "One of us must be wrong."

"Everyone, wait," Sora said, holding out an arm. "What did she look like?"

Tum Tum watched Brouben carefully. If he'd seen Nesilia, and he didn't immediately recognize Sora, then it must have been after she'd hopped bodies. The Prince didn't hesitate before his description like a liar might. Tum Tum knew his fair share of tall tale-tellers. One stood right behind him.

"Skin, milky, creamy, white as fresh-fallen snow," Brouben said. "Hair to match. Eyes the color of death."

"Not impossible," Sora said softly.

"He saw her after she *poofed* over to Sigrid?" Whitney asked.

"Now we know where she disappeared to," Lucindur said.

"But why White Bridge?" Tum Tum asked.

"Couldn't tell ye, but I feel Sir Torsten might know more," Brouben said.

"Sir Torsten?" Whitney said. "You know Torsten?"

"Aye, and ye?"

"We're the best of pals," Whitney said. "How is the old, stiff bastard?"

Brouben laughed, settling a bit, and taking another sip. He turned his mug upside down and let the last drop fall into his mouth.

"Sounds like ye know him, all right," he said.

"Did Torsten see her, too?" Sora asked.

"He can't see anymore, Sora," Whitney said, as if proud of that knowledge about the famous knight.

Brouben ignored him. "We all did. Men, dwarves, even the gray skins. She killed the famous rebel, Muskigo, in cold blood."

"Muskigo Ayerabi?" Sora asked softly. Tum Tum thought he saw a twinge of sadness pass over her features.

Brouben nodded. "Did him in like he were a child."

"Then ye told yer father?" Tum Tum asked.

"And that's why he made the decree?" Sora asked, saying what everyone was thinking.

"Aye, I told him," Brouben said. "Took a beatin for it, too. Told me to shut my yiggin mouth if I knew what was good. Said that he'd know if the gods were back, cus Meungor himself would stop by for a drink, and dragons would come crawling back out of our arses."

"Perhaps if someone from the outside…?" Lucindur said.

"Ain't expectin me father to care what some foreign bard has to say. And especially not ye, Dwotratum. Yer a deserter, an outcast, and we got strict orders to throw any deserters back to the snow."

"What about me?" Sora asked. "Before Nesilia was that white-skinned upyr, she…" Sora swallowed hard. "She was inside of me."

Brouben laughed.

"This isn't funny, half-pint," Whitney snarled. Tum Tum cringed at the insult. He understood Whitney wanting to defend his lass, but they stood before a Prince who could have every clanbreaker in the Three Kingdoms on them in a heartbeat.

Brouben's face went hard for a moment, then he said, "Yer serious? Ye got proof?"

"Other than my word and the word of these with me? No," Sora admitted.

"Without proof, it won't do much good with me father. We ain't exactly seen eye to eye, our people, for a long time. Some want to trade more, some want nothin to do with ye surface dwellers at all. Ye know how it is," Brouben said, looking to Tum Tum, "or ye did, before ye never came back."

"Why am I not surprised?" Whitney groaned.

"Whitney, now's not the time," Sora scolded. Then, turning back to Brouben, who looked like he'd just about had enough of insults, she said, "I'm sorry, your Highness. He's just a bit *on* edge."

"We all are," Tum Tum added.

"The truth is, if we don't do something, Pantego is in trouble—anything beyond Pantego is in trouble."

"We've got to talk to your father."

"Pretty please?" Whitney said.

Brouben stood and did his best to stomp forward. It was a bit sloppy, and he tripped more than once, but soon he was right in front of Whitney, glaring up at him. He may have been short, but he was stout and would squash Whitney like a bug if the thief wasn't smart.

"Ain't no way yer gettin in to see me father unless it's at the hands of the clanbreakers," he said.

"You mean arrested?" Lucindur asked.

Brouben nodded.

Everyone went silent. And then, like he did so many times, Whitney broke the silence. Only, this time, it was to unveil one of his rare strokes of genius.

He held out his hands and said, "Then arrest us."

"What?" Tum Tum and Sora said at the same time.

"Arrest us," Whitney repeated.

"He's right. That's the way in," Lucindur said.

Tum Tum stroked his beard. "Hmm, not a bad plan. Someone's gotta get through to the king. If ye couldn't do it, maybe we all could together. We need to talk to him."

Brouben remained quiet as he returned to his keg, filling his cup to overflowing. Then, he cleared his throat and said, "It came to blows with me and me father... ye'll find yerself in a pit. But ye know what? I think ye should, too. I saw Nesilia's power with me own eyes, and he didn't care. I never seen a thing like it..." he shuddered. "Someone's got to get through to him.."

Then his attention turned to Whitney. "Especially someone as imposing as this flower-picker. Then again, knowing my father, he'll likely just say 'It's yer problem, not ours.' And after what I saw out there at White Bridge, he may damn-well be right."

"I see sarcasm extends beyond all cultures," Whitney said. "Look, Brouben is it? What do you have to lose? We corroborate your story; your dear old dad realizes he was wrong. Easy peasy."

Brouben rolled his shoulders and tossed back his drink. Then he cracked his neck. Tum Tum could see the frustration written all over his face beneath his bushy beard. The stubbornness of dwarves knew no bounds. Especially dwarven fathers.

"Fine. Me favorite brother is still in Yarrington, and there be no way to reach him like this," he said. "I'll help ye, but more likely, it's yer funeral."

"Meungor's hairy arse, that's great news!" Tum Tum clapped his hands. "Oh, and me Lord. There be one thing more."

"What now?"

"We also need to convince the King to give us the, uh… the Brike Stone."

Brouben's eyes went wide as saucers, just as expected. The great treasure of Brotlebir, being taken away. Any dwarf would scoff at the idea, but the thought of it actually accomplishing something rather than sitting in a vault—he hoped that'd be enough to convince a man as honorable as he knew Brouben to be.

XIV

THE THIEF

Whitney hadn't mentioned it, but he'd been there before—Balonhearth, the heart of the Three Kingdoms. Of all the destinations, in all his many travels, Brotlebir and the Dragon's Tail mountains topped the list as the least enjoyable. Aside from ale—and even that tasted like sewage—there were simply no redeeming qualities. It was cold, bitter, stark, bleak, harsh, and a million other words to say he'd rather be anywhere else.

And, worst of all, surprisingly, there had always been very little to steal. Outside of the vaults of kings, apparently. Dwarves loved their gold, mining it, hoarding it—and that meant they had more currency than anything actually worth taking. If Whitney wanted gold bullions, he'd have sold all the things he'd ever stolen.

It had been a long time ago when he'd been in Brotlebir. Shortly after his time spent with the silent monks—an adventure he'd rather leave far behind in his distant past—he'd ventured south to the Dragon's Tail through subterranean paths, not unlike the ones Tum Tum had just led them through. However, unlike those, the ways dug by ancient beasts were dank and dirty. In comparison, they'd walked through a palace.

Though he hadn't exactly snuck in that time, he hadn't been welcomed with open arms either, and he sure-as-Exile didn't want to stand before King Cragrock. Not again.

Dwarves had memories like none other. It was said that a dwarf could remember the individual divots in a cave they'd been in only once, fifty years ago—that, in darkness, they could identify their pickaxe from amongst dozens by nothing more than the feel of the handle's woodgrain.

And as he looked around, Whitney realized dwarves weren't much for change either. The place was precisely as he'd remembered it. Even the handcuffs.

"Are these things really necessary?" Whitney complained.

"This was yer idea, flower-picker," Brouben said.

"You say that like it's insulting. I like flowers."

Although there were more passages, deeper caverns, and new statues erected for some such warrior or whatever, all-in-all, Balonhearth was the same oversized cavern coated in veins of silver and iron it had always been. Nothing impressive, at least not to someone as well-traveled as Whitney Fierstown.

"This is beautiful," Sora marveled.

"This?" Whitney scoffed under his breath.

"It has its beauty, though I prefer the sky," Lucindur said.

"Exactly."

Sora ignored him and said, "But I agree, Your Highness. Do the cuffs have to be so tight?"

"Right?" Whitney said, stretching his fingers.

"Keep quiet," Tum Tum said. He kept his head down and in shadow, doing his best to play the part of their dwarven escort along with Brouben. He'd have fooled Whitney any day.

Looking up, Whitney admitted it was *a little* impressive. He couldn't begin to imagine the time it would have taken to carve out such a place. The mountain was at least five thousand feet high, and almost every bit of it was hollowed out, with stone homes tucked away in every nook. Each home and shop was meticulously crafted with intricate designs. The floors, although only stone like the mountain itself, were smooth as glass. Wooden carts zipped all over on rails held together with iron bars and rivets, carrying dwarves and their newly-mined treasures every which way. He couldn't understand how they climbed the many tracks, some almost at a complete vertical incline, but they did.

Dwarven engineering, he thought.

"Hey, keep up back there!" Tum Tum hollered, having now made his way in front of them. He sounded all cheery just from a few moments with his people. He slapped his own thigh. "We shouldn't be beatin you with these stubs."

"This way," Brouben said.

The Prince looked like any other dwarf Whitney had ever seen. Wide as he was tall, yellow beard he could tuck into his belt. But the one difference was his armor looked to be worth an entire Glass town. All thick plating made of dark dwarven steel and golden embellishments. It probably hid his gut; such was the fate of a Prince. Never expected to do anything—just sit around getting fat, waiting for daddy, the King, to kick the bucket.

"I'd feel far more comfortable with all of this if we had Aquira with us," Sora said.

"Yer wyvern will be safe," Brouben assured them. "There's no way ye'd be gettin ye to the king with a dragonkin in tow. This was the only way."

"I know," Sora agreed. "I just feel bad."

Whitney watched Sora, sadness in her eyes. He wanted to find a way to keep that precise look from shadowing her features ever again. After they defeated Nesilia, he'd do it. Whatever it took. A lovely house in Yarrington or Panping. A farm out in the country—whatever she wanted, she'd have.

"Oi! What's this!" shouted a dwarf up ahead, waddling their way.

"Found them sneakin round in the tunnels," Brouben said. "Takin em to see me father."

"Yer takin petty intruders to see the King?" the dwarf said, eyebrow raised. He had the look of a guard—Whitney knew guards.

Brouben hesitated but quickly recovered. "Ye questionin yer prince?"

"I—uh," the guard stammered. "It's just… unwanteds usually just get thrown in the dungeons til we got time to execute em."

"Execute?" Whitney said, voice cracking.

Brouben elbowed him hard in the gut. "Shut up, ye flower-pickin shog-shucker."

Then he turned to the guard. "King's decree—no one in. No one out. Entry's locked up tight with Gargamane the Gold himself watchin it. Don't ye think the King would wanna question the party who managed to sneak in unseen? Never mind, don't answer that. Yer opinion don't matter. And if ye wanna keep your position, and ever have hope of bein a clanbreaker, shut yer trap and move clear."

The guard's face scrunched up like he'd been gut-punched. "Yes, sir, yer Highness, sir."

After the guard stepped aside, Brouben shoved Whitney and motioned for Tum Tum to bring the others.

"Are you sure about this," Lucindur said when they were safely out of earshot.

"Have I ever steered you wrong?" Whitney asked, slowing long enough for them to catch up.

Sora and Lucindur both began speaking, but Whitney cut them off before they could respond.

"That's enough of that," Whitney said, coaxing them all closer. "Listen, I've been up there before, to the King's throne room. He doesn't like me much."

"You don't say?" Sora interjected.

"I can't imagine why not," Lucindur added.

Whitney rolled his eyes and continued. "He's a stubborn old bastard, and if he didn't listen to his own son, you really think he'll listen to a dwarven reject? Sorry, Tum Tum."

"I'd be more offended if it wasn't true," Tum Tum sighed.

"We need a contingency plan in case, no, *when*, he says we can't have the stone. Took enough to convince his son, and he seems to be the sane one here."

Brouben didn't acknowledge him. It had taken them nearly the entire trek to this point to convince him that the Brike Stone was necessary. But Sora could be mighty convincing when she wanted to be. She'd put out the whole damsel-in-distress vibe warriors like Brouben swooned for.

Eventually, Brouben agreed after hearing how close they'd come to beating Nesilia last time. Though, he made them promise to do their best to return it. Which, of course, they all agreed to. Though Whitney knew that wasn't going to happen. No way. They'd trap her in, and toss her into a wianu's gullet, sending her right to Nowhere with poor Kazimir...

"Who would be foolish enough to reject a chance to save the world?" Lucindur asked.

"A dwarf," Whitney muttered.

"Now that I might take offense to," Tum Tum said. Brouben agreed.

They passed by guard after guard, and even with the circulation to his hands being cut off, Whitney was glad for the disguise.

Execution? he thought. *For trespassing?*

"We should at least give King Cragrock a chance to hear us out," Sora said.

"I agree," Lucindur added.

A look of concern passed over Brouben's face.

"I ain't too sure the gravity of this is hittin ye like it should," he said. "I already told me father what I seen at White Bridge. If he ain't listenin, he ain't listenin—and *he ain't listenin.*"

"Still…" Lucindur said.

Whitney clenched his jaw, then exhaled slowly through his teeth. Looking at Sora and Lucindur, he said, "You two don't know dwarves. The ones out there are one thing, but in their tunnels? They love watching us squirm. They won't help."

"That's as cruel as calling me knife-ear, Whitney," Sora scolded.

"It's not. Not at all. It's called being… uh… forward-thinking. All I'm saying is that if he rejects us, they'll have the vault doubly secure, and we'll never get back in. You really want to risk that?"

Sora's lip twisted, but she didn't answer.

"He ain't wrong," Tum Tum said, looking to Brouben. Again, the Prince agreed.

"I suppose he has a point," Lucindur said.

"Exactly!" Whitney exclaimed, the cavernous hall carrying his voice and earning the attention of a few passersby.

"Exactly," Whitney repeated, lower. The others leaned in to hear him. "This is the world we're talking about," he went on. "Do we really want to chance it to the compassion of dwarves?"

Brouben spun on him, cheeks flushed as plums. "Look, I'm only listenin to ye for one reason… I heard Torsten Unger credit ye with a thing or two—"

"He *what?*" Whitney asked. "I mean… yeah. Torsten and I go way back. Best friends, as a matter of fact. Saved him from sure death more than a time or two."

"Only reason I'm trustin ye," Brouben repeated. "The way a man fights says everything about his character, and Torsten is honorable as they come."

"Ah, his only flaw."

Brouben scowled. "Now, what's yer plan then?"

Whitney turned to Sora. "Remember all I taught you? Lesson fifty-two, always be prepared."

Sora broke into a grin as she shook her head. "Not your lessons again."

"Yes, my lessons. Now, are you ready for one more?"

"Fine. For getting Nesilia out of my head, you get to take the lead this one last time. But if you get us in trouble…"

"Oh, with him, there'll be trouble," Lucindur lamented.

"Ah, so you do know him well," Sora said.

"Ha ha, very funny, everyone," Whitney said, feigning laughter.

"But, I guess it doesn't matter who's mad at us if the world ends," Lucindur added. "Whatever it takes to stop Nesilia and save the ones we love, right?"

Whitney affectionately rubbed shoulders with her. He could imagine she was thinking about Talwyn as much as he'd been thinking about Gentry. They had to save them, and the rest of the world. "I knew I liked you. Now, listen here…"

They leaned in, and Whitney revealed his plan. They'd already gotten arrested by Brouben to gain access to the throne room. Now, they'd let Tum Tum carry out his part of the plan: petition the King with the truth of Nesilia's return. But Whitney added another component. He was all but sure diplomacy would fail. It would come down to his quick hands and nimble boots. Sora and Lucindur would distract the dwarven King and his guards while Whitney escaped his cuffs and snuck into the vault to steal the Brike Stone himself.

"That's the plan?" Sora said. "That's barely an idea."

Whitney pretended to be hurt, but it wasn't hard. "After all the things we've been through, you still doubt me? Sora, if your hands weren't bound behind your back, I'd have thought you stabbed me in mine."

"Oh, get over yourself," Sora said, smiling. "You know how many times luck has factored in?"

"Perhaps, but she's a lady, and unlike you, she's kind to me."

"I don't like it," Brouben said.

"I didn't expect you to," Whitney said. "But you've already tried to convince your father, right? If he denied you…"

"Me sneakin ye up to see me father is one thing. Me playin part to yer stealin—that's another altogether."

"You said it yourself," Whitney said. "Nesilia is back, and she's going to kill us all. What's a silly stone worth if the whole world ends?"

Brouben scratched his cheek. "I still don't like it."

"I still don't expect you to."

"My father will prolly have his clanbreakers kill ye on the spot."

"I'm not easy to kill," Whitney said.

At that, everyone grew silent until Sora said, "How are you going to break out of these? They are tight."

"Remember when we were reunited in that dwarven fortress?" Whitney asked.

"Sure, wasn't that long ago in my time."

Whitney swore internally. "Six years in mine," he said under his breath. Then louder, he said, "Well, if it hadn't been for Torsten's gauntlets, I don't know how I would have broken out of that cell. That's not a good position for a thief to be in. So…"

He shifted his hand slightly, and a thin sliver of metal slid out from beneath the sleeve of his tunic.

"Is that a—"

"I'll never be without a lockpick ever again." Then, looking at Lucindur, he said, "Really, it was in the wagon with Darkings and Rand Langley when I realized something had to change, and I couldn't leave things to chance any longer."

"Clever," Lucindur said.

Whitney nodded once. "Thank you. It's nice for my genius to be acknowledged."

"He always takes it too far," Sora said to Lucindur.

"So, I'll escape, and then you're up."

"Yeah, well, I'm not sure how you want me to distract them. 'Using my *assets*' isn't going to work against dwarves."

"Rule number eight-hundred-nine: be creative," Whitney said.

"Skipped a few there, didn't we?"

"I wasn't going to wait around for you forever. I kept teaching, you just weren't there to listen."

Sora rolled her eyes. "Well, how do you propose we distract them?"

"You are both powerful magic users," Whitney said. "I'm sure between the two of you, you can manage something. Dwarves may not care for how you look, but abilities are assets too, and dwarves *love* shiny magic."

"It would not be wise for me to use my particular brand," Lucindur said. "It might clue Nesilia in on our whereabouts, and her monsters trawl these underground places. We may not be in Glinthaven anymore, but I still don't want the blood of all these people on my hands."

Brouben looked as if he wanted to ask a question, but instead said, "Ye've got my thanks for that."

"Right you are," Whitney said, clapping his hands. "I guess it's down to you, my Panpingese Princess."

"No pressure," Sora said.

Whitney glanced up at Tum Tum, whose eyes looked like someone had stolen his last gold ingot.

Whitney knew the dwarves had their pride, and if Tum Tum thought for even a moment that Whitney didn't believe he could be successful in convincing the dwarf king to hand over the stone, it would crush him like a mineshaft cave-in.

Yes, Whitney knew dwarves. That bastard Grint had sent him on this fateful path toward being forced to become a hero, after all. "Steal the Glass Crown," he'd challenged. And who was Whitney to say no to a challenge? He couldn't regret what happened since though—at least not all of it—because it led him back to Sora and without her at his side, he wasn't so sure why he'd care to save the world in the first place.

Whitney also knew Kings. He'd stolen the Glass Crown off one's head—almost. They were brash, and arrogant, and above all, selfish and greedy. There was no way, no matter what evidence Tum Tum could give—and there was precious little of that—King Cragrock was going to give up his most rare and prized possession. The legendary, preserved heart of a real dragon. If it wasn't all a sham… the thing would make the Glass Crown seem worthless.

Whitney's specialty was separating people from their most valuable things. Looking again to Sora, he realized he'd even done it to himself when he'd lost her. Never again. Come Pantego, the Gate of Light, or the hellish pits of Elsewhere, Sora and Whitney would never be apart again.

"Tum Tum," Whitney said. "This isn't about you, you know? We just can't chance the King writing off your tale as a lie and… *executing us.*"

"Are you all that tired from walking?" Tum Tum said, changing the subject. But Whitney got the point. Tum Tum was full of integrity and he was smart. He wouldn't let something as silly as pride keep them from changing the world for the better.

"Their legs are soft from ridin horses everywhere," Brouben remarked.

"We got a plan," Tum Tum said. "Now, let's do it."

Brouben led them onto a platform attached to a rail system. In its center was a seesaw contraption that, when pumped, would send the cart screeching along the tracks.

"Gimme a hand with this, Dwotratum," Brouben said. "We're a bit short on hands since the war in the south and the plague of goblins and grimaur in the mines. I'm thinkin it's a bit why my father is so disinclined to listen to reason about you-know-who."

"A Prince and an outcast, huffin and hoin to King Lorgit's throne with three fake prisoners in tow," Tum Tum said. "I can hear the songs now."

They both laughed, and each grabbed a wooden bar.

"Hold on," Tum Tum warned, raising his hand in Whitney's direction.

"To what? Our hands are bound!" Whitney had barely finished his sentence when the platform lurched and sent him stumbling a few steps. They were off at a quick clip, faster than Whitney would've expected of something so old.

The track groaned under their weight, but soon, the cart was off and on its way.

"These are quite ingenious contraptions, my lord dwarf," Lucindur said. "We could use them back home."

"If ye could build em, have em," Brouben laughed.

"Oh, I missed this, I have," Tum Tum said. He closed his eyes and leaned into the rushing air.

"You missed careening through sharp rocks on rickety wood?" Whitney said. "Gods and yigging monsters, I should have stayed behind."

His eyes fell upon Sora again, who stood in the opposite corner, taking in the sights and sounds of Balonhearth. It was like a dream that they were back together after so long, and now, they'd have one last heist together. One more big ta-da to bid Whitney's illustrious career as a thief farewell. Either they'd succeed, save Pantego, and be hailed as heroes forever, or they'd fail, and it'd all go up in glorious flames.

Either way, Whitney would steal that stone.

As they bounced along the tracks, steadily climbing up toward the Iron Bank and King Lorgit Cragrock's throne room, the whole city splayed out beneath them, Whitney tried not to puke.

From so high, the many veins of precious metals looked like a spreading disease. Below, giant braziers burned, smoke billowing up and through ventilation systems, carrying itself out into the crisp, cold Brotlebir air. Zigzagging staircases rose on all sides, connecting the many-tiered city. The track zipped around columns thicker than a giant's belly. So close to braziers, Whitney felt the sweat on his brow evaporate.

"Been awhile," Tum Tum whispered.

"Never have I seen anything more beautiful," Sora said.

"I'll admit, it is stunning," Lucindur said.

"Now you're on her side?" Whitney asked.

"Hey, Glinthaven ain't nothin to balk at neither," Tum Tum said.

"Over there," Brouben pointed. "That's where Dreligar Bottom-snatch was born."

"Bottomsnatch?" Whitney snickered.

"Aye. That be nothing to laugh about. Dreligar killed ten dozen frost giants with naught but a stick and the tooth of a dragon."

"There are no more frost giants," Lucindur argued.

"Or dragons," Whitney added.

"Not anymore," Brouben agreed with a knowing smile.

They traveled further up the mountain. Several times, Whitney found his bound hands gripping the cart with enough force to crush the wood. He was sure the dwarves built the thing well, but he wasn't confident they'd taken riders of his height into consideration. As it was, the railing only came up to his hip. One swift turn and he was liable to topple right over, and without hands to stop—

"Get ready," Brouben said, pointing and interrupting Whitney's worries.

Whitney followed the dwarf's outstretched finger to a gargantuan rock carved in the shape of a dwarf's head hanging from the ceiling. A deeply recessed, winged crown sat atop the head, overlapping with thick locks of hair. From a long, stone-carved beard, which braided itself around a natural stalactite, water issued down into a pool in Balonhearth's central hall. Below, dwarves scurried around like ants, swimming, and bathing in the waters.

"King Andur," Tum Tum said under his breath, staring up at the dwarf head. He didn't mask the awe he felt at the sight of the King's visage. "He be the first of us to call this place home."

The cart closed in on the King's open mouth. Mist soaked them all —which felt nice after the heat of the many fire pots lining the track. An instant later, they were shrouded in darkness, zooming through the King's throat.

Sora had inched over to Whitney and caught him off guard. He didn't mind. She pressed close to him, and he nestled back, but when he glanced over, he saw that fear had crept over her features. She appeared as pale as a Drav Cra warlock.

"I feel like we shouldn't be here," Sora whispered.

"Oh, stop," Whitney whispered back.

"I'm serious. Like, really shouldn't be here."

"Ye shouldn't," Brouben agreed, apparently listening in. "But if what ye say is true, and I think it be, then my father ought to hear it from yer own lips. And if he won't listen, I gotta trust the thief the Master of Warfare himself seems to trust."

The idea of Torsten trusting him brought a balloon full of pride to Whitney's chest.

An orange light flickered just ahead, and the cart began to slow as

Brouben yanked on a lever. The squeal echoed like a dying zhulong, and the vehicle stopped just as the cavern opened into a circular room. Statues of Meungor the Sharp Axe, god of the dwarves, lined the room as if holding up the ceiling.

"You're up," Whitney said to Sora. "Stick to the plan," he said to everyone else.

As the cart halted entirely, Whitney backed into the far corner. He peered over his shoulder to where the track continued through darkness until it exited through a hole at the base of the large head and dipped back down into the city proper.

One step over a small gap would take them off the platform and into a giant cavern featuring the skeleton of a dragon nearly as large as the room itself. It was curled up like a sleeping dog, spine tracing the wall in a semi-circle, head on one end, barbed tail on the other. Even though Whitney knew it was dead, it was a terrifying sight.

A large, iron gate wedged within its ribs. Guarding it on each side were two dwarves—four in total—wearing solid black armor adorned with foot-long spikes.

"Clanbreakers," Brouben confirmed.

In the darkness, Whitney slipped his lock pick from its hidden compartment and made quick work of the cuffs. They fell, and Whitney winced as they clattered to the rock below the suspended tracks. However, no one seemed to notice over the shrieking of the cart's wheels and the whine of the rails.

Tum Tum disembarked first, followed by Brouben, and Lucindur. Finally, Sora shot a quick glance at Whitney, and he shooed her.

She took a step toward the platform and missed. As she tumbled, one leg in the gap, the rest of her body hitting hard onto the rock, Whitney almost reached for her, but she winked at him from the ground and blew a kiss.

That was believable, Whitney thought. *I really am a great teacher.*

Sora groaned, writhing, arms still secure behind her back. Tum Tum and Brouben tried to pull her up, but she stayed down, rocking back and forth on the ground. The clanbreakers turned their attention from Whitney just long enough.

"Ye okay, Girly?" Tum Tum asked.

While everyone was focused on her, Whitney flipped himself backward over the cart and landed deftly on his feet.

Their voices were faint, but Whitney could immediately hear them asking if she was alright. He stayed low and made his way through the ditch that held the track in place. Finding a dark corner, just at the edge of the room, Whitney pulled himself up. He could still see the clanbreakers. Now, they were fully intent upon Sora and the others, but neither moved.

Whitney heard a faint flapping sound. It grew louder until something bigger than a bat tore through the darkness toward him. It rose from the opposite direction they'd come from. With the massive dragon skeleton so close, Whitney's mind began speaking impossibilities until finally, the creature came into view.

"Aquira!" he whispered as loud as he dared. "You really can understand, can't you? Good girl." He'd whispered instructions for her to join them before Brouben forced them to leave her behind, but she'd been such a pain since Sora returned, he doubted she'd show up. But, he knew he could use her help.

She landed on Whitney's outstretched arm. "Stay quiet, now, okay?"

She puffed her nostrils, and together, they crept along until they reached a flat spot well-shielded from their view, and thrust himself over the ledge. Belly crawling a bit, he watched as Tum Tum finally helped Sora to her feet.

She started walking again, perhaps a little too well.

You're still injured, Sora, Whitney thought hard, as if he could will it to her mind. But no one seemed to notice.

"I don't think anything is twisted," Lucindur said.

"No, I'm feeling better," Sora said. "I think I was just surprised. I'm sorry for the shock. I can't believe… I'm usually more stable on my feet."

She wiped her eyes. It sounded like real tears.

She's become quite the actress, Whitney said to himself. *She'd do great in the Troupe.*

Then again, Sora had plenty of reasons to cry real tears.

The thought of the Troupe, of Gentry and Talwyn back in Glinthaven, made Whitney picture the faces of everyone he'd ever known and cared about. He hadn't even realized how many there were —Torsten, annoyingly pious as he might be, Kazimir… he'd died for Sora. How many centuries had he lived on Pantego, only to be killed by Gold Grin? And whose fault was it?

Mine.

His mind drifted to others in Troborough like Hamm and Alless— though he'd never given in to her romantic advances, she still meant something. There were so many more, many long gone, dead in the razing of Troborough by Black Sandsmen, and the destroying of Fake Troborough by the demons of Elsewhere. But all of them were real to him, nonetheless.

"We're gonna make it," Whitney whispered to Aquira. "This is gonna work. It has to."

XV

THE KNIGHT

They stood within the main tunnel leading into the heart of the Tal'du Dromesh. Torsten thought he knew what a gathering of thousands sounded like until he heard the racket of Latiapur's people above, feet pounding, shaking off dust from the ceiling. A cacophony of chattering voices rumbled like the waves.

Torsten couldn't tell, within the mess of noise, whether they spoke favorably. Not that it mattered any longer. They were here, and in a short time, the marriage would be official. He had to trust in the future Queen that those who remained in Latiapur were those who most believed her. He had to trust that those who remained might see the victory that this was.

From a people in rebellion to the kin of a new, mighty Queen.

The tunnel walls shook louder. King Pi flinched.

"They are eager for peace," Torsten said.

"Or foaming at the mouths," Lord Jolly countered. Torsten glowered at him, and Jolly rolled his shoulders. "I jest. You're making their leader Queen of the world. I'm sure they're eternally grateful." He leaned over to whisper in Torsten's ear. "Just like the Drav Cra, eh?"

"Ignore him," Torsten said.

"I simply see all sides of every picture, as is my sworn duty." He bowed low to King Pi and backed away.

"I'm not making her be Queen," Pi said. "Was this not *her* idea?"

"An idea solidified the moment she met you," Torsten replied.

Torsten marveled at the boy, amazed by how little he had to look down at him these days. Pi was the picture of royalty. A polished steel chestplate with the Eye of Iam emblazoned upon the center covered his snow-white tunic. It puffed out at the elbows and shoulders, making him appear larger than he was. An armored skirt fell to his knees, the plated strips lined by angular crystals that refracted every bit of light around them. And, of course, the Glass Crown sat proudly upon his dark, feathered hair.

It seemed ages ago now, but Torsten remembered Liam wearing something similar on the day Oleander came of age, and they were wed in the Yarrington Cathedral by Wren the Holy.

"You look so much like him," Torsten remarked.

"Everyone keeps saying that," Pi said, then frowned. "All I can remember is him stuck in a chair, raving—"

"That wasn't him, Your Grace. The Liam I knew would have been prouder than you could imagine. To be here, impressing a Queen on your first meeting, after all you've been through. His accomplishments may be favored by bards for songs, but yours will be equal."

"I remember the first time he rode into Crowfall," Lord Jolly said. "The way his armor caught the white light of snow clouds. We Northerners are rarely impressed, but my wife thought Iam himself had ridden through the gates."

"I think we all did. His enemies, too."

"*He* wouldn't have been possessed," Pi said softly. "He would have resisted."

"No," Torsten rebuked. "We've seen how strong Nesilia is. No child could have resisted."

"You don't know that."

"I do. I'm only sorry it took me so long to realize your struggle." Torsten knelt and held him at arms' length. "You don't need to be your father, Your Grace."

"Nobody can be," Lord Jolly added. His words didn't help, but Torsten could tell by his tone that he was trying to. Northerners weren't known for warmth, not even in their sentiments.

"True," Torsten said. "Pantego doesn't need another Liam. You can only be King Pi Nothhelm, and the bards will sing songs of your name for ages to come."

"They sing for every King, no matter what they'd done," Pi said.

"That may be so. History will remember your father as the greatest general the world has ever known. Still, it will remember you, I swear it. You told me once, in the castle gardens, how you would aim for peace. Perhaps such things aren't what make the best songs, but they make the best kings. I see that now."

"And hey, claiming victory in a second God Feud won't hurt," Lord Jolly added.

Torsten smiled. "No. No, it can't."

The corner of Pi's lips lifted slightly as he nodded. "Thank you. Both of you. For everything you've done for my Kingdom. I hope you're right."

"We are," Torsten said.

"It's our job to be," Lord Jolly added.

Pi straightened his back and dusted off his outfit. "Okay," he said. "I'm ready."

"You really are, aren't you?" Torsten asked as he cinched Pi's chestplate tighter. Then, standing, Torsten nodded to the Shieldsmen lined up on either side of them, and so began their slow march.

The crowd reacted as the first of the Shieldsmen emerged, more dust than ever pouring from the ceiling. Pi never flinched again. Not once.

Torsten wished Oleander could've been alive to see this. Not Liam. The thought of his only son with a Shesaitju might've sparked another war, but Oleander would have approved. In fact, Torsten imagined her loving Mahraveh like her own child. A woman that could be all the things she wasn't, who could fight like she always wished to, and how she did at the end.

Creating a woman that never was, aren't you, Torsten? he thought.

Light from the open gate filtered in as they approached. The high sun was impossibly bright so far south, but it was custom—a King should be married under Iam's clearest gaze. Already, Pi was making history. The first King to marry anywhere but atop Mount Lister.

Then, Torsten noticed a disturbance in the ranks. Someone pushed their way back toward them.

Torsten stuck his arm out in front of Pi and stepped forward, other hand reaching for the grip of *Salvation*. Then he saw why none of the

Shieldsmen cared to stop the intruder. Lucas Danvels stopped in front of them, panting, and barely with the energy to bow.

"Sir Danvels, what is it?" Torsten questioned.

"My Lords. Your Grace." He paused to catch his breath, then looked straight at Torsten. "You need to see something."

"You do realize what's happening right now? Can you not handle it?"

Torsten's mind raced back to the day of King Liam's funeral when another Shieldsman—Rand Langley—interrupted with reports of the Shesaitju having razed a dozen villages on the outskirts of the Glass. He tried to ignore the omen.

"Of course, Sir." He leaned in and whispered, "Please. I don't want to cause alarm, but I need to speak with you privately for a moment. I would never do this unless it was urgent."

"Always something," Torsten grumbled, clenching his jaw. Then, he turned to Pi. "Sir Danvels has an urgent matter I must see to."

"Torsten, you must be out there," Pi insisted. "You're on my Royal Council."

Torsten regarded Lucas, and the young Shieldsman appeared like he'd seen a ghost. Months ago, Torsten may have scolded him, but they were both at White Bridge and in Panping. Lucas was right, he wouldn't do something like this unless it was urgent.

"I'll join you shortly," Torsten said. "We can't delay or show any sign of weakness. The sun is at its zenith. Iam's blessing is upon us."

Pi took his arm. "Sir Unger."

"It'll be fine, Your Grace," he said. "If the Black Sands' sages are as wordy as Dellbar, the sun will be set by the time we reach the vows."

"He's right," Lord Jolly agreed. "Come along now, Your Grace. Your safety is more important than anything, and Sir Unger would never risk it."

Torsten fixated on the pleading eyes of his King. He was too young to be married. Too young for any of this. Still, Torsten could see that he was ready. The young King who'd endured so much trauma before the crown fell upon his head was now prepared to bear the weight of leading while Torsten served as his shield.

"Look after him, Lord Jolly," Torsten said. "As your brother would have."

"Always."

Torsten offered Pi a slight smile and a bow before managing to tear his gaze away and follow Lucas down a branching hallway. The line of Shieldsmen parted for them, and soon they were alone.

"This better be important," Torsten growled.

Lucas didn't answer. Instead, he picked up his pace, forcing Torsten to a jog just to keep up. They rounded another corner into a tunnel leading to a series of cavernous rooms within the undercroft.

"Lucas!" Torsten barked, clutching his wrist.

"He's here, Sir Unger," Lucas whispered, spinning toward Torsten.

"Who is?"

"Rand Langley. The Shesaitju guards found him standing at the gate asking to speak directly with you, and brought him straight to me."

Torsten froze. The last time he'd seen Rand, he was curled up in a cell, haggard and pathetic, and begging to go after Sigrid. Then, Rand had called upon a blood pact to free her, and they disappeared. Whether or not he knew that Nesilia was controlling his sister's already cursed body, wasn't clear in Lucas' description of what had happened.

"Torsten, if he's here…" Lucas went on.

"We don't know anything," Torsten said. "He could be coming to atone."

"Or for her."

"*She* has an army. Send scouts out across the Black Sands—"

"They've already been dispatched," Lucas interrupted. "Glassmen and Shesaitju alike."

"Well done," Torsten said. "If Rand came alone, we have to know why."

"I agree. He's being held close."

Torsten glanced around the corner, back down toward the main hallway. The last of Shieldsmen escort went by. The ceiling quaked more intensely than ever from the crowd above. He couldn't believe anything but a dwarven engineered structure could withstand such abuse.

"Quickly," Torsten said.

Lucas led him a short way through the grids of tunnels beneath the grand arena. It was almost entirely empty until they reached one of the combatant waiting rooms. Three Glass soldiers stood right outside, since no more Shieldsmen could be expended. They saluted as Torsten and Lucas approached.

"He's inside?" Lucas asked.

The guards nodded.

"Wait here," Torsten told Lucas.

"Sir Unger, I—"

"Last time you were with him, he nearly killed you. I need him calm."

Lucas opened his mouth to protest, then conceded.

The guards opened the door, then shoved aside a layer of seashells hanging on strings. They clattered as Torsten swept in. During their last meeting, Rand had been so devastated he couldn't even stay upright. Presently, he stood in the center of the room. His beard was thick and messy, his eyes drawn back from over-exhaustion. The rags he wore were the same as those which Torsten found him in on White Bridge—still stained with Bartholomew Darkings' blood.

"Sir Unger, you came!" he exclaimed, eyes like saucers, but at least they weren't black with possession. He took a step forward, but Torsten's glower sent him cowering to the back wall.

"Not this time, Rand," Torsten said. "I've given you my sympathy, my help, but an assault on any of my Shieldsmen is an assault on me."

"I didn't mean it, I swear. It was her, everything. All her."

"You demanded a blood pact on Sir Danvels!" Torsten roared. "After he brought you food and water. After he watched you, made sure you didn't cut your own wrists. Maybe he should've let you."

"I thought I was helping Sigrid…"

"And what about the Kingdom that you swore to shield from all evil? Perhaps if you'd stayed, I'd be able to look at you. But you ran again when Nesilia nearly killed us all. Deserter to redeemer and right back to deserter."

"I know… I know…" he sniveled. He stared at the floor, tears running down his cheeks. Then his gaze snapped upward, bright with energy. "But I'm here now. I want to… I *need* to help."

"It's too late for that, Rand. Maybe you didn't know, and it was all an accident, but it doesn't matter now. Your sister became an upyr, murdered Queen Oleander, and then surrendered her body to Nesilia."

"Sigrid is still inside of her, Torsten! I know it."

"I was there," Torsten said. "I fought her, watched her kill. There was no hesitation. Nesilia was in complete control."

"She turned my sister into a monster..." Rand wheezed. "I didn't believe it, but I know it's true. I... I have to help stop her."

"No. You've done enough, and I have done enough protecting you. You'll be brought back to Yarrington, where you'll be punished for crimes against our Kingdom. It's time the people learn the truth about Rand the Redeemer."

"I can fight!" he said. "You know I can fight. Let me help, and when we save Sigrid, I'll lock myself in a dungeon myself, I swear it."

"There is no saving her."

"That's not true," Rand argued.

"All the legends say that a man or woman must accept becoming an upyr. It's a choice, Rand. One she made, with horrid consequences."

I know my sister, and even if she lost her way or became an upyr or whatever you all think... this isn't her."

"It is now."

"Then, we have to destroy her!" Rand approached Torsten to plead.

Torsten promptly shoved him so hard his back slammed against the wall. All air evacuated his lungs and crumpled to the floor, a pathetic mess of a man. Perhaps he always had been, and Torsten was too blind —even then—to see it.

"I can't have her remembered for this..." he wept, sucking in raspy breaths. "I can't... I'll do anything, Sir. Anything."

Torsten clenched his jaw. His hands balled into tight fists. But as he watched Rand floundering, his stance softened. He could never escape the fact that Rand had been broken while Torsten was exiled by Oleander.

"Enough of that." Torsten sighed.

He moved to the wretch and grasped him by the arm to get him upright. "Now, get up," he said. "You'll never fight with us again, but you can—" As Torsten lifted him, Rand suddenly resisted. And not like a person having a breakdown, but a focused surge of strength.

Torsten's shoulder came down, and as he pushed Rand off, his enchanted blindfold was torn from his face.

Torsten swung a mighty fist, meeting only air. He swung with the other arm, and as he did, exposed his flank. Something sharp stabbed through a weak point where Torsten's plated armor cuirass met—one only a former Shieldsman would know about.

"I'm so sorry, Torsten, but she needs me," Rand whispered.

Torsten caught Rand by the forearm. What Rand wouldn't have known about was that Torsten now wore zhulong skin beneath his metal armor, a gift after White Bridge. The blade barely pierced his flesh. He smashed his heavy boot down on Rand's foot, causing him to squeal and pull away. The blade fell out, and Rand broke free, hammering Torsten in the back with an elbow. As Torsten fell forward, Rand stole *Salvation* from Torsten's back-sheath.

"Stop him!" one of the guards shouted.

Torsten heard sounds of struggle—grunting, then the clanking of metal. One of the guards shrieked.

"Get off him!" Lucas yelled.

Torsten heard it all. Lucas charged, and his body slammed into Rand's. They flew across the small room, *Salvation* scraping across the floor. Lucas cursed like no Shieldsman should as Torsten heard the familiar sound of a fist crunching against Rand's face.

"I'll kill you!" Lucas screamed as he punched again and again. Torsten didn't need eyes to know who was winning.

"Lucas, don't," he said through clenched teeth. "We need to know what she needs. I—" His words trailed off as he collapsed to one knee and clutched his side. The left half of his body where Rand had stabbed him went suddenly numb.

Torsten heard the *thump* of Rand's body dropping.

"Sir, stay awake," Lucas said, near him now, voice shaking, struggling to help keep him from lying down. "Help me with his armor!"

Torsten gripped some part of either Lucas or the other conscious guard and squeezed. They yanked his body this way and that to remove his armor and get a better look at the wound.

"It's not deep," Lucas said. "Your leather kept it from—"

"My blindfold…" Torsten managed to squeeze through his lips. Now, his fingers went numb and lost grip. His left foot felt like dead weight. Torsten has been stabbed enough times to know that he should be in pain, yet, there was none.

"My blindfold!" he repeated.

"Get that!" Lucas ordered.

The two other guards tripped over themselves, and a few moments later, Torsten felt the familiar feel of his sweat-soaked, enchanted blindfold being pulled over his head. The world formed before him in swathes of white and black, light, and the absence of it.

"I swear... we checked..." one guard stammered. "He had no weapon."

"What is this?" Lucas asked. While supporting Torsten with one arm, he examined what looked like a long talon in the other. He clearly didn't recognize it, but Torsten did.

"It's a grimaur talon," Torsten said.

Even speaking was difficult as the paralytic toxin expelled by a grimaur scratch moved through Torsten. It wasn't deadly, but it would be enough to stop a man's motor functions. Only Torsten's size and the fact that he'd caught Rand before he could stab too deep kept it from completely immobilizing him.

"The King... Rand is working with Nesilia..." Torsten shoved off and lumbered toward the door. His left side was now entirely numb, and his right limbs felt like they were tied to anchors. He staggered out into the tunnel and hit a wall, where Lucas caught him again.

"Sir, you need to lie down," he said. "I'll get a healer."

"Get me to the King!" he shouted.

Lucas looped under his shoulder and helped him down the tunnel. With every step, Torsten expected his feet to give out. He could barely feel them, only a slight pinpoint of pressure.

"One of you help me!" Lucas yelled back at the remaining guards.

"What about him?" one asked.

"He's not going anywhere."

"Watch him anyway," Torsten demanded.

One stayed with Rand, the other reached Torsten and helped them along. Torsten was glad his eyelids had been burned off; otherwise, he wouldn't have been able to keep them open. His blessed sight allowed him to stay cognizant.

They turned once, then again into the central passage. By then, Torsten's right foot dragged slightly, and both Lucas and the guard groaned from the stress of carrying him. Now, there was no dust falling from the ceiling. The crowd was silent as they headed straight for the arch leading outside.

"Torsten!" Rand bellowed.

They all stopped and looked back.

In the chaos, Torsten had forgotten his weapon—how could he have been so careless?

The traitor stood, carrying *Salvation*, coated in the blood of the guard they'd left to watch him. It would have been threatening if he wasn't propped up on the wall, his vision lagging from head trauma, and holding a weapon too heavy for his emaciated frame. More blood dripped from his mouth and a cut over his eye, courtesy of Lucas' beating.

Rand's features suddenly transformed from rage-filled to concerned. "You need to run," he said. "You all need to run."

"Enough of this," Lucas growled, then turned to the other guard. "Get Sir Unger outside. I'll deal with the traitor."

Torsten tried to speak, but the effort it took just to open the left side of his mouth made a coherent word challenging to form. Lucas stepped out alone and drew his longsword.

"C'mon, Sir," the guard groaned, struggling under Torsten's weight.

Torsten looked back as he was slowly dragged toward the arena.

Lucas charged Rand and had him on the defensive, the loud clangor of their blades echoing across the empty undercroft.

Torsten's neck muscles gave out, and his head drooped. Through the sunny opening, he could make out the figures of those partaking in the wedding ceremony. He saw Pi, across from Mahraveh, standing atop a low pedestal, so they were the same height.

They held each other's hands. A cloth bearing the Eye of Iam wrapped them together, while Dellbar the Holy spoke to an entranced and silent crowd.

Adrenaline flooded Torsten's system upon seeing them. His left fingers twitched as he started to regain tingling sensation.

"My King!" Torsten forced himself to scream. It was still slurred.

All eyes snapped toward him in the archway. Before Torsten could do anything else, a deafening *boom* shook the very earth. The struggling guard lost his grip, and Torsten collapsed.

His head hit the packed sand first. Then, all he could hear were screams...

XVI

THE CALEEF

Mahi's bare foot slapped down in the shallow stream of water encircling the Tal'du Dromesh arena. The crowd silenced in a heartbeat. She gazed up and around at all the thousands of Shesaitju eyes fixated on her.

Throughout the boisterous walk out of the undercroft, showered in dust from the pounding feet throughout the stands, Mahi remembered fighting on these very sands. She remembered the adrenaline pumping through every muscle, the fire in her bones, the bloodlust. The quiet changed that. It unnerved her. Made her hear the steady *thump-thump* of her heart between the distant cawing of gulls and the waves pounding the beach and stone on the other side of the arena's southern rock wall.

Her gaze shifted downward toward Tal'du Dromesh itself. Serpent Guards and Shieldsmen stood at arms around the circumference and within the stands at every entrance and aisle. Their alternating gold and silver armor, and pink and gray skin, would have seemed otherworldly if not for what was in the center of the sands.

King Pi stood there, dressed in elaborately crafted armor, a light blue cape flowing from his back and draping around his feet to hide the low pedestal, making him appear taller to the crowd.

Or is it for me? Mahi wondered.

During the only meeting they'd had prior to this, seated alone at the feast, they'd talked openly and candidly. He hadn't seemed self-conscious about anything. Quite the opposite, actually.

Behind him stood the High Priest, bare white robes cascading down his body like snow-capped mountains. A shorter distance away was one-armed Lord Jolly and a few other noble-looking Glassmen who'd made the journey. Torsten was inexplicably absent. Though, even only knowing him so briefly, Mahi imagined he was somewhere, high up in the boxes, watching for the safety of his King.

Across from the Glassmen stood Bit'rudam and Tingur. Sages dribbled nigh'jel blood along Mahi's path and toward the center, humming prayers in Saitjuese. Others stood atop the rocky dam, facing out to the Boiling Waters. Over it, the angled sails of two warships could be seen, the fabric bright against a backdrop of looming storm clouds. Thunder rumbled in the distance, also now perceivable with her people quieted.

Within the Tal'du Dromesh, however, the sun was bright and hot. If there really was an Iam, it was hard to deny he was watching.

"And so, your rebellion ends, Father," Mahi whispered to herself. She closed her eyes and breathed in the moment, salt spray from the sea and all. Then, drums broke the horrible silence, and she strode across the sand.

Memories ran through her mind, of all the countless ceremonies held in this hallowed place by Caleefs of old. Tournaments, executions, funerals—none were so momentous as this. She wasn't nervous, though it remained strange to hear her heartbeat so clearly, pounding along with the drums and no other sound.

Pi watched her on approach, his chin lifted proudly. His lips were straight, and his expression stern, but Mahi had been around enough young men. Could he do what was required to consummate their marriage by Glassmen law after the sun fell? Could she?

Bit'rudam wore a similar expression, likely concerned over the same thing, being brave, even though Mahi knew he had to be agonizing on the inside. She knew she'd made the right choice having him be her guard. If Pi grew large like his father and violent like his mother, Bit'rudam wouldn't hesitate to stab him in the back.

All those thoughts and more assailed her mind until she stopped directly across from King Pi. Dellbar the Holy put on a weak smile, the lines around his lips far more profound than his age would indicate.

"You look stunning, my Lady," Pi said. Again, his tone was confident, though difficult to read. Mahi knew how she looked in her outfit and makeup—like a goddess. Any other young man Pi's age might have been drooling, but not him. It was all so business-like. She couldn't even tell if he meant the compliment, only that he intended to flatter her.

Mahi smiled and nodded.

"Friends. Allies. Men and women of the Glass and Sands. What a fortuitous day, here, beneath the vigilant Eye of Iam," Dellbar pronounced, loudly as he could.

He seemed in better spirits than at the feast. The winds swirling within the arena should have muffled his voice, but instead, it projected far beyond Mahi expected it would. Judging by the vision of the man, she'd expected little more than a whisper.

"And the Lord of the Sea, graciously inviting us to walk upon sands where, in his honor, so many have spilled their blood," Dellbar added.

Mahi couldn't help but note the improper use for her god's name.

"The God of Sand and Sea," Pi corrected, gently, so only they three could hear.

Mahi's breath caught. Dellbar cleared his throat.

"Yes, of course, my King," Dellbar muttered, then raised his voice. "A rift has existed between our lands for far too long. Yet all are here, in the name of love and unity. In the face of death and curses, these two young souls are intertwined by a history of miracles."

"Our Caleef is the only miracle!" barked a man from the crowd.

All eyes snapped up to see an older Shesaitju man standing in the middle of the lower level. No sooner was he revealed than Serpent Guards were on him, dragging him away, squirming and shouting in Saitjuese.

"Afhem Babrak is right about her!" yelled another, across the arena. A few others rose to join that man in protest, and they too were removed, though in a far more aggressive manner.

Before any more dared speak, the Serpent Guards made a show of force. They emerged from all the arena entry tunnels along the concourse's edge, slamming their weapons down in unison. A deafening *clank* echoed, followed by a growl of thunder from the nearing storm.

Dellbar winced. Mahi peered down, expecting the same from Pi, but his attention had turned to the west archway into the arena undercroft. Concern rippled across his features, but when he turned back to Mahi, he was back to his young, intrepid self.

"Yes, and so…" Dellbar cleared his throat again. He regarded the sun, blinded eyes unaffected, then circled them with his fingers. "It is with great pride and honor that I present beneath Iam's vigilant gaze, these two brave leaders. Pi Nothhelm, the Miracle King, Lord of the Glass Kingdom and Herald of Iam's Light; son of Liam Nothhelm the Conqueror. And Mahraveh of Saujibar, Caleef of the Black Sands, daughter of Muskigo "the Scythe" Ayerabi, and champion of the Tal'du Dromesh."

Dellbar reached into the folds of his robe and produced a small vial filled with Black Sand.

"Your hand, Lady Mahraveh," he instructed.

She glanced over at Bit'rudam and Tingur. The latter nodded her along while the former watched without really watching. Mahi extended her hands, and Dellbar opened her fingers, so her palm faced upward.

"In your hand, you hold your land," he said as he uncorked the vial and poured the dark sand out over her palm. She welcomed the feel of the grains against her fingers and within the grooves of her hand. It felt like home.

"My King, your hands," Dellbar went on.

Mahi noticed Pi peer again toward the west entry to the undercroft before he, too, followed the instructions.

"In your hand, you hold your land," Dellbar said, pouring a vial filled with tannish-red colored sand. Having only seen her own black sands, and the pure white sands of the M' stafu Desert to the north, Mahi had never seen sand like it and imagined it had to be from the coast off Yarrington.

"And so those lands, in your names, will be as one," Dellbar said. He lightly positioned their hands, one atop the other, with Pi's in the upper position. Mahi resisted a bit out of instinct.

"It is said that Iam's greatest gift to us is the light which guides our way from above," Dellbar went on. "But I don't believe so. That same light allows the wicked to prey, and the vengeful to find their quarry. It is why we of the priesthood do not see with our eyes, because in truth, Iam's light comes from within. His greatest gift to Pantego… is love."

Dellbar produced a cloth that glowed like a nigh'jel, as if covered in luminescent paint. In its center, stitched in pure white, was the Eye of Iam. Dellbar raised it to the sky, the sunlight catching its folds and glinting.

"And love will blossom here today," Dellbar said. "Beneath Iam's vigilant Eye, two souls have found their light. And now, in heart, mind, and land, they shall be as one." He began to wrap the cloth around their sand-filled hands, then tucked the remaining fabric.

The grains shifted and blended. She could feel the gazes of her people fixated on her, judging her every move.

"Just as these sands could never be separated, so shall you two be."

Mahraveh stared down at their hands.

"Do you, Pi Nothhelm, King of the Glass, take Caleef Mahraveh of Saujibar, as your Queen and wife? Will you swear, in Iam's name, to be true to her, to foster her light, and to protect her with all that you are until the Gate of Light greets you?"

Pi's cobalt eyes stared straight into Mahi's. A hint of fear now showed in them, but only for a second. He blinked, likely thinking she'd see it as a sign of weakness. Instead, Mahi welcomed it. It would be weakness to deny what he was feeling, and for a boy locked in a castle all his life, she was as foreign to him as he was to her.

The sand continued trickling through his fingers as they remained merged with hers. Blending them thoroughly would take time. But they both were clearly willing to try.

"I do," he said, soft, but firm.

Dellbar then turned to Mahi. "Do you, Mahraveh, Caleef of the Black Sands, take Pi Nothhelm as your King and husband? Will you swear, in Iam's name and on the Eternal Current to be true to him, to foster his light and to protect him with all that you are until the Current takes you."

Murmuring began as he mentioned the Current. It surprised Mahi as well. She noticed the slight smirk tug at Pi's lips as Dellbar spoke it, and realized that it had to be his doing. From what she knew, his father would have cut out his own tongue before uttering such a thing, ceremony or not.

"I do," Mahi stated proudly so all could hear.

No sooner were the words through her lips than an incoherent shout echoed from the western entry of the undercroft. They all looked that way and spotted Torsten Unger standing in the opening. Blood covered his side as he leaned against a Glass soldier, hardly able to stand.

His eyes went wide. An earsplitting crack rang out, and the ground shook, throwing Mahi and Pi. Pi fell off his pedestal, and hands bound together dragged her with him.

The entire crowd screamed but were soon drowned out by a guttural bellow that was far from human. Shieldsmen and Serpent Guards ran to the King and Queen. Mahi scrambled to lift herself and Pi to their feet, tearing the cloth tied around their hands in her efforts, spilling the mixed sands.

The ground quaked again as the dam made of immense boulders at the south end of the arena blew apart along with the warships moored just beyond. The rocks fell loose, some heaved up into the stands, crushing people there. Wood splintered and shot out like arrows, and through the many growing breaches in the rock extended what looked like massive tentacles.

They thrashed and tore, breaking apart more rock. Seawater and debris gushed through, assisting them further. The storm offshore was now closer than what seemed possible in so short a time.

Mahi saw the embodiment of evil rise over the breaking barrier; soulless black eyes and a maw filled with thousands of razor-sharp teeth. One massive wave sent it tumbling into the arena, limbs flailing.

Guards were pulverized, crushed, their armor doing absolutely nothing to protect them. More thrashing tentacles sent others through the air. As water cascaded in, one of the warships snapped in half against the rock. It was impossible to tell if there was more than one of the beasts.

"Run!" Mahi shouted.

Pi froze, staring. That subtle show of fear turned to full-on terror. She grabbed him and ran for the arena walls.

"What is that!" he screamed.

She had no idea how to answer, even if there'd been time.

In ancient times, sailors told stories of great sea beasts like giant octopuses called Current Eaters. Still, Mahi had always thought them things painted on maps to turn travelers away.

She and Pi reached the wall, the sound of rushing water and terrifying roars at their backs. Lord Jolly was on one side, his sole arm around blind Dellbar the Holy, guiding him to safety, if there was such a thing. The stone wall surrounding the sands was tall, with the top half coated in spikes. Impossible to climb for a reason.

"My Caleef, this way." Bit'rudam waved them over.

It was now clear there was more than one of the things, and Tingur stood facing the legendary beasts as if he could do anything to slow them.

Bit'rudam barked orders and Serpent Guards formed at the base. Without hesitation, they launched one up. His chest plunged into the spikes and pinned him there in sacrifice. Then, they started lifting people over, using his body as a shield against the spikes. Thankfully, he had no tongue with which to scream.

"Sir Unger!" Pi yelped. Mahi grasped the King's hand as quickly as she could, stopping his attempt toward Torsten and yanking him back toward Bit'rudam instead. Torsten Unger laid on the sand nearby, both hands digging to drag himself toward them. Floodwater slowly filled in around his face.

"My Caleef, you first!" Bit'rudam said.

"No, take them," she replied.

Before he could respond, she sprinted for Torsten. Without him to lead the Glassmen, fighting Nesilia would prove even more challenging.

The floodwater had neared her knees by the time she reached him. A Current Eater had caught onto the side of the arena and clambered up the stands, devouring and mashing everything in its path. Stone blocks, which had stood for thousands of years, were torn loose and flew every which way.

"Sir Unger, get up!" Mahi yelled.

She knelt and wedged her arm beneath him. Luckily, he was mostly out of his armor, or he would be sinking like a rock in the rising water.

"She played us for fools," he mumbled. "She wanted this."

"Nesilia did this?" Mahi asked, peering back at the dam. With every passing second, its integrity was further compromised. Waves and ship debris surged over and through it, filling the arena, sloshing onto the stands and causing the crowds to slip or fall in.

"Who else," Torsten said.

Mahi continued digging her way beneath him and groaned. "Sir Unger, you have to get up!"

"Can't move... I..."

A Current Eater roared so loudly, Mahi's very bones chattered. A large wave carried another, and it smashed through what was left of one warship and into the dam, blowing it fully open.

The coast of Latiapur was one of sharp bluffs with shallow beaches forming along it at low tide and very few treacherous paths up. Until now, the water rarely rose more than a few meters up the dam. The sea had been rough from the storm, but this was something else. She'd never witnessed the tide so high or winds so fiercely focused on a single spot—nor had the memories of all the Caleefs within her. Warship sails became thin shreds as if the very air was filled with knives.

"Mahraveh!" Bit'rudam screamed.

She glanced over and saw him waiting for help from the Serpent Guards. Pi and Lord Jolly were busy hefting Tingur's heavy body over the guard who'd sacrificed himself upon the spikes. Dellbar the Holy sat behind them on the stands, catching his breath while the mostly Shesaitju crowd fled in a panic.

"Go, now!" She grabbed his waist and hoisted him up.

The rushing water gave him no choice but to go with it. The guards helped him the rest of the way, and soon after, they were pounded by the sea. Mahi took a lungful of air before she too was overtaken.

She clutched Torsten's hand and swam as water engulfed them. Her father had taught her never to tire herself fighting the current but to wait and ride it until it settled.

The Current always wins, he'd said more times than she could remember.

But her father had never been drowning in a place like this.

Mahi flipped over and saw that they zoomed toward the spike wall. She released Torsten, using the momentum to shove down, then pressed her feet on the wall between dagger-sharp edges. She pushed off as hard as she could, tackling Torsten, so their backs struck the smooth, lower portion of the wall once the current overtook them.

They were pulled back out in the undertow. Through the murky water, Mahi saw the dark mass of a Current Eater hurdling toward them. Submerged, it wasn't so clumsy. All its tentacles were tucked behind its bulbous head as it dashed forward, toothy maw opened wide and aimed straight for them.

A stout, gray-skinned figure plunged through the surface and banged into its side, knocking it off-angle. The beast's head crashed just adjacent to her and Torsten, black blood swirling into the water as the spikes stabbed it.

Mahi found herself lost in a flurry of tentacles, lucky none crushed her head, though many pounded her flesh. She clasped one of its suction cups, which really seemed to upset it. It whipped into the air, and once she emerged from the water, holding up Torsten's body was no longer so easy. Her elbow stung as his weight bent it back. Air blew across her face and made it difficult to draw the breath she so desperately needed.

"Let go!" someone yelled.

She listened without thinking, getting a quick glimpse of Torsten falling onto the concourse below. The tentacle swung back up, and Mahi dared not let go. Instead, she flung herself around it, finding her footing on the lumpy meat of its top side.

Another tentacle lashed at her, its tip as sharp as the Current Eaters' teeth. She ducked under it, then sprang up, hopped over another, and leaped toward the stands.

"Mahi!" Bit'rudam screamed as she soared above him. He stole a spear from a guard and hurled it. One of the beast's tentacles was pierced just before stabbing Mahi, harmlessly slashing the base of her dress instead as it recoiled.

She tucked into a roll upon landing and didn't have long to react. If this Current Eater was a mindless servant to Nesilia, that certainly didn't show. It perched over the side of the arena, the water now filled all the way to the lower stands. It unleashed an earsplitting roar.

The Serpent Guards shoved by Mahi to attack it, slicing at tentacles that slapped down all around, impaling some, crushing others, and sweeping out legs. Dozens of frantic members of the crowd were caught in its wrath as well.

Mahi dropped to all fours as one wet limb whipped overhead, then scrambled low to Bit'rudam and the others. Her extravagant and constricting dress tore more and more with each vigorous motion, allowing her to move unencumbered.

"My Caleef, we have to get you out of here!" Bit'rudam yelled.

She quickly took stock of everyone. Torsten was on his hands and knees wheezing. Dellbar stood over him, glowing hands upon his back as he whispered a silent prayer. Lord Jolly had Pi backed into a nook between two rungs of stands, arm extended to guard him. Gone was any semblance of Pi's bravery, and Mahi couldn't blame him. Many veteran warriors who'd come to watch the marriage ceremony were equally panicked, and some had already escaped.

"Where's Tingur?" Mahi asked.

"He jumped in to save you," Bit'rudam replied.

Mahi peered over the ledge at the raging beast. The guards kept it occupied as they were picked apart. Its many tentacles acted as much like a shield as they did daggers, and even if they could find an opening, it was too immense for them to deal any real damage. Above all, it was careful never to expose the back of its head where she imagined its brain would be. It was smart, as well as dangerous.

She didn't see Tingur anywhere.

Behind it, across the arena, another Current Eater ascended the stands, slaughtering everything in its path. A third had its tentacles around the edge of the structure where it transitioned into the dam, ripping the walls apart and widening the breach to allow for even more water to pour in. The storm cast everything behind it in darkness, a wall of driving rain and whipping wind somehow planted right outside the arena.

"We have to save him!" Mahi yelled.

"We can't," Bit'rudam argued.

"He—"

"You can't, my Caleef. You and the King must survive."

Mahi bit her lip, eyes darting back to the raging waters, then nodded. "All right. Get them, everyone. There's an exit this way."

Bit'rudam jumped onto a lower bench and yelled, "Defend your Caleef!"

Most of the people in the arena were either trampling each other to escape or petrified, but a few courageous warriors trickled down to help.

"My King, we have to run," Lord Jolly said.

He pulled Pi free by the hand just before the nearest Current Eater exploded out of the water toward them. Its weight compromised the arena wall, and it tumbled back into the water. The tip of one of its tentacles stabbed into Lord Jolly's calf and hoisted him into the air.

"Release him, you unholy beast!" Torsten roared.

Everything happened so fast, Mahi hadn't even seen Torsten recover, yet there he was. He tore a glaive free from one of the Serpent Guards, knocked Dellbar aside, and brought the blade crashing down on the end of the tentacles.

Mahi's guards had little luck piercing the beast's thick skin. Not him. The giant Shieldsman cleaved it in two in a single stroke. Lord Jolly fell free, and the tentacle lashed back, spewing out blood like a garden fountain.

"Take him!" Torsten yelled. "Take the King!"

He seemed dizzy as he moved, but he grasped Pi by his cape and shoved him toward Bit'rudam. Dellbar ran to Lord Jolly in the opposite direction and helped him up the stands, higher and beyond the Current Eater's reach.

Torsten whipped the blade around, slashing another tentacle. He couldn't move fast, and every attack seemed off-balance like a warrior suffering heat fatigue. But she'd never seen anyone strike with such raw power—not even Babrak.

Inspired by a Glassman acting so bravely, more Shesaitju stirred to protect their Caleef, leaping onto the beast. It shook them off like ants, but the distraction worked.

Mahi took the petrified King's hand, then offered Bit'rudam a nod. Her protector summoned the remaining nearby Serpent Guards to them, and they took off around the concourse. One tentacle raked a few in, but Torsten earned its attention back, his efforts even drawing Shield-smen to him from all around that portion of the arena.

"I swear, this wasn't us," Pi huffed as they ran.

"I know that," Mahi answered.

Bit'rudam reached a wide ramp leading out of the stands and waved for them to hurry. Serpent Guards shoved dozens of fleeing Shesaitju aside to clear a path. Some fell, others tripped, and another of the Current Eaters rampaged toward them from the south side of the stands, its roars like thunder.

Or is that really thunder?

Mahi glanced south, and the thick, dark veil of clouds remained paused at the breach in the dam. Rain fell in angled sheets on the strong gale but moved no closer, and bolts of lightning coruscated throughout the blackness. As they flashed, Mahi saw silhouettes of large, rectangular shapes sticking out from the waves.

"Long live Afhem Babrak!"

Mahi heard the words before she saw where they came from. She shoved Pi away, then whipped around and caught a Shesaitju man jumping down at her from the stands above.

A shiv carved out of loose stone drove toward her chest. Her elbow caught the attacker in the throat, loosened his grip, and she wrenched his forearm back to stab him through the eye with his own weapon.

Bit'rudam tore him off her. Mahi ripped the shiv free and flung it over her protector's shoulder, hitting another loyalist to Babrak in the shoulder. Serpent Guards swarmed the man and gutted him, then formed a circle around her, bashing more fleeing civilians aside.

"No, the King!" Mahi yelled. "Protect my husband!"

The words sounded foreign from her lips, and her cries were drowned out by the added chaos. Bit'rudam and the Serpent Guards marched down the exit aisle with her in the center, keeping everything and everyone away. Pi was stuck on the outside of them, jostled this way and that by the rushing throng.

Mahi pushed Bit'rudam aside and ran back to help him, and that was when she saw it. The shapes within the hovering storm came into focus, and at their lead was a Shesaitju warship. A giant figurehead in the form of a sawfish stuck out from the prow. Angled sails were painted with the crest belonging to the Trisps'I—Babrak's afhemate.

A man so large it could only be him stood upon the bow, watching. Beside him was a red-robed woman. She seemed to be hovering, but the rain made things blurry, and her hands were raised toward the sky with bolts of lightning jumping to them, somehow causing her no harm.

"Pi, get to the Boiling Keep," Mahi called.

"I can help…" he stammered. "I want to help."

"You will. But first, get to safety!"

Before she could order a Serpent Guard to stay with him, the nearest Current Eater flattened all those caught in its path, cleaving a mass of stone away from the arena. Bit'rudam clutched Mahi and tugged her back into the protective circle. More people fell into a mad scramble in the undersized exit, and Mahi made eye contact with Pi for but a moment before he darted away, lost in the heap of flailing bodies. From the corner of her eye, she noticed Babrak—the man who'd taken so much from her—raise his fat arm. From such a distance, she could only imagine his grin as he let his arm fall.

The robed woman besides him did the same, streams of lightning dying at her fingertips as the rain, wind, and clouds suddenly dissipated. More ships by the dozens were revealed as if from nowhere, all Trisps'I. The raging sea calmed as well, allowing them to safely sail through the beach while waves radiated outward that would keep the Latiapur navy at bay.

Hundreds of arrows darkened the sky, fired from archers upon the decks. The sun vanished behind them. They were aimed without prejudice. Even the Current Eaters would be caught in the volley.

Serpent Guards threw themselves over Mahi as they hurried her down the exit ramp. She couldn't see a thing, could only hear the zip of the arrows falling, and the chorus of screams, rent flesh and clacking stone as they landed.

Now, Mahi knew without a doubt.

Her new enemy was capable of feats unlike any she'd ever witnessed. And her family's oldest enemy, Babrak, had no honor. He'd aligned himself with Nesilia, and through the guise of a dark magic storm, attacked Latiapur from the sea, where it was thought to be impenetrable.

XVII

THE MYSTIC

Sora limped along, barely having to put on any performance at all. She'd planned to fake a fall anyway, but she'd actually caught her ankle as they disembarked the cart.

Out of the corner of her eye, she watched as Whitney skulked along the dark edges of the room, careful to not make a sound.

By now, they'd all recovered, and Brouben stood at the head of them, speaking quietly to a guard wearing armor black as night and covered in long spikes. Brouben called them clanbreakers—they looked as fierce and violent as any dwarf Sora had laid eyes on.

An onslaught of memories blasted her, of Nesilia's destruction of those poor dwarves called the Strongirons. Using Freydis and the Drav Cra, she'd been merciless, cutting down so many just to prove a point. Now, without Nesilia's callousness, fear gripped her heart at the thought of being captured and perforated by the clanbreakers.

What if anyone made it out alive and blamed her?

In Yarrington—even Winde Port, they had rules. The guards wouldn't run them through with their swords, even if they'd been caught performing any of Whitney's stupid cons. They'd have been arrested sure, maybe thrown in a dungeon for the rest of time, or in the worst case, chop off their heads in front of a crowd, but at least then they'd have been prepared.

Here though, Sora wasn't so sure. Whitney had always said the dwarves valued gold above all else, and that guard had mentioned execution for simple breaking and entering. She wouldn't be surprised if they had the right to kill first and then interrogate the corpse.

I'm sounding more like Whitney every day, Sora thought.

"Father!" Brouben called as an old dwarf shuffled through the gate leading to what appeared to be a barred vault situated within the ribcage of the dragon skeleton.

This must have been King Lorgit Cragrock. He wore a bright red cloak, but the end of it was a patchwork of other fabrics—various colors and patterns. He looked like he'd always been old. His hair—which seemed to be making a determined retreat from his forehead—was nearly white as the snow they'd trudged through to get to the mountain. Deep chasms in leathery skin were buried beneath thick, furry brows. A gray beard climbed up his cheeks almost to his eyes and fell over glinting chainmail, every link crafted from gold. He was frail—not skinny. From the look of things, no dwarf was skinny. And just like the colossal dwarf head they were now inside of, he wore a golden, winged helm.

"Brouben, what's it now?" he asked, a voice as weary as he looked. "What's this ramshackle group of humans ye got with ye? Prisoners? Since when do we bring prisoners to the throne room? Take em to the dung—"

"Fathe—" Brouben cleared his throat. He was already at work, undoing everyone's shackles. "King Lorgit Cragrock, please forgive the deception, but I needed to get em to ye. These are me friends... new friends. They've got somethin to say."

The King stopped, cocking his head to one side like a confused puppy. "Are me eyes growin old, or is that Dwotratum Goodbrew?"

"Aye, that be me," Tum Tum said, stepping forward.

Sora held her breath as the King glared at Tum Tum. She wasn't sure Cragrock had the strength to punch Tum Tum, but if looks could kill...

The King approached slowly, eyeing Tum Tum the whole way. "Ye've got nerve returnin here after so long," he said.

"And I don't do it lightly," Tum Tum said. "There be trouble. Much of it. And I be thinkin, there's no one better to face the trouble head-on than me own King."

King Lorgit laughed, but it was filled with fire. "Do I look like Pi Nothhelm to ye?"

Tum Tum looked taken aback, but Sora saw it coming. The old adage seemed true. *A dwarf never forgives nor forgets.*

"Did ye think I'd kept a room for ye?" Lorgit spat. "Ain't ye even wondered where yer father were—may he drink with Meungor. Ye swore me off as yer King long ago."

"Not true, me King." Tum Tum managed to squeeze the words out, but Sora could see it plain on his face, the news that his father had died was clearly a shock. She was grateful Tum Tum fought the urge to ask what had happened. There'd be time for that if they all lived. If not, he'd be able to ask his father in person.

"Now yer callin me a liar?" Lorgit stroked his beard with his many-ringed hand. There was silence, long and agonizing. He looked at Brouben, then back to Tum Tum. "Ain't got nothin more to say."

Lorgit then turned his back to Tum Tum.

Sora scanned the room for Whitney. If the dwarven king returned to the Iron Bank so quickly, Whitney would have no chance to execute the heist. Sora and Lucindur would need to enact the next part of their makeshift plan immediately.

"We traveled a long way," Lucindur said, doing an excellent job of just that. Her voice was soft but commanding, same as it always was.

It amazed Sora how such a slight woman could practically demand the attention of anyone in any room across Pantego. It was a talent Sora hoped to learn. Whitney had told Sora a lot about his time with the Pompare Troupe during his endless stories on the way back from the Citadel. He'd said that Modera and Fadra may have run the Troupe on the outside, but honestly, it was Lucindur. She knew how to unite people, care for people, and scold people when necessary. Even in Sora's short time with the woman, those things were evident.

Sora just wasn't sure how much of the woman's magic played a role in things.

Lorgit stopped but didn't turn around. Lucindur, apparently, took that for an invitation to continue.

"You're truly the last hope we have, Your Grace," she said.

With those last words, the pride Sora knew all dwarves to possess kicked in. Perhaps, Lorgit had seen through his son's flattery, but Lucindur spoke with such confidence, Sora almost believed it.

Lorgit spun, almost a smile on his face. But Sora misread his intentions.

"Ain't that convenient," he said. "Ain't heard a word from ye Glintish folk until just weeks ago when one of yer own came here under the banner of the Glass, and now, here ye are again. I gave ye an army, and what did ye do with it?"

Just then, Sora caught sight of Whitney slinking along the tail of the dragon skeleton. The fact that Aquira sat upon his shoulder completely shocked her. Somehow, she knew that was his doing, but she couldn't worry about it now.

She and Whitney locked eyes, obviously both thinking the same thing.

A Glintish under the banner of the Glass requesting an army? Sounds like Torsten.

"I'm sorry, Your Grace, but I don't know what you're referring to," Lucindur said.

Brouben cleared his throat. "Father, I told ye. We were out—"

"Outmatched?" Lorgit said. "In all me years alive, I ain't never seen a man outmatch a dwarf. And yer tellin me them gray-skins found a way to slaughter—"

"As I told ye, Father—"

"Don't ye say it." Lorgit's face was the color of a ripe plum.

"How do ye expect me to defend meself if ye keep tellin me not to talk about it?"

"I ain't lookin for defense; I'm lookin for quiet!"

The request was granted apart from what was surely an involuntary harrumph from Tum Tum.

Whitney motioned for Sora to do something.

"Your Grace," Sora said, improvising. "What is this about? If I might ask."

At the same time, Brouben said, "Father, I don't think—"

"By Meungor's shinin axe, yer finally right on a point," Lorgit interrupted. "Ye sneak these flower-pickers in, disguisin them as prisoners—in me own throne room! Yer lucky I don't have me clanbreakers shred all of ye on the spot."

"I'm sorry, Father," Brouben said. "It seemed the only way."

"Only way for what? They want more of our warriors killed in their squabbles?"

"Warriors?" Sora said. "Your Grace, we don't need soldiers…"

"Then spit it out," Lorgit said, interrupting Sora. "What's an outcast and a horde of outsiders doin in my home?"

Whitney let out a sharp raspberry, then covered his mouth with his hand. Sora sucked in a breath, doing her best not to look at him, hoping everyone else would do the same. Thankfully, no one seemed to notice.

"I sent me own son to Yarrington to help those fools govern their coin," Lorgit said. "Seems like it ain't done nothin good. Ye ain't here for soldiers, then yer here for gold."

"They ain't here for gold neither," Brouben said. "Please, listen to them. If ye won't listen to me…"

For a moment, Lorgit calmed, and just as he was about to speak, Sora did.

"Nesilia, the Buried Goddess—"

"For the love of all shog-shuckin, yiggin horse-lovin—Enough already!" King Lorgit shouted. It was a strange sound coming from such an old man, deep, resonant.

The clanbreakers edged forward at the outburst from their king, undoubtedly ready for violence should it come to it. Perhaps they were even hoping for it.

Sora watched as Whitney used the distraction and continued the climb further up the dragon skeleton. At first, Aquira looked skittish, as if afraid of the great beast that was her ancestor. Sora's heart nearly melted as Whitney turned his head, nuzzling against her for a moment. However, then her eyes drifted to the armor-clad warriors below them, faces forward. She wondered how they could possibly fight in that getup, and hoped she wouldn't learn. Two slits were carved out of their helmets for eyeholes. They didn't even look like they could turn, much less see what was beside them.

That boded well for Whitney as he crept along the dragon's spine toward the spot at the crest of the beast's back where Lorgit's throne sat. No less than ten large braziers similar to those in the main hall kept the throne room lit. That also meant if anyone turned around, he'd be shining like the sun atop the dragon's back.

Sora cringed as he leaped nimbly from bone to bone until he was safely hidden behind the king's massive throne and waited for his next move. It was quite the feat, she had to admit. To do such a thing so quietly as he had—perhaps he wasn't exaggerating *all* of his tales. She smiled, then remembered her face and cleared it of emotion.

"Your Grace," Sora said, taking a place next to Lucindur. "Your son tells the truth."

"And what do ye know?" Lorgit said.

Sora was confident the word "knife-ear" was sure to follow, but it didn't. She supposed that was a mark in the positive column for the dwarven King.

"Yer people have been just as quiet as hers." He pointed to Lucindur.

"All the more reason you should believe something important has occurred," Sora said.

A look washed over him that made Sora think he might be considering it. Until he spoke.

"Ain't a thing more important than preservin this mountain and me people. Now, if that be all, ye can find yer way back to the warmth, and feel lucky I don't have yer heads taken from yer shoulders."

"Father, ye can't expect us to simply sit back while the world ends," Brouben said.

"That's precisely what I mean us to do. Ye don't know what yer triflin with, boy."

What did that mean? Did Lorgit know more than he was letting on? Sora chewed her lip and considered Nesilia's previous tactics with the Strongirons. Had she gotten to Lorgit and secured the Three Kingdoms as her own?

"Excuse me, Your Grace," Lucindur said. Brouben put a hand on her arm, but she yanked it away. "With all due respect. We were there."

Lorgit glared at her. There was something there in his eyes, emotion thick in the air. Though, Sora couldn't place it. Anger? Pity?

"There?" the King asked.

Lucindur hesitated, but to her credit, it wasn't for long. "Nesilia and her whole army… we saw her."

The King, however, didn't pause for a second. "Aye, and I'm tellin ye, ye saw wrong."

"I promise, we didn't," Sora said, her heart heavy. She'd seen from the eyes of the goddess herself. "We saw it, right after her army ravaged the Strongiron Kingdom in the East."

"More hogwash." Lorgit waved his hand in dismissal. "Whatever trouble the Strongirons be in, they did it to themselves. Prolly stirred up the nest of forgotten beasts. We've seen our share. Those soft-bellies never know when to stop diggin."

Sora considered telling him that she was there, but that truth might get them killed sooner rather than later. He clearly didn't care for a rival dwarven kingdom so far away, but they were all dwarves in the end.

"Father…" Brouben tried again to reason with the King.

Lorgit turned to his son, a look of disapproval on his face. "Ye think ye know these folk?"

Brouben didn't answer.

"The place now called the Glass Kingdom… ye know what we call it?"

"Morrastreaudunimum," Brouben answered without a moment's hesitation.

"That's right. Morrastreaudunimum will always be Morrastreaudunimum no matter how many times those flower-pickers change its name. Been that way since before King Andur Cragrock, me great-great-great-great-grandfather, brought our folk to the mountain just to avoid ye filthy humans." The King's features turned soft. "Don't get me wrong, I love Balonhearth as any good dwarf, but ye know this weren't where we was supposed to be."

Brouben shifted, and Sora could feel his discomfort.

"Before the Drav Cra rode south on their chekt—foul, smelly beasts," the King continued, "our people were all happy down there. Warm weather and all. We built the place those flower-pickers now bury their Kings. Built most of their castle too, and that damn bridge ye have so many wild stories about. Then, the bastards turned on us. Used their chekt and dragons against us until they nearly got those creatures extinct like so many others. Drove us north to here."

He motioned with his hand.

"Father, what does all this mean?" Brouben asked.

"It means we are resilient," Lorgit said. "Strong. Ain't no way no one, goddess or not, gonna be drivin us from our home again. We learnt."

"But Father—"

"No buts. We be traders and merchants, Son. We know a good deal when one comes along."

Deal?

The king turned without another word and started back to the Iron Bank. Above, Whitney pulled himself behind Lorgit's throne.

Below, the clanbreakers returned to the gate, armor clattering.

Sora couldn't breathe. Had Lorgit struck a deal with Nesilia? If he had, they were in more danger than they'd thought. The glint in Lucindur's eye told Sora she was thinking the same thing.

If they had any chance of surviving, Whitney would have to move soon. His chance, slim as it was, was now gone. One of the clanbreakers on the right pulled on the gate of the Iron Bank, and it squeaked as it opened.

"She got to ye, didn't she?" Brouben said, voicing Sora's own thoughts. His words were barely more than a whisper, hard to be heard over the roar and crackle of the many fires, but it made Lorgit stop dead in his tracks in the middle of the threshold.

"I never thought ye, me own father, King of the Three Kingdoms, to be a coward," Brouben continued.

With that final word, the clanbreakers tensed, and Lorgit turned. "What did ye say?"

"Deaf, too? Yer a coward," Brouben repeated, slowly, emphasizing each word. "She's got ye by the balls, and ye can't grow em enough to get away."

What are you doing, Brouben? Sora thought. *You're going to spoil the whole rotten plan!*

"Stop talkin, now," the King practically growled.

But Brouben ignored him. "Ye don't get it. Are ye gonna kill me? We're all gonna die just like the Strongirons if ye don't step up. Because they're all dead, we can't ask them what did it, but why would these people lie? We're all gonna die without ye. All of us. Them, me, ye."

Lorgit didn't speak, he just waved his hand dismissively and turned.

"Ye don't deserve the crown," Brouben said. Cold ice covered everything in the room. "Me brethren been sayin it for years, but I always told em they was wrong. But ye don't deserve to be King of the Three Kingdoms. Ye don't deserve to be my father."

King Lorgit cleared his throat and flattened his beard. "Take him to the deep mines," he ordered his men. His voice was serene, calm, collected. "All of them. Chain em up and don't give em a pickaxe. Let's see if they can hit quota with their fingernails and sharp tongues."

The clanbreakers stomped forward, and Sora tried with all her might to think. She had to do something.

The memory of her first grift alongside Whitney exploded into her mind. It had been Sora waiting for Whitney that time atop the Jarein Gorge. She remembered the feeling well, praying to whoever that he would leap out from his hiding place behind that rock in time to save her from the vile deeds Grint Strongiron and his gang had in mind for her. Funny how many things came back to dwarves, and specifically, the Strongirons.

That snapped Sora to attention. She locked eyes with Whitney, who peered out from behind the throne. She gave him the faintest of winks, then looked within. She remembered her anger as Nesilia made her watch while she slaughtered Grint's own brethren, as if Sora herself wanted it. And that anger fueled her reach into the ever-present well of Elsewhere, now more prevalent than ever. Her hand wagged just the slightest bit.

The cavern quaked.

The clanbreakers broke stride, rushing toward their King.

Heat sprouted up from the many basins around the room, including one hidden within the dragon's skeleton. Sora hadn't intended it, but the flames threatened to make a roast giant's meal of Whitney. The dragon bones chattered; the braziers erupted, shooting flames every which way. Tendrils leaped from their pots and drew a line between Whitney and Aquira and the others, clanbreakers included.

The clanbreakers grabbed the King as he stumbled.

"What's the meanin of this!" Lorgit cried.

Brouben took advantage of the opportunity, hurrying to the mouth-piece of a large horn situated at the eastern wall. It soon became apparent that it would act as a bell tower, warning the whole city of danger.

The sound it made was so resonant, the walls trembled.

"Father, come on!" Brouben shouted as the flames crept toward Lorgit.

The King stared at the flame, awestruck. "I thought I listened well… Why?" he said to himself. Sora had no idea what he was talking about.

"Father, we can settle our differences later!"

King Lorgit snapped to and nodded. The clanbreakers grasped him and rushed toward Brouben.

Sora didn't relent. Even as her head grew fuzzy from exertion and her skin became pale and cold. She couldn't keep this show up much longer, but Brouben rushed everybody onto the same cart that brought them up to the throne room just in time. Lucindur grabbed Sora and helped her on, then held her upright. They exchanged a knowing glance.

This time, as the cart took off, there were five extra passengers—four if you consider Whitney wasn't with them. Tum Tum and Brouben took the lead on the seesaw once more and began pumping. Everyone else did their best not to get stuck by the clanbreaker armor.

Sora breathed in and out slowly, letting Lucindur's gaze calm her. Then, under her breath and covered by the many sounds around her, Sora whispered, "Go steal a stone, Whitney. And come back to me."

XVIII

THE THIEF

I t was official: Whitney had never seen so much gold in one place in his entire life. Actually, he wasn't sure he'd ever seen so much gold if he'd added it all up. King Lorgit Cragrock was rich. No, Barty Darkings was rich—Lorgit Cragrock had the wealth of a god. No, ten gods. Shog in a barrel, all the gods.

Whitney hadn't had time to make sure Sora made it out of the King's throne room. He didn't have time to think about his own escape either. He had just dropped through the dragon skeleton's ribs as soon as the others had loaded onto their cart. Hearing the sound of a cart pumping through the tunnels gave him solace to know that he'd be alone to do his deed and that Sora and the others would be safe below, within the city. Right now, though, none of that could be his concern. He needed only one thing: the Brike Stone.

Looking down at his hands, Whitney could've sworn they were glowing gold in the reflection of the stuff. He took a few timid steps, careful not to disturb anything. Coins were strewn everywhere like a metal carpet. Just one bagful from this place would set Whitney up for life.

Then again, just one of the coins would cover the remainder of his life if he didn't get that Brike Stone and stop Nesilia once and for all.

Chests, overflowing with gold and jewels, surrounded him. What looked like the newest of them hadn't even been unloaded from a wooden wagon yet. It bore a familiar crest, a bundle of grapes, though Whitney couldn't remember where he'd seen it before.

"This is something else, huh, Aquira?" he said.

The wyvern chirped in response, then flew up ahead a ways.

He pressed forward after her. Piles and piles of treasure threatened to bury them both—truly enough to keep all Pantego living comfortably for many years. It was impossible to tell the breadth and depth of the chamber, the glow and gleam of everything was so disorienting. When he made it to the end of the room, he saw an opening on his right and walked toward it.

"Come on, girl."

Inside was something more akin to a palace sleeping quarters than something that should've been found inside a vault. Indeed, a bed rested at the crest of the half-circle wall on the far side. Whitney nearly laughed out loud when he saw it, expecting a small version of a human bed. Instead, it was huge—big enough for ten of the dwarven King to sleep in without bumping into one another, even if they all had a fitful night.

Torches burned in sconces on the stone walls, light dancing like Talwyn on a stage. Whitney assumed it to be the right side of the giant stone-carved dwarf head he was inside of. The furniture was all made of stone as well, dressers carved out of the walls themselves. Whitney could only wonder how the drawers opened and shut.

"Let's find out, shall we?" he said to himself and to Aquira, if she was even listening as she zipped around.

Approaching the nearest one, he cracked his knuckles and wiggled his fingers. He ran a hand along the edge, feeling for any traps or alarms. Finding nothing, he tried to open the first drawer. There was no handle, and it was so finely carved, not even his fingertips could fit into the almost invisible lines.

"Curious."

He placed his palm against the face of the top drawer. He slowly felt for any inconsistencies, anything that might hint at a secret button or release mechanism. Still, he found nothing.

"Any ideas, girl?" Whitney asked Aquira.

In response, she flew from her perch on his shoulder and landed on the top of the dresser. He watched her, expecting something, then felt stupid for doing so.

"Smart but not that smart, I guess."

She snorted once, a dismissive sound if he'd ever heard one, then reached down with her front limb, which was attached to her body by membranous wings. She gave the drawer face a gentle push. There was a click, then the drawer shot outward toward Whitney. It stopped, and he helped it the rest of the way.

"I stand corrected," Whitney said. "You are so much more than anyone credits you for. Except maybe Gentry."

Aquira made a sad sound.

"I know. We'll see him again soon. I promise. And maybe he'll still have some of those peanuts you like so much, huh? All right, now, let's see what's inside."

There were six such dressers, each one with four drawers filled with clothing and keepsakes that Whitney could've sold to any merchant in the realm and used the proceeds to live in luxury. He now regretted never pursuing dwarven kingdoms in his younger, thieving days. They did have stuff worth taking, just, only their Kings.

What he didn't find was anything that even slightly resembled the stone Tum Tum had described. He searched under the bed—or at least he'd tried to. The bed, too, was carved from stone and permanently affixed to both the back wall and the floor. There wasn't even a mattress on it, meaning the King slept on a slab of cold rock.

"Sounds about right for dwarves," he remarked.

The walls were mostly bare except for tapestries, all of which hid nothing behind them. The art within the Glass Castle had depicted great battles—kings against kings, gods and goddesses at war, but these were something else altogether. They bore the visage of frothy ale, each one in a different style container.

Whitney shook his head.

"C'mon, Aquira. Think," he said, just as much to himself. "Sora's distraction won't keep them away for long,"

There were no other doors in the chambers. Or was there?

He gave thoughtful consideration to the nearly flush drawers. From where he stood, in the center of the room, the dressers looked more like solid blocks of stone. What if there was a door somewhere with similar characteristics?

As if Aquira had read his thoughts, she started circling the room. Whitney watched her, floor to ceiling, inspecting every inch of the place. Finally, above the bed, she hovered in place.

"Find something?"

She puffed.

She was pretty high up. High enough that Whitney couldn't reach the spot, even standing on the bed.

"What is it?" he asked. She puffed again. "Oh, right. Words. How would a dwarf get up there if I couldn't?"

Aquira shoved her back legs against the wall. Nothing happened.

"No, not that," Whitney said.

She did it again.

"It's not working, Aquira."

She screeched, swooped down, and hit Whitney on the shoulder, then flew back up and did it again.

"Hey! Watch it… oh!"

In a moment of realization, Whitney reached out and began pushing on the wall, moving his hand with each failed push. His fingertips brushed something—a slight depression in the otherwise perfectly smooth walls. He pressed, and the sound of stone shifting was his reward.

Not only did a door appear next to Aquira, but smaller slots opened in line with one another like a ladder.

"Dwarven engineering," Whitney said.

He climbed and lifted himself onto the ledge. The passage was short, built for a dwarf. The doorway was dark, and the room inside even darker. It reminded him of Bliss's lair, just more organized. And no spiders or egg sacs. He hoped.

He swallowed the lump in his throat and pulled his daggers from his belt, one in each hand. Many people had weapons that were special and unique to them, but not Whitney. He couldn't even remember where he'd gotten these particular blades, and if he lost them, he'd just pick up a couple more.

Putting one foot inside, Whitney peered around the doorframe, and his heart leaped into his throat. He swung his daggers furiously, sparks jettisoning in every direction as the metal struck dwarven armor. He stumbled backward, nearly slipping off the ledge onto the hard bed below. Then, a feeble laugh escaped his lips when he realized it was just that—armor. There was no dwarf inside, just a mannequin holding a flashy set of armor which now looked like it had been through its first skirmish.

"Hold it together, Whitney," he said under his breath. "You're acting like this is your first job."

His first job hadn't been anything special. Sure, he'd stolen plenty of things in Troborough growing up, but early on, he'd been commissioned by a fence in Westvale to rob a noble. It turned out the nobleman was kind of a big deal. Whitney had been successful, though, and that's all that mattered.

This, however, might have been the most important job he'd ever taken. This wasn't about worthless trinkets or priceless gems. This was his chance to prove he wasn't just the World's Greatest Thief, but the World's Savior.

"That has a nice ring to it, huh, Aquira? 'Whitney Fierstown, Savior of the World."

Aquira made a noise that sounded far too much like a raspberry to be anything but, and Whitney followed her within.

Feeling the wall, he noted they were in a hallway. The deeper he went, the less light poured in from the room below. His hand touched something—an unlit torch. Snatching it from its holder, he thought to return to the king's bedroom so he could light it on one of the others. That thought was stolen from him as Aquira blew a swift breath of flame, and the tip caught with a dull roar.

"You are quite the useful little devil," he said. "Glad I thought of you sneaking to me."

With a torch lit and held out in front of him, Whitney could see the tunnel for what it was. Utterly unremarkable.

"All right, where are you, oh, Stone of Brikey goodness?" His last word was cut off as a soft click met his ears.

"Shog," he whispered.

Sure, this wasn't Whitney's first job, but he certainly was acting like it was. It truly had been a while in his time. He slowed himself down.

He'd encountered traps like this before. The plate in the floor would trigger some kind of defense, be it arrows, boiling pitch raining down from above, spikes jutting out from the walls or some other horrible method of death. The trap wouldn't spring until Whitney removed his foot. The trick would be finding the source of the defense before moving.

"Aquira, I need your eyes."

One thing no one would have accounted for was a wyvern accompanying a would-be thief.

"Just like in the bedroom. Check the walls. If you see anything strange, anything at all, let me know."

A short while later, Whitney heard her screech from the darkness ahead.

"Find something?" he called.

She responded in what he assumed to be the affirmative.

"I can't see you." He leaned forward with the torch as far as he felt comfortable doing, wincing the whole time.

He heard wings flapping, then Aquira appeared in the cone of light emanating from the torch. She stole the torch from his hands with her teeth and returned to her former position.

Now, Whitney could see what she saw. He'd been right. Arrows or something like them would shoot out of four holes situated in a diamond shape in the wall on the opposite end of the hall. They were positioned knee-to-waist-high—which Whitney realized was chest and head height for a dwarf.

"Keep the light there," he instructed Aquira.

Gauging the exact placement of the holes was difficult. It was also taking a big chance that Whitney could move fast enough even if he knew precisely where the arrows would strike.

"Okay, Aquira. See that hole in front of you?"

She moved a bit to the left.

"Yes. That one. I want you to hold the torch in front of that hole. Make sure your legs are out of the way. Do you understand?"

She puffed.

"I'm going to dive to my right. If I press up against the wall, and you block that one, I should be safe."

Even hearing his own words struck a bit of terror into his heart.

What if there was another grouping of arrows that would shoot from the other direction? What if something got Aquira?

No, she looked all over. If that's all she found, that was all there is.

"You ready?" he asked.

She puffed.

After a deep breath, Whitney looked down at the plate below his boot. He whispered something. He wasn't even sure what. It wasn't a prayer, but it was as close as he'd get.

"On the count of three, okay?"

Here goes nothing.

"One. Two. Three!"

He threw himself to the right with every bit of strength he could muster. With the torch so far away, he couldn't tell how close he was to the wall, but it didn't matter, he needed to get low and far, fast. As soon as his foot left the trigger switch, he heard a loud *ka-thunk* followed by Aquira's alarmed cry, then felt air rush past him as the three remaining arrows blew by, one just barely scratching his left leg.

"Aquira!" he shouted, rushing to his feet.

Ahead, the torch lay on the ground, fire still burning, but there was no sign of the wyvern.

"Aquira!" he shouted again, rising. He started toward the torch, then thought better of it. If there was another trap and Aquira was injured, he'd likely find himself in Elsewhere permanently. He decided to crawl, feeling every inch of the floor as he went, searching for even the slightest imperfections in the dwarven-carved stone.

He reached the torch without a problem. A giant spear protruded from its base, just as it was meant to do. Crawling further, he found Aquira lying just outside its circle of light. She was breathing and close to the wall, eyes open but twitching.

Whitney cradled her. "You okay, girl? Did you hit your head?"

She blinked her two sets of eyelids, obviously recovering from the shock. He also noticed that it wasn't an arrow that'd been shot, but a miniature spear. The force of it must have been enough to blow her back into the wall. It was far bigger than the arrows he'd expected, and Whitney was thankful she'd held on long enough to keep the missile from eviscerating him.

"That-a-girl," Whitney whispered. "That's it. You're okay."

He held her close and rose. She breathed softly against his chest, her frills opening and closing along with her shallow breaths. Anything worth booby-trapping was worth stealing—in most cases, at least. In this one, Whitney hoped it would be the Brike Stone.

He gathered himself and started off again. At the end of the hall, where the arrow holes were, the tunnel turned to the right. Light poured out through an opening about forty meters or so down. He had to guess they'd left the dwarf head throne room and were now in the heart of the mountain.

Still taking it slow, Whitney pushed forward. Aquira seemed to have almost fully recovered physically, but still seemed quite shaken.

When he reached the next room, it became immediately apparent that the light was less from the torches and more from their reflections on countless amounts of gold. The first room, which made Whitney think King Lorgit to be the richest man alive, was absolutely destitute compared to this.

Aquira chirped.

"Glad you're feeling better."

High stacks of golden bullions were stacked a dozen meters tall all around him. For the briefest of moments, Whitney worried that if even one of the towers toppled, it would crush him beneath the weight. Then, he thought that dying under a pile of gold might be preferable to whatever Nesilia had planned.

Whitney whistled. "Would you look at all this? We could liberate every man, woman, and child in the Panping Ghetto. Then again, there's probably no Panping Ghetto left in Winde Port."

A low growl emanated through the room, making the words catch in Whitney's throat. Then, he heard the sound of shifting coins, and two glowing orbs appeared in the darkness between two columns of ingots. It moved toward him, slowly. The growl came again, and Whitney took a step back.

"Who—wh—what's there?" he stammered.

The response was a sharp bark. He'd heard a sound like that before with Torsten the first day they'd met.

Dire wolf.

Amazingly, that day, setting off to battle with the world's most evil warlock and a vile Spider Queen were fun times compared to the woes of this day.

"Easy, boy… Easy," he said. "We're friends…"

The further into the room Whitney went, the less he could see, like something was sucking all the light from the room. However, the orbs that were its eyes grew larger. Then, suddenly, it broke through the darkness and was fully visible in all it's vicious, slobbering glory.

Aquira rose, but she faltered in the air and slammed down on the floor, flopping around like a fish out of water. Poor girl was still dazed from the spear trap. Whitney bent and scooped her up.

The wolf broke into a run. The coins beneath its feet were tossed around like dust on the Glass Road.

"Shog…"

He squeezed the dagger in his free hand, then realized it'd be useless. But those spears that had just about skewered him wouldn't. He turned to run, and just then heard a metallic *snap* and *clank*. The dire wolf was yanked backward to the ground.

"You're chained up," Whitney said, his voice quavering. "Yes, you are. Oh, what a good little boy." Though his voice was gaining a bit of strength, his knees were still wobbling. He laughed. "You're chained up!"

The wolf stood and snapped at him again, but Whitney waved the torch, and it retreated slightly.

Relieved, Whitney gave his weak knees a break and collapsed to the floor. "Gods and yigging monsters, Aquira, I thought we were dead." He laughed again, then said, "Okay. I need your help again." He stroked her back. "You feeling up to it?"

She nodded and puffed, then turned and growled back at the dire wolf who, although chained, looked like he was ready to spill their guts to the floor.

"We need a plan."

Whitney looked around at a room similar to the first. In addition to the towering stacks of gold bars, piles of trinkets cascaded over the sides of chests. But one thing was different. The only reason to chain up a wolf was to protect something, and Whitney now saw what it guarded.

"The Brike Stone," he whispered.

He followed the chain to a ring that was connected to a podium of sorts. Darkness engulfed the area like a plague. Even so, the stone was far larger than Whitney had expected—the size of his fist or greater. Unlike the stories Tum Tum had apparently heard, the blood-red stone emanated no light of its own. It was just a dull, dead thing that seemed to absorb all the light around it—the petrified heart of a dragon if the stories were to be believed.

"It's frightened of the fire," Whitney told Aquira. "You know what to do, right?"

Without another word, Aquira hopped down to the ground. She was half the massive dire wolf's height, but with her wings expanded, she cut quite the intimidating figure. Especially as she blew flames in a wide plume. The dire wolf leaped back but returned immediately to snarl after the fire dissipated.

Walking a circle around the wolf, keeping it at bay with his lit torch, Whitney split the beast's focus. It didn't know whether to watch him or Aquira. Confused is exactly how Whitney wanted the creature. He could have Aquira enkindle it, but if that melted the chains before the beast died, they were done for.

Every time the wolf got close, Whitney waved the torch, and it hopped back. Then Aquira blew a small wisp of flame in its direction, and it leaped the other way. It bent low, hackles up, scared.

Whitney was nearing the podium, which held the Brike Stone. Suddenly, his flame was snuffed out like magic. He swore, threw the dead torch to the ground, but dared not take his eyes off the dire wolf. It showed yellow teeth, thick saliva on black gums, and darted for Whitney. Aquira roared and shot a focused line of fire that nipped the wolf's tail. It spun around, giving Whitney the opening he needed.

Turning his back, he was at the mercy of the dire wolf. Mercy he didn't believe the creature would have should it spin to find him stealing the very thing it was meant to protect.

The chain pulled taut, slightly shaking the podium. Behind him, he could hear the sound of jaws snapping and wings flapping. He reached out slowly, letting his fingertips graze the cold hard Brike Stone. Upon its icy touch, he felt like his very soul was coming undone. He took a deep breath, closed his eyes, and clenched it tight. Then, he drew it to himself. He couldn't breathe. Immediately, he regretted it. The ground shook, the walls clattered, and before he knew it, the dire wolf was back on him.

Darkness now surrounded Whitney despite Aquira's attempts to give light. For so long, he'd said he had a plan for the day he would perish, and in a vault full of someone else's gold, being torn to shreds by an overgrown dog wasn't it. But if the last six years taught Whitney anything, it was that you don't always get what you want.

You can damn well try to, though, he thought.

He lowered the Brike Stone into his cloak pocket and spun. The feeling vanished, and Aquira's flames returned just in time to turn the wolf's attention once more.

Whitney ran, barely dodging the beast's razor-sharp fangs. Aquira flew above, raining flames down between them to keep it at bay without risking melting the chains.

Calculating the distance, Whitney guessed he was almost to the place where the chain would snap tight, and he'd be safe from the wolf. When he got there, however, he heard a slight strain and then the distinct sound of dozens of metal shards flying in every direction. The chain had snapped... into pieces.

Whitney turned, knowing he had no choice and no defense. He put his hands up in a weak attempt to slow the attack, but it wasn't necessary. As the dire wolf dove for Whitney, one of the golden towers toppled over and crushed the thing, eliciting a sharp yelp.

He looked up to see Aquira hovering above it all, a mischievous grin on her snout, if that were possible.

"Wha-ha," Whitney laughed. "Ha. Wha… Ha!" He had no words, just a series of vaguely happy sounds. There was no time to celebrate. The ground still shook, and with or without Aquira's help, the other towers were just as likely to come crashing down. He ran, avoiding the newly-created mound of gold, and Aquira swooped in beside him.

One after another, the towers clattered to the ground. The sound was loud and incessant, and Whitney could hardly think. When he saw the opening to the tunnel, he went to dive but pulled back just in time when he saw a glint of gold in his peripheral. A second later, the shaking stopped, and a pile of gold ingots blocked the entrance into the treasure room.

Just like that, he was stuck.

He tried to sift through the gold bars, but they were heavy, and there were a lot of them—at this rate, it would take him well into the night. By then, King Lorgit might have figured out Sora's involvement in the fire. He might already have.

"Shog in a barrel," Whitney swore. He turned back to the room, now more like a mountain of gold.

Aquira made a clicking noise and moved in front of him. He watched her throat inflate, and a plume of flame shone in her mouth. He pulled her back by the tail. She snapped and nearly took his hand with it.

"Hey! You melt that in a room this small, you'll turn us into soup with it," he explained.

She backed away, hanging her head in shame.

"How could they even get all this in here through that hole in his bedroom?" Whitney said aloud. "There has to be another way out."

Without hesitation, Aquira was reinvigorated. She shook out her frills and took flight. Whitney did his best to follow, but without wings himself, he was forced to crawl up and over numerous peaks and dip into just as many valleys. It took more time than he'd desired, but he finally found Aquira zipping around some distance away. The room was far more extensive than he'd previously thought.

Aquira screeched. Looking up, he shouted, "Did you find an exit?"

Whitney followed her calls. If she could have responded, the answer would have been, "Sort of."

Whitney was now staring at a ten-meter by ten-meter hole in the ground. It appeared to be like a dumb waiter with a set of ropes leading up and around two pulleys at the top of a stone shaft.

"I guess that answers the question of how they got this all in here." Whitney closed his eyes, and sighed. "Only one way out, and that's down."

He leaned over. It wouldn't be the first time he'd done something like this—escaping the tower of the Whispering Wizards came to mind —but without gloves, that rope was going to smart.

He turned back to the room and approached the closest pile of coins. "Just a few," he said, swiping up a handful of them and shoving them into his pocket. "For my troubles."

XIX

THE TRAITOR

"Torsten!" Rand shouted from down the tunnel.

His elbow, propped against the wall, helped him wield Torsten's claymore. King Liam's weapon had been re-designed for a brute Torsten's size, but it was the first thing Rand grabbed after coming to and choking the life out of the guard they left behind. The man hadn't stood a chance.

When Nesilia gave him the mission to remove Torsten from the equation before their magic-aided, naval ambush, he thought it'd be difficult. But then he saw him—the Shieldsman who'd pretended to be his friend, all while lying about Sigrid. The Shieldsman who'd abandoned him to face Oleander's wrath alone.

The truth was, the grimaur talon he'd been provided slid into Torsten's side all too easy. Rand only wished he was able to stab deeper and truly take Torsten down. Hampering him would have to suffice.

Torsten and his entourage stopped to look back. Rage twisted the features of Lucas and the other guard, but not Torsten. Even while fighting the toxin, he looked ashamed. Sad. Like how Rand's father would regard him every time he lost to Sigrid in some manner of competition. Or every time he came back, bruised from a fight with the kids at school.

And at that moment, Rand's own ire waned. His heart plummeted. He knew what was coming… he could feel the subtle vibrations of the floor beneath him that only he knew had nothing to do with the crowd above.

"You need to run," he said. "You all need to run."

"Enough of this," Lucas replied.

He turned to the guard and whispered something. As he did, Torsten's lips quivered like he was trying to speak, and his muscles wouldn't comply. Rand had been drunk enough plenty of times to understand what that felt like.

Rand stared at him. Torsten had betrayed his trust, but had also trained him, picked him out of all the King's Shield recruits who'd tried to rise from Dockside. Helped him see the better parts of the world.

Lucas pushed Torsten toward the exit; toward what was coming. Then, fearless, he turned to face Rand. He drew his gleaming longsword and set his jaw.

"It's time for you to die, traitor," he growled.

Brandishing his weapon, he charged. Rand shifted back into a fighting stance and lifted Torsten's claymore as high as he could. His legs remained a bit woozy from the beating Lucas had put on him back in the cell.

"I'm trying to help," Rand implored.

"You've done enough of that!"

The young Shieldsman came at Rand with reckless abandon. It was obvious. This wasn't about defending Torsten or fighting a traitor, but because Rand had offered his life as a blood pact to attract Sigrid.

Young and foolish, that's what Lucas was. Perhaps Rand wasn't actually much older beneath his scrubby beard, but he'd faced enough adversity for a thousand lifetimes. Lucas' charge left openings for numerous countermoves. Rand easily had the upper hand against such a raw opponent, if only he wielded a weapon suited for his size. With *Salvation*, he could only manage to parry the first attack. Using a defensive, high-elbow stance, he defended against a flurry of strikes that pressed him down the tunnel and back toward his cell.

"You were a Shieldsman!" Lucas screamed, swinging hard.

Rand blocked, but the force sent him reeling against a wall. Out of training for so long, he wasn't as strong as he'd been. As his muscles strained against the attacks, his anger returned.

The King's Shield truly was nothing like the legends, as it had been under Sir Uriah and the Wearers of White who'd preceded him. The Order had failed Rand just as much as he'd failed it. Failed their Kingdom.

Sigrid had clearly seen that, to give Nesilia control. The Glass Kingdom was unfixable and needed to be purged. Ruined by a sick King, a mad Queen, and a cursed, petulant child who couldn't even grow a beard, let alone think for himself.

"And you're a fool!" Rand yelled.

He countered fast and thrust the blade, but just then, the ground trembled. It sent them both staggering, barely able to stay on their feet. When the violent tremor ceased, a low, gushing sound replaced it, growing louder with each second.

"The sea," he said to himself.

Nesilia really did it.

Stories of unconquerable Latiapur filled tomes, and in mere minutes, Nesilia and her new allies were able to make history bow its knee.

"I'll kill you!" Lucas growled, recovering quickly. He slashed, leaving a shallow incision on Rand's left arm as he spun away.

"I told you all to run," Rand said, panting.

He dropped back into a defensive stance, but the ground quaked again and shook enough dust off the walls and ceiling to have them both in coughing fits. The sound of flooding seawater grew louder and more distinctive, like standing behind a waterfall.

"Because that's all you know how to do," Lucas said.

"No. I just refuse to die without talking to her again."

"She's dead!" Lucas shouted.

Chunks of stone fell off all around them. Booming crashes from above reverberated, and Rand had no idea what they could be the result of. And then, they both stopped as they noticed the far-off arena entrance and the water raging through it, spitting foam as it sloshed against the walls.

Amidst the distraction, Rand reared back and swung as hard as he could at the wall. The blow resulted in cracking off stone, another cloud of dust, and shooting sparks at Lucas' face. Then, he did what everyone thought he did best.

He ran.

Lucas gave chase, shouting drowned out by the deluge pursuing them. Having been brought down from the city gates with a bag over his head, Rand had no idea how to get out of the undercroft except through the flooding arena. However, the Glass Castle had many warrens and tunnels connecting one place to another and even auxiliary entries for servants and supplies. He hoped he'd find the same here.

"You won't get away again!" Lucas barked, voice now nearer.

Rand ducked, but not before feeling Lucas' blade shave hairs from his scalp. Too close.

"You're crazy!" Rand shouted. "You're going to get us both killed."

He skidded to his knees, then flipped over to raise the claymore in time to block Lucas' next attack. Their blades locked, and Rand's jaw clenched as he resisted Lucas's upper position.

"So be it," Lucas said, seething. "You won't deceive Sir Unger any longer!"

"He deceives himself, trusting a broken Kingdom."

"Only in trusting you." Lucas slid his blade free of their entanglement, allowing Rand's to slice his forearm as it dipped so he could gain an opening. His sword crashed down toward Rand, but not before the flooding water rushed around the corner and struck him in the back.

Lucas toppled forward, giving Rand the chance to grab his weapon hand and push it aside. The heavy current then heaved them across the floor, and they both lost grip of their weapons.

Unarmed, they tangled, punching, kicking, and biting. Rand wasn't sure what he hit, stone, or his opponent, only that the current was unreasonably strong and that the water rose fast. Both were shoved against a wall at the end of a tunnel. By then, they were no longer fighting, but flailing for the surface, desperate for air.

Rand and Lucas broke through at about the same time, and they both caught sight of one another, then, the giant claymore stuck in the hinges of an open cell door.

Lucas kicked, then dove for it. Rand did the same. They groped through the water, the hilt shifting in the wild current, and every time one of them managed to get a finger on it before the other pulled them away. Soon, they were both pulled beneath the surface again.

Rand popped up and quickly landed a fist on Lucas' chin with a wild punch. Lucas reeled, and Rand grasped him by the shirt, wrenching him back into a choke lock. His arm squeezed Lucas' throat as he took frantic elbow after elbow to his ribs. Rand clenched his teeth and held on until the blows softened, both by Lucas losing his strength, and the pure volume of water closing in around them.

Lucas's neck started to lilt. His arms went limp, stretched back by the current. Rand kicked his feet, fast as he could to keep his mouth above the rising water, but he continued to squeeze, just in case.

Then came a deafening *bang*.

He found himself blinded by an explosion of stone and debris. Water sloshed and splashed, and a shockwave hurled him. He tumbled in the water, stopping at a crease between the wall and floor, where a hefty chunk of stone fell on his foot and pinned him.

The arena's outer wall had come crashing down, breaking open the street above the tunnel. A shaft of light pierced the water, revealing the sky and providing more light so Rand could see his own leg.

He grabbed and yanked. A layer of leg skin scraped off against the abrasive surface, but he managed to free himself. The saltwater burned the fresh wound while he kicked for the surface.

Clambering up the rubble while more floodwater rose with him, he reached the square surrounding the arena's north side. Lucas' hand gripped his leg, fingers digging into the wound.

"You won't—"

Rand silenced him with a kick that sent him back into the rising water, then pulled himself over the broken ledge. Feet stampeded all around him. Hundreds of Shesaitju civilians fled the arena, while others dressed like warriors approached from around the city.

The city's infamous Serpent Guards surged out of the main entrance in a tight formation. Shieldsmen here and there leaked out of other archways.

Rand shook out his foggy head. Any of them might recognize him, or worse, Torsten might spot him. He hadn't gotten enough of the toxin into him to completely knock him out, and Torsten was bigger than the average man.

So, Rand pushed to his feet and fell in with the crazed throng. The sounds emanating from the arena sent chills up his spine. Crushing stone. Screams. Roars that could belong to nothing but the same tentacled beast he'd watched his sister's body upon in Yaolin City.

He wasn't sure where to go next. Then, he spied what looked like King Pi fleeing with the rabble, guided by one Serpent Guard. The boy-King of Glass. The boy who'd died in the arms of a wicked mother who'd punished everyone around her, and then rose from the dead to cause a devastating war.

His chestplate was scratched and dented, white clothes torn, and his hair disheveled, but there was no question it was him.

"Remove Torsten from the equation," Nesilia had told Rand before she dispatched him, wearing the body of his sister. "Without him commanding the Shield, the boy-King, and Latiapur, are sure to fall. Then, the seat of Glass will come undone."

"Why not kill him?" Rand had asked.

"Because I want Torsten—a man of the most unshakable faith—to watch his failure with his blessed vision. I want he who thought himself able to stop my return atop Mount Lister to know it was my doing."

Rand might've failed to render Torsten completely useless, but if he could take Pi out himself, Nesilia would get what she wanted anyway.

Then, maybe, she'd release his sister.

Then, maybe, Sigrid could have her life back.

XX

THE KNIGHT

Dellbar the Holy rubbed Torsten's back and whispered in his ear, beseeching Iam, begging their God to retake control. On his hands and knees, after Mahraveh saved him from the floodwater, Torsten could do naught but listen to the chaos erupt.

But he was lucky for his leather zhulong armor—at least the beasts from the Black Sands were good for something. The grimaur toxin had already dwindled in his bloodstream, and sensation slowly returned to his left side.

In his peripherals, he spotted Lord Jolly being torn away from King Pi. Torsten didn't hesitate. He pushed Dellbar aside, robbed a Serpent Guard of his glaive, and brought it crashing down on the tentacle of a beast he'd thought to be a thing of Panpingese lore.

Blood, cold as death and black as night, splashed his face as the creature reeled. Torsten stumbled forward, the weight of the weapon and the effects of the toxin keeping him off balance. Lord Jolly collapsed beside Dellbar, and Pi ran to Torsten.

"Take him!" Torsten yelled. "Take the King!"

He shoved King Pi at Mahraveh and the other Shesaitju warriors, then slashed again at the monstrous creature. The resistance as his blade cut through its flesh was unlike anything he'd ever experience. Like chopping stone. The force of it ripping through the other side sent him down to his knees. Another tentacle kissed his chest and sent him flying up into the stands.

"Torsten!" Lord Jolly shouted, running to his aid.

He got Torsten to his feet, both of which he could now almost feel again. The wianu's strike seemed to knock some sense into his compromised body. And with that, came the impossibly bright lines of pain tormenting his torso. Rand's stab wound was the least of it. To see to the injury, they'd removed his chestplate, and without it, the beast's hit had easily fractured a rib or two.

"Torsten, what in Elsewhere happened to you?" Jolly questioned.

"Nesilia baited us all," he said, throat still sore as the muscles re-acclimated. "Leaders of armies and countries defying her, all of them together."

"I knew the ceremony should've been in Yarrington!"

"Then maybe—" Torsten lost his train of thought when he heard Dellbar, still muttering, "Iam help us. Iam take me," under his breath, while he crouched behind stands, tracing his eyes again and again.

"Lord Jolly, listen to me," Torsten said. "You need to get Dellbar out of here alive and reach Hornsheim. He must rally the priests."

"You're worried about him?" Lord Jolly asked. He pointed to the flooding arena. "Even with one arm, I know how to fight on the water. We need me here."

Torsten shook his head. "Iam chose him. If he dies, even in the face of destruction, the Order will convene to replace him. We will need all of Iam's shepherds and their flocks. Take the west exit. Lucas and my horses are the fastest in the realm. Fetch them from the city's stables."

Pi and Mahraveh were headed to the northern ramp, and it was better not to bring everyone together for Nesilia to pick off again. Pi had an entire contingent of Serpent Guards and the hero of Nahanab to guard him.

"And you?" Lucas asked.

"Me? I am the shield that guards the light of this world," Torsten said, reciting the final vows of a Shieldsman.

The monstrous wianu was half-upon the arena's lower concourse, fighting off Serpent Guards and Shieldsmen alike on a path toward Pi and Mahraveh. Its giant tentacles swung wildly, breaking apart stone and skewering grown men like their armor was made of parchment. Through Torsten's blessed vision, the entire thing appeared as one ugly mass of shadow. Absent light, like Nesilia had been.

Torsten launched himself high, kicking from one stand to the next, landing on top of the creature's head and driving the glaive down into its left eye. It got stuck only about a forearm's length in, but he twisted it from side to side, earning distressed screeches.

"Sir Unger, are you insane!" Sir Mulliner shouted. He and a cohort of Shieldsmen arrived from the western side of the arena, busy helping to organize the retreat of those civilians seated there.

"Keep its attention!" Torsten ordered.

A flurry of tentacles all zoomed toward him. He loosened his grip and slid off the side of the monster's head, dangling adjacent to its maw. The stink gave what he'd experienced in that Panpingese inn a run for its autlas. It snapped at his feet while fighting off Sir Mulliner's men.

Torsten pushed off a set of teeth, narrowly avoiding losing a foot. Then, he broke the glaive in two, swung back in, and shoved its broken shaft into the top of the sea creature's mouth, keeping it from biting down. Unlike the thing's outer skin, this flesh was soft, and the jagged edge sank right in.

Recovering quickly, Torsten pushed back, dropping from its maw and landing back in the stands. Sir Mulliner was there to help him while the monster flailed around like a mad boar until the shaft shattered in its mouth. It swallowed the sharp, wooden shards without any hesitation.

"Protect the Master of Warfare!" Shieldsmen echoed, forming a wall in front of Torsten with heater shields. Torsten glanced left toward the central exit Mahraveh and Pi had been heading for. A flood of people shoved down the generous passage, which now seemed all too narrow. Another of the wianu approached them from the opposite side of the arena. A third devoured those who'd fallen into the waters, plucking others off the walkways with its long tentacles.

They made it, Torsten thought.

"Retreat!" he called out. "In Iam's name, Mulliner, get everyone out of here!"

The Shieldsmen broke rank immediately. They were young, probably more terrified than he could even imagine. He was too. Possessed people were one thing, but these legendary monsters were pure evil.

The one he'd injured propped up above Torsten, using its tentacles like legs, covering him in cold shadow. Its head turned, so its one remaining eye stared directly at him. Torsten's heart was a heavy stone and felt like it was trapped in a vice as he froze there. All the other sounds of death and chaos were muted.

Even Torsten's fear melted away. He felt only crushing and immeasurable sadness. Pain, as if he'd lost everyone and everything he loved all at once. He could do nothing but focus on the eye and discover that it wasn't soulless like how it appeared; it was filled with pain and rage and suffering. It was precisely the absence of light, of Iam's grace.

The wianu descended upon him, ready to devour, shadowy tendrils extending around him.

Then, it screeched.

Barbed Shesaitju arrows peppered every inch of its backside, some sneaking through its tentacles to clatter on the stone around Torsten. It must've absorbed more than a hundred—enough to bring down even the mightiest beast.

Not this one.

The distraction, however, allowed Torsten out of its soul-crunching gaze. It also guarded him against a barrage of arrows that would've shredded him with his lack of armor.

He ran up the stands. There was no time to whisper a prayer as he grabbed a shield off a fallen Shieldsman, chest caved in by a blow from the monster. Glancing back, he saw Shesaitju ships sailing into the flooded arena. Somehow the approaching storm broke right at the breach in the dam, guiding them in on a robust and focused current.

He'd never been one for naval warfare or ships in general—that was Lord Jolly's purview—but none of it made sense. The Boiling Waters were said to be treacherous and violent, with safe access routes pathed out to existing docks like the one King Pi had arrived on. A fleet couldn't merely approach, miss a labyrinth of razor-sharp rock, and avoid being spotted.

And then Torsten saw her... On the bow of the lead ship, floating over the deck, streaks of energy crackling over her fingers, a mystic. Torsten had fought in the Third Panping war, and it was like he was thrown back in time, the way her red robe seemed to ripple in a wind that didn't quite match what he felt.

At first, he thought it was Sora, back again at the least expected time. But this woman was old, ancient even. He could tell, even from so far away. He didn't have time to study her much longer. The wianu went into a rampage, its tentacles slapping and breaking apart Tal'du Dromesh with new fury. Another across the arena was struck by arrows and lost its grip on the stands. It tumbled down in a mess of dust before splashing in a heap.

The Shesaitju archers arriving with the fleet nocked more arrows and let loose another volley.

"Retreat!" Torsten screamed. "Back to the Keep."

He sprinted up the stands, long legs taking him from one row to the next. Shieldsmen and stragglers throughout the place ran for whatever cover they could find as well. His acute hearing picked up the thrum of another volley fired. He dropped into the space between two levels— amidst bodies already skewered by the first salvo—and raised his shield. The three-pronged projectiles battered against it. It took all his strength to hold it up, considering the injuries he'd already sustained. One arrow stabbed down, missing the flesh of his foot by the length of an eyelash. Others tore through a group of Shesaitju women and children nearby.

There was no strategy for the attack beyond instilling fear. Wasting arrows on innocents and remnants? The last fell and Torsten sprang up, his arms sore at every joint. Unable to carry the shield, he was forced to drag it up to the top row of the arena. He peered back as often as he could. Straggling Glassmen and Shesaitju were picked off one by one. The ships all approached the lower concourse, the wianu leaving them be and instead, continuing to rage and break apart centuries of history. Zhulong statues broke free and tumbled down the entire height of Tal'du Dromesh, crushing and maiming as they went.

And so Torsten did the same. He reared back with the shield using two hands and bashed the base of one of the still-standing statues. Once, twice, using his mass and might until the stone broke. He wedged the shield behind it and gave it a shove to send the massive statue bouncing down the stands.

It crashed through the bow of one of the invading ships. Wood splintered everywhere and at least a dozen gray men were thrown into the water. The one ravenous wianu still swimming lost control, devouring many in a single gulp.

The mass of archers had stowed their bows to prepare for the invasion, but a handful dotting the masts of the nearest ships fired arrows up at him. Torsten deflected them with the shield, nearly slipping from the upper ledge. He glanced down. The long drop was sure to break his legs, if not bring death. But nearby, damage from a rampaging monster caused a portion of the arena wall to fall, bashing through the square and revealing a part of its extensive undercroft. Water surged the rift like it had an appointment.

It was a longshot, but Torsten had no choice. He skirted the top row toward the arch nearest the break, arrows whizzing by his head, or glancing off his shield. He struck the statue at that arch until another arrow grazed the back of his calf. The thing started to wobble loose, but he couldn't wait for results.

Torsten dropped the shield, removed his blindfold, squeezed it tight in one fist, then threw himself off the top of the arena toward the water-filled opening.

Blindly, he plummeted, air rising all around him. He had no time to be nervous. But Iam made his leap true, and Torsten's fall broke in salty water. Water rushed up his nose and filled his mouth, completely disorienting him. He flailed to find anything to push off of, and his finger sliced against something sharp. He pulled it back, but as he patted around more, he realized that it was a sword stuck somehow between two metal rods, or a cell.

Torsten knew that smooth groove down the center of a claymore blade anywhere—impossibly smooth, perfectly balanced. Even as his lungs struggled, he pulled himself to the side of it until his back hit a surface. He wrapped his blindfold around it, then pushed off with his feet.

Stone shifted, nearly crushing his arm as it ripped a portion of his sleeve. The flat of the blade slipped forward and slapped the top of his boot. A pair of hands grasped the back of his shirt and heaved. The next thing he knew, he lay upon a ramp of rubble extending from the hole in the Tal'du Dromesh square. He huffed for air, hacking up water.

"Sir Unger, you're alive!" Lucas said, coughing as well.

Torsten slid the sword up the stone, then tied his blindfold back on. The thing was soaked, blurring his vision—light and shadow bleeding over one another.

But he was alive, thank Iam.

"I suppose I am," he said. "How did you—"

"Rand got away, Sir," he groaned as dragged himself farther up the rubble. "I failed again."

"We have other things to worry about."

Torsten flipped over and searched for *Salvation*. After locating it, he used it to push up to his knees, aiding Lucas as well. The chances of him finding that sword in all this mess, it gave him a spurt of hope that Iam was still with them.

Markless Shesaitju men and women stampeded all around them, running for their lives, screaming. Zhulong tusk horns bellowed throughout Latiapur, summoning warriors. One voice, however, rang louder than all things—that of Caleef Mahraveh across the square.

"Here, we fight for our city!" she yelled, standing atop a zhulong so all could see her in her shredded but still sparkling golden clothes. "Stand with me, warriors of the Black Sands."

"Stand with your Caleef!" her guardian Bit'rudam echoed. Then, he barked orders in Saitjuese.

Torsten pieced together the blurred figures as the hot sun quickly dried out his enchanted blindfold. Serpent Guards fell into formation around Mahraveh, armed to the teeth, facing the entries of the Tal'du Dromesh. Shesaitju warriors fell in around them throughout the square, those without weapons handy wielding whatever they could get their hands on.

Torsten approached the familiar faces, while Lucas struggled to keep up. He looked as bad as Torsten imagined he did himself.

Sir Mulliner stood with a pack of Shieldsmen, brow furrowing with disbelief when he saw Torsten nearing.

"I thought you were done for," the Shieldsman said, breathless. His tanned skin was coated in blood, dust, and grime, as were all the other Glassmen.

"You're not so lucky yet," Torsten replied. "The King is supposed to be holed up in the Keep. We have to get to him."

"We have to survive first."

"Sir Danvels, we'll handle here," Torsten said. "You reach the King."

Metal clattered and men chanted. Torsten looked back and saw the rival Shesaitju army amassing around the entry arches of the arena. Many painted their gray faces with stark white lines like skulls. The patterns were indicative of the far eastern and island afhemates he'd fought against in the wars.

"Go, Lucas!" Torsten demanded. "And don't return without him." He clutched the weary Shieldsman by the shoulder and shoved him toward the markets before he could protest. Then, Torsten turned to the enemy, tightening his grip on *Salvation*.

"Shieldsmen!" he bellowed. "The Black Sands stand with us in the light. We are the shield that guards Iam's Kingdom. Stand with them until the bitter end!"

The Shieldsmen pounded on their chest plates. He could hear their nervous breaths, their unsteady footsteps—they, and all the Shesaitju allies standing with them. Only the faceless Serpent Guards stood in eerie silence.

A large portion of the arena's upper level crumbled as one of the wianu clambered over it. Its midnight black eyes peeked over the crest, and then, it unleashed a bloodcurdling roar. At that, the enemy army charged, rushing out of the archways in the thousands.

Torsten twirled *Salvation* and dug in to face them. "Iam is with us, my friends!" he shouted. "For our King!"

XXI

THE CALEEF

Surrounded by Serpent Guards, Mahi was transported out into the square beyond the curved entry colonnade of the Tal'du Dromesh. They led her to the mass of Shesaitju warriors who'd been patrolling the city. Now, they surrounded the arena to see what was happening and why all the markless, merchants, and cowards fled.

"What is—"

Mahi snatched the spear from the hands of the approaching commander addressing her from atop a zhulong. She elbowed aside the Serpent Guards around her and whipped back to face the arena.

"My Caleef, you must get to safety!" Bit'rudam said, taking her arm.

She shook free. "Safety is for the King. Babrak has gone too far this time." She pushed off with the spear to stand atop the zhulong. She turned back to its rider. "Go to the stables and get any man or woman old enough to fight mounted."

He nodded and hopped off, summoning a few other warriors to run with him.

Then, perched atop the beast, Mahi raised her spear and shouted in Saitjuese, *"The traitor comes! Stand with me, my people. In the name of the God and Sand and Sea and his true Caleef, we must hold his city!"*

She didn't tell them that their God was dead.

The Serpent Guards immediately formed lines on either side of her and raised their weapons. More warriors fell in behind them, heeding the commands of their leader. Zhulong horns bellowed from former afhems, directing the formations. Even some unarmed civilians caught in the retreat were inspired to stop and stand with them.

For a moment, Mahi was glad the stripping of their stations was mere ceremony. Without them to lead, there would've been confusion.

"You saw what they have," Bit'rudam protested, refusing to join the other guards. "Mahraveh, you must get to the Keep with King Pi. We'll set up a second defense there in case—"

"In case what?" Mahi growled. "If Babrak wants to fill the streets of this sacred city with blood, then let it be more of his own."

The ferocious roar from a Current Eater within the arena drew their attention. Babrak's army had arrayed themselves beneath the arena's entry colonnade.

Mahi felt sick to her stomach. These were her own people, prepared to ravage Latiapur. All because an angry, pis'truda of a man refused to bow to a woman as his Caleef. Everything else fell from her memory. Pi, the marriage, Nesilia—she just wanted to kill Babrak.

"My father fought on those sands!" Mahi screamed. "I fought on those sands! It was not the marks we earned that made it mean something. It was our hearts. As Shesaitju. Babrak would destroy that!"

Her people voiced their agreement.

Across the square, Babrak's army riled up in their own manner, their leaders probably telling them lies about how Mahi had stolen her title. How she, Yuri, and her father had planned all of this, as if what she'd endured when she hit the Boiling Waters and met Nesilia face to face could've been planned.

"He will lie and say I destroyed our history," Mahi continued. "But we don't need afhemates. We need only to flow in one Current. The souls of those who perished on those hallowed sands stand with us!"

Her people broke out into raucous cheering, cursing Babrak—all but the Serpent Guards who stood firm and silent as always, and Bit'rudam, fretfully watching her. Their opponents did the same as their numbers amassed within the Tal'du Dromesh.

"One Current," Mahi said to him, softly. "I must stand with them. Besides, we have with us the man whose battle with my father ended in a draw." She nodded down the line of their forces, toward where

Shieldsman gleamed in their pearly armor. Torsten stood in their lead, somehow escaping the arena after helping them.

"Then none shall get near you, my Caleef," Bit'rudam said. Without waiting for an invitation, he hopped onto the back of her zhulong and laid his weapon across his lap.

"Circle flanks!" he ordered. "Drive them toward the serpent's fangs, and we'll cut them to pieces."

Not all the Shesaitju in their makeshift army understood his tactics. Still, enough former afhems were amongst them to relay the orders. Fanning out from the core of Serpent Guards, the ranks curled in, forming a U-shaped broader than that of the arena. When the enemy charged, they'd be funneled toward Mahi's best warriors before they even realized it.

She hoped. They could do little else to prepare before arrows started zipping over the arena walls. Then, without so much as a war cry, Babrak's army charged.

Hundreds of angry, gray faces rushed at her. Mahi clenched the shaft of her spear and prepared to kill however many she needed to. Ever since her reincarnation, staying calm had been an easy thing. It came with the onslaught of memories and the knowledge of what she was. Yet, Babrak changed that. Rage fueled her. Bit'rudam's chest heaved against her back as he, too, prepared in his own way to battle his own kind.

The forces crashed upon each other, and her zhulong bashed the first wave aside with its mighty tusks.

Then hers and Bit'rudam's blades went to work. They were like one artist painting the same canvas with two brushes, flowing this way and that, never clashing, always in sync.

Torsten barked orders across the battlefield. His men plowed through the enemy ranks in a wedge formation, driving more toward the Serpent Guards, whose sickle blades and fauchards twirled without relent, dousing the stone in blood. The Glassmen didn't move with the same grace, but Mahi had to admit, their tack was effective. They, themselves, were like a herd of angry zhulong in their heavy armor and giant shields.

Mahi had sacrificed so much to stop the infighting between her people, yet here they were again. It all seemed so inevitable. Two clashing tides, only one to prevail. The old ways and the new.

Their lines held in places, collapsed in others. Brave citizens of Latiapur flung vases and wares from the markets at the enemies—anything that could do damage. They weren't archers, but it was better than nothing. From a numbers standpoint, now that most of the city's army had arrived, Mahi had the advantage. Especially when her commander came from the stables with a horde of zhulong-mounted warriors, barreling toward the enemy's east flank through the afhem housing district.

Mahi stabbed a man's chest, then ripped her spear out and slashed another across the jaw.

They brought this upon themselves, she told herself. *Babrak did this.*

Her zhulong took a spear to the hide and bucked so hard it snapped the weapon. Bit'rudam beheaded the attacker with one smooth stroke, while Mahi took down a warrior aiming for his back. Then, her attention returning to the arena, she spotted Babrak watching through an arch at the arena's upper level.

"Come and face me, you worm!" she shouted up, spinning the spear above her head and slicing it down through an enemy soldier's shoulder.

The zhulong cavalry crashed into Babrak's forces, trampling them like ants. Babrak didn't seem fazed in the slightest by the sudden turn in tide. He grinned directly at Mahi, then spun and lumbered away. In his place, hundreds of archers filled the open arches of the Tal'du Dromesh.

He'd waited for all of Mahi's forces to converge, then gave the order. Barbed arrows, loosed from high ground, lanced down in straight lines, maintaining full velocity, and peppered the battlefield. Babrak didn't seem to care who they hit.

Bit'rudam screeched, and Mahi glanced back. Her heart jumped, but only for a beat. He'd been clipped on the thigh. Nothing serious. Mahi yanked on the zhulong's wild mane to turn herself toward the attack, swatting away one arrow and dodging another. By the time the last of the volley fell, men on both sides groaned everywhere. Shesaitju arrows weren't built for range, but they shredded like no other. They were meant to intimidate with brutality. And it worked.

"Caleef Mahraveh, it's time for you to fall back!" Torsten called out, fighting toward her. His massive sword cleaved a man in two while a Shieldsman moved along at his side, shield raised to deflect arrows.

"He's right," Bit'rudam moaned. An enemy warrior grabbed at his injured leg to pull him off the zhulong. He kicked the man away, and Mahi finished him.

"Find the King at the keep," Torsten said. "We need you…" he paused as an enemy charged him. His mighty blade swung in a wide arc, catching the man off guard with his range and gashing his gut. Other enemy combatants circled Torsten, keeping their distance as they watched their ally fall to his knees, cradling his entrails.

"We need you both alive!" Torsten finished.

Mahraveh bit her lip. But before she could respond, the distant roars of the Current Eaters rampaging within the arena were no longer so distant. She noticed Bit'rudam's eyes widen with unfamiliar terror in her peripherals. All three of the legendary beasts broke through the side of the Tal'du Dromesh at the same time, masses of razor-sharp tentacles slashing everything in their paths. Massive chunks of stone and lengths of columns blew off the walls with them, flattening Shesaitju on both sides as they landed and rolled.

Babrak, self-proclaimed man of the people, brought everyone together so he could heartlessly sacrifice whoever he needed to. The horrifying Current Eater, which landed in the center of the battle-ground, roared, its spittle and stench dousing the square.

Mahi didn't fear it, but her zhulong did. She felt its muscles tense before it tucked tail and bolted. It turned so abruptly, Bit'rudam was thrown aside. She would've joined him if she hadn't grasped a handful of its mane with one hand.

The beast rampaged through her army, and it wasn't alone. The zhulong cavalry was driven into hysterics as well, squealing in terror. Mahi had been around the creatures her entire life and had never heard them release such a sound. She attempted to calm hers, to no avail. So, she tried to leap off onto a market stand canvas, and as she did, one of the Current Eaters bellowed again, and her zhulong made a sharp turn.

Her foot twisted, getting caught in its stirrup. She hung off the side as the zhulong bounded down alleyways. She tightened her core, crunching to avoid hitting buildings, all while trying to tear free.

Another zhulong raced in front of hers and broke through a stand. The canvas awning collapsed atop it, forcing it into a wild spin. Its tusks stabbed hard into Mahi's mount, and together, they spun. Before Mahi knew it, she was careening through the air, landing hard against a rock formation.

Rubbing her dizzy head, she worked her way to her knees, and from her low vantage, saw the battle she'd just been ejected from. Once the Current Eaters had entered the fray, everything changed. Their tentacles raked everyone aside, showing no prejudice—Serpent Guards, Shieldsmen, everyone had to fend for themselves.

She clambered higher up the rocks to get a better view. Her presence alone would help nothing. She needed to devise a strategy and fast.

The crest of the formation didn't offer any answers. It did, however, allow Mahi to see over the bluffs to the Boiling Waters, where Latiapur's defensive navy had somehow not noticed the approaching fleet. Her ships converged toward the mouth of the arena where the attack had originated.

Waves pushed out in a straight line from that point, rocking her fleet violently. One slammed into the bluffs. Another's sails were ripped to shreds. One of Babrak's warships sailed toward the palace, somehow unaffected, that same mystic on the front holding her arms out wide.

Waves didn't naturally behave in such a singular manner. They weren't only big, but forceful, radiating off of the ship like magic.

Mahi turned back to the city, where one of the Current Eaters broke through further and rampaged through the markets. The thing was pinned with hundreds of arrows and still hadn't slowed.

Destruction rained down everywhere. Chaos in the streets, barbed arrows in the sky, mythical monsters, cartwheeling through Latiapur, a place where no battle was to be done outside of Tal'du Dromesh. The old ways were officially over, but Mahi was afraid of what the new would genuinely look like.

That was when Mahi realized… no strategy could get them out of this. The enemy's magic could manipulate even the waves.

So, she ran along the ridge of the bluffs, hopping from point to point, racing toward the Boiling Keep. Hundreds lived there, and bells within the high dome bellowed as the city remained on alert. It was time for them to signal retreat and get the King to safety.

Mahi squeezed through a narrow pass in the rocks, then leaped down to the palace steps where warriors posted in the palace were set up in layers to prepare a final defense.

Mahi grabbed a former afhem. "Call a retreat," she ordered. "Everyone. The entire city."

"My Caleef, we can hold the Keep," he protested.

"We won't. Is the King inside?"

"The Glass boy?" the former afhem asked, not masking his disdain. "Not at all."

Mahi grunted in frustration. "North. Tell everyone to flee north by land." The Current Eaters were sea creatures. As little as Mahi knew about them, she had to believe that land was their best option for escape.

"To what end, my Caleef?"

"White Bridge." Then she turned and shouted, "Abandon the city! Abandon Latiapur." Her voice carried to the dock lifts where soldiers prepared to descend and take more ships out to their doom.

She yelled it to warriors, to the few posted Serpent Guards, to servants and dockworkers.

Abandon Latiapur... Words she never thought she'd utter, words her father nor any of the proud afhems ever would've dreamed of until their ranks were broken entirely, and they were forced to surrender like Sidar Rakun.

Shoving aside the entry gates, Mahi shouted louder than ever. She swept into the entry hall and was surprised to find it full. Dozens of sages were present, kowtowing toward the imagery carved on each column, praying in Saitjuese. Some had nigh'jel blood dripping from their wrists as they sacrificed the creatures to the Current. Some clutched prayer bracelets made of varied shells.

"Everyone, to the city gates," Mahi demanded. Unlike the warriors and servants, none budged. Across the room, however, she saw that a young Shieldsman—the one who'd arrived with Torsten—clutched one sage by the folds of his robes and appeared to be threatening him.

"Shieldsman, have you seen King Pi?" she asked. "We must abandon the city."

He dropped the sage and turned to her, face bruised, eyes wide with panic. "Sir Unger said he'd be here, but nobody has seen him. None of these useless priests will say anything!"

Mahi regarded the sage recovering on the floor. "You all have to leave as well."

"We cannot, My Caleef," the sage replied softly, calm as ever. "Our lives were offered to serve he or *she*, who inhabits this palace. We will never abandon it."

"You'd rather die?" Memories from other Caleef's flashed through Mahi's mind. It was faint as always, but she could see sages remaining put while generational storms ravaged Latiapur and King Liam's army marched outside, the only other times the city had been emptied. None ever ran.

"On the Current, we never die," he said.

Mahi clenched her jaw. The floor quaked as the roar of a Current Eater rang out, and it continued to wreck through the beloved city. The sages didn't even wince.

"You stubborn men," Mahi said. "She's come here for her brother. She wants the Current. You'll die for nothing."

"Only the God of Sand and Sea can control it," the man said.

"Caliphar is dead!" She shouted, pushing him off. They looked at her like she was crazed. "Then at least make yourselves useful and get everyone out of the Keep. All of you can stay to die, but we need every willing man and woman alive."

"Yes, my Caleef."

"All of you. Go."

The sages rose upon her request, each of them scattering into the halls. Even Mahi had no idea how many people lived in the palace. She never needed to. She'd never wanted the service that so many so willingly offered just because of her title.

"They don't matter," the Shieldsman insisted. He pushed by one and clutched her arm, and not even her glower could back him off. He didn't seem to care. "Where in Iam's name is the King. If you did—"

"What would I gain from harming him now?" Mahi hissed, yanking her arm away. He was lucky they needed everyone they could get. "Have you checked the throne room?"

"It was locked, and none of those fools would let me check."

"I can get in. Search his temporary quarters; I'll check there."

His lip twisted. She could tell he didn't trust her in the slightest, but after a few long seconds, he offered a reluctant nod and headed toward the western stairwell.

Mahi pushed through the scrambling sages across the golden floors of the vast entry hall to the great doors of the throne room. If they'd been locked, they no longer were.

Passing through the doors, she froze almost immediately. Babrak stood near the coral throne, running his hand along the arm. He remained oblivious to her even though there was no way he hadn't heard the doors creak. A few sages lay dead on the floor, their blood making iridescent puddles on the gold floor and streaming toward the Sea Door like a drain. Pi's body wasn't present amongst them, nor were any of her warriors.

"You," Mahi spat.

Babrak turned, sneering. He had Mahi's spear—which she'd left balanced across her throne—gripped in both hands, spinning it to test the weight. His spiked leather armor hugged his oversized frame. His neck was the size of a man's thigh, and fresh scars from his battles with both Mahi and Muskigo covered the parts of his torso that were exposed.

Worse than it all, however, was that his skin was coated in nigh'jel blood, making it black like hers. The coat was lumpy, sloppy, and peeling off in spots, but his intent at claiming Caleefdom was clear. Again, everything else in her life faded away. The battle, the King— everything. There was only him.

"How did you get here?" she asked. She spread her feet shoulder-width to keep her base beneath her and slowly shuffled in. Her eyes darted from side to side, checking the spaces behind the columns encircling the area to ensure they were alone.

"There are many secret routes throughout the city a child like you wouldn't know," he replied.

"Not smart to come alone."

"Somehow, I knew the Current would lead us both here." He tested the tip of Mahi's spear with his finger, drawing a pinpoint of blood.

"You destroyed everything we stand for."

"I saved what we stand for!" he snapped. "While you and your father erased history and joined a war against a goddess with no concern over us."

"She'll destroy us."

"She's giving me Latiapur."

"A city that no longer has inhabitants."

He sighed, gaze dropping to the ground. He actually looked remorseful, which made Mahi's blood boil even more than she thought possible.

"A small price to pay to rectify so many wrongs," he said softly. "But we will be all the stronger for it. She, sister of the God of Sand and Sea—who has abandoned us—has named me Caleef. Helping destroy the Glass for her is a fair trade."

"You didn't even want to rebel."

"I didn't want to lose," he corrected. "Now, we can't. They'll drown on their own greed, and from the ashes, the Black Sands will rise! Don't make the same mistakes as your father, Mahraveh. Surrender your title, and you can be a part of it. You can stand at my side as—"

"As your whore?" she interrupted, fuming.

"As my *Queen*. Think of what we could do together. All Pantego will tremble. This vengeful goddess? After she wipes the Glass away, even she couldn't stand against us."

"No, Babrak. I will take you with my bare hands, and you will face the Dagger of Damikmagrin. You will be wiped from this realm for all eternity, and not even that is a fate worthy enough."

His remorse deepened as he nodded. "You are your father's daughter."

"No, I am Caleef."

Babrak regarded the spear one last time, then tossed it longways in Mahi's direction. It rolled across the floor, stopping against her foot. She didn't bend to grab it. Not with him in the room. He couldn't be trusted to a fair fight.

"Take it," he said.

"I don't need a weapon to kill you," Mahi replied.

"My Caleef!" someone shouted, throwing open the throne room doors. Bit'rudam hurried to her side, angling his sickle-blade in front of her. "Mahraveh, everyone is in full retreat. We have to go."

"Not without him dead," she said.

"What a lovely reunion," Babrak laughed. "You'll both find I won't be so easy to beat without a cowardly ambush."

"Mahraveh, go! I'll handle him," Bit'rudam said. "The Serpent Guard awaits you."

"We'll take him together. It ends today."

"Two on one?" Babrak clicked his tongue. "Now, that's not fair, is it?"

His grin stretched from ear to ear. Electricity crackled through the Sea Door as if lightning somehow struck from below. Then, the red-robed mystic rose through, hands glowing with raw, magical energy. Her eyes were black as Mahi's own skin, expressionless, like that of the Current Eaters.

"So, this is the child that our brother chose to carry his flame?" the mystic said, her voice laced with an ethereal quality. It echoed from every direction. "She's so scrawny."

"They're mine, demon," Babrak said.

"Demon? I'm so much more than that." The ancient-looking mystic's already cold glare darkened. She hovered above the Sea Door, embers floating all around her. Then she snapped her finger, and a wave of fire erupted forth.

"Mahi!"

Bit'rudam rammed her out of the way. She couldn't feel the elements through her Caleef skin until then, but the mystical fire was so hot. Her spear remained on the ground and immediately was reduced to ash, the blade liquified.

"Coward!" Mahi screamed as her hands scraped along the floor.

"We need to go!" Bit'rudam said. Getting his arms around her, he lifted and dragged her toward the exit. As he did, the mystic again unleashed a swath of magical destruction.

"No, they're mine!" Babrak protested. He went to block her, but she waved her arm and flung him aside with an unseen force. Her other hand then extended, and lightning coruscated out.

Bit'rudam threw his blade up, absorbing the electricity and delaying the surge enough for them to get out. The rest of the magic splashed against the throne room doors. Mahi managed to close them just in time.

"Come on," Bit'rudam yelled.

Mahi glanced back, and the doors burst open with a gust of wind as strong as any storm she'd ever encountered. She and Bit'rudam were thrown forward, barely able to stay on their feet.

Blood-soaked Serpent Guards rushed in and formed a line, crouching to brave the gale. Mahi found her balance behind them. The mystic floated within the entry. She barely seemed drained at all, even after using so much of her strength disguising an entire fleet within a storm of her creation. In all the legends of the mystics Mahi had heard, they were never capable of so much magic without rest.

Armor clattered as the Serpent Guards prepared to face the woman. Mahi glared straight at Babrak.

"Congratulations, Babrak," Mahi called to him. "You will be King of nothing."

He only stared, silent. The mystic stretched her slender fingers and rolled her neck. Her feet lowered to the ground, and she breathed in deeply as her arms extended in front of her.

Mahi saw no more. Bit'rudam pulled her out of the palace, and only the sounds of the mystic's magic could be heard.

No screams.

Only the *jangle* of armored bodies dropping.

XXII

THE MYSTIC

The fire above still raged. Since the moment their cart parked back in the main hall, Sora, Lucindur, and Tum Tum had been treated with abuse, being shoved and prodded. King Lorgit kept silent the whole time, and barely seemed affected by his throne room being in flames, which troubled Sora.

His clanbreakers flanked them on both sides. They were as disciplined as any Glass soldier, but Sora imagined under all that armor, they were infinitely more fierce.

Sora felt trickles of water on her skin as mist rose from the large pool in the center of Balonhearth, catching the downpour from the mounted dwarf head above. It practically sizzled off her, skin still hot from her magic, like her very blood was on fire.

All around them, merchants, tinkers, traders, and miners by the dozens passed by. All watched as an odd set of humans were rushed along by the King himself. It must have been, to them, quite a sight.

Sora found it odd that there were no women in the lot.

"Tum Tum," Sora whispered. "Where are all your women?"

"What do ye mean? They be everywhere!" He added a quick wink at Brouben.

Brouben, in turn, tried to quiet them, but it didn't work.

Sora gave Tum Tum an incredulous stare.

Tum Tum nodded toward one. "Right there. And there. And walkin toward us here. Don't look now; she's a good-lookin one."

Despite Tum Tum's instructions, Sora followed his motions and saw a dwarf lumbering in their general direction.

"I said don't look." Tum Tum palmed his forehead.

"That's… that's a female?"

"Aye, ain't she just!" Tum Tum elbowed Brouben, whose face went red. Brouben quickly composed himself, glanced toward his father, who strode ahead of them with determination.

She had long, blonde, braided hair and a matching beard that cascaded down to her ample belly. Resting on her shoulder, she clung to a giant water tankard Sora assumed would be used to help put out the fire she'd created. She had droopy eyes and a bulbous nose that covered her mustache like an awning. One thing was sure: there was nothing to distinguish her from the men.

"Ye almost had me fooled," Lorgit finally said, the first words he'd spoken since the incident in the throne room. The only good thing about it was that it allowed Sora to not respond to Tum Tum.

"Almost," Lorgit punctuated.

"Father—" Brouben said before being cut off.

"Quiet ye, before ye get strung up as well," Lorgit said, stopping the group and spinning on his son. "Ye gotta rise pretty yiggin early to fool the Ruler of the Three Kingdoms."

Clanbreakers closed in to ensure no one tried anything stupid. The King weaved through them like a needle and thread, eying each one with condescension. Sora and Lucindur kept silent, knowing that anything they might say would have consequences. Lorgit stopped right in front of Sora.

"Ye think I don't know that was ye?" he asked. "Panpingese mystic."

The accusation didn't catch Sora off guard. She'd learned how her heritage made people behave, like she was always the enemy. And the word 'mystic' came out of his mouth like poison.

"Your Grace, I don't know what you're talking about," Sora said. "It was Nesilia—the Buried Goddess. Had to be."

Lorgit laughed, though it sounded more like a death wail, wet and gurgled. "We were a part of many wars, my dear. While men play games, killin this king, usurpin that throne, the dwarves watch it all. Ye know how old I am?"

Sora shook her head.

"Neither do I," he said. "Been that long since I popped out. Sometimes, I wonder if I be older than Meungor himself. Problem with men be that they only see the future as far as they can chuck a stone. Dwarves… let's just say we can throw pretty far."

"Father, what is this about?" Brouben asked, then shrank back when the King eyed him.

"I told ye, Morrastreaudunimum was ours, and we want it back. We spent a long time watchin those flower-pickers tear the place to pieces for no good reason. Done. We be done watchin. Look up there," King Lorgit said, pointing to the smoke pouring from his throne room. "Just another example of man's destruction."

"That was the work of the goddess!" Brouben protested.

Lorgit shook his head. "See all those carts already on their way, tanks of water at the ready?"

Even as he said it, Sora noticed the workers all scooping more water from the fountain into large steam-powered contraptions with hose pipes attached.

"She told us about ye," King Lorgit said, turning again to Sora, his voice barely a whisper. "Said ye'd try to burn us all alive if we let ye."

Sora's heart sank, and her stomach dropped. *She* could only mean Nesilia. Her suspicions were confirmed. Lorgit had struck a deal with the goddess. But when? If it had been when Sora's body was occupied, she'd have had some memory, no matter how vague. And it couldn't have been after, not with the reports they'd heard of Nesilia's whereabouts.

"Almost didn't believe her," Lorgit went on. "Said she was servin the Buried Goddess, and doin her work, and that if we stayed out of what's comin, we'd be safe for all eternity. That her fight wasn't with dwarves."

"I promise you, whoever told you that is lying," Sora said. "Nesilia slaughtered the Strongirons to send a message."

"It don't matter. I gave her the only message that does. That I know it's all horse shog. All the work of mages and witches, making up stories about goddesses to fuel more war. I told her that we dwarves are done getting involved with yer kind, and we didn't need some witch asking us to make more deals. Nearly had her killed on the spot, Arch Warlock or not."

Freydis, Sora realized, accompanied by a chill up her spine. "King Lorgit, you can't trust anything she told you," she blurted.

"And I can trust ye, mystic?" he spat. "Ye lied from the start, posin as prisoners. Well, ye got yer wish. Yer gonna rot in the dungeons til yer nothin but bones—or…" He looked around. "Maybe I should take yer heads right here and deliver em to the Warlock just to send a message of me own." His voice got louder, intent upon everyone hearing him. "A reminder that when King Lorgit Cragrock says, 'No one in. No one out,' it means *no one!*"

"Father, please listen to me," Brouben said for what must have been the fiftieth time. He didn't look enthused. His father's words were clearly weighing heavily on him.

"Ye think me a fool, don't ye?" Lorgit looked at Sora. "Well, I heard what happened on the pass, too. My loyal commander, Garga-mane… he saw yer filthy powers with his own eyes. Ain't no denying it."

"Father—"

"Get movin," Lorgit growled.

The clanbreakers responded in kind, shoving the three of them along. Brouben followed like a lost puppy, unsure of what to do.

"What now?" Lucindur whispered.

"I should have killed that wretch when I had the chance—hanging Whitney over the ledge like that." Sora felt her blood roiling below the surface.

She gazed up at the smoke still pouring from the mouth and nostrils of the large dwarven head encapsulating the dwarf King's throne room. She could imagine the dragon bones, charred and burning. She knew Aquira was impervious to flames, but that was her skin. She wondered what fire would do to her bones. Then she found herself overwhelmed with worry for the wyvern… and Whitney.

"That was smart thinkin," Tum Tum said, obviously looking, too. "Don't matter what he says."

"That *was* you?" Brouben whispered.

Sora blushed, realizing there were good dwarfs too, and like her own people, their kings and queens didn't represent each individual. "I'm sorry," she said.

"Sorry? Shog-shuckin brilliant it was," Brouben said. Then, lowering his voice, he added, "I meant me words. Me father ain't worthy of the title or that throne no more."

Lucindur shushed them. She was right, there was no telling who might be listening. Though it would be hard to imagine anyone hearing anything with all the hustle and bustle of dwarves working to extinguish the fire. Cart after cart rumbled up, hauling massive tanks of water and thick, sturdy dwarves. The rails all rattled, people shouted, and through it all, King Lorgit and his clanbreakers trudged along like nothing was wrong.

Sora thought about what she'd done up there and how easily the fire had bent to her will.

She hadn't needed to draw blood. There were no command words like she'd learned in the Red Tower anymore, either—which had been true ever since Nesilia left her body. The power surging from her wasn't like it used to be. Up there, in the throne room, she hadn't felt Elsewhere calling—Elsewhere was weak now compared to her.

A few minutes passed as they all watched the carts, occasionally earning a prod by one of the clanbreakers. By now, the first of the brigade reached the throne room, and steam could be seen taking the place of smoke.

"Ye think he'll be able to do it?" Tum Tum asked.

Sora was still fixated on the zooming carts, but when no one answered, she returned her attention to her friends.

All eyes were intent upon her.

"Me?" she said.

"Aye, who else?" Tum Tum chuckled. "Ye known him the longest, ain't ye?"

Sora supposed he was right, but not truly. "Maybe in number of years... but both of you have spent more time with him, especially lately. Lucindur, you traveled the last several months on the road with him. All the time."

"A fact I needn't be reminded of," she said with a sly smile.

"And Tum Tum, you've probably heard as many stories—or more —than I have. You know his... exploits. And you also have the unique perspective of what it means to…" She lowered her voice. "… steal from the Iron Bank."

Tum Tum shook his head, cleared his throat, and tried his best to look innocent. "I never done the sort."

Sora smiled now, but hers was as mirthless as they come. "The last thing we'd stolen together was a ship from an upyr. That didn't go very well."

"I was there, Lass, and that's talkin kindly about the event. But here's the cold truth of it: if that boy can't get what we came for, we ain't got any hope, anyway. It be this, or we gotta come up with a whole new idea before the whole world goes up in flames."

"Shut your ale holes," one of the clanbreakers said, giving Tum Tum a shove. Sora was surprised it had taken so long.

They were beyond the city's grand hall now, and moving toward a particularly dark passage. It was nothing like the streets of Panping or Yarrington, and so far removed from a place like Myen Elnoir that they could hardly be considered in the same class. Balonhearth was all one color: slate gray. Gray walls, gray ground, gray ceiling, gray buildings. It was all the mountain, every bit of it.

Jutting out beside them, small homes lined the path if it could be called a path. The closest thing Sora could use to describe the city would be an ant mound or hornet's nest. Deep pockets or alcoves housed more "buildings" although they were really just a few walls carved into the side of the rock.

She felt like eyes were watching them through the short, squat windows, and probably were.

They all let a moment pass before Lucindur whispered, "So, *what now?*"

"I don't know," Sora admitted, and the words pierced her like knives. "I never was the plan-maker. That was Whitney's job, terrible as he was at it."

"You know, I don't know if that's true," Lucindur said.

"It is. I just followed his lead—"

"Not that," Lucindur said. "The part about him being horrible at it. Do you know how many times that boy saved my life or someone else's?"

She wasn't wrong. Whitney had saved Sora many times as well. If it hadn't been for him, would any of them be alive? Even Torsten Unger would likely be dead if not for Whitney's hairbrained schemes.

"Those're the dungeons," Brouben offered, pointing at the darkness ahead.

"Shog in a barrel," Sora said.

"Shhh, you hear that?" Lucindur said.

"Aye, she's even startin to sound like the thief," Tum Tum said.

"No, not that," Lucindur said. "Listen."

Sora didn't hear anything, but she felt something rumble beneath her feet. *Then* she heard something; the voices of every dwarf in Balonhearth questioning what was going on as the ground began to shake beneath them. It intensified until they were all thrown to the side.

"What's this!" Lorgit shouted. He whipped around and stuck a finger out at Sora. "This your doin, witch?"

Each of the clanbreakers drew their weapons.

"It wasn't me, I swear!" Sora said.

Brouben gave her a look that said, "Are you sure?"

Small rocks cascaded down while goods from various shops toppled off tables and shelves, crashing against the ground. King Lorgit took two violent steps toward Sora, no doubt ready to deal some punishment. But then, a tremor sent him reeling, and he hit his head on the stone wall. His clanbreakers rushed toward him.

"This is our only chance. Go!" Sora shouted.

No one hesitated, not even as they heard shouting behind them, nor when they heard the clattering of clanbreaker armor. They shoved through crowds, sending many a dwarf scrambling. The mountain itself was heaving, and Sora found it hard to run in a straight line. Her ankles kept buckling, and she worried that they'd snap in two, especially after she'd already twisted one in the throne room.

She had to push the pain aside. Their pursuers were closing in.

"Run!" Sora said, and picked up the pace.

Sora and Lucindur's long legs carried them far faster than any of the dwarves, Tum Tum and Brouben included, but even her dwarven companions outran the armor-encumbered clanbreakers. Everyone else was too caught up in the earthquake to worry about them.

They ducked between two buildings and took a breather. An instant later, the shaking ceased, and they were left alone in eerie silence.

Then, murmurs broke out in the distance, and Sora said, "Where do we go?"

"Follow me," Tum Tum said, and stay low… try to blend in."

They emptied out of the alley, and Tum Tum skidded to a stop. There stood Gargamane the Gold.

"Stop there, Dwotratum, and I won't run ye through," he said.

Tum Tum swore, but Sora had had enough. She strode right up to the dwarven commander.

"Like you did last time?" she asked, bold as one would expect the daughter of Liam the Conquerer to be. "You're going to move aside, or you won't see tomorrow."

Her threat was real. She could feel the fire welling up in her, begging to be released and char his little dwarven bones. And worst of all, she liked it. The dichotomy between the old Sora and the new, goddess-scorned Sora was jarring, even to her.

Gargamane reached for his weapon, but Sora didn't give him the chance. She focused her energy on Gargamane's sword, and as soon as his hand hit the hilt, he yanked it back like he'd stuck it into a bonfire.

He squealed, then his face contorted to a mixture of anger and fear.

"Ye ain't welcome here, witch!" Gargamane growled.

"I don't want to hurt you any further, but this whole city is mad," she said.

"Mad? Ye think I don't know ye did that up there?" he asked. "King said, 'No one in. No one out' and it looks like he was right."

Brouben stepped forward, but Sora threw her hand up.

"We've come with everything but tangible proof that the Buried Goddess is back," she said, "and your coward of a King can't be bothered to be a part of it."

Gargamane looked to Brouben. "Yer gonna sit by while she talks about yer King and father?"

"Just listen to her," he said, though, lacking the vim of a Prince giving an order. Clearly, he was still conflicted.

Sora took another step toward Gargamane and said, "Are you going to let us pass, or do I need to do to your armor what I just did to your blade?"

Gargamane looked around. Sora didn't dare take her eyes off him, but she knew what he was seeing. Chaos, destruction, and that was just a tiny sliver of what Pantego would look like if they didn't succeed in stopping Nesilia.

"What happened to the Strongirons?" Gargamane asked, quietly. "That weren't the Drav Cra—or at least, not them alone?"

Sora breathed a sigh of relief. Perhaps, some of these people were open to reason. "As I said on the pass, the rumors are true. You've seen the grimaurs and goblins infesting the mining tunnels—I may not live here, but I know it's not normal. The Buried Goddess leads not only the Drav Cra, but all manner of beasts, and we need to stop her."

"Me own cousin is a Strongiron," Gargamane said, head to the ground. "Was one… I never even got to say goodbye."

"She's right, the grimaurs, goblins, all of it… Nesilia's controlling them," Lucindur said.

Gargamane looked around again.

Sora almost felt bad for him, until his attention suddenly became hyper-focused and he shouted, "Aye! Over here!" Then he looked at Sora and smiled. "They sure took long enough."

Sora glanced over her shoulder and saw an entire continent of clanbreakers heading their way. They were still a great distance off, but they'd be on them in no time.

"Ye shog-shuckin bastard," Tum Tum swore.

"Ye don't know what yer doin," Brouben said.

"Ye gonna burn us all, witch?" Gargamane asked.

"I don't need to," Sora said. Then, in one motion, she thrust her hands forward, and a gust of hot air exploded from them, hitting Gargamane square in the chest. The dwarf went flying, tumbling hind over teakettle until he slammed against a nearby home.

Then, Sora turned and sent another shockwave at the ground right in front of the clanbreakers. A large crack zig-zagged across the rock, tripping them up and crumbling the wall beside it, veiling them in dust.

Sora turned back to the others. "Let's go!"

XXIII

THE TRAITOR

Rand swam through the chaos of the Latiapur markets. He had no weapon, but as a Glassman, he looked like an ally. That didn't make it easier. Citizens of Latiapur ran from the arena in a frenzy while warriors ran toward it. Rand didn't have to see to know some were being trampled.

Market stands broke. Canvas shredded and drifted in the air. Goods rolled across the stone and floated in puddles. Food stores were squashed. The Shesaitju were lucky that they rarely used fire for lighting. Otherwise, the whole place might have gone up in flames like Dockside had, even with all the water. As it was, enough dust and sand was kicked up to make visibility extremely poor.

Rand had to squint and block his face just to see anything, all while bouncing off bodies left and right. He threw someone aside and finally spotted Pi's slight, white-clothed frame again, weaving through the crowd with his guard to the right.

Rand veered in that direction when a bloodcurdling wianu roar sent the masses into more of an upheaval. A heavyset man bashed into his side, and Rand went sprawling. He scrambled to his feet, searching through legs for Pi.

There he was... A squealing zhulong had trampled his guard, leaving him on his own. The young King stood, gawking at the pulverized body. Then, another zhulong darted by. The scared little boy rushed into the nearest alley.

Finding his footing, Rand continued after Pi. He couldn't try and blend in anymore, there were too many people. Pushing, shoving, he made it to the alley. Another wianu roared, and a booming *crash* shook Pantego and heaved him against a wall. Every part of him was still sore from the clash with Lucas, but there was no time for a break.

"Move!" he barked at a woman and her daughter running down the alley.

A frightened zhulong blew through the clay wall of the building to his right, canvas stuck to its tusk. Rand whipped around, grabbed the girls by the back of their clothes, and yanked them to the ground, so it didn't crush them.

He didn't wait for gratitude.

Pi vanished around the corner on the far side of the alley. Rand pounded dirt and sprinted as fast as he could. With every moment that passed, the din of war and destruction grew. It made what the cultists had done to Dockside seem like a child's prank.

He emerged into a smog of dust that scratched his throat. More Shesaitju ran on this narrow street, though it thankfully wasn't nearly as crowded as the markets. Rand searched from side to side, then saw the King only a cart's length away, against a wall, chest heaving. Blood and dirt coated his thin cheeks.

"My King, we need to get you out of here," Rand said, approaching cautiously.

Pi glanced over but didn't make eye contact. His gaze darted in every direction, toward every scream, squeal, or roar, toward the terror-stricken zhulong trampling through anything in their paths.

"My King, please," Rand insisted.

Pi swallowed audibly, then reached out and grasped Rand's hand, still not looking. His touch startled Rand, even though he expected it.

Is it really this easy? Rand wondered. Throughout history, all the tales of regicide came with epic stories and otherworldly assassins, like what his sister had become. The kings never willingly took the hands of their killers.

Rand snapped out of it and studied his surroundings. There were too many people around to risk it here. He had no idea who any of the Shesaitju were or if they'd recognize what was happening. And no matter what, Rand had to survive this. Seeing Sigrid again depended on it.

"This way!"

He clasped tight and dragged Pi across the road. They dodged a zhulong, mounted by a warrior who couldn't control it. Shoved by more people. Rand occasionally glanced back to see massive wianu tentacles thrashing over the dust.

The words "Retreat!" echoed over screams of death. Fleeing Shesaitju warriors appeared in the distance. A handful of Shieldsmen were with them, pearly armor like beacons against the all-brown-and-black city.

"Come on!" Rand pulled left down another alley then another until they reached a small clearing.

"Which way?" Pi asked, squeezing Rand's hand so tight he could hardly feel his fingers.

Ahead, a blackwood fence was being pounded from the other side by more scared zhulong, locked in their pen. Otherwise, they were on a backstreet with only a child crying on a balcony above and a blind beggar trembling behind a blanket. In a city under attack, this was about as alone as he could get without a plan.

"Sir Unger told me to get to the Keep," Pi went on. "Which way is it?"

Rand closed his eyes and drew a deep, grating breath.

He's just a child, a part of him said within.

He started a war, answered another. *Got thousands killed.*

Rand's free hand quaked uncontrollably. He himself had done many things he wasn't proud of for the sake of his Kingdom and sister—killed men, hung women, including the one he loved. Never a kid, though. Even if Pi was starting to look older, that's what he was.

"Answer your King," Pi yelled, pushing against Rand's side.

Rand shoved it all out of his head and pictured him and Sigrid sitting on the docks of Yarrington. Pictured her soft, freckled skin, and the way her wild, red hair never seemed to stay still.

Before he knew it, he stood behind the boy, his arm wrapping Pi's throat and constricting. The boy immediately retaliated, but Rand withdrew against a wall to brace himself and wrenched Pi's arm behind his back.

Pi had truly grown bigger, though, and his bony elbow caught Rand in one of the wounds Lucas had left him with. His grip loosened, and Pi's head slid down enough for him to sink his teeth into Rand's arm.

The King broke free but didn't make it two steps before Rand grabbed the neckline of his overly elaborate cape and tore him back. He hit the ground hard, the wind fleeing his lungs with a loud gasp. Rand jumped on top of him, both hands throttling the boy like he was tying off a rope to dock.

Slapping, kicking, Pi did everything he could to break free. Rand closed his eyes as he squeezed, feeling the boy's windpipe beginning to collapse beneath his fingers. He remembered all those awful moments of his life. Everything he'd lost—his sister's eyes as he told her he'd return for her…

As the resistance lessened, Rand peeked once through his eyelids. The sheer dread in Pi's crystal blue eyes arrested him. His mind was reminded of those poor souls Oleander had forced him to hang. To Tessa, a handmaiden he'd cared dearly for, begging him to ignore his duty, begging him to stop.

She'd offered that same feeble look before he'd hanged her. He heard the rope creaking while she swung in the wind, left to be food for gallers. Now again, someone who wasn't his sister had him playing executioner.

"What am I doing?" Rand asked himself. He staggered away. His hands peeled from Pi's flesh, grits of sand sticking to both his and Pi's sweat. The boy gasped and coughed, squirming to get free.

All Rand could manage was to gape at his trembling hands, the hands of a young boy from Dockside who wanted to grow up and become a great Shieldsman who looked out for the small, defenseless people of the world. Even if they were the King.

"Sigrid couldn't—"

Pi cut him off with a heel across the jaw. He pulled free, still coughing and clutching his brushed throat.

"Help me!" the boy rasped and tried to run.

Rand lunged and grabbed him by the sleeve. "The Boiling Keep isn't that way," he said. "I'll show you. I won't hurt you."

Pi punched at his arm, the exertion making him hack. Rand caught a kick in the shin this time and bit his lip to fight against the burst of pain.

"I won't hurt you!" he said.

"Get off of me, traitor!"

"I'm not—"

The sleeve ripped, and Pi stumbled onto his rear. At the same time, a shadow fell over them, cast by a wianu rising high over the stables. A zhulong thrashed as it was strangled by its tentacles high in the air, on its way to being dropped into the monster's oversized maw.

Pi scrabbled to stand. The penned zhulong went into a frenzy and slammed against the fence until the blackwood snapped. Rand didn't think. He bolted forward as they stampeded out onto the street, grabbing Pi and hoisting him over his shoulders. He evaded one of the charging beasts right before it bashed into the side of another, both mewing in pain.

He caromed off their collapsed bodies and sprinted. Pi fought every step of the way, but Rand felt stronger than he had in months, at that moment, doing the right thing. Pi may have been a cursed, troubled boy and the daughter of a monster, but how many times had Rand been scolded by teachers for acting out of line, or beating down a street rat for saying something inappropriate to Sigrid?

I won't kill him, Rand decided. *Only destroy the Crown.*

A zhulong bumped him in the side and sent him right, spinning out of the way of another one, all while Pi pounded on his back. Behind them, the wianu roared again and rampaged, feeding on zhulong like a feast had been laid out for it. Dust swirled. Bodies of the city's retreating populace dropped in the stampede. Rand wasn't sure where he was going, only that he had to keep running. They were now trapped in the middle of a street, no building to duck into, as if that would matter.

A second before he felt it, he heard it. A beast snorted and rammed Rand from behind. He hit the sand-coated stone and skidded, scraping his elbows and knees. Pi tumbled off his shoulder. The boy looked up, petrified. Rand dived under the legs of a zhulong racing by, passing beneath it just in time. Then, he grasped Pi to help him up. They were nearly to their feet when a hoof crashed down upon Rand's neck.

His head hit the stone, and he saw stars. Pi was somewhere beneath him, squirming to get free. Another hoof hit, and another. Before Rand knew it, pain exploded from every part of his body, and he couldn't move.

It felt like drowning. Dust choked him, caught in his throat, and he couldn't scream; couldn't even draw breath because every time he did, another hoof pounded on his back.

Pi's body ceased to wriggle underneath him, and before Rand knew it, the stampede ended. He rolled over onto his back, struggling for breath. Every inhalation stung. Every exhalation stung worse. The stifling veil of dirt, sand, and Iam-knows-what-else lifted enough so Rand could see the people running past. He couldn't manage to turn his head, only peer through his peripherals.

"My King!" a deep, familiar voice bellowed as Rand lay there, gasping.

Rand expended as much energy as he could to rotate his head toward the sound, and saw Torsten kneeling by King Pi's broken body. The Glass Crown lay beside them, surrounded by hoof prints and broken into countless shards.

"Sir Unger, we have to go!" Sir Mulliner shouted. In the center of the avenue stood a wall of Shieldsmen and Serpent Guards. They slowly backed up while providing cover for the retreat against Babrak's invaders. Their armor was so covered in blood and grime it no longer shone.

"No, no, no…" Torsten sniveled. "My King, wake up. I won't lose you, too."

Rand didn't understand. He'd absorbed the brunt of the trampling zhulong. But as Torsten shoveled his hands under Pi's body and lifted, Rand realized something. Pi looked smaller than ever, wilting like a dry flower over Torsten's arms, fragile. His clothing, perhaps, had made him seem larger. If he wasn't dead, he was close to it.

Rand took solace, though barely, knowing that if Pi was dead, he hadn't killed him in cold blood; hadn't crossed that line of no return... but he may as well have.

I crossed that line a long time ago...

As Torsten's feet shuffled in his efforts to lift Pi despite his own wounds, all Rand could hear was the creaking of rope. That same infernal sound that plagued him into drunkenness back in Yarrington returned in full force.

Creak, creak, creak, went the strained ropes tied around the throats of those he'd hanged. He could smell the death of their decaying bodies swinging in the wind.

"Rand?" Torsten muttered, his tone dripping with disbelief.

Rand could hardly turn his head enough to see the face of his old mentor. The pity Torsten wore in his expression when last they met was gone, replaced by heartbreak. Or was it rage? Probably some combination of the two that made Rand's already aching heart feel like it had sunk out between his shoulder blades.

"I… I… didn't…" he muttered. Forming even the simplest words hurt all over. He shook his head, and every time it felt like a knife-point pushing against his spine. "I… couldn't…"

"Sir Unger, the Caleef is safe, we have to go," Sir Mulliner panted, sprinting over. The Shieldsman stopped, eyes going wide. "Is that the King?"

Torsten didn't answer. His attention remained on Rand, and he stayed completely silent. Sir Mulliner looked the same way, and his features corkscrewed with anger.

"Rand Langley? I heard what you did at White Bridge, you traitor!" Sir Mulliner raised his sword and charged. Torsten stepped between them.

"No," Torsten said, low and measured.

Sir Mulliner panted like a wild beast, knuckles whitening as he squeezed the grip of his sword. Rand had met him in training but didn't know him well. But it was like Torsten said, he'd harmed Lucas, which meant he'd harmed them all.

"Let him live his few last moments knowing what he's done," Torsten went on. "Better yet, let him survive knowing. Let him live forever."

Sir Mulliner lowered his weapon and spat. Then, placing his hand on Torsten's shoulder, he guided him away. Just like in the tunnel, Torsten glanced back, and now Rand knew that it was indeed heartbreak gripping his expression. He looked like Sigrid had every time Rand came home, too drunk to stand up.

Torsten stopped and turned fully, ignoring Sir Mulliner's protests.

"The Sigrid I knew would be ashamed," Torsten said. "But you got her killed, too."

And then he was gone, Pi draped across his forearms. At the gates, Shieldsmen lined up, side by side with Serpent Guards, covering the retreat. The Glassmen formed an unbreakable wall of shields while the Shesaitju used polearms through the openings. They'd die eventually, but waves of their enemies crashed against them and were torn to pieces.

A worthy sacrifice, unlike Rand's.

His head fell back. Darkness closed in around his vision, but not as far as he hoped. He didn't die. He merely lay there, unable to move, each breath agonizingly painful.

Creak, creak, creak.

"What a shame." The otherworldly voice of a woman spoke after what could have been hours. At first, Rand thought it was Nesilia until the pale, dour face of her mystic pet appeared. She hovered over him with her continually vacillating form. Behind her, one of the wianu rose on all its tentacles to eclipse the sun. Its black, soulless eyes fixated on Rand.

The mystic touched down. The mystic scooped up the Glass Crown, letting the shards fall between the gaps in her long fingers.

"Yet, perhaps not a waste," she snickered.

She swept in front of Rand and joined the wianu in staring directly into his eyes. "You want the end now, don't you?" she said. "You pathetic, fragile creations always do."

Rand's lips quivered as he tried to reply, but he couldn't. He could only watch more of the fractured Glass Crown fall from her hand to be buried in the sand for all time. Forgotten.

"Don't worry, it's not your time yet, little one," she said.

She leaned over him and pressed her palm against his chest. Then, muttering under her breath, her hand started to glow, bright and golden like the rising sun. Energy surged through Rand's limbs. Blue smoke rose. His bones popped as his tangled limbs and broken ribs straightened. His neck cracked left, then right. His lungs inflated, and air rushed down his throat.

He shot forward, gasping. The mystic stroked his back, hushing him like a crying infant.

"There you are," she whispered. "You can't die yet, Rand Langley. How then would I ever be able to control my sister?"

XXIV

THE KNIGHT

Every part of him hurt, but Torsten walked, clutching the reins of the zhulong over which he'd secured Pi's body, refusing to ride it. For two days, the survivors of the ambush on Latiapur marched through the sweltering heat of the Black Sands.

Solemn. Weary. Defeated.

No one would ever know what happened to the dozens who stayed behind at the gates, bravely covering the retreat. Lucas had to be amongst them, as he hadn't been seen since Torsten dispatched him to find Pi, all too late.

Torsten found strange peace in the knowledge that his and Lucas' horses were also missing. They'd either broken off their hitches and ran, or Dellbar and Lord Jolly had indeed made it out alive.

Torsten had promised that chestnut mare her retirement. Just yet another failure...

The Shesaitju managed to herd many of the frightened zhulong so they could help the exodus. Torsten accepted only a single beast to transport Pi. He wanted to feel the burn in his arms and legs as he climbed and descended the dunes. He deserved it. He should've been there in the arena when all hell broke loose. Right at King Pi's side like the shield he was meant to be. Instead, Rand Langley's final betrayal was complete. He'd caused them to be separated and gotten Pi killed.

Whether or not Rand did it with his own two hands, or it was the result of a stampede, Torsten couldn't be sure. The boy's body was too bruised and bloody to tell. All Torsten knew was that it would take more than a miracle to bring Pi back to life again this time.

And while he lay across a zhulong, wrapped in blankets to keep out the heat, his bride yet lived. Mahraveh hadn't spoken since joining up with everyone, not to her guardian, who commanded the defense of the women and children marching with them. Not to Torsten. The most she'd offered was a sad look as she passed by and saw Pi's remains.

Shouting from up ahead slowed the migration. Shesaitju mounted on zhulong raced by, and as Torsten ascended a dune, he saw the small settlement in a clearing below, beside a rocky outcrop. Rather, what used to be a settlement. Charred structures and a few lonely palms surrounded a small oasis.

Bit'rudam had gone ahead, taking the cavalry on a sweep meant to ensure that more enemies weren't waiting to ambush them.

"This used to be my home," Mahraveh said, stepping up beside him. She, too, had refused a mount. "Saujibar. I learned most of what I know about fighting on these very dunes."

Torsten turned to face her. She looked every bit as battered as all of her newly homeless people. Her resplendent dress might as well have been rags.

"I'm alive because of you," Mahraveh said.

"And he's not," Torsten replied. He had no eyes. Otherwise, she'd have seen tears welling in them, but his expression must've revealed everything. He couldn't fight it. Couldn't manage a brave face.

She shook her head. "You sent him with me. I shouldn't have gone after Babrak, I shouldn't have—"

"No. The King's Shield failed him. I failed him."

"Your people won't believe that. Babrak wanted me because of my deeds, and Pi died for it."

"He wasn't a child anymore. He chose to marry you, here, in the name of peace."

"Will that matter?" Mahraveh asked.

"Will anything if Nesilia wins?"

Mahraveh exhaled through her teeth. "I should have killed Babrak when I had the chance," Mahraveh said. "Now, Nesilia has more allies."

"There are plenty I should've killed earlier, as well," Torsten answered. "I didn't. I desperately tried to see the light in them. Now, look where we are."

Mahraveh stepped closer and ran her fingers through Pi's hair. Torsten choked back tears he couldn't release. The boy actually looked peaceful, lying there. He'd fought so much just to live a normal life, to grow into the man all of Pantego hoped he would be. He did it in spite of Redstar, Nesilia, Liam, Oleander, even Torsten.

Torsten wondered if he and Oleander were finally together, without pain, without sadness. Still, he knew if there was any justice, those two would not find rest on the same plane.

"He was nothing like the rumors said," Mahraveh whispered. "I am honored to call him husband. I know what protecting him meant to you. It's how my father looked at me. I swear to you, Sir Unger, we will destroy Nesilia in his name. Whatever it takes."

Torsten swallowed against a dry throat. His lips were so chapped they'd already begun cracking and bleeding. "I don't know how much more I have to offer," he said, voice trembling.

Bit'rudam's voice echoed across the dunes, shouting something in Saitjuese.

"They found someone," Mahraveh relayed. Bit'rudam yelled some more. "A Glassman with one arm," she went on.

"Kaviel," Torsten whispered. He handed the zhulong reins to Mahraveh, offering her little choice but to take them. "Don't let him out of your sight." Then, looking back to Sir Mulliner and the other Shield-smen, he nodded for them to follow.

He never found it easy, moving through the sand. Maybe it was his size. The supple surface shifted beneath his every step, and his giant feet kept sliding outward, but he managed.

The heat, however, was a different story. By the time he reached the clearing of the ruined village, he was panting and sweating from every pore. He had to pause a short distance away from Bit'rudam to rest against a blackwood palm and catch his breath.

"No wonder they all kill each other," Sir Mulliner said as he caught up, also short of breath. It was much too hot for plate mail. He took a deep breath. "Who could be happy in a place this sweltering?"

"We're not as thin-skinned as you," Bit'rudam said, approaching on zhulongback. "The man requested to speak with Sir Unger. He's lucky it's daytime, or the wolves would already be feasting on him. As it stands, he's lucky to not have encountered sand snakes or pit lizards. The desert is not forgiving."

"Get your filthy hands off me!" Lord Jolly protested. Torsten leaned around the zhulong and saw him kicking at Serpent Guards. His hair was unkempt, his face coated by dirt and dried blood. His fine robes were tattered and equally stained. One of the guards managed to flip him and wrenched his only arm behind his back, shoving his face down into the sand.

"What in Iam's name are they doing?" Torsten asked. He went to step forward, but Bit'rudam trotted his zhulong into his path.

"He could be working with Babrak," Bit'rudam said.

"He's on the Royal Council, you dumb pound of shog!" Sir Mulliner barked, half-drawing his sword from its sheath. The other Shieldsmen joined him.

"As was your Yuri Darkings," Bit'rudam argued.

"He was at the ceremony!" yelled one of them.

Bit'rudam reached for his own weapon. "And now he's here. Maybe, he helped Babrak ambush us. Maybe all you pink-skins did." He barked something else in Saitjuese that didn't sound friendly. Lord Jolly protested even louder.

Mulliner stomped forward and growled, "Easy to say from atop one of your oversized swine."

Bit'rudam hopped down and puffed out his chest. "I don't need anything to take you down."

"Would you both stop it and get out of my way," Torsten yelled. He grasped one of the beast's tusks and pushed it aside so hard it squealed and nearly knocked Bit'rudam over.

Bit'rudam rattled off commands in Saitjuese, and at least a dozen Serpent Guards formed a line in front of Lord Jolly. Their dark eyes were the only parts of their faces visible beneath their horrifying masks. And even with their heavy armor and the heat, they barely breathed.

"You would dare draw your blades at him?" Sir Mulliner asked. His defense of Torsten was more surprising than anything, at least until the man reared back and punched Bit'rudam across the face.

They were both trained enough to know to disarm each other's weapon hands first. Since they couldn't fully draw them, they wrestled each other to the ground, rolling in the sand, punching and kicking.

The Serpent Guards started to march forward. The Shieldsmen armed themselves and did the same. One went to help Mulliner, but Bit'rudam was fast as a viper. He rolled free, kicked the interloper in the chest, then ducked under Mulliner's punch. He caught Mulliner under the armpit, flipped him over, and fell upon him.

"Get off him, in the name of our Ki—" Torsten stopped himself before he finished the word. Just the act of nearly speaking it caused his chest to constrict.

Sir Mulliner caught Bit'rudam in the jaw with a wild haymaker and scrambled free. He reversed the attack, climbing onto Bit'rudam and kneeing him in the side once, and when he tried to again, a spear lanced through the air, shaving his cheek.

Sir Mulliner staggered backward, dabbing at the fresh line of blood on his face. "You… you…"

Mahraveh arrived, parting the Shieldsmen, the zhulong carrying Pi in tow. Behind her, thousands of her people followed, all of them witnessing a skirmish break out between the elite soldiers of their respective kingdoms.

"My Caleef, I…" Bit'rudam spat out a gob of blood and fell into a bow.

She passed by him and Mulliner, and to the spear she'd thrown. It was lodged in the neck of a pit lizard that had been baking in the sun on the coast of the oasis.

"Bit'rudam, take the guards and sweep the rest of the village," she ordered. "We'll rest here in what little shade there is and keep moving at sundown when it's cooler. I must believe that it's the heat that has the commanders of *my* army acting like children."

Bit'rudam's cheeks flushed. He stammered over a response, then started issuing orders to the Serpent Guards. They promptly sheathed their weapons, fanning out across the ruins and leaving Lord Jolly lying in the sand, coughing.

"You could've killed me," Sir Mulliner said, incredulous.

"If I'd wanted, you'd be dead," Mahraveh replied. "I only mean to feed my people." She rocked the spear one way to jar it loose, then tore it free. Her response stunned the abrasive Shieldsman to silence.

"Sir Unger…" Lord Jolly rasped as he used his one arm to prop himself against the tree. Even that little exertion left him wheezing. "You made it. And you're all still getting along, I see."

Torsten forced himself to ignore everything else and rushed to the Lord from Crowfall. As he did, he noticed that another handful of pit lizards rested in the shallows of the oasis, their forked tongues hissing as they prepared for a meal.

"Where's Dellbar?" Torsten asked.

"Good to see you, too."

"This is no time for jokes. Where is the High Priest?"

"We could only calm one horse enough to ride. I sat with him for a while, but the heat had the thing's heart racing. Too much weight. I let Dellbar keep all the food we scavenged out of the stables, and he went out on his own."

"You sent a blind man alone across the Black Sands?" Torsten asked, incredulous.

"Sent?" Lord Jolly chuckled. "The drunkard didn't leave me much choice. He said, 'Iam will guide me,' and that I'd 'only slow him down.'"

"What a damned fool."

Lord Jolly shrugged, "Hey, at least he left me someplace with water… if those damn reptiles will ever let me get close. My throat feels like Elsewhere."

Torsten walked to the water, and the pit lizards backed away, not daring attack a man his size. He scooped up some water in his palms, intending to bring it to Lord Jolly, but he gulped down a mouthful first.

"If Dellbar doesn't make it, we won't have enough of the church with us to help," Torsten said as he approached with two palms full of the fresh, warm water.

"Have faith, Torsten," Jolly said. "He does."

Torsten angled his hands for Lord Jolly to drink. The nobleman didn't seem to care at all how demeaning it looked for a man of his stature to be lapping from another man's hand.

"Faith…" Torsten repeated as he did, low and brooding. He was running low on it. Iam had shown Himself and saved them at White Bridge, but hadn't made His presence known since, even when Pi, King of His chosen Kingdom, was killed. Maybe, He really had expended all

His being that day, manifesting in Dellbar. Perhaps, now, they were entirely on their own to save His kingdom.

"Sir Unger, who is it?" Mahraveh asked.

He wheeled around to see her approaching, a crowd of Shieldsmen at her back, gawking. Torsten imagined they'd never seen a woman like her. He hadn't.

"It's our Master of Ships," Torsten said. "He made it out alive."

"I'm thrilled to see you survived, my Lady," Jolly said. "Where's the King?"

Torsten shot Mahraveh a dour look. Again, his chest grew tight, and for the first time since their escape, Mahraveh's expression went rife with sadness, as if what had happened had only then sunk in. She bit her lip and stared down at the dark sand.

"By Iam…" Jolly whispered, only needing to look at them to realize the truth.

"Everyone, get your rest," Mahraveh said softly. "We don't have long. Babrak knows how to cross the desert."

"They aren't coming after us," Torsten replied.

"You don't know him. Babrak burned this place to the ground once before. He won't care that we have women and children with us. When they catch up, he'll hit with everything they have."

"But Babrak isn't in charge. Look behind us, nobody's coming except your faithful. Nesilia wants us alive. She wants us all back in Yarrington for her arrival."

"How do you know?" Mahraveh asked.

"The dead aren't entertaining enough for her," Torsten said. "She wants a crowd to bear witness to her glory, right beside the mountain where Iam damned her for eternity."

"Then we'll destroy her there," Mahraveh snarled, her dark eyes burning with conviction. Torsten wasn't sure what to say. Nesilia had an army of possessed men and women, a mystic commanding power Torsten couldn't believe, the Drav Cra and their warlocks, and legendary beasts able to control the seas. Even Liam had never gone up against such overwhelming odds.

Mahraveh strolled by him. "Just get some rest, Sir Unger," she muttered, resting her hand upon his shoulder. "Those of my people still with us will follow me to the end. But yours will be lost now. They may no longer have a King, but they need their commander."

Saujibar no longer had much to offer in the way of amenities. Sand had swept through even the ruins of the remaining structures, burying them. Barely enough remained to provide shade, even the trees were scant.

Torsten and the Glassmen claimed one on the far side of the oasis, so as to avoid any more trouble. Many thousands filled in the rest of the area, clinging to the low ridge for cover.

Water was in plenty, and the survivors of Latiapur desperately needed it. Food, not so much. There had been no time to grab supplies, so all they had were the pit lizards that Mahraveh's men hunted out of the oasis and dunes. Markless women were busy cooking and rationing them out. Enough for every person to each have a bite, if that. It wasn't much, but it would have to do until they reached a major settlement.

Torsten couldn't stomach any. He could barely get water down, and listening to his men complain about how hungry they still were or how chewy the lizard meat was, had his blood boiling.

Torsten stared at Pi's encapsulated body, lying in the sand like a rolled-up Breklian rug in the shadow of the resting zhulong which had carried him.

The first time Torsten buried him in the Royal Crypt, he'd been sad, but more so for his family—his mother. However, since Redstar's grip on the boy had waned, Torsten had grown close to him, learned how smart and capable he really was.

The Glass Kingdom hadn't only lost a King, Pantego had lost a boy that would've become a great man. One who bore all the best aspects of his famous parents and was only beginning to scratch the surface of his untold potential.

"Are You watching?" Torsten asked the sky. The sun reddened as it slowly fell across the dunes, making the black sand glow a deep purple. "Is this what You want?"

Silence answered him.

"Figures," Torsten growled.

"Look at them, Torsten," Sir Mulliner said as he hobbled over, nibbling on his chunk of lizard meat to make it last longer. He plopped down beside him. "Plotting away. We're inviting the hornets into the nest—not the best analogy, but you know what I mean."

Torsten followed the man's finger. He pointed to Mahraveh, staying in the wreckage of the largest building in Saujibar. It looked like it'd been some sort of mansion. However, now all that was left were crumbling clay walls and portions of a broken blackwood structure. She sat on one, sharpening a new spear while talking with Bit'rudam and some others who appeared to be former afhems. Serpent Guards kept anyone else away, forming a square around the ruin.

"How in Iam's name did they not see that fleet coming?" asked another Shieldsman.

"No wonder Liam crushed them," said one more.

"It's like they wanted to get our King killed."

Torsten whipped around, fist squeezed tight, ready to knock the head off the man that'd said that. The Shieldsman flinched, and Torsten somehow managed to compose himself while, in his peripherals, he saw the wind rustling the fringes of Pi's covering.

"I'm just saying," the Shieldsman said, shrugging. "Our King is gone, and his brand new wife is sitting over there without a scratch on her."

"I know I won't kneel for her," added another.

"No way."

"Relax boys, it's the *King's* shield for a reason," Sir Mulliner spat. "The foreigners can find their own new home. Yarrington isn't hot enough for them, anyway."

"Enough, all of you," Torsten said, quietly fuming. "Our King isn't even in the ground yet. This was his choice. To marry her. To make her his Queen, so that we might have a chance against what's coming."

"Sea monsters and Shesaitju?" a Shieldsman spoke. "That sounds like their enemies, not ours."

"I promise you, they are one and the same. They didn't get King Pi killed. We did by not protecting them, for not doing our job. We are the Shield... As far as I'm concerned the only people here unworthy of reentering Yarrington are all of us."

None replied out loud, just a few muted grumbles as they all returned to prior conversations.

"Not the best way to inspire loyalty," Sir Mulliner said to Torsten as he scooted closer.

"I shouldn't need to," Torsten bristled. "Everyone knows what we're up against."

"We know what we saw. 'Nesilia, reborn.' But they're all right. All we saw were the enemies of our supposed new Queen."

"And did you miss the mystic sailing with them? Or beasts made of pure darkness? Uriah and I really did fail this Order if you're all so blind. If only Lucas…" Torsten stopped. With all of the starvation, thirst, and dramatics, he'd forgotten about the young man who'd helped him when no one else would.

He wasn't with them, which meant he was either hiding in Latiapur or dead. The other option, Torsten didn't want to imagine. Who knew if Nesilia might guide more demons of Elsewhere to claim people. He could only hope Lucas would be strong enough to resist.

Sir Mulliner opened his mouth to respond when he was interrupted by Lord Jolly, still leaning on the other side of the tree. His eyes had been closed, but clearly, he wasn't sleeping.

"She's not Queen of anything," Jolly said.

"What are you talking about, old man?" Mulliner asked. "They spoke the vows before Dellbar the Holy. We all heard it."

"It's almost like Nesilia was waiting for that exact moment," Torsten added. "What joy she'd take watching us tear each other to pieces."

Lord Jolly sighed loudly. "You Shieldsmen really are out of touch. I guess not being able to get married makes you forget certain… things."

"Would you just say whatever it is you want to say?" Mulliner said.

"The vows mean nothing if the marriage isn't consummated before the Eyes of Iam," Jolly said.

Torsten turned to him. "So it'll be annulled?"

"I apologize for the crudeness, but unless she managed to get King Pi's pants down while the arena was flooding, in the eyes of our King-dom, nothing happened."

Mulliner snickered. "That's right. Nobles and their rules. Do you think they realize that?" He nodded in Mahraveh's direction.

"If they don't, we can't say a word until we get them to Yarring-ton," Torsten said. "No matter what she is to us, we need this army."

"Only if I get to be the one to tell them," Mulliner said.

Torsten scowled, and Mulliner shrank back.

"So, the throne will remain empty," Torsten ruminated. "Pi was the last of the Nothhelms. We have no King left to shield."

"The last direct descendant of Liam, sure, but not the last. Liam's father was a purest and did what he could to cleanse the bloodline. Liam's war against his brother didn't help either. But there are distant cousins bearing the blood of King Autla, no matter how diluted."

"Governor Nantby was a fifth cousin, I believe," Mulliner remarked.

"I fear his fate is worse than death," Torsten said.

"Not only him," Jolly went on. "Lord Eveliss, Duke of Marimount goes back a few generations. Lord Rapheusto Messier in West Vale… and more. Liam's father sent all his relations away from Yarrington because he didn't trust them nearby."

"But the Jollys were already in the bitter North." Torsten sat up. If he had eyes, they'd be wide open. "Wardric told me once. The first of your family's name was brother to the wife of King Autla and vowed to defend them against the Drav Cra barbarians for all eternity. It's true, isn't it."

"An age ago, yes."

"Better you than another foreigner," Mulliner said. "Though, Oleander might have scared Nesilia off, eh?" he nudged Torsten in the side, and even though he wanted to be mad, Torsten couldn't help but chuckle.

"Maybe that's why she waited so long to return."

"You'll find the nobility of Yarrington a much tighter circle than either of you imagined," Lord Jolly said, clearly not amused. "Many families more powerful than mine claim relation. With the throne empty, they'll all come crawling out of the weeds to start the next great dynasty."

"Well, like Torsten says, if Nesilia wins, none of that will matter," Mulliner said.

"It will if we win," Torsten replied. "But we can't let any of this get in the way of this war. We need the forces of every fortress and city west of the gorge helping us defend Yarrington."

"Then Caleef Mahraveh must be told the truth," Lord Jolly said. "Otherwise, they'll see her only as an occupying force."

"Leave her to me, and I'll leave the court to you," Torsten told Lord Jolly. "A King has died. We will declare observation of his passing in the name of Iam, through to the next Dawning. By then, we'll either all be dead, or the Glass Kingdom will be reborn."

"Perhaps, either way, it's time for it to end…"

"That isn't funny, Lord Jolly," Mulliner said.

"It wasn't meant to be."

He groaned as he stood, then strode over to the oasis for some water. Torsten watched him go. He was a knowledgeable man. Not overly impressive in any way, but loyal. A friend to the Crown who left Crowfall the moment he was summoned to help guide King Pi.

"You know it'll be your choice," Sir Mulliner whispered.

"What?" Torsten asked.

"The King. Master of Warfare. Wearer of White. Whoever the King's Shield and the Glass army support, nobody else will be able to raise an army substantial enough to take the throne by force."

Torsten drew a long, ragged breath. It was true. After the war against Muskigo, and all of Liam's before that, Pantego's population had suffered. Maybe a city like Westvale could raise enough people to fight, but they'd be conscripts, not an army.

His gaze drifted back toward Pi's body. He caught Mahraveh watching them, probably discussing their next move as well. As if any of it mattered.

"Let's survive first," Torsten said. "We've lost enough already."

XXV

THE MYSTIC

Tum Tum led them through the city like he'd lived there his whole life. Through alleys and caverns, and great halls filled with columns as tall and thick as the oldest trees she'd ever seen. It was impressive. Sora supposed the stories were true, the dwarves had minds like their treasure boxes. Once something went in, it would never likely leave.

Presently, they stood in a quaint living space. Each piece of furniture was a permanent fixture carved out of the floors and walls—chairs, sofas, tables. Nothing looked remotely comfortable to sit on, and the table was far lower than any Sora would be able to eat at.

"Me pa's house," Tum Tum said, the slightest tremble to his voice. "S'pose'n he won't be needin it no more."

Sora knew that feeling well. Loneliness.

"I'm so sorry for your loss, Tum Tum," Lucindur said.

Sora stared through the small window, hoping they'd truly lost the clanbreakers. Several dwarves in armor patrolled the city, and some of them actually appeared to be urgent about something. Sora wondered if there was already a kingdom-wide search party. Neither Lorgit nor Gargamane was likely to ignore her attack.

"Loss," Tum Tum said dismissively. "Haven't seen him in a long time. It's sad, but he wouldn't have accepted me back, anyway."

"Odd customs your people have," Lucindur said.

"Ye should be talkin!" he shouted, though his tone spoke of joviality. "I just left yer land, and it was queer as a snake in flight."

"You don't think this'll be the first place they'll look for you?" Lucindur asked.

"Don't think anyone would be stupid enough to stay in the city, do ye?" Tum Tum said, smiling. "They'll be lookin in all the possible exits, not some rundown old shack."

"Still can't believe me own father would be so callous to abandon the outside world," Brouben said, chin to his chest.

"If the King tells the truth, it's understandable," Sora said, still focused on the scurrying guards. "My people stole your lands. Destroyed your world. Drove you out."

"Yer people?" Tum Tum said. "Yer people have suffered the same injustices as me own."

"Let's not be coy, Dwotratum," Sora said, turning toward them.

The use of the dwarf's real name gave him pause, but only long enough for Sora to continue.

"I'm as much a woman of the Glass as anyone born in Yarrington," she said. "You've spent more time in Panping than I have."

"So, ye a mystic, then?" Brouben asked.

"Not in the sense you might be thinking," she answered. "Though my mother was a powerful one."

Tum Tum and Lucindur shot looks at one another.

"I thought ye didn't know who yer parents were," Tum Tum asked.

"I didn't… not until recently." She pushed her hair behind her ear. "But that's not important right now, is it?"

"Aye, mystic or not, that's some power ye got," Brouben said.

Sora smiled as she sat on one of the hard, stone chairs by the table. "Just tricks I've picked up."

"Ever modest, Sora is," Tum Tum said, taking her spot at the window, looking out for guards. "All right. So what be the plan?"

Sora's smile faded. "I don't know."

"This all seems like a bedtime tale," Brouben said. "Don't feel real."

"Sounds like your people have strange bedtime tales as well as customs," Lucindur said.

"Greater truth ain't never been told!" Brouben said. He strode forward and grabbed Sora by the hand. "Ms. Sora, on behalf of my people, I'm sorry for how ye been treated."

Sora thought back to all her encounters with dwarves, starting with Grint. Most of them weren't memorable for good reasons. But then she regarded Tum Tum, standing by the window. Since the moment she met him in Winde Port, he'd been kind and helpful. He took care of her while she sulked on Kazimir's ship.

"You're not all bad," she said, placing her own hand atop his. "Thank you."

"We've got to find Whitney and get out of here," Lucindur said, breaking the moment.

Tum Tum swore, looking out at the city beyond. The chaos had stopped, but now, the streets filled with dwarves prattling on about the event, cleaning up the results. Guards marched by in a constant flow.

"No way we're goin out there right now," he said. "The thief's on his own."

"Anyone sees him, he's dead on the spot," Brouben said, joining Tum Tum at the window.

"He is not dying," Sora said matter-of-factly. "I'll lay waste to this place if I have to."

"She's scary," Brouben whispered, though loud enough for everyone to hear.

"Sora, dear," Lucindur said, "are you all right?"

Sora thought back to the feeling she'd gotten just before unleashing her fury on Gargamane. How she'd done it without even hesitating. Brouben was right. She was scary. It scared her, too. However, she also knew that without her power, the chances of them ever getting out of Balonhearth were slim. And what if they did?

Out of the frying pan. Into the fire, she thought.

"All right?" Sora laughed mirthlessly. "I think 'all right' is the last thing any of us is, don't you? What are we supposed to do, Lucindur? We're stuck inside a mountain with an army after us. Whitney and Aquira are out there without even the knowledge that they are being hunted down—"

"Some things are just out of our hands, Girly," Tum Tum said.

"Not this," Sora said. "This is my problem, and I'm going to fix it."

"Your problem?" Lucindur scoffed. "Last I checked, this was all our problems when we agreed to take on Nesilia, together."

"You weren't the one possessed by her. Made to look on while she slaughtered the Strongiron—" Sora noticed Brouben in the corner of her eye and stopped herself. Luckily, he was focused on the window while they argued amongst each other.

"But it isn't your fault," Lucindur said. "None of it."

"That's right," Tum Tum added. "Not even what happened on Kazimir's ship. That wasn't even yer magic."

"I know," Sora said. "Whitney told me it was the Sanguine Lords. But, I just can't help thinking I could've stopped it."

"I saw them Lords—nothin but mist and smoke. Wasn't no stoppin it ye could've done." He took a seat beside Lucindur. "Ye know what's the worst?"

Lucindur and Sora eyed him suspiciously.

"When someone fightin gods and yiggin goddesses thinks they're weak for havin lost. Ye know what makes em gods, eh? They're shog-shuckin gods!"

Sora chuckled again. This time, she felt a little relief, but it was gone just as quick.

"I fell right into her hands, again," she said. "That vile woman, Freydis… she was the one he saw. Nesilia sent her here already, and we just walked right into it."

As if having a sudden realization, her attention snapped to Brouben. She stood, hands balled into fists. "Did you know Freydis was here?"

"No idea," he said.

"Are you playing us?" Sora demanded.

"I swear. She must've come when I was on me way back from White Bridge. How could I not've seen this?" He groaned.

"Stop all this blaming," Lucindur said, placing her hand on Sora's shoulder to sit her back down. "You didn't ask for Nesilia to possess you, Sora. None of us knew she'd sent the Drav Cra warlock here."

Sora supposed Lucindur was right. There was no way for any of them to know that King Lorgit had been turned. And he had been. Even if he thought staying out of things was his choice, Sora knew the fear that Freydis could inflict upon people, and it was evident in his eyes when he spoke of her.

Even if they'd known Freydis had been here, what could they've done anyway? The Brike Stone was their only hope.

Then a thought hit her.

"Why did she do that?" Sora asked.

"What?" Lucindur said.

"Why did she send Freydis here, of all places?"

"What are you getting at?" Lucindur asked.

"Ye think she knew about the lot of ye bein after the stone?" Brouben asked.

Sora shook her head. "I think if she knew that, she'd have just taken it herself."

"Or destroyed it," Tum Tum added.

They all nodded in agreement.

"She might have sent her followers all over Pantego to gain more," Lucindur said. "To build her army."

"Mmm, perhaps," Sora assented her agreement.

"However," Lucindur said, "I don't think there's any help to be had by questioning such things or worrying about who's on her side now. We need a plan." She took a seat across from Sora and removed the salfio, her enchanted musical instrument, from her back.

"Right, but what if she's expecting this? All of this? What if we are just enabling her plan?" Sora bit her lip. "You think Whitney is okay?"

"He's always okay," Tum Tum assured her. "Like a plague ye can't rid yerself of."

Sora closed her eyes and took a breath.

"It was a joke, Lass, I swear," Tum Tum said. "Truth is, if that dirty thief's successful, his little plan might've saved the whole yiggin world."

"When," Sora said. "*When* he is successful."

Tum Tum left his post by the window and placed both palms against the table.

"Right, so that be it, huh?" he said. "I say we move forward like he's already done it."

"What do you mean?" Sora asked.

"I mean he ain't failed none of us yet, has he? Yiggin Exile, I bet that quake was his causin too! The next step be to find Nesilia, aye? Well, how were we gonna do that?"

Sora's stomach sank. She knew everyone would be counting on her to somehow tap into the Buried Goddess' thoughts and find her, wherever she was. But even in the time it took for them to travel from Glinthaven to Balonhearth, Sora hadn't seen any signs of Nesilia. Even her dreams had been pleasant.

They looked to her, nonetheless.

"She's in Yaolin, right?" Sora said, thinking it out for herself.

"She *was* in Yaolin," Lucindur corrected. "That was weeks ago. If we were able to make the trip here, she could have made it halfway across Pantego by now. Probably further with her abilities."

"Restricted by the upyr host, though," Brouben offered. "I've seen her."

"Right, so she can't go out into daylight," Sora said. "But when she was… me, she traveled from Winter's Thumb to Brekliodad completely underground. We have to assume she could do the same now if she wanted to. Maybe that's why she wants the Three Kingdoms on her side."

"Damn," Tum Tum swore.

"I'm sorry," Sora said, head bowed. Then, looking up, tears forming, she said, "I've got nothing."

She could see the disappointment etched on their faces, but like any good friends, they comforted her. Brouben, too, even after she'd snapped at him, telling her they'd figure something out.

But what if they didn't? Part of her wondered if her fear of Nesilia was keeping her from being able to tap in. It was a genuine concern that, by allowing her mind to be totally freed, she would find herself right back in Nowhere and under Nesilia's control. It might've been selfish, but Sora would rather be dead than be back in that place.

Then, she realized that it wouldn't just be her that would be dead if she couldn't find Nesilia. Whitney would die too. And Aquira. All of them. Everyone in all of Pantego and anything beyond—all dead because of Sora's fear.

"We could just wait," Tum Tum said. It sounded like a question.

"For?" Lucindur asked.

"Beats me. Her to strike, or attack, or whatever she's plannin?"

"We can't do that," Sora said. "By then, it might be too late. By all accounts, she's already gathered her army. She has Queen Bliss and all the demons. There won't even be a fight."

"She's right, it might already be too late," Lucindur said. "We will need a solid plan in order to get close to her."

"Didn't ye say she came to ye in yer dreams?" Tum Tum asked. "Can't ye do that again?"

"I can't control it," Sora said. "And what if she can see into my mind and learn about the stone? What if opening up to her like that lets her take control of me again? I..."

Lucindur gave her arm a comforting squeeze. "We can't risk the unknown."

Sora swallowed hard. She knew what needed to be done. Instead, she just didn't want to do it. Thoughts of Nowhere tortured her. The thought of getting stuck there again, so close to Nesilia—it was more than she could bear. But everyone was counting on her.

"This could be our last chance," Sora said.

"For?" Lucindur followed Sora's gaze to her salfio.

"Let's find her."

"And risk her and her army of monsters finding us first? What about all these people?"

"You mean the people who just tried to have us killed for trying to save them?" Sora asked. "They can take care of themselves... or not."

Sora couldn't believe her own words. It was that feeling again inside of her, that new, ruthless version of herself that she could only imagine was leftover from when Nesilia was in there. Or... was Nesilia *still* in there?

She pushed the thought away. There was no time for it. Whether she liked it or not, this was the way.

"My fire didn't cause the distraction we needed," she said, counting off on her fingers. "Whitney is sneaking through the vault with no idea that if he's found, they're going to kill him on the spot. King Lorgit thinks Nesilia will leave him be."

"And?" Lucindur said.

"So let's show him that she isn't and bring her monsters here."

"Oh, I like this one," Tum Tum said.

"What's this about monsters?" Brouben asked.

Lucindur pointed toward the city. "You are really going to let these people fend for themselves? We know what my power does. This place will be crawling with her slaves in seconds."

"We're running out of choices."

"It's not so simple," Lucindur said.

"None of it is," Tum Tum argued. "Don't mean we can't try."

"The clanbreakers won't be able to stop us in the chaos. And maybe, just maybe, it'll convince Lorgit to help us."

"People will die," Lucindur said.

"They'll die anyway!" Sora argued.

"Stop," Tum Tum said firmly, standing on the chair and drawing all of their attention. "This ain't yer home, or mine any longer. If we do this, knowing what it'll bring, then it be up to Brouben to decide."

Sora and the others all looked to the Prince, whose attention had returned to the many dwarves roaming the streets outside the window. He watched his people with a thousand-meter-gaze.

"Yer sayin ye have a way of finding Nesilia, but it'll reveal where we be?" Brouben asked.

"Yes," Lucindur said. "It draws her creatures like moths to a flame."

"Goblins. Grimaurs. Probably worse," Sora added.

"And she'll wanna come get ye?"

"Without a doubt."

He exhaled slowly and scratched his beard. "So, the Three Kingdoms can either wait around for her to turn on us or maybe, join the fight today."

"Nesilia only cares about getting to me," Sora said. "All she'll know is that we're hiding here. She won't have to know your people are even involved."

"And yet, we should be," Brouben said. "Ye say Nesilia slaughtered the Strongirons to send a message, and for whatever reasons, I trust ye. We dwarves pride ourselves on bein excellent judges of character, me father excluded."

"I tried to tell em that," Tum Tum chimed it.

Brouben took another long moment of reflection, then nodded firmly. "If this be what it takes, then I say, find her. We dwarves are built for fightin. Let her monsters come, and we'll show them the might of the Dragon's Tail."

"Perfect," Sora said.

"Are you sure?" Lucindur asked.

"Ye keep forgettin, I saw what Nesilia can do," Brouben said. "Only reason I'm back here is to warn me father, and he threw me out like the trash. We've gotta stop her, no matter what it takes. We either fight today or die tomorrow."

Tum Tum slapped Brouben on the back. "Glad to be back by yer side, brother!"

"Glad to have ye back. Just wish it were under different circumstances."

Lucindur shook her head. "I don't know. We should wait until we were in a more defensible position before showing our cards. Until we have the stone, at least."

"I'd think in a mountain like this, surrounded by warriors like these dwarves," Sora said, eyeing Brouben, "we won't find a more defensible position."

"She ain't wrong there," Tum Tum said.

"Nope," Brouben agreed.

"Be that as it may, my magic only works if I have something that belongs to the one we seek," Lucindur said. "Being as how she is a goddess, I doubt she left one of her possessions lying around."

Sora's stomach turned over. That's exactly what Nesilia had done. Sora was her possession, and she'd left her, empty and alone. What other choice did she have, but this? She didn't know how to access their link to each other or the implications of doing so. She couldn't even be sure if the vision Nesilia last gave her of Yaolin was actually just a dream. Or even if Nesilia was showing her lies. This time, they had to be entirely sure, and Lucindur's powers would allow that.

"Me," Sora said, low.

"What?" Tum Tum and Lucindur replied together.

"She possessed me, mind and body. If you can't use me to find her, you won't be able to use anything."

"That seems dangerous," Tum Tum said.

"And what isn't dangerous?" Sora asked. "We are talking about gods and goddesses and the end of all life. Brouben is risking his own people for us. This is it. This is our chance. It's now or never."

"What about Whitney?" Lucindur asked.

"If he don't get that stone, we are all dead anyway," Tum Tum reminded them.

"He's right," Sora offered. "And maybe Whitney needs our help for once. We give him a real distraction. If he can't get out with the stone during this, then what kind of thief is he?"

"She's right," Tum Tum returned, grinning.

"So, it's settled. We find Nesilia, we find Whitney, and cause chaos in the city enough for us all to escape."

"What if she comes herself?" Lucindur asked.

It was a question Sora hadn't considered. Until then, she figured it would just be more goblins and the like.

"Let's not think about that," Lucindur answered herself, beating Sora to it. "It's a fine plan as any."

"Only one we got," Tum Tum said. "Whitney would be proud."

"Right. Okay, so how do we do this?" Sora asked.

Lucindur looked nervous. "Tum Tum, we need quiet and privacy."

It was a simple request said with kindness, and Tum Tum took the hint, rose, and grabbed Brouben by the arm. "C'mon, me old friend. Let's go stand guard. Tell me everythin about yer fight with the goddess, and I'll tell ye mine."

Brouben looked around nervously, then conceded. Together, they moved into an adjacent room.

"Maybe me father's got some of his old weapons still in here. I could use a new hammer," Tum Tum said as he closed the door.

When they were gone, Lucindur said, "My gift. Lightmancery... Have you ever seen it in practice?"

She hadn't. However, Wetzel's lessons, although not comprehensive, were sufficient. She'd learned about all kinds of magics from all over Pantego, both old and timely. There hadn't been much about the Glintish folk in his books, but enough to know what Lightmancing entailed.

Sora shook her head. "No, but I've read of it."

"Right. Well, in practice, it can be... jarring."

"I used to cut my hands and arms. I understand the risks, Lucy." Using the name Whitney had given her provided slight comfort. It was silly, but Sora would accept all the comfort she could. "But what choice do we have?"

Lucindur nodded. "Right you are. Okay, now, I want you to close your eyes and relax."

After a long, deep breath, Sora closed her eyes, and panic overwhelmed her. Darkness had been taunting her for as long as she could recall since the Citadel. It was almost like she could feel Nesilia reaching out for her mind, teasing her, in control. Her eyelids shot open, and she was breathing heavily.

"Sorry," she said. "I just need a second." She didn't want to let Nesilia in again, didn't want to give her that power, even if it would help accomplish the same goals as Lucindur's magic. *They* needed to be on the offense this time. Nesilia couldn't be given a chance to deceive.

"Take your time," Lucindur said, tuning her salfio.

After a few deep breaths in through her nose and out through her mouth, Sora nodded. "I'm ready."

"Keep breathing and clear your mind," Lucindur told her.

Lucindur strummed her salfio. The notes were beautiful, reminding Sora of the sounds which echoed through the streets of Glinthaven. Actually, it reminded her so much of Fabian "Feel Good" Saravia, her favorite bard that would frequent Troborough's Twilight Manor.

This time, she didn't close her eyes but watched as little dots of light sped through the air around them. It was gorgeous and mesmerizing. Faintly, she heard Lucindur singing, but the words hardly mattered.

The next instant, Sora witnessed bright, colorful light swirling all around her. She had the sensation of falling, but it wasn't scary at all. It was relaxing, wonderful, beautiful. Over the years, she'd experienced many things magical—fire from her hands, mending wounds, and far darker things while under Nesilia's control. She'd been to Elsewhere and back again, but nothing felt quite like this.

A moment later, she stood in the middle of a boundless plain full of tall grasses and wildflowers. It was chilly, but not cold. A gentle wind sent her hair and kimono flapping, but it was nice. Before her stood nothing but greens and yellows, browns and oranges—a serene landscape where birds and animals could live harmoniously, swooping in and out, leaping from stalk to stalk.

But there were no animals. Nothing living, as if all had been terrified of what was to come.

A lone tree stood, tall and proud. Even in summer, it had no leaves, but the trunk was thick as a zhulong.

Her breath caught when, beyond the tree, she noticed a plume of black smoke billowing. It was a sight she'd seen far too many times—a village in flames. Then, she heard it—the shouts of the villagers, cries of anguish as their loved ones burned or bled to death in the streets. She thought back to all those she'd known and lost in Troborough at the hands of the Black Sandsmen.

It was amazing how quickly the threat of the Shesaitju disintegrated when something as violent and capricious as the Buried Goddess was at large.

Without delay, she started toward the village, unsure if she was seeing the past, present, or even future in this vision created by Lucindur's magic.

A dark shadow cast itself over the prairie some distance off, and Sora looked above and beyond to find its source. A gasp, stifled by her hand over her mouth, echoed. It was no shadow but an army. She ducked low, letting the tall grass hide her, then slid behind the tree and waited.

Her breath came in, stunted and sharp. This was a familiar feeling, a familiar fear. She didn't even need to look to know what she would see.

Nesilia, the Buried Goddess, would be at the head of that army like a king off to battle in the warm days of spring.

She didn't know if she could die in one of these magical visions, but she wasn't keen on finding out. She tried to steady her breathing. Peering around the tree, she saw two faces she knew intimately. Nesilia and Aihara Na. In truth, it was the Spider Queen Bliss, Nesilia's sister and the One Who Remained. Once enemies, now they led an army of creatures so vile it brought the taste of vomit to Sora's tongue.

Spiders by the thousands gathered around Aihara Na, rolling over the grasses like waves in the sea. Goblins, grimaurs, and even more monsters followed behind them—things Sora didn't recognize. Though, what horrified her more than any of it were the legions of humans serving them, their eyes entirely black and wrapped in pulsing, black veins. And not only them, but wolves as well, the possession twisting them into something hellish.

Sora swore. They were heading right for her, and she wasn't

convinced a simple cover like the tree or grass would hide her, and it certainly wouldn't mask her scent from the beasts.

"Stay calm," she said, but couldn't heed her own advice.

The worst part was that she'd located Nesilia, but what good did it do?

If only she knew which village they'd just razed. Were they in the North near Westvale?

The weather hinted that they were farther south, perhaps where Lilith's Mill used to be? Had they continued the work across the great plains that the Shesaitju had started? There was just no telling.

Sora's own thoughts made her sick. In that village, so many people would be dead and injured, their homes and businesses gone, and she thought of it so flippantly.

No, she had to tell herself. *There's nothing you can do about saving this village, but you can still save the world.*

Save the world. As if that were such a simple task.

The sounds of the army were now upon her. With her back to the tree, she was still well-hidden, and as long as they kept to the other side, at least they wouldn't see her, but it was only a matter of time before one of the hounds smelled her.

But could they smell her? She wasn't really there, was she? The body produced a smell, but what of the spirit? Was she corporeal there? If only she'd taken the time to ask Lucindur questions instead of relying on fuzzy memories.

Whitney had been corporeal to her when he found her in Nowhere, but Nowhere was a realm of the spirit. This... this appeared to be Pantego in its natural state.

Once again, looking beyond the treetrunk, Sora saw Nesilia, but she couldn't hear her words even though her mouth moved. Sora had to get closer. She'd trained with Whitney long enough to know how to move unheard, but would it work here?

She shook her head, trying to dispense of all negative thinking. She had one shot at this. One chance to find Nesilia, to learn of her plan, and to get the Brike Stone—which she could only pray and hope Whitney had found—to wherever they might be able to stop this once and for all.

Before she could change her mind, Sora slipped out from behind the safety of her hiding place and snuck toward the mass of evil that was Nesilia's army. Through the grasses she went until, finally, she found herself flanking Nesilia. Her heart beat in her throat.

"I want to devour them," Bliss said. "Eviscerate them, one by one, while the others watch."

"Anger only causes mistakes," Nesilia said. "You must learn to exact revenge cooly, and calmly."

"For a thousand years, I've inhabited a body vaguely like this one." She extended her arm, where an oversized spider crawled up toward her hand. "We are always calm as we spin our meals."

Nesilia snickered. "When we get to Yarrington, there will be plenty to eat."

"Yes. Iam's followers are soft and ripe. I wish you'd let me have a taste of the one we've captured."

"He has his role to play, as does my host's brother."

Yarrington? Sora thought, focusing on the one word in their discussion that mattered.

Sora was crouching and walking, keeping pace with the army. Then, her foot found a hole in the soil, and she tripped. She was careful to make no noise, but when she rose, she was staring directly into Nesilia's eyes.

The Buried Goddess didn't charge. She merely sneered and whispered, "I see you."

XXVI

THE TRAITOR

Rand Langley walked the streets of Latiapur. What was left of it, at least. After the stampeding zhulong and the raging wianu, it looked like it'd been struck by a tidal wave as tall as Mount Lister. A roar echoed from the water-filled arena. Rand winced. Even all these days later, a line of Shesaitju warriors marched from it, bound at the wrists. One by one, they were fed to the beasts if they refused to bow before the warlord called Babrak. And the women and children? Their fates were far less swift.

Rand could barely stomach the sounds of Babrak's army ravaging the survivors. The Shesaitju weren't known for their kindness to those they defeated. Pi was lucky he died when he did.

Nobody here is lucky, Rand told himself.

A scream reminded him of that, and his face screwed up as he climbed the first step up the palace.

"Come along, little human, she's here," the mystic Bliss summoned, wagging her finger as she soared a circle around him. Then, she soared up, the bottom of her frayed robe wriggling like tendrils of fire.

"I'm coming," Rand grumbled. *At my own yigging speed,* he thought. The mystic may have breathed life back into him, but his body felt as battered as ever, and his legs like anchors dragging him down upon each step.

He tried not to look at the two warriors on the ridge to his right, arguing and playing tug-o-war over a women's dress, her still in it. He tried to ignore the fresh blood marking the polished stone of the steps slick, seeping into all the elaborate carvings along its surfaces.

I told them to run, he reminded himself. And the small voice at the back of his mind replied, *it was already too late.*

"Smile little Glassman," Babrak said to him. The big man stood atop the stairs, hands folded behind his head as he stretched his full belly. Flaking black paint coated every inch of his skin. It was an odd thing, and something Rand wasn't sure the former afhem even realized, how he'd painted over history—all of his many tattoos representing his tribe, his family, his Kingdom… all of it was gone.

Rand wanted to smack the satisfied expression right off his face. He, the conqueror who had done nothing, who now enjoyed the fruits of the Boiling Keep. Without Sigrid and Nesilia, he'd still be in his little corner of the desert complaining that a woman took the position he coveted.

"Why in Elsewhere would she choose to help you?" Rand spat.

"Excuse me?" Babrak answered, his features drooping into a deep scowl. Rand only then realized that he'd said that out loud and not in his own head.

"She wants to make a better, new world," Rand went on, deciding to commit to the jab. "You seem like more of the same."

Babrak stopped stretching and lumbered forward. He may not have been fit, but he was massive. Terrifyingly so. At least Rand would go down fighting. Better than being trampled like a coward and a traitor.

"Who do you think you are, boy?" Babrak sneered.

"Someone with eyes."

Babrak reached out and held his tremendous hand just over the top of Rand's head. "The witch says you're untouchable, but I could crush your skull like a rotten bellot."

Rand sucked in a breath. His blood boiled. "Do it then," he whispered through his teeth, and he meant it. He'd seen the future and would welcome death.

Babrak's brow furrowed as Rand leaned into the giant man's grip. The tips of his fingers dug into the sides of Rand's head.

"It'll be one less outsider," Rand went on.

The lump in Babrak's throat bobbed. Then, sneering, he pulled his hand away. "You Glassmen have truly lost it. Good work killing the boy-King, though. How very brave of you." He turned and entered the Keep, his laughter echoing within the courtyard.

Rand let out a mouthful of air. He blinked and looked around. For a moment, he'd forgotten where he was, and all the terrors of war surrounding him. A few seconds hearing the screams and cries of the victors sacking a city that was once their capital reminded him.

He followed Babrak inside, only to find the man absorbing the adoration of the palace sages. Everyone else in the city suffered, but not these ball-less fools. They kowtowed in a line leading to the throne room, foreheads touching the sand.

"So, now you all see how we have been deceived," Babrak spoke as he crossed the room, rotating slowly to address them all. "Mahraveh was no Caleef, just a scared little orphan without her daddy. And now, she abandoned all of you here to die. A true Shesaitju would have fought to the death!"

He unleashed a deeper, heartier chortle, one that made Rand's blood start to boil. Then, he stopped before one of the bowing sages, knelt with all the great effort it took for a man his size and lifted the baby-faced man's chin with one finger. The sage trembled.

"Don't be afraid, my child," Babrak said. "The Current is with us. The usurpers are gone."

"Do you ever stop blathering?" Bliss asked, appearing from behind a golden column. Her half-spectral being floated around Babrak, and then fluttered to the doors of the throne room.

Babrak forcefully removed his finger, and the sages chin fell, bouncing on the floor. "I appreciate the help, witch. But I think it's time that you leave my city. We have a lot of work to do."

"That wasn't the arrangement," a voice carried. Rand's heart stuttered upon hearing it. He could never forget that voice, even if it wasn't exactly Sigrid's. He pushed by Babrak and found Nesilia lying horizontally across the coral throne with her feet up on the armrest. Then, he stopped.

The body of a sage lay on the platform before her, throat cut open.

Nesilia held a goblet filled with liquid that was dark like wine, but much too red to be. She stirred it once with one of her long fingers, sucked it, then brought the rim to her mouth. Her dark eyes flickered as she sipped, then she licked the remnants from her lips.

"I must say, more and more, I grow to enjoy this body," she said. "And they call this state of being a curse. Perhaps I should have left the Sanguine Lords intact. Clearly, they weren't as worthless as so many other gods."

"I hope you don't mean me, dear sister," Bliss said as she swept fully into the room, playfully swerving around the columns.

"You again," Babrak said to Nesilia, terse. "I think you found the wrong seat."

Nesilia took another long, indulgent gulp out of the goblet, then swished it around in her mouth. As she did, she reclined to make herself more comfortable.

"I needed to get off my feet," she said, mouth stained. "Speeding around Pantego all night in this body is... exhausting. And finally giving our cowardly brother the fate he deserved really took it out of me." She let her head sag back over the armrest and stretched out her legs.

"That throne is not meant for the likes of you," Babrak said. "Get. Up."

Nesilia rolled her head to the side, cracking a few vertebrae.

"I said get up!" Babrak roared.

Nesilia sighed. "If you insist." She swept her legs one after the other and pushed off to her feet. Then, in a flash, she was behind Babrak. She gave him a shove in the back, and he flew forward like he was no bigger than a child. He stumbled over the lip of the Sea Door.

Right as he dropped, Bliss flicked her fingers, and a vine grew from the floor and lashed his ankle. It heaved him back up, and dumped him on the floor, huffing for air.

"You think you can do that to me?" Babrak hissed as he got to his hands and knees. However, all the former bravado was gone.

"I think I just did." Nesilia strolled by him, taking her time, hips swaying, ankles crossing over one another with each step. "I may have promised you that chair in exchange for helping me, but I didn't promise you'd be alive when you sit in it," she said. She kicked

Babrak in his belly, and he flipped up, back smashing against the coral throne.

"Now, stay there like a good dog and be quiet."

Babrak coughed in response.

"And you." Nesilia whipped around to face Rand. From behind, she was Sigrid. Maybe with white hair and more confidence in her gait, but she was his sister. As those dark eyes locked on him, however, ice shot through his veins.

"M… m… me?" Rand stammered.

She approached him, and he instinctually found himself retreating toward the wall without realizing it. "Impressive work, killing King Pi," she said. "I would have enjoyed dangling him in front of Sir Torsten, but you did what you could for a puny mortal."

"I didn't…" Rand swallowed. "I didn't kill him."

"That's not what it looked like to me," Bliss said.

"I didn't."

"Take credit where credit is due, Rand Langley." She clapped her hands, and the sound made him leap out of his boots. "Well, if I can't use the King, I suppose the knight's friend will have to do."

"His friend?" Rand asked. "His... who?"

"The scrawny one. I don't know his name." She tapped her forehead. "Lucian, or whatever."

"Lucas," Rand muttered.

"Yes, that's it. Torsten seems to care for him. Though, maybe not as much as he seems to care for you." Her glare hardened, and Rand's throat felt like he'd swallowed a stone. She leaned in so close he could feel the frost on her breath, smell the blood. "From what I hear, he found you red-handed, lying on the street and left you to live. Now, why would he do that?"

"He left me to suffer."

"To suffer?"

Rand nodded meekly.

Nesilia stared for a few long moments as if letting the information settle. Then she sneered. "Of course, he did. Everyone must pay for their sins against a god who's sinned more than any other. What a fool."

"Why do you care about him?" Rand asked.

"Because he represents everything wrong with this world!" she bellowed. Again, Rand cringed. "Because he believes with all his heart that he can stop what is coming, just as he stopped Redstar. And he would throw you to the wolves to do it, I promise you that."

"What if I deserve it?"

"Now, now, Rand Langley," Bliss said, winding her way behind him. "You're not going soft on us, are you?"

"Have you looked out there?" he asked. "Is that the change you want to bring? Is that your world? Because all I see is the same suffering and death as ever. I can't believe that Sigrid would want that."

"The forest burns before it grows."

"Not if it's all ashes!" he barked.

He didn't mean to, the words just came exploding out of him, even seeming to catch Nesilia off guard. He shifted his feet, preparing for her to strike, but she didn't. Instead, her shoulders hunched, the way Sigrid carried them. Her dark eyes softened to the green Rand had known all his life.

"Stay strong, brother," she said. The hard dockside accent of his sister returned. *Brother*. He'd heard her say that word thousands of times. It sounded exactly like her.

"Siggy?" he asked softly. He stepped closer and cocked his head to the side to get a better look at her eyes—at the flecks of green filling the irises. "Is that you?"

"It is."

He reached for her cheek, and she leaned into it like one would a warm pillow after a harsh winter's night. "You're really in there?"

"Always."

"Sigrid, I'm…"

She pressed a finger to his lips and hushed him. "I'm not angry with ye anymore. I just want ye to stay strong. The world we'll be makin… it's gonna be perfect. Simple. Gone with all the complexity and borders, all the things we only think we care about. There'll be only the people worth carin about."

Her words went in one ear and out his other. All he could focus on was her accent that he never thought he'd hear again. The same one that the Glass Castle had trained out of him.

He stared, wondering what to say next. What could he say next?

And then her eyes reverted to the all-black of Nesilia, and her back straightened.

"No," Rand said, grasping at her shoulders. "No, I need to talk to her."

Nesilia swiped him away.

"Please, I'm beggin ye!" Rand pled, his own accent reverting to his lowborn childhood in Dockside.

"Your time with her will come," Nesilia replied. She backed away and left Rand's arms dangling, tears rolling down his cheeks.

"For now, it's time to start the change," Nesilia continued. "Right now, all our enemies are gathering together in their perfect little city by the mountain I was damned to."

"Better than a dark, damp forest," Bliss said.

"Say that again, and I'll send you right back," Nesilia hissed.

Bliss bit her lip, then floated away, grumbling.

"I thought so," Nesilia said. "They gather only to die. And so, enough games. It's time to oblige them."

"We're taking Yarrington?" Babrak asked. Rand had almost forgotten the fat slob was there. He'd made himself comfortable on the throne, though his expression spoke of bitter embarrassment.

"*I'm* taking Yarrington. Torsten Unger believes that even without a King, he can stop me. Others rally to him because of it. And so, I will break him first. The glass spire will shatter all around him, and he will see that the god he loves is a lie. Iam's Kingdom will fall."

"About time, Sister," Bliss said, swooping back around. "I was beginning to worry you enjoyed toying with them a bit too much. Let me do it. He helped kill me in the Webbed Woods."

"No, I need you for another. A mystic."

Bliss chuckled. "Of course."

"No, for Torsten, my host's brother will do." She turned back to Rand. "Go to the dungeons and fetch his friend, Lucas. Take care of him. Keep him fed. I want him healthy for when we drag him in front of the Yarrington walls and show Torsten how weak he and the followers of Iam truly are."

Rand looked around at the others in the room. The three most powerful beings in Pantego and they all seemed to be salivating over taking Yarrington. He imagined its peoples' screams, and so instead, he forced himself to remember the creaking of the ropes he'd slung over the walls. And he imagined those walls falling, crumbling like they so deserved.

"What are you going to do with Torsten?" he asked.

Nesilia grinned. "You'll see."

XXVII

THE THIEF

Whitney stood atop a large, hollow box. He'd made it down the rope, and his hands weren't going to thank him for it. They were raw and bloody in places, rope burns on his arms and legs, but what choice did he have? There was no other way out of the dwarven King's treasure room.

Aquira stood beside him, and they both looked down about fifteen feet through a small gap where the wooden box and the stone shaft containing it failed to meet each other. It appeared to be exactly what Whitney thought it was—a very large dumb waiter. He remembered using Darkings' system so long ago, but this was massive in scale. It made sense considering its intended use—hauling big loads of treasure to be stored for whatever it was dwarves stored treasure for. They were like dragons of old, rumored to horde gold because they liked how it sparkled.

Whitney supposed he couldn't be one to cast judgment. He'd stolen and buried priceless items all over Pantego with little intention of ever digging them up unless he absolutely needed them. But then he had, and though the mystic robe got destroyed, it proved that he hadn't been stupid.

Presently, he snuck up to the edge of the box and laid down, then dragged himself as far as he dared. Four clanbreakers stood guard, just like they did at the other entrance to the Iron Bank within the throne room.

"What to do, what to do," he whispered.

Aquira made a little sound and slinked up closer.

Whitney glanced her way, then backed up.

"There's barely enough room to squeeze through there," he said. "And even then—four spiky metal dwarves against you and me? I don't think we'd stand much of a chance."

Aquira puffed, her form of acquiescence.

"Well, we have to do something."

He looked up, back where he'd come from. There was no way of getting back up there, even if he did chicken out. Side to side was nothing but solid stone. Up was just black as far as he could see.

He peered over the ledge again. Down was a definite no-go. There was no doubt in his mind that he'd be dead in an instant if those clanbreakers saw him.

"Unwanteds usually just get thrown in the dungeons until we got time to execute em."

Whitney swallowed hard upon recalling the dwarven guard's words.

He thought about sending Aquira out first as a distraction, but that wasn't fair to her. For all he knew, there would be dwarven archers posted along the many tiers, waiting to unleash deadly projectiles.

"What are we going to do, Aquira?" he asked. "Sora is waiting for us somewhere—I hope."

He couldn't shake the thought that Sora had been discovered as the culprit behind the attack in the throne room. Maybe that shog-brained Gargamane had warned the King of the would-be trespassers. All Whitney knew was that he had the Brike Stone, and now they needed to find Nesilia and hope it actually worked like the bar guai had. He was no expert on the magical power required to bind a goddess.

Yet another trinket that may or may not be worth the sweat it took to get.

He felt the box shake beneath him, then heard a slight whimper.

"Aquira," he said without turning around. "What are you doing? Aquira?"

When no response came, he spun and nearly slipped off the edge from surprise. A small, green, humanoid creature wearing a bone mask of a long-beaked bird stared back at him, holding a squirming Aquira.

Sickly yellow eyes pierced through the shadows cast by the mask, never leaving Whitney even as the goblin struggled with the wyvern.

"You let her go," Whitney said, pulling his daggers.

Another goblin dropped beside the first, followed by yet another. Soon, four of them stood shoulder to shoulder, and when Whitney dared to look up, he could see the glinting eyes of a dozen more.

"Shog in a—"

A goblin thrust a spear at Whitney, and he narrowly avoided its tip, slapping it down with his dagger. The creature pulled it back and tried again, but still, Whitney was faster.

"What do you want?" Whitney asked as if the thing would respond.

It did respond, but in the form of more violence as it whipped the spear shaft horizontally. The wood cracked against Whitney's arm, and it sounded like broken bone until he looked down and saw half the weapon on the floor.

"What's goin on in there?" came a shout from below.

"Help!" Whitney shouted, not caring if he was discovered. He'd take his chances with the clanbreakers if it meant escaping the goblins alive.

"What are ye doin?" the voice called again. "How'd ye get in there?"

The same goblin charged Whitney while another one yelped.

"Never mind that!" he shouted back. "Goblins!"

Aquira was finally free and clawing at her former captor's mask. The goblin went down under her weight, but Whitney didn't have time to see the outcome. His own battle raged as a second goblin joined in. Whitney struck out with his dagger and felt resistance as the blade dug into scaly flesh. He felt warmth as a black ichor cascaded over his hand and wrist. Its scream was accompanied by mechanical grinding sound and the feeling of movement.

The box beneath them was moving.

They rose within the shaft. It shifted sporadically, sending Whitney staggering. Whitney was surefooted, but the goblins were more so, and now had another advantage.

The rest of them had reached the platform, and Whitney found himself facing six foes on his own. Aquira had her struggles with nearly as many, but she made quicker work of them, zipping and breathing contained streams of fiery death. The smell of burning meat was sickeningly sweet, like something Franny would have cooked the Pompare Troupe.

Whitney dodged one goblin, tossing it into the wall behind him. It made a satisfying *thunk* and dropped through the gap. He glanced up at another goblin chewing on the dumb waiter's rope.

"Cut that out!" Whitey shouted, but he immediately regretted the distraction. The next attack landed, a goblin's fist catching him in the throat. He gasped, feeling like his windpipe had collapsed. His vision went blurry and could only see Aquira in front of him and feel the heat of her flames.

There was a time when he believed goblins to be cute little Wildland-dwelling reptiles—little more than pests for travelers crossing Pantego. Now, he saw them for what they were… savages. They truly were fit to serve Nesilia's evil will.

Arms wrapped him from behind, wrenching him back and forth. He fought, but it was becoming increasingly more difficult. He saw darkness creep into his periphery, and his chest heaved. A sudden flood of air inflated his lungs. It burned, but he sucked in, letting the oxygen do its work. Still struggling to see, he threw a leg backward and kicked his assailant's kneecap. Its grip weakened, but it didn't let go.

Then, something sharp dug into Whitney's shoulder, and instinctively, he threw his head back. It definitely connected with a goblin skull, but in doing, caused the creature to tear a chunk of flesh from his shoulder with its needle-like teeth.

Whitney let out an agonized cry. More and more goblins were upon them now, as if attracted to the blood. It was chaos, and he could barely tell what was happening until suddenly, there was a *snap* and the ground fell away beneath him.

They were free-falling, all of them.

An explosive *boom* sounded, and pain coursed through Whitney's back and legs. Splinters tore through him; larger chunks even downed a few of the goblins, but Aquira still hovered, untouched, above.

Whitney, however, lay on his back, staring up at a hole, wood shards stabbing out in all directions. Somewhere in the distance, there were more screams, but all that mattered was getting away from these goblins.

Aquira screeched, swooped, sliced. Whitney tried to stand but felt like he'd been stampeded by a zhulong herd. Then, a synchronized roar brought hope as spiky, metal blobs rolled in around Whitney. His head swiveled, frantically watching the group of clanbreakers tear into the goblin horde. They worked as a single unit, shredding the enemy to bits.

"Op! Op! Op!" one called.

"Ep! Ep!" shouted another.

They flopped around like fish out of water and let their spikes do the dirty work. Black blood and green flesh showered down, and Whitney covered his face.

It went this way for less than a minute before the entire interior of the box—what was left of it—was filled with dead goblins and ichor.

While the clanbreakers were distracted watching the remaining goblins scurry up the shaft, Whitney pushed himself to his feet and made a break for it. He raised a hand to signal to Aquira, but pain radiated from his shoulder.

No wonder I'm light-headed, he thought as he looked down to see his own blood pouring down his neck like a gurgling fountain.

"Aquira!" he shouted instead, and she zipped behind him.

Soon, they were within eyesight of the main city. It was pandemonium, dwarves everywhere, goblins, too. Something had happened.

The Brike Stone?

It was the only thing that made sense. He stole the Brike Stone, the ground shook, and goblins showed up.

It didn't matter. He needed to find Sora and the others.

"Let's go!" Whitney shouted to Aquira as he ran through the crowd. Each step was torture as even the slightest bounce made his shoulder throb. But he pushed through the pain until a goblin charged into him, full speed. Whitney hit the ground hard, he lay there, groaning. The wily little creature was about to pounce when Aquira intervened with a long blast of flames that charred the goblin like meat on a spit.

"Thanks," Whitney said, struggling to rise.

He absentmindedly patted his pockets.

"Yigging Exile," he said. The Stone was gone. "Find the stone!"

Aquira took off to look for it, but Whitney saw it in a goblin's dirty grasp. "There!" he shouted. The thing was mesmerized by the gem, but its eyes looked pained. He considered waiting to see what kind of effect it would have if held for a length of time but worried it might only have a limited use and somehow be rendered worthless.

Whitney rushed the creature. He closed his fist, ignoring the pain from the rope burns and raw palms. The goblin looked up, startled, and instead of hitting the stupid thing, Whitney grabbed the stone and pulled. His heart wrenched upon its touch. His throat seemed to be closing, and he heaved.

"You little… no good… thieving…"

It yanked back, blubbering something incomprehensible, but Whitney was stronger. The Brike Stone came free, and he toppled, landing on his backside. He saw the goblin soaring through the air above him and managed to pull his dagger a second before it landed on him. Its teeth chomped near his face, snapping and barely missing his nose. Whitney shouted for Aquira, tried to get his blade up, but the goblin had his arm pinned down.

Whitney stared up at a cracked bone mask, more than half of the creature's reptilian face visible. Its skin appeared to be dripping off like dark green sludge. Saliva poured from its open maw, the smell of it like week-old fish. A gobbet of flesh hung from its forehead, and thick black ooze dribbled out of a deep wound.

Though he couldn't raise his dagger, he got his other hand free and slammed the goblin in the side of the head with the Brike Stone. It rolled off him, not dead, but clearly stunned. Whitney rose and ran again. He heard Aquira above him but didn't take the time to look. He shoved the stone into his pocket, and relief washed over him.

"This is nuts," Whitney said. "We've gotta find Sora and the others and get the yig out of here!"

He'd expected it to be challenging to find them in such a dense crowd, but he hadn't considered the noticeable height difference. He spotted Lucindur's tall, Glintish frame almost immediately. Sora was beside her, surrounded by a wheel of mystical flame.

"Sora!" He kept calling for her while he did his best to not trample the dwarves.

They were fighting too, it seemed. Aquira made a beeline for them and engaged in the conflict.

With Aquira back with Sora, Whitney was left to focus on not dying. Goblins were everywhere. Blood and black ichor literally flowed through the streets like rivers.

Is this all from the stone? Whitney thought again.

If it was, at least that was confirmation that they'd taken a step closer to taking Nesilia down. However, that also meant they might not live long enough to see the plan come to fruition.

A goblin dropped down in front of him from somewhere above and slashed. Ducking, Whitney narrowly avoided a sharp set of claws. His head swam, though, the constant loss of blood from his shoulder wound proving to be severe. The goblin came at him again, and Whitney rolled backward, then perched on one knee. The motion had saved him, but he was now so dizzy he saw two of the attacker... no, there *were* two of them now.

"Shog," Whitney swore, closed his eyes, and prepared to receive the next blow squarely.

But it didn't come. When he opened his eyes, he saw a blur of black and gold.

"I dunno if this be yer fault, but ye ain't dyin before I get answers," Gargamane the Gold said as he tore the goblins to shreds.

Whitney wasted no time while the dwarf engaged. "Thanks!" He said as he stumbled toward Sora.

When Whitney caught up, he saw Lucindur jab what looked like a dwarven short sword into a goblin's eyeball just as it was about to swipe at Sora from above. Tum Tum drew large swaths around himself with a warhammer while Brouben chopped the enemy to bits with his big axe.

Sora whipped around and blasted a goblin over Whitney's shoulder with a ball of flame, nearly singeing his eyelashes. He fell back, and seconds later, Sora was there to help him up.

"Are you okay?" Sora asked, staring at his wound.

"Never better," he panted. "We've gotta get out of here."

"No kidding," Sora said, sending another burst of fire at the mobbing goblins.

Whitney watched, stunned. He knew she had power, but to see her throwing around fireballs like they were bales of hay on the farm was different. He was used to her having to slice herself to summon even the faintest bit of magic, then being immediately drained.

"Brouben, how do we get out?" Lucindur called.

"Follow me," he said, driving his axe blade through the skull of his latest victim.

He led them past the many houses, each having to battle as they went. The closer they got to the great hall's exit, the thicker the crowd. When they reached the main stairway, Brouben stopped and threw up a hand. Before them was a mass of dwarves and goblins all entangled in warfare.

"Not that way," Brouben said. "Ain't gonna happen. C'mon!"

He changed course and took them through a series of tunnels just like the ones they'd originally entered through.

"Glass Queen's sparkly tits, this is madness," Tum Tum said. "How did those beasties get into Balonhearth? Place is a fortress!"

"Its my fault!" Whitney said.

"What?" Sora said. "No, it's not."

"It is. I grabbed the stone, the world started shaking, and the goblins showed up."

"That's what that was," Lucindur said.

"Ye got the stone?" Tum Tum asked.

Whitney pulled it out as they ran. The blood-red stone sapped the light from the whole tunnel.

"Wow," Sora said, reaching for it.

He tossed it back into his pocket immediately. "You don't wanna touch that."

"Whit," Sora said, grabbing him by the arm. He turned to her. "I'm glad you're okay."

"'Okay' is a relative statement," he said. "I'm pretty woozy from blood loss."

"Don't be such a baby," she said, smiling broadly. She leaned in and kissed him.

"Now I'm really woozy," he said, throwing his hand over his forehead.

Sora laughed and placed her hand over his wound, closing her eyes. Whitney winced, but a feeling of cool comfort flooded him as blue smoke rose from the spot. When she removed her hand, he was miraculously healed. And she didn't even faint.

"There," she said. "Good as new."

"That's some trick," Brouben said.

"Thanks," Whitney muttered.

"We gotta get goin," Brouben said.

They pressed forward around a corner, down a ramp. They were running, but there was no indication anything was following them.

"I think we lost them," Tum Tum said as if reading Whitney's thoughts.

"Still think we should run," Whitney said.

They all picked up the pace.

"This was us," Sora said. "She knows where we are."

"Nesilia?" Whitney said.

"Who else?" Tum Tum growled.

"Lucindur did her thing and sent me somewhere. There was a village on fire. Nesilia saw me in the vision. I came to and not a minute later, the whole mountain was crawling with goblins."

Whitney swore.

"We knew this would happen," Lucindur said, voice dripping with regret. "Using my magic."

"It was my choice, my lady, and mine alone," Brouben said.

"It could be worse," Whitney argued.

"Halt right there!" a voice shouted from behind.

"Ye couldn't keep yer mouth shut?" Tum Tum said.

Whitney looked over his shoulder to see Gargamane the Gold and his men following behind.

"There's an exit. Up ahead," Brouben said.

"Did we at least find out where she is?" Whitney asked Sora as they ran.

"No, but we know where she's headed. Yarrington," Sora said.

"Yarrington?"

"She's headed straight there, surrounded by an army, set out to destroy Iam's beloved Kingdom. I know her mind, Whitney. I can… feel it. Revenge is all she wants. She's consumed by it. Distracted. It will be the best place to get a jump on her."

"Shog in a barrel," Whitney said. "We have to warn Torsten, then. Make sure they're ready to fight and win us an opening."

"Our thoughts exactly."

"I only wish it weren't so far…" Whitney said.

"Are ye really gonna complain about a long walk?" Tum Tum asked.

"I need to get ye away from him first," Brouben said, thumbing back to Gargamane.

"Speaking of, are we almost there?" Whitney asked.

"Right here," Brouben said. They came to a stop at a small vertical shaft with a ladder leading upward.

Sora sent a fireball back through the tunnel. It wouldn't really hurt the clanbreakers in their armor, Whitney didn't think, but it would buy them some time.

Whitney held his breath for a moment. He didn't know what would happen once they crawled up that ladder, but he knew what needed to happen here. He grabbed Sora and kissed her deeply, one hand on each of her cheeks. When they were done, he said, "I don't know what I'd do without you."

"All right, all right. There'll be plenty of time for that if the goddess don't kill ye." Brouben motioned to the ladder. He tossed Whitney a key. "Up ye go."

"What is this thing?" Tum Tum asked as Whitney climbed. "Ain't never seen it before."

"Hatch leads up to Groblegrook's blacksmithy," Brouben explained. "Always thought he was crazy for wantin it to be in the valley, but he said the steel gets its hardest when it cools in the snow. Guess it's a good thing. Once ye get out, go south about a day's journey. Ye'll soon recognize the area if ye've got any adventurin under ye."

"What—yer not comin?" Tum Tum asked.

Brouben placed a hand on Tum Tum's shoulder. "These be my people, and I be their Prince. I can't leave em like this. Not when I caused it. I'll rally those loyal to me and drive the beasts back into the darkness, away from you lot. Besides, someone's gotta hold off Gargamane and his clanbreakers."

"But your father—" Lucindur began.

"Will do what he thinks he must. And so, will I. I belong here, defendin til death."

"Sounds likely," Whitney said from above.

"Aye, but I'll die soakin in the blood of the enemy, not hiding away like gold in a vault. Ain't a better way to go."

"I can think of many," Whitney said. "But it's your life."

"Thank you," Sora said to Brouben, taking his hand and staring straight into his eyes. "Make things right with your father. I promise, you won't regret it."

"Let's hope Nesilia's claws aren't in too deep," Brouben said. "He was a brave man once."

Whitney noticed Sora's features darken at the thought. "Sora, we gotta go!"

Gargamane was shouting again, this time incensed by the flame.

"It was good seein ye again, old friend," Tum Tum said.

"And ye," Brouben replied. "If Meungor gives a shog or two, we'll meet again. Otherwise, I'll see ye for a pint in his halls."

"Rock below, rock above," Tum Tum said and mimed toasting his goblet.

"To Yarrington," Whitney said, throwing open the hatch. "I can't wait to see how much Torsten has missed me."

XXVIII

THE CALEEF

The Black Sands were harsh and unforgiving. Even with the water they could gather in Saujibar, and food scavenged from Nahanab, many didn't survive the trek. Especially the children and those markless who'd grown so used to the luxuries of Latiapur.

Bodies were left behind for the gallers and the wolves. Mahi hated every moment of it, but the limited supplies and access to shade needed to favor their army. Not a single warrior was expendable against Nesilia's darkness. Especially now that Mahi had seen firsthand what she was capable of.

But, finally, they'd cleared the M'stafu Desert, where the black sand swirled away into the white. Where the air was cooled by moisture and a draft blew in from Trader's Bay. The Wildlands, as Torsten Unger had called them, was now behind them as well. White Bridge was not far.

Mahi unfurled the cloth wrapping her half-bald head and breathed it in. She longed to feel the kiss of the wind on her skin but knowing it was there would have to suffice.

"I never thought I'd be so happy to leave our lands," Bit'rudam said, riding another zhulong at her side. Mahi wanted to ditch hers like Torsten had, but she knew it was foolish. She needed all her energy for the fight to come.

"Babrak's lands now," she said.

"They'll never belong to him. We'll destroy this Nesilia, and then we'll drive him out, I swear it, Mahraveh."

"One fight at a time," she said.

"I know, but… how can you be so calm about this? He was one of us."

"Because he's aligned with a monster," she said. "First time he steps out of line, he's dead. And you know him. That won't take long."

"It will not feel as good if we are not holding the blade."

"And yet, he'll be dead," Mahi said, giving her zhulong a kick. It trotted ahead, leaving Bit'rudam to consider things.

There was truth to what she'd said, but that wasn't all. She was calm. Remarkably calm. And it was likely because the further away from Latiapur and the Black Sands they traveled, the more her memory cleared.

In Latiapur, she had to continually fight back the surge of blessed memories from Caleefs past. She hadn't even realized how incessant it was until now as her head quieted. This was a blank slate, where few Caleefs had previously ventured.

She raced by the horde of marching people. Torsten offered her a nod, still leading the zhulong carrying his King's body. His people glowered, though said nothing. Everyone was far too exhausted by then to argue.

But at least Torsten was right about one thing. Babrak's army never pursued them. Even as Mahi crested the nearest hill and glanced back, they were nowhere to be seen. She wasn't sure what that meant, but if Torsten was right about Nesilia's arrogance, it would be what undid her.

She should have slaughtered us all when she had the chance, Mahi thought.

Seconds later, an arrow split the dirt a few feet in front of her. Her zhulong squealed as it spun away, and she reached for her new spear. Armor clanged as Serpent Guards ran to her aid, forming a wall before her and unsheathing their weapons. Torsten mounted the zhulong along with Pi's body and hurried her way.

Mahi didn't flee. She soothed her zhulong with soft strokes behind her ear and stood proud, staring across the field of crusted dirt, toward a trench of wooden spikes filled with Glass archers.

The line of them had their bowstrings pulled taut, while the man who'd fired stood, awestruck, staring at his hands. The arms of the others all trembled as they held, waiting for orders from commanders who seemed as dumbfounded as they were.

"Don't fire!" Torsten yelled, waving his arms as he raced by. Bit'rudam charged out of nowhere, his zhulong skidding in front of Torsten's and sending it onto its hind hooves. Torsten grasped to hold Pi's body on.

"My Caleef, fall back, it's an ambush." Bit'rudam said, whipping around.

"Get away from him!" Sir Mulliner roared. He charged from seemingly out of nowhere and barreled into the side of Bit'rudam's mount. Mahi couldn't imagine how much hitting the side of the muscular beast must have hurt, considering he and the other Shieldsmen had ditched much of their plated armor by then to combat the heat.

Mahi rolled her eyes. While arguing broke out behind her and more Shieldsmen and Shesaitju arrived, tempers flared. She spurred her zhulong forward, remembering the stories of the last battle here. How one stray arrow fired by Nesilia cost hundreds their lives. All because their two Kingdoms couldn't trust each other. *Wouldn't* trust each other.

"My Caleef!" Bit'rudam shouted. She heard what sounded like a punch, then the squeal of a zhulong. Its hooves crunched dirt behind her.

"Relax, Bit'rudam," she said. "It was an accident."

"How do you know? This could all be—"

"Because they won't shoot me," Torsten said. He rode up behind them, and as Mahi glanced back, she noticed the lines of opposing forces preparing to skirmish at the crest of the hill.

"I don't always need your protection," Mahi addressed Bit'rudam.

"I know, I—"

"And you don't always need to apologize. Now, go and tell everyone to put down their swords so we can cross White Bridge."

Bit'rudam stared silently for a few seconds, then bowed his head. "Yes, my Caleef." He hurried away without letting her see the shame painted on his cheeks.

"Sheath your swords!" Lord Jolly shouted as his horse trotted up.

"They've all been through a lot," Torsten said to Mahi.

"And we haven't?" she replied.

He grunted in response, then turned back to his men. "Sir Mulliner. Lord Jolly. Keep everyone in line, or so help me, Iam."

"My pleasure," Lord Jolly replied.

Sir Mulliner responded only with a grimace and a half-nod.

Torsten then nodded Mahi along toward the Glass army's camp, and they set off alone. The eastern spires of White Bridge rose high above them, the tops charred and broken apart. Trenches with spiked walls were dug in a large radius off the entry, filled with archers and the army's camp.

All around it was a dirt field with patches of trampled grass. One swathe of the dirt was a much darker color than the rest, and tips of stray arrows that hadn't been cleared away glinted in the afternoon sun.

"That's where my father died?" Mahi asked, knowing the answer.

"It's where we all would've died if not for Iam," Torsten said.

"Where was your god in Latiapur, then?"

Torsten bit his lip. "I'm not sure. Where was yours?"

"Hiding. Or dead. Doesn't matter."

"How could that not matter?"

"Because in the end, this is our world. Not theirs. Just as no parent should own the future of their child, they don't own ours. We all have to work together, Sir Unger. That..." She pointed back to their exhausted forces, Bit'rudam and Sir Mulliner still bickering while others tried to pry them away. "...can't keep happening. They need to start seeing we're all in this together."

"That's why your father arranged that marriage. Or, rather... you did."

"Still, we need honesty between all of us. Otherwise, one more stray arrow will finish Nesilia's job for her." She couldn't help but think about how she wasn't being entirely honest. The idea for the marriage had been inspired by Yuri Darkings. But anyone knowing that might have called it all into question. Especially after all the evil he'd done to both the Glass Kingdom and her people. Some secrets had to stay buried for the good of everyone.

"I couldn't agree more."

She held her gaze on him for a few lingering moments. He seemed earnest, but ever since they left Saujibar, she felt something different in him. Without eyes, it was hard to get a true read of him, but there was no denying it—he was hiding something.

"Good," she said, then sped her zhulong away.

By then, the Glass archers had lowered their bows and stood at attention. "Sir Unger, we've been awaiting you since the scouts arrived," the garrison commander said, donning the armor of a Shieldsman. He pushed through his ranks, then struck his chest and bowed at the waist.

"And yet you fire an arrow at our royal guest?" Torsten questioned.

"I'm s… so sorry, my Lord," a lowly archer spoke. He fell to his knees before them and groveled. "I meant to hold… I… I…"

"He saw you alone first and thought the worst," the commander said. "Every night, someone walks right up to our defenses. They don't answer. Don't care about warning shots. One even took an arrow to the knee and simply limped away, cackling."

"They're possessed by demons of Elsewhere," Torsten said.

The archer's face lost all its color. The commander swallowed hard. "I see…" he muttered. "And… how do we know you're not…" He swallowed again, eyes darting in Mahi's direction. "You know…"

"Because we answer," Mahi said. "And you'd be dead already." Even more color drained from their faces, along with all the soldiers within earshot.

Torsten sighed. "The Light is with us, brother."

"And the King. Is he really…" he didn't dare finish the sentence.

Torsten looked to the dirt as he patted the wrappings of Pi's corpse, tied across the front of his zhulong. "He is finally at rest. But I know, deep in my heart, that he would want revenge for what was done. Nesilia will pay the ultimate price."

"That's not bein what Dellbar the Holy said," an archer with an accent Mahi understood to be from the impoverished parts of Yarrington voiced.

"He passed here?" Torsten asked. He drove his zhulong through the ranks, causing them to part and reveal the man who'd spoken.

"Aye. Few days back, he did. Said if we all stayed here, we'd die here. Then, he rode right on without sayin much else."

"I'm sure you misunderstood him," Torsten said.

"No, I was right there. Took his horse for some water."

"Then you won't mind fetching more for them." Torsten pointed toward the mass of survivors. He clapped. "Everyone, on the double. As much as you can get from the lake. Food, too. I want our stores emptied for our people."

"Those ain't our people," another soldier said.

Torsten's zhulong stomped right up to the man before Mahi could do the same. He glowered down, towering over him from atop an already tall steed. The soldier slinked back. Torsten hopped down and approached the man, still taller, even off his mount.

"They are now," he growled. "Everyone, get moving. That's an order."

The ranks broke, and soldiers scurried in every direction. Torsten waved back to Mahi's army, and when she did the same, they marched onward. Then, Torsten led Mahi through the camp, toward White Bridge itself. As they moved, people started to notice the body-sized wrappings on Torsten's zhulong, and broke out into muttering and whispers.

"Is that the King?"

"We're doomed."

"Iam really has abandoned us."

All the enjoyment of Mahi's mind being silent went with it. She could tell how each remark irked Torsten to his core. His shoulders looked to be bearing the weight of this entire bridge.

There were stories about the place. A great bridge built by legendary dwarves out of immense blocks of stone, reinforced with some precious metal from the mountain near Yarrington. She'd expected more. It was massive, sure, and the damage to its spires didn't help, but it still had nothing on the Boiling Keep.

"We'll set your people up west of the bridge," Torsten said. "There's a clearing and a small support village for the soldiers here. They'll have to cram together, but at least it'll be safe."

"And separate from your people," Mahi remarked.

Torsten's jaw clenched.

"Sorry, I didn't mean anything by it," Mahi said. "I'm grateful for everything."

"You lost your home, Caleef Mahraveh. You have nothing to apologize for."

The breath caught in her throat. The way he said it, so straightforward. So honest. She hadn't even really thought about it that way yet, but he was right. First Saujibar, then Latiapur, even her afhemate. Every home she found in places and people seemed to vanish.

Will Yarrington now be more of the same?

"Now it is your time to rest," Torsten went on after she didn't answer. "I'll prepare a small convoy that will take us to Yarrington ahead of the army so that Pi can receive a proper burial and defenses can be prepared."

"You can go ahead, Sir Unger," Mahi replied. "I'll stay with my people."

"Our people now."

"You don't need to keep lying," she said.

"About?"

"I know the marriage is worthless without consummation. It will be annulled, which means I'm no longer a Queen or a Caleef, just a wanderer leading loyal wanderers."

Torsten's features twisted with concern. "Mahraveh, that's—"

"The truth, Sir Unger. Speak it, and so will I."

Torsten stopped his zhulong, then led them to the wall of the bridge, where the rush of water from far below reminded Mahi of the ocean. At least it drowned out some of the murmurings. As her people approached, it became less about Pi and more about "untrustworthy foreigners."

Torsten exhaled slowly. "You're right. In the eyes of the Church of Iam, the marriage isn't real. And west of this gorge, those are the only eyes that matter."

"I was wondering how long it would take you to tell me," Mahi said, feigning a smirk. It all seemed so wrong to talk about with the cold body of her unofficial husband lying right behind her.

"In the spirit of honesty? We can't afford to lose your army."

"And you won't," Mahi assured him. "We will fight alongside the Glass Kingdom until this is over. You have my word. *If* your people will let us."

"They will, or they'll die. But your father burned down many villages west and south of here when he rebelled. Killed the family of a lot of these people."

"And your army didn't do the same to mine?"

"It doesn't matter. We're in the Glass now, not the Black Sands. All we can hope is that they'll put aside the past so we can all fight together. It's what the marriage was meant to do."

"They'll listen to you," she said.

"By Iam, I hope so."

"Make them, Sir Unger. Make them, and we will all fight Nesilia until our dying breaths for taking our homes away. All I ask is for one thing."

Torsten turned to face her, his blindfold hiding any true expression. "And what is that?"

"After Nesilia is gone, you'll help us take Latiapur back from those loyal to Babrak."

He lifted his hands and circled his eye-sockets with his fingers. "In the name of Iam, if there's an army left to do it with, you have my word."

"That's not it. The Glass Kingdom will relinquish all claims to my lands. There will be no more tribute. No more bowing before a Glass King. We will be free to be our own Kingdom."

"I can't promise that."

Mahi set her lips in a straight line. "You have to."

"I can't!" he blurted, squeezing the parapet so hard a chunk of loose stone along the top slid free. "I am not King."

"You'll advise the next one."

"Mahraveh, I don't have any idea who the next one will be. That boy was the last of the Nothhelms. The last of the family I swore and failed to protect time and time again. The next King would be wise to have me hanged so I can't fail again, but until then, I will serve. So, I can't promise you anything. Not freedom. Not an army. Only that if we win, *I* will help you take your city back from the men that helped kill Pi."

Mahi didn't realize her hands had been balled into fists until she looked down. She drew a measured breath. It was hard to be angry with the man. She'd lost everything. Clearly, so had he. And one thing was for certain, if they won, Pantego wouldn't be the place she knew as a child.

Panping was a leaderless mess infested by demons. Her home was ruled by an imposter. The West was without a King and about to come under siege by monsters and all the evil of Elsewhere.

"Okay, Sir Unger," she said. "I understand. But I'm going to hold you to that. Who will need an army when I have the man who tied my exalted father in a duel?"

Torsten released an exasperated chuckle. "Who, indeed?"

Sleep was as hard to come by in the safety of White Bridge's shadow as it had been in the desert. Mahi had to break up a number of arguments between her people and the Glassmen.

Especially with Torsten and Lord Jolly gone. They'd left with Pi by horseback before nightfall, intending to ride non-stop to Yarrington where his body could be preserved, as were their ways. Mahi couldn't question it any more than why she'd resigned her father's body to driftwood and sent it out into the Boiling Waters.

With them absent, however, the Shieldsman named Sir Mulliner was left in charge. Which didn't help at all.

So, Mahi found herself strolling along the crags of the Jarein Gorge alone with her thoughts. The rock this far north was different—rougher and easier footing. She climbed to a low clearing overlooking the river at the bottom of the gorge, where the light of Pantego's moons could barely penetrate.

She found a lonely apple tree growing out of a patch of grass. The fruit wasn't ripe, tiny and pathetic, but it would provide shelter and a bit of comfort. It was there she finally decided to lie down. Away from noise, away from all the people who couldn't put aside their prejudices to fight a common enemy.

She watched the moons slowly arcing across the star-speckled sky, and for the first time since before the eve of her failed marriage, she dozed off. She drifted in and out, but she hadn't even realized how tired she'd been. Even in a body blessed by her god, she was still mortal.

Branches rustled, stirring Mahi awake. Her eyes snapped open, and she saw a shadowy, feminine figure lurking around the other side of the tree. She was so tired she'd left her spear stabbed into the ground across the clearing, behind the stranger.

The woman picked a piece of fruit off the tree. She examined the fruit, rotating it in both hands as if she'd never seen an apple before. Of course, that was when Mahi realized she hadn't ever seen one growing in the wild either. Only stuffed into crates by traders in the Latiapur markets.

"I remember when I helped create these," the woman said. Her voice was familiar, sultry, with an ethereal quality like that of the mystic, yet was different. Intoxicating almost. Mahi wanted to make a break for her weapon but found herself too entranced to move.

"This is a dream," Mahi said.

"Maybe. Maybe not." The woman finally decided to bite a chunk out of the apple. It was too dark to see her expression, but she nearly gagged before tossing the fruit over her shoulder and off the ledge. She wiped her hands together. "Disgusting."

"Who are you?"

"You know who I am." The woman turned and stepped into the light of the moons. Her hair was so white it was nearly silver. Her face was pale and freckled, but clearly belonging to a woman from Yarring-ton. All except for eyes that were dark as midnight, dark as Mahi's own enchanted skin.

"Nesilia," Mahi spat. She sat up, digging her fingers into the dirt and preparing to attack at a moment's notice.

The Buried Goddess spread her arms wide. "In the flesh… well, not my own."

"Dream or not, I'll still kill you!" Mahi kicked to her feet and rushed her. She aimed for the throat first and laid a blow before Nesilia could defend. Then she rolled around behind her, grabbed her spear, and plunged it forward into the woman's stomach.

Mahi grunted and shoved the blade through with all her might. It burst out of Nesilia's back, but the woman didn't budge in the slightest. Her lips merely curled into a wicked grin.

"No, you won't." Her hands shot forward, lightning-fast. They broke Mahi's grip on the spear, throwing her against the tree in one smooth motion. Then, Nesilia yanked the weapon out and rolled her neck.

"You are impressive, though," Nesilia said. She admired the dark blood staining the spear, while Mahi stared at how the wound in her gut healed all on its own. "I suppose my brother's final act in choosing really wasn't so dreadful."

"So, he is gone?" Mahi asked.

"As gone as I was. Here."

She tossed the spear over, and Mahi jolted forward to catch it in mid-air and commence a new attack. This time, Nesilia dodged her every strike with ease. She was like the air, impossibly fast. Barely even trying.

"Would you relax?" Nesilia asked.

"Not until you're dead!" Mahi came at her with a flurry of blows. Nesilia evaded them all but backed up toward the ledge right where Mahi had her. Mahi feigned a slash, then curled back to thrust with the Serpent Strike her father had taught her, which had won her a victory in the arena.

Nesilia was gone in a blink, and Mahi found herself nearly tumbling until her enemy grasped her from behind by the clothes and yanked her back. She slipped onto her rear, once again losing grip of the spear. But she recovered quickly and reached for it. The moment her hand wrapped the spear, Nesilia's foot fell upon it with a crushing weight, not befitting her size.

"Do you ever stop?" she asked.

"You killed my father!" Mahi abandoned her pursuit of the spear, pushing herself into a roll that swept out Nesilia's legs. Her knee came crashing down toward Nesilia's chest, then the goddess was gone. Nesilia was suddenly in front of her and smacked Mahi across the face with the back of her hand.

It felt like a sledgehammer and sent her soaring across the clearing into the cliffside, then tumbling down onto the dirt. The taste of iron filled her mouth. She spat up blood and tried to stand.

Nesilia vanished again and appeared behind her, knee against her spine so that her face was smashed against the dirt. She leaned over to whisper in Mahi's ear. Glinting tips of upyr fangs drew close.

"I did kill him," Nesilia whispered. "He thought no god could touch him, and I squashed him like a bug. Isn't that what my brother taught your people to respect? Strength? Who is stronger than me?"

"You're a coward, hiding in that body, here in the shadows," Mahi hissed.

"Oh, I promise you. I'm not hiding. I came here for you. Not to kill you, but to make you an offer. Babrak was merely a tool. A means to an end. To destroy the sad world Caliphar built in the Black Sands. But you, my dear Mahraveh. You are a jewel."

"I would never fight for you if that's what you're going to ask."

"And smart as a whip!" Nesilia exclaimed. She let her weight off and began to pace. Mahi was so weakened, her muscles burned just in an attempt to get to her hands and knees.

"No, Mahraveh," Nesilia went on. "You have far too much self-respect to do that. The most powerful woman in the world for a week. A champion of my brother's favored arena. By all means, you could be a true goddess yourself, not this… sham." She waved her hand in dismissal.

"I'll show you a sham." Mahi mustered every ounce of energy she had and begun to rise.

"Sit. Down." Nesilia snarled, her tone echoing across the crags of the canyon. Her voice struck Mahi like a shockwave and sent her back against the rocks, holding her there.

"Can't you see?" she continued. "I will make a new world, for the strong. Like us. It won't matter who birthed them, or their family, or what is or isn't between their legs; only what they can do."

"At what cost?" Mahi said through her teeth.

"The only cost. Why stay on the losing side? Your god is gone. Iam means nothing to you nor his Kingdom. Stand with me, or stay out of my way. Do either, and when this is finished, you'll have your Kingdom and so much more. I'll let you cut Babrak's heart out yourself."

The pressure released from Mahi's muscles, and she collapsed to her knees, gasping for air and feeling to see that her heart still beat. She drew a few more beleaguered breaths, then glared up at Nesilia. "I don't need your help to do that. I'll kill you. Then I'll kill him, then anyone else who hurt my people."

"*Your* people," Nesilia scoffed. Then she clicked her tongue and shook her head. "What a shame. What an awful shame."

She turned her back and walked to the ledge, staring down at the water, completely unafraid that Mahi might sneak up on her. Mahi recognized the move. Men in the arena did it when they knew they had the fight in hand. Sometimes, their arrogance cost them, but this time, Nesilia did have the upper hand. Mahi could barely move.

"Well, my dear," Nesilia said. "My offer stands until the moment your heart stops beating, and you meet the fate of your father. Even if you fight against me. Any time you change your mind, I'll be ready. There are so few humans on this rock worth paying attention to, but you truly are one of a kind."

Mahi sucked in another breath, her lungs stinging. "Well, I..." The words died on her lips when Nesilia vanished with a gust of wind like she'd never even been there at all.

"My Caleef, who are you talking to?" Bit'rudam asked from above while she bent to retrieve her spear.

She glanced up and saw him standing atop the cliffside. "Nobody," she said. "Just a bad dream."

"About Latiapur?" He hopped down a few rocks, then slid down the sharp slope to her level.

"About many things." She squeezed the weapon's shaft and stared down where Nesilia had been. The river gushed along, though she could barely see it. A few seconds went by in silence until she heard Bit'rudam's heavy breathing right behind her.

"I'm sorry about how I've been acting with them," he said.

"You should be."

"I just see the way they look at us, and now we're here, and I..." he sighed. "There's no excuse. It's not my place."

"We all need to be in this together, Bit'rudam."

"I know."

Mahi spun to face him. "Sir Unger thinks Nesilia wants an audience, but he's wrong. She just wants us all to be together, looking into each other's eyes as she ravages us. She's a monster that just wants to feel the pain."

Bit'rudam reached for her hand, hesitated, then went all the way. "Mahraveh, is everything all right? I haven't seen you look this rattled since before you fell."

"Just be quiet." She threw her spear aside and grabbed him. She didn't think twice. Her lips pressed against his, and she squeezed him into her so she could feel the heaving of his chest.

He pushed off, breathless. "But your marriage."

"I said, quiet."

She kissed him again, silencing him, forcing him onto his back. Finally, he stopped resisting and kissed her back under the shadow of the apple tree.

XXIX

THE PRIEST

Glayton Morningweg had gone by many names. His father called him lazy more than anything. But a blacksmith's life was never for him. His mother called him sweetheart, as mothers are oft to do, and he loved her for it, even though he never felt like it fit.

As a child, he'd had cruel tendencies.

Sister Ulture, who taught at the school he went to, smacked that right out of him. She always called him stupid.

And so, he ran away. Then, alone in the bitter North in the dead of night, cursing Iam, his God revealed himself in the form of brilliant, vivid lights dancing in the arctic sky. A rare occurrence, so he'd learned.

And thus began his pilgrimage to Hornsheim, the site where Iam was said to have birthed Pantego's first life. There, serving as a monk, he'd earned a new name when his own eyes were taken from him.

He returned home as Father Morningweg, priest of his village, Fessix, only to find that his parents had already passed on. That didn't stop him. In their name, he served Iam and taught his flock that faith would protect them.

All this until Redstar and a horde of Drav Cra proved that wasn't true, and named him Faithless. His entire village was slaughtered but for a single boy, and Father Morningweg was left father to nobody.

A wandering priest.

A drunkard.

A man who needed no name.

From that moment, he'd waddled through life in a haze.—back to his younger ways of caring for nothing and no one. Then, fate or Iam played a cruel trick, making him the personal priest of a horrible gangster named Valin Tehr. Absolution in exchange for the money to stay drunk.

It was there, in a dungeon no less, that he met Sir Torsten Unger, and everything changed. He bore witness to a man who'd been faithful to a fault, who never let it waver, even when it cost his eyes and dignity. A man who, right then, was finally ready to crack.

And so, after years of cursing Iam's name, Morningweg prayed. He expected nothing, but then, Iam gave Torsten the ability to see again. Glayton thought it was Torsten's faith that earned such a blessing but nobody would hear him.

From a priest without a church, he became High Priest of Iam, presiding over the entirety of the Order. A man capable of miracles, he was now named Dellbar the Holy after a far more famous high priest of old.

It was quite a story, even he would admit, but he wasn't the same man whose church and people had been burned down right in front of him.

He'd drifted along the path laid before him, doing as he wanted to, speaking as he wanted to. No, the man who was now Dellbar the Holy continued doubting that Iam cared for one second about his pitiful life.

Then the Buried Goddess rose on the fields outside White Bridge, and for the first time in Dellbar's life, Iam made his presence known. Not through signs or miracles, but his very being.

He became more than an idol for faith. And in doing so, more than the perfect Father of Light he was thought to be. Dellbar saw in his God the same emotion that had gripped him every time raiders came to his village. He saw in Him everything that made humans so flawed.

Fear.

Even when Iam's presence left him, and Dellbar was a mere mortal again, that fear remained. Because in that ensuing silence, he knew, as Iam knew, that was it—their God's last gasp to defend His children against His own horrible mistake.

Dellbar then knew in his heart that Iam… God… was as human as His own creations.

As said, it was quite the tale. It had to be, considering the ambush of Latiapur hadn't even made it into the epic. Even he could hardly believe the journey as his horse dragged its weary hooves up the road to Hornsheim.

He'd run out of food the day before, and his stomach was in all-out rebellion already. His vices had gotten him used to being full. Water, he could at least scrape from the light dusting of snow that reached this high region, even in the summer months. Still, he was sure that as the monks and sisters living in the small village at the foot of the monastery looked at him approaching, they'd never seen a man in such rough shape. He couldn't see himself with his useless eyes, but he could imagine.

Just as he could picture all of Hornsheim from his first visit long ago. The modest stone hovels of the lower members of the Order were all gathered around a grand well, the water warmed by a crystal prism absorbing sunlight. More of them hung from posts on the road, casting infinite rainbows across the pavers arranged into the shape of the Eye of Iam.

It was quiet, its inhabitants all carrying supplies up to the monastery built into the mountainside. Its central tower carved out the peak of a low hillock so light could always filter through the open top down to the altar at its heart. Two wings curved out from along lower ridges, dotted with hundreds of little windows, each the sleeping quarters of a man or woman of the cloth.

The quiet always reminded Dellbar of a cemetery, but he had to admit—now that he was older—there was something serene about the place. A settlement of thousands without any traders hocking wares. The Glass Kingdom provided all that they would need to live here in exchange for faith and knowledge. A sanctum in the truest sense of the word.

The clop of his horse's hooves echoed. So did his own ragged breathing.

"That's the High Priest!" he thought he heard someone whisper. He wasn't sure how they'd recognize him. Only the chain of Eyes of Iam around his neck might have given it away.

He and his horse gave out together, and the beast tipped over. Dellbar's shoulder slammed against the stone, and his leg was crushed beneath it.

He heard shouting next. Felt hands wedging their way beneath him and lifting him.

"Iam…" Dellbar muttered. "Show yourself. Stop… hiding…"

"*I'm not,*" came an answer. It didn't sound male or female, it didn't even sound like a voice. More like a feeling. "*I am here, Glayton Morningweg. I have always been here.*"

Glayton… Dellbar hadn't been called by that name for decades. He wasn't sure anybody even knew it.

"Yet You left after White Bridge. You let Nesilia…"

"*I let her do nothing,*" He replied. "*And I did all that I could to slow her.*"

"That can't be true. Everything. Our entire lives. We dedicate them to You and… that is how You repay us?"

"*Even when the Light erases the darkness, there is always shadow. One cannot be, without the other.*"

"I don't know what You're talking about."

"*The God Feud. To end the fighting. To purge the darkness. It took everything I was. Just as it took everything I am now to intervene at White Bridge.*"

"And what about my home?" Dellbar growled. Intervene. The word caught him by surprise because it was what people praying always begged for. Divine intervention. For Him to intervene in their problems. Fix them. Even though Dellbar knew that wasn't how faith worked, it was what they always wanted. What he'd always wanted…

"What about intervening then?" Dellbar questioned. "All those people died right in front of me, begging for You. And You did nothing."

"*One town, or the world… I had to wait. I saw it coming, but I can see no more as My energy fades. Even this conversation is beyond—*"

"No more riddles! I felt Your fear that day. What does any of that have to do with Nesilia? Would You really let her destroy everything in her rage? Give me the strength to fight her again."

"*It took so much Light to erase the darkness. Nesilia… My love… she thought I'd left her for eternity, but I simply couldn't reach her after the end. My Light brought peace, and the darkness grew within her. Letting her go was My greatest mistake."*

"That doesn't help us."

"But it does. You seek to erase her army. Light and darkness, we live or die together. Bound, eternally. One cannot be without the other. And one cannot die without the other. Put faith in the Light, and fade to shadow with them. It is the only way."

"You're not making any sense! Help us!"

"My word is true. I wither now. Helpless to do anything but watch. It's in the hands of My children now... Erase My mistake. This world is yours... "

"Iam!" Dellbar screamed. Only this time, the word screeched through his lips, and his body bolted up. His throat was so parched and hoarse it stung.

Soft hands promptly patted his stomach and pressed him back against a cushion.

"Your Holiness, there you are," an old man said. "You're awake."

"It was a dream?" Dellbar asked.

"A dream? Sure, it must have been, Your Holiness. They say you and your horse collapsed outside, and you must have hit your head."

The way the word *Holiness* rolled off the old priest's tongue like he'd had a taste of rotten stew, Dellbar knew this was real now. None of the elders had been happy to select him as High Priest, but after the miracle of giving Torsten his sight back, they had no better choice.

"I need to get up," Dellbar said. He pawed to find the floor, then flattened his palm against the cold stone and pushed. The priest gently pushed him back down.

"No, you need to rest. And drink water. I don't understand, how is it you came to be this way?"

"Do you all live under a rock? Latiapur was a trap! The city has fallen, and our army is in retreat to Yarrington. We must signal the Order. Every priest and monk and sister in Pantego must hurry to the capital at once." He leaned up again. This time, when the priest fought it, Dellbar clutched his wrist and twisted. The old man's soft bone creaked as he released a pathetic whimper.

"Yarrington?" asked another elderly man, shuffling in from Dellbar's left. "What use would we have there?"

"To help fight the Buried Goddess, you dolt." Dellbar unhanded the first priest and shoved him away.

The man groaned, then said. "More with that lunacy? Her cultists were thwarted at Mount Lister."

"I saw her myself," Dellbar said.

"In another dream?"

Dellbar overheard a few chuckles.

"All these rumors and lies are the work of her followers. We mustn't fall prey to them. We answer Iam's call here.

"No, you'll die here," Dellbar said.

"Your Holiness," the most elderly-sounding voice yet began, the title sounding even more pitiful from his lips. "You are young…"

Dellbar scoffed. Young… he carried more than four decades upon his shoulders. Just because he wasn't knocking on the Gate of Light didn't make him young.

"…and I believe you will grow into a High Priest worthy of your predecessor," the man continued. "But rumors of all types of madness spread every day. If it is true that we were betrayed at Latiapur by the heathen Shesaitju, then we must pray for the safe return of our brothers."

"It has nothing to do with them!" Dellbar shouted.

"Unfortunately, it always does these days. Now please, you look like Elsewhere frozen over. Get some rest. I could have one of the sisters fetch you wine if you'd like?"

More snickers sounded from the old lechers. Dellbar bit his tongue, then shook his head. "Just water."

"Good. I'm glad to see you all right, Your Holiness. When you rode up… we feared the worst. Perhaps a chance to… uh… clean your body will be good. Hornsheim is here for you. May the Light of Iam shine upon you always."

"You think…" Dellbar couldn't finish. Instead, he started to cackle. It wasn't surprising. Secluded up here in the mount, led by men without eyes, of course, they thought it was Dellbar's drinking that brought him here. Only suppliers and traders brought news, and they were in short supply with Nesilia in power across the eastern mainland.

"Your Holiness," came a soft voice, then a knock at a door. "I have water for you."

"Bring it in," he said, waving.

The sister neared, and he heard the tray rattling.

"Please," he said. "Can you place it in my hand? Those insufferable old bats are right about one thing, my head is killing me, and my ears are ringing."

She gently placed the cup in his hands like she was afraid of breaking him. Then she bowed away. He stayed there, feeling the cool droplets course along his fingers as they dripped down the side.

It was clear she was frightened of being around him. Ever since being named High Priest, he'd been on the road amongst soldiers, or in Latiapur with foreigners. He hadn't spent any time amongst the people or with his Order, but this was how they saw him. A drunk. A man, chosen by Iam for reasons they didn't understand, and deep down, resented him for.

Nearly as much as he resented himself.

"I should've kept Lord Jolly with me," he grumbled. "Who'd ignore him?"

"What was that, Your Holiness?" the sister asked.

"Nothing. And please, just Glayton." He lifted the water to his lips and took a few sips. It was cold, like everything else up here. Stinging his throat all the way down like a rope of icicles.

"I… uh… Glayton?"

"Oh, right. I don't know why I said that." That was a lie. Even still, the words spoken to him by Iam in his dream resonated within him. Deafening. "Dellbar," he went on. "Father Morningweg. Whatever you'd like. Anything but '*Your Holiness.*'"

"Yes… Father…" she said, ample hesitation before choosing which name to use. He heard her footsteps leaving, then stop. "Father, are you all right?"

"Would you be, with death and darkness closing in from every direction? Whatever you overheard, it's all true, Sister. I'm not drunk. I haven't touched wine in… months now. Oh, how I wish I even had the desire."

"Well, that's very good, Father."

"Is it? If nobody will listen to me anyway, why care?"

She stepped up again, and her footsteps were harder, more confident. "I was there, in Yarrington, when you caused a miracle. Then, at

White Bridge… Sister Nauriyal, I'm sure you don't remember. You just seemed like you were in so much pain… I hope you're better. My father, he never stopped drinking."

"Bartholomew Darkings' daughter? I remember. I'm so sorry you had to witness that."

"So am I…"

He sat up. "That means you saw what happened. Iam—"

"No, we were behind the gates. But we heard many things. That you summoned the power of Iam's Light in another miracle to defeat a cursed upyr. Some said Nesilia attempted to rise again. I'm not sure. When we returned here, everyone figured it was soldiers telling grand tales. They do tend to exaggerate."

"Yes, they do." He braced himself, then pushed to his feet. Blood rushed to his head and made him wobbly, but Nauriyal quickly raced to his side and took his arm.

"Your Holin… Father, you shouldn't."

"I'm fine. Just hold my arm. Young Nauriyal Darkings. Another child of Iam who doesn't belong here and who nobody would ever believe, thanks to a father she didn't choose. What if I told you that all the stories being told of White Bridge happened, all at once. And that the only lie is that I performed a miracle. *I* didn't do anything at all."

"Don't sell yourself short, Father. I've been with the church for a year and honestly… you're a breath of fresh air."

He smiled. "Then, you clearly haven't smelled my breath." He started to walk, leaving her no choice but to loop his arm and guide him.

"Father, please, I don't want to get in any trouble."

"You won't. As your High Priest, I order you to accompany me, Nauriyal of…"

"Bridleton."

"Ah, there, I believe I knew that, didn't I? You know, they sent a letter to me to take up the priesthood there once."

"And?"

"I didn't answer. Far too warm for my blood."

They reached the opening. He could tell by the sound of footsteps and the chilly draft.

"Here, Father. Your staff." Nauriyal unfolded the fingers of his right hand and placed it inside. He gave it a few good taps. An unremarkable stick or an ornate staff adorned with a crystal orb worth more than a small village—it didn't matter. It all worked the same for him, and this particular cane with its Eye of Iam carved into the top earned him a shred of beleaguered respect.

"Thank you. But please, stay with me. I need you to take me to the Chamber."

"For what?" Nauriyal asked.

"We need to gather all of the writings on demonic possession that we can find."

"Demonic… possession?"

"Yes, my dear. While these old men have been locked up here praying and worrying about the Shesaitju, the Buried Goddess has been quite busy breaking open and emptying Elsewhere. She's possessed thousands of men and women in the East… and I fear, killed thousands more."

"That's insane."

"Quite. Yet still, undeniably true."

Her grip on his arm tightened. She said nothing but continued leading him down Hornsheim's stone halls. Every clack of his cane echoed loudly against the stark, unadorned walls.

Hornsheim was designed for blind old men with walking sticks. A simple layout, easy to memorize. Dellbar could remember it from even back when he was but a lowly monk and still had sight of his own. He didn't need Nauriyal to help him find the stairs down to the Chamber of Light—a library buried beneath the central altar. It was nice to have someone with him, however. Made him look like he was just trying to stretch out his limbs while he recovered.

Every soul who passed greeted him with a 'Your Holiness.' They stopped and bowed and, he imagined, circled their eyes in prayer, even if they didn't respect him. It helped him understand why the elders who fought to be named the next High Priest coveted the position so. A lifetime of dutiful service and serving the whims of their unseen God… it was a chance to finally *be* seen.

Dellbar listened as they moved, ears attuned to even the tiniest of sounds. By the way voices carried upward, he knew they passed the central altar. A low chorus of murmured prayers rippled like waves along a beach.

Then stairs, lots of stairs, spiraling down into the earth. The irony wasn't lost to him that the Holy Order kept their most prized writings down where their enemy was buried.

He was reminded of Iam's words from his dream. *"One cannot be without the other."* The simplicity of that statement astounded him. Despite bearing witness every single day to nightfall, the church existed to bring Iam's Light to all corners. Even the holiest of days, the Dawning, celebrated the rising of the sun from a year's last night.

"He had to mean something else," Dellbar said to himself.

"Who did?" Nauriyal asked.

"What? Nobody."

"Do you always talk to yourself?" she asked. While the words sounded rude, her tone didn't. It was an honest question from an honest person. A woman who never hid her horrid origins even when nobody here would have asked.

"No different than praying."

"Father!" she yelped.

"What?" he said. "Do you really believe Iam has the time to listen to all of us?"

"You're a very unusual High Priest, do you know that?"

"Well, how many have you met?"

She fumbled over an answer. Not long after, their feet slapped down on a rough surface. The chill down in Hornsheim's undercroft was unmistakable. Not only books and scrolls dwelled down here, but crypts for hundreds of people of the cloth who'd spent their lives in service dating back to the God Feud.

All the knowledge they might have known, preserved only by a few who wrote things down. Dellbar almost wished he was an ancient necromancer that could bring them back to life and interrogate them. How did they defend against dark magic when such a thing was prevalent—when mystics performed experiments that defied all sanctity of life?

"Sister Nauriyal, what are you doing here?" asked yet another old man. Keeper Jorlin, was his name. Around even when Dellbar was young. The way his voice wheezed through his lips, he was probably around when half the tomes were written.

"Keeper Jorlin, His Holiness, High Priest Dellbar has asked me to collect all writings on…" She cleared her throat and looked to Dellbar, who nodded. "…Demonic possession."

"Has he? And what need would anyone have for those?"

"More need than collecting dust down here," Dellbar said.

It was now Jorlin's turn to clear his throat, and his had far more phlegm. "Those are prohibited texts. I—"

"Will adhere to the wishes of your High Priest. I assure you, it is Iam's work."

"I… yes, Your Holiness. Sister Nauriyal, would you care to help me? They should be in the backroom. And please, grab the torch, but be careful with it around the old parchment. These old eyes aren't what they used to be."

"At least you have them," Dellbar remarked.

Jorlin muttered someone under his breath. Nauriyal hesitated to let Dellbar go, but he shooed them along and leaned on a column to wait. He didn't last long. Noticing a rhythmic *clank* echoing from down a hall, his tired legs began limping that way.

He tapped his staff along the floor in time with the sound until he found a path where the unmistakable sound of iron on stone grew louder, only, nobody mined down here.

"Aye, ye can't be down here!" a man shouted from a bit up the hall, his accent distinctly of South Corner, Yarrington.

Dellbar didn't stop. "I could say the same to you. I know a man of Iam when I hear one."

"We're here—" The man released a strange, gurgling sound. He fell to his knees hard. "Your Holiness, I didn't realize."

"Stand up. That's quite all right."

"You must be here to examine the expansion of the western crypt," he said, speaking fast like nervous men commonly do. Someone from South Corner likely hadn't ever spoken with a noble in all his life, and while Dellbar wasn't noble in any sense of the word, his title put him on the Royal Council.

"Sure," he said.

The mason started to lead him, the *clack-clack, clack-clack* growing ever louder. "Was supposed to be a crew of dwarves hired by that new miniature Master of Coin." He chuckled at his own joke. "But they never showed so, we're it. Taking a little longer than expected…"

"Good work takes time."

"That it does. At least they sent a giant with us. Makes things easier with him hacking away at the rock."

"A giant, really? Way down here?" The corridor expanded into a large chamber, judging by how his words carried. And it was a bit warmer from heat emitted by an unclear number of masons.

"Yeah, he—"

The mason was cut off by a deep, cavernous voice. "Mister Father Morningweg?" a giant said, lumbering over each syllable in every word as if they were a real challenge. A whiff of foul breath soon followed. The giant tossed aside an oversized tool with a crash and a flurry of yelling from human masons. His footsteps shook the earth as he stomped over. The vibrations disoriented Dellbar, and before he knew it, a pair of hands the size of tree-trunks wrapped around his back. Surprisingly enough, the giant's touch was gentle.

"Me haaaaaaappy I seeee you," he said.

"You too…" Dellbar strained to say. Even a gentle giant crushed the air out of his lungs. Then, seeming to notice, the giant let go.

"Remember meeeee?" he asked, backing away so that his wretched breath washed right over Dellbar's face. "Remember meeeee?"

"Of course! It's… uh… Ahl… Ul…"

"Uhlvark!" the giant exclaimed. "You dooooo. I tell all I know you. The High Priest." Those last words were said with more reverence than all the priests combined had mustered.

"Yeah, yeah," the mason groaned. "You two seem like best friends."

Of course he remembered the giant that Valin Tehr kept locked up in his underground arena, forcing him to kill just to eat. He was impossible to miss. He didn't, however, remember them ever talking. Though, he imagined that was more thanks to his own drunken state than a dull giant making up stories. They were honest beings, often to a fault.

"Uhlvark, it's good to see you again," Dellbar said. "And under much better circumstances. Clearly, Iam's Light favors you."

"Uhlvark here to build."

"Well, hitting rock is certainly better than hitting people."

"What was that?" the mason asked.

"Nothing!" Uhlvark blurted. "He said nothiiiing." His feet slammed across the rock, as he moved away from the sounds of the workers. "I don't like to remember thaaaaat."

"Mmm, yes," Dellbar said. "My apologies. I don't like thinking about certain things too."

"Like whaat?"

Dellbar scratched his chin. He hadn't noticed until then how sloppy his beard was getting. He was beginning to look like a proper High Priest, gray beard longer than ever.

"Oh, plenty of things," he said. "Like what the chances are that you and I should wind up underground in another series of dark, stale tunnels."

"Hmmmmmm." Uhlvark plopped down with a rumble that nearly flung Dellbar from his feet. "I not know."

"No, me neither." His head fell back, and he chuckled. An idea popped into his head for how he could convince a bunch of old, comfortable men to leave the only place they'd ever known. A mad one, but these were mad times. Most of his stay with Valin Tehr was a blur, but he did recall the virility of the giant. How he could crush a man's rib cage with the poke of a finger or break a spear in half like a splinter.

"Uhlvark, how would you like to perform a special project?" Dellbar asked.

The giant leaned forward, the puff of his nostrils all too loud. "Special?"

"Yes, in the Chamber of Light. I could use your help with something."

Hours went by. Dellbar sat outside, enjoying the warmth of the sun as it refracted through a crystal onto the side of his face. He was on the lip of Hornsheim's well, scooping up a bit of water, surprised by the temperature. It met his lips and felt like Iam's own touch. Said to be the purest water in the Kingdom, Dellbar had to admit it really wasn't half bad, considering it wasn't wine or ale.

With his other hand, he patted the top of the tomes and scrolls he'd gathered from the Chamber of Light. Dozens of them. Enough to fill a small cart pulled by a mule or two.

Somewhere in them were answers to how to banish a demonic spirit that had already possessed a being. Or, the answers were somewhere in the heads of one of the elder priests who no longer thought of anything beyond their own concerns. Though, Elsewhere being broken open meant even what once worked might not this time.

He heard Nauriyal approaching before she spoke. She had a certain way about her gait. A strut. Not like the sisters who'd grown up in service of the church, but like one who'd found it late.

"Is it done, Sister Nauriyal?" he asked.

"Yes. I've told everyone to convene out here by your word," she said. "Do you plan to tell me why?"

"You don't like surprises?"

"I'm not sure. I've never experienced a good one."

"Ah, well... I've always been a fan. That... flutter in your heart when you aren't sure what to expect. Sometimes it's raiders or ambushing armies, but other times, it's a friend knocking on your door to wish a happy birthday."

"And are you..." she paused. "Wishing someone a happy birthday?"

He smiled. "Not quite. Now come, sit. You've been a great help so far." She didn't move quickly, but eventually, she sidled up next to him.

He listened.

Footsteps gathered along with whispers, large groups of them, filing in from all over the monastery. Down steps in the mountainside, up from basements.

"Your Holiness, what is this about?" asked one of the elder priests who'd woken him earlier. They all blended together.

"You really should be resting," said another.

"If only there was time for rest," Dellbar said. He turned his head in Nauriyal's direction, and without needing to be asked, she helped him stand. He then poked the cart of tomes with his cane. "In here, are all the writings we have on possession. A tool of the fallen and the wicked who wish to return to a realm they've already left behind."

What rose wasn't a collection of murmurs, but jeers, outward hostility.

"You removed them from the Chamber?" an irate priest barked.

"Keeper Jorlin, you let him do this?" scolded another.

"I didn't give him a choice," Dellbar said.

"The sunlight could damage those pages! They aren't even covered."

"Then get me a blanket," Dellbar said.

"This isn't a game, Your Holiness. Please, you aren't thinking straight. You have—"

"To rest," Dellbar interrupted. "Because I'm the drunken High Priest none of you wanted. But you see, as much as I'd rather not have this title, I do like one thing about it. It reminded all of you that we don't exist for our own interests. Our sacred duty isn't to choose who gets stationed in which city or decide which Lord favors who. It is to spread the goodness of Iam, to show the people of Pantego how to bask in His Light.

The oldest priest laughed. Dellbar recognized the voice. Father Pengelly, the one favored by a vast number of the priests to have received the title Dellbar stole. "Your Holiness," he said with rotten vim. "I think we know what our jobs are."

"You don't," Dellbar said calmly. "None of you do. I didn't. Darkness rises outside this haven, and none of you have heard or will listen. What wisdom is there in that? What help is there in that? We're comfortable in our faith because it isn't tested. Light surrounded by more light is nothing but light. If light never encounters darkness…" He let the words linger.

"We are doing our duty," the old priest said.

"Not like the men who march on the battlefield, or those of us who fought against the mystics."

"I fought the mystics," Father Pengelly said. "I did what I had to in that war. Where were you? You have no right—"

"And now you rest for a lifetime. I may be many things, and a skeptic was one of them, despite my robes. But Iam came to me at White Bridge, and I have seen what evil we face. Demons, fallen goddesses, and beasts forged by shadow. And I can stand here and spend days trying to convince all of you that we don't have to sit around here praying in order to help. But that we *can* help. Iam wants us to help."

"Okay, okay, we're listening," said the first priest, voice dripping with sarcasm. "Tell us, Dellbar. Tell us all what you have seen without eyes. Tell us what happened in Latiapur after *you* sanctioned the marriage between King Pi and a Shesaitju without consulting anybody!"

"No, I won't waste my time. You'll all see soon enough. Right now, you're taking everything you might need, and we are marching to Yarrington. And all the gallers we have will be dispatched to every church west of the gorge, telling those priests to go to Yarrington as well."

Father Pengelly scoffed. "Everyone single one of us?"

"Not just the priests," Dellbar said, ignoring him. "Every monk. Every sister. We will decipher these texts, and we will help stop Nesilia before it's too late."

In unison, the priests release an exasperated sigh. It almost sounded somber.

"It's very clear we've made a mistake," Father Pengelly said. "You can't be trusted with this honor that we have bestowed upon you."

"Like I said, there is no time to convince or argue." He aimed his face at the sky, and a few harsh words were aimed at him. Then, the earth quaked. A few priests let out nervous laughter. Then, it shook again. And with a third time, the sound of stone splitting echoed across the valley like thunder.

"What is this!" Father Pengelly shouted.

Dellbar didn't answer. He merely listened. The cracking augmented, and the shaking increased. Panic flourished all around him. And then, some of the monks and sisters started shrieking.

"The central tower! It's breaking apart."

Father Pengelly charged at him and grasped Dellbar by the collar, missing a few times as panic clearly hampered his senses.

"Dellbar, what is the meaning of this!"

The loudest crack yet sent a chunk of stone tumbling down the tower, breaking to pieces on the rocks below. Everyone gasped and crouched for cover, even Father Pengelly. Dellbar straightened out his robes and kept listening until Uhlvark's cavernous voice rang out.

"Mister Father Morningweg!" he called out from the direction of the tower's comprised entrance. "Mister Father Morningweg, I done it!"

His footsteps banged along, more screaming coming as he and the masons bounded through the gathered crowd of holy men and women. Behind him, parts of the tower kept breaking apart, and Dellbar knew it wouldn't be long before it partially collapsed in on itself, burying an ancient altar with it.

A low price in the grand scheme of things, eh, Iam? he thought.

"Dellbar, what is this madness!" Father Pengelly demanded.

"A few comprised columns in the foundation, thanks to my good friend Uhlvark, and even the oldest tower comes down," Dellbar said.

"You're insane!"

"Probably. But now, none of you cowards have a place to be comfortable in. Nothing to keep you here instead of marching with me to where we can make a real difference. Hornsheim can be rebuilt. Altars can be rebuilt. Even books can be rewritten. But our world cannot exist if all the light is snuffed out, and we all took a vow never to allow that to happen. By Nesilia's hand, or any other... not even our own."

Another bout of yelling was interrupted when more of the tower collapsed. The bang was as loud as those in Latiapur when Dellbar witnessed the true horrors of war. Now, maybe these soft people might have a taste of that, too.

"Gather everything," Dellbar said. "We move immediately. And no dawdling or Uhlvark will get you moving for me."

"Faaaaaast to Yarrington," Uhlvark said. "Got to save Pantego."

The grumbling and complaining was like music to Dellbar's ears. For the first time, he truly enjoyed being High Priest. Even if history might remember him as the worst one ever. As a mistake. As the man who destroyed holy Hornsheim. He couldn't have expected different.

"And Nauriyal," he said, hoping she hadn't moved yet. Her cries of shock had been lost amidst all the others. "You're in charge of watching over all the texts. Priest or not."

XXX

THE CALEEF

Mahi stood at the edge of the Jarein Gorge, staring into the deep abyss Nesilia had nearly thrown her into.

"The army is entirely on the western side of the bridge, as you commanded," Bit'rudam said, climbing up to meet her. She glanced down, and he hid a bashful smile. "We're ready to move on your command."

"Good," Mahi said succinctly. Bit'rudam stopped by her side, and he scanned the gorge.

"Are you sure this is going to work?"

"For years, my father would talk about taking this bridge," she said. "About how it was the key to western Pantego. He knew that when the day came we owned this bridge, it would mean that we won."

"Well, we're here now."

She turned to him, deep regret bleeding across her features. "He was wrong."

He took her hand. "Yet."

She allowed herself a smirk, then pulled away. Not hastily, or with shock like all the other times, but gently, because this wasn't the time for emotion to get in the way of anything.

"No, but he does." She nodded down the ridge, hearing Sir Mulliner on approach before seeing him. He seethed with rage, cursing her from afar even though the wind was too loud to hear him yet.

"What in Iam's name is going on!" Sir Mulliner shouted. Mahi looked down the ridge where Sir Mulliner struggled to clamber up the rock in his needlessly heavy armor. He seethed with rage after sleeping in late and missing her plans, thanks to a night of arguing.

"Sir Unger placed her in charge," Bit'rudam snapped.

"Well, he's not here." He reached the landing and stopped to gather his breath. "What in Iam's name are you doing?"

"Slowing Nesilia down." Mahi turned back to the valley. The idea had come to her when she awoke beside Bit'rudam. White Bridge was the fastest means of reaching Yarrington from the east, where a curtain of dark clouds signaled her stronghold. At first, she'd considered piling debris as high as castle fortifications in its center, but she'd witnessed the mystic Nesilia had under her control. She'd burn right through it.

What Nesilia would never expect, however, was for the ancient bridge to be torn apart. It was said to be unbreakable, built by dwarven masons thousands of years ago after a battle of the God Feud split the earth. Latiapur was also supposed to be unconquerable from the water. Her father, unbeatable in battle.

Mahi knew now better than ever that unbreakable merely meant that nobody had ever tried hard enough.

And so, before dawn, she'd had her men gather all the debris and heavy chunks of stone from damaged towers on either side of the bridge. They'd bound them in chunks. At the same time, she'd divided their zhulong herd in half. A few hundred on the western side, a few hundred on the eastern. Each was lashed to ropes and then tied to the bridge.

Those on the eastern end led to flat points lower into the valley. They would never be able to get back to them—a sacrifice even Bit'rudam argued against, but Mahi knew it didn't matter. So many of the beasts would help little in defense of Yarrington. Not with the Current Eaters on Nesilia's side that would just turn them into terrifying instruments of destruction again.

On her mark, she'd tear down Nesilia's best route and buy them just a little more time to prepare.

"Slowing Nesil—" Mulliner stopped himself and observed the same sight Mahraveh was fixated on. His brow furrowed. "You can't mean?"

"She does," Bit'rudam said. "We will destroy White Bridge and force her to go around."

Mulliner stared, dumbfounded. Then, he broke out into laughter. "You can't be serious. You're going to rip down the bridge that's stood longer than both Yarrington or Latiapur?"

"I am," Mahi said.

Mulliner stomped forward, sticking his face right in front of hers. "I don't think so," he said, low and threatening. Bit'rudam moved in, but Mahi stuck out an arm.

"And why is that?"

"Sir Unger himself took this bridge back from the Drav Cra. It's the best way across our Kingdom and some… foreigner… isn't going to undo that. What if the people still in the east try to flee this way?"

"They're too late."

"Too late!" he laughed scornfully. "Too late. I'm sorry, little girl. You don't get to march in here, destroy our history, and sentence our people to die. I don't care what Torsten says."

"And that's exactly why he didn't leave you in command," Bit'rudam said.

Mulliner leaned in closer. "No, he did it so you lot would keep thinking you're special."

"Don't you see, or are you blind as one of your priests?" Bit'rudam continued. "The King's Shield is gone without a King to shield. You have no authority here."

"I have all the authority here!" He pushed forward, and in a flash, Mahi ducked and swept his legs out from under him in one smooth motion. He hit the rocks hard, and her knee pressed against his neck, turning him sideways, so he faced the bridge.

"Ancient feuds, ancient ways, and ancient things need to die if we're going to beat her," Mahi said. "Sentiment can't matter."

"Well, it's a good thing we feel nothing for this bridge, then," Bit'rudam said. "Except remembering how the Glass troops crossed here to invade our home."

Mahi glared at him. "Sentiments. Can't. Matter. Torsten put me in charge because he knows that as well. And we will either honor the sacrifices caused by cutting off this route, or we will fail them. It's as plain as that."

She let off him, and Mulliner rolled away, coughing. "My men won't go along with this. I'll have them arrest every single one of you in the name of the Glass."

"While you slept, I already convinced the ones who matter," Mahi said. "Now, sit there and watch. And maybe, when we're finished, you can decide to join this war like the rest of us who realize that all these old Kingdom names no longer matter."

Mahi studied his stunned expression for a few seconds, then turned and climbed to the ridge's highest point. She raised her hand, and immediately all of her men looked to her. Beastmasters to drive the zhulong, Serpent Guards, and Glassmen alike on the bridge prepared to do her bidding.

"I hope this works," Bit'rudam said.

So did she. She wished that the blessing of the God of Sand and Sea could allow her to summon the force of the river at the bottom of the gorge and send it crashing through the bridge. She wished that the Walled Lake would rise up and swallow everything whole like one of Nesilia's vile Current Eaters. She wished for the blessing offered by anything but vague memories of the past, or numbness to the wind.

But as she had always known, since the day her father left her to go start his rebellion, she could rely only upon herself.

"It will," she said.

She swiped her hand, and the beastmasters starting shouting and whipping the poor zhulong. The hundreds of them scattered around the gorge wherever they could find footing and began to pull, squealing as their hooves dug in.

Nesilia had her magic, but Mahi had the raw strength of the Black Sands—centuries of creatures bred in the harsh environment.

As the beastmasters got louder and more aggressive, the zhulong pulled harder. Some on lower ridges lost their footing and slipped off the ledge. Their weight, squirming as they dangled, would only help.

They were loyal beasts to a fault. Mahi knew most of her people wouldn't be able to watch as they exerted themselves so much that many of their hearts would fail. She didn't dare look away. She owed them that much...

Bit'rudam climbed next to her and stood by her side. This time, he didn't dare try and take her hand, but his presence was welcome none-theless.

"This is insane," Mulliner said.

Mahi ignored him and kept watching. Waiting for the thick, arched stone of the bridge to show any sign of slipping. History said it was reinforced with glaruium, and she would now put that rare metal the Glass Kingdom so revered to the test.

Their metal, her beasts.

More zhulong screeched and slipped. The beastmasters kept pushing, and now, she could hear the pain in their voices. They'd given their lives to raising these creatures—her warriors, too—all to teach them how to join in on the Shesaitju tradition of war and killing each other.

At least now, they'll help save us.

"There! Did you see that?" Bit'rudam exclaimed,

She did. It was faint, almost imperceptible, but the very bridge itself tremored like a shiver up a person's spine when winter's chill begins to take.

She swiped her hand again, and the men positioned on the bridge got to work. They shoved and lifted, heaving the bundles of heavy debris over the bridge's side, letting them drop. Then, they fled for the western cliffs.

The ropes extended their full-lengths, then jerked up, the force tearing some, debris plummetting to the waters below. But those weighty bundles were also attached to the damaged towers flanking the bridges. Loose portions of the towers were ripped free, crashing down upon the bridge where the zhulong were already pulling.

Mahi was no engineer, but she treated it like a battle, like a strategy her father might draw in the sands when she was younger. Exposing weak points in the formation, then exploiting them until the enemy ranks broke, and had no choice but to retreat.

Zhulong kept pulling, releasing horrid sounds that would plague Mahraveh's dreams forever. Loyal to their own deaths. More of the towers came apart and smashed, stone on stone echoing like they were inside a sand storm.

Mahi's fingers twitched—a meager show of anxiety she didn't want to be seen but also didn't think herself capable of. The muscles in her back and neck tensed. Bit'rudam was on his knees, squeezing a chunk of rock and praying, though it sounded more like begging.

Then it happened. A deep, reverberating *crack*. Dust shot out of a portion of the perfectly cut and arranged dwarven blocks of stone. Most debris from the towers crumbled inward, and that crack became tangible.

The bridge had begun to slip. Mahi didn't think stones shifting could be so beautiful, but it was almost like the Boiling Waters and its frothy waves. It cracked and fell, the bridge coming apart in swathes, dragging those poor creatures unlucky enough to be latched to it to their deaths.

Mahi wasn't sure how long the deconstruction of ancient work took. To her, it felt like many minutes, but it could have been seconds.

Piece by piece, block by block, the center of White Bridge was ruined until the gap left between the two deeper parts of its arched structure was nearly as wide as the gorge itself. Impossible to cross.

If her father could have seen her, then, she couldn't imagine how proud he'd be. However, he was the furthest thing from her mind as the last chunks of stone fell loose. Only one thought pervaded. Nesilia.

"Your move," Mahi said.

XXXI

THE KNIGHT

Sir Torsten Unger had returned to Yarrington in many fashions: victorious after battles alongside King Liam, flower petals lining the streets and horns blaring. Ashamed, locked in a cage after killing one of his own men outside Winde Port. Blind, after Redstar had been thwarted atop Mount Lister, and Nesilia was thought to be stopped.

But never in pure defeat. Not like this. It didn't strike him until he saw the glass spire soaring into the horizon, but they'd stared the power of a goddess in the face and were routed. Fully.

By now, word would have spread not only of his loss but of the Black Sands' as well. Just as he'd heard rumors along the road of the worsening fate of Panping, of the horde of monsters and men trekking west across Pantego, eyes set upon the White Bridge and the capital city beyond.

And only then did it truly hit. Months ago, he'd marched away from Yarrington, thinking he would be ending two wars with one fell swoop. Instead, he found a third and realized that, while Kingdoms warred and weakened each other beyond repair, real evil lurked in the darkness, ready to strike.

Panping had already been claimed. That vast and beautiful countryside, neutered of its defenses by Liam's last great war. They'd had no chance against demons and worse. Now, thousands of Black Sands warriors joined Nesilia's ranks, undone by infighting.

Now, Torsten knew. Yarrington would have to be their last stand.

"Are you ready for this?" Lord Jolly asked as they stopped before the main gates.

"Can anyone ever be ready for this?" Torsten replied.

"No, but someone has to be."

The main gates swung open to permit entry to Torsten and his small entourage. What a pathetic sight it was. Traders and grimy citizens crowded the plaza, eyes filled with fright. They whispered about failure and wondered where the rest of the army was.

Torsten knew how it looked. He'd ridden ahead with such a small number of men, they probably thought that's all that remained. The truth wasn't far off.

"Lord Wearer, what happened?" asked a much-too-young guard stationed at the gate. There weren't even enough soldiers to keep the masses at bay, to keep the prying eyes from looking closer.

"Move aside!" barked one of the Shieldsmen riding with Torsten.

"Did the Shesaitju betray us again?" asked another.

"Where's the rest of them!"

On and on, the questions rolled, each more horrifying than the rest. And with each step Torsten's zhulong took across the stone, the terror gripping the faces of his people deepened.

Lord Jolly accompanied him so that they could not only begin planning defenses but so Pi's body wouldn't decay any more than it needed to before the Master Physician could preserve it for the crypt. Now, Torsten knew that was a mistake. More playing into Nesilia's hands, if he weren't careful. She'd sown so much fear that Yarrington was liable to tear itself apart from the inside. And a people without will were ripe for her demons to possess.

"The rest of our army is coming," Lord Jolly said, with all the pomp and circumstance of a practiced dignitary accustomed to skewing the truth. "The Black Sands stands with us now."

"Against what?" someone from the growing mob asked.

"Is it true? Has the Buried Goddess really returned?" spoke another.

"Did she take Panping?"

"Is the King truly dead?"

"Has Iam abandoned us?"

"Enough!" Torsten bellowed, his voice carrying like the bells of Yarrington Cathedral. "All will be made clear in time."

"That's our King!" someone shrieked. "Under here!"

Torsten felt a tug and whipped around on his mount. A shaggy-looking Docksider peeled back the coverings to reveal Pi's foot. Torsten drew *Salvation* and slashed, the blade stopping mere inches from the man's throat.

"Get back!" Lord Jolly demanded.

Gasps rattled all over. Women wailed. Men voiced their rage. Torsten squeezed *Salvation's* handle so tight he thought the metal might bend. In that moment, he understood why Queen Oleander could have grown to resent her subjects, why Liam probably did—at least when they weren't cheering for him.

All these people who'd only seen Pi from afar, if ever, carrying on as if he were their own son.

Yet, every eye in the entire city fell upon Torsten, pleading for answers, begging to feel safe. He recalled something Liam had once said to him in a war camp outside of Crowfall during a campaign against the Drav Cra. Torsten was barely a squire then, and on a rare occasion, his great King came to sit by the fire beside him and soldiers.

Torsten had been so awestruck, he said nothing, but Liam never had a problem speaking with the silence.

"Not a soul wanted this war, you see," he'd said, his breath reeking of wine. Back then, Torsten imagined that wasn't the case but finally allowed himself to admit Liam's shortcomings to himself.

"But it isn't a King's job to play their subject," Liam went on. "It's my job to show them what they should believe. To lead them like a flock of lost sheep to pasture. And they love victory. They feed off it. And that hunger will bring Pantego together in the name of Iam, the one true God."

As Torsten held his sword to that man's throat, he realized something. He had returned to Yarrington in defeat before. After that campaign. Liam called it a victory because they'd killed a powerful chieftain and claimed his daughter—Oleander—but it was a lie. They marched north to stop the Drav Cra raids forever, rather than bolster northern defenses. To completely eradicate and assimilate the northerners into the realm of Iam. And they hadn't.

The harsh conditions of the tundra and their enemies' knowledge of the land had sent them retreating after Liam took Oleander for his own. He'd only made his people *believe* that was a victory. Made Torsten believe it. And for a few years, their northern cousins were too weak to raid successfully, so it continued to feel like a victory. But then, Liam led his men on another war in the name of Iam, and by the time the raids started again, the people had forgotten.

He'd inspired them to hate a new enemy. And one by one, they despised everyone who wasn't them. Drav Cra, Shesaitju, Panpingese mystics—it was all the same. And if the latter were still allowed to exist in the east, maybe they could've resisted Nesilia's takeover instead of falling prey to her.

Can they really be so wicked if that's the case? Torsten wondered, for some reason, drawn to his memories of how he'd treated Whitney's friend Sora. *Could war and hate really be Iam's will?*

"Torsten, don't do anything rash right now," Kaviel Jolly warned in a harsh whisper, eyes fixed on *Salvation*.

His voice drew Torsten back to the present, and the blade moved away from the haggard man's throat. He gasped for air as if he'd been plunged underwater. The plaza remained in stunned silence, layers of it so thick, Torsten's neck started to itch. These people had never been without a King. Nor their parents, or their parents before that. For millennia, a Nothhelm had sat upon the throne.

Now, they looked to him for answers, and he had none. He drew a deep breath. "Show them what they should believe," Liam had said. And right then, Torsten decided he would do the same. But not how Liam would've done. Torsten would show them what to believe by giving them the truth.

"Everything you've heard is true," Torsten said. Not from the fortifications of the Glass Castle, but right among Yarrington's people. Poor, rich, it didn't matter. They all gathered here together, desperate for guidance.

"Our King's marriage to the new Caleef of Latiapur was a trap." Immediately, came protestations against the Shesaitju. Torsten held out his palm while Jolly tried and failed to calm them. "But not laid by the Black Sands! Their intent for peace was genuine. No, it was Nesilia, the Buried Goddess. It's true. She has returned and has now taken Yaolin

City as her foothold. Her army is vast and dark and threatens to swallow us all if we don't stand together."

The silence returned. Even the few whispers of shock coruscating through the people seemed like explosions.

"And in her treachery, the Buried Goddess took the life of our young, generous King," Torsten continued. His voice cracked a bit, and he seized a moment to gather himself. "He will join his family at the Gate of Light."

"Who will be King!" someone shouted.

"I won't bow to that Shesaitju whore!" screamed someone else, and raucous cheering followed. The crowd swelled like a wave, making Torsten's mount nervous.

"It doesn't matter who is King or Queen!" Torsten yelled. "Not right now. The Nothhelm dynasty gave us this grand Kingdom. Kept us safe for more years than not."

"And where are they when we need them most!" another citizen called out, earning a chorus of cheers.

Torsten struck his chest. "In our hearts! Always in our hearts. The last of their line gave his life to bring together an army that can face the coming darkness. Pi died a hero, and we mustn't forget."

Rumblings of agreement buoyed Torsten's spirits, but they were fleeting. The fear settled back in. These weren't soldiers. They weren't fighters. They were people told that if they served their Kingdom and lived a good life, King and God would protect them.

"Iam has abandoned us!" a woman shrieked.

"Dead with the Nothhelms."

"Left us to darkness and closed the gates."

"No!" Torsten yelled. He guided his zhulong up the incline of the Royal Avenue so he could face down upon the square. His heart raced. He wasn't used to giving speeches to these types of people. It was somehow more nerve-racking than thousands of battle-hardened soldiers.

"Iam is with us," he continued. "Always with us. And He Himself saved us at the White Bridge only months ago." Torsten's hand went to his face, and he rubbed the fabric upon his eyes. It felt dirty and smelled far worse, but he feared what might happen should he clean it.

"I saw it with the very sight He blessed me with. One last miracle…

But He is weak now. It falls to us. We must protect the city, the King-dom, given to us by Iam and his chosen Kings, or we will not live to see another age. So, I say, let Nesilia come. It doesn't matter who our King is now, let her bring whatever horrors she can muster.

"She thinks Yarrington is ripe for the taking, but she doesn't know its people. My skin may be brown, but this is my city. I suffered here. Lost here. Loved here. And it is here, in the name of Iam and of King Pi the Unifier that we will build a new era upon Nesilia's corpse!"

Torsten thrust *Salvation* into the air, breathless. A complete and utter hush responded to him. It felt like it lasted forever. Then, one of the Glass soldiers by the gate started to cheer. Then another. And another. It was infectious. The crowd erupted, cursing Nesilia, hailing their city, and, most of all, honoring their fallen King. Torsten said no more. He turned his zhulong and headed toward the castle.

A smirk touched his lips as he heard the hollering on either side of the street. He reached back to pat Pi's remains.

"Now, there is a send-off worthy of a King," Jolly said. "Well done."

"It will have to do for now," Torsten said.

They only made it one block before Torsten's heart sank, and his smirk vanished. *Did I twist the truth too?* he wondered. He believed in everything he said, but there was one part of his speech that irked him. The promising that Iam was still with them. He'd seen no such evidence since White Bridge. Even that feeling in his chest that had stayed with him since he'd found his faith for the very first time felt faint, distant.

All he had to go on was the fact that his blindfold still had the power to make him see.

Am I lying to myself?

The gates of the Glass Castle's fortifications cranking open ruined any further chance for doubt to seed. Shieldsmen, guards, and workers alike waited eagerly within the forward court, even a young stablehand, barely old enough to lift a sword.

Not only those, but the entire Royal Council that hadn't been in Latiapur also stood by the entry. A mixture of young and old, all equally inexperienced. King Lorgit's son, Alfotdrumlin, even stood among them. Torsten had nearly forgotten about that arrangement, figuring early on, after what happened at White Bridge, that the dwarven king would've recalled his youngest son.

"Sir Unger, Lord Jolly, what's happening out there?" asked Casper Brosch, the Master of Scrolls.

"Nothing," Torsten said.

"Sir Unger merely provided the people a reason to believe," Jolly added.

Brosch's features darkened. He stepped forward, moving around the side of Torsten's zhulong, where the truth was clear as day. "By Iam…" he traced his eyes and bowed his head. "I was hoping by the reception that the messages we'd received were false."

"Unfortunately, every word was true," Torsten said. The stablehand ran up to help, unsure how to treat a zhulong. Torsten dismounted on his own, and the beast just stood there, unmoving, as the kid pushed on its hide. The poor creature was probably shell-shocked from its new environment.

"Nesilia has taken Latiapur after forging an alliance with a usurping afhem named Babrak," Torsten went on. "Caleef Mahraveh and a bulk of her land forces made it out alive and will arrive soon. Their fleet is… decimated. And our young King fell during the fighting. I saved him once, but I wasn't strong enough to do it a second time. I… failed."

"We were betrayed," Jolly said over him, so his last statement went unheard. "And we will have our vengeance."

Torsten heard a few of the handmaidens weeping. They'd spent most of their time with Oleander, but nobody else in the castle would have spent more time in Pi's presence, preparing his outfits, cleaning his quarters.

At the same time, the Royal Council forced their own exaggerated reactions. Master Fenwick, Master of Husbandry, howled toward the setting sun as if he'd been stabbed in the gut. Torsten didn't blame them. None had known Pi long or well enough to genuinely care for him. They were simply carrying out their jobs all before it sank in that they were now counsel to a Crown without a head to sit on.

"Master Pymer, under there is the body of our King." Torsten pointed to the wrap on the back of his zhulong. "He is…" His throat got tight.

"Do what you can to prepare him to join his family," Jolly ordered the Royal Physician. "He'll be laid to rest once more in the grave already dug for him."

The man strode over and peeled back the top of the wrappings. Torsten didn't need to see Pi to know how he likely looked. Abijah Pymer's retch told enough. "I'll… uh… do what I can," he stammered, then whispered a prayer under his breath.

"Lord Unger… uh… Sir," spoke a small voice. Torsten glanced left, then down, to see a little face, the stablehand, caked head-to-toe with dirt and shog.

"Yes?" Torsten asked.

"Do you think that, maybe… uh… maybe in the same grave, our King might, you know, come back to life again?"

Torsten sighed and pressed his hand upon the boy's shoulder, so much larger, his fingers stretched down over his shoulder blades. "I think we've truly lost him this time," Torsten said softly. The boy's chin fell to his chest. "But who are we to doubt the will of Iam?" Torsten added.

At that, the boy's face lit up. "I hope he does. He was nice. He would always drop an extra bronzer after I brought him his horse to ride."

"And you should hold onto that memory. Use it. Fight with it."

"With all due respect, Sir Unger, he's just a boy," said Taskmaster Lars. "He won't be fighting." It had been a long time since Torsten had seen the old wretch, roused from the bottom quarters of the castle barracks. His white whiskers were as messy as a rat's to boot. But he was good at his job. Had been since Torsten was a young man. Keeping track of all the troops' training schedules, names, retirement benefits— it was a man everybody liked to pretend didn't exist.

"Unfortunately, my friend, he might," Torsten said. "We all might. Make no mistake, I have seen what Nesilia is capable of, and it will take every single one of us to resist."

His gaze arced across the faces of the nobles, all immediately changing from feigning sadness to real, intense fear.

"But, first. We prepare," Jolly said. "I'm from the far North. We've been through far worse."

Jolly earned a few reticent chuckles. Torsten watched as soldiers helped the Master Physician remove Pi's body from his mount. They carried it toward the lower entry into the castle's undercroft like he was a fragile ceramic vase. As if gentleness mattered any longer.

Torsten couldn't help but wonder, as the stableboy had, if maybe this wasn't the end. Surely, Iam wouldn't let his chosen line go out like this? But he knew, deep down, that wasn't the case. The Nothhelms had distilled their bloodline over generations, eliminated rivals, sought perfection. It only made sense that, eventually, the blood ran out.

Focus, he told himself. *It doesn't matter what comes next if there is no next.*

He shook out his head and started off toward the castle entry. The Royal Council followed along behind him like baby ducks.

"Has any word come in from his Holiness, Dellbar?" Torsten asked.

The Master of Scrolls cleared his throat. "He was with the King, was he not?"

"Damn," Torsten swore, taking that as a "no."

"During the attack, I dispatched him and Lord Jolly to Hornsheim to rally the priesthood and bring them here, but they were separated. Nobody has heard a word from Dellbar since."

"He's fine. I'm sure of it," Jolly said. "The man's hardy as an ox. But I'll send search parties as soon as we're done here."

"Priests?" the dwarven Master of Coins scoffed, from far in the back of the small group. "Yer sayin there's to be a battle, and yer invitin priests?"

"We need everyone," Torsten said.

"Oh, what a Commute this be turnin out to be," Al groaned.

Torsten reached the maw of the Throne Room and stopped. The Glass throne sat across the hall, lonely, no guards lining the long carpet leading to it. What did they have left to defend?

He turned and pointed to the Master of Scrolls. "Brosch, send gallers to Hornsheim on multiple routes. Nesilia has an army of grimaurs, there's no telling where they patrol." He turned to Fenwick. "Then, with the gallers, riders, both, to Westvale and Fort Marimount. They are nearest to us. Any man of fighting age they can spare is to be summoned here, along with all rations and arrows."

Torsten reached the throne and paused for a moment. For so long, Liam had sat there, when he was around—even when his mind wasn't.

Then, Pi, the massive chair, making him look so small. A Nothhelm, for all its existence.

Exhausted from just about everything, Torsten sat on the dais, back to it. Knowing how he'd failed its owners was too distracting, and the Kingdom needed him one last time.

"Sir Unger, did you hear me?" Master Fenwick asked.

"Sorry, what was that?" Torsten asked.

"The Lords of those cities are proud. They've long been loyal to the Crown, but sending all their food and defenses when we're at war? I'm not sure they'd go for that. Especially—"

"Especially what?" Torsten snapped.

"Especially when there is no…" The man's eyes drifted toward the empty throne, then back. "… King…"

"Tell them that if they don't comply, they will be stripped of their titles and their holdings," Lord Jolly proposed.

Leurevo Messier, Master of Masons and son of Westvale's presiding governor, stepped forward. "I'm not sure we have the authority to do that."

"They'll listen, or we will all die!" Torsten didn't mean to shout, but his volume made all the nobles wince except for Jolly, who leaned comfortably against a column. It echoed across the mostly empty hall. Dealing with men like these was the bane of Torsten's existence. He preferred the battlefield, but with so many others absent, somebody had to do something.

"And what about Crowfall?" Messier addressed Lord Jolly.

Kaviel Jolly was the Master of Ships, himself. He took a moment to consider it. "If Nesilia's army is coming, we have to assume the Drav Cra are with her. Crowfall has stood for hundreds of years, and it will remain. We Jollys are sturdy folk. Crowfall will hold Winter's Thumb as long as she can, but I'll request that they send half their food stores by ship."

"Half?" asked the Master of Stores. "I'm not sure that's advisable. They need it all for the harsh winter. And what if there is a siege?"

"Make no mistake, Master Westerly. Nesilia's target is Yarrington," Torsten said. "This is personal for her. Extra supplies in Crowfall help nobody. We will deal with re-distribution *after* we win.

"He's right," Lord Jolly said. "Besides, if Crowfall lends full support, Westvale will follow. It's how it's always been."

Master Westerly bowed and backed away, though didn't look convinced in the slightest. Neither did any of the others.

Torsten faced the chubby, dwarven Master of Coin. "Lord Alfotdrumlin. Have you spoken with your father? I know our agreement was only for eliminating Drad Mak and defending White Bridge, but we'll come to a new one. We must get King Lorgit to send us your brother's army and more."

"I'm not for thinkin that'll happen," Al replied.

Torsten punched the polished marble of the dais so hard his knuckles split open. The dwarf winced. "Empty the coffers! Offer the Royal Family's jewels, their clothes, everything. How do none of you understand that it doesn't matter what we have now if we lose everything?"

"It's uh… not that," the dwarf stammered. "Me father hasn't answered a thing since I got here. I hear they shut down the city completely after the battle at White Bridge. No communication."

"Typical dwarves, hiding in their holes when things get scary," Master Brosch said from behind the pack.

"Say that to me face!" Al barked.

Torsten's glower silenced both of them before things escalated.

"He'd go silent, despite your brother himself witnessing Nesilia's true power?" Lord Jolly asked.

The dwarf rolled his stocky shoulders, then blew a raspberry. "Me father has left his own son here and locked me out. What do ye think?"

Torsten cursed under his breath. "Well, keep trying. We could use the help of dwarven engineers to bolster our defenses. For now, use some of the jewelry to ensure the support of our nearest lords. And pay every inn and brothel and place with beds ahead of time to house folk from neighboring towns on the route from White Bridge. Fettingborough, Troborough, Grambling, I want the people here, not feeding Nesilia's army."

"Aye, I'll do that. I'll be needin to have the effects appraised first—"

"There's no time," Torsten said. "Jewels are your people's specialty.

By luck and happenstance, you're stranded here, managing the coffers of a kingless kingdom. Estimate, and get the job done."

His beard parted as he opened his mouth to respond, but nothing came out. Instead, he nodded.

"Now, we must begin preparing defenses," Torsten said. "Lars." Torsten looked around and didn't see the Taskmaster anywhere. "Lars!"

The withering old man appeared across the Throne Room, by the entry, peeking in.

"Yes?" he croaked.

"Work with the Royal Blacksmith, Hovom Nitebrittle. Every set of armor, every weapon made of glaruium, toss them into the Torrential Sea. Steel and iron only. Once that's done, begin outfitting every citizen of Yarrington of age with whatever we have."

"I'm sorry, I know defenses are your prerogative, but why would we discard our sturdiest armor?" asked Messier.

"Because Nesilia was buried in that mountain. She has command over the metal and would use it against us."

"That's absurd," Messier argued.

"I've seen it—felt it, myself."

"But what would the Shieldsmen wear?" Brosch added.

Torsten bit his lip. Then he stood, looking out over the inexperienced and tiresome Royal Council, and the empty Throne Room. Beyond them in the entry hall, soldiers and Shieldsmen had gathered to try and listen. Most were too young to have armpit hair. Few had seen a battle, and mostly those who had died in Latiapur

"There is no King's Shield any longer," Torsten said, voice shaking. "For there is no King to shield. We failed in our duty, and as Wearer of White, named by the late King Pi, I will disband the Order."

He could hear the gasps of shock from the soldiers outside the Throne Room. Some even started to trickle in, kicking etiquette to the curb.

"We have no advantages in this coming war," Torsten said. "No glaruium armor or weapons. No Order of legendary warriors. All we have is each other. And if we stand together, we can beat back this darkness."

He wasn't sure what he'd expected in reaction to that, but it wasn't what happened. The people in the entry hall gasped again and parted. Torsten and the Royal Council looked on in confusion.

Then, a horse raced through them, right into the Throne Room, it's fur-covered hooves indicating it was northern breed. The sigil on its rider's boiled leather armor and his thick beard revealed the same.

The horse skidded to a stop on the slippery surface, and the man dismounted so fast he fell onto his side. Blood stained his sleeve and the horse's neck. Dark circles ringed his eyes, which were completely bloodshot. Men rushed to help him, but he pushed them out of the way and scrambled toward the throne.

He barely made it before his legs gave out and he fell to his hands and knees. There, he remained, trying to speak but unable to catch his breath.

Lord Jolly pushed everyone out of his way and grabbed the man by the collar with his only arm. "What is it?" he asked. "Speak!"

"It's…" the man huffed. They waited patiently. "It's Crowfall, my Lord. The Drav Cra they… I don't know what happened. But they took the city."

Torsten sank back onto the dais. He stared, forlorn, at the paintings filling the vaulted ceiling, telling stories from the origin of the Glass Kingdom after the God Feud to now. All the great kings and their legendary victories. And he wondered if there would be another victory to paint up there, or if it'd all come crumbling down.

"Sir Unger, what do we do?" one of the councilmen asked. It didn't matter who. The same question seemed to echo off all their lips.

"We prepare," Torsten said, sitting up, gaze flitting toward Jolly, who was now on his knees, running his one hand through his hair. "For our war has already begun."

XXXII

THE SERVANT

Freydis stood at the bow of a Drav Cra longboat, squinting against the wind and the driving snow. She'd sailed these waters many times, but this time was different.

This time, she was Arch Warlock.

This time, she was Nesilia's first in command.

And she wouldn't waste time with trivialities like Redstar always had. Sowing fear into the minds of his enemies. Playing games. Seeking relics.

No, Freydis sailed as her people were meant to—as a conqueror. With all the tribes united under her command by word of the Goddess herself, expanding the fleet so her entire army could cross the strait was easy.

Many grumbled, afraid to head back south into the warmth of summer, into the lands where they'd been betrayed, losing Mak and so many others. Those who grumbled loudest earned vines around their hearts.

Then none complained.

"Do you see, Redstar?" she sneered to herself. "All it took was faith in her. All you cared about was yourself."

"Crowfall nears!" one of her scouts shouted from the crow's nest.

Freydis dragged her hand hard across the rail, tearing it open on the rough wood. She drew on the fresh blood, digging deep into the connection to Elsewhere. Nesilia said it was emptied of souls, and

Freydis could feel it. There was so much latent power for her to draw upon.

She waved a bloody hand in front of her, forcing the snow and the fog to the side, giving her a clear view. And there it was, the dark stone walls of Crowfall. Built onto a series of sharp hills like a crow's talon, the low points gave the city an added natural defense thanks to high positions for archers.

Only the most foolish dradinengors in history had attempted to raid the city proper, each of them dying. Nearby towns and villages—even the outskirts of the city—fell prey to the Drav Cra all the time, but Crowfall's walls had never been breached. The Jollys had kept the place safe for generations.

No longer.

Freydis reached again into the reserves of Elsewhere and launched a ball of flame up into the white sky. The men rowing at her back stopped, and all around her, the Drav Cra longboats followed their example, forming a line across the calm water.

Bells chimed. Glassmen scurried around their city like ants. Archers gathered atop the parapets of the tall walls. What little was left of their fleet after the war in the south sprang to action, letting down their sails and loading in soldiers for defenses.

"Sacrifice as many as it takes," Nesilia had told her. *"They must learn that the North is ours."*

Freydis listened to the bated breaths of the warriors filling the ship behind her. They were eager to raid, chomping at the bit like the dire wolves caged up beside them, ready to kill those who thought themselves superior.

She lifted her sliced hand, the blood dripping down her pale arm, and then let it fall forward. All at once, shouting in Drav Crava sounded from the dradinengors on the other ships.

Young men and women walked to the bows, all of them, faces painted red and white. They were a new wave of warlocks, recently indwelled. Some were weaker than others. Some were nearly worthless in this new flock, but all together for the first time, they would be unstoppable.

Freydis drew her jagged knife, lifted her unscathed palm, and sliced it straight across. All the other warlocks throughout the fleet followed her lead—three to a ship, with one on each giving their own lives by stabbing themselves through the chest while the other two cut their hands. A worthy sacrifice.

And as their blood poured out, so too did the power of Freydis and those left living. As one, they raised their bloody palms toward Crowfall and drew on Elsewhere. The bells continued to chime as the waters before them started to ripple.

Freydis smirked. *So much power.* It was as if she could feel the weight of the sea in her fingertips. Lone chunks of ice floating about, leftover from winter, broke apart from the vibrations. Her ship rocked violently, all the warriors forced to hold onto whatever they could.

She didn't.

Now, the water yanked on her like a magnetic force. Her heart raced, blood pumping through her limbs as fast as it could. In her peripherals, she could see some of the young warlocks falling to their knees, unable to handle the magic flowing through them.

Black started to close in on her vision, but she held firm. The sea didn't just ripple now, it raged. Spiky waves rose and fell, running on opposing currents that could never occur naturally. One of their longboats was caught on it and pulled up ahead before being capsized.

Still, Freydis held. Blood now gushed out of her hand, making her entire arm numb up to the shoulder. Her legs grew weak, shaky. One of her men must have noticed because she felt hands on her back, struggling to keep her upright.

And then, the sea budged. Freydis collapsed to her knees and released a breath she hadn't even realized she'd been holding. Gasping for air, she watched as the water before their ships rose into a tidal wave as tall as the walls of Crowfall itself and raced toward the city. Freydis' fleet was drawn along in the undertow at speeds beyond what rowers might be capable of.

Terrified shouts from Crowfall's commanders echoed. The bells grew louder. Freydis could see none of it over the wave, only imagine. Imagine the water ripping through their oversized ships that compensated for their lack of magical ability. Imagine the drowning soldiers, burdened down by too much expensive armor to breathe. Imagine the fortifications crumbled to dust and detritus by the sea itself.

And that's exactly what happened. Portions of the wall broke apart, flooding the lower sections of the city. The wave ravaged their ships, and her longboats finished them off at ramming speeds.

She was too exhausted to move, but she remained kneeling on the ship's bow, even after it scraped onto the docks along with the dozens of others. The Drav Cra army charged off. What remained of the Glass archers picked off many from above, but not nearly enough. The dire wolves were let loose and clambered up the rubble to tear them to pieces.

Without the walls, the Northern Glassmen were too compromised to resist. Her people swarmed them, even with all the city's defensible high points. And her army wasn't alone.

While they charged, Wvenweigard finally arrived from the east with a throng of chekt. It was a long route around and through the mountains, and it looked like some of his forces didn't make it, but there were enough.

The warlock charged out in front atop one of the great beasts, flinging fireballs at any Glassmen in their path. A horde of grimaurs flew with them, dicing up the archer's positions on that side of the city.

Crowfall had stood in the hands of the Glass Kingdom since their first King—that feckless coward who'd abandoned the Drav Cra for weakness and warmth—sent men north to defend it against people who had once been family, now proclaimed by them to be worthless savages.

That great city, once untouchable, now, in mere minutes, had fallen. Exhaustion tugged at Freydis, but she watched and listened with a smirk on her lips… until the screams stopped, the bells stopped tolling, and all that was left were the screeching grimaurs.

XXXIII

THE THIEF

Sunlight refracted through the glass spire, blinding Whitney even at such a distance. He'd never found Yarrington to be all that impressive—not after seeing places like Myen Elnoir and Brek-liodad—but that didn't mean it couldn't be beautiful.

He hadn't been back to the Glass capital since that crazy battle atop Mount Lister, where Torsten had lost his sight, and Whitney had lost Sora. He'd met Lucindur soon after when the Pompare Troupe's juggler died during Nesilia's cultists' rioting. It astounded Whitney the way events tended to strike one another like flint, the sparks bouncing from one thing to the next, setting flame to unintended targets.

More and more, he felt like a pawn in someone else's game. Gods and goddesses, no less. Like he was nothing, just an insignificant speck on a world so vast, not even he had seen half of it.

If he followed the trail from his imprisonment for stealing the Glass Crown, he'd find Sora, lose Sora, find Sora again, then lose her and find her all over. He wasn't even sure that was it if he counted seeing her in Nowhere. Enough to make his head spin off his shoulders. That job had sparked so many things, and it had all led them to this place.

They'd been walking for a few days after having found carriage rides through Westvale and further south to some of the fringe towns, stopping only to resupply. It hadn't been a comfortable journey, but it was better than being in the far North, frozen to the bone, and chilled to the core.

"My feet are killing me," Whitney complained. He couldn't help himself.

"We heard ye the first dozen times," Tum Tum said. "Ye wonder why we call ye flower-pickers."

"I don't wonder, and I still don't think it's insulting."

"Suit yerself."

They kept walking through colorful hills, and Whitney fought every desire to actually pick Tum Tum a flower, snickering to himself and then wiping his face of the smile every time the raven-haired dwarf peered upward.

"It's nice to see the city," Sora said. She stopped to dig through her bag and passed around a water skin. "Despite all the horrors that have taken place there."

"That old place?" Whitney said, taking a swig and giving it to Lucindur.

"So, this be Yarrington?" Tum Tum said. "Ain't impressed."

"You're just trying to get me back for thinking Balonhearth was a rubble pile," Whitney said. "Won't work. I don't like this shog hole, either."

Yarrington stood on the horizon like a beacon of hope, or bastion of despair, all depending upon one's name and status. Acres of farmland surrounded its tall, stone fortifications. Within, was a blanket of thatch homes that slowly became more substantially built the closer they got to the castle. At the base of the mountain, Old Yarrington and its many mansions threatened to give the castle a run for its money. In the north and west, the city butted up to the Torrential Sea and Mount Lister, respectively. Natural defenses. Dockside alone should have dissuaded attackers—no one in their right mind would want to go to that sewage dump, and to think, that used to be the nice part of town.

"Ah, yes. The place where the high and mighty look down upon the lowly, eyes filled with Iam's grace," Whitney said, circling his eyes. "Good to be back."

"You love it," Sora said.

Whitney shrugged. "Beats Troborough."

He'd never admit it out loud, but he missed that little farm town and hope that someday, he'd return.

"I still don't know exactly what we are supposed to do when we get there," Lucindur said.

It was an excellent question, and Whitney had been mulling it over for as long as they'd been on the road. Sure, they had the Brike Stone—horrifying little thing—but they honestly didn't know what to *do* with the Brike Stone beyond repeating what they'd done in the Citadel with the bar guai. Typically, Whitney would have a portion of a plan, and fate, or whatever power, would develop the rest of it on the spot. This time, however, with the Buried Goddess looming over them and threatening all of existence, Whitney felt a smidgeon of concern.

"First, we'll find Torsten," he said, making believe he had it all thought out. "Besides being thrilled to see me, there's plenty he needs to know." Whitney gave Sora a knowing glance, and she lowered her head.

He drew close and nudged her with his elbow. "It's going to be fine. Remember, this is Torsten."

"That's exactly why I don't think it'll be fine," she said. "Perhaps you don't remember our time spent with him. It wasn't exactly pleasant. 'Witch,' I believe, was the term he used."

"Torsten loves you."

They crested a hill that looked down into the Haskwood Thicket, and all Whitney could think of was himself bound up and being dragged down the road by Torsten on their way to slay their first goddess in the Webbed Woods. That gave him hope that they could do it again.

The Glass Road pierced through trees and farmland, and they followed it through the hills until they reached the fields outside the Eastern Gate. And there, Whitney found something new to a city he thought he knew every nook and cranny of—a dark mass milling around.

"What in Meungor's shiny, bald arse be that?" Tum Tum said.

"Are those… people?" Whitney asked.

There could be no doubt about it. Thousands of people filled the pasturelands just outside of Yarrington, suffocating crops. They didn't appear to be hostile or any of Nesilia's forces, just good, hard-working farmers and merchants.

As the party got closer, the sound grew deafening. Tents were like tiny arrowheads sticking up from the ground. Campfires burned, sending up puffs of smoke. Above, Aquira screeched, then soared ahead a bit to try to get a better view.

"Don't go far!" Sora shouted.

"She'll be fine," Whitney said, knowing the wyvern was more than capable of handling herself. They had a new respect for each other after the Iron Bank. At least, he did, and he hoped she did too.

"What do you think that's all about?" Sora asked.

"Beats me," Whitney answered. "Let's find out."

The city looked closer than it was, and Whitney did his share of complaining along the way, but eventually, they stood at the outskirts of the still-growing crowd. Blankets of travelers poured in through the Thicket, from the east and south.

"There're so many," Lucindur said. "Are they… homeless?"

"It's almost like a pilgrimage," Sora said.

"For what, though?" Tum Tum asked.

"Hey… is that," Whitney said, standing on the balls of his feet. "It is! Hamm!"

Before she could protest, Whitney grabbed hold of Sora's hand and dragged her through the throng toward some of the newcomers.

"Hamm!" he called.

"Whitney, slow down," Sora said, but he didn't listen.

He did, however, hesitate when he saw who was with Hamm. Alless—but not the Alless Whitney had spent so long with in Fake Troborough. No, this was the Alless he'd grown up pining after, who was now twice his age and looked it. Still, her eyes were kind and inviting.

"What's wrong?" Sora asked.

He shook his head. "Nothing. C'mon."

After shoving their way through irritated mobs, Whitney tapped the Twilight Manor's big bartender on the shoulder.

"Aye?" Hamm said, turning to them. Then, his eyes locked onto Sora.

"Sora?" he said in utter disbelief. He waited a moment for Sora to respond, and when she smiled, he gave her a big hug. "Sora, it is you! You look to be doing well!"

Whitney almost scoffed out loud. If Hamm only knew.

"And you," Sora said.

"And who's this you're with?" he asked her.

Whitney's mouth almost won the race with his heart to the bottom of his stomach. Hamm, however, didn't let the joke go too far.

"I'm kidding! Whitney Fierstown again! Get in here," he said, pulling Whitney into a bear hug. "It's been a while. Fancy meeting you out here of all places. I thought you'd have been back to the Manor by now. Seen what we've done with the place after those gray skins burned her down. And now we're supposed to shake their hands like nothing happened?"

Whitney put a hand through his hair. "I saw it not too long ago while I was traveling with my troupe. Was uh—keeping a bit of a low profile, you understand—was still new with the troupe. It looked great though!"

"I see," Hamm said, the disappointment on his face palpable. "Well, you remember Alless."

Hamm beckoned Alless forward, and she curtsied.

"Yeah. I… of course…" Whitney could feel his face turn red.

"That's how all the young bucks act around her," Hamm said. Then, turning to Alless, he said, "Isn't that right?"

Alless smiled. Like her eyes, it was kind and inviting.

"Oh, hey… stop me if you've heard this one," Hamm said with his typical charm. "What's the difference between a Westvale whore—"

"Hamm," Sora interrupted. "I'm sorry, but what's going on here?"

"You don't know?" he asked, only a little deflated at not being able to finish the joke Whitney had heard and told a million times.

Sora shook her head.

"The King's dead," Hamm said.

"Again?" Whitney asked.

Sora punched his arm.

"Dead? King Pi?" she asked. "You're kidding? What happened?"

"No one's telling us, but it can't be good if we're all here," Hamm said.

"Right," Sora said. "This can't be normal. Everyone traveling from so far for the King's death? Forgive me if this is disrespectful, but no one really even knew Pi, did they?"

"Aye. You're right. This ain't just for the King's death. Master of

Warfare called for us all to seek refuge in Yarrington. Said an army's marching on the capital."

Whitney gave Sora a look. She returned it.

"Then, shouldn't everyone be sent *away* from the capital?" Whitney said.

"That's what I said," Alless added.

"No safer place than in those walls," Hamm said, pointing to the city.

"I suppose," Alless said.

"Some say, a horde of demons is coming," Hamm went on. "Others, the Shesaitju under the usurper who betrayed King Pi. All I know is, I watched them let in a mob of them traitorous gray skins. Marched right past us, through the gates, and said they were allies, while we're all left out here."

"We certainly weren't expecting this," Alless said, gazing out over the field of people. "What is this? They invited us all here to what—sleep in the fields? I'm of the mind to turn heel and march right back home."

She said it with that same sass Whitney had come to expect from her, and for a minute, that young Alless appeared in all her fury. Then he remembered that he barely knew the real woman at all. In fact, this might have been his first time ever talking to her directly.

"Don't do that," Whitney blurted, knowing full well why Yarrington would want everyone within the safety of its walls. Torsten was attempting to shield them. But how could he explain to all these simple folk that the army wasn't from Shesaitju or Brotlebir, or any enemy they'd ever heard about before?

"He's right. Settle, Alless, dear," Hamm said with a steadying hand. "Something's gonna come of this. I'm sure of that."

Alless furrowed her eyebrows.

"I–uh. Yeah, I don't know. Look, Hamm, uh… Alless… we should get back to our friends. I'm sure we'll run into you again before all this is through. If they say they want us inside the walls, I'm sure there's a reason. Just… stay safe, okay?"

Hamm and Alless now wore the confused looks and exchanged glances. "You, too," they said at the same time.

"This isn't good," Sora whispered as they headed back.

"Well, you didn't think it was a party, did you?" Whitney replied.

"Don't think I didn't see the way you looked at her, Whitney Fierstown."

"I—you—That's what you're concerned about?"

"I'm kidding. But I certainly hope I look so good at her age," she said. "If I live to see her age."

That brought a somber quiet to the rest of their journey back to where Lucindur and Tum Tum waited. They returned just in time to see Aquira descend and find a perch on Sora's shoulder. The crowd around them screamed and distanced themselves. With all the guards stationed by the gates, none were out here to do anything about it.

Sora scratched the wyvern's head. Then, as calmly as if she were ordering a drink, she said to the others, "King Pi is dead, and I'm guessing Nesilia had something to do with it."

"Wait, what?" Whitney said, turning to her. "How did you get that?"

"You didn't?"

"I... I didn't... not?" he said, not wanting to sound ignorant. "Hamm said something about Shesaitju betrayals. We know they're good at that."

"You don't think this is a coincidence, do you?" Sora asked.

"I don't know about coincidence, but I didn't jump to *that* conclusion."

"So, what—you think the world is about to end, the last Nothhelm King dies, and she had nothing to do with it?"

"Slow down, both of ye," Tum Tum said.

"Yes. Tell us—who was that, and what did you learn?" Lucindur asked.

"That was a friend from our hometown," Whitney said. "He said the—what did he call him?"

"Master of Warfare," Sora supplied.

"Right—you think that's... it's gotta be, right?"

"Who else would it be?"

"Yeah, but he's blind—"

"What are ye two blabbering about!" Tum Tum shouted.

"Sorry," Sora said. "We think Torsten Unger, the new Master of Warfare, apparently, called everyone in the realm here to prepare for the attack. But I don't think most of them know exactly what's coming."

"Well, that is one way to get everyone killed," Lucindur said.

"Hey, now. This is Torsten we're talking about," Whitney said. "He wouldn't get people killed… on purpose."

"You think he has a plan?" Sora asked.

Whitney patted the lump in his pocket—the Brike Stone.

"Not like the one we have, I doubt," he said, still hoping his confidence would inspire a real plan of his own. "We've gotta find him. He clearly needs us... again."

"How?" Sora asked. "In this mess, we'd be lucky to even find the front gates."

Whitney surveyed the landscape. "Gates are that way. We should start off, then."

"That's it? Just waltz right up to the gates and hope someone opens for us when they're makin all these people wait?" Tum Tum asked.

"You got a better idea?" Whitney asked, looking at each in turn. "Didn't think so," he said when no one responded. "Now, come on. If I know Torsten—and I do—he'll take one look at me and haul us in for a banquet."

"You're delusional," Sora said, laughing.

"This is no time for laughter, Sora," Whitney scolded, then smiled and took off toward the gates, practically dragging the others in tow.

"You don't think this Torsten fellow of yours has summoned my people, do you?" Lucindur asked, not even trying to hide the worry in her voice.

"Sure hope he has," Whitney said without thinking. "They could use all the help they can get."

"I'm sure your daughter is fine, Lucindur," Sora chimed in.

"Oh, right," Whitney added, thinking about Gentry. "You know what? I'm sure he knew they'd be safer there in Glinthaven. Nesilia is headed here. Plus, I don't see many of your people here."

He was right, of course. There were plenty of pink-skinned men and women, from seemingly all over western Pantego, but sparse few brown, gray, or any other colors present.

The crowd thickened now that they were pressing toward the gates, making it hard to push through. Rumors and theories about what was happening flew around. Whitney recognized accents from Westvale, even a handful as far up north as Crowfall, or south as Winde Port.

"What if this isn't about safety at all?" Lucindur asked.

"She's right," Tum Tum said. "If he be smart as ye say he be, he's buildin an army."

Silence prevailed for a moment before Whitney said, "All the more reason to leave Glinthaven out of it. You saw those folks; none of them could swing a sword if their lives depended on it—present company not included."

The look on Lucindur's face told Whitney he wasn't fooling her. Rarely did she appear worried, but the emotion was clearly etched there on her pretty face.

They soon came to a cloud of white robes, priests by the look of them, eyes burned out, all old and grumpy-looking. So many, in fact, Whitney wondered if every last holy man and woman on Pantego had arrived for whatever this was.

"Must be full inside if even the priests are bein forced to wait out here," Tum Tum said.

As they continued to shove through, more than a fair share of those who could still see jumped when they caught sight of Aquira. Some circled their eyes in prayer as if warding off a demon.

"Relax," Whitney said. "Haven't you ever seen a wyvern? Geesh!"

Aquira retreated, burying her muzzle into Tum Tum's hood.

"Father?" a voice said. There were so many 'fathers' present, but for some reason, this voice broke through the din. "Father Gorenheimer?"

Sora turned first to view a sister of Iam hurrying toward them.

"You've got to be kidding me," she said.

"What?" Whitney whispered. "Who's that?"

"Father Gorenheimer! I've looked for you all over Hornsheim," the sister said. "I thought for sure you'd be there during such trying times —Blessings of Iam! Your eyes! It seems Torsten Unger wasn't the only one to receive a miracle."

Was she talking to Whitney? He was at a total loss. His eyes? Based upon Sora's reaction, he figured he should know this woman, but he didn't recognize her at all. Then, he realized she must have been the victim of one of his many grifts.

He swore internally, then took a breath.

"Oh-oh!" Whitney said. "Father… Father Gorborhibbon—you must be thinking of my… my brother!"

"Brother?" the young lady said.

"Yes, yes. He went onto the priesthood. Twins. Identical. New name, everything."

"Is that so?" the young lady asked.

"Sure is," Whitney said. "Me? I'm a vagabond. So sorry to disappoint."

Before the young lady could speak again, Whitney rushed everyone along.

"Who the yig-and-shog was that?" Whitney asked Sora when they were safely out of earshot.

"You really are oblivious sometimes," she said. "Nice save though. Twin? Do people actually believe that?"

"You've just witnessed the answer yourself, my dear. So, who was that?"

"Nauriyal," she said.

"Hmmmmm."

"Nauriyal from Bridleton?"

Whitney thought for a moment. "Nope. Nothing."

"Nauriyal Darkings, daughter of Bartholomew Darkings, the governor of Bridleton!"

"Shog in a barrel. You've gotta be kidding me," Whitney said.

"That's what I said."

"Man, I forgot about that one." He laughed to himself. Sora's scowl didn't wane. "What? Six years in Elsewhere, remember? I remembered everything about you, at least."

"Oh, golly. Aren't I the luckiest." Sora rolled her eyes.

"Are ye two done playin social club? We got a world to save," Tum Tum grumbled, pushing forward to make a path. "Look out! Comin through. Comin through!"

There wasn't much complaint from anyone as they noticed Aquira and the stocky dwarf elbowing hips and thighs.

"I guess we should follow," Lucindur said, passing them by as well.

"After you," Whitney said to Sora with a flourish of his hand.

Just then, horns sounded, loud and crisp, and playing a royal fanfare. Whitney followed the noise to the ramparts above the front gate. They were still pretty far away, but the dark-skinned, well-armored man standing over the entrance couldn't be mistaken.

"Torsten!" Whitney said.

The horns died down, and Torsten began to speak, though they were so far back they couldn't understand a word of it. That added to the confusion as everyone around them began to complain that they too couldn't hear what the new Master of Warfare had to say.

"This could've been better thought out," Whitney remarked. "Let's try to get closer."

Everyone else had the same idea, which made it like a school of fish swimming upstream. Countless complaints filled the air, and suddenly, it made sense to Whitney why they didn't just let them all in. People were a pain.

"We're baking out here!" a man shouted.

"You let gray scum in ahead of fellow Glassmen?" barked another.

"We're never going to get close enough," Sora said as they ran into a blockade of complainers.

The people may as well have been holding torches and pitchforks. They'd feel differently when Nesilia's demon army arrived. They'd all be grateful for the refuge then.

Look at me, taking the side of the nobles, he thought. *Who am I?*

A commotion rose behind them, and a gruff voice said, "Move aside. Move aside. High Priest coming through."

The voice belonged to a middle-aged priest who looked half-dead and used a white cane topped with an Eye of Iam to guide his steps. He smelled like his not-so-white-anymore robes had been soaked in rum, but he didn't appear drunk. Unlike other priests, he wore no cloth over his eyes, just let the gruesome holes in his head out for all to see.

Several other priests joined him, as well as monks and sisters of Iam, Nauriyal, too. One member of their holy group stood above all the others, though—a literal giant with a crooked nose and missing teeth, and a face like an anvil.

"Moooove," he droned, voice like wind through the deepest cavern.

"Follow them," Whitney whispered as the group pushed by.

Hiding within the holy company, Whitney marveled at how the people parted without question. He wanted to believe it was because of the man claiming to be the High Priest, and a few people did indeed circle their eyes and bow. Though, he imagined it was more due to the giant and his thunderous footsteps and a desire to not be crushed beneath them.

In Yarrington, you saw them from time to time, working the docks or on a construction site. In the towns and villages surrounding, however, they were pretty rare. Troborough occasionally had some pass through, employed by troupes or merchants. Still, he imagined a lot of these folk would have gone their whole lives without ever seeing a real giant.

It wasn't long before Whitney and the others were closing in on the gates. Torsten had just finished giving his speech with the words, "Everyone will be allowed inside in due time. Trust in Iam, and He will protect us."

The people up front who had been able to hear didn't seem at all pleased, pushing against the Glass soldiers lined up before the entry like a wave. More than a few brought up the fact that Shesaitju had been allowed in before them, and that such disrespect indicated the Nothhelm line was truly gone.

"What else do you think he said?" Whitney asked.

"Maybe the truth for once," Sora said. "Now that would be a new look for the Crown."

"Well… nobody is wearing the crown right now."

The robed man who claimed to be the High Priest and his giant companion stopped before the gate, and their easy ride toward the entry ceased. Whitney bumped into some brawny farmer's back who had the same idea.

"Some help please, my dear Uhlvark," the High Priest addressed the giant.

"Nooow?" the giant replied.

The High Priest nodded.

The giant lifted his leg as high as he could, then brought it slamming down. The mud from so many trampling feet made him stagger and catch himself on the wall. Guards looked on in confusion.

Torsten was in the midst of turning away but stopped when he heard the resounding stomp. He returned to the parapet and looked down. The sight of the white cloth over his eyes stole the words right off Whitney's tongue. His old friend looked like a priest, like Father Drimmond, the version of Torsten from Elsewhere.

"Sir Unger," the High Priest shouted, without facing up. He couldn't see, so Whitney supposed it didn't matter where he looked. "Is that you up there?"

"Your Holiness!" Torsten shouted back. He circled his eyes over his blindfold. "You made it. I was beginning to fret." It looked like he was staring right at the group of them, though.

The High Priest hurriedly circled his own eyes, but it was sloppy.

"Worry not." He spread his arms and gestured to the priests surrounding him. Whitney noticed then that many of them appeared less than pleased to be there. "I bring all Iam's Light with me. Let us hope it's bright enough."

"It has to be. Open the gates!" Torsten shouted. "Let the company from Hornsheim in."

At this, the crowd lost all semblance of passivity, shoving toward the gates so much that the Glass soldiers drew their weapons.

"Stay back!" they ordered.

Whitney and the others used the distraction to sneak back into the group. Just as they were about to pass the raised portcullis, he felt a hand grab his cloak and yank.

"Oi! You! What's your business here?"

Whitney turned to see a scar-faced guard, big and brooding.

"We're with them," Whitney said and started forward. Again, he was jerked back.

The guard stared him down. "You're with the priests?" he asked.

"No, they aren't," Nauriyal said without even a second glance.

"Oh, c'mon!" Whitney protested as he was shoved back out into the maddening mob, the others not far behind.

"Torsten!" Whitney shouted up. He called again and again until finally, Torsten's bald head peeked over the wall and stared down. This time, it was exactly like he looked at Whitney.

"Torsten, it's me—your very best friend, Whitney Fierstown!"

"You've got to be kidding me," Torsten said, loud enough to hear.

"That seems to be a theme," Whitney muttered to himself.

"I know who it is," Torsten said. "I can see you."

"You can—what? Never mind..." Whitney said. "Just let us in."

"Not a chance," Torsten said. "You can wait your turn like everyone else."

He quickly vanished again.

"Well, that's that!" Tum Tum threw up his hands in frustration and began turning away.

"Wait a second," Sora said to Tum Tum. This time, she called for Torsten. Seconds later, he reappeared.

"What now?" Torsten growled.

"Sir Unger, it's me, Sora. Maybe you don't remember me, but we have grave news and believe we can assist in…" She took a moment to gather her thoughts. "Please, hear us out, Torsten. We think we can stop *Her*."

"Sora…" Torsten said, barely loud enough to be heard, but Whitney saw her name on his lips. Then, louder, Torsten said, "Fine. Let them in."

Whitney smiled, turned to the others, and said, "And that's how it's done. I told you we were close."

"Aye, close like piss and shog," Tum Tum said.

Whitney bowed to each guard in the line, taking a bit longer on the scar-faced one. They mostly ignored him and reformed their blockade for all the angry folk waiting on the fields.

"The Master of Warfare is Glintish?" Lucindur asked.

Whitney wrapped his arm around her shoulder. "Oh, Lucy, you have a lot to learn."

"And you have a lot to learn about women," Lucindur said, before shaking him off.

Lucindur looked back at Sora, and Whitney realized she'd fallen behind them. She didn't seem upset, just deep in thought. Her very posture was strained.

He couldn't blame her. Here they were, Yarrington, where this whole awful adventure had begun, and where, now, it would come to its end. And if they failed, the entire world would too.

No pressure. No pressure at all.

XXXIV

THE KNIGHT

Whitney Fierstown. He was the last person Torsten wanted to see in a time of crisis. Sure, they'd come to terms with each other in their previous meeting, when Torsten lay bruised, bloody, and blind from the fight with Redstar atop Mount Lister. But trouble seemed to cling to the thief like a shadow.

Worse yet, he was back with Sora, the very blood mage who'd caused all of Winde Port to burn down with her vile, uncontrollable powers. At the time, he thought she'd been sent there by Iam to turn the tide of battle when all hope seemed lost. Just as she had when Torsten battled Redstar for the first time in the Webbed Woods.

Now, he saw it differently. Sora was a precursor for dark magic returning to Pantego as Nesilia regained her foothold. From Redstar to the return of mystics like he'd witnessed in Latiapur to the creatures of Elsewhere itself.

Torsten pushed through the square toward Uhlvark, whose bulbous head rose high above the crowd. Shieldsmen wearing leather and iron helped Torsten make his way. Anything but glaruium. Under the Royal Blacksmith Hovom Nitebrittle's guidance, soldiers had already gathered every bit of glaruium-reinforced armor and weapons and tossed them into the Torrential Sea.

The metal, like so many things in the realm, had gone from blessed by Iam to cursed by Nesilia. Touching the cloth wrapped about his eyes, Torsten almost prayed he wouldn't be next.

The mob in Yarrington's markets grew daily. There wasn't enough room in the city for everyone, especially with the Shesaitju being accommodated in the castle grounds. Better that than them out in the open with all the townsfolk who'd lost their homes and families to them in Muskigo's rebellion.

Another nagging thought beat on Torsten's brain. Was he as naïve as Pi had been when he allowed the savage Drav Cra into the castle gates? Were these people any different? Enemies somehow turned ally in the face of an attack. The irony wasn't lost on him that these were precisely the enemies Pi had entreated Redstar over.

He shook the thought away. Had to. This was the only chance against an enemy they had no natural hope of beating. Besides, at least they weren't slicing themselves open in the courtyard and watching as their blood filled the cracks on hallowed ground.

But still, Torsten thought to himself. *In the castle?*

The inns—filled. Cathedral halls—filled. Every home in Yarrington was to house as many as it could, by royal edict—whatever that meant without a King. Even the mansions of Old Yarrington were forced to help. Some of the nobles resisted, citing precisely that—there was no King—but Torsten had no problem bashing their doors down.

He didn't need to keep everyone happy. Just alive.

Still, complaints and rumors spread through the mob like wildfire. From people saying the dwarves were attacking to others claiming that Mahraveh and the Shesaitju had usurped the throne. Torsten tried to be truthful, that the Buried Goddess had returned and marched on them with an army of demons and rebel Shesaitju, but the more people arrived from outside the city, the more lies came with them. He'd even heard rumors that some ancient goblin king had returned from the dead to turn Pantego into his own kind.

Again, it didn't matter. As long as they knew that war was coming. It was just taking forever to get them all into the city. Every man of age had to be sorted out and ushered to the armory, then fitted in preparation to defend the city. And not every man *wanted* to fight.

They didn't have a choice.

It would have all been easier with Pi around, but this was where they were.

"Toooorsten," Uhlvark's unmistakable drawl hung on the air as

Torsten bulled through yet another crowd of conscripts saying they'd never fight alongside a gray man.

The giant jogged at Torsten, a string of drool on the right side of his toothy grin. His boisterous footsteps cracked stone and scattered the mob.

Before he was crushed in the giant's embrace, Torsten stuck out his hand. Uhlvark slid to a stop, regarded the gesture curiously, then gently squeezed Torsten's palm with two thick digits.

"It's good to see you again, Uhlvark," Torsten said. He shook, and immediately regretted it as the giant shook back and nearly ripped Torsten's arm out of the socket.

"I ran into an old friend," Dellbar said. He stopped in front of Torsten and traced his eyes.

Torsten did the same. "I hope you found what we were looking for."

"I hope so, too. If nothing else, I brought a pack of angry priests." He laughed solemnly, nodding toward the group of white-robed men following the path the giant had cleared for them. Sisters and monks helped guide them along, while others pulled carts filled with tomes.

"Good."

"We'll see," Dellbar said. "What of Lord Jolly?"

"He's fine. He relayed your message and is busy taking stock of our naval forces." Torsten took a deep breath. "But the King—"

"I heard," Dellbar interrupted. "I only hope his betrothed-to-be is still with us."

Torsten nodded once. "She's helping Lord Jolly. And she knows that the ceremony was worthless without consummation."

"She is wiser than her years dictate."

"That, she is."

Dellbar took a deep breath. "And so, here we children of Iam stand, kingless. I must say, even poets couldn't have written a more fitting end."

"Your Holiness, don't speak like that. At least, don't let anyone hear it. We have to believe that Pi's death won't be in vain."

"Spoken like a true man of faith," Dellbar said, wearing a withering grin.

"The city will hold," Torsten added.

"It has to," Dellbar agreed.

A brief period of silence passed between them until Torsten said, "You look exhausted. The Cathedral has been prepared with bedding for all of you. Get some rest. We have a battle to prepare for."

"Rest." Dellbar chuckled and laid his hand upon Torsten's shoulder. "Wouldn't that be nice?"

Torsten snorted in agreement, and then Dellbar whistled Uhlvark along. The giant followed like a stray dog while the rest of the priests and men and women of Iam joined them. Torsten's attention was caught by a familiar face amidst the white-clothed. Bartholomew Darkings' daughter offered him a coy smile.

"Torsty Cakes!" Whitney exclaimed, catching Torsten off guard. The thief threw his arms around him from the side.

Torsten clenched his fists and prepared to push Whitney away. He held back. Instead, he returned a light embrace, and when they parted, Whitney was left beaming ear to ear. Any other time Torsten would have desired to slap the look right off the thief's face, but not now. He couldn't remember his last time seeing a smile like that.

What did he expect? Whitney was an enigma, an eternal optimist who also found a way to complain about everything. The man could grin like a child on Dawning morning when the entire world was at risk of ending.

"Whitney Fierstown, it's been a long time," Torsten said.

"Even longer for me," Whitney replied, making no sense as usual. "Are you a priest now?"

"What? Oh, this." He tugged on his blindfold. "It allows me to see."

"It does, doesn't it?" a Glintish woman said, emerging from behind the thief.

Torsten's next words caught in his throat. She was gorgeous, a true beauty amongst ugly things. Oversized, gold pendant earrings hung from her ears while a colorful dress clung to her like hope in the midst of a storm. And strapped across her back, something Torsten had not seen in many years: a genuine Glintish salfio. She was nothing like the Glintish immigrants Torsten knew from Dockside. And her skin... It was smooth and shiny like melted dark chocolate, flawless.

Even more than Whitney's embrace, his Glintish companion caught him by surprise. Then, without regard for having just met him, she leaned in and studied Torsten's blindfold. He fought the urge to back up. An expression twisted her delicate features as if to her, it looked like more than a bloodstained, white cloth.

"I can almost feel the magic radiating from it," she said, reaching out to touch it. "It has its own melody."

"Not magic," Torsten said quickly, his throat tight.

"Right," the woman said.

"And you are?" Torsten finally found the words to ask.

The woman pulled her hand back. "So sorry, I'm—"

"This is Lucy," Whitney said. "She's a friend. And that short fellow is Tum Tum. He's a dwarf."

"Me Lord," the dwarf said, nodding.

"And oh, I'm sure you remember Sora." Whitney stepped to the side, revealing the blood mage, Sora.

"Sir Unger," she said, performing a perfect bow. "It's good to see you again."

Like Whitney and the Glintish woman, she caught Torsten by surprise. Though, not in the same way. He'd seen her at the gates, knew she was there.

But, something was different about her. She seemed older, more mature. Not in appearance, but in the way she carried herself. Her eyes even. The young blood mage he'd known so shortly seemed to care about every little thing, eyes darting around as if hiding something. She always had her arms tight to her side, obscuring the scars on her hands and forearms. Her stance had been slouched, protective.

Not this Sora. She stood tall and proud, unveiling a figure that could have given Oleander healthy competition. She wore what appeared to be an authentic Panpingese kimono, and her eyes were focused with intense purpose. Her arms... Torsten's blessed vision sometimes made it difficult to see details, but to him, it seemed like there were no scars on them at all. Just smooth amber-toned skin.

She looked not like a raged blood mage prone to losing control but like a true mystic.

"I'm not so sure it is," Torsten admitted.

"Oh, don't be like that, Torsten," Whitney said. "She's come a long way since the Webbed Woods! You should see her in action. No cutting herself." He stuck out his tongue in disgust. "Just pure, mystic power."

"That is exactly what I mean," Torsten said, then turned to Sora. "You aren't the first mystic I've seen lately. The last killed far too many of my brothers in Latiapur."

"Then it's a good thing Sora's here."

She stepped in front of Whitney and stared at Torsten straight on. She seemed taller now, too.

"You wanted to tell me something?" Torsten said. "Get on with it."

"That mystic must have been Aihara Na," Sora said. "You may have fought her a long time ago. In secret, she carried the Order after Liam destroyed it. She even trained me… but that was before she fell to Nesilia's promises."

Torsten didn't even try to hide his distaste for the subject.

"There's more," Sora said.

Torsten grunted for her to continue.

"Aihara Na isn't Aihara Na anymore. She's been possessed by Bliss —the One Who Remained."

"Bliss is dead," Torsten said, words truncated.

"So was Nesilia."

He grunted again but bobbed his head. She made a good point. Everything she'd just told him should have surprised him, from the Mystic Order enduring to another goddess returned, but nothing did, not anymore. And maybe that was what had changed about Sora. Not her so much as him. He no longer saw her powers as the root of evil. Not now that he'd seen evil in its purest form. Sora couldn't choose the curse she happened to be born with.

"They're working together now," Sora went on. "And they're coming to destroy Yarrington and everything in Iam's Kingdom. Though, it seems you already know that."

"She's made it pretty clear," Torsten said.

"Well, we can stop her," Whitney proclaimed. "We came close once already."

"I'm sure you did." Torsten let out a sigh, but as his gaze passed across the strange group of adventurers, he witnessed absolute sincerity in each of their expressions. The Glintish musician's eyes had an especially honest quality to them. If she were supporting a lie, she was the best actress Torsten had ever seen. Even the dwarf nodded enthusiastically, foregoing the grumpiness typical to their kind.

For once in his filthy life, Whitney wasn't just boasting. Torsten wondered how many times in these many months since White Bridge he'd begged Iam to present a miracle, begged Him for a sign that He was still with them.

Were they it? Was Whitney Fierstown Torsten's answer to prayer? Torsten shuddered at the thought.

"We have a lot to catch up on," Torsten said.

"Oh, Torsten, my old friend." Whitney patted him on the back. "You have no idea."

XXXV

THE TRAITOR

Rand strode through the portal of White Bridge, the gates left wide open. He didn't look behind him at the pillars of smoke, dotting the horizon from all the settlements they'd passed through. He had to keep moving straight ahead. It was the only way.

At least, metaphorically. For, the grand bridge where, just months ago, Rand had lost so much, no longer stood. He didn't think it possible, but the white stone had been completely destroyed. Chunks of it filled ledges all the way down the ravine, shining in the moonlight. A few large pieces even poked through the gushing water of the river far below.

All Rand could picture as he stared down was Caleef Sidar Rakun, whom he'd been tasked to protect, plummeting. Another failure on his long list, growing ever longer. Not failing his sister—whatever she was —was all he had left.

"Clever girl," Nesilia said, the hint of Sigrid's accent just one ripple of her ethereal voice. She stepped up beside Rand. "The Glassmen have always been so attached to their antiquities. I never thought they'd allow one to be so utterly ruined."

"I'll destroy her," the mystic inhabited by the goddess Bliss spat as she soared out over the gap. A chilly breeze that had no business in summer accompanied her.

Rand's muscles tightened as, first, he heard the giant spiders following her, then saw them. They clambered over the broken stone, between his legs, and up the demolished towers flanking them.

"Now, now, sister, there is no need for dismay," Nesilia said.

Rand recoiled further from hearing the word 'sister,' as he had every time since they all began their march west together. Sigrid was his family. Not this witch, to whom darkness clung like a fungus.

At least they were rid of the insufferable leader of the Shesaitju sect, which had thrown its allegiance behind Nesilia. Babrak seemed to be everything Nesilia spoke about wanting to rid this land of—entitled, traitorous, unworthy. But she'd promised he had a role to play when she dispatched him and a fleet of Shesaitju and Panpingese ships to hit Yarrington from the sea… from Autlas' Inlet… that place where he and Sigrid had grown up, spent so much time together.

"My pets cannot fly," Bliss said, fuming. She glared at Nesilia. "You said that when you visited the Caleef here, the bridge remained intact."

"So, we go around," Rand proposed. "Through the mountains. You told me yourself, the dwarves will stay out of things. They know now this isn't their war."

"And yet they harbored the rogue mystic," Bliss said.

"They were being hunted by that weakling Lorgit when they used the Lightmancer," Nesilia said. "Meungor's little vermin are no concern."

"And where is she now?"

Nesilia moved to the edge without answering. She stopped, the moons painting the side of her face a soft amber. She inhaled deeply.

"I do not know," she said, a smile touching the corners of her lips.

Bliss *whooshed* in front of her. "And you smile? They nearly destroyed you last time, and you smile? Who knows what they're plotting?"

Nesilia closed her eyes, her simper deepening. "Sora fights our connection. Oh, she fights it with every ounce of her being. Her friends don't know. Perhaps she doesn't even know. That's why they used the Lightmancer and nearly got themselves killed. Fear will be her end. If only she would let go, she'd be more powerful even than that creature whose form you now occupy. *Ancient One*." Those words were said with mockery wet upon her tongue.

"Then I'll take her next," Bliss sneered.

"You won't touch her," Nesilia said, terse. "Sora belongs to me, as will all of Yarrington, soon enough."

"Then now much longer must our vengeance be delayed!"

Nesilia sighed. "You never did have patience, my loathsome sister. It remains your greatest flaw."

"And you care too much about what others think." Bliss circled her. "Sora. Caliphar. Mahraveh… Iam. Here I am, the sister you never wanted, the one Iam turned you against, working with you, side by side. Who gives a damn what they think? We are all Pantego needs."

"You've spent too long living alone amongst the spiders."

"And whose fault is that?"

"Whose fault was it that I was buried beneath that cursed mountain?"

Bliss sank back, chin jutting out. Rand watched them argue and tried to keep up, but it was difficult. He knew legends of the God Feud, of Bliss and Iam and Nesilia, and so many others. But the versions changed slightly depending on which church you lived near. And when these two spoke, it was with layers of context. Millennia worth. It made him feel impossibly small.

"Exactly," Nesilia said. "We cannot show this world how it has been lied to if they're all corpses." She turned to face Rand, making him twitch. "Like Rand here. He sees that we are freeing this realm, as does his sister."

Rand swallowed the bile forming in his throat. More and more, the dark eyes worn by Sigrid's body were beginning to seem entirely unfamiliar.

"The mountain pass should only add about a week to our journey," he said.

"Maybe if we could move during the day," Bliss remarked. She soared back through the open gates and onto the plains. Instantly, Rand felt warmer.

"No creativity, that one," Nesilia said. She extended her long fingers across Rand's cheek, and the chill returned. Still, he closed his eyes and nestled into them, picturing all those days back in Dockside. "Where Bliss sees a dead end, I see opportunity. And it's all thanks to where she buried me."

Rand opened his eyes, and now, Sigrid's face was right in front of him.

"Like I said," she went on. "I am inevitable. Now, go and rest, Rand Langley."

"But it's nightfall," he whispered, voice faltering, so close to the monster who looked so much like his sister. "We have to keep moving while it's safe for you."

"You'll see."

She gave his cheek a gentle push toward the exit. He backed up slowly, watching as she knelt by the edge of the fractured bridge, wind slinging her hair like a thousand tiny whips. She pressed her palms upon the stone, and Rand thought he felt the ground beneath him rumble.

One long stride at a time, he left her as instructed. Rand supposed he could use the rest. For so long, they'd moved during nighttime, resting during the day. That's how it'd been. The possessed people had no problem sleeping with the sun up. Apparently, they, too, needed to rest the bodies they controlled. Though, they wouldn't even lie down. Just stand, eyes closed, still as timeless statues.

Her army awaited at the gate like loyal hounds. The dark-eyed, possessed humans each glared at him as if through a single eye. Even the hundreds of former cultists in the red robes and porcelain masks, who'd willingly given their bodies to Elsewhere, just stared.

Dire-wolves-turned-demonic-hounds snarled and slobbered. Spiders burrowed. Goblins piled up loot from the towns they'd passed through, clicking in their strange language. Grimaurs screeched and picked at each other overhead, fighting over meat scraps.

Rand averted his gaze. He knew that Nesilia needed an army to carry out her vision, he only wished it wasn't this one. Nobody talked. Everything ate wild meat, uncooked, raw. And he couldn't help but think back to his Shieldsmen training, the camaraderie with the other trainees, whispering secrets while Torsten or some other senior member of the Order gave a lesson. The private jokes between them.

He'd joined the Shield to make his home a better place, and instead, found the brotherhood was what kept him. Until it all fell apart, and they forsook him.

Maybe this is where I belong, he thought to himself.

There was no Torsten here to be his mentor, his hero. To be everything Rand ever wanted to be, only to ultimately deceive him and use him as a tool. At least Nesilia was honest. She hadn't looked straight into his eyes and lied that his sister was dead like Torsten had. No, she told him the truth, had even shown her to him.

Everyone else… they were all helping the plague of greed, false faith, and decadence, which had driven Pantego into countless wars. This army was her tool to wage the last war Pantego ever needed to see. And on the other side of the darkness would be the light that Iam had lied to the world about.

It had to be.

"Is she coming?" Bliss asked, materializing in front of him. He was too busy with his own thoughts to even be startled this time.

"She says to wait," Rand replied.

"Wait? All her scheming and plotting, it never changes. I swear, if I was in charge, Yarrington would already be soot."

"But you're not," Rand dared say.

"All because Iam *chose* her. Like Iam even matters anymore."

"Then go, face her. You're Bliss, the One Who Remained. I know the stories, how you buried Nesilia after all the other warring gods were cast out by Iam. Then, he punished you by damning you to the Webbed Woods to live as a beast."

"And you're not as dumb as you look," Bliss muttered.

He glared up at her, stepping forward into the cold of her form. He whispered, "So, you can do it again. Take control. Or, did you really just stab her in the back like a coward while Iam was away?"

Her lips pursed. Lightning crackled around her fingertips. Spiders emerged from the dirt and encircled him. He didn't give ground.

Bliss leaned in, then released something akin to a growl, and vanished with a wisp.

Rand shook out his hands and inhaled deeply as the spiders burrowed away into the sides of the gorge. Her, he didn't trust in the slightest. While part of him wished she'd just let him die in Latiapur, he had to see this thing to its end.

He continued through the horde of beasts and mindless men to the back, where a cart remained guarded by possessed Shieldsmen who'd been captured in the battle, men he'd known. Their dark eyes and veins coruscating around them brightly contrasting the white of their armor.

Demons had possessed their bodies. Like the others, they didn't converse, but they gave something familiar to be around. Sitting nearby with a fire, he could almost feel like they were back in the Glass Castle courtyard, together.

"Why are we stopped?" asked a weak voice. Dirty hands wrapped the bars of the iron cage atop the cart, and then, moonlight illuminated the nose poking through.

Rand regarded the sad state of Sir Lucas Danvels—a pathetic excuse for a Shieldsman if there ever was one. Which reminded Rand that the home he pictured no longer existed and would now be destroyed by that fat Shesaitju brute and his people. There was nothing special about the Order. Torsten had allowed so many to perish, they became a slipshod crew of young liars and thieves. Honorless dregs.

Men like Lucas, who, like Torsten, had been happy to sit across from Rand and tell him that Sigrid was dead even though she was out there, transformed into an upyr, alone and scared. Until Nesilia found her and gave her purpose.

"Does it matter?" Rand asked. He rummaged through his supplies to find something to eat. He had nothing to cook, so Shesaitju pit lizard jerky would suffice, as it had every other night.

Lucas squeezed his head through the bars to try and get a look at the surroundings. His Shieldsman armor rattled, loosely fitting on his weakening muscles. Rand knew how heavy and constricting the armor was. It was slow torture to leave him in it, all while he crouched in a cage too low to stand or even sit straight. He deserved no better.

"Is that White Bridge?" Lucas asked.

"Quiet." Rand tore off a chunk of the dried meat and tossed it through the bars as if to an animal. Lucas tried to catch it, but it slipped through his fingers and bounced out into the dirt. Lucas sat back with a loud *thud*, not even attempting to reach for it.

Rand sighed. He stood, found the piece on the ground, and slid it back through the bars. "You're lucky I need to keep you alive."

"For what?" Lucas asked. In the darkness, Rand heard him crawl across the cage, then devour the jerky.

What a weakling, Rand thought. A true Shieldsmen like he was trained to be would have refused food and water, would have let themselves rot rather than be held captive by an enemy.

Rand returned to the fire and tore a piece off the tough meal with his molars. It was better than training rations, at least.

"Fine, ignore me," Lucas said.

"Now you're starting to get it," Rand said.

Lucas gave it a few seconds, then slid back to the bars. "You know, Sir Unger was only trying to protect you. He knew you would do something crazy in your state of mind, and he was right."

"Good for him."

"I think you're an embarrassment. The only lie you're a part of is the one we told Yarrington so they wouldn't be ashamed. Rand the Redeemer. Even saying it out loud is ridiculous. You're a traitor to everything. Most of all, your sister."

"You know nothing," Rand growled.

"I know she's a slave to Nesilia. I see her walking through the night, and there's no human left in that stride. She probably gave herself up to the Buried Goddess because she's as weak as you."

"Shut up!" Rand screamed. Without even realizing how he got there, he banged on the bars of the cage. "You know nothing. Just sit there, and be quiet or I'll—"

"What?" Lucas interrupted. His impish smirk spread into the moonlight. "Kill me? You can't. Because you're her slave, too, and apparently, she wants me alive."

"But she doesn't need you with all your parts, does she?" The satisfaction of hearing Lucas swallow sent Rand back to his seat. He poked the fire with his boot, a spray of embers swirling up through the darkness. He watched them dance, wishing they'd swallow him whole.

"Reminds me of Dockside after Nesilia's cultists made it burn," Lucas said.

"Purged like a forest fire," Rand replied.

"Is that what she told you? What about how it was Torsten who cut Valin Tehr's head from his shoulders before that fire let him take Dockside over for good?"

"The Shield let him fester there. Torsten was just finally doing his job. When I first joined, I begged them to look deeper into the Vineyard. But he called it an 'unnecessary evil.' Sir Unger wouldn't even meet with me about it. I had to talk to that old rat, Lars."

Lucas' voice softened. "Torsten wanted to do something. I know it. It just wasn't simple."

"It should have been. That's what Nesilia will change. No more gold ruling over everyone. No more powerful noble families deciding who lives and dies. No more wars for which to send children off to die."

"Did she tell you that while her cultists danced over the bodies of our friends and neighbors?"

Rand gnawed off another piece of jerky and chewed.

"I met you when I was younger. Did you know that?" Lucas asked after another bout of silence. Rand would've moved, but he'd already spent so many nights alone. The possessed Shieldsmen just continued staring forward. Their all-black eyes didn't even reveal where they were looking.

"You were just a guard," Lucas went on. "My parents run a bakery down near the harbor. Someone broke in and stole some bronzers from their register. You were assigned the case. You found the thief and returned everything he hadn't already spent. I was still young, but I remember being amazed."

Rand chuckled.

"What's funny?" Lucas asked.

"I remember that. I never caught a soul. Just wasted three nights looking after Captain Henry told me to let it go."

"That's not true. I watched you hand my parents a bag of autlas."

"My own earnings. I felt so bad when they cried, and seeing their pitiful son staring at me behind the counter with sad, wet eyes, I gave them my weeks' pay and lied that they were safe."

Now it was Lucas' turn to sit in silence.

"I guess I'm not surprised I did it. That's what we're taught. To lie when there isn't any answer. Keep the peace at all costs."

Lucas edged closer to the bars. "Rand, that kept them going during the Third Panping War when so many Docksiders marched off. They prayed for you that Dawning, hard as I'd ever seen them pray. Prayed you'd be in charge one day and make Dockside a brighter place."

"Soon, maybe I will be."

"With them at your side?" he gestured toward the mindless husks of Shieldsmen. "Hey! See? Nothing. Just like your sister, they aren't who they used to be. Might as well be dead."

"Can't you see?" Rand said, finding it in himself to ignore the comment. "Your parents were robbed because they couldn't defend themselves. They were too weak. And all my lie did was help them feel safe, like anyone gave a yig about two bakers from the armpit of the Kingdom. If they'd been stronger, they'd have gutted the thief themselves."

"And we'll live like the Drav Cra?" Lucas said. "Raiding and pillaging and kneeling to whoever's got the biggest axe?"

"We already do that. The nobles needed Dockside as much as we did, and even more than we needed them. They built their homes on our broken backs, tossing us a pittance that we so willingly gobbled up. They pillaged our souls for gold. Because Iam blessed them to be born in Old Yarrington, they deserved it. Right?"

"I'm not saying Yarrington is perfect," Lucas argued. "I've seen it at its worst."

"At least the Drav Cra are honest about it. No games, no lies. Sigrid worked at a tavern and never once let a man touch her. If a thief tried to take anything from the place, she'd have castrated him right there. And she lived just like your soft parents when she should've been a Queen."

"You can't believe that."

"How could I not? You bow before names and titles and gold. A Mad Queen who hanged innocent people for no reason. A king who screwed whoever he wanted, and called for war in the name of Iam. The god, they say, wanted only peace during the Feud—who supposedly stayed out of it." Rand blew out a raspberry. "You followed a meek boy who started a war, leaped from a window in cowardice, got himself killed in Latiapur when I tried to save him!" Rand's voice had risen to a shout. His fingers dug into the log he sat on, bark cramming under his nails.

"And a murderous goddess is better?" Lucas said. "Pi is dead. The Nothhelms die with him. Do you really think this will be a better replacement?"

"Can't be worse," Rand grumbled.

"Then why did you try and save the King, if that's really true?"

"My sister wanted him alive."

"Don't lie to me."

"I'm not," Rand said through his teeth. He focused on the fire, but couldn't stop the flood of memories. Him, lying in the wet sand with the King's battered body beside him. Sir Unger, looking down on him in disgust and disappointment.

Lucas sighed. "It's not too late, you know?"

"For what?"

"To be redeemed. To earn that title."

"I didn't ask for it. That was Torsten, deceiving people yet again. Because Iam forbid a Shieldsman be capable of doing what I'd done. How dare I go against the Crown to try and save my sister. And yet, for refusing to be okay with hanging handmaidens, they called me a deserter."

"Nobody wishes things were different more than Torsten," Lucas said. "Can't you see that? It's why Nesilia keeps you around, because she knows you're his soft spot. Just how she knew you'd once again get close enough in Latiapur to stab *him* in the back."

"No. It's for my sister."

"She's gone."

"She's not," Rand said, anger carving deep gashes in his heart.

Lucas grasped the bars again. "You can still make things right, Rand. Iam's light is always there. Maybe His Kingdom did lose its way. It stopped offering forgiveness and started demanding blood. But we can change that."

Rand shook his head. "Iam abandoned this world. Left us to fight over what was left of it."

"You know that's not true. You saw Him, on this very field, saw him drive Nesilia away. I heard what happened. I see it in your eyes now. You watched it."

"I watched a drunken priest do a magic trick." Rand dismissed him with a wave as he stood. "I've had enough of you."

"No, you haven't," Lucas said. "Who else will you talk to now that you've thrown in with monsters. Does this really look like the army of a liberator?"

"More than Liam's ever did."

Rand kicked the logs, sending up smoke, embers, and flames, then stormed off. Even the company of goblins was preferable to a Shield-sman who thought he knew anything, who'd been blinded by false promises of glory and God's favor.

He heard Lucas hollering in the background, growing desperate as he lost his chance to play on Rand's former loyalty and maybe get himself an extra meal or two. Rand knew the tricks. He knew how thieves in dungeons would try to endear themselves to the guards. All lies and distractions.

A deep rumble started in the distance, near the bridge. Then, the ground quaked, rocking him to his knees. None of the possessed budged in the slightest, and Rand shoved through them to return to his sister. Goblins and spiders skittered away. Grimaurs took flight, snapping at one another as they rose.

Rand drew his sword and shoved a tremendous Panpingese man out of the way.

"What happen—" He skidded to a stop when he saw.

Nesilia remained kneeling by the edge of the bridge, only, the fractured pieces of it all now floated across the wide valley. Hundreds of them, from the tiniest chip to a chunk that could carry a giant. One by one, they shifted into place, reforming the bridge which had once connected west and east Pantego.

Bliss appeared at Rand's side, mouthing only the word, "How?"

Nesilia remained with her hands upon the stone but looked back. He'd never seen this version of his sister so self-satisfied. Echoes of Sigrid when she used to beat him at well, anything, filled his brain. It made him look away.

"The dwarves who built this bridge had reinforced the stone with glaruium," Nesilia said. "Thanks to you burying me under the only mountain where it's found, Bliss, it listens to me."

Bliss didn't answer. She flew out and swirled around the loose pieces, still filling into the impossibly complex puzzle of reversed devastation.

"You see," Nesilia went on. "Patience. Everything happens for a reason. They thought they'd bought themselves time by destroying history. But the past cannot be forgotten. And it cannot be forgiven."

Her eyes fixed on Rand, and he froze. Was she talking about his conversation with Lucas? Could she hear them?

"Come now, my pets," she said. "Yarrington awaits."

She stayed where she was. Rand realized that the bridge didn't merge or repair completely. All the cracks remained visible as if she were holding them in place only temporarily. As creatures began to cross without any fear of it crumbling beneath them, Rand realized she was.

A grimaur pecked at his ear as it swooped by, and he swatted at it with his sword. Then he, too, began to march. They were close now. He, also, was close. To the end of this nightmare and seeing Sigrid on the other side.

The Glass Kingdom be damned. The whole world be damned. It was broken as is. Filled with cruelty and suffering for no good reason.

"But we can change that," Lucas said.

And his sister would.

She had to…

XXXVI

THE KNIGHT

"**S**ora was *what*, by the Buried Goddess?" Torsten asked, incredulous.

He scanned the Shield Hall and saw more than a dozen faces equally aghast as he was. He ignored the irony that the north wall of the room was an open balcony overlooking Mount Lister—the very place where Nesilia had been buried in the God Feud.

Everyone with an essential role in Yarrington's defense was present, seated or standing around the thick, stone table, including Whitney and his group, who claimed they could stop the goddess.

Torsten had caught them up on what had happened since he'd left Yarrington for White Bridge, along with everyone else. From Nesilia's return in the body of an upyr to the ambush at Latiapur where Rand Langley completed his betrayal. Then, Whitney did the same, telling all about a journey to the upyr Citadel to save who he just claimed to be Nesilia's host prior to Sigrid.

If it weren't for the other companions, especially the Glintish woman called Lucindur, Torsten would have believed the tale to be just another wild exaggeration by the self-proclaimed "World's Greatest Thief."

"Possessed by her," Whitney said blithely, as if that were a routine event in his insane life. "Keep up, Torsten. We broke her mind free using an old mystic relic, and nearly contained Nesilia's power in time to destroy her in the mouth of a wianu, when Grisham "Gold Grin"

Gale showed up and ruined it all. He killed… Sigrid's master… and caused the bar guai to break. Then, Nesilia escaped into Sigrid's Upyr body."

Torsten didn't respond. His gaze fixated on Sora, who sat beside the thief, quietly staring down at the table. Tum Tum and Lucindur stood behind them, and they were the only ones who didn't have their jaws ajar.

"And you brought her here?" Mahraveh asked, stealing the question straight from Torsten's mouth. She and her lieutenant, Bit'rudam, sat across the room.

"Yes, *and*?" Whitney asked, shooting daggers at her with his eyes.

"Need I truly say it?"

"Truly," Whitney said with as much sarcasm as Torsten had come to expect. "And then, Torsten can explain why the castle is filled with you gray skins? Or did the King not just die in your hot, crusty desert?"

"I second that," Sir Mulliner muttered.

"We have pledged our spears to the defense of this city," Bit'rudam snapped. "Who are you to question anything?"

"Oh, I don't know… perhaps one of the inhabitants of Troborough —do you remember that place? You might remember it as one of twelve Glass villages that now looks like piles of ash," Whitney said. "Weren't you there? I swear I saw you there, killing children."

"How dare you!" Bit'rudam pushed out his chair. Mahraveh stopped him with a raised fist.

"My father did what he thought he must, for our people," she said, firm and steady. "As yours have. As your former Wearer or White did when he burned down my village. It is behind us now."

"Shog, it is!" Whitney protested. He placed his hand over his heart. "And Torsten Unger would never burn down a village. I'm offended you'd even accuse him of that, right, Torsten?"

Bit'rudam opened his mouth to yell, then stopped himself. His features crinkled in confusion.

"He doesn't mean me," Torsten said. "Sir Nikserof Pasic."

"But you're… and…" Whitney threw his hands up in confusion. "I can't keep up with this city. How many Wearers does that make now? And you… you can see, you can't see. You're Wearer, you're nothing, you're in charge. By Iam, it's been a mess since I left."

"Stop!" Torsten's large hand slammed down on the table. Pieces from the modeled version of Yarrington in its center toppled from the vibration. "None of this matters. You brought Sora here and didn't think to mention that at the start of your story? It's bad enough you worked with the very upyr who killed our Queen!"

Whitney shrugged. "It wasn't relevant until we got to the part where we saved her.

"It couldn't be *more* relevant," Torsten said.

"And hey, those upyr hated Nesilia as much as we do. The enemy of my friend is my enemy, or however it goes."

"I agree with Sir Unger," Mahraveh said. "The Buried Goddess is a deceiver to her core. I've met her."

Hearing that finally seemed to break Sora out of her blank stare. She eyed Mahraveh curiously, but still remained quiet.

"How are we supposed to know she isn't in the mystic still?" Bit'rudam said. "Just as she controlled the one who drowned Latiapur?"

"Gray skin or not, that's a valid point, Torsten," Sir Mulliner said.

"Wait, I'm lost," Lord Jolly chimed in. "They were with Nesilia when she took over Sigrid's body, and then Rand summoned her to us with a blood pact on the late Sir Danvels?"

"We don't know he's dead," Torsten said.

Jolly conceded the point with a wave of his hand.

"I don't know what's so hard to understand," Whitney groaned. "Yes, and yes. And we need to get close to Nesilia again so that we can wake Sigrid up inside her own head using Lucy's Lightmancing, then bind Nesilia inside of this."

Whitney reached into his pocket, pulled out a gem, and plunked it on the table. With his enchanted vision, Torsten couldn't perceive color in all its magnificent shades, but for him, the gem seemed to be draining all the light from the room. It was midday, the hot summer sun blaring in through the open wall, and yet now it felt like twilight.

A handful of people gasped, flinching, and backing away.

"What in Iam's name is that?" Lord Jolly demanded.

"They brought it here for her!" Sir Mulliner barked.

Master of Rolls Caspar Brosch, however, moved closer and whispered, "Curious."

Bit'rudam placed himself in front of Mahraveh, hand on the grip of his scimitar. Whitney tried to argue. Tum Tum too, but the shouting intensified until Torsten wasn't sure who was saying what.

"That be me father's Brike Stone," whispered Al. Their dwarven master of coin stepped forward from the corner where the more unnecessary-for-defense Royal Councilmen lurked. But, even in the face of the end of all things, contractors, smiths, and all the citizens whose work would help prepare the city for war required the gold from Yarrington's coffers.

"My thoughts precisely," Brosch said, still at a whisper.

"The what?" Sir Mulliner asked.

"My father's greatest treasure. Said to be the heart of the last dragon, after his ancestors tricked it into tradin its soul for our riches." He made his way around the table and reached out for it.

Whitney slapped the dwarf's hand away and said, "It's ours."

"How is that possible?"

"We uh… borrowed it. From yer father," Tum Tum said. "Yer Alfotdrumlin, right? Lorgit's youngest? He be an old frie—"

"My father would never give that up," Al said. "Not to a friend. Not to his own sons. He believes the power of the last dragon has allowed him to live all these centuries."

"It's bad enough with a mystic, now they threaten to draw the Three Kingdoms into war against us?" Lord Jolly said.

"We'll give it back," Whitney argued.

"You don't give anything back," Torsten couldn't help but retort.

"They are clearly attempting to fool us," Sir Mulliner said. "They should be locked up in the dungeons."

"We speak the truth," Lucindur implored.

The fighting and accusing continued. Torsten hushed and begged for everyone to quiet down, but he should have known better, filling a room with peoples and races, all of which had slighted each other for centuries. Nesilia had cornered them and transformed Yarrington into a tinderbox without a trusted King to keep the peace.

Was Sora the fuse?

The two dwarves pushed each other. Whitney pointed a knife at Sir Mulliner and Lord Jolly. Mahraveh bit her lip and glared at Sora with malice. Bit'rudam, the same. The too-young Royal Council members joined in for the sake of not feeling left out. Lucindur, for what's it's worth, attempted to calm things.

Sora continued to sit quietly, not engaging, out of the argument. Torsten knew she had Whitney wound around her fingertip. He was a thief, but he wasn't malicious. If she was a pawn of the Buried Goddess, she could get him to do anything.

Then, everyone went suddenly silent when Dellbar the Holy grasped the outlandish gem and rotated it in his hands. Torsten wasn't even sure when he'd managed to sneak over so close. Though, he was used to him stumbling drunkenly into things. He still wasn't used to the sober version of the High Priest.

"Hey, don't touch that!" Whitney yelled.

Dellbar turned on him. He hadn't eyes with which to glower, but the grisly holes in his face got the job done. Whitney fell right back into his chair.

The High Priest clasped the stone with both hands. He shuddered for a moment, his face wrinkling deeper. Then, without a word, he sauntered calmly to the great window framing Mount Lister. Every eye was on him now. He stopped there, facing out for a few seconds, and Torsten's superior hearing allowed him to hear Dellbar mutter in a pained voice, "In the hands of Your children now, eh?"

He chuckled to himself, shoved the stone into his pocket, then turned. Only, it wasn't to the entire room. He focused on Sora specifically. "So, that's how we destroy Nesilia?" he said. "We tear her and the upyr apart with Lightmancery, and bind her in this?"

"Yes," Sora answered.

"Hmph. As simple as it is not. It is said that dragons once served as the messengers of the gods until the Feud claimed so many, they went extinct. I can feel the power emanating from this. Whether or not it is what legends say, it can only restrain her for a short time."

"We hope," Lucindur added.

"It has to," Sora said. "There won't be another shot at her with something else. If we can't separate her from Sigrid and bind her, we'll all die."

"How do you know that?" Torsten asked. "We can withstand her army. Dellbar and the priests will figure out how to banish her demons. We can hold."

"We can't," Sora said.

"We can."

"You know that we can't," Sora attested. "You of all know. We've all seen parts of her army, and when it's all here? Even Liam the Conqueror couldn't survive this. Our only hope is destroying her, and that stone gives us the best chance."

"Exactly," Whitney said, boasting a proud smile. "So, by all means, if you all have something better hiding in Yarrington's coffers like a spare bar guai or the kidney of a god, let us know." He drummed his fingers on the table. "No? Nobody? Thought so."

"So, what? We're going to leave our future in the hands of a potentially possessed mystic and a thief?" Lord Jolly said, a sly smile on his face. He glanced at Casper Brosch, the Master of Rolls, who still looked shocked from the sight of the stone. "Do you think I didn't ask for the records of Whitney Fierstown before coming in here?"

Whitney perked up and leaned forward. "What did they say?"

Jolly ignored them. "I've already lost one home this week, I will not lose another."

"I agree," Mahraveh said.

"And me," said Bit'rudam.

"Ah, *now* we all care about lost homes," Whitney said.

"If me father was on the fence and now joins her over this, I won't be able to talk him down," Al added. "And no offense to any of ye fine people, but this ain't me home to die in."

Whitney groaned so loudly it bordered on performance. "Oh, would you fools all stop it? I didn't get chomped at by a wolf, nearly burned alive, and get half my shoulder chewed off by goblins to not use that stone."

Torsten raised a hand to preemptively stifle the opposition that would inevitably come from Whitney letting his opinions be known.

"If you're all right, and telling the truth," he said, "then what's your plan for getting close to Nesilia. She conquered Latiapur without even showing up. Her mystic, or sister, or whatever that red-robed witch is, seems perfectly capable of carrying out an attack. Plus, now with Babrak on her side, and her new Arch Warlock leading another Drav Cra horde south, how do you possibly plan on getting near to her?"

Whitney jammed his elbow onto the table and pointed. "I'll tell you how…" His words trailed off, and with his other hand, he scratched his chin.

"She'll come to us," Sora said.

"Yes," Whitney said. "This is ridiculous. If you all knew who Sora was, you'd be on your knees, not—"

"Don't." Sora laid her somehow-unscarred hand upon Whitney's shoulder and did what Torsten thought impossible—silenced the thief in an instant. She stood.

"It's true," she continued, now to everyone. "Nesilia possessed me when I attempted to enter Elsewhere and break every law the mystics should stand for. She thought we were kindred spirits. Both abandoned time and time again. Both misunderstood. Called by names we never asked for. Unloved. Forgotten. There was a point I even thought she was right…"

Her hands trembled as she spoke, and Torsten noticed the embers dancing at her fingertips. His own slowly reached for *Salvation*, which leaned against the table beside him, ready to do whatever was necessary if the worst was to come.

"I had to watch as she used my body to please herself." After several gasps, she continued. "I watched her turn a psychopath named Freydis into her latest beloved weapon while she slaughtered Drav Cra not loyal to her. Then, she destroyed an entire city of dwarves simply because they were in her way."

She gazed down at Whitney, and a weak smile formed. He bit his lip.

"I had to watch while she surrounded the people I love, with every intention of killing them, too." Her voice cracked slightly. "And then Whitney and his friends—my friends—helped break me free. They reminded me how wrong Nesilia was before I gave in."

She looked at Torsten, then across the table all the way to Mahraveh. "So no, I can't prove to any of you that Nesilia isn't in my head, because I can't prove it to myself. Everywhere I look, she's there, her horrors like a shadow on my mind. I looked into the eyes of pure wickedness and hate, and they were my own. And that is exactly how I know that when her army comes for Yarrington to wipe every shred of Iam's existence from this world, she'll come for me first."

Sir Mulliner grunted. "Exactly what a pawn would say. Invite her right in."

"Quiet," Mahraveh snapped, breaking a long silence.

"How dare you—"

"I looked into her eyes as well," Mahraveh said to Sora, ignoring Mulliner. "I haven't slept since. Generations of memories clog my head at all times… and yet, her eyes are all I see."

"Oh, now you believe her?" Mulliner groaned.

"I have to agree with Sir Mulliner," Lord Jolly said. "We can't stake our survival on a prayer that Nesilia will senselessly expose herself. You go ask my family if Nesilia needed to be in Crowfall when that witch your 'body' helped train broke open our walls like an acorn."

"It's not a prayer," Sora said.

"You can't know that."

"She does," Dellbar stated, stepping forward. After his long silence, Torsten had almost forgotten about him. But when he spoke, Torsten was reminded of Wren before Redstar got ahold of him. There was vim and vigor in his tone.

"Nesilia will come for Sora for one simple reason," Dellbar said.

"And that is?" Mulliner asked, fully out of turn.

Dellbar looked at Sora. "Because she rejected her. Right?"

Sora swallowed hard, then nodded.

"She spent an eternity buried," Dellbar went on as he slowly rounded the table. "Her hate rising with every Dawning. And then she found a woman as powerful as she was unknown. And you rejected her. Not like Torsten or Mahraveh, who were raised their entire lives on their own faiths, with their own families to love. You were the orphan, far from home, and even you rejected her like she believes Iam did. For him."

Dellbar punctuated the sentence by placing the Brike Stone down in front of Whitney. The thief had been so enraptured that he yelped. Again, the light was sapped out of the room. Then, the High Priest took Sora by the shoulders and positioned his blind eyes straight in front of hers.

"She wants you, for who you are," Dellbar whispered. "But you aren't where you're born, or where you come from, or what you've done. Destroy her for hatred and vengeance, and you'll become exactly what she wanted you to be. You'll never win. Do it, instead, because you understand her more deeply than any of us here can ever know."

Sora's lip quivered. A tear rolled down her cheek. Dellbar wiped it with one finger as if he wasn't completely blind. Then, he stood, wearing a thin smile, and gave her arms a squeeze before using his cane to tap toward the exit.

"Where are you going?" Torsten asked.

"I think I may have finally figured out how we banish her demons," Dellbar said.

"We need you here."

"You don't."

The High Priest reached the doors and knocked with his cane. Guards outside pulled them open, and like that, he was gone.

Torsten swore. The drunken version of Dellbar made far more sense.

Sora collapsed back into her chair. Whitney, the man who never shut up, remained silent, consoling her by rubbing her hand. It had been a year of strange sights for Torsten, and somehow, that felt like one of the strangest. It also erased nearly all the doubt in his head over whether or not they could be trusted.

He knew that look in Sora's eyes. The pain of being violated. Having her entire life stolen. He'd seen it once, long ago, in the eyes of a girl taken from her tribe and brought to Yarrington. In Oleander's eyes. There was something else there, in Sora's eyes—something he couldn't place…

"Remind me again, how was he chosen to be High Priest?" Sir Mulliner asked.

"Because, for once, the charlatans in Hornsheim trusted in Iam," Torsten retorted.

He couldn't believe the words he'd spoken about his church, and yet, there they were, hanging on the air. And Torsten meant it. Dellbar had been a breath of fresh air from the start, with no worry for politics or gold. He barely wanted to be alive.

"I like him," Mahraveh said. "And he's right. Sora is here, whether we like it or not. If she's telling the truth, it's our best shot. Nesilia spoke to me to try and lure me to her side, but she made a mistake. My father taught me to sense the weaknesses in everyone around me because even friends can become opponents like that." She snapped her fingers. "For Nesilia, this isn't a mad, murderous quest. It's personal."

"It is," Lucindur agreed.

"Have I mentioned how much I love the Shesaitju?" Whitney remarked.

A chuckle snuck through Torsten's lips. Lord Jolly looked like he'd heard a horrid curse.

"I suppose, I would have loved to be there to see father's face after he found the stone missin from his vault," Al said.

"Aye, I wish we could've, too," Tum Tum said. "But fear's got the best of him now. It was a sad sight to see."

"That explains why he's ignored any attempt to contact him," Torsten said. "But it doesn't matter. Here. This room. This is what we have to stand against the goddess: two knights, a mystic, a Caleef, a thief..." He continued like this, regarding each as he spoke their titles. "We might not all trust each other, but that's the truth of it."

"Hear, hear!" Whitney hollered, banging on the table and sending more of the little figurines and carvings sprawling.

Even Sir Mulliner showed a hint of amusement, then said, "What a ridiculous group."

"She's hurt us all," Mahraveh said, standing. "Some deeper than others. My home. My father. I will do whatever it takes to stop her." She moved to the model of Yarrington. "She may have revealed her weaknesses, but she's also not a fool. She planned and built her army before rushing here for vengeance. She won't come near the fight unless we draw her. I think if we—" She stopped and looked to Torsten. "May I?"

He nodded her along, all while wishing Pi had lived. They would've made an impressive pair one day.

"What do you propose?" Torsten said

Mahraveh pointed to Dockside and Autla's Inlet. "Put me in charge of defending the waterfront."

"Are you sure that's smart? We know from scouts that Babrak's fleet is sailing around from the south. He'll try to taunt you. We shouldn't repeat Nesilia's mistakes."

"This isn't personal, I promise. If we win, Babrak dies either way. But we all need to win. Nesilia might try to flood out the low-ground around the harbor, like in Latiapur. My people are used to fighting on the water."

Torsten looked to Lord Jolly, the Master of Ships.

"I can think of no one better," Kaviel Jolly said. "My ships are at her command."

"Thank you, Lord Jolly," Mahraveh said.

"She will have many Current Eaters with them," Bit'rudam said. "Wianu," he corrected when everyone looked at him quizzically.

"I'm sorry, that sounded plural," Whitney chimed in. "How many of those monsters does she have?"

"Enough," Torsten said.

"We'll need one to devour the Brike Stone after we bind her," Sora said. "The more, the better."

"Sora, I love you, but that's the craziest thing you've ever said," Whitney replied.

"No, I like it," Mahraveh said. "Your blacksmith, Hovom Nitebrittle and I had an idea when I helped him toss all the glaruium armor into the water. He wasn't sure you'd like it."

"All plans must be heard," Torsten said. He turned and found the old blacksmith standing amidst the Royal Council, quiet as always. Hovom may not have been on the Council, and he certainly didn't dress like it, but he'd been around for a long, long time. There was no one Torsten would trust more in regards to outfitting his army.

Hovom cleared his throat. "Well, we thought it might be wise to ignore saving Dockside and South Corner and transform them into a death trap. It is, as Mahraveh said, the lowest point of the city."

"Abandon nearly a third of Yarrington?" Sir Mulliner asked in disbelief.

"In a sense."

"Turn it into a weapon," Mahraveh clarified. "Nesilia will attack with raw power again. The buildings there are the most brittle. Hovom thought maybe we craft chains, as many as we can, and lash all the structures together, pulling with my zhulong. In the harbor, we'll create a snare of barbed iron."

"I got the idea from the Shesaitju arrows," Hovom interjected.

"Yes, and every strand they pull on," Mahraveh continued, "will not only work to destroy their hulls but will bring buildings crashing down upon them. We can arrange it to purposefully funnel them to strong points. If the chains are durable enough, they could even slow the wianu, and then I will make sure to capture one alone."

"You?" Whitney scoffed.

"Me," she said firmly.

Whitney swallowed hard and stayed quiet.

Hovom agreed. "We can't use glaruium, but they'll be strong. I'll see to that."

"How do you expect to prepare so many chains in so short a time?" Lord Jolly asked.

Hovom was a large man. Perhaps not Torsten's size, but not small by any description. He turned his gaze to the floor. "I hope I was not out of line, but I already have blacksmiths throughout the city working on it."

Torsten eyed the man for a moment, then smiled.

"Well done, my friend," Torsten said. "However, this will shrink our area of defense as you hold them off. That'll mean tighter confines. More innocents and soldiers clustered in the high city. An easier target. There are no walls between South Corner and the rest of the city."

"But we'll slow them," Mahraveh said. "I know Babrak. He'll press an imagined advantage like a rabid boar. We can blockade routes out of Dockside, and defend choke points here, here, and here."

"I'm with them," Lord Jolly said. "I took stock of our naval forces after Winde Port and Latiapur. We won't have a chance at stopping their fleet, they'll roll right through us. So, we can use that. Send out ships manned with a barely workable crew, merely to lose and retreat. Load the ships with oil. While the crews escape on rowboats, they can set fire to their former vessels. We'll block the enemy with flames and iron."

"Dockside, too. Once the chains snare them, we'll burn the whole district if we have to."

Torsten cringed at the thought of South Corner engulfed. Though he hadn't lived there in a very long time, that would always be home. He scratched his chin.

"Okay, so we do that," Mulliner said. "That's just one of her many armies."

Torsten stood and skirted the table toward the model. "Freydis and the Drav Cra will march from the north. If she has the savages organized—even if she doesn't—they'll be a mighty foe."

"Yarrington's walls are tall and thick, many times that of Crowfall," Lord Jolly said. "They won't fall so easily."

"They'll rely upon her magic to break through," Torsten said.

"So, we let her," Sora said. "Make her confident enough to get in range."

"We're already letting them flood Dockside," Lord Jolly said.

"Freydis is the key to everything. I need to kill her. She's too strong for anyone else to take, but that's how we draw Nesilia in. Freydis is the sister Nesilia never had, the one follower who never abandoned her, or went out on their own like Redstar. Who loved her."

"What about the mystic?" Torsten asked. "You say it's her sister-goddess, Bliss?"

Whitney blew a raspberry. "They hate each other. They're just working together for convenience."

"Sounds familiar," someone from the Council grumbled. Torsten didn't bother to find out who.

"He's right," Sora said. "If I take out Freydis, Nesilia will come for me."

"Hmm," Torsten thought aloud. "Drav Cra, Shesaitju, they're human—them we can fight if they get in. Nesilia's demons, they might infest us all. So, I will mount our main defenses here at the Eastern Gate. I'll make myself very visible in leading. Nesilia will think that's our focus."

"So, let me get this straight," Sir Mulliner said. "We burn Dockside *and* South Corner, and surrender the Northern Mason's district—which is vitally close to the castle and Old Yarrington, I might add. Then, we put our leader on display, all to try and capture Nesilia with a magical stone?"

"He's smart, Torsten," Whitney said, pointing. "Really smart guy."

Austun Mulliner sat back in his seat. "I just want you all to hear how insane this is."

"We lose in a fair fight," Mahraveh said. "We all know that. So why fight one? We have to play to their weakness, which is that they don't think we stand a chance."

Torsten returned to his seat, staring at the model the entire way.

What would Liam do? he wondered. The unexpected, sure, but he'd trust in Iam. This plan, however, required trust in many gods and peoples.

Maybe, Torsten hoped, that was the point of all of this.

"One problem," Whitney said, raising his hand.

"What?" Torsten asked.

"We can't put Nesilia in this…" Whitney picked up the Brike Stone and stuffed it into his pocket, beckoning the light to return. "… Without Lucy's Lightmancing. We have Sora, whose connection to Nesilia should let her in, but as soon as Lucindur starts, every creature in Nesilia's army will come after them. That means grimaurs from above, goblins from below. Wolves." He shuddered.

"It's true," Lucindur said. "They'll be drawn to me like moths to a flame."

Every word out of her mouth fell on Torsten's ears like a symphony. And when she looked at him, his heart skipped a beat. Was this the ancient, forgotten power of Lightmancery? He'd seen tales written about it in tomes, but that part of Glintish history had long since vanished, back when the mystics rose to power.

"So, Sora kills Freydis, Nesilia hopefully comes after her," Torsten said, running the plan through his mind out loud just to make sure it wasn't as crazy as it sounded in his head. It was, but that didn't matter. "Then, she retreats back to the castle, and that's where we take her. Lucindur and Sora will be safest there while entering Sigrid and Nesilia's mind."

"Once Freydis is gone, I'll send Aquira to ring the cathedral bells, and we'll all know it's time."

"What is an Aquira?" Mulliner asked.

"A wyvern," Sora replied.

Mulliner exhaled through his teeth. "Of course."

"Hey, she may only be a wyvern, but I trained her to be sneaky," Whitney said. "She can handle it."

"*You* trained her?" Sora said.

Whitney crossed his arms. "Yep."

"Then it's settled," Torsten said. "We make our stand in the Throne Room and pray all the great kings of old are there with us to protect the Lightmancer."

"She'll have me by her side," Tum Tum said.

"And me," Whitney said.

"And what's left of the Serpent Guard," Mahraveh added. "If she's the key, we'll need our best warriors defending her while she uses her magic."

"Then it should be the Shieldsmen," Sir Mulliner attested. "You dissolved our Order, but we're still the best in Yarrington."

"The best of all of them," Torsten decided. He gazed up at the finely carved chunked of stone comprising the Shield Hall. "This castle has stood since the dawn of Iam's Kingdom. Where better to make our last stand against her?"

XXXVII

THE MYSTIC

Since the moment she'd arrived in Yarrington—even before that, when she'd gained her first view of Mount Lister casting its shadow over the city—Sora had one lingering thought. She knew it was silly; she hadn't even known the man, much less cared for him, but blood was blood. A mystic knows that if they know anything.

Walking through the Glass Castle dungeons gave her the chills. Though, it might've been the cold. It was freezing, as if part of the punishment endured by the prisoners was to suffer a slow death by frostbite.

"You've gotta think," Whitney whispered beside her, "if it's this easy to sneak *into* the castle dungeons, it can't be too hard sneaking *out* either."

"I still don't understand why we are in the dungeons to begin with," Sora said. "I thought the Royal Crypt was inside the mountain? It feels like we are going away from it."

"Just a figment of your imagination. Things get confusing when you're underground."

Nesilia had been in Sora's head for so long that Sora could almost imagine what the goddess would've said if she heard that sentence. *Imagine how confusing things would be after thousands of years underground.*

Right here, Sora thought. *She was buried right here, only much, much deeper.*

Sora, however, stayed quiet and trusted that Whitney was leading them the right way.

They passed dozens of cells—most of which were now empty. Torsten had given the command for even the prisoners to be given weapons and serve in the defense, under strict watch by former Shieldsmen. He'd said anyone capable of fighting needed to fight, criminal or not. Without the aid of all, there'd be nothing left for anyone. Sora supposed he was right, but that didn't change how scary it was that so many who'd just been locked up were now running around Yarrington with sharp blades.

But she'd come to trust Torsten. His mind for war was keen, and she had to admit, the strategy they'd all developed sounded far better than any she'd have thought up on her own. The Shesaitju Caleef, too. Mahraveh had a collectedness to her as uncanny as her pure black skin. And at the same time, eyes that spoke of ferocity even Nesilia should fear.

This city was in as good hands as possible.

And Sora was thrilled she'd be the one to take down Freydis. A fire burned inside of her that had nothing to do with Elsewhere or magic. She wanted to see Nesilia and anyone who'd pledged allegiance to her, dead. She'd wrap vines around that warlock's throat, tear out her tongue and silence her once and for all.

A chill ran through her at the darkness of her thoughts.

"Are you okay?" Whitney asked.

"Mmm-hmm, fine," she said quickly. "Just get us to the crypt. I don't like this place."

"Wow, the all-powerful mystic is afraid of a few unoccupied cells."

"Shut up," Sora said.

"What do you think of Torsten's plan?" Whitney asked.

Sora thought about how to answer. She couldn't even believe she'd gone from a young girl, locked up in the basement of the town witch doctor to having just been seated around a table with the Royal Council, generals, and god-queens.

"It's about as good as we can ask for," Sora said.

"I don't like that it has to be you who goes in with Lucindur," Whitney replied.

"You know it has to be."

"I still don't like it. And that Shieldsman? Mulgibore? What is that guy's deal? And a greedy little dwarf as Master of Coin? It's like they plucked the whole lot of them out of a Royal Carnival. Who'd have thought that, in that room, the most sensible would be a priest and a Shesaitju?"

"Who'd have thought the Buried Goddess would rise again to kill all of us?" Sora said.

"Honestly? I could've called it."

A sudden clang of metal sent Sora stumbling away from iron bars and into the stone wall behind her. A pasty hand reached through, grasping for them. Dirt caked its knuckles and fingernails, and dark liver spots dotted the length of the arm. Sora followed it in the darkness to the haggard face of a woman who had seen far better days. Gray hair, gray cheeks, brown teeth, and eyes covered by shadow.

"I see you," she said.

The bars clattered again as the woman made another lunge.

"What?" Sora said back.

"I. See. You." The voice was unfamiliar and cold. What followed the words was a shrill cackle that sent Sora and Whitney both skittering away from the cell. A cold shadow followed them down the hall.

"Sheesh, what a freak," Whitney said, shaking his whole body out like he'd just been covered in ants.

"Did you hear her?" Sora asked.

"Yeah? So, what?"

"'So, what?' So, what is that's what Nesilia said to me in Lucindur's vision. 'I see you.'"

"Yeah? Right, and just now… that woman also *saw* you," Whitney said, chuckling nervously. "She's just a batty old kook left down in the dungeons for too long, so even the soldiers didn't want her. There's nothing to worry about. We are safe here, for now."

"For now" was what Sora was worried about. How long did they have before evil armies were pounding at the city gates—Weeks? Days? Hours? No one knew exactly, and she feared none of them would be prepared, not really. Maybe they'd all faced Nesilia in some form or another, but none of them had shared a body with her. They had no idea what she was truly thinking, truly capable of.

"Oh, look," Whitney said, tearing her from her thoughts. He

pointed up. Webs were strewn from the stone wall at the joints of the ceiling, across and through the iron bars. "Why is it that all of our dates seem to involve spiders?"

"Date, huh?" Sora said. "Is that what this is? Not exactly traditional."

"Am I ever?"

"Are you sure you know where you're going?"

"This isn't my first time," Whitney assured her. "Besides, do you have somewhere better to be than here, with me, on a romantic walk?"

"Old crones and dark dungeons. So romantic."

He wasn't wrong. Sora had learned to enjoy every moment she was given, especially those by Whitney's side. They'd been apart for so long it still felt like a dream, him, there, next to her. At that moment, she felt his warm hand clasp hers, instantly stealing away the chill from her bones.

He squeezed, and so did she.

They walked the rest of the way to the Royal Crypt in silence, but it was a good silence. It might have been the longest Whitney had ever stayed quiet while being awake. Actually, he even talked in his sleep most nights, so it might have been a record all around.

"Here we are," he said after a time Sora didn't want to end. "The Royal Crypt, creepiest place in the whole world."

They stood within a cave mouth a bit larger than a standard doorway. Beyond it, the stone went from the rough, jagged dungeon to impossibly smooth and intricately carved walls and domed ceilings. Sora didn't bother to examine any of the etchings. Again, her focus was singular.

"Would you mind…"

Sora didn't even finish her sentence before Whitney cleared his throat.

"You know—why don't I… uh… I'll hang out here and keep watch. Make sure you aren't disturbed. Are you okay to go in alone? Dead bodies… yuck."

Sora smiled. For such a self-centered dolt, Whitney had become quite thoughtful.

"Sure. You stay here. I won't be long."

"Right, then," Whitney said, kissing Sora's hand before letting it go.

She turned back to the crypt. It was quiet, and eerie, and felt very much like she'd just walked into an infirmary, or the royal library—like they should've been whispering. She took a few tentative steps forward, then turned and said, "Thanks."

Whitney shooed her onward.

Her heartbeat sounded like drums, drawing back a small memory of the Earthmoot celebration in Drav Cra.

She ignored the tall statues in the crypt's center, kings and queens who were unfamiliar to her, relics of a history that was no more. She ignored the upright glass coffins, recessed into the walls, encircling the room. Then, she came to one she recognized. Pale, white skin, half her face covered in a porcelain mask—the Mad Queen, Oleander Nothhelm.

She looked like any other Drav Cra, only infinitely more beautiful. Perhaps, this was the most beautiful woman Sora had ever seen. Then, Sora remembered the countless stories of the Queen's cruelness and that notion melted away.

Beside her was a small boy. Couldn't have been older than a teenager. A mop of black hair swooped across his eyes, both covered with gold autlas, Eyes of Iam side facing out, like all the others. His skin looked wrinkled and withered.

King Pi. Her half-brother.

He looked even younger than she remembered him being on the only other time she'd seen him, floating atop Mount Lister, writhing under Nesilia's control. She figured it was the goddess' presence then that added to his looking older. Now, probably the most powerful boy who'd ever lived was dead... again. The only thing differentiating him from every other who'd come and passed was, instead of being food for worms, he was eternally memorialized in a glass casket.

She hadn't even noticed she'd stopped, so lost she was in her thoughts of the boy she didn't even know.

After a deep breath, she pressed on, still not having found what she came for. Three more steps took her to the place she'd been thinking about for days.

All the stories told of a man covered in rippling muscle, hair dark as night, and a chin like hardened steel. She saw none of those things but could imagine them well. The corpse's hands were clasped over a metal rod. It looked odd, and when she looked around at all the other kings, gripping swords, she wondered what it signified.

However, even in death and frailty, King Liam Nothhelm looked every bit the conqueror he was named to be. Though she couldn't see his eyes, covered by coins like his son, she knew them. Every time she stared into polished metal or a still pond, she saw them. Amber, not unlike the autlas now covering them. Like sunshine in darkness, she knew those eyes well, and saw them, even now, where his eyes should be, in her own reflection cast upon the face of Liam's glass casket.

She considered sitting, then chose instead to fold her arms against her chest. Finally, she resolved to just standing there, arms at her sides. She took a deep breath, let it out, then tried to find her voice.

"What do you say to a father you never knew? Did you…" Her words got caught in her throat, and she felt stupid. What did she care if a dead man she'd never even met heard her words? Like he could hear anyway. She glanced over her shoulder and didn't see Whitney. At least knowing he wasn't listening in made it a tad easier.

Sora cleared her throat and continued. "Did you… did you miss me? Did you even care that I was alive somewhere and being raised to be the very thing you lived to destroy? You tried to keep me from embarrassing you. Is that it? A King waging war against mystics, only to create a child with the most powerful mystic in Pantego. What a legacy to leave. A stain."

Sora heard Nesilia's sing-song voice in her ear, taunting her. *Forgotten…*

"But I wasn't," Sora continued. "I wasn't a stain. I was a child. A baby. Full of potential and possibilities. But you couldn't be bothered to ruin your reputation, so you got rid of me. Sent me to a crazy old man… a crazy old man who loved me more than you ever could have, but had no idea how to show it."

The thought of Wetzel, dead like the many corpses around her, shook her more than she expected it could. It was like knowing who her father was, really seeing him before her for the first time, made her appreciate the excuse for one she was given.

"But now he's dead, too," she said. "Because of you. Because of your stupid wars over stupid gods who don't give two shogs about us. All they care about is themselves. Their names. Just like you."

She wiped away a tear, then laughed. "Stupid," she whispered. "This is so stupid. I'm just here to say…" She drew a deep, trembling breath. "I forgive you. For whatever that's worth. I don't know why, but I forgive you. I wound up right where I was meant to be."

She placed her palm against the glass and left it there a moment. Only then did she notice the embers floating around them. She couldn't control it, and for once, she didn't try to. She let her be herself. The glass crackled, and the reflection around her hand warped and fractured.

"Torsten, you're being ridiculous!" Whitney shouted.

The outburst startled her, and Sora spun to see the two of them, Torsten, with his claymore half-drawn and Whitney chasing after him.

"Torsten, stop," he said. "Just let me explain."

"There's nothing to explain," Torsten said. "I trusted you, and now I find you down here… doing what?"

Before she even realized it, Sora was backing away from the charging, towering man. She'd seen him angry, but this was something else.

"Get away from that casket!" he roared. He was now right before her. She saw pain in his eyes as he grabbed her arms, one after the other, turning them one way and then another as if inspecting them. That was when Sora realized what he was doing.

"Get your hands off her!" Whitney shouted.

"No, Whit, it's okay," Sora said.

"It—what?"

"Torsten, it's not what you think," Sora said, taking inspiration from Mahraveh in how to appear impossibly calm at all times.

"Says every criminal who has ever been locked up in that dungeon."

"And this time, it's true," she said.

"I saw the flame. Is that why you were sent here? To possess these preserved bodies of kings and queen more worthy than any of us? To turn our very heroes against us?"

"No, that's not it."

"Then what are you doing down here?" Torsten demanded. "Tell me. Show me that I wasn't a fool to, once again, stake our entire existence on a blood mage and a thief."

"I'm just here..." Sora really didn't know how to answer the question. Part of her didn't even know.

For longer than she could remember, Sora wanted—needed—to know who her birth parents were. She'd never been told Wetzel was... of that, he'd always been honest. Besides, it wouldn't have been long before she realized her skin color, ears, and so many other things were different from the old man.

She could remember long nights, lying in bed, or out behind Wetzel's shed, staring at the stars, wondering who her parents were and why they'd abandoned her. Now that she knew...

"To pay my respects," Sora said.

"To a King you never knew?" Torsten retorted. "Tell the truth."

"Torsten, old pal, you're making a mistake," Whitney said.

Torsten turned on Whitney. "You made the mistake. Coming back here. Bringing her." He jabbed a finger toward Sora.

"*She* is our best hope at beating Nesilia," Whitney argued.

"And how do I know we didn't just invite Nesilia right into the castle?" Torsten said. "That's the whole plan, isn't it?"

"You're out of your mind," Whitney said.

"How do I know she's really gone?"

"Torsten, would I lie to you?" Whitney asked.

Both Torsten and Sora answered at the same time, "Yes."

Torsten turned to appraise Sora, and she raised her hands in a display of surrender.

"Look, no magic, okay?" she said. "I'm not down here, cursing the Kingdom or anything. I just needed to see him."

She pointed to Liam, sure there was no way to get out of this without being honest.

"That doesn't make sense," Torsten said. "What business could you possibly have with King Liam?"

Sora exchanged a look with Whitney and let out a sigh. As she considered the ways she could possibly explain, Whitney blurted, "She's his daughter. Well... bastard I guess? Can a girl be a bastard?"

Torsten stood, mouth agape as if he were about to speak, head turning from Sora to Whitney and back again.

"Preposterous," he said. Then, he seized Sora by the arm again. This time, he wasn't merely inspecting. "We don't have time for Whitney's games."

Sora had tried to do this calmly. It probably would've worked if Whitney hadn't blabbed his mouth like usual. This time, at least, he was just trying to protect her, as if she needed protection. She focused on the blood flowing through her veins, through the arm Torsten held. She didn't call forth flame, but she let it burn on the inside.

He pulled away and yelped. Though his hand blistered instantly, he still used it to draw his sword, but he couldn't lift it high. "Lying witch! I trusted you both like a fool. You're worse than Rand."

"And you thought he'd changed," Sora said to Whitney. Then she reached out, waved her hand over Torsten's, and after a puff of blue smoke appeared, Torsten's hand restored itself. He stared down at it in disbelief, all while hoisting the blade higher.

"It's just a misunderstanding," Whitney said. "Please, Torsten, listen to us. It's true. I saw it myself in the Well of Wisdom."

Torsten's face went slack, like he was speechless.

"I didn't believe it either," Sora said. "But I saw it, too. My mother, the Ancient One before Aihara Na, and Liam. They had a child."

"Not just a child. *You*," Whitney clarified.

"My mother didn't die in the war. She died giving birth to me, and Liam knew how it would look after dedicating the entire Kingdom to wiping out the Mystic Order. So, he smuggled me away, pretended I never existed, and then sickness stole the memory."

Torsten staggered back, his sword slipping loose and clattering loudly on the stone. His eyes darted between Sora and the casket behind her.

"Sora... you..." he stuttered. "No..."

"A part of me wishes it weren't true," Sora said. "But it is. It's what drew Nesilia to me, but it's what I now realize makes us different. I wasn't forgotten. They hid me, sacrificed their love for me, to protect me. Liam destroyed the entire Mystic Order even after their surrender... to protect me."

"And yet I get in trouble every time I tell the tiniest fib," Whitney remarked, earning a scowl from Sora, which shut him right up.

"No… No. He did it in the name of Iam," Torsten said, shaking his head.

"He did it for Liam," Sora said, "as he did everything. For *his* love, for his first daughter, and the first woman he ever truly cared for."

"This is…" Torsten said. "This is not possible."

"You know that's not true," spoke a voice from across the crypt. Everyone whipped around to face an older man wearing leather over-alls. Sora recognized him from the war meeting.

"Iam's shog, what is this—a party now?" Whitney said. "We try to get a moment alone."

"Hovom," Torsten said. "What are you doing here?"

"You were there, as I was," Hovom said, striding into the crypt. His gait was wary, cautious, as if he knew Torsten could be unpredictable in this state. "In Panping, after the war, didn't you find it curious why Liam himself remained there for so long after it ended when any other general would have sufficed?"

"He was plotting the transition of power to Governor Nantby. Plan-ning the succession. Unraveling the mess the mystics had left. Like any great leader."

"You can't be so naïve, Torsten." Hovom stopped a meter or two from them. His hand wasn't on his blade, but Sora got the distinct feeling that it could have been in the span of a heartbeat. But the man was old—not frail or fragile, but old enough. And if the stories were true, even in Torsten's handicapped state, he was amongst the greatest fighters in Pantego.

"Liam was a great leader," Hovom said, "but he wasn't a great man."

"Watch your tongue, Hovom."

"The Ancient One during the Third Panping War. What was her name?"

"No," Torsten said, shaking his head even harder this time.

"Sora Sumati," Hovom said.

"I won't believe it."

"You think that a coincidence?" Hovom asked.

"It's simple, Torsty. Older Sora and Liam had a baby," Whitney added, motioning toward Sora.

"Then Liam didn't know!" Torsten barked, spinning on Whitney.

Sora stepped in front of Whitney, who had been standing between her and Torsten like a shield. "Do you think so little of my kind that you believe that if he knew of me, I wouldn't be here any longer?" Sora asked. Then leaving no room for argument, she said, "He knew."

Sora turned to face Liam's casket.

"He knew and chose to protect me," she said. "Now, I understand why. Men like you would have had me killed just to preserve Liam's legacy as Iam's champion."

"We are not murderers," Torsten said.

"Another lie," Hovom said. Then, when Torsten turned on him, the blacksmith raised his hands placatingly. "I don't mean you. I mean all of us. We've spent so many years doing 'the work of Iam' that I fear we failed to stop and ask Iam Himself if we were doing his will at all."

"Iam wishes all to experience His light and love—"

"By slaughtering them if they refuse?" Sora asked.

"Look, Sir Unger. I know this is hard to grasp, but I believe her," Hovom said. "I may not have ever been a fighter, but I repaired Liam's armor, Uriah's armor—anyone of importance. The blacksmith in a war camp hears all. King Liam had many dalliances. Uriah knew it, too. And no visits with Yaolin officials went longer than his with the Ancient One. Even as Uriah questioned why she and the surviving mystics were kept around so long."

Sora watched as Torsten's features darkened with realization. He said nothing, but it was there. Only, she couldn't tell if the news had broken him or set him free from a lifetime of adulation for an imperfect man.

"We were close friends, Uriah and I. Shared stories many would be ashamed of while I repaired his armor or shared a drink. When we returned from the war after the Mystic Order had finally been eradicated, Liam was torn, broken. Now, I understand why."

"My mother showed him their value, but they would have never let the daughter of the Ancient One go," Sora said.

"I believe it was the beginning of the end for him," Hovom said. "Uriah and I didn't see him for many weeks, after that, and even when we did, he wasn't the same. He spent most of his days in the stables with that Whitehair he brought back for Oleander."

Hovom's eyes went wide as if he had a sudden realization. "He named the horse Sora too, right?"

Torsten shook his head again though his face confirmed that it was true.

"That sure sounds like a guy who was lovestruck," Whitney said.

"It's true, Torsten," Sora said, stepping forward and placing her hand on Torsten's arm. "We don't need to tell anyone. I don't want anything, I swear it on my life. But down here, surrounded by the kings you vowed to protect, you deserve the truth."

Sora stared him straight in the eyes, making sure he would see the amber there, the source of which Sora had discovered after so long. She may have been given every other feature by her mother, but her eyes… those belonged to Liam.

Torsten silently stared back for a few long seconds, then yanked his arm away. He stammered for words, but none came. Instead, he shoved by Hovom and left the crypt, failing even to retrieve his dropped sword.

A deep hush followed him, as if his leaving sucked all their words until, as usual, Whitney broke the quiet.

"That went well," he said.

XXXVIII

THE KNIGHT

Torsten quietly roamed Yarrington's streets like he used to before things became so confused and confusing. Celeste and Loutis hung high above, but it didn't feel like night. Not with all the activity. It barely felt like the city where he'd spent nearly all his life.

Lines wrapped every street corner, people waiting for rations. Poor, nobles, soldiers, and conscripts—all had to wait their turn. The siege hadn't even begun, and they were treating things like it had.

And Torsten knew things would get ugly. People cursed and scuffled in alleys, some even out in the open, yanked each other out of the queue. The soldiers posted to keep the peace were equally starved and irritable, which didn't help. Yarrington was a big city, but not this big, especially with South Corner being evacuated. You couldn't walk more than a few feet without bumping elbows. The rats in the sewers had more space.

Torsten looked right. The city's defense catapults were being set up along the eastern fortifications. Spare blacksmiths and carpenters hammered on the joints. Carts rolled in arrows by the thousands, along with tar and rocks to be dumped upon invaders from the ramparts above. Some even looked to be stones chipped off the Glass Castle itself.

Nothing was sacred any longer, and rightly so.

The soldiers were too busy to even acknowledge Torsten. Sir

Mulliner was up over the gate, barking orders to conscripts who barely knew how to wield a sword, let alone dig proper trenches around the city.

Torsten kept walking, the protests and complaints from confused Glassmen like a dull roar from every direction. He'd told the truth of what was coming, but he barely believed it, let alone humble villagers from the countryside. They'd understand when they saw Nesilia's horde. Until then, Yarrington would suffer.

There weren't enough beds. Families had to share single bedrolls in some homes. Barely enough food and water. Not even buckets for shog. The streets stunk. Closets became bedrooms. Women and Children cried as soldiers went door-to-door, recruiting able-bodied men to serve in the defense. Those who hid were punished, publicly. It was the only way.

Torsten rounded into the Northern Mason's district, another area having its inhabitants removed, forcefully and otherwise. A dwarven mason crew on scaffolding worked by a small span of wall, hacking and whittling to purposefully weaken it. That was where they'd let Freydis think she broke through.

It led into a small square, surrounded on all sides by workshops and homes with plenty of windows. Spiked barricades blocked all roads leading out. Unlike Dockside, nearly all was stone here, so fire wouldn't spread. But they piled hay and tinder where they could, and gave every archer arrows and torches. The smoke and chaos would provide Sora her opening to take Freydis down.

Torsten didn't feel good about surrendering yet another portion of the city. After all the initial bedlam of the ambushes, the lower city would be completely breached. And if their plan to kill Freydis and draw Nesilia out failed, a full retreat to the castle would be their last hope.

They'd die fast instead of slow. At least there was that.

Torsten shook his head to dispel the negative thought.

The plan will work. He repeated those words in his head, but the notion didn't stick. For it to work, he had to rely on Sora. To trust her. After what she'd just told him, he wasn't sure what to think.

Either she really was the bastard daughter of Liam Nothhelm and had inherited his ability for unorthodox strategy, which allowed him to conquer more than half the known world. Or, she was as much a liar as the thief she loved. A servant of the Buried Goddess to sow doubt in Torsten's mind.

He found himself climbing the steps to the Yarrington Cathedral without even realizing it. From the high ground, he could see just how busy the city was. Torches marched like tiny ants in every direction, around every corner of Yarrington.

Behind him, the Grand Plaza of Old Yarrington itself—some called it Yarrington Square, and some Cathedral Square—was most crowded. Tents coated the stone like snow. Thousands of refugees from South Corner, Dockside, and Northern Yarrington were packed into them. The stench reminded Torsten of Valin Tehr's dungeon.

The mansions along the Royal Avenue were crammed as well. Shadows lurked behind every single window.

Torsten had never seen anything like it. With Liam, they were always on the offensive. Yarrington was always at peace. He wondered if this is what Yaolin looked like when Glass armies surrounded it and let the mystics drive their subjects to starvation. Living like cattle stuffed in muddy pens, soldiers, like farmers, keeping them herded.

The conditions had most resigned to their fates. Any man leftover was old and crippled, and the women focused on keeping their children fed. But patches of the slums roared in protests, their chants filling the night air. Some thought this was all a ploy by the nobility to eradicate Dockside and ship them off.

They had to spare a large portion of Glass soldiers and former Shieldsmen to oversee the evacuation. South Corner and Dockside were shog holes, but the people were territorial—proud of their heritage. And the Shesaitju couldn't be seen dealing with the inhabitants, lest Yarrington burn itself down and save Nesilia the trouble. Though, that was the plan, wasn't it?

It was bad enough to have former enemies occupying the castle. Their assistance had to be contained to prepping the harbor itself.

"Sir Unger, my home, they took my home!" an enraged woman squealed from the markets, Docksider accent heavy on her lips.

Torsten lowered his head and shoved by. She grasped at his sleeve.

"Yer from there! Don't let them take our homes."

Seizing her wrist, Torsten peeled her away, but as he turned, he saw the swaddled infant in her other arm, and all he could come up with to say was, "I'm sorry," before pushing on through.

She wasn't the first to beg his mercy and wouldn't be the last. The moment she uttered his name, eyes of the starving and homeless fell upon him like ravenous wolves. The crowd swelled in his direction, screaming and hollering. Guards did their best to calm them, but it was no use. Emotions were too high.

Torsten found his way to the doors of Yarrington Cathedral and slipped inside. Pounding fists echoed, but Shieldsmen within held the doors shut. Of all places, the Cathedral needed to be kept secluded from the madness.

Not because it needed to be kept clean. Though having Yarrington retain some dignity in these trying times wasn't a bad thought. But it wasn't Iam's way. Churches and Cathedrals were built sturdy, and all across Pantego, they'd long served as havens for those with nowhere else to go.

However, the Cathedral was already filled with priests—all of Hornsheim, there and waiting. Only at the selections of High Priests were so many men of the cloth together in the same place, but then, it was *only* priests. Now, hundreds of sisters and monks filled the place. Their beds between every arch, every side altar, every pew.

The cathedral was as packed as any Dawning morning.

Only nobody was praying. They all survived no differently than the rabble outside. Waiting for food and water. Complaining about the conditions. Snoring loudly.

There was so much clamor that, for once, Torsten's footsteps didn't echo on the polished marble. And just like outside, most didn't notice his presence. He felt like a ghost in the aisle, not stirred by faith and conviction like his previous visits to the beautiful edifice that was the home of his God. A part of him couldn't help but know that Iam had given all He had left to provide them this last chance to show they were worthy of being His favored children.

He stopped at the front pew, directly before the altar, the very same place he'd sat when Dellbar was anointed High Priest. Moonlight pouring in kept the great crystal Eye of Iam bright and shining. The only part of the Cathedral left untouched. The altar itself was covered in unfurled scrolls and dusty tomes. Words in languages ancient and modern filled them. It looked like Pi's mad scrawling when Torsten found him that night, long ago.

The words the boy had used then tortured his mind. *Buried... not dead.*

Torsten sat, scrunched between two sleeping monks. His legs were sore from walking the city. His brain ached from all the madness outside, and from their planning, and most of all, from the thought that Liam's line wasn't dead, but endured in the blood of his most-worthy, dark-magic-wielding adversaries.

Sighing, Torsten reached up and removed his blindfold. The world became black, and for the first time since returning to Yarrington, he felt like he had a moment to himself. He could focus on his breathing, and all the din of the cathedral's inhabitants melted away.

He didn't pray. He didn't ask anything of Iam. He simply sat. And he wasn't sure how long he was there before he heard a familiar voice.

"Searching for answers?" Dellbar asked.

"Searching for anything," Torsten replied.

Dellbar chuckled, then gave a sleeping monk a whack with his cane. The man cursed, then noticed who it was and apologized profusely. Dellbar sat beside Torsten, and Torsten couldn't help but be reminded of when he and Wren the Holy sat like this, many times before.

"Sometimes it's pleasant not to see, isn't it?" Dellbar asked.

"It is." He clutched the enchanted blindfold and held it up. "You want it?"

"It doesn't work for me."

"Right. Iam chose me to be His eyes, His shield, and His sword." Only then did Torsten realize he'd left *Salvation* in the Royal Crypt.

"You place too much responsibility on those broad shoulders, Torsten," Dellbar said. "Have you ever wondered if, perhaps, He gave you your sight back simply because you never deserved to lose it?"

"No. And you don't believe it, either."

"Too true. There has to be a plan, doesn't there? That's the way of the Glass Kings. Here by His mandate, to carry His word."

"Have you lost your faith now? After all of this?" Torsten asked.

"Quite the opposite. I've just stopped trying to hear Him, and started to actually listen."

"And what does He tell you?" Torsten asked.

"For one, He answered how we can dispel Nesilia's demons before they possess all of our bodies. And I may not care about much, but I would like to die in control of my own self. I felt helpless once, lying on the floor in my church as Redstar's savages slaughtered everyone around me. Never again."

"I can agree with that." Torsten turned to face him, though he let himself remain blind. "How will it be done?"

Dellbar drew a deep breath. " 'Light and darkness, we live or die together. Bound, eternally. One cannot be without the other. And one cannot die without the other. Put faith in the Light, and fade to shadow with them. It is the only way.' "

"Is that scripture? I've never heard it."

"No. Iam spoke to me in Hornsheim. In a dream, or directly, I'm not sure."

"Does it matter?"

Dellbar gave Torsten a pat on the leg. "Now you're getting it. No, it doesn't at all. And I didn't understand it at first until your friend showed us his cursed stone."

"He's not my friend," Torsten muttered.

"He has to be. He's here. We may fail, Torsten. I've accepted that, and you must as well if we have any chance. And better to die beside friends than in a city full of strangers."

"Have you been drinking again?"

"I think the people out there need an ale much more than I do."

"Or three." Torsten let out a chuckle with him. That was Dellbar, able to see the light and dark in any situation, at the same time. Torsten had missed him in Latiapur when he seemed out of sorts, but this was the High Priest Yarrington needed right now. One who could accept the awful fact that Torsten's brain refused—they could lose.

"So, how does banishing her demons work?" Torsten asked.

"So long as the gates of Elsewhere remain open, it's a temporary solution," Dellbar explained. "But it is as Iam said. 'Put faith in the Light, and fade to shadow with them.' And so, we who have dedicated our lives to his Light can absorb the demons after their hosts are killed."

"And be possessed yourselves?"

"Holding the Brike Stone showed me the way. In that moment, when we are full of darkness, we must let go. Bind them in our souls with faith, and be banished with them to the furthest recesses of Elsewhere, where it could take Iam-knows-how-long to escape again."

"I'm not sure I'm understanding," Torsten said.

"You are," Dellbar said. "You just don't want to hear it, but you have to listen. To dispel them, we who have willingly given our eyes to see only with His, must go with them."

"So, you must die?"

"In a sense."

Torsten shook his head. "And those who have already been taken… what about them?"

"They're already gone."

"Sora isn't," Torsten argued.

"And do you have hundreds of magical artifacts as powerful as a bar guai or a dragon's cursed heart lying around?"

Torsten bit his lip.

"Then why do we even need the stone?" he asked. "We'll gather all the priests together. Ignore the rest and banish her."

"She is no mere demon, Torsten. It will take extraordinary power to hold her. And just as the Brike Stone must go with Nesilia, the light we hold in our hearts is our weapon against the others. It is our magic. It is how priests of old healed or summoned shields of blinding light. Maybe the magic comes from a different place, but it's the same. Magic is in the blood, and faith flows in ours."

"You know that's not true. Their magic comes from Elsewhere."

"A domain created by Iam to hold his enemies."

"No," Torsten said. "The mystics are born with the curse that allows them to draw on Elsewhere's dark power. Anyone can be a priest of Iam."

"Can they?" Dellbar asked, a hint of playfulness to his tone. "Would they? Or do only some find that unfillable hole in their hearts that can only be filled by undying, dutiful faith in His power and Light? I wonder if that Sora girl felt the same before she summoned fire to her fingertips?"

"Why are you bringing her up?" Torsten asked quickly. "Did she talk with you?"

"You brought her up."

"I… oh." He leaned in closer and lowered his voice. "She's not who we thought she was, Dellbar."

"I didn't think her to be anything but an ally in our most desperate time," Dellbar replied.

"I don't mean that."

"Though Mahraveh seems to approve, and the girl is an excellent judge of character, wouldn't you say? You get that sense from her right away."

"Not any of that." Torsten swallowed back his suddenly dry throat. He leaned in even more, forehead against the side of Dellbar's head just to make sure he was as close as could be. "If I tell you something, will you promise, here before Iam, to keep it between us?"

"I doubt Iam is listening in."

"I'm serious."

"Of course, Torsten," Dellbar said, as earnest as Torsten had ever heard him. "Since I found you wasting away in that cell, I value nothing more than our conversations."

"Well…" Torsten swallowed again. Now his throat stung like his body was rejecting even saying the words aloud. His lips parted a few times, only for nothing to come out. But Dellbar waited patiently, listening, as he'd said he'd learned to do.

"Sora claims to be the bastard daughter of Liam Nothhelm and Sora Sumati, the last known Ancient One of the Mystic Order." He was breathless by the time he forced it all out. His stomach turned over. His hands beaded with sweat.

"Does she?" Dellbar laughed.

"Ridiculous, right?"

"Less ridiculous than a shred of cloth giving a blind man the ability to see."

"You believe it?" Torsten asked.

"I didn't know the man," Dellbar said. "Or the woman. Or their daughter. She told you this?"

"In the Royal Crypt. Right in front of his family."

"And what did she ask for?"

"She told me not to tell anyone," Torsten said. "That she didn't want anything."

"Yet, you told me."

"That's not fair."

"Relax, Torsten. I'm not judging you. All I wonder, is why lie about something you want nothing out of?"

"To distract us, because Nesilia is still in control of her."

Dellbar let out a low murmur of acknowledgement. "Perhaps. What do you think? Not in here." He poked Torsten in the side of the head. "But when you listen to your heart."

"I don't know," Torsten admitted. "The thing is, I've learned that Liam wasn't the man we all saw."

"You mean he wasn't God incarnate walking around with a sword?" Dellbar said. "Instead, he was a simple man, flawed like all men, who got sick and died, like all men?"

"I know he never loved Oleander. She was a prize to him, nothing more… like a rare horse brought home from Panping." His heart plummeted as he spoke that last sentence, but he knew it was true.

"My question for you is, whether or not Sora is who she says she is, do you doubt that Liam has other bastards out there? I've had a lot of books read to me these past two weeks, both from Hornsheim, and the Castle libraries. My predecessor noted some peculiar things."

Torsten sat up. "About a Panpingese daughter?"

"No," Dellbar said. "But enough for me to believe that whether she is or isn't his, I doubt she's the only one. And if so, why not her? Wouldn't the king of kings fall for an enemy as powerful as he was? Much as Iam loved Nesilia."

"You believe the lies spread by her cultists?"

"I believe what I felt that night when He looked at her through my eyes," Dellbar said. "So, I ask you again, what do *you* believe?"

Torsten's fingernails dug into his palms. As if learning about Liam's sordid past wasn't enough, now the High Priest spoke of love between Iam and His foulest enemy—the same things Redstar had said. The same truths lying beneath the lines of all the stories of the God Feud that generations of priests refused to acknowledge until it felt like heresy to imagine them. But now, after so much, Torsten could see that. But Sora?

"I don't know," Torsten said again. "I can't… I can't see the lines of her face or the color of her eyes, not anymore. And I can't remember how they looked when I met her with my own sight. I don't know if he's in there."

"Then, why worry?" Dellbar said plainly. As if it were that easy.

"If the Nothhelm line isn't dead—"

"It is. Whether she's his or not, she's as legitimate as Pi and Mahraveh's marriage. Who cares where she came from? The Kingdom you loved is dead, Torsten. You aren't fighting for it any longer. Just walk outside and look around."

"Then what will it be?"

"When you know, you'll know." Dellbar took Torsten's hand and gave it a firm squeeze. "Stay strong, my friend. These people may not have a King, but right now, they have a leader." He let go, dusted off his robe, and stood. "Now, I have some priests I have to convince to sacrifice their lives. And *you* need some sleep."

Torsten grunted. He listened as the tapping of Dellbar's staff faded. He, as usual, made about as much sense as he didn't. Speaking in riddles came naturally to High Priests. It must have been the position— countless people looking for answers that it turns out, they probably didn't have.

One thing was for certain, however. Truth or not, Torsten couldn't let Sora distract him. Maybe she was still under Nesilia's control, but that meant the Buried Goddess already knew everything they were planning. All Torsten could do was have faith that the last kind of person he ever thought he could trust, could be trusted.

He'd gone down to the Royal Crypt to speak with his King one last time and instead, found her. Like Dellbar said, maybe it was time to leave them all behind, anyway, to dedicate their final days to what was good about Liam and his bloodline—bringing people together. They never did it kindly, not until Pi, but still, here they all were.

"If You are still out there," Torsten said, aiming his face toward where decades of visiting this very spot told him Iam's altar would be. "I'm listening."

Then, he tied his blindfold back on so he could see all the hapless priests roaming and with no idea yet what was coming. He'd have to trust them to keep the demons from spreading throughout Yarrington as their host bodies fell.

Who didn't he have to trust? Mystics, thieves, Black Sandsmen.

One mistake, and the world ended. There was no retreat like in one of Liam's campaigns. There was no surrender like his enemies had done. Torsten was back in Valin Tehr's arena, fighting a giant. Survive or die.

He was about to stand when he felt a tap on his shoulder.

"Uh, Torsten." Whitney Fierstown slowly shuffled out in front of him, not wearing his usual carefree expression, but looking as grim as Torsten probably did.

"What?" Torsten asked.

"You dropped this." Whitney knelt, and Torsten noticed that he had *Salvation* balanced across his palms, presenting the blade like a knight to his King. The blade had been reforged, but the hilt had been wielded by Liam himself. The thief could've sold it, used the earnings to buy a whole town somewhere far away where Nesilia might never reach. Yet, here he was, looking like a damned fool.

"Get up," Torsten said, gripping the handle and lifting it high. The refracted moonlight coming through the Eye of Iam made the steel glint. "I thought you'd keep it."

"That's really what you think of me, isn't it?" Whitney asked.

"Isn't that what you want people to think?"

"I... what... you're welcome." Whitney groaned and turned to leave. Torsten grasped his arm and stopped him.

"Thank you, Lord Blisslayer."

He smirked and plopped right down next to Torsten on the pew. "Ha. You still remember my old name."

"Fierstown doesn't count as a new name, you fool."

"It does the way I use it this time."

Torsten wasn't sure what he meant, but somehow, he understood. Whitney's expression bore conviction that could've only been found in one who's made peace with his past. He'd seen it on the faces of many great men before they died.

"We didn't mean to tell you that way," Whitney said. "She made me promise not to tell anyone, I swear. I told her she should be Queen, and she nearly bit my head off."

"You really love her, don't you?" Torsten asked.

"Huh?"

"I'm not trying to argue or make a point. I'm simply asking."

Whitney kicked his legs out and crossed them in the air, then let them crack down on the marble floor. "Yeah… this old horse is finally hitched."

"Then you should be with her. Not me. Spend as much time as you can together, because it may be all we have."

"Hey, what happened to 'we won't lose?'"

"A friend let me see again."

"Well, we won't. So, Sora can have a few hours by herself." He put his arm around Torsten's shoulder, barely able to reach the far side. But damned if he didn't try. "I'm here to make sure my old pal is okay. We really do swear not to tell anybody. It's not my secret, anyway."

Torsten turned, his eyeless stare boring through Whitney—a thief who'd say anything to get off. One who'd pose as a priest or lie to a King. But at this moment, he was being completely sincere.

"You know, of all the insane things that have happened since the day we met. Having you here, ready to fight and die for someone you love… that is the most surprising," Torsten said.

Whitney averted his gaze. His throat bobbed as emotion clearly got the better of him, but Torsten didn't draw attention to it.

"What can I say?" Whitney asked. "I'm evolved."

Torsten laughed.

"So, you promise you're not mad about Liam?" Whitney asked. "I only took Sora down there because she needed it. But she's okay now. We won't go there again."

"I'm not mad," Torsten said. "I'm not happy. And I truly, truly, don't want to talk about Liam. So, would you do something for me?"

"Anything."

"Would you pray with me?"

"Anything *but* that."

Torsten laughed, then grew serious once more. "Everything we know is coming to an end. Why not take the chance with me?"

"Because it's hogwash."

"Then take the chance. Just once, sit and pray with me, Whitney Fierstown. The former World's Greatest Thief. Or are you scared?"

"All right, you're going to pull that card. That's fine. That's fine." Whitney removed his arm from Torsten's back, circled his eyes, and dropped his head. "I'll play your game, *former* Wearer of White. But Iam better close his ears."

XXXIX

THE CALEEF

The Yarrington docks were a jarring reminder that Mahi was not in Shesaitju lands any longer. From the yellow sands by the northern coast to the distinct lack of finger-like rocks jutting out of the sea, everything was so… different. Everything, except the hectic, crazed men and women dashing along the piers. Those, apparently, were everywhere.

However, now more than ever, there was a reason for their manic behavior. Mahi's destruction of White Bridge wouldn't hold Nesilia's forces back long. There were passes to the north, through dwarven territory—and Nesilia had already proven she was unafraid of the dwarves.

Presently, longboats cut the waves from one side of Autla's Inlet to the other, dragging with them massive, barbed chains. On the shore, teams of beastmasters whipped zhulong into action, doing just the same. Uhlvark, the High Priest's giant friend, helped on land, attaching the chains to the watchtowers and lighthouses along the coast.

In the waters, out beyond the makeshift jetties, Lord Jolly orchestrated the larger ships, each overflowing with vat after vat of whale oil. Mahraveh marveled at his leadership. These Glassmen weren't fools as she'd been led to believe they were her whole life. Different, perhaps, but not by much more than their skin color or chosen deity.

"Pull!" Bit'rudam shouted, his voice cutting through the rest.

She'd been watching him as he worked, barebacked and sweating, more than a little ashamed at her thoughts during such a tumultuous time. She hadn't loved since Jumaat, and she doubted that's what this was now. Still, she couldn't help but wonder what it would've been like to have lived a normal life, here in the Glass capital, without all the infighting and politics she was so used to back home.

Would she have been wed already? Bearing children of her own?

It does not matter, she thought. *You are the snake. You are the Caleef.*

Behind her, a skirmish broke out just beyond the docks on what they called Port Street. It wasn't the first and certainly wouldn't be the last. The Docksiders had been restless since they'd been informed that their home would be used as kindling in an attempt to stop the attackers. Many complained that there was no need for an invading army if they, themselves, were to destroy the city. To the credit of the Glassmen, none offered the slightest inkling that it was Mahi's plan.

She wasn't surprised by the protesting and riots as Glass soldiers dragged many people out of their homes. They'd decided it'd be best if no Shesaitju were seen doing anything but working in the water. They earned enough curses and hateful stares from the locals. Mahi walked along the docks, watching as Torsten's men held the angry locals at bay. They'd done an excellent job so far, keeping the peace, but it wouldn't last much longer if something wasn't done. To tell so many thousands to evacuate their homes, taking only what they could carry, and find refuge at a church all the way across the city… they were lucky there wasn't a full-on civil war.

Still, she understood. As shoddy and unpleasant as this corner of Yarrington was, she'd come to learn that people were fiercely defensive of their homes. She'd have killed every Glassmen alive when they'd burned down her own village. But that was before she gained the perspective of a thousand years of conflict.

At the same time, she found herself impressed by her own people beyond compare. They worked tirelessly, despite being underfed and sleeping on hay like zhulong in a crowded stable. It was almost like they'd forgotten about what had happened in Latiapur. Gone was the mourning and complaining, now replaced by sheer determination to survive.

Bit'rudam wiped sweat from his brow with his forearm and crossed the deck to where Mahi stood. He snatched up one of the many water-skins hanging from posts along the docks.

"How is it going?" Mahi asked.

He turned, startled as first, as if he hadn't even seen her there. Then, he did a little bow and said, "My Caleef, it is going well. The Glassmen around here know their way around water, I'll give them that at least."

Mahraveh nodded. "I agree."

"Lord Jolly has his ships ready for flame, and now they work to create the blockade. Our people, with the help of others, have successfully strung up over one hundred chains, and the rest will be done by the end of the week. It is slower work the further out we go. If we hope to impede the wianu, we must go deep and cover every route."

Mahi looked beyond him to a group of Shesaitju women braiding rope. "And them?"

"Ah, yes. That was my idea," Bit'rudam said. "Large nets to hang from the chains in an effort to further deter the sea beasts. We won't have time to craft enough chains. They can spare no more smiths."

"A fine plan," she said. "As good as any when fighting gods."

Those words carried with them a weight she hadn't intended. The memory of Latiapur, although temporarily out of mind, would linger with them forever. They hadn't stood a chance and looking around at all her men now, she wondered if the same were true.

Mahi gazed out over the sea, then followed the breaking waves to a sandbar on the southern end where a lone figure sat in the water, ignoring the waves as they crashed all around.

"If you'll excuse me," she said to Bit'rudam.

"Of course, my Caleef."

Bit'rudam grazed her arm with intent before he returned to his work. She didn't scold him, even if they were out in public. They could all die soon. There wasn't enough time not to enjoy the small things, and she enjoyed so little these days.

Mahi walked the docks, passing a dilapidated church, several tiny shacks, and one building that looked entirely out of place. Balconies wrapped its exterior, beautifully carved wood creating elegant arches.

Even in the midst of filth, beauty can be found, she thought.

She stopped in a green patch, her naked toes curling in the grass, a feeling mostly unfamiliar to her. She wished she could have experienced more than the vague sensation. The trees here, like the one she stood under now, were so unlike those back in the Black Sands. The shade would have felt nice, too, if things like temperature mattered to her any longer. She even wished she could feel the wind blowing in from the ocean, whipping her braids. She could only smell the salt. At least, that reminded her a bit of where she came from.

From there, she watched the figure in the sandbar, who was clearly lost in thought. Sora, the mystic, was unique, but Mahi couldn't help but feel she'd found a kindred spirit after the meeting in the Shield Hall. Not many others would know what possession by a god felt like. As a matter of fact, the only other person she knew who would was now dead, minutes after pledging himself to her in holy matrimony.

In the distance, a wyvern swooped down, breaking the water's surface and then rising with a fish flapping in its teeth. The miniature dragon-beast flew toward the shore, ultimately landing beside Sora and wasting no time getting to work on her meal.

Mahi followed the jetty to the sand bar and slowly made her way to Sora. As she got closer, she noticed the glowing orange speckles hovering around the mystic's fingertips. She cleared her throat, not wanting to experience the consequences of surprising her.

The wyvern looked up, but when Sora didn't respond, Mahi cleared her throat again. This time, it elicited the reaction Mahi had hoped for, causing Sora to turn.

"Oh," she said, rising, water dripping from her soaked clothing. Long, dark hair was matted to a face that was misted with saltwater. She swiped at the strands, tucking them behind her pointed ears.

The wyvern chirped, took a small hop closer to Sora, then went back to her meal.

"I didn't aim to disturb you," Mahi said. "And I understand if you'd rather be left alone."

"I—no, not at all," Sora said. "It is nice to have company in a city so large."

"Where is your friend, Whitney?"

Since they'd arrived in Yarrington, Mahi hadn't seen the two separated.

"He had some… uh, business with Sir Unger," Sora said.

Mahi didn't like the sound of that, but resolved to allow them their privacy. As long as it didn't interfere with the battle, it was no concern of hers. She was a stranger in these lands, after all.

"Good," Mahi said. "And who is this?"

Sora bent and scooped up the animal.

"This is Aquira," she said. "She's a wyvern."

"Yes, my father taught me about them. Though I've never seen one. May I?" Mahi extended a hand toward Aquira.

Sora looked genuinely surprised at the request, as if most people were terrified of the thing. Then after looking to Aquira, likely to gauge her response, said, "By all means."

Aquira shrank back only slightly at Mahi's touch. Then, she pressed her head forward and into her palm.

"She prefers women," Sora said. "And she seems to like you."

"Yes, well, she is beautiful and ferocious. Just like her owner. Has she been with you long?" The words immediately returned to her own ears, and she regretted them. They'd just been together in the Shield Hall when Sora shared of her time spent possessed by the goddess. Unless Aquira was there with her, which was doubtful, Sora had been away from the creature for a very long time.

Sora must have noticed the look on Mahi's face.

"It's okay," Sora said. "Before Nesilia took me, Aquira brought me great comfort for many months. She was all I had."

There seemed to be more to the tale, but Sora's words trailed off as she stared down at her companion.

"I know what it feels like," Mahi said. She allowed a moment for her words to register with Sora before continuing. "I didn't always look like this, you know. My people, they all consider this some great gift from our God. But I…" She kicked her foot in the water. "I can't even feel the waves against my feet. Or the wind against my brow."

"Sometimes, a lack of feeling is advantageous."

"Yes, perhaps," Mahi said. "In the castle, you said Nesilia made you do things you did not wish to do. I, too, have been forced to act in ways I would have never desired."

Visions of her afhems being scarred and maimed at her command passed through her mind's eye. The look on her father's face as the skin was sliced from his scalp. Even though he understood, his heartbreak couldn't be completely masked.

"What is it?" Sora touched her ears. "I understand being different. If I'm being too forward, I'm sorry. Just… the blackness of your skin. None of the others—"

"For you, Nesilia took over on the inside. For me and every other Caleef, our God alters the outside too. This…" She stroked a finger over her flawless, black skin. "This is the blood of a thousand nigh'jels, though it does not wash off. The sea itself first threatened to kill me, tossing me to and fro like leaves upon the wind. Then, it offered itself to me in fullness."

"I'm sorry," Sora said.

"Yes, well, this too shall end soon," Mahi said. "But you… you have a unique perspective of this upcoming battle. You have felt her mind. We Shesaitju believe that you learn another's mind through battle, and we have yet to fight. All I know is that she killed my father."

"Muskigo, right?"

Mahi noted the way she said it. Like his was not a name she'd merely heard from the war.

"You knew him?" Mahi asked.

"Briefly," Sora said. "In Winde Port, when everything changed. I got trapped in the city. Everyone around here calls him a monster, but he was kind to me. Protected me." She scratched the wyvern's chin. "And Aquira."

Mahi sighed and nodded. "He could be as hard to read as the ocean. But the things he chose to protect, he did so with the ferocity of a dragon."

"I can see him in you. Strong, resilient, unwavering." Sora's gaze turned toward the ground, and her features darkened. "I guess we all can't help but be like our fathers."

"You say that like it's a bad thing."

"I don't know what it is."

Mahi could again tell there was more history there, but she didn't press. "Well, what a strangely small world it is that we would meet here… a Panpingese woman in Yarrington, with a soft spot for my rebel father."

Sora chuckled. "Strange, indeed."

"So, Sora the mystic, against this enemy who slew my legendary father like he was no challenge at all. Do we have a chance?"

Sora appeared to be mulling the question over while she stared off toward Mount Lister. Mahraveh had never seen anything like it. The Shesaitju deserts had dunes, even some large ones, and the cliffs near Nahanab were tall and steep, but she didn't think anything of such magnitude could have existed. If its peak hadn't been sheared off, it would have touched the sky and beyond.

Finally, Sora spoke, pulling Mahi's attention back. "I have to believe that if there's any force on Pantego that could stop her, it is here, in this city. With your Serpent Guards, Torsten's knights, and the magic at our disposal, there could be no greater hope."

"Is it true, then—what was said about your battle in the north?" Mahi asked.

"It was hardly my battle," Sora said with a small laugh.

"Poor choice of words, but the question remains. Had it not been for the meddling pirate, would Nesilia truly be gone?"

"I can't say for certain, but that's how it appeared," Sora said. "She was definitely caught in the bar guai. It wasn't until the stones broke and released her presence that we lost."

"Resourceful, that thief of yours, isn't he?" Mahraveh peered across the waters at the docks, once again letting her eyes linger upon Bit'rudam. "You are lucky to have him, and him, you."

"I'm sorry about what happened with the King," Sora said as if the two were in any way related. Though, Mahraveh knew the mystic had no way of knowing just how shallow an arrangement the marriage had been. Mahi had hardly known the boy before they stood before the Glass priest. Even though he was the start of her newfound respect for the pink men, she'd only known him for a matter of days, and that wasn't enough to qualify as anything more than moderate interest.

Sora kept talking, but Mahraveh's attention remained on the wharf where something new was taking place. Three Glass soldiers stood with Bit'rudam. The look on her commander's face spoke of dire news.

"What is it?" Sora asked, apparently noticing as well.

"I'm not sure, but it doesn't look good."

"Let's find out," Sora said. "C'mon Aquira."

The wyvern obliged, begrudgingly abandoning its seafood to land on her shoulder.

They followed the coast up the jetty until they arrived at a small stone staircase leading up to the docks. Before long, they stood with Bit'rudam and the soldiers, Sir Austun Mulliner, present among them. She may have found a new respect for Glassmen, but that one, she preferred to stay away from.

"Dire news, Mahre—my Caleef," Bit'rudam said. Then, he looked to Sir Mulliner.

"Mahraveh," he said. It wasn't exactly reverence, but there was a measure of respect in his tone. "Despite my protestations, even I must admit that your plan to disrupt Nesilia's travels by destroying the bridge was smart—however, it didn't work."

Didn't work? How could it not have worked? Mahi, herself, was there, and she saw to it that White Bridge lay in ruins at the bottom of the gorge. What was left of it could hardly have been called passable.

"Speak plainly," Mahi said.

"We don't know how, but we've received word by scouts that Nesilia rebuilt the bridge and has crossed with her entire army and are on their way through the fringe towns."

"Rebuilt it? That's impossible. It would take years to construct."

"I don't know, but she did it."

"She doesn't play by our rules," Sora said, then swore. "They won't be long then."

"No," Mulliner agreed. "A couple of weeks at most. One if they push. Sir Unger has already been informed. Even the women are being called upon to help with preparations. These chains, they're it. We need every blacksmith arming our people now."

Mahi surveyed the inlet, and the many things still left to do. Time was no longer on their side. Nesilia had made a seemingly impossible countermove, yet Mahi wasn't surprised. Like she'd said to Sora, Muskigo wasn't even a challenge for her, and he'd nearly brought the Glass Kingdom to its knees.

She racked her mind, hundreds of years of history through the eyes of other Caleefs for ideas. A new strategy that might work. Some new weapon. None came, as no one had ever faced anything like this.

This was it. The war of ages had arrived. And she wasn't afraid, no. She was ready. Even after everything Nesilia had said to her, trying to tempt and taunt her, she had no doubt. This, right here, the tip of the spear, was where she belonged.

"Then we'd better get to work," Mahi said. "And fast."

XL

THE KNIGHT

"We all know the plan," Torsten said.

"Kill a goddess," Whitney chimed in. "Easy peasy."

Mahi lifted an eyebrow his way. "You are a very strange man," she said, earning a grin from the former dastardly thief.

"You have no idea," Sora said.

"Sir Unger," Sir Mulliner intoned, arriving at the Shield Hall's entry, slightly short of breath. "They're all here. The Drav Cra, the Shesaitju, and Her."

"Then it's already begun," Torsten said.

"The end of an age," Dellbar added. "Win or lose."

"Glory or grave," Whitney said, voice chipper.

Torsten looked around the Shield Hall; at the stone-hewn table built for the first King of Glass, and the statues of Wearers come and gone, men Torsten respected above all others. He turned to the large window and the view of Mount Lister, where he'd spent so much time ruminating. He could still picture Liam, Uriah, and other great knights standing around the table. Great and legendary men, who'd inspired the songs of bards across Pantego. The company was much different now, but it was all they had.

He pointed at Mount Lister and the Royal Crypt. "It all started right there, just beneath that hill. Its where she was buried and where she possessed our late king. Let it end here as well."

"Hear, hear," a few voices said.

Mahraveh's destruction of White Bridge had failed. Torsten could only hope that wouldn't be a foretelling of what was to come. They had all the time they ever would. Yarrington was as ready to fall as it ever would be. Ready to fall, so that Pantego could live.

"Hovom, bring them," Torsten said. He waved to the door, and the Royal Blacksmith entered, carrying a cloth bundle that clattered as he moved. Laying it upon the table, he unfurled the end to reveal a cluster of swords and daggers, all beautifully fashioned with gold and gems. Royal weapons.

"Iam's golden shog, those are pretty," Whitney said. He reached for one, but Torsten's glower stopped him.

Dellbar let out a soft chuckle at the comment but said nothing.

"These," Torsten said, "are the weapons of our buried kings."

"Those forged without glaruium, at least," Hovom added.

"You raided graves for these?" Whitney reeled his hand all the way back. "Even I don't do that."

"Today, they will stand with us, here, in the city they built as a shrine to Iam beside the holy mountain."

"A little on the nose, don't you think?" Whitney said.

Sora nudged him.

"A beautiful gesture," Lucindur said, offering Torsten a warm smile.

"We need all the help we can get," Torsten replied.

"The Caleefs are all with me," Mahraveh said. "And my father. He fought to destroy this city and everything its people stood for. Now, we fight to save it."

"I grew up with stories of the evil of this place," Bit'rudam said. "Today, it is an honor to be here with all of you."

"They ain't so bad, huh?" Tum Tum said.

"Indeed," Mahraveh said.

"Well, isn't this adorable," Whitney said as he strode around the table, hand hovering over the weapons as if he were a salesman flaunting his wares. "But how are a bunch of old swords going to help? I mean, they are sharp, sure... but will they kill an upyr goddess?"

"Funny you should ask," Hovom said, his voice soft but commanding. "Their blades have all been reforged using silver."

"Silver," Sora said at the same time.

"It's true," Torsten said, sliding *Salvation,* newly dusted with silver, out of his sheath and placing it on the table before them. "We don't only fight Nesilia, but the body she inhabits. Our respective people fight for their very lives, but if we in this room fail, it'll all be for naught. If the Buried Goddess is near, do whatever it takes to plunge the silver into her and slow her down. Give your lives if you must. Everyone, take one. I believe you will all find weapons comfortable for use."

All eyes fell upon Torsten, and he nodded them along. Whitney shrugged and dove in first, taking two matching daggers once owned by King Remy. Then, one by one, the others took from the pile. A dwarf, a Lightmancer, a Shesaitju—they grasped the weapons of Kings.

This was Torsten's last act as Wearer of White, to bring this hodge-podge group of strangers together and make them feel like a King's Shield of their own.

Hovom had left the room while everyone selected, then returned and approached Mahraveh.

"My Lady," he said. She turned to him. "Our kings never used spears, but Torsten tells me you are proficient with one of these?" he said. "I had one crafted for you, modeled after a historian's text on the first Afhem of Ayerabi. It's imbued with a silver tip."

Mahraveh received the spear and gave it a spin.

"It's perfect," she said, looking to Torsten.

Sora went last. Reaching for a small blade, she hesitated. Hovom moved up beside her. "A fine choice. *Faith* belonged to King Autla himself—the first king of Glass, and the first in the Nothhelm line. They say, he plunged it into the heart of the first Drad who attempted to conquer his lands."

Whitney blew a raspberry. "Look at the size of that thing. He probably just used it to open letters."

Sora slowly wrapped her fingers around the grip, then glanced up at Torsten. His breath caught for a moment. A mystic holding the legendary blade, *Faith,* was a sight he never believed he'd see. But if she genuinely was a Nothhelm by blood, it belonged with her. Though he hadn't yet come to terms with that possibility, he couldn't allow his feelings to get in the way. To win, they needed Sora. Perhaps, more than anybody there.

She lifted the weapon to the light and turned it over. The pommel was an eye of Iam sculpted out of crystal. The grip, a map of Yarrington burned into the leather, detailing Yarrington's origin at a scale only the finest artisans could achieve. And the blade, while recast in silver, curved like a dragon's fang.

Her wyvern leaned over from its perch on her shoulder, then chirped.

"I guess it is pretty," Whitney remarked, leaning likewise.

Sora bit her lower lip, then looked up at Torsten. They nodded at one another before she looped its sheath around her waist. After that, nobody spoke a word. They all silently stared around the room from one pair of eyes to the next as the gravity of what was to come sank in.

"May we all meet at the Gate of Light," Dellbar said, breaking the eerie silence.

"Or right back here," Whitney said. "I've got a feeling Iam wouldn't let me in even if I knocked and asked nicely."

"He would," Torsten said. "You are the greatest hero Pantego never wanted, Whitney Fierstown. All of you are. Today, the Buried Goddess falls for good."

"Aye!" Tum Tum chanted, alone.

A few others followed, but no chorus of cheers came, as would fill the war camps before Liam's great battles. The solemn silence returned, and after a handful of firm, knowing looks, Torsten said, "Prepare for battle."

He turned and headed for the exit. On his way by Sir Mulliner, he took him by the pauldron. "You held me to account when I didn't deserve the White Helm. We may not have a King to shield, but it has been an honor and a privilege, my friend."

"I was right then. I'm honored now," he said, returning the gesture. "If Liam is up there, looking down. His legacy is safe in your hands." He closed his eyes and looked up. 'We are the Armor of Your Holy Kingdom. Our lives are given freely under the sight of your Vigilant Eye, so Your children may thrive in this world You have blessed us with."

"'We are the right hand of Iam," Torsten said. "The sword of His justice, and the Shield that guards the light of this world.'"

"We finally fulfill our oaths," Mulliner said.

Torsten grinned. "Took us long enough."

There was no more to say. Torsten had been the enemy of nearly everyone in the Shield Hall, or their fathers. Only Sir Mulliner had tossed him into a dungeon cell and forced him to atone. And the hard, dour Shieldsman would never know how much that loyalty to what they stood for meant to Torsten.

He glanced back one last time as the others bade farewell. Whitney held Sora in an embrace, not bothering to fight back his tears. She buried her face in his shoulder, Aquira tangled in her hair.

"I don't want to leave you," Whitney said. "I don't like this."

"It's the way it has to be," Sora replied.

"I still don't like it."

"Well, trust in me." Sora pulled her head back and kissed him. It was an awfully effective way to keep the man quiet, but Torsten could tell every ounce of her being was poured into that kiss, which might be their last.

The others bid farewell also, in their own ways. Even strangers embraced, showing love for former foes.

Yes, they were ready. And so was Torsten. In fact, he was oddly calm as he moved through the castle, past all the defenses being established in order to protect Lucindur. Blocked doors. Spike traps. Layers of Serpent Guards and former Shieldsmen at choke points—all to buy her as much time as possible when they made their move.

He was calm as he emerged into the entry courtyard, filled with archers and more barriers. Conscripts were still being armed. Commanders barked orders from on the walls, moving these untrained, terrified men into position. Most were shaking. But now that the armies of their enemies had arrived, nobody protested. They'd seen the hordes of death and knew it was time to fight or die.

Shieldsmen saluted as Torsten passed through the castle gates. Carpenters still hammered at spikes along the wall's base. Men atop the ramparts yanked on pulleys to heave barrels of arrows and rocks for catapults. And out on the streets, armored men marched in every direction. Their clothing and armor didn't match like Liam had always insisted upon. These men wore anything that could be scrounged up. For every Glass soldier in shiny iron, there were others in furs pilfered from what Redstar's Drav Cra had left behind, shoddily crafted leather hauberks—anything.

To Torsten's left, all the way down in Old Yarrington, mansions were shuttered and filled with women and children. They huddled on the streets, in the tents around the Cathedral, everywhere Torsten could see. They, too, were armed, mothers with pitchforks and children with hammers and the like. Priests walked among them, praying in clusters as they all made their way to the Eastern Gate to stand with Torsten against demons and worse.

Whatever it took, it would be done.

Torsten marched down the Royal Avenue toward the markets, desperate to remember things as they were and not how they would become. But it was already too late. Homes became abandoned outside Old Yarrington, sanctuaries for archers now. All the taverns and shops he'd passed countless times before—silent. As were so many things, it was eerie. Never in his life had this strip of the city been so quiet.

Then, he reached the market square—the heart of their defense against Nesilia's monsters. The catapults were all loaded, manned throughout the square. Thousands of archers filled every foot of space. Legions of soldiers waited behind the gates, no real idea of what was to come. The front line carried the heater shields of Torsten's Order, though, they weren't all Shieldsmen. The giant, Uhlvark, helped pin heavy wooden beams behind the gates as extra reinforcement.

Making his way through the sea of iron and Glassmen, Torsten received shaky salutes from every direction. He could smell the terror in their blood. He could hear the muffled cries as they bid farewell to loved ones. And most of all, they could feel the cold.

Even though it was summer, as Nesilia approached, her dark cloud from Panping spread. Snow flurries floated through the air on the brisk breeze kissing Torsten's cheeks. But that was Nesilia. No need for stealth any longer. No hiding behind the faces of friends as Redstar had done. She'd announced her arrival with the very flourish they'd hoped would be her undoing.

Torsten climbed the Eastern watchtower, up to the ramparts, and stepped out to the landing above the city's main gates. His hands clasped the stone ledge, and he gazed out, his blessed vision allowing him to see despite the darkness Nesilia had drowned the city in.

Nesilia's army didn't just stretch across the horizon, it was the horizon. From the southern woods to the lower slope of Mount Lister—a mass of blackness. Creatures and possessed men with no need for torches. Even from so far away, he could hear the otherworldly growls and cackling.

Further north came a break in the army, then the Drav Cra. They seemed civilized compared to their allies, but equally terrifying. Torches lit the massive furry legs and long curved tusks of chekt. Dire wolves snarled, dancing at their feet. Berserker warriors, shaking with anticipation, finally had a chance to avenge their late Arch Warlock.

Never, in all Torsten's life, had Yarrington seemed so small. And while he wasn't high enough to see all the way west to the harbor, Shesaitju horns rang out, signaling the approach of the enemy fleet.

"By Iam," Torsten whispered to himself, circling his eyes.

He looked left, then right, at all the archers witnessing the same. Their fear was palpable. Even with so many present, the silence was thick and tangible. Torsten could hear the staggered breathing all around the city. Even those who proudly wore Glassmen armor—trained soldiers. Nobody prayed or cried. Instead, they were stunned into silence.

Nesilia's army marched at a slow pace, almost purposefully, as if she wanted to amplify the sense of terror. Knowing her, that was indeed the plan. With every minute, more of them flooded through the Haskwood Thicket and into the open farmland around Yarrington, the sea of blackness ever-expanding.

"She sure knows how to make an entrance," Dellbar said, using his cane to move up beside Torsten.

"If only you could see it," Torsten replied.

"Don't need to."

Turning to him, Torsten noticed priests taking up intermittent posts throughout his own army. "Are they ready?"

"No," Dellbar said. "But is anyone truly ever ready to die?"

Torsten exhaled slowly, the supernatural coldness stinging against his teeth.

"Are you?" Dellbar asked.

"Close enough." Torsten's fingers squeezed the stone, then he leaned out over the wall and yelled, "Nesilia! Show yourself!"

A wave of hissing and sinister laughter responded. They began to chant something in a language Torsten didn't know. Beside him, and all over the city, soldiers shuddered at the sound. He could feel their fear. Hairs all over his body stood on end, but he bit back his terror and stood taller.

"Are you too cowardly to face me yourself?" he called out.

The demonic refrain grew louder. He could hear it above him, behind him—all around. The soldiers whispered in dread and searched all around, hopeful, he thought, that someone might tell them to drop their weapons and surrender. Torsten didn't take the bait. His gaze remained fixed until the dark army split at the middle.

Nesilia strolled through the center, out into the open. In the darkness, he wasn't sure if anybody else but he could see, but there she was. The mystic Sora and Whitney claimed to be Bliss floated at her side, the hem of her red robe whipping like tendrils of flame.

The two stared directly at Torsten, only, they weren't alone. To Nesilia's left marched a man all-too-familiar. Rand Langley, decked out in full Shieldsman armor, as if he was all that remained of the Order Torsten had abandoned. Unlike the others, he looked to the ground, so Torsten couldn't see his face, but he knew it was him.

This man whom Torsten had trained, fought beside, trusted… somehow he had survived being on the brink of death in Latiapur.

"Just because he is lost, doesn't mean you must join him," Dellbar said.

"I should've made sure he was dead." Torsten's lip twitched as he withheld his rage.

"Killing our King wasn't enough for you, Rand?" Torsten shouted down.

Nesilia, Bliss, and Rand stopped just out of range of arrows. Rand said nothing, simply continued staring at the earth.

"Rand Langley has seen the truth of this world," Nesilia replied, her voice echoing from all directions, just as the demons' had. It was as booming as it was sultry, each syllable causing some of Torsten's soldiers to wince. "He seeks to purge it of liars and thieves."

"He can't speak for himself?" Torsten answered. "Or have you possessed him, too."

"Rand is here of his own free will."

"Just like the cursed army at your back?"

Nesilia laughed. "They were, all of them, cast out and forgotten by your God. Just as you abandoned poor Rand."

"No, he chose his fate," Torsten said. Rand's gaze momentarily flitted up before returning to the dirt. "I offered him everything. Every chance."

Nesilia reached out slowly and brushed long fingernails across Rand's cheek. "And he chose family," she said. "Something you would never understand. You, who worshipped killers and liars simply because of the Glass they wore on their heads. Weak men. Perverted men."

"Great men!" Torsten countered. "And they will be here with us when we destroy you."

"Destroy me?" Her laugh bellowed like thunder, shaking the ground. Even Bliss joined her.

"Let me torch him, sister?" the possessed mystic said.

"Not yet."

The mystic swooped forward. "Please? I remember the feel of his sword in the Webbed Woods. Oh, how I would like to make him feel the same pain."

"I said, not yet." Nesilia took another step forward, earning a flinch from everyone atop the ramparts, even as far away as she was. She grasped the spirit-like mystic by the back of her robes, causing them to become physical, and ripped her back.

"You dare—"

Nesilia turned, and whatever look she gave her sister, the mystic seemed to fade momentarily.

"Will Iam come to save you again?" Nesilia asked, flicking her gaze back up, toward Dellbar. Then, she closed her pure black eyes and inhaled deeply. "No, I can barely feel Him. He's left you all to yourselves, just as He left me. Your loving God, as there for you in the end as your drunken parents were."

"Enough games, Nesilia!" Torsten roared.

"One more game." She looked back and snapped her finger. Some movement followed in the mass of shadows, and then, two possessed men wearing cultist robes and white masks dragged someone forward. "Let us see how deep your love for your soldiers runs."

Torsten wished he could squint so he could see further. Still, his heart thumped against his rib cage.

"Believe nothing she says," Dellbar whispered.

"Would you all hurry up," Nesilia hissed. She flashed away, using her upyr speed to grab the figure. In mere seconds, she returned to her position and shoved a man to his knees.

"Lucas," Torsten mouthed the name. The young Shieldsman looked up, his face caked with dirt and blood. He wore torn rags, loose on his now emaciated figure.

"Another Shieldsman you left behind," Nesilia said. "Tell me, is this the Word of Iam? Abandon those you love."

"Let him go!" Torsten yelled.

Nesilia grinned. "Happily. All you need do is walk down here and give yourself over, and young Lucas can take your place."

"Torsten," Lucas rasped. He could barely lift his head, but he pushed himself to do it. Even just for a second. "Don't listen to her."

"Come now, Torsten," Nesilia said. "He was your friend. He saved your life."

Torsten's hands quaked. His throat grew dry.

"Think of his poor parents, hidden behind the worthless walls of your city," Nesilia went on. "Don't they deserve one last moment with their beloved child? Like Rand did, with the woman he loved before your Queen made him hang her!"

Nesilia snapped, and a gust of cold air chilled Torsten's heart even more than it already was. Nesilia looked to Rand, and he drew his longsword.

"It's in your hands," Nesilia said. "You chose, Torsten Unger. Your life, or his?" She nodded Rand along.

"Do it," Bliss demanded, swooping in front of him.

Rand stepped forward and extended the sword over the back of Lucas' neck. Still, he looked toward the ground, his grip shaky.

"Rand, stop this!" Torsten yelled. "She's not your sister anymore. You have to see that. You have to fight this."

"You are blind as ever, Torsten," Nesilia said. "I protect his sister as nobody else would. I'm giving her everything. Rand could walk away at any time, yet here he stands because he sees you all for what you truly are. Show him he's wrong!"

Torsten pushed away from the wall, but just as he went to turn, Lucas struggled to raise his head again and cried, "Don't." He shook his head. "Don't."

Nesilia strode in front of him and cradled his head as she looked back toward Torsten. She dug a fingernail into the soft spot beneath his eye, and Lucas fought back a whimper. "Listen to how brave he is. Is he not worthy of life? Show your people that you are different, Torsten. Do it."

"Rand, listen to me," Torsten said, his voice cracking. "Whatever you've done, don't do this. Don't let her make you exactly what Oleander did."

"The blood pact must be fulfilled," Nesilia cackled. "Rand knows that. It's you, Torsten, only you, who can take young Lucas' place. You can save him, as you failed to save Pi. As you failed to save your Queen and your King. As you failed to stop my return. Every step of your pathetic life has been a failure. But here I am, offering you a chance at redemption. Be the propitiation for your peoples' many sins."

With all that he was, Torsten wanted to walk down and do as she asked, to give Lucas that chance at survival he so deserved. And yet, he remained still, frozen atop the walls.

"Our people need *you*, not me," Lucas rasped. "Not me."

Torsten could hardly control his breathing. He knew Nesilia's game. It was the same one they were trying to pull on her, to bait her by taking one she cared about. All she wanted was for Torsten to walk out there and die in front of all his people, to fill their hearts with dread, because that was what she fed on.

"She'll kill you both," Dellbar said. "You know that."

"Do I?" Torsten asked.

"You rejected her. And here, in the shadow of Mount Lister, where she was buried, all who betrayed or rejected her are her enemies."

"Make your choice, Torsten Unger," Nesilia said. "Make your choice. As Iam did."

"Rand," Torsten pled. "You took the same oaths he did. You stood, upon that mountain, and swore to shield this city. You swore it!"

Rand remained silent and fixed.

"I knew you were a coward," Nesilia said. "So eager to cast everything away for a few more measly seconds of breath. Let all of you see the heart of your leader, so flawlessly sculpted in the reflection of Iam. Very well. Rand, my dear. Show our friend that there is a price for cowardice."

Rand's grip tightened on his sword as he raised it high above his head. Still, he looked at nothing but the ground. His hands betrayed the slightest tremble.

"Thank you, Sir Unger…" Lucas said weakly. "For the honor of serving."

"Do it," Nesilia said.

Rand's sword twitched, but it didn't fall.

"Be with me, Lucas," Torsten said. "You're in Dockside, at your parents' shop. Your mom just baked your favorite pie. Your father sold all his stock to a noble family for Dawning morning."

"Would you do it already, boy!" Bliss barked.

Still, Rand hesitated.

"They see you coming home, and they smile," Torsten went on. "They're proud of the man their son has grown to be."

Lucas closed his eyes and smiled.

At the same time, Nesilia shouted, "The Shield is dead!" and whipped around, slicing her hand across the air. Torsten momentarily lost his view behind her, and then he saw Rand. His blade had fallen, Lucas' head with it. And the traitor stood, looking shocked, staring at his hands, as if he couldn't believe the blood that was on them.

Torsten turned away, offering a feeble prayer under his breath. Dellbar did the same. But Nesilia's malice had the intended effect on the rest of Torsten's army atop the walls. They unleashed no gasps nor cries. They were just drowned in a deepened layer of dread and silence.

Nesilia calmly strode over Lucas' body, away from the wall. She looked up at Bliss.

"Okay, sister," she said. "Now, you may have your fun." Then, her gaze moved across the rabid ranks of her horde. "All of you, the time has come. Tear Iam's Kingdom down to dust and ash, and from the rubble, a new age shall rise!"

With that, the silence ended.

Drav Cra horns sounded from the north. Shesaitju drums beat in the west. And straight ahead of Torsten, Nesilia's monsters unleashed a cacophony of terrible cries as they began to charge, loud as an avalanche.

Nesilia stopped beside Rand and whispered something in his ear as he remained, staring at his own weapon. Only then did he finally lift his head and regard Torsten.

Torsten didn't give him the satisfaction of returning the gaze. Turning to Dellbar, seething, he said, "That man is truly lost."

"So were you when we met," Dellbar replied.

"And now, I am found." Torsten drew *Salvation*, turned to face over the wall and down to the city square, and lifted his blade. "Soldiers of Yarrington, stand with me!" he shouted. "Let us send Nesilia back where she belongs!"

A trickle of cheers sounded throughout the city. Not the eruption Torsten hoped for. Nesilia had driven her talons of fear in deep. At least, until Dellbar leaned over, clasped his hands over Torsten's, and whispered something.

Pure, white light shot through Torsten's sword. It was warm, but Dellbar held him steady as the light rose and bloomed like a beacon on the darkest nights, leading sailors home.

"Iam stands with us," a soldier blurted.

"His light is with Torsten!"

"He will shield us."

More murmuring and cheers echoed from throughout the defenses. And somehow, even though the light allowed a clearer view of the hellish monsters bearing down on the city, seeing them for what they were made it less terrifying.

The surge of energy was palpable. Whether it was fight or flight taking hold, or true faith, it didn't matter.

"The Buried Goddess tries to prey on your fear," Torsten shouted, "but only because it is she who is afraid! Because she knows, in her black heart, that we are the light of this world! Iam is in each of you, my friends. His strength, it is yours now!"

Now the explosion of cheers came. Fists pounded on armor. Spears and shields banged against the stone.

"Archers, nock!" Torsten commanded.

Other former Shieldsmen at intervals throughout the army relayed his orders. All down the fortifications and in the square, archers drew arrows from full quivers. Some were barely trained, taking many attempts to set their bowstrings. Many had shaky hands, a few accidentally misfired into nothing. Others were proper soldiers of the Glass, still as statues.

All aimed together upon the same wave of evil.

The very earth quaked as Nesilia's army neared.

Light from Torsten's blade waned, but now, the enemy was close enough. There were no siege engines of any sort to help break through or mount the walls, only a mass of hate. Possessed people sprinted at full speed—cultists, Glassmen, Panpingese—anyone caught in Yaolin when Nesilia made her move. Black-eyed dire wolves nipped at them. Goblins shrieked, hurling rocks from slings at the wall. They fell harmlessly, but the patter sounded like violent hail, and Torsten could only imagine what those down in the square thought as they heard it.

"On my mark!" Torsten called out. He leveled his blade toward the two nearest ex-Shieldsmen commanders on his left and right. They nodded. "Loose!" he screamed as loud as he could manage, letting his blade fall. "Loose!"

The thrum of his army's arrows being fired was like wind through the Jarein Gorge. They zipped down from the walls. Arced up from behind. Catapults *whooshed* as their ropes were released, launching massive chunks of stone.

Just then, Bliss appeared. She hovered high over the horde, beyond the reach of the arrows, her hands stretched toward the sky. Dark clouds swirled above her, crackling with arms of lightning that flashed down toward her until she, herself, was wreathed within the storm.

The horde ran straight toward the blanket of arrows without fear, but Torsten kept his sights on the mystic-goddess. A quick break in the storm revealed a sneer. Then, the wind settled, followed by a prevailing silence.

"Dellbar, watch out!" Torsten tackled the High Priest as a bolt of lightning exploded from her fingertips. A swathe of arrows was reduced to ash by the violent lighting before they could reach the horde, others were blown off course, sent straight back into the stone. The bolt exploded into one of the rocks launched by a catapult, right where Torsten and Dellbar had been, sending bits flying every direction like tiny knives.

Torsten's ears rang as he rolled himself off the High Priest.

"Sir Unger, I've got you!" a soldier said, hoisting him up by the shoulder. Seconds later, something smashed across the man's chest, and he flipped back and over the wall.

He looked up at a wave of grimaurs, blotting out the moons as even the arrows couldn't do. Their screeches deafened him to the thrum of more arrows and catapults being fired, though now, their organization broke as men fired toward the sky in a panic. Only, the grimaurs didn't dive on this first pass. Instead, they dropped more objects like that which had hit the soldier. Some hit with a clank atop shields in the square, but others squished like popping egg sacs when they struck stone. They were heads. Gruesome, decapitated, human heads from across Pantego, some so rotten they nearly evaporated on impact. The stink was almost worse than the sight.

Torsten swallowed back the contents of his stomach and rushed to his post, crossing the corpses left courtesy of Bliss' lightning strike.

"Get somewhere safe, now!" Torsten told Dellbar. Before the High Priest could protest, a host of former Shieldsmen grabbed him and marched away. Then, Torsten yelled to the archers, "Ignore the grimaurs. Focus on the ground. The ground!"

He reached the parapet and saw Nesilia's swarm bounding toward the spiked trenches dug around the city. Hellhounds tripped and tumbled in, howling. Nimble goblins cleared it with ease and started to climb the stone with their sharp claws. And the possessed people… they didn't even care. They fell and were skewered by spikes, but made no sounds of pain. With the trenches slowing them, arrows rained upon them. Still, even as they were pierced like pincushions, they felt nothing.

Some lost the blackness in their eyes, and the specters of their demonic possessors soared up over walls to possess their next targets. This was Nesilia's plan. They aimed for the weakest men first, those untrained who'd never fought before. Torsten watched, awestruck, as one plunged into the heart of a conscripted archer.

The man's eyes went black, and he wheeled around, firing an arrow over Torsten's shoulder. He charged and slammed his fist into the man's jaw. The body crumpled to the ground, alive but unconscious. The cackling demon whisked back into existence again, and Torsten brandished his blade.

"This is our world!" Torsten roared. He swung at it, and the blade passed directly through its spirit form, earning a fiendish laugh.

"You cannot resist us," the demon whispered. Its voice engulfed him like a cloak. In him. Around him. Its dark specter rose, and it felt almost like his blood had stopped flowing.

Torsten noticed a young priest running up behind it. He was probably barely old enough to have traded his sight for Iam's.

To his knees, he fell, lips trembling as much as the hands he used to grip the Eye of Iam pendant dangling from his neck. He prayed, maybe not to be brave, but that no longer mattered. He prayed because he had to, and within his hands, a light bloomed.

Torsten sensed the demon's fear first, as if it were his own, and then, its essence drained away into the priest's pendant. The man remained on one knee, no longer praying, but holding the light as more demons were pulled into its aura. Hundreds of the foul things soared through the air, their cries like Elsewhere itself. The color fled the priest's dark skin. He scrunched his face and held on, more and more demons from the fallen possessed sucked in until the light burst. All that remained in its wake were ashes blowing through an empty robe.

Spinning, Torsten saw more priests giving themselves, as if for the first time, realizing their truest callings. They dotted the fortifications like bright white lanterns—priests snaring demons in their holy light before they could jump to possess soldiers atop the wall.

Not every evil being was caught, though. Fighting broke out as men everywhere were overtaken. Still, Dellbar's gambit proved to be working. At least, it would, if they didn't run out of priests before Nesilia ran out of possessed. And she had many, many thousands more. The horde, still charging down below, seemed endless.

"Hold the walls!" Torsten yelled. "In Iam's name, hold the walls as long as you can!"

The possessed were relentless. Their bodies filled the spiked trenches, forming bridges of skin and flesh. Hundreds crossed and smashed against the walls, where others climbed on top of them, creating piles of death to serve like ladders.

At the deeper pit of spikes before the city gates, Bliss summoned dark magic and shifted the earth to fold over. As she did, the large spikes were launched at the outer portcullis with the force of fully manned battering rams.

A grimaur zipped down, and Torsten hopped back just before clipping its wing. Another sank its talons into a nearby archer and launched him off the wall into the fangs of hungry dire wolf hellhounds. His screaming ended when they ripped him in half.

Torsten nodded toward a commander in the eastern watchtower. Bells tolled. Buckets of boiling oil were dumped from it, and the other lookouts, torches along with them. Fire flared like veins of iron down the walls, singeing goblins climbing the stone and laying waste to piles of dead being used as ladders.

"S-s-spiders!" a voice squeaked from down in the markets.

Torsten could hardly keep up. It was true. Down in the square, massive, many-legged servants of Bliss burrowed from the ground. It was the Webbed Woods all over again. The biggest came first, then smaller ones flooded through as if the streets themselves had come alive.

One sprang onto the arm of a catapult, and as it attempted to launch, the weight caused the rock to fall too early and smash into the interior of the city gates, crushing a portion of the reinforcement.

Archers on the wall lost discipline and turned to fire down at the spiders.

"Over the wall!" Torsten shouted. Before he could again, a blur of movement in his peripherals spun him, and he cut a goblin down.

Their incoherent language assailed his ears as the tiny lizard-men scrambled over the ramparts. Torsten deflected a small spear, then he kicked one of the beasts into a group. Nearby archers were forced to draw their short swords and join the melee.

Without hesitating, Torsten shouldered through them and ran for the enemy horde. The now-empty pots of boiling oil hung on ropes, and Torsten dived, catching one and swinging.

His bulky frame slammed into the piling of earth and corpses rising against that portion of the wall, breaking it apart. He held on with one hand even as the stress threatened to rend his arm from his shoulder.

A grimaur plunged and sliced the rope as Torsten attempted to climb back up, sending him onto the lower death-pile. Blades in the hands of black-eyed men and women slashed at him. He parried and stabbed. A hellhound snapped at his wrist, but his armor endured, and he flung it against a wall.

The grimaur rushed down at him, talons first. Torsten kicked a possessed man down the pile with his heel. As the grimaur closed in, Torsten sprang away, timing it to grasp the thing's legs in a bundle and be hoisted into the air. Unable to support his weight, the beast flapped a short bit before sputtering. Torsten let go and got his off-hand over the ledge of the ramparts.

Goblins and hellhounds attacked his dangling feet, and Torsten swiped *Salvation* in wide arcs to keep them away. His brothers-in-arms heaved him up, and as Torsten rose, he spotted Bliss, floating at the gates, twisting the earth before it into a lance of rock and spikes that pummeled the gates and wall.

The soldiers got Torsten over the ledge while a goblin grasped his ankle and stabbed at his armor with its bone knife. He rolled onto the parapet, palmed the reptile's head, and crushed its skull in his mighty grip.

Then he stood, shouting, "Shoot at the mystic! Everyone, take her down!"

Orders were impossible to issue in the mounting chaos. Nesilia's forces invaded at multiple levels. Still, enough heard and turned their bows upon Bliss.

It seemed that her ability to have the projectiles phase through her took some focus, and as she avoided the volley, her earthen battering ram began to fall apart.

She screamed, releasing a shockwave of wind that sent all the soldiers atop the wall flying back. Torsten braced himself against the torrent, dirt whipping against his cheeks.

A loose bow caught against his ankle, giving him an idea. He remembered the war in the east—that mystics could only draw on Elsewhere so much before exhaustion took its toll. And like Nesilia, Bliss was limited by her possessed body.

Torsten sheathed his sword, snatched a clump of arrows out of a fallen soldier's quiver, and fitted one against the string. Archery had never been his strong suit, but every Shieldsman had trained in it. And even if it was a lesser skill for him, that still made him superior to half the archers they had.

He stood and fired.

His arrow caught Bliss on the shoulder and actually sank in. There was no blood, but she screeched as if in physical pain. A second later, she reverted to her ethereal state, and the projectile fell through.

"You fool!" she boomed. "You can't defeat me!" With another scream, she flung a ball of flame.

Torsten, predicting the reaction, had already taken off down the wall. He ducked and weaved through his soldiers as they battled to hold their positions. In each arched opening, he stopped long enough to fire an arrow at Bliss.

She continued to howl and hurl fire, angry at the man who'd helped destroy her prior form. Vengeful, just like her sister Nesilia. And in doing so, Bliss was draining her magical reservoir, pushing her current body because she didn't know its limits.

Torsten struck her once again in the gut, then slid to duck into a watchtower. He checked his quiver to find it empty. He peeped over the ledge, and Bliss was nowhere to be seen. Her ram summoned from the earth had crumbled entirely away.

"That will buy us some time," Torsten muttered.

He forced himself to his feet and reached for *Salvation* so he could rejoin the melee. His men were doing an admirable job holding back the goblins, and the points where possessed dead were piled high enough for more of Nesilia's army to scale.

As Torsten turned toward his central post, a tattered, red robe wavered in front of him. Bliss' hard, emotionless face smiled a heartless smile. He wasn't sure he believed she was truly Bliss until then. Her eyes may have now been black instead of that vibrant purple they'd been as a giant spider, but they were indeed hers.

"You're all alone this time," she said. "Nobody can save you."

Her hands extended, and lightning coruscated out. Torsten lowered *Salvation* in time to absorb the bolt, but the shockwave sent both him and it flying back over the wall.

Luckily, he landed on the thorax of a giant spider, bounding off and rolling to a stop near a pile of rubble. He could hardly see straight.

Couldn't settle his jaw enough to speak. His hands twitched from the lightning, dancing in his veins.

Feet stomped all around him as soldiers battled. The tiniest spiders swarmed his body, then his face—thousands of legs crawling all over him. They bit at his blindfold, his armor. He couldn't even breathe.

"Tooorstennnn," a voice echoed. At first, he wondered if it was Iam, finally calling him home. Then, the creatures coating him fell away, and a great hand wrapped his waist.

Uhlvark's pockmarked face appeared over him, one eye closed as if studying Torsten. He flicked away another spider as if it weren't the size of a wagon wheel. Then, he lifted Torsten onto his feet.

"Do your feeeeeet work, friend Torsten?" he asked.

"They do indeed, Uhlvark," Dellbar said.

The High Priest strolled closer, using his cane to navigate the growing field of flesh. With his other hand, he dragged *Salvation* across the stone, too heavy for him to lift.

"I believe you dropped this?" he said. "The wall isn't lost yet. My priests surprise even me with their bravery.

Torsten shook out his head and straightened his blindfold so he could see. His muscles still spasmed, but standing felt increasingly normal with each passing second.

"Dellbar, retreat to the castle," Torsten ordered as he reclaimed *Salvation* and used it to find balance until he gathered his bearings.

Dellbar considered it, aiming his empty eye sockets toward the sky. "Yes, I believe you're right. I'm needed there."

"Uhlvark, take him to the castle!" Torsten ordered.

"But, I here to fiiight." Uhlvark's giant head looked between them, spit flying and lips flapping.

"Dellbar needs your protection!" Torsten said. He steadied a hand atop the giant's massive arm. "And I need him, alive."

Uhlvark snatched the High Priest up with two hands, gently as he was capable of. "Must saaaave friend!" He repeated over and over as he lumbered back up the Royal Avenue toward the castle.

Torsten spun to face the city gates and the madness still there. His men were holding. Against the tide of darkness, they stood their ground. Grimaurs plummeted from the sky, punctured by arrows. Spiders lost limbs and clicked their chelicerae in fear. Bliss had taken her best shot, and Torsten had endured. Though she was missing again.

"Hold steady, men!" Torsten shouted as he strode forward, emboldened by his luck. "Reform ranks. Second battalion, to the walls." He pointed to a forward commander. "Brace the gate. Hold them off!"

Even as terrified as they were, soldiers snapped to action, and morale soared as they'd survived Nesilia's first wave. Fresh reinforcements climbed the walls and joined the archers to keep the tide of battle on their side. More wooden beams were jammed into the stone behind the inner gate, re-bracing it.

Nearby, an ancient-looking priest without a hint of hair drew on his light. With as long as he'd served Iam, it grew bright enough to shine like a small sun. Demon spirits were drawn to it by the dozens.

"The darkness cannot drown the light!" Torsten yelled. "We will hold, we will—"

The words trailed off when Bliss appeared above the wall. Her form was so faint she was barely visible, but her compassionless grin didn't wane. In that briefest moment, Torsten remembered what Dellbar had said, that the darkness and light couldn't exist without the other.

At the same time, the ground below that brave, old priest crumbled, and a giant spider burst through, crushing his frail chest between its jaws. Freed demon spirits burst forth, zipping into the soldiers around them. Some fell to their knees, grasping their heads as they fought the possession. Conscripts gave in quickly.

"Kill them!" Torsten screamed. "Take them out!"

So far across the square, his commands fell on deaf ears. He took off, shoving through a crowd of his own men, slashing down every beast in his way. The newly possessed soldiers ambushed those around them, stabbing and biting at throats. One, however, tossed his weapon aside and ran toward the great crank which opened the gate.

"Stop him!" Torsten yelled as he pushed something aside. A grimaur zoomed at him, and he ducked right before the toxic talons slashed his throat. "Stop!"

He sprinted again, but the possessed man already had his hands around the lever. The gears for both inner gate and portcullis shrieked.

Ripping a short sword out of the hands of one of his own men, Torsten flung it. His aim was true, the blade soaring through the ranks of his soldiers before stabbing through the possessed man's arm. As the man fought to remove the sword, Torsten drove his shoulder into him, and they both crashed into the wall behind him. But as the body slumped, the man jammed his other arm into the crank, leaving the gate slightly ajar.

That's all it took.

"Close the gate!" Torsten yelled, stuck in the clinch with the possessed soldier. "Close the gate!"

The front line of soldiers ran to close it, others to try and free Torsten and the jammed body.

Simultaneously, spiders, possessed men, and beasts shoved into the gaps in the gate, mobbing it in seconds. Priests stationed all around the square banished the demons as they gave up their possessed bodies, but it was too late. The horde pushed and shoved until the portcullis was clogged.

The iron gates soon followed. A wave of flesh and madness smashed against it, and the soldiers trying to push it closed not only struggled but failed. A final gust of magical wind blew it wide, and Bliss appeared in the open entry, arms spread as her seemingly permanent smile.

"Shields, steady!" Torsten ordered, squeezing his way to the front to lead the defense. "Do not lose heart. We will hold this gate!"

He stopped before the first row of shield-bearers, his grip on *Salvation* tightening.

"Why do they wait?" stammered one of the terrified soldiers around him.

Torsten wondered the same. Bliss's ethereal body floated, and behind her stood a host of possessed cultists, black eyes like onyx behind their expressionless masks. Hellhounds snapped, foaming at the mouths. Goblins hissed.

"Why even resist?" Bliss asked. "We will take this city." Spiders crowded around her, filling the ceiling of the tunnel through the thick fortifications. Their skittering legs matched the pace of Torsten's heartbeat.

"Then we will take the next," she went on. "And every statue, every church, every letter written about Iam shall be wiped from existence. All these millennia later, the God Feud will finally end!"

"Yes, sister, it will," spoke a familiar voice. The swarm parted, and Nesilia stopped beside Bliss. Rand followed close behind her.

Torsten's heart flipped at the sight of the traitor. His jaw clenched. But Rand didn't return the look. His thousand-meter gaze aimed straight ahead. He was lost in his mind somewhere, like when Torsten found him so long ago, drunken and ready to end his own life.

"Ah, so now you show up to gloat?" Bliss spat.

Nesilia flashed out of view, appearing behind Bliss a second later and plunging a knife into her back. The mystic's body dropped to the ground and vacillated between spiritual and physical form. The spiders screeched in reaction, collapsing from the ceiling and writhing on the ground. Their legs curled into tight balls, twitching.

Lightning crackled around her, but Nesilia seemed to absorb it, her bright eyes flickering an electric blue as she jammed the dagger in deeper.

"Thank you for breaking this city for me," Nesilia said.

"Sister… what…" Bliss moaned, her spirit form slowly separating from the Aihara Na's body. Nesilia clutched her throat as if to bind them together just a bit longer.

"Did you really think I'd let you see your vengeance?" Nesilia hissed. She pointed toward Mount Lister. "This is where you buried me. Right there!"

She twisted the knife, even as magical elements slashed out from Bliss' fingers. Nesilia's upyr body resisted them, even seeming to be strengthened by them.

"Now, I will bury you there. The One Who Remained." She scoffed. "*You* will watch for all eternity as I claim my world. No longer am I the Buried Goddess. I will gladly relinquish that title to you, sister of mine." Nesilia glanced up, straight at Torsten, and bared Sigrid's upyr fangs. "Enjoying yourself, Torsten? I'll be right back."

"Sister, no," Bliss groaned. "You can't—"

Nesilia winked, then vanished in a haze of dust, dragging Bliss with her. The spiders continued their shrill cries, legs spasming in agony. The rest of the horde, however, remained, with Rand left in their lead.

"You see what she is now, Rand!" Torsten shouted. "She's no liberator. She is rage, and vengeance, and hate."

Rand looked up but said nothing. The horde stormed around him.

Torsten and his legion braced themselves for the crash of iron, tooth, and talon. They were dug in now, fighting to hold out as long as they could while the endless masses flooded the city.

The ground trembled, and Bliss' distant cry echoing from the north squelched even the clatter of war.

Torsten had to buy Sora as much time as possible to find a way to take down Freydis. To find a way to draw in the Goddess who he now knew held grudges for thousands of years.

XLI

THE THIEF

Whitney felt helpless in the Throne Room, listening to the distant rumblings of war. He'd been sequestered there with Tum Tum, told to protect the Brike Stone, and keep Lucindur safe until the time was right. To him, it felt like they were being punished, made to sit in time-out while all the real warriors fought the battle. He knew it wasn't true, but at the same time, he resented it.

The Throne Room was empty save for them. The castle, although filled with Shieldsmen and Serpent Guards, watching every entrance and dark hallway, felt equally abandoned. Just empty rooms and haunting memories. He could recall the first time he'd been there, under much more joyful circumstances.

He, Sora, and Torsten had just returned from the Webbed Woods where they'd killed a goddess, stopped Redstar, and saved the world. That was the day he became Whitney Blisslayer, and in light of current events, it all felt like a sham.

No one had killed Bliss. No one had stopped Redstar, and they sure as Exile hadn't saved the world. If anything, they'd set off a chain reaction, which all led to this moment. Bliss was right outside, slaughtering people—in a new body, sure, but it was her.

Whitney fought back the feeling of despair, threatening to bury him. He had to do something.

"You know what we are, right?" he asked. "We are the children during family workday who are told by their father that he's got 'a very important task' for us to do. They just don't want us to get in the way."

"Speak for yerself," Tum Tum said, spinning his warhammer. "They be savin the best for last."

"Whatever."

It really did feel like a complete farce. Of the three of them who'd been in the Woods that day, Torsten went blind, but still, he'd killed Redstar on the Dawning, and he walked away with enchanted-yigging-sight. Sora had been possessed by the Buried Goddess, but she would still have the chance to kill her, and she'd come away from it with godlike powers.

What did Whitney get?

Not only had he not killed Bliss, but that meant he didn't truly earn his ennobled name. And to top it all off, he got to spend six years wallowing in Elsewhere.

Whitney grumbled as he climbed the dais. There was a time his head would have rolled before his boot even hit the step. But now, there wasn't a soul in the place to care. Like the throne meant nothing at all.

No King. No Kingdom. Just live or die.

He plopped down on the Glass Throne, looking around skeptically like the Shieldsmen posted beyond the doors might come pouring in at any moment. No one did. Not even Lucindur or Tum Tum said a word about it.

"Even this doesn't feel remotely like I'd expected it to," he said, knocking on the armrest with his knuckles. "Hard as a stone and slippery." He groaned and theatrically slid down the seat until he was slumped on the floor.

"This was partially your plan, you know?" Lucindur said, calm as ever, from her perch on one of the Royal Council chairs, hands folded in her lap, salfio on the seat next to her.

Whitney let out a sigh. On his back, staring at the beautifully painted, vaulted ceiling telling grand tales of old, he let his fingers play over the Brike Stone in his pocket. As much as he hated to admit it, Lucy was right. This was how it had to be. But, while they waited there, listening to the echoes of walls crumbling, men dying, and gods laughing, Sora was out there in the thick of it, hunting an

Arch Warlock. He had no way of knowing if she were safe or even alive.

"You weren't there, in the Webbed Woods," Whitney said. "We were so stupid to think that would be the end of anything. It was the beginning. We awoke the gods."

"Are ye admitting to doin somethin stupid?" Tum Tum asked, chuckling. "I never thought I'd see the day."

"Sounds more like he's taking credit for all of this to me," Lucindur said.

"Sora was brilliant," Whitney said, ignoring them both. "You should've seen her. She turned that dumb Redstar into a blubbering fool. Torsten sliced Bliss from neck to navel. It was disgusting, all those little spiders pouring out. And me… I got wrapped up in her web like an idiot."

"I thought ye killed the bitch?" Tum Tum said, snickering.

"Forgive me for interrupting your reminiscence, Whitney, but what's this all about?" Lucindur asked.

"You should've seen us coming home," Whitney said, still ignoring her. "Our smiles were falling off our faces. 'We killed Queen Bliss. We stopped Redstar.'"

"To be fair, from what I hear, ye would've done just that if Torsten would've killed the bastard," Tum Tum said. "Damn knights and their honor."

"That's the point though. It was three of us versus two of them. Now, it's what—us versus a bunch of goddesses and their armies? You think we have a chance?" Whitney asked as yet another growl echoed from the battlefield, followed by the floor quaking. Little rocks and dust fell from the ceiling. "I've spent the last six years… well—whatever—bragging about killing a goddess who is right out there, right now, destroying a city that has never even been attacked."

Lucindur rose and approached Whitney. He didn't see her, but he heard her footfalls.

"Get up," she said, kicking him.

"Hey!" Whitney complained and rolled a bit.

She kicked him again and again. "Get up!"

Whitney scrambled down the dais, finding his footing. "Fine, fine! I'm up. I'm up."

Lucindur followed him down the stairs. She moved a hand toward his shoulder, and he flinched.

"My daughter is three thousand kilometers away, and I don't know if I'll ever see her again," she said. "You may not have killed Bliss or stopped anything, but you didn't have an angry, protective mother on your side last time."

"But—"

"No buts. We will win this thing."

"How do you know?" Whitney asked.

"Because I *will* see Talwyn again," she said. Then, she whispered, "I have to."

"And ye didn't have a dwarf with nothin left to lose, neither." Tum Tum grinned a big toothy grin as he stepped up beside them.

Another *boom* filtered in through the walls. Whitney winced.

"I need to go out there," he said. "Sora might be in trouble."

"And she might not be," Lucindur added. "She is more powerful than any of us. If she is in trouble, we all are. You cannot save her this time, Whitney Fierstown."

"Maybe not. But I can try."

Lucindur grabbed his arm. "You cannot stop this on your own."

"We'll have our chance, lad," Tum Tum said. "In the end, it'll all come down to us."

"And if it ends with the castle coming down on us?" Whitney asked.

Tum Tum shrugged.

"We should at least be in the crypt," Whitney said.

"Sure," Tum Tum said, laughing, "let's go to the mountain where the last God Feud took place, surrounded by dead kings, somewhere south of where Nesilia was buried. That sounds safe."

"You're right," Whitney said. "That's exactly what we shou—"

The ground shook and sent Whitney sprawling against the stairs. He got to his hands and knees just as another tremor rocked the castle.

"Shog in a barrel. That's it." He knew where he needed to be, and it wasn't hiding in the castle.

He rose, dug his hand into his pocket, and grasping the Brike Stone, fought against the feeling that his soul and body were going to be torn away from each other. As he pulled it out, all the room's light seemed to evaporate like rainwater on a hot day.

He tossed it to Tum Tum. "Hold onto this. I'll be back," he said.

The dwarf was left with no choice but to catch it. The moment he did, he froze, gawking at it silently, like his brain had stopped working.

Lucindur strode forward and whisper-shouted as if the big bad army might overhear her, "Where are you going?"

Whitney stopped at the side entrance, the place where the Royal Council was meant to enter.

"If a castle full of the best soldiers this place has to offer can't keep you safe, an exaggerative thief won't do much better," Whitney said. Then, without another word, he cleared the threshold and tore off to the only place in the castle he knew he'd be able to get a glimpse of what was happening on the outside.

He passed many guards who objected to his leaving the Throne Room, but who were under strict orders not to leave their post. They were there to keep people out, not in.

It took focus to remember where the Shield Hall was in such a labyrinth. Still, familiar landmarks told Whitney he was headed in the right direction. After a few more turns, he finally burst through the war room's door.

He was met by a Shieldsman, sword extended outward.

"Mister Fierstown," the soldier said. "What are you doing here?"

Mister? Whitney thought. When had he ever been called anything other than 'thief,' or 'hey, you!' in this damnable castle.

He cleared his throat. "Just doing my part, Sir..."

"Hystad, sir. Is there something I can do for you?"

"Just keep... uh... keeping the keep safe," Whitney said.

Sir Hystad finally sheathed his sword and returned to his post beside the large window.

Whitney took two steps forward until he stood beside the massive planning table upon which sat many carved figurines spelling out the precise plan Torsten and the Shesaitju princess—or whatever she was—had devised. As Whitney pored over it, he wasn't even sure it was a good plan, but it was the best they had.

He looked around at the statues of so many Wearers of White, wondering if Torsten's visage would be represented there someday. Then, he found himself hoping it wouldn't be too soon.

"What do you think of Torsten?" Whitney asked the Shieldsman.

"Sir Unger?" Sir Hystad repeated. "Best there is."

"We're all about to die, Sir Hystad," Whitney reminded him. "There's no better time for the truth."

Sir Hystad laughed nervously. "Well, hah. He's... he's a bit of a grump sometimes." Then, he stood tall and said, "But still, the best there is."

"Can't argue with that," Whitney said.

Whitney walked just a bit more, and there, directly in front of him, was a statue he hadn't noticed when they'd been planning. Sir Uriah Davies—the face Redstar had stolen in the dwarven ruins and the Webbed Woods. For Whitney, it felt like so long ago that he and Torsten embarked upon that grand adventure, getting captured at Oxgate. Eventually, they both escaped, albeit at different times. Whitney was shocked Torsten had ever forgiven him for that.

Under his breath, Whitney echoed Sir Hystad's sentiments. "Best there is."

His attention returned to Sir Uriah Davies' sculpture. The sight disgusted Whitney. To think that the memory of such a valiant warrior had been so stained by evil...

"Yigging Exile," Whitney said, almost a whisper, "what am I, some kind of hero?"

Then, he turned and started toward the balcony overlooking the Northern Mason's district to his right and Mount Lister to his left.

"Yeah, maybe I am," he said.

"Sir?" the soldier said.

Whitney ignored him.

Far below the balcony, the city's northern fortifications still stood, doing what little it could to protect against the enemy's various magics and brute force. As soon as they broke through, it was just a shallow strip of homes, then up the sharp hill Old Yarrington was built upon, and they would be at the rear of the castle.

It was then that Whitney considered the incredible arrogance of whoever had built the castle. To leave such a wide opening on the exterior of the fortress showed how sure they were that no one would ever breach the city. Looking to his right, where the Drav Cra's gargantuan, hairy mounts slammed over and over again into the wall, Whitney doubted the Glass Kingdom's intelligence.

He leaned out, hoping to catch sight of Sora, but only saw the vast army and what could've been remnants of Sora's magic flame petering out in the muddy fields. The rumbling appeared to have come from catapults. The fields north of the city were strewn with boulders.

Everything shook as the Drav Cra used their chekt like battering rams, with barely enough archers posted in the area to make more than a display of defense. Not that they could've accomplished much. Freydis and other warlocks outside flung balls of flame and exploding ice, keeping many from aiming—incinerating others.

All while each chekt caused clouds of dust, and drove the Glassmen upon the ramparts to their knees. Whitney's eyes combed the ranks but still didn't see Sora anywhere. He did, however, recognize Sir Mulliner, barking orders for his men to retreat down the stairs and prepare the city ambush. Then, just as they'd cleared the parapets, the wall came tumbling down with a sound like thunder. However, it was precisely part of the plan, in the exact location the dwarves had been working so hard to compromise. It was just what Torsten had expected.

The opening led the Drav Cra army into a funnel where the shield-bearing ranks of Mulliner's men made quick work of them. At the same time, archers waiting in windows unleashed barrage after barrage. Wherever Sora was, she unleashed fire upon them, and Whitney even spotted tiny Aquira zipping around blowing more flames.

It was a blood bath and every Drav Cra who entered died just as quickly. The one thing Torsten hadn't accounted for were their giant mounts.

Massive vines grew out of the ground and pulled the breach in the wall wider, allowing one chekt to squeeze through. It stomped across the left side of Mulliner's ranks like a boulder through a barley field. Men were flattened beneath their hairy feet. A building full of archers came down as its tusks raked across the first floor. That was when Whitney finally saw Sora. She leaped across a rooftop, her fire lashing out like a whip around the beast's throat. She jumped to the street, slamming the thing down face-first where it could be killed by many blades.

But the damage had been done.

Just like that, the northern defenses were partially breached, and Drav Cra filtered through the ambush. Mulliner and Sora still had the upper hand, but the enemy had the numbers, and the warlocks continued to use their magic vines to widen the entry. Eventually, they'd be overwhelmed.

Whitney swore again.

Sir Hystad shifted uncomfortably behind him, obviously having witnessed the same thing.

"Aren't you going to go help them?" Whitney asked.

"I have my orders."

"Yeah, well, some orders aren't worth keeping," Whitney said, turning his attention back to the foothills of Mount Lister just behind where the bulk of Freydis' army was positioned. According to Torsten, that was where the crypt had split open when Pi was resurrected and possessed by Nesilia. Whitney had been in the city during that time, just before setting off with the Pompare Troupe. He had a vague recollection of the upturned earth, thinking it would have been best to fill it in with stone and forget about it altogether.

However, that was before he and Sora went down there to visit Liam. Dwarves were supposed to be the best, but Whitney had witnessed their shoddy craftsmanship. At the time, he didn't know what it meant or why he should care, but now…

He took off at a sprint, knowing precisely what role he was going to play in this thing. He checked his new daggers as he ran. Whitney knew they were laced with silver, prepared in case he was the one to drive a crippling blow to Nesilia in her upyr form. For now, it was just another blade for which to kill humans and monsters—and Whitney didn't like killing.

The dungeon stairs passed beneath him three at a time, and he didn't bother to stop when he got to the bottom, just allowing his momentum to carry him into the iron bars of the first cell. He pushed off and ran in darkness, knowing there would be nothing but a straight hall. He swiped at spider webs that covered him and passed by only a few occupied cells. Their inhabitants grasped for him, all saying the same words that had Sora so freaked out on their previous visit.

"I see you."

Whitney just continued by, still unsure if they were possessed like the men he'd seen in Panping, or just mad loons not even fit to help in the fight. It didn't matter. The dungeon soon opened up into the Royal Crypt. He didn't know why, but he felt such a strong sense of urgency that his stomach roiled. Seeing those great beasts breaching the walls, even though it was part of the plan, had Whitney uncomfortable. Sure, they were *supposed* to break through, but they weren't supposed to slaughter the whole of the front lines in a matter of minutes. Knowing Sora was down there didn't give him any comfort either. Freydis wasn't charging. She was being smart, remaining at a distance, and using her magic to benefit her army, rather than driving the attack.

Stopping in the mouth of the entrance, Whitney scanned around, seeing the many statues, and a new one built for Liam just across from his casket.

That wasn't the reason he was there, though. He'd seen something when he and Torsten were arguing. Not many would have noticed it, but Whitney prided himself in being observant. It was the mark of any great thief. He figured out how best to enter and exit every place he ever visited. He needed to know how to get in to reap his reward and escape the guards if they were to interrupt the caper.

Just above Liam's new statue, a thin seam in the new stone forming a small dome for the altar allowed the tiniest sliver of light. Whitney cracked his knuckles and rolled his neck.

He moved to the statue and peered up. It was three times his size, but there were plenty of crevices for climbing. He tested the handholds on Liam's stone greaves. Once he was convinced it was sturdy enough, he grasped and pulled himself up. One hand after the other, placing his feet where his hands had just been. Next was the stone belt, and then the cuirass.

Finally, he stood upon Liam's shoulders, took a moment to consider the metaphorical implications of it, then he started the climb to the crown upon the old King's head. It was fashioned just like the one Whitney had stolen. Whitney patted the statue.

"Sorry, old man," he said.

Reaching the top, he stretched his arms only to find he was still an arm's length away.

"Shog in a…"

He looked around, desperate for something to give him that little bit extra.

Upon his last visit, each of the kings had been holding weapons. But now, most had empty hands, those weapons appropriated by Hovom Nitebrittle to be used in the battle—some of the metal contained within Whitney's daggers, he figured. One body's hands, however, weren't empty. King Liam held a thin, iron pole.

Whitney knew Torsten now used Liam's old blade, but that was taken long ago when Hovom had the luxury of time. It seemed he'd used that opportunity to give Liam something to rest his hands upon until the sword was returned. Where all the other kings were slumped over and leaning against their caskets, Liam was upright like the proud man he was said to have been.

"Torsten is gonna kill me," Whitney said, shimmying his way down.

Before he could change his mind, he wrapped his cloak around his elbow and drove it through King Liam's casket. Glass shattered and splintered, spraying outward. Whitney felt tiny cuts along his cheek and neck but had no time to care. He grabbed the pole and pulled. Unexpectedly, it held in place. Whitney pulled harder, and the pole came free, dragging Liam's body with it. Whitney leaped out of the way just before the corpse fell upon him.

"Blech," he said. He sloppily circled one eye with his free hand and backed away.

Then, just as he'd done when leaving the Whispering Wizards' Tower many moons ago, he placed the pole in his teeth like it was the Splintering Staff, and started his ascent. The staff had been a light wood, and this iron pole, though thin, was far heavier. But Whitney managed. Once at the top, he whispered encouragement to himself and stabbed the new portion of the ceiling.

A few chunks of stone toppled down, bouncing off his arm and the statue below.

"Best masons in the land," Whitney scoffed. "Are dwarves good at anything?"

He jabbed it again, and more came loose. He continued until he could see the sky beyond. Dirt and grass poured onto his face. He kept at it until there was a hole large enough to pull himself through to the surface, though he was going to have to jump for it.

He looked down and dropped the pole. It took a few seconds before landing with a resonant *ping*. It was a long way if he missed the leap.

It wasn't as if he hadn't made bigger jumps with longer falls, but if he missed this one, Sora's life was at stake, too. He wasn't sure why he felt that way. She was more than capable of handling herself, but something inside of him said they'd vastly underestimated their enemy—if that were even possible.

He closed his eyes, inhaled, then opened them again and pushed off the highest point on Liam's crown. His fingers found purchase... in loose soil covering the rebuilt sections of the crypt. The dwarves hadn't even packed it solid.

Immediately, he began slipping. He clawed at the dirt, feeling no stone at all. Scrambling, pulling and scratching, dirt dribbling into his open mouth, he felt an elaborate root system and seized it. Pieces broke off, getting in his eyes, but he was able to get a good enough grip to climb the rest of the way out.

He wiped at his face. Rubbed his eyes. Spit.

He stayed there on the ground for a bit, letting himself breathe. The air felt cold against his sweat-soaked face even though it was summer. And it was dark—way darker than any night other than the Dawning. The moons were just a soft haze in the sky, providing almost no light at all.

He got the impression it was nothing natural. However, Whitney could still see the horde of Drav Cra warriors and dire wolves gathered before the wall, pushing inside little by little. The breach in the wall was now much more significant than planned for, with remaining chekt able to rumble through and level buildings with ease.

Behind them and to the west, Whitney could make out Freydis and other warlocks punishing the city with their magic. Now that the opening no longer needed their prying, they flung elemental projectiles over the walls with no care for who they were hitting—friend, or foe.

The enemy flowed through the breach and broke Sir Mulliner's ranks in full, leaving a bloody, fiery massacre behind as the melee tore throughout the district. Others used the body of a dead chekt to scale the wall itself and fight for the parapets to claim high ground for their magic missiles.

They'd planned to lure Freydis close by simulating an overwhelming victory. Instead, the opposite had happened. They'd drawn the bulk of her army away from her.

Whitney surveyed the fields for Drav Cra stragglers. A plan was brewing, and he needed some new clothes.

XLII

THE CALEEF

Mahi had heard her father's stories about the fleet from Abo'Fasaniyah, the former home of the Babrak Afhemate. However, she'd never seen it in full until now. She wished that were still true. Babrak and his people had always claimed that their naval forces outmatched the al'Tariq afhemate. They were right. Strikingly so. Even before Awn'al al'Tariq's horrible accident upon the seas, there was no way the fleet of Mahi's predecessor could have been larger than this. From where she stood, a level above the docks, it looked like a solid wall moving toward them. So much more than was present in Latiapur.

"There are so many," Bit'rudam said, voicing what everyone was thinking.

"Our defenses will hold," Lord Jolly said.

"You know that's not true," Mahi said, no room for argument in her tone.

"Perhaps," he said, "but it will buy the others time."

The vibrations of war had already begun to echo across the city. Things didn't sound good at the walls, either. The sky was as dark as Mahi's skin and equally unnatural. Others complained of the cold, uncharacteristic of this time of year, though Mahi couldn't feel it.

"Right, then," Lord Jolly said. "It has been a pleasure coming to know you, Caleef Mahraveh. And you, Bit'rudam. My prayer is that Iam sees fit to see us through this battle, but if not, the Gate of Light doesn't sound so bad. Nor does your Eternal Current. Fight with honor... when you can. But, no matter what..." He stabbed a finger toward Autla's Inlet. "Kill them first."

"Yes," Mahi agreed. "A lovely sentiment." She bowed her head to the one-armed Glassman and tugged Bit'rudam, leading him by the hand toward a regiment of their archers.

Having fled Latiapur with such haste, they hadn't had time to gather many barbed arrows, but the Shesaitju were no strangers to the power of fire. They would use the simple arrows Torsten was able to provide, but their tips were wrapped tight in flammable cloth. The ships that managed to break through the initial line of defense, and also made it through the barbed chains crisscrossing the inlet and lower Dockside, would be met with flying torches.

The arrows wouldn't travel the same, and Mahi's men would be at a disadvantage, but she hoped the sheer number of them would help.

Surveying her army, each of them more fearful than the next, she couldn't blame them for their trepidation... and they didn't even know Caliphar was gone, along with the Sirens. They were on their own unless Iam decided to show. In the hands of a god who'd caused her people far too much suffering.

"Are you ready?" Bit'rudam asked her.

"Nesilia offered to have me lead her army. Instead, I am here, fighting alongside strangers we must call friends. To defy a god is to welcome death."

"I won't let her touch you."

"I know you won't. But, like Lord Jolly said, would the Eternal Current not be welcome, after all of this?"

"I wouldn't know," Bit'rudam said. "But I will trust your word."

Mahi placed her palm against his chest. "Today, trust this. Let it guide you. It is all we have left."

He raised his hand to cover hers and let it linger for a few seconds. Time seemed to pass slowly as he felt her breathing. Then he whispered, "I hope that's not the truth." He stepped back and bowed as if to beckon Mahi to go ahead.

She stepped up to the front of the warriors stationed in the middle of the docks. Each one snapped to attention, longbow to their side, and chin high. From this angle, they looked even more terrified. She looked beyond them, to the Glass forces lined up on Port Street, under the command of Sir Garihad Yuliz. The man was young, as many of the Glass leaders appeared to be, and those they commanded... They weren't soldiers... not all of them. Many were commoners with weapons they barely knew how to hold. But these were their allies now, for better or worse. Mahi would let them find their own ways of motivation. As for her men, she only knew one thing that would give them the strength needed to carry out today's battle.

"I know this is not our land," she spoke, "but we will fight like it is. You saw what happened to our great city. If this one falls, the Current will never return us home to take back what is ours."

There were murmurs, but not even Mahi could make them out.

"This enemy wishes to divide us, just as we have been for so long. She offers false promises, even as she murders our children. But now, we all must survive together. Though I may not be the Queen of Sand and Glass as I was to be, is it not a wonder that glass is made when sand is put under flame? Could it not be that we are one and the same, deep down?"

"Yes, Caleef," they all said together. None of them sounded convinced.

She'd already given this speech to the other groupings and would have to give it a dozen times more, and none could be done with less vim than the last. It was vital that each of these warriors felt the weight and gravity of this day.

"We fight not for King or Queen, but for all life upon Pantego." She pointed to the fleet upon the horizon. "It may be Babrak out there, that cowardly pis'truda, but he fights for Nesilia, the Buried Goddess. The one who saw to it that our God of Sand and Sea is not here with us today."

The murmurs now became loud grumbling.

"What are you doing, Mahi?" Bit'rudam asked.

"That's right," she said, ignoring Bit'rudam. "I was there when Nesilia swallowed Him like the sea gobbles up the beaches; when she buried Him like she had once been."

The look of confusion upon the soldier's faces was evident.

"I don't think this—"

She cut Bit'rudam off. "Winning this battle may be our only chance of bringing Him back. Let us show Him that He will not be forgotten. No, this day isn't just for us, nor for the Glass. Today is a battle for our very God. For all those who dance upon the Eternal Current. For all those who one day will. If we do not win today, our spirits will wander like lost wolf pups. This cannot be."

"Yes, Caleef!" They all said, louder and with more conviction this time.

"Fight with all the rage of the sea!" she shouted. "Kill them first!"

She left them in a frenzy of spirits and began toward the next group of archers. Bit'rudam stayed behind, leading the men in a pre-battle prayer. They had no sages after they'd all stayed behind in Latiapur, but he did his best. Even though they now knew Caliphar would not hear them, they repeated his words with such respect, and she could tell, they meant every last word.

They *would* rise upon the tide by the guided hand of God. They *would* cast down the enemy like a rip in the current, dragging them to the depths of darkness. The sea *would* feast upon their flesh and spit their carcasses out upon the rocks. This would *not* be the day they met their end.

Mahi spoke the same words to each of the front lines throughout Dockside, and each received them the same way. It bolstered their faltering resolve to know that they fought for something bigger than themselves.

By the end, Mahi almost believed it herself. Almost.

But she'd been too close. She'd seen it—the end of all things. She knew that Caliphar wouldn't be returning, not even if they won. The Sirens were gone, and she was His last voice in this realm. Things would never be the same.

She considered the memories of all the former Caleefs and found herself wondering if that was such a bad thing. There'd been so much infighting and war that, perhaps, a fresh start where her people were no longer under the boot of the Glass, but hand-in-hand, might be best. There may not be a King—she may not be their Queen—but that didn't mean something new and wonderful couldn't sprout from the horrors of the world's end.

Horns sounded from the north end of the docks, tearing her from those thoughts. The sound indicated the first of Babrak's ships had reached their blockade. A sudden inferno blazed upon the waters as the soldiers out in the water lit barrel after barrel full of whale oil. Small explosions sent shards flying everywhere. She could hear the hysteria, even from there, as Babrak's men realized what was happening.

As little men on little boats rowed away and back toward the docks, Babrak's ships slowed, and for a moment, Mahi felt encouraged. Until she heard it, a loud *crack* before something massive tore through the sky.

Barbed, metal bolts, large enough to tear through the hull of any ship at sea, did just that, shredding Glass vessels before any of them could fully realize their purpose as explosives. The Glass blockade had stopped a few of Babrak's ships, and it was only meant to buy time. But as the bomb-ships crumbled, the already dark sky darkened further from a volley of enemy arrows peppering the inlet. They came down upon the fleeing Glassmen, and their screams could be heard above everything.

None survived. It was as if Babrak had expected the defense, and Mahi realized he might have. It was similar to the tactic the Glassmen had used in Nahanab. Still, it was only meant to slow them down, and by the look of it, it was working, forcing them to waste crucial arrows and reveal the signature ballistae weaponry of Babrak's fleet. Once meant to hunt large beasts that would threaten their fishing hollows, they'd been transformed into vicious weapons.

The first of her archers, positioned to the north of the inlet, let loose upon Babrak's stalled fleet. They would fire, then duck behind shanties while they prepared for their next salvo. The cluttered area of the city made their ranks disorganized, but that also made them unpredictable to the enemy.

Mahi ran back to where Bit'rudam stood. "Prepare shore defense," she said. "Take out as many as you can with the flying torches, and then fall back. Lure them in and set fire to the docks."

Sacrifice the few, her father had always said. She'd thought it heartless, but now, she understood better than ever.

And she was ready to be sacrificed. They all were.

Dashing past the lines of archers, she climbed the low bluffs on the north to where Lord Jolly stood, watching with his spyglass.

His cheeks were red, and sweat poured down his face despite the bitter cold.

"I'm sorry," he said, lowering the spyglass and averting his gaze. "That should have been more successful."

"It was," Mahi said. "In Nahanab, the *first* time our people saw such a tactic."

She didn't mean for it to come out with such venom, but it did nonetheless.

Lord Jolly turned, shock upon his face. It immediately turned to anger. "And what would you have done?" he snapped. "I didn't hear you voice an objection in the Shield Hall."

In her past life, Mahraveh would have responded in like manner, but now, possessing centuries of wisdom passed down from great men of strong character, she withheld her ire.

"You're right," she said. "I didn't. This is no time to be at each other's throats." She turned to the approaching army. "And look, it did work upon a number of their vessels."

It was true. From at least three of Babrak's larger warships, men leaped off and swam through fiery waters to the safety of other ships. Many didn't make the journey, as Mahi's archers picked them off. The initial defense wasn't a complete loss. Though, for every ship thwarted, another ten pushed on.

"Blackwood doesn't burn so easily," Mahi said.

"Now what?" Jolly said.

Babrak's men returned fire, but they were nearly out of range, and Dockside offered cover they didn't have out on the water.

"Now, we hope our chains hold," Mahi said. "And when they do not, we fall back and let the fires of war consume them along with Dockside."

Lord Jolly nodded. "Those things are devastating," he said, his face returning to a static position. He, no doubt, referred to the ballista missiles that still tore ships and soldiers apart.

"They are, but Babrak can't help but waste his arsenal," Mahi said. "He has no idea what's coming. They approach the shallow water. Now!"

Babrak's lead ships cut the waters, and the sound of splintering wood against iron couldn't be heard over the din of flames, screaming, and humming arrows. Mahi, however, saw it. As did Lord Jolly. The unnatural darkness caused by Nesilia was their undoing, making everything below the surface of the trap-laden inlet invisible.

All throughout Dockside, zhulong attached to heavy cranks pulled, tightening the chains and bringing them to hull height. Jolly let a small smile play upon his lips, but Mahraveh knew better. She waited, watching as Babrak's lead ship slowed abruptly, and soldiers were flung off the deck.

Their minor victory was short-lived as a sudden explosion from the sea brought giant tentacles with it. They grasped the ship, dozens of them. In a display unlike anything either of them had seen before, the ship rose from the surface and came back down just beyond the initial, underwater barrier of chains. Its hull was damaged, but not disabled.

One ship after another, the Current Eaters did the same. Some ships fell victim to the traps, but not nearly what was expected.

Jolly swore.

"Those are no mere beasts," Mahi said.

"We are fighting gods," Lord Jolly agreed.

Mahi brandished her spear. "They will be upon us shortly. Do you intend to die today, Lord Jolly?"

He shook his head.

"Nor I." She clapped his good shoulder. "Your men fought valiantly. I suggest you fall back with Sir Yuliz and await landfall. Now, it's my turn to send Babrak to the Currentless Realm."

She scaled down the bluff until her bare feet met the docks again.

"Archers, ready!" she shouted. Her command trickled down the staggered line all the way to the south. They all lowered their arrows into fire pits. The sound of bowstrings going taut reverberated through the air.

She met eyes with Bit'rudam across the harbor for but a second as she stalked behind her men. This was it. This was her final opportunity to show that the Shesaitju were the greatest warriors in Pantego, that Liam only conquered them because they forgot what it meant to stand united.

She looked out to the sea and saw him. Babrak, large as ever, stood upon the prow of his flagship. A menacing looking fish with a sharp nose was carved into the prow of his ship, and the grin he wore made her sick. Never before had he been uglier than at that moment. He looked every bit the part of the villain, stretching his arm forth. She noticed then that he had his archers ready as well, with more arriving as Current Eaters heaved more ships over the chains.

"Fire!" Mahi shouted, and she watched Babrak's men do the same.

Missiles joined in the air like two opposing forces. Many glanced off each other, there was such a number. Babrak's volley landed just short of the docks, and her own missed as well.

"Ready!" she shouted again. "Fire!"

Her arrows went up, and a second later, so did Babrak's. This time neither would miss. She stood there as barbed arrows rained down all around. She didn't flinch, she didn't move. The *thunk, thunk, thunk* diverged with the cries of her men.

"Ready!" She could hear Bit'rudam shout. She echoed to her men as well.

There was a hesitation to their pull this time.

"Ready!" she shouted again. "Fire!"

Their flaming projectiles landed upon Babrak's fleet. Blackwood was durable, but all the oil they'd dumped in the inlet and on their ships throughout the false blockade served as kindling. The flammable stuff was everywhere, catching on masts and sails, flaring on debris throughout the water. Those men who'd given their lives to feign a naval defense didn't die in vain.

Bit'rudam continued calling out commands to his archers. They moved as they shot, using the city for cover against Babrak's return fire, all while enemy arrows and ballista ravaged Dockside beyond repair.

Mahraveh had seen enough from her side. She rushed forward.

"Shoot that thing, now!" she shouted to one of her archers, pointing at the Current Eater. Without hesitation, the warrior took aim and fired. His arrow plunged through the eye of one of the Current Eaters as it rose above the surface.

"Aim for the beasts!" she shouted to everyone.

Her men shifted their focus. After a few volleys, the Current Eaters disappeared beneath the surface. Babrak's ships continued forward, cracking against the chains and further catching fire from the flaming debris. Left and right, the harbor-adjacent buildings and docks which held the chain's anchors broke and pulled, dragging rubble and zhulong with them. Dozens of blackwood hulls came undone, and ships took on water.

Still, thanks to the Current Eaters, Babrak's army was close enough to land for many to swim. Other ships endured long enough to carry men closer, driving hard against the chains. A strong wind fully filled the sails, and the buildings began to topple. All part of the plan to funnel Babrak's men in through central Dockside.

With the Current Eaters out of sight, Mahi's men now refocused on the enemy soldiers. There were so many overflowing the inlet now, they could aim anywhere and find one. But Shesaitju warriors in a coastal afhemate like Babrak's were trained for naval combat and wore light armor. Those in the water dove down where arrows couldn't hurt them, with trained lungs that allowed them to hold their breath for minutes at a time.

Mahi's forces' flaming arrows continued to burn through the hard Blackwood of the second wave of ships as barbed arrows pounded Dockside. A ballista fired from a sinking vessel near the front of the formation. The massive bolt lanced over Mahi's head, crashing through a wood building. Debris and detritus spewed out, and Mahi dove before a shard crushed her. Others weren't so lucky.

As she scrambled back to her feet, she realized they'd done all they could at range. Babrak's surviving ships were close enough to see the whites of their warriors' eyes. Swimmers reached beaches and jetties near Bit'rudam's side of the inlet, forcing his archers to abandon their bows and engage in close combat.

"Draw swords!" Mahi shouted just as one of the flaming ships smashed into the docks straight ahead, splintering through it. If there was confusion before, now there was utter chaos. Babrak's men leaped from the deck and into Dockside.

Mahraveh unstrapped her new spear from her back and charged. She windmilled around, clipping two soldiers as they disembarked. One stumbled backward and into the water, and the other dropped to one knee. He didn't let the attack slow him, swiping at her with a polearm of his own.

Sir Yuliz's Glassmen finally joined into the battle, forming shield walls to repel attacks as more battered ships crashed into the docks.

While enemies debarked, trilling their tongues, Mahi's reserve archers fled to the many flat rooftops deeper into the city.

Mahi jabbed the butt of her spear into her opponent's throat, then staggered forward as she was hit from behind. She turned and stopped her attack just before the tip of her spear buried itself in one of her own people's forehead, locked in battle with one of Babrak's men.

She looked around for Babrak as more ships crashed, and swimmers from sunken vessels invaded the shore but saw him nowhere.

Across the harbor, Bit'rudam held the southern end valiantly. His sword flashed, swiping enemies off the dock. Others stabbed spears into the water as swimmers tried to climb. Crashing ships allowed Babrak's men to pierce the defenses in areas, but a fallen lighthouse cut off the northern route and kept Mahi and her army from being overwhelmed.

The Current had turned in their favor.

Mahi even began to wonder if, perhaps, this wasn't just an extended defense to buy time for the others, but an opportunity to completely rout Nesilia's naval force.

Then, as if Nesilia was purposefully inflating her hope just to spite her, the Current Eaters returned. Giant, wet tentacles slapped down all across the inlet, stretching ten meters or more and raking across shanty buildings, turning them to rubble with hardly an effort. Archers perched atop them fell to their immediate deaths. Men in the streets below were crushed as well.

Some of the great beasts clambered out of the inlet, collapsing docks everywhere, but they were so immense that they simply skittered up anyway. Many were slowed by the heavy chains which entangled them, but others dragged them like huge whips. The warriors caught in their paths were shredded and crushed.

In an instant, all hope vanished. In the face of the monsters who'd ravaged Latiapur, her front lines fell into a frenzied retreat.

"Fall back!" Mahi cried out as she joined her men. "To South Corner. Abandon Dockside!"

At her orders, all the remaining archers kicked over buckets and barrels of oil being used to ignite their arrows. All throughout Dockside, torches were lit to initiate the blaze.

Enemy arrows zipped past Mahi's head as she ascended the stairs leading to Port Street, where their next stages of defense were situated in the form of Glassmen with shield barriers, and mounted zhulong cavalry, the last they had left. Stacked debris and barrels would force Babrak's troops down certain roads where attackers were ready. They'd crafted a maze of death throughout South Corner's already disorganized streets.

She was almost up to the top when in the corner of her eye, she spotted Babrak. He lumbered off his flagship, which was fully collapsed against the docks. Fire from the hull licked at his boots, but he didn't seem to care. His mighty warhammer caught a fleeing Glassmen in the back. Warriors armored falsely like Serpent Guards flooded out behind him.

"Babrak!" Mahi shouted.

She turned to charge him when a tentacle smacked down in front of her. She stabbed at it, but it rose only to fall again in another place. When it lifted, Babrak was gone again.

Mahi clenched her jaw but thought better than to abandon the plan for vengeance. She wasn't Nesilia. So, she crossed Port Street and gave the signal. Glassmen stationed upon the higher portion of the city fired more flaming arrows to set piles of tinder and hay ablaze along with the spilled oil. Soon, the fires raging throughout Dockside became an inferno, so many of the buildings made from dry and cracked wood. Enemy screams saturated the air. The flames rose high in front of Mahi as she fell into ranks and glared through the fiery haze.

Now came stage two. All the smoke made visibility poor, especially in the darkness, and only she, Bit'rudam, Sir Yuliz, and their respective warriors knew the best paths through South Corner.

A silhouette burst through the orange veil, sword high and slashing down. Mahi ducked and rolled back, then brought her spear up through her bent knee. The *Scorpion's Sting* caught the attacker in the heart.

She pulled her spear free and shouted, "Hold the line!" Her army braced for the enemy charge, but none came, only mad, screaming stragglers. Mahi bolted away and down a side street to reach a position where she could survey the situation and ensure things were unfolding to plan. While her army held South Corner, she had to snare a Current Eater, all while keeping it alive and from killing everything around it.

She soon came upon the most elaborate building in the district. It still stood, untouched despite the blaze. She climbed to the balcony, using the grapevine-carved railings as hand and footholds. From there, she saw Babrak's men waiting to climb over the fiery rubble throughout the city. Instead of charging, they fell back and gathered behind the Current Eaters, and whatever zhulong riders they were able to successfully deliver to shore.

Some of the Current Eaters were missing limbs and pouring black blood, dying. Others were so wrapped by the chains they were stuck in the water, releasing wicked screams as they pulled with all their might and tore apart more of Dockside to get free.

The uninjured ones rose like black storms against the night sky. Fire seemed to do nothing to them. They tossed rocks and chunks of building out of the way, clearing paths so Babrak's army would be able to charge alongside them in overwhelming masses.

Burning Dockside had backfired. It created space between their armies, allowing them to regather after the initial losses, thanks to monsters that couldn't have been adequately prepared for. How could anyone have guessed they'd be intelligent and resourceful enough to do what they'd done?

Their roars split the night, thunderous, terrifying—a feeling Mahi thought she could no longer feel tugging at her. She watched, helpless as Babrak reappeared, issuing orders for where his men should gather. More climbed up from the inlet, now with time to rest after a long swim.

"Mahraveh!" Babrak the Usurper shouted at the top of his lungs, voice echoing as dread stole over her entire army. "Come out, come out, wherever you are!"

XLIII

THE MYSTIC

Half a dozen of the gargantuan chekt tore through the Mason's District north of the castle. No one had considered their substantial strength when planning this little trap. Maybe they didn't know about them. Crowfall had apparently fallen fast, with only nearby scouts to tell of it. Sora wasn't sure it would've mattered, but she'd spent so much time under Nesilia's control in the harsh white tundra of Drav Cra, she should have known better.

Now, she watched as Sir Mulliner's men were trampled underfoot. They had no hope. Not even as Sora threw fireballs toward the beasts. A few were slowed by her magic, but she was limited—if she unleashed her full power, she'd incinerate the Glass soldiers as well. The best they could offer was Aquira zooming in and out of the fray, blowing flames into the creatures' eyes, hoping to blind them long enough for one of the soldiers to land a killing blow. Sora would have to trust her little friend to stay alive. Her skin was tough and wouldn't easily succumb to an arrow strike.

Their entire plan hinged upon the Arch Warlock leading the charge, but with Freydis pulling up the rear, she was more dangerous than ever. Vines burst from the ground all over the battlefield, but not small ones like Sora had seen her use before. These were the girth of any tree trunk in the Webbed Woods and then some. They carved great fissures in the landscape, dragging men inward to death. The chasms also jeopardized the integrity of not just the city walls, but small avalanches were already beginning in the foothills of Mount Lister.

Sora stood upon the walls, enduring every shake and quake, eyeing the battlefield and trying to determine her best course of action. She could stand there, throwing fire and immolating the enemy unto whichever god they wished, but her magic wasn't inexhaustible. She would need to reserve her strength for Freydis.

"Sora!" Sir Mulliner shouted. He strode across the ramparts, slowing when he reached her. The man looked like... well, like he should. Under Torsten's leadership, this man might have seen battle, but never anything like this. None of them had.

"Sir Mulliner," Sora said solemnly.

"This is a disaster, and it doesn't sound like anyone else is faring any better," he said, quiet enough that his men might not have overheard. "Torsten's defenses have broken. Dockside is already in flames. We're not going to be able to hold them off much longer."

"We have no choice," Sora responded. "Look out there. There's an entire army between us and Freydis. I need your men to clear the way."

"My men can barely hold the streets, much less press the attack beyond the wall!"

Sora followed his gaze to the northern battlefield, then to those within the city.

"We have to take out those chekt," Sora said. "They are all that's stopping us within."

"With what, our good looks?" Sir Mulliner said, though there was no humor in his tone. "It's taking everything just to not get crushed like ants. Not to mention the wolves."

The *dire* wolves...

They were ruthless, and now that many of them were possessed by hellhounds, those vile dogs Sora and Whitney had fought in Elsewhere, they were even more vicious. As with every other thought, she *had* to push this one away. She couldn't be distracted.

"If Torsten died today, who would replace him?" Sora asked. She let the question linger, knowing the former Shieldsman would understand. Then, she continued. "I have my job." She pointed to Freydis. "Your men are to occupy these forces while I put an end to that witch."

Sir Mulliner's face turned to a stone-cold resolve. "There was never any hope of winning this battle, not traditionally," he said more to himself than to her. "We need to cut off the head, so the snake might die."

"Exactly," Sora said.

"Then that's what we'll do." He turned to his archers and began to direct them all to take out the chekt, even if it meant the walls were scaled and more city streets were taken.

Sora didn't hear the rest. She was too occupied with watching the massacre unfolding before her. She had to stop Freydis—the proverbial snakehead. She knew she had to do it. If not her, then no one.

The Arch Warlock stood alone, high upon a foothill, overlooking a field of thousands, surrounded by a pile of dead… children? The bodies were small, even though they were painted like warlocks. Were they part of the new stock of Drav Cra magic-users—sacrificed to provide the power to tear open Yarrington? Sora had watched children be offered to Nesilia while at the Earthmoot, and now, their very blood seemed to be swirling in the air around Freydis.

Below Freydis, Wvenweigard, Nesilia's loyalist warlock apart from Freydis, used his own magic as he advanced on the walls, raining shards of ice down upon Mulliner's archers. His face, Sora could see, and beneath the white and red paint—if that was paint and not blood—there was the joy of battle. It sickened her.

It didn't just sicken her, it enraged her.

Glassmen fired back at him with arrows, but Drav Cra warriors gave their lives to protect him, and he continued forward. He'd soon finish what the chekt started and break her army's front lines.

She returned her attention to Freydis in the distance. But now, she wasn't alone. Another nasty, pathetic Drav Cra warrior was with her. Sora fantasized about lopping off both their heads. Now was her time to move. But as she planted her foot on the wall, she stopped.

The newcomer was behind her, and he was… sneaking? Crouched and low to the ground, he inched toward Freydis, each hand gripping a glinting blade. It was a familiar posture, one Sora had seen many times before. Her breath got caught in her throat for an instant, then…

The Drav Cra warrior plunged a blade into Freydis's back, cutting her attacks short. Vines dropped and fell all over the battlefield, crushing her own men. Then, the warrior stabbed a second time, higher, closer to her neck. Even from there, Sora could see the blood.

"Oh, Whit," Sora said, realizing both who it was and the horrible mistake he'd made. The only chance he had was to kill her instantly. Now, her powerful blood was seeping out all over Whitney's arm.

Sora felt a familiar tingle within her own blood. She used to think it was Elsewhere, but now, she wasn't sure. Whatever it was, it was like magma shut up in her bones, begging to be released. And this time, she didn't think she would argue.

Freydis spun on Whitney and slapped him hard. Whitney went down, but Sora didn't see anything else. She let out a primal roar, sprinted, and leaped down from the wall, landing on the hairy back of a chekt.

She kicked its rider off, and the beast bucked in a frenzied attempt to shake Sora off, too. However, Sora gripped its thick hair and refused. Then, with one hand, she grabbed hold of the reins and slapped them hard. The beast responded by rearing its front legs, then smashing down. It whipped its head to and fro, but somehow, Sora still held on. Then, pressing a hand against its neck, Sora closed her eyes and willed the creature to obey her. She'd never tried anything of the sort, but something within her said it would work.

At once, the chekt calmed.

With her hand still firm, Sora guided it. With all the ferocity in which it attacked Yarrington, it now turned its ire upon the Drav Cra. Two mammoth tusks ducked low and rose, goring Sora's enemies and sending them soaring through the air. Its giant feet crushed and smashed. Freydis' army didn't even know what was happening. Soon, confusion was evident, but it was too late. The dead piled up around her.

She was outside the walls now, exposed and caught within it all, but something was different. She couldn't see anything but blood and flame. Black blotches moved in front of her, silhouetted against a fire that hadn't been there before. She didn't even think about it as she hurled her magic. Fireballs exploded all over the grassy plains. Out of the corner of her eyes, she could see her arm wreathed in flame.

With that hand, she shot thin lines of fire. Like arrows, they tore through the horde of painted faces.

Without mercy, she charged. Each step sent Drav Cra warriors to Elsewhere or Skorravik—their supposed resting place—it didn't matter to her. All she could think about was Whitney knotted in mortal combat with the Arch Warlock of the Drav Cra—Nesilia's chosen champion on this plane.

Sora had seen first-hand what Freydis was capable of. She knew that Whitney could already be dead. But she also counted on Freydis and her twisted sense of humor, her inability to end things quickly. She liked to play, just like her master.

A warlock stopped before her chekt—barely old enough to be in her teens. She drew a blade in a long line between her unformed breasts. Naked and bloody, she raised both hands, palm out, and a mess of vines grew around the chekt's feet and tripped it.

It fell forward hard, tusks breaking against the hard ground, crushing the child warlock serving Nesilia with her life. Sora was flung off, but she had height and momentum on her side now. She summoned a powerful gale, catching her limbs and clothes, and lifting her above the Drav Cra army.

As she landed close to the foothills where she'd seen Freydis, she heard confused Drav Cra clamoring behind her. She looked back to see Wvenweigard storming toward her on a pathway made of ice, his own men pushed to the side. He slid, blood-covered hands contorting into tight balls, two fingers extended on each. Another sphere of ice careened toward her.

She raised a fist, and a wall of flame formed, melting the projectile before it reached her.

Wvenweigard skidded to a stop in front of her.

"Our Lady offered you everything," he said. Genuine sadness coated his features. Perhaps a hint of jealousy as he raised bloody hands to attack and shouted, "Everything!"

Sora didn't have time for Wvenweigard, and she didn't have time to rest. She cut her hand in a sharp gesture, horizontal with the ground. A blade of fire followed her movements, hitting Wvenweigard square in the chest and throwing him back into the Drav Cra trying to keep up.

Sora used the opportunity to rush toward the foothills where she could now see Whitney and Freydis squaring off. As expected, the Arch Warlock was toying with him. Five meters above the ground,

Whitney hovered, due to her foul magic. Freydis swiped her bloody hand to the side, sending Whitney flying toward the jagged face of the lower rock hills.

Sora stretched out her own hand, palm flat and vertical. Another blast of wind sent Whitney onto softer ground, just stopping his head from splitting open on rock.

Freydis whipped around.

"You!" she cried.

Freydis raised her fist high in an upward motion, blood was already streaming across her forearm like a spiderweb. Sharp icicles stabbed through the ground where Sora stood, but Sora easily rolled out of the way. It was as if she could feel them before they struck.

She retaliated with a strike of her own, and the grass around Freydis' feet grew longer and twisted, holding the Arch Warlock in place, just as the warlock child had done to her chekt. Then, Sora drew her sword and charged.

"You use tools of metal when such power is at your mercy?" Freydis said. "Our Lady said you were the most powerful."

Freydis clenched her fist, and a droplet of blood splashed the ground. The grass holding her withered upon its touch. She extended her hand to the side, then swung toward Sora. Rocks spewed from the field and slammed against Sora's shoulder, disrupting her attempt to cleave Freydis's head.

She took the hit in stride, using its momentum to carry her into a roll. When she stood, she decided to take a page out of Freydis' book. She looked inward, embracing her power, and the mass of earth beneath Freydis broke free, tossing the warlock backward.

"Now that is strength!" Freydis admired after she hit the ground. "What about this?"

She twirled her hands, and thick vines wrapped Sora's midsection, forcing her arms to her side. Freydis stood, grinning as she clenched her bloody fingers.

But she made the mistake of thinking that, like her, Sora needed her hands for magic. That she needed anything but her mind. She knew nothing of the raw power that burned within. Sora would have to enlighten her.

She thought of fire, and fire came. It burned away every remnant of the vines, and for the first time, Sora saw terror etched upon Freydis' face.

"It's over, Freydis," Sora said. "You chose the wrong side."

A loud screech distracted them both as Aquira darted down behind her at Wvenweigard, who had managed to catch up.

"Kill the imposter!" Freydis shouted and pointed toward Whitney, as if unaware that Wvenweigard was under attack. Then, while Sora was still distracted, Freydis darted forward and drove her jagged knife through Sora's shoulder.

Sora cried out and slammed a fist forward, knocking Freydis back. She pulled the dagger free and tossed it to the ground. She didn't need to draw on blood any longer, but that molten fire within came roaring back in full force. Sora screamed, and a pillar of flames shot up from the ground but dissipated just as quickly as Freydis blocked it with a sheet of ice. Freydis then drove her own fist into Sora's chest, just below her open wound.

Sora flew back, feeling like her ribcage had compressed into her heart.

Freydis charged forward and struck Sora again. "She said I couldn't compare! Well, look at us now."

Sora was hit with a barrage of elemental magic. It all happened so fast she couldn't even figure out what was happening before she was flat on her back.

"Sora!" Whitney cried out, a reminder of what was at stake.

Sora kicked upward and caught Freydis in the chin just as the warlock was about to mount her for another attack. Then, rising, Sora turned to see Wvenweigard fighting Aquira, flinging spikes of ice and unable to catch her. Now, Whitney had joined in. There was no way he would survive. Freydis may have been using him as a plaything, but Wvenweigard wouldn't hold back. And neither would the Drav Cra warriors closing in on all of them.

Sora growled, something bestial-sounding that came from deep inside. The darkness crept in on her vision once more, and flames and shadows danced.

"For once," she said, extending her hand, "that bitch was right."

Fire poured out of her like a thousand hearths. Like ten thousand suns, it engulfed Freydis, making the fires of Winde Port look like a mere match. The Arch Warlock tried to fight it, conjuring ice and water, but both melted and evaporated as Sora refused to relent. She screamed, unleashing every ounce of rage which had filled her since her earliest memory. She heard the voice of every man, woman, and child calling her knife-ear, telling her she was worthless. She saw the face of every mystic, taunting her within the red tower. Then, she saw Nesilia.

Her roar contorted into a single word. "Move!" she shouted, then hoisted the other hand and raised another pillar of flame beneath Wven-weigard. Whitney jumped back as the fire overtook the warlock.

Sora felt herself growing weary but refused to let up. Somewhere within it, Freydis screamed until all noise other than the roar of flames stopped.

Sora collapsed to her knees.

Whitney rushed to her, Aquira following.

"Are you okay?" he asked.

"I'm—Frey—"

"They're dead," Whitney said. "Really, really dead. Aquira, you're up. Fly to the cathedral and give the signal!"

Aquira screeched, nestling against Sora's side.

Sora nodded. "Go."

The little wyvern took off into the night sky, and Whitney helped Sora to her feet. A contingent of Drav Cra charged them, ready to avenge their Arch Warlock. Then a terrible scream echoed that definitely didn't belong to Freydis. Terror and sadness unconsciously clouded Sora's mind.

The warriors stopped, staring up at Mount Lister in fear. A rumble started in the distance. They turned to flee, but the earth shook, splitting rock. An explosion of light emanated from Mount Lister, and a crack coruscated down it toward them.

"What's that?" Sora said, weak.

"Hold on!" Whitney shouted.

Suddenly, they were falling.

Caught in a wild landslide, they plummeted. Rocks split off the walls around them, battering them. They slid, but the ride wasn't smooth at all. Sora felt as if they were going into the very depths of Elsewhere.

XLIV

THE KNIGHT

"Hold the line!" Torsten screamed as Nesilia's army crashed against the shields in front of him. He stabbed and thrust *Salvation,* but every possessed body that fell was immediately replaced by another. Torsten's ranks gave up ground fast. It actually felt like a tidal wave slamming into them, even with the spiders gone.

It didn't take long for the shield wall to be compromised either. Dire wolves, which Torsten had now started thinking of strictly as hellhounds—no natural animal left within them—pounded over the formation with no care for their own survival. Grimaurs slashed down from above. Demons body-hopped and attacked from behind before priests could absorb them, and as the number of remaining priests dwindled, that happened more and more often.

Darkness, in conjunction with dirt kicked up from trampling feet, made it impossible to see far. Torsten's world was reduced to the allies and enemies directly around him. He dodged talons and blades, hacked and slashed. Bodies smashed into him from every direction. There was no room to parry or fight anything one on one.

A hellhound soared over the men and tackled him. Claws ripped off one of his pauldrons before he plunged his sword through its chest. As he went to stand, a host of goblins jumped on him and stabbed away, mostly connecting with armor.

He flung one. Smashed another against a stone wall so hard it left his own shoulder burning with pain. He spun, only to find a black-eyed cultist charging him. The man gripped Torsten's throat with unnatural strength, and a knife raced toward his head.

Torsten bashed the man's arm down, freeing his neck. The knife grazed his flesh as he dipped out of the way, grasping the cultist's robes and hurling him at more possessed. He staggered, rasping, desperate for a fresh breath of air as the stifling dirt swirled around the markets. He needed to get free, but couldn't.

Even as he tried again, a grimaur dove onto the back of a soldier in front of him, digging in. Torsten swung and de-winged it, but the paralyzing agent in its talons petrified the victim. Shouldering by, Torsten narrowly avoided a slashing sword, then gutted something, the chill of a demon being freed overwhelming his senses. In this murk, he couldn't even tell if any priests were left down here.

Finally, he managed to fight his way to the edge of the fray.

"Sir Unger, the markets are overrun!" Sir Pimpero Bali yelled.

A hatchet landed in the man's neck, leaving his head hanging by a strand. His body collapsed.

Torsten swore and huffed to catch his breath.

He started up the slight incline of the Royal Avenue, and he turned to look upon the chaos. There was no order. They'd been overwhelmed on multiple fronts. Archers could no longer help as enemies surged over the walls. Not that they could've aimed without risking hitting one of their own, anyway.

We've bought as much time as we can, Torsten realized.

All he could do now was have faith that Sora had upheld her end of things, drawing in Nesilia by revealing her presence in dramatic fashion. And that Caleef Mahraveh had held back the waterfront invasion, and somehow managed to capture one of the wianu.

"Retreat!" Torsten screamed. "To Old Yarrington. Retreat!"

Sadly, most couldn't. The men still fighting across the markets wouldn't even be able to see which way retreat was. The archers on the walls struggled for their lives. And now it was against more than monsters. Torsten spotted the pale skin and markings of Drav Cra berserkers, charging in from northern Yarrington. They'd broken through as well.

Commanders relayed Torsten's orders, and those that could retreat did. Nesilia's quicker monsters broke out of the mob to give chase. Archers posted in the windows of shops and homes along the route let fly.

"C'mon, Sora," Torsten whispered to himself as he broke into a jog up the hill. "We need you."

It almost felt fated that Yarrington should be in the hands of the daughter its greatest king had apparently rejected. Was Iam playing a joke all along?

Suddenly, somebody emerged from an alley and tackled Torsten from the side at full force. His knees cracked the stone, but years of battle had honed his reflexes. He twisted as he went down, elbowing back and catching the attacker's chin. When his torso hit the ground, he'd freed himself enough to duck out of the way of a heavy gauntlet that split the stone pavers beside his head.

Torsten pushed off on his elbow, whipping *Salvation* in a wide arc with one hand. His assailant jumped back, the quick counter shaving a thin line across the man's breastplate. Rand stood before him, longsword drawn, blood pouring down his face through a straggly beard not befitting of a Shieldsman.

"You coward!" Torsten roared.

"Torsten, you—"

Before Rand could finish the sentence, Torsten was on his feet and rushing him. Rage fueled each swing of his sword, knocking Rand off balance as he did his best to parry. Before he could break Rand's grip with another strike, the traitor grabbed a retreating conscript and pushed him at Torsten.

"It wasn't enough for you to get our King killed?" Torsten said, stalking forward. "You had to drive your sword into the throne itself?"

"You don't understand!" Rand replied, hoarse.

"Lucas was a good man. Everything you never could be!"

Torsten pressed again. His claymore gave him superior reach, and he trounced Rand with raw strength. Clearly, he hadn't been training. His face and neck were as gaunt as the crazies spending a lifetime in the dungeons.

"I didn't want to kill him," Rand said. He blocked, and the force sent him staggering.

"Tell that to the blood on your hands!" Torsten raised his sword, but before he could swing, a hellhound came out of nowhere and bit his arm. *Salvation* dropped.

Rand recovered and stabbed forward, but Torsten yanked the beast down, and Rand hit it instead. When he released the heavy animal, it dragged Rand with it and pulled the sword from his grip.

Torsten ripped his arm free of the beast's clenched jaw, a fang stuck in his bare wrist. The momentum sent his fist crashing into the side of Rand's face. A second left hook sent him flying through the window of a bakery.

Glancing up and down the street, Torsten saw the chaos rushing up the avenue. Spiked logs were lit on fire and were now rolling down, crashing through the enemy ranks. Cavalry at the top prepared for a charge. Under heavy attack by grimaurs, the archers on rooftops fired almost aimlessly.

Torsten bit his lip, then scooped up *Salvation*.

"Lucas' parents had a place just like this," he said. "Now it burns, thanks to your master's army."

He moved through the shop's entry, and Rand jumped at him from behind. His gauntlet cracked against the back of Torsten's bald head, and he staggered into the counter. Rand quickly clutched Torsten's blindfold and pulled. Torsten held it, but without two hands couldn't get a good angle with his sword.

Another earthquake hit. Like with Bliss, a primordial howl echoed along with it. But this time, it wasn't Bliss. It shook the room enough to rock them both into a wall and knock them apart.

"What is she doing?" Torsten asked, peeling himself off the ground.

"I don't know," Rand replied, using the counter to try and stand.

Torsten pointed out the window, where the battle raged. "Is that her freeing this world?"

"I don't know!" he screamed.

"You knew when you killed my friend!"

Torsten charged, and Rand caught his hands. Torsten's shoulder rammed into Rand's chest and planted him onto his back, splitting the wood floor.

"You betrayed your people!" Torsten shouted as he punched the Eye of Iam sculpted into his Shieldsman chestplate. "You betrayed your king." He punched again. "You betrayed me!"

The third blow splintered the wood right beside Rand's head. The weakling writhed to get free. His arms lay back flat, and he coughed up a gob of blood.

"All your blame for Oleander and you became the executioner for something so much worse," Torsten said, voice quaking. Again, he had Rand at his mercy, and he couldn't bring himself to do it, no matter how much he hated him.

"Torsten…" Rand gurgled. "She took control of the glaruium in my armor. She did it. She brought the sword down."

"Liar!" Torsten snarled.

Rand shook his head. "It doesn't matter. It doesn't… I—I don't know if I would have done it myself anymore. Or if she made me. I don't know. I—I just want to see her…"

"Your sister?" Torsten replied. "You've betrayed her memory worst of all, Rand Langley."

"No, I talked to her!" Raising his voice sent him into a fit of coughing. "I talked to her. This is what she wants. She's saving our world."

"You know that isn't her."

He squeezed his eyelids shut. "It is. It has to be."

"It isn't."

Torsten shoved off the floor with his fists, retrieving *Salvation* on his way. He squeezed the grip, staring down at the pathetic excuse for a man. He'd left him like this in Latiapur, and, somehow, he'd come crawling back like a rat. If he'd killed him then, Lucas might still be alive. But he knew that wasn't true. Nesilia used Lucas to taunt Torsten, and if Rand hadn't been the one holding the sword, it would have been someone else. Rand was a tool. Nothing more.

That was how Torsten knew Rand's Sigrid didn't remain in any capacity. Not in her upyr form. Not in Nesilia's mind. No sister would ever use a brother in such a way. Rand groaned as he dragged his body and propped up against the counter, his crushed armor constricting his movements.

"Just do it," Rand moaned. "End it already. I don't want to live anymore. Not like this."

Torsten hoisted *Salvation*. He could see hope in Rand's eyes that it might finally end. Instead, he rested the blade against his shoulder and moved to the doorway. He could hear sobbing behind him, but that was the least Rand deserved.

Madness awaited outside. The cavalry had charged down, trampling goblins and possessed men, but the Drav Cra had halted their charge. A giant, furry beast rampaged through the market, its tusks killing ally and enemy.

Above the clamor of it all, Torsten heard the familiar bells of Yarrington Cathedral chiming. He remembered the plan. When Freydis was dead, Aquira was to fly up and ring those sacred bells.

"Please…" Rand rasped, crawling into the threshold of the bakery shop's doorway.

Torsten glanced back at the traitor and his broken body. In that moment, all he could feel for the man was pity.

"I'm no executioner," Torsten said, and then rushed out. He stuck to the shadows of the overhangs, but it was impossible to avoid a fight. Horses rumbled by. Arrows glanced off all around. Buildings burned. Others crumbled.

He'd allowed Rand to steal his focus for the last time. Former Shieldsmen arrayed at the top of the hill, at the archway welcoming citizens to Old Yarrington. It was broken in the center, the sign hanging from one side. The Shieldsmen covered his approach. All those who retreated from the markets flowed through the castle gates and mounted its walls.

Old Yarrington was located upon a bluff, but grimaurs were already terrorizing the civilians hunkered down in mansions, and beating at the windows of the Cathedral.

"Sir Unger!" Sir Mulliner said, approaching the gates with a regiment. "You made it."

"Barely," Torsten said. He stopped to gather his breath. "Sora. Did she do it? Is the warlock slain?"

"I'm not sure. She chased her out beyond the walls, and I—I… I had to call a retreat. We collapsed the northern stairs to Old Yarrington. The heathens will have to go around, but it won't buy long."

"You did well," Torsten said. "Pull all defenses to the keep. Hold, as long as you can."

"Yes, sir. Where are you going?"

"To the Throne Room, to end this."

"What if she failed?" Mulliner asked.

Torsten seized him by the shoulders and gave a firm shake. "I have faith, my friend."

Sir Mulliner nodded, and not a second later was barking orders throughout the courtyard, prepping the castle for the maelstrom of death that was to come.

Torsten rushed into the courtyard, where he found Uhlvark sitting by the fountain, arms around his knees, chin to his massive chest.

"Uhlvark, my friend, are you okay?" Torsten asked. "Where's Dellbar?"

The giant splashed a bit of water and stuck out his lower lip. "Friend Dellbar say he has to go to crypt alone. No Uhlvark."

"Then I'm sure he had a very good reason." Torsten moved to his side and pointed back at the gate. "Do you see those doors? When the retreat is through, the enemy is going to try and break through them. You can help hold them closed. No matter what. Do this, and you'll protect everyone."

The giant perked up. "Even friend Torsten?"

"Especially me." Torsten gave him a pat, and the giant seemed invigorated. Torsten didn't even mind that the clumsy thing broke the fountain's dragon statue as he used it to stand.

If the age was truly ending, what was one more relic gone?

XLV

THE CALEEF

With Babrak's army charging into South Corner, Mahi was left in Dockside, surrounded by death and Current Eaters. There was no opportunity for ambush. Bit'rudam and Lord Jolly called for charges, and an all-out, bloody war between the now-equally-matched sides initiated.

Out in the inlet, bodies floated, carried upon sloshing waves produced by flailing sea creatures. Ships burned, sending thick, black, and putrid-smelling smoke into a sky just as dark. Whale oil continued to burn with no regard for the water surrounding it. Even in Trader's Strait, Mahi had never seen such an inferno dancing upon the sea.

She closed her eyes. Is this what they'd become? Those were her people out there, even those belonging to Babrak. How could any of them have chosen to follow Nesilia? What could she have promised that was worth all this?

No matter what she'd promised, death is all that's been delivered, Mahi thought.

She stood, back to a city on fire, looking out beyond the Current Eaters who continued to ravage the docks and surrounding buildings. Turning, she opened her eyes. The fires burned hot, but she didn't feel them. Before her, Dockside was little more than smoking cinder. The death throes of the Shesaitju bombarded her from every direction. Sadness overwhelmed her, knowing that each voice, regardless of which side they were on, belonged to a Shesaitju brother.

Yarrington in flames. It was what so many of her ancestors, including her father, had spent much of their lives dreaming of. Even the memories of the Caleefs within her mind echoed the sentiment. Now, seeing it in fruition, it made her sick.

She took slow steps, eyes traveling the tragedy enveloping her. She wanted to jump back into the battle, join her people, embarrass Babrak with a loss, but she had a job to do. She needed to capture a Current Eater, and the ones rampaging into South Corner were surrounded by allies and enemies. Too many chances for it to go wrong. She needed one isolated. No chance for interference.

Her thoughts were interrupted by a voice.

"Dijent!" came the cry in Saitjuese. *Help.*

It called again, and Mahi followed the sound to a warrior lying on the stairs leading toward South Corner's market district. He was surrounded by licking flames. His gray skin was charred and bloody. His hair, if he'd had any before the battle, was singed off. And his legs… they were shredded gore, torn off, one at the knee and one at the hip. As he bled, he cried, begging for help.

It was one of the enemies, one of Babrak's traitors. She stood over him, her face betraying no emotion.

"Caleef, Saiduni'min feydlik, dijent," he said. *Please, help me, my Caleef.*

She continued to stare down, wondering how this man could have the audacity to call her that after what he'd just taken part in.

"Please," he said in common.

She took one step forward, then knelt.

"You've brought dishonor to our people," she said.

He didn't answer. Just closed his eyes. Tears mingled with sweat, and he struggled to open them again.

"*You've brought dishonor to our people,*" Mahi repeated, this time in Saitjuese.

"And may the God of Sand and Sea forgive me," he said with an effort.

"Because of your actions, he may be unable to," she answered as she drove her spear between his ribs and into his heart. She twisted as she removed it, his eyes going wide. She wondered what he'd see next. Blackness? Nothing at all? Or would he somehow float upon the Eternal Current, even without Caliphar or the Sirens to guide him?

Then another thought struck her. Would he see Iam—the God of the Glass to whom so many of her people had feigned worship of for all these years?

She rose, letting the blade drag across the man's tunic, cleaning it of blood as if it wouldn't just get sullied again.

With the number of dying warriors littering the docks, she could have spent all day there, bringing ease to their agony. The battle, however, continued to rage just beyond the flames. She could hear it all over the city, and as more enemies swam ashore throughout the docks, they would gain an advantage. Her people were engaged in mortal warfare, fighting for lives where the future was a question mark. All while Babrak remained with his honor guard at the rear, issuing orders but too cowardly to join the fight.

A part of her still begged her to charge in and take him on alone. But her job here wasn't done. And as more and more of the exposed Current Eaters disappeared below the waters, she knew she needed to move quickly. If her allies managed to trap Nesilia, they weren't sure if one of the monsters would be willing to devour her. She needed to leave one without that choice.

Finding a spot on the docks least affected by the fires, she struck down an enemy climbing up, then dove headfirst. She hit the water and felt it against her skin, one of the few sensations she could experience. Like she was one with the sea. Eyes open, she searched, but it was dark. The fires burning on the surface created eerie, disorienting shadows.

First, she was looking for any Current Eaters that would pose a threat. Secondly, she needed one alive... and trapped. If they all escaped, there'd be precious little hope of defeating Nesilia. The entire plan now rested upon her shoulders.

She heard everything underwater with such clarity, as if the Current itself spoke to her. What she didn't hear was the voice of her God. He remained silent, missing, dead. More bodies hovered below the surface. Some swam for land. Others were riddled with arrows or had the weight of armor dragging them downward. Eyes were stuck open, accusing, staring at her like this was all her fault.

Something brushed against her leg, startling her and forcing her to breathe sharply. Coughing, she pushed toward the surface. She grasped for anything, finding a dead Glass soldier. She used him to float until he began to sink. Water evacuated her lungs, and she returned her focus to whatever touched her. Diving again, her head swiveled but saw nothing but darkness. Until…

Everything lit up like the brightest noonday sun, except it was bright green. Suddenly, swooping all around her were nigh'jels. She reached out, let her hand brush one of the jelly-like creatures. It was a piece of home in this foreign place, and somehow, confirmation that she was right where she needed to be.

Her elation was immediately cut short as two giant orbs glinted in the distance. A plume of bubbles rose, and with it, eight massive tentacles. She could also see her target—a ship she knew to have one of Babrak's hunting ballistae on board.

She kicked with a fury, zipping around floating bodies and chains. At the same time, the Current Eater shoved off, and it covered the distance much quicker. At this rate, there was no chance of her reaching the ship before becoming entangled with the beast. If it came to that, there was no chance she'd survive.

She saw the surface, but was afraid to break through, knowing that as soon as she did, she'd lose sight of the thing… but she would eventually need to breathe. She swam, fast as she could, growing ever closer to the ship. At first, she didn't see it, but she felt it. The gentle ripples coming from beside her, just outside of her peripherals. Another Current Eater approached from her right, this one even closer. She spun, tore her spear from its place upon her back, and readied for an in-water battle.

Darkness overwhelmed her, disorienting her until she realized the nigh'jels had rushed from her side. They were swarming the Current Eaters, disrupting their charge, and buying Mahi the time she needed. She couldn't hesitate. She wouldn't waste this opportunity.

Her hand grasped the wood of the ship, smooth and unclimbable. But then, she saw a hole in its hull, water rushing in. She swam for it, following the rip of the tide. Just as she was about to enter, a giant, slippery head broke the surface beneath her, lifting her high above the waters. Tentacles slapped and slashed, barely missing her in a vain attempt to remove her skull. Like the practiced warrior she was, she regained her composure and used the attack to her advantage. She needed to board the ship, and this thing was taking her right to its deck.

A tentacle came at her, and she stabbed, drawing thick, black blood. It screamed, primal, raw. Another raced toward her from behind, and she ducked just before it could do its damage. She slashed again. Then, looking over her shoulder, she found the ship wreckage. Shaky and rocking back and forth upon the thing's head, she steadied herself and pushed off, landing hard on the wood deck. After a roll, she came back up with her spear poised for battle. But she saw nothing.

Then, all at once, the ship rose, thrusting Mahraveh to the ground. She slid from one side of the deck to the other, shoulder slamming into the center mast on the way. The vessel came down hard, and Mahi went airborne. Her stomach flipped, and then she plummeted until she slammed the deck, her face leading the way. She tasted fresh blood in her mouth and knew she'd lost at least one tooth.

Scrambling to her feet, she brandished her spear this way and that, guarding against any unseen attack. When she was sure none was coming, she rushed to the side of the ship where the Current Eater would be and drove her spear into one of the tentacles that still draped over the railing. Hot blood gushed out. She pulled it free and pierced the creature again and again. But it didn't stop. It barely slowed down as, now, its head appeared over the railing. Those eyes—giant globes that begged her to cast herself into their depths—looked like bottomless pits. Spit-coated teeth like scythes spread apart, stained with blood. A stench like rotten fish and fetid beer assaulted her, and the sound of thunder threatened to deafen her.

Another tentacle rose, this one with a chain attached to it, wrapped around it and digging in with many barbs. The chain swung, crashing through the main mast and scraping across the deck.

Mahi turned and ran toward the prow where she knew the ballista would be. The ship lurched, and it took all her focus to stay upright, but she managed. Reaching the ballista, she slid on her knees to a halt. The weapon was empty, a body slumped over it, and she saw no munitions of any kind nearby.

Swearing, she spun. The ship lurched again, and she heard a clatter. Her head snapped toward the noise, and she spotted the ballista missiles sliding around, a couple dangling through the railings on the port side. Fighting to stay upright, she rushed over, and as she reached them, one fell through, leaving only three.

Mahi swore. She could achieve her goals with three, but it would be a tight victory if one at all. Right now, however, she had one focus, to end this Current Eater before it ended her.

With that thought lingering, a second head popped up behind her and slammed into the ship on the other side. Suddenly, she was caught between two Current Eaters like two dogs fighting over one bone, and she was the bone. The ship rocked back and forth and sent her stumbling toward the middle.

She snatched up a ballista bolt before getting tossed away and used the momentum to bring her with force toward the first Current Eater. She jumped, letting the missile lead the way. It glanced the creature's head, causing quite a large gash. It wouldn't be enough. Her feet landed on the railing, and she teetered, trying to find balance. Before she could, her solar plexus was met by a wet, slapping tentacle. She skidded across the ship before a backward summersault allowed her to regain her footing.

The Current Eater retreated, but she knew it wouldn't be for long. She broke into a sprint, still carrying the missile. It was heavier than she'd expected.

Waves swelled high, soaking the deck, but Mahraveh's bare feet had no trouble on the blackwood deck. It felt natural. It felt like home.

She reached the ballista, pushed the body off, and cranked the wheel until the string was taut. Then, placing the bolt in the slit, she rotated, aiming it at the second Current Eater. Its maw opened wide as it roared. Three tentacles, large enough to be monsters all on their own, ascended into the dark sky and slammed down with authority, breaking the deck in half.

Mahi held steady. She took aim, and just as she was about to fire, she felt a tentacle wrap her ankle, and she was upside down a second later.

The first monster had recovered and was now back on the offensive.

You are the snake, she heard in her head as she was heaved up into the air. It was her own voice, but it sounded so much like her father. *My sand mouse…*

"For Muskigo!" Mahi shouted, letting out her rage.

She tucked her belly and bent at the waist. Grasping the beast's appendage with one hand, she redrew her spear from her back and whipped it around. The tip of the tentacle sheared off, and Mahi fell. She landed hard on her back. Air rushed from her lungs, but she didn't stop. She stood, stabbed, and stabbed again. The deck was now saturated with black ichor, slippery and sticky at the same time.

One of her strikes landed just above the creature's mouth, the other just under its eye. While it was distracted, she rushed back to the ballista. The second Current Eater loomed over her, having ravaged through the other half of the ship, about to devour her. She fired the ballista straight through its still-open mouth, the teeth already closing in around her. The bolt burst through the back of its head in a fine spray of gore.

She released the ballista and jumped, her back bashing against the ship's railing as the thing's teeth clamped inches away from her. The sound of it wheezing was like a winter storm. That hole, causing the creature to be unable to draw breath, would eventually be its demise. But it wasn't going down easy.

Thrashing, it shattered more of the ship, and one tentacle collided with the ballista. The weapon broke free from its foundation and was cast into the sea.

"No!" Mahi shouted, grasping futilely as if she were strong enough to catch it.

To make matters worse, the broken ship was sinking fast.

The other Current Eater recovered, striking again with its chained tentacle, and Mahi dove, narrowly avoiding the barbed metal. It gave her an idea, but she knew it might kill her.

As the tentacle whipped back around, she grabbed hold of it, letting it land against her belly, luckily finding a non-barbed length. More air rushed out of her, but she held on, wrapping both arms over the top of the appendage. The chain rattled at the end, and she rode the momentum.

When the tentacle reached its zenith, she mounted it like a zhulong. Then, she waited, patient until the time was right. Spotting the last link in the chain, she thrust her spear through the hole and drew the chain to herself. Grasping it tightly, she then leaped into the depths of Autla's Inlet right before the roaring monster could drop her into its mouth.

The saltwater stung her many abrasions in a way she hadn't expected, at least not since becoming Caleef. The waters burst with green light as the nigh'jels quickly rejoined her like a living shield.

Mahi swam, still holding the end of the chain. She stayed close to the Current Eater's gigantic, squishy frame, weaving in and out of undulating tentacles, doing her best to pull them together. Thanks to her Shesaitju origin, she was a good swimmer. But not good enough. A limb bashed her back, and she shot down toward the monster's rising mouth.

Its teeth snapped at her, but nigh'jels rushed in and veiled her movements, allowing her to escape before being sawed in half. She pushed off one, rising with the chain, then hit a floating chunk of wood and pushed back down.

The creature flailed wildly, slapping nigh'jels away. But it was too late. Mahi had half of its tentacles bound, and the other half were injured from battle.

They reached and grabbed at her, but soon, with the nigh'jels still swarming it, disorienting it, confusing it, and blinding it to Mahi's position, those too were disabled and caught up in the chain. The barbs dug in, staining the waters with inky blood. It looked like strings of yarn as it flowed through the green-washed waters.

As soon as she could, she took the loose end of the chain and lugged it against her shoulder toward Babrak's ship. She looped it around the prow, a carving of a large fish with a long, jagged nose.

Nigh'jels lifted against her soles and helped her reach the deck. The ship was half-sunken but too large to be entirely submerged in the inlet. She retrieved another ballista bolt, dove, and used it to jam the chains around the stump of the foremast.

Then she collapsed, lungs begging for air, stinging and heaving. From there, she watched as the Current Eater fought her web of chains. Unable to use its tentacles, its head was pinned against the prow. Wood creaked as it struggled, but the more it did, the more her makeshift pulley-system kept it in place. So long as the missile held, it couldn't get leverage to pull free even with its incredible strength.

Finally able to catch her breath, she rushed to grab anything else she could find to help keep the chains jammed. As she did, she looked back at the city. Many of the sea beasts had been caught in the inferno and lay screaming, a bloodcurdling sound. Others were torn apart by the chains and left dead. Others still fought with Babrak, rampaging through South Corner and her people. One could even be seen in the distance, climbing the southern walls of the Glass Castle.

Between it and her, all her army and Babrak's warred. She couldn't help them, only watch; only hope that in that mess of smoke, fire, and killing, Bit'rudam was still holding steady. Buying time for the others.

She held the chains, making sure the Current Eater stayed put, and she watched, waiting to see Torsten, or Sora, or anyone rushing toward the inlet with Nesilia as trapped as the beast before her.

All she could do was pray that they would have as much success in their own efforts.

Only, she didn't know who to pray to.

XLVI

THE MYSTIC

Sora searched from side to side. When the dust settled, she was given a view of a familiar room. Glass caskets were propped up on all walls except the one they'd just broken through. Statues of Kings were toppled and broken. Drav Cra warriors caught in the collapse groaned.

"My Lady, you came…" a voice rasped. Sora followed it, and moonlight filtering in through the devastated ceiling illuminated Freydis. She lay on her back, body shriveled as if she'd given every ounce of her blood toward trying to survive Sora's onslaught. Barely breathing, but somehow still alive.

"And you failed me, my dearest servant," a soft, seductive voice spoke from the shadows. Sora knew it too well. "Don't be scared. You will be avenged, and then, you will be replaced by one more worthy.

A silhouette appeared over Freydis, but Sora couldn't see Nesilia clearly in the darkness. She squeezed Freydis' throat, lifted her to her mouth, and drank what little blood she had left. Then, she dropped the desiccated corpse to the stone.

Sigrid's form stood tall, her shadow facing Sora. Then she vanished.

"Ah, my other body." Her voice echoed through the crypt, cold, and heartless. "Such convenience, this place. It's almost as if ordained by some… deity."

Sora groaned and extended her hand, slapping aimlessly, hoping Whitney was there. Alive.

"Oh, sweet Sora," Nesilia said. "Everything horrible that has ever happened to you was his fault, and yet you still cling to him like a lost child."

"Shog off," Sora said.

"He *is* rubbing off on you, isn't he?" Nesilia laughed.

"I killed your servant," Sora taunted. "She chose you and failed. Just like you will."

"Where are we?" Whitney moaned, then coughed.

"Such a good question for such a dumb fool," Nesilia said.

"Hey," Whitney argued, but it was clear his heart wasn't in it.

Sora still couldn't see him from where she was. He must have rolled into another chamber of the crypts in the slide. She pushed to her feet and stumbled a few steps. Between the fall and that immeasurable use of magic to defeat Freydis, her head spun, and her stomach ached.

"We are exactly where we need to be," Nesilia said. "So close to where I spent the last several thousand years, and where my dear sister now resides, rest her soul. Oh, who am I kidding? She has no soul."

"You… killed Bliss?" Sora asked. "Your own sister?"

"Buried, not dead," Nesilia jested.

"Good. Because in my experience, she doesn't stay dead anyway," Whitney remarked.

"Bliss would have done the same to me if she got the chance," Nesilia said. "But she never had any vision. I used her for her talent for breaking things apart, and now, she will watch for eternity as I reclaim my world."

"Oh, I do enjoy a pair of loving siblings," Whitney said.

"You're a monster, Nesilia," Sora said. "Maybe, if you weren't busy betraying your sister, Freydis would still be alive. And you talk about others abandoning the ones they loved?"

"Freydis was meant to stand on her own," Nesilia hissed. "My world has no room for the meek."

Sora could now see Whitney, standing just a few meters away near the altar to Iam. He turned in a slow circle, looking for Nesilia just as Sora was. Sora took a few steps toward Whitney over crumbled stone. She embraced him.

"It's goddess killing time," Whitney said, wielding his daggers.

"Touching," Nesilia said, appearing in the center of the room. Moonlight filtered in through a hole in the ceiling just above King Liam's broken statue. It illuminated Sigrid's body, almost glowing a soft silver.

At the thought, Sora palmed her silver shortsword. The temptation to plunge it through Nesilia's stolen heart was strong, but she knew it would accomplish nothing. Furthermore, it might cause Nesilia to re-enter Sora or even Whitney, and both options were out of the question.

"Sigrid," Whitney said, stepping forward. "Don't you remember me? We had good times together with old Kazzy, no? Remember when you tried to eat me, and I screamed?"

"What are you doing?" Sora whisper-shouted.

"I don't know."

Nesilia tilted her head like a dog, and in a heartbeat's span, she had Whitney in her grasp. She lifted him by his collar.

"The things my host once tried and failed to do would be as simple as breathing for me," Nesilia said. She licked Whitney's face, tasting his blood. Closing her eyes, she moaned with delight. "Sweet Sora, you took my beloved Freydis from me. It's only fair he join her."

"Put him down, Nesilia!" Sora warned, squeezing the sword and circling around to her side.

"If you say so," Nesilia said before launching Whitney across the room with a single flick of her wrists.

Whitney landed in a heap by the dungeon entrance. He didn't move. Didn't make a sound.

"If you've hurt him, I will—"

"You'll what?" Nesilia stalked toward Sora. "What will you do? You gave up so much for that pathetic little thing. Love... You could have had it all!"

"I could have had it all, and the best you could give me was a wrinkled old pirate?" Sora countered. "If that's your idea of blessings, I think I'll stick with Iam's curses."

"Don't you dare speak that name," Nesilia said. Dust fell from the ceiling, and Whitney stirred. "Iam is gone. Caliphar is gone. Bliss is gone. All that remains of the Feud is me. Forgotten, just like you, but now I stand in victory over them all!"

"Look around you. This is victory? Queen of nothing. Goddess of nothing."

Nesilia smiled, then turned back toward the center of the crypt.

Sora took the opportunity to glance toward Whitney. She didn't know if he was okay, but at least he was breathing.

"Look at all of these pathetic Kings," Nesilia said. "Your *family*. I wonder, did you tell Torsten who you really are? You think they would accept you? An outcast. A bastard? They'd hang you and bury you with your little secret."

"There's a difference between you and me, you know," Sora said, still not looking at Nesilia.

"Mmmm. Is there?"

"You were forgotten, but I never was," Sora said, now focusing her gaze on King Liam's casket.

"Is that so?"

Sora finally stepped down from the pile of stones. "You see, I was hidden. Protected. Because of love, I was placed in the care of another. Someone who would watch over me."

"So cute," Nesilia said. "By him?" She pointed at Liam's casket. "He loved no one but himself. Just like his precious Iam. He didn't care about you. He only cared that no one finds out about you. With that, he would've been so disgraced."

"You're wrong," Sora said. "You don't know how to care about anything but yourself. Freydis. Bliss. Me..."

Out of the corner of her eye, Sora saw Whitney stand, still wobbly. Inside her mind, she begged him to stay down, to not try anything stupid. Where he was, in his state, he was safe. For now.

"All failures," Nesilia said. "All weak. Relying on others to clean up their messes."

"Freydis loved you."

"And I, her," Nesilia said, solemn. "Which is why I'm here. Despite how she failed, the one who took her shall feel pain you can't imagine... yet. I will take the one you love, and rip him to pieces." Her sights landed on Whitney, and she flaunted her fangs with a hiss.

"As always, you're wrong." Sora focused her remaining strength. Within her mind's eye, she could sense the flow of blood through her whole body. She called upon its power, one drop at a time. She recalled how she'd seen Nesilia do it when she'd taught Freydis to burrow through the ground to slaughter the Strongiron dwarves. Sora used the memory. Though this time, she didn't burrow, she called the stone down.

Like it had happened in the Webbed Woods when she beat Redstar, Sora's eyes shone bright white, light exploded from her, and her face twisted into unnatural forms. She could feel her pulse within her every fiber. The crypt shook, rumbled, quaked. It wasn't like uprooting a small chunk of earth as she'd done to Freydis.

Nesilia had no time to realize she was being buried once more until the stone above her collapsed. Statues were crushed. Caskets destroyed. The history of the Nothhelm dynasty was shattered in an instant.

Sora knew it wouldn't kill Nesilia. She didn't need it to. She just needed it to buy enough time for their escape. To get to the Throne Room where the others would hopefully be waiting to carry out the plan. And she had no doubt now. She'd pissed Nesilia off enough that she would chase.

Giant rocks crashed all around them. Mount Lister had now joined the battle in full, still reeling from whatever Nesilia had done with Bliss.

When Sora reached Whitney, she grabbed him and pushed him toward the dungeons.

"Are you okay?" she asked as they staggered through the archway.

Even now, she could hear the stones behind her moving, Nesilia breaking through.

"I was just about to retaliate," he said.

Sora smiled. "Come on."

"Fine, I suppose you can have this one."

XLVII

THE THIEF

Regaining strength, Whitney tugged on Sora's hand as they rushed through the dungeons and back upstairs to the rear entry of the Throne Room. After her explosion of power to slow Nesilia, Sora seemed weaker even than Whitney. It appeared to be a struggle, her just holding Aquira.

"Let us in, let us in!" Whitney shouted to the guards posted there. There were at least two dozen of them, with shield and longswords, ready to clog the passage.

"Nobody in," the lead one said, a former Shieldsman by the looks of him. It was impossible to know now that Torsten ditched their armor, but they just had a… look... like they thought they were better than all the other brave warriors around them.

"Nobody in? I was just in there!" Whitney shrieked.

"We have our orders."

"It's the yigging dwarves all over again," Whitney said under his breath, clenching his fist. Now it was Sora's turn to gain strength again. He had no idea how she managed after all she'd done, but Sora pulled herself ahead of him before he cursed the guards and their parents and their parents' parents.

"Nesilia…" she panted. "Is coming…"

The Shieldsman's eyes went wide. Others behind him muttered amongst each other in fear.

"I-I'm sorry, b-but nobody gets in," the man finally decided.

"Now listen here, you sorry pile of steaming shog," Whitney said. With her eyes, Sora begged him not to make things worse, but guards were his speci-al-ity. "The Buried Goddess is on her way here. Do you all want to be the reason that the world ends?"

More muttering came from the group.

"Do you?" Whitney went on, sticking his finger in the man's chest. "Sir Unger has entrusted us with saving Pantego. And her, do you know who she is?"

Sora nudged Whitney in the ribs, as she had all too many times in their relationship. One day, he'd tell her how her bony elbow actually really hurt, but only when he got tired of the pain reminding him they were finally back together.

She drew her small blade halfway from its sheath, the rasp earning the attention of the guards. The elaborate, gold and jeweled hilt had a crystal Eye of Iam for a pommel.

Whitney wasn't sure why he hadn't thought of showing the gifts.

"We're with Sir Unger," she said.

The Shieldsman looked back, then sighed. He stepped aside, and the rest joined him. "Don't make me regret this."

"C'mon," Sora said, wasting no time.

Whitney stood on his toes and stared the Shieldsman straight in the eyes. "A shame, how far your Order has fallen." He shook his head. "A yigging shame." Then he followed Sora.

"Yer all right, Lassie!" Tum Tum exclaimed, waddling over to hug her.

"We feared the worst," Lucindur said, joining him.

"Yeah, yeah, we're all fine," Whitney interrupted before anyone said anything else useless. "Perfect. Dandy. Lucy, are you ready to play?"

"My salfio is right here." She patted the strap over her shoulder.

"Well, get it off your back! Nesilia is coming. Right now, she's—"

The main Throne Room doors swung open, Whitney spun around so fast he lost his footing and slipped. Torsten appeared in the entry, gripping *Salvation,* which was as covered with mud and blood as his ever-grim face. And Whitney had never been happier to see him.

"Finally, someone who might take things seriously!" Whitney said as Tum Tum helped him up.

"I heard the bells," Torsten called. "Is it true? Is the warlock dead?"

"Oh, she's dead all right," Whitney answered. "Fried to a crisp and worse. Oh, and Nesilia's yigging pissed."

"She came after us through the crypt," Sora said. "I—I…" Her head sank. "I collapsed it on her, but it won't delay her long."

"Then we better be ready," Torsten said, not even missing a beat at the news of his beloved crypt being destroyed.

"Thank you!" Whitney threw up his hands. "Finally, someone who gets it. Now, Tum Tum, where is the Brike Stone?"

"I put it down right over there." Tum Tum pointed to the throne. A cloth covered what Whitney assumed to be the blood-red stone. It sat on the seat of the throne, bathed in an aura of darkness. Around the stone, even the glass of the throne, polished beyond reason, reflected nothing. It was dull, colorless.

Whitney grasped the dwarf by his collar. "I told you not to let go of it!"

"We were right next to the thing," Tum Tum said. "I tried holdin it, but it hurt. Made me start thinkin of things I'd rather not be thinkin bout."

A scathing response died on Whitney's tongue. The dwarf's expression spoke of horror, and Whitney knew those dark thoughts. He had them every time he touched the stone. Only, they barely affected him because he'd had all those thoughts and worse during a six-year stay in Elsewhere itself.

"I've got it." Whitney hurried over and snatched it off the throne. Even through the cloth, despair assaulted his brain. Thoughts of losing the battle—of everyone and everything dying. But he'd learned that when the claws of darkness start to dig in, all you can do is smile.

Across the hall, Torsten barked orders. Soldiers flooded through the front doors, men who looked like Shieldsmen along with the terrifying Shesaitju Serpent Guards. The faceless, tongueless killers were scarier than even the stone in Whitney's palm.

"This way, Milady," Torsten said, ushering Lucindur away from the throne and toward an expanse of gray stone wall farthest from every entrance.

"Thank you," she said, flashing a reticent smile as she unfurled a sheet, then kneeled upon it. She strummed her salfio once, finding the perfect tune, and the note resonated all the way up the towering glass spire in the center of the room.

The soldiers formed ranks all around her, Glassmen and Shesaitju alternating—a force that would make enemies tremble. Everyone except Nesilia that is.

"Are you okay?" Whitney asked Sora, who remained standing by the throne, staring at it. Was she wondering what could be? Or perhaps, listening to the soft refrain of screams and destruction echoing from beyond the castle walls as thousands laid down their lives to protect this room.

"Sora?" he whispered.

She shook her head. "It's nothing. I'm fine."

"You're scared to go into her head," Whitney said. "Scared of the darkness." He clasped her hand, the Brike Stone within smothering them in their own shadow as if they were in a tiny room together. "Don't be. Embrace it. Show her she's nothing compared to you. Because, you know what? She isn't. You're Sora of Troborough, daughter of kings and mystics, and the woman who stole the heart of the World's Greatest Thief."

He flashed her a grin, and Sora threw her arms around him, pressing her lips against his. The Brike Stone showed Whitney images of her death over and over again as they touched, but he didn't let go, because he knew there was no way in Elsewhere he'd ever let that happen.

"If ye two lovebirds don't mind!" Tum Tum called, barely visible through the wall of soldiers save for his oversized hammer.

"Right," Sora said with vim and resolve that Whitney hoped meant she really was ready. It's not like the entire future of the world was resting on her shoulders or anything.

They rushed through the soldiers, and Sora sat directly across from Lucindur and Tum Tum, who stood guard beside her. Whitney drew his daggers and stood by her side.

"It ends today," Torsten said, unwavering.

"One way or another," Whitney added.

Torsten nodded to Whitney and all the others, then moved to the front of the formation. And then, there was eerie quiet. The kind that made Whitney itch and want to say something uncomfortable as if by reflex. Only, in the face of what was coming, he couldn't.

Death wails sounded like Elsewhere's wind coming from every direction outside of the room. Each time, making Whitney's muscles tense.

A high-pitched screech nearly made him shog himself until he realized it was only Aquira bursting through a stained glass window high above. She landed upon Sora's shoulder, squawking again as Sora scratched her chin.

Something crashed through the door just outside the Throne Room, the one leading toward the dungeons where Nesilia would be soon following. There were more cries, then, seconds later, none.

"Lucy," Whitney managed to force through trembling lips. "I think it's time to start."

"I—I agree." She strummed a chord. "Relax your mind, Sora. Let the music flow over you, through you."

The door blew off its hinges, a body bursting through and sliding across the marble. The white-haired form of Nesilia's upyr body crouched over it, twisting the corpse's neck at an unnatural angle as she drank from its throat.

"I'm beginning to enjoy the taste of your people," she said, her voice swirling about the Throne Room like a serpent's hiss. "Perhaps I'll keep some around. Enjoy feasts right in this hall like your corrupt Kings."

She let the body fall with a *clank*, then licked her lips as she sauntered forward. "This is something beautiful, isn't it?"

She looked upward toward the painted ceiling.

"Except that," she said, pointing. "Iam casting down some hideous beast to the depths of the mountain. Who developed this depiction of me?"

Whitney recalled the murals upon the walls in Redstar's ruins—the first time he'd seen the Buried Goddess represented as anything other than a monster.

"And Iam," she laughed. "Of course, he would be nothing but a blinding light to your people. You worship a god without even caring what he looks like?"

She shook her head and focused on those assembled in the room. No one spoke.

"Look at all of you. Gathered here to die." Her gaze snapped toward Sora. "I'm so disappointed in you. Did you think it poetic? Burying me?"

"I thought it was what you deserved," Sora said.

"Perhaps," she said. Her face went rigid, and she rushed across the room with blinding speed.

"Now!" Torsten thundered.

Lucindur's fingers started to pluck, sounds like the ocean washing across a beach. Pleasant and harmonious in a moment when chaos and suffering ruled. Whitney watched as her eyes rolled into the back of her head, wondering if he, too, looked like that when he went under the Lightmancer's spell.

Nesilia fell to one knee, grasping at her head within meters of the guards surrounding Sora. Her upyr speed would have had them all cut to pieces in no time, but Sora's connection seemed to be enough to slow her.

"Fools," Nesilia growled. "Attempting this pathetic move again? It won't work."

Torsten glanced back at Whitney. "When you see the opening, get that stone in her hands."

"I'm really better at taking gems *out* of hands," Whitney replied.

"Now, isn't the time. Take her!"

Torsten brandished his claymore, and together with the Shieldsmen and Serpent Guards, they charged. Nesilia may have been hampered by the magic, but she still wasn't completely useless. She drew Sigrid's own Breklian knives and sprang to action.

She deflected and stabbed, mowing through the guards one at a time. It may not have been with lightning speed, but still, other than Kazimir, it was unlike anything Whitney had ever witnessed. She couldn't be hit.

Her shoulder collided with a Glass soldier's knee, toppling him. As he fell, she gashed his throat while, at the same time, ducking under Torsten's mighty swing, bending backward in a manner that seemed impossible while sliding forward. As she twisted, she flung a knife at Lucindur, still seated. But Tum Tum had guessed right and jumped. It caught him in the leg with enough force to hurl him, spinning against the wall as if he'd been hit by a catapult.

"Tum Tum!" Whitney screamed. He clutched his silver daggers and went to join the slaughter when a deafening crash above sent him diving, hands over his head. Glass throughout the spire shattered, raining down like sharp, deadly hail.

A wave of grimaurs flowed through, flocking down in a tornado of talons and screeching. Whitney knew why. As always, Lucindur's power drew them, and he abandoned his charge to rush back to her. Aquira darted up, blowing flame to keep them at bay, but there were so many. They spread around her blast, others diving at her, sending her fleeing.

"Defend the Lightmancer!" Torsten ordered right before Nesilia caught him in the chest with an elbow. His chestplate cracked, and he flew back against the Glass Throne, causing a crack right up the center. Nesilia attempted to advance but was stalled by Lucindur's magic once again, staggering back with her hand over her temple.

"Is this all you have, Sora?" Nesilia said, eyes and lips twitching as they shared an unheard conversation. "A tired-out old trick that barely worked the first time? Maybe I was wrong about you. You are weak. Sigrid wants this at badly as I do. All she has known is suffering, thanks to this castle. We will bring it crumbling down!"

A Serpent Guard stabbed at her, but Nesilia recovered quickly and caught the blade between her hands. She broke the shaft, took the spear herself, and skewered three guards with it.

Before Whitney could see any more, a group of soldiers closed in around Sora and Lucindur, creating a shell of shields. Grimaurs pounded against the steel like thunder, a storm all around them. Talons broke through and incapacitated some, but more guards with shields filled in. Eventually, they'd run out.

Whitney glanced at Sora, her eyes twitching, chest heaving. She was no longer at peace under the spell but struggling. Nesilia was fighting back, almost like she'd expected this feeble attack. Maybe she did. Maybe, she'd wanted to gather all their leaders, all those who'd wronged her, like pigs for the slaughter.

Hitting the floor, Whitney crawled through the legs of the guards. A grimaur squawked at him, snapping its razor-sharp beak. He rolled away from it, and someone stepped on its wing. It turned to free itself, and Whitney stabbed it through the eye, then emerged into the torrent.

Tum Tum had roused now. "Die ye foul beasts!" he bellowed as he leaped, swinging his hammer like a madman.

Whitney sliced a wing. Then a tail. Then, one grimaur smashed into his side. He fell back, grasping one of their ankles to keep talons from stabbing into his face. A violent blast of flame incinerated the thing's head, scorching Whitney's brow and hair. He turned over to avoid the heat, and things went suddenly dark. It only took a moment to realize the Brike Stone had fallen from his pocket.

He scampered to grab it. A grimaur plunged for it as well. The moment before either could grab it, however, Aquira zipped by and scooped it up. The grimaur crashed into the floor at full speed, its neck snapping.

"Nice one, Aquira!" Whitney cheered. He popped up, ready to keep fighting, but Aquira made a sound he'd never heard—a curdling squeal from deep in her gut that sounded more pained than proud.

She sputtered across the room, a ball of darkness and fire swirled together like a precious orb. She hit the wall, flapped a few times, and without the Brike Stone in his hand, forcing him to very dark thoughts, Whitney came up with them on his own. They hit him much harder.

"Is that the toy you brought to stick me in this time?" Nesilia asked as she snapped the neck of a Shieldsman with a sharp twist.

Grimaurs suddenly swarmed Aquira, only, they couldn't get close. Fire spewed out from the wyvern, not only from her mouth but all over. Vicious, violent pillars poured from her, burning through walls, singeing columns, melting glass.

Whitney couldn't believe his eyes. With the Brike Stone in hand, Aquira wasn't oppressed by sorrow but transformed. The form of an elemental dragon entirely made of fire broke free. Where her heart would be, the Brike Stone pulsed blood red as she now swept across the room, reducing a whole cluster of grimaurs to ash.

"The heart of a dragon," Tum Tum whispered, extending his hand to catch the ash of the very beasts he'd been battling.

Whitney marveled as the elemental beast that was Aquira circled up the spire, melting the hide and feathers from grimaurs as well as the debris falling from the devastated spire.

"Aquira, you clever girl!" he exclaimed.

He whipped around to face Nesilia. Many of the guards had the same thought. This was their opening. Whitney charged at her, and by then, Torsten had recovered to join him.

"Perhaps, you should have spared your sister," Torsten taunted. "Your arrogance will be your undoing."

Nesilia licked her bloody lips. "No. More fun for me."

Whitney swiped at her, met only air. In that brief moment, as he came around again, two guards were collapsing to the ground, dead by her hand. Torsten swung as well, a downward slash. She flipped back, landing behind a Serpent Guard and sinking her fangs into his throat before tearing it out.

"Do you hear the sounds outside these walls?" she asked as she dodged and blocked with ease. "That's Iam's Kingdom meeting its inevitable end. How many times will all of you fail? Iam needed new heroes."

Torsten missed an attack. Whitney timed it perfectly—they were best friends after all—and slid in low as a Serpent Guard also stabbed. Nesilia dipped back, below Whitney's swiping dagger, causing him to just barely shave her side. The skin steamed as silver made contact.

She whipped around, bearing her fangs in a feral hiss as she seized Whitney by the throat. His airway closed in an instant as her knife sank toward Whitney's eye. This wasn't the way he'd planned to die, but he'd take it. Nesilia's rage toward he-who-stole-Sora-from-her drew her focus.

The knife, however, stopped a fingernail's length from him. His heart stopped. Her hand shook. She winced and grimaced.

"Get. Out. Of. My. Head!" Nesilia screamed.

More glass from the spire shattered but turned to droplets of slag by Aquira's fire. A loud, misplayed chord sounded from Lucindur's salfio before a wave of energy from the instrument broke the connection between her and Sora. Both barely clung to consciousness. The shockwave sent Whitney flying back out of Nesilia's grasp. White spots danced across his vision. Guards fell too.

Torsten alone, however, was large enough to withstand the blast. His claymore raced toward Nesilia's head. But with Lucindur's spell broken, the full extent of powers returned. She dodged it with no room to spare, grabbed Torsten's arm on the downswing, and snapped the bone, even through his armor.

Salvation fell free, and as it clattered on the floor, she stomped on the blade with her heel, breaking it in two. A second blazing-fast move sent a kick into Torsten's midsection, and he was sent rolling across the room into a column.

"Is that all?" she asked, laughing. "All the great heroes of Pantego, this was all you could muster against me? How pathetic." Guards closed in around her one second and the next, all were on the ground, grasping at bleeding throats while she crouched between them, fresh blood upon her teeth and nails.

Aquira roared. Any other time, the sound would have made Whitney proud. She blasted the last grimaur out of the way, and her fiery form dove toward Nesilia. A single flick of a knife and it struck the Brike Stone, knocking it away. The elemental dragon broke apart, and from it fell Aquira, one of her wings torn. She slammed the floor and slid to Tum Tum's feet. The dwarf bent and lifted her into an embrace. He sucked in through his teeth. Smoke billowed off Aquira's flesh. She must have still been hot, but to the dwarf's credit, he didn't let her go. The Brike Stone landed near Lucindur without bouncing, far heavier than it appeared. Light flickered and began to draw itself toward the stone.

Nesilia clicked her tongue. "I'm so disappointed. I saw so much potential here. A part of me thought that, perhaps, some of you might stick around to forge this new world at my side."

"We'd… never… join… you," Sora moaned, barely able to pick herself up.

"Oh really? Then where is beautiful young Mahraveh?"

"She's destroying your uncaged beasts," Torsten moaned. His first attempt to stand failed.

"Is she?" Nesilia cackled. A guard charged her, and she caved in his chest with a single blow. "She and I had a nice chat before this. If I had to gamble, she's already turned against you, slaughtering all of your precious followers in my name." She closed her eyes, lower lip quivering with ecstasy. "Yes. She will be a worthy servant. Unlike you!"

Whitney lunged from the ground, but he was too far away. The few guards remaining around Sora and Nesilia were killed in an instant.

Then Nesilia stood right in front of Whitney, Sora on her knees before her.

"I learned a bit about this body," Nesilia said, addressing Whitney directly. "It is said that the blood of a mystic empowers it beyond belief. And well… my sister's ghastly body hadn't enough power to offer much. Sora is a true mystic now, isn't she?"

"Whitney…" Sora whispered. Fear flooded her face as Nesilia kneeled and sniffed her neck as Kazimir once had, like she were a Dawning Feast.

"Don't touch her…" Whitney said. He clenched one of the daggers and swung. Without a chance to counter, Nesilia stole the blade and stabbed it down through the center of his hand so hard the blade jammed into the marble and pinned him down. He screamed in agony as she pushed it deeper.

"How will you steal anything without this?" Nesilia asked.

"Stop it!" Sora shouted. A wave of elements exploded from her fingertips, and she bolted to her feet. Ice, burning coal, sleet, stone, it all landed harmlessly upon Nesilia. Sora was simply too weak, and an upyr too resistant to her magic.

"Enough," Nesilia said. She shoved Sora back to her knees and wrenched her head to the side. She leaned down to her ear. "I offered you everything, and you chose this laughable excuse for a man. This *thief*."

"Sigrid," Sora whimpered. "If you're in there, listen to me."

"She couldn't hear you before. She won't now." Nesilia bit the side of Sora's neck and drank from her, holding her upright as she did. Her eyes twitched with delight. Sora's fingers jerked, fire dancing upon them, but unable to summon. The color fled her cheeks. She didn't scream, didn't cry—but the sight of her pained face was unbearable.

Whitney could do nothing. Nobody could. They were either too injured or dead. And the horrid sounds from beyond the castle told of a similar tale. Wianu roars were close now—recognizable in their awfulness. The shrieks of people fighting and dying seemed endless.

"Let go of her!" a new voice growled.

Nesilia released Sora and stumbled. Steam poured from a silver-induced wound on her back. This strike hurt her. Her face contorted like she'd never experienced anything like it. Her jaw dropped in utter shock, and she slumped to one knee.

Sora collapsed forward, and Whitney embraced her with one arm. His other hand remained pinned by the knife. "It's okay," he whispered. "I have you." As her head lolled over his shoulder, her blood all over him, he peeked.

He expected to see brave and mighty Torsten standing behind Nesilia. Instead, he saw another familiar face. Sure, it was gaunter and more bearded than it had been on their last adventure together, but this was Rand Langley—deserter of the King's Shield, no doubt. For some reason, he wore all the armor of a Shieldsman except a breastplate. And in his grip, coated in black upyr blood, was half of Torsten's broken sword.

"Rand," Nesilia spat, turning on him. He backed away slowly, nearly tripping over a body. "You couldn't help but be the traitor you've always been, could you."

"You're wrong," Rand said. He looked around the room, destroyed and filled with dead and broken bodies. Torsten crawled for a fallen weapon. Tum Tum was crushed beneath a mound of grimaurs. Aquira chirped in pain. Lucindur cradled her salfio, barely able to breathe.

"My sister wouldn't have wanted this," he said. "I'll never see her again." He swung at Nesilia, but her hand shot forward to catch his forearm. She squeezed and bent it back until Rand lost his grip. Blackness oozed out of her back and from her mouth as she then forced him down and rose to her full height before him.

"You're right," she hissed. "You never will, because your pathetic life has come to its end."

Whitney gave Sora a look while they talked. He didn't need to tell her the plan. It was like they shared a mind.

In one smooth motion, Sora lunged and drew her silver shortsword. It took everything she had, but she slashed the back of Nesilia's knees. She collapsed forward, and as she did, Torsten raced to grab Rand and drag him away toward Lucindur and Tum Tum.

Nesilia remained on her hands and knees, steam and black blood shedding off her. Sora crawled toward her. Nesilia started to laugh.

"You should have aimed for the heart," she said. She raised a fist and punched the floor. The force made the marble ripple like water and threw Sora back. The knife pinning Whitney tore free with it, and he rolled over, clutching his hand and groaning.

"I always knew you'd be the one to save me," Nesilia said as somehow, she stood. "Your mystic blood. I can feel it coursing through me. Your mortal tools can do nothing against me."

Slowly, but impossibly fast for any human, her wounds started healing. Whitney knew it shouldn't be possible based on everything he'd learned from Kazimir. Silver should have caused her injuries to heal like any other person. But Sora's blood was strong, and she'd had plenty of it.

Nesilia cracked her neck. "I think… I'll kill you all now."

As she vanished in a blur, a beautiful chord chimed. Whitney glanced over and saw Lucindur, barely able to move and with Torsten supporting her. He lifted her one arm so she could strum her salfio. Rand sat before her. Both their eyes rolled back into their heads.

XLVIII

THE TRAITOR

Rand looked from side to side. Last he remembered, he was in the Throne Room. He wasn't sure why he ran there after Torsten left him battered in that bakery. Something deep inside called to him, like when he used to know his sister was in trouble with vagrants down in Dockside.

It wasn't hard to enter. He was human, after all, dressed like a Glassman, without possessed eyes. And nobody was defending the gates after what Nesilia did to those inside. He knew he should have aimed somewhere fatal when he went after her, but it was hard enough to bring himself to stab Sigrid's body.

Now he was here. It was then that he realized he had no idea where "here" was. Was that his final failure? Was this the afterlife?

"Hello?" Rand asked, his voice carrying.

Everything was white. But as he started to walk, shadows took the shape of buildings and streets. He saw the Glass Castle rising high above them, even taller from down in sunken Dockside.

That was where he was. He recognized the couturier on the corner. Spinning a slow circle, he noticed that the entire district was empty. But not only that—every building burned. He could smell the seared wood and ash, taste the smoke, and feel the heat.

He coughed, then shouted. "Hello!"

No one answered.

His weary feet carried him along Port Street into the thicker smoke that forced him to cover his eyes. The blaze wasn't spreading or destroying, just crackling in place. He turned down the stairs toward the North-End Harbor. Stopping by the water and searching from side to side, he spotted a lone figure seated down on the dock, veiled in smoke.

"Hey!" Rand called out. He started to jog, his feet bare against the wooden planks that'd given him so many splinters as a boy. In fact, he was now dressed in rags as he used to then.

"Hey, what are you doing! Can't you see the city's burning?" He kept pushing through until the smoke cleared. His heart skipped a beat, and he skidded to a stop, no doubt earning one of those infamous splinters.

It was Sigrid sitting just in front of old Gunter's oyster stand, which was also on fire.

His Sigrid.

"Let it burn," she said. Then she raised a fishing rod and cast her line into the inlet.

"Sigrid, is that really you?" Rand whispered.

"Ye never were very observant, big brother. It's a miracle that ever ye made Shieldsman."

Tears welled in Rand's eyes. He couldn't even feel himself walking, but somehow he wound up directly behind Sigrid, watching as the breeze tossed her curls. And they were red as the fire across all of Dockside, not upyr-white as he'd come to know them in recent days.

"They must not have had high standards." He half-laughed, half-sniveled.

Sigrid's fishing rod jerked. "Got one."

She struggled for only a few moments, and then like the expert Rand knew, she pulled in a fish. He shuffled up next to her and slowly crouched, eying her in disbelief the entire way. She held up the fish to observe.

"What are you going to do with it?" Rand asked.

"Nothin," she said. "Absolutely nothin." She gave it a wriggle, then unhooked the line and tossed it back in.

"Sigrid, is this a dream?" No longer able to control himself, Rand clutched her shoulder and turned her to face him. Her stunning green eyes looked back, only, there was no light in them. It made her almost unrecognizable, despite her appearance. The Sigrid Rand knew could always make his days seem brighter—cheer him when all the world seemed to be ending.

"No," she said. "It's the purge. The real one. Not the one that got me killed the first time. Do ye want to see the spot where I bled out? Where that controllin wretch Kazimir found me?"

Rand sat and let his legs dangle over the water.

"I should've never left you here with them," he said. "I know that now."

"Yet here we be. Can't be undone, it can't. Just like that Tessa of yers can't be brought back to life. Or any of the people ye killed."

Rand bit his lip. "No, they can't. But this? We have to at least put the fire out."

"Why? What did any of these people ever do for us? Force us to murder. Make us work so they can toss a few bronzers our way and move on? Let em all burn with it. Maybe somethin better will grow from the ashes."

"You know it won't. Not with her in control. I see that now. I know you do too."

"Can't be worse." She turned away and started fixing another worm on her hook.

"It can be. I promise you, it can."

"What do ye care anyway? All these people, they cursed and betrayed ye, then call ye the traitor. Even Torsten, coming day after day to check on ye. Where was he when Valin took us? Where was he when I died on the streets? They abandoned us all."

"That's not you, Siggy. That's Nesilia, taking over your thoughts."

"It ain't her. They're all food, Rand. No different than the fish." She cast her line in again.

"You're lying to yourself. Look at you; look at your hair." He ran his finger through one of her curls. "You're no upyr in, wherever this is. You're you."

"Go back to all the people ye chose over me, Rand."

"No. I'd rather let them all burn than leave you again. It was the worst mistake I ever made—not following Oleander's orders when I knew it was wrong. Not deserting the shield. Leaving you. And I'll stay here an eternity if that's what it takes to show you how sorry I am."

She bobbed the fishing rod but said nothing.

"The world sent us both down paths we never wanted," Rand went on. "But it's not too late to make a difference."

"There's no redemption, brother, don't ye understand that? There's no changin what we done. The people we killed, they'll always be dead."

"I know. I know. You're right. Redemption is a dream, and I don't want it. I don't care what they think of me anymore. Let them blame me for killing a King, and you, for a Queen. All I care about is what you think of me."

"I think yer a gods-damned coward," she snapped.

"I am," he replied, choking on the lump in his throat. "But I'm here."

He stroked her hair again, and this time, he noticed how she struggled to not look at him. Her head tilted slightly into his palm before she straightened out.

"I made you terrified. Valin made you a prisoner. The upyr made you a monster. Nesilia made you something so much worse... All I want is for you to be you again. The sister I loved. The sister I—I..." He choked up again. "The sister I looked up to all my life, even though you were younger."

Sigrid's throat bobbed. She lowered the fishing rod, and the line went slack, but still, she didn't turn.

"The truth is, my dearest Sigrid," Rand said. "Without you, I'm nothing. I'm a coward—worse even. A deserter, a traitor—all of it. Without me, you're still the strongest woman I've ever known. So, I sit here, begging you to realize what I did the moment you caught our first dinner. You never needed anyone—not even our parents. And you don't need Nesilia."

Sigrid sniffled. Then, just as Rand was about to keep going, she turned and threw her arms around him. It caught him off guard at first, but as his head fell against her shoulder, it was the pillow he'd always needed.

"I just want to stop bein so angry," she whimpered.

Her chest heaved against his. Her heart raced. Rand squeezed harder and let himself feel everything, tears running down his cheeks as he fought to breathe.

"I know," he said. "I know, Siggy. But don't blame the world. They don't know what they're doing. Just blame me. Only me."

Rand peered through the strands of her messy hair and saw the fire throughout Yarrington starting to extinguish. Embers flurried all over the horizon in a way that he found surprisingly beautiful. It was like they were dancing to some unheard melody. He could almost imagine the notes… like from a Glintish bard playing her salfio.

"I forgive ye, brother," she whispered into his ear, and never was there a sound sweeter.

"And I'm here for you, Siggy," he replied. "Whatever you want to do."

"Let the world, let Nesilia, let all the monsters and the men fend for themselves. I'm done fightin…"

XLIX

THE KNIGHT

It was a split-second decision. While Nesilia reeled, first from Rand's attack, and then Sora's, Torsten could have gone for a blade. Instead, he grabbed Rand and saved him from the fury of his enraged master.

He didn't do it to save Rand. It was something from Whitney's story that spurred him—unbelievable as that was. Using Sora's connection to Nesilia through Lightmancing hadn't worked, but when they tried last time, it was Whitney's connection to the body Nesilia *stole* that gave them a chance, not the goddess, herself.

That was Rand.

"You should have aimed for the heart," Nesilia spoke, and a burst of energy helped throw Torsten and Rand forward, close to Lucindur. Just where they needed to be.

"Torsten, you…" Rand muttered as Torsten rolled him over and dragged him even closer. His eyes pled for forgiveness that would never be offered.

Torsten shook his head. "You can save your sister, Rand," he said. More than once now, he'd had the chance to kill Rand and get revenge. Part of him wanted to, but another… it felt the mercy of Iam's light.

"Lucindur, this is Sigrid's brother," Torsten said, sitting Rand across from her. "We need you one last time."

"I can't…" Lucindur groaned. "I can't."

"You can." Torsten released Rand and crawled to her. "I believe in you." He cradled her broken body, lifting the salfio into place and holding up her arm. She was so exhausted from Nesilia breaking free, her muscles barely seemed to work.

"Pantego needs you now," Torsten said, ignoring whatever Nesilia was saying. She was irrelevant now. He knew what needed to be done —why he'd spared Rand all those times when every part of him wanted to put him out of his misery.

Lucindur closed her eyes and drew a ragged breath. "Talwyn..." she muttered as she moved her fingers into place on the strings of her instrument. Torsten held it upright and supported her arms the entire way.

"You can do this," Torsten urged.

"I think I'll kill you all now," Nesilia said.

"Sigrid, you have to be in there," Rand sniveled, the Brike Stone lying right beside him. "Please... don't..."

Nesilia made her move. Torsten had been in countless battles, and his heart had never stopped like it did then. He held his breath. He'd have closed his eyes if he had eyes to close. He focused, feeling the muscles of Lucindur's forearm tense as she strummed a chord, as if channeling his own strength into her.

When he breathed out, Nesilia was directly in front of them, the Brike Stone in her grip. She'd squeezed it so hard in that fraction of a second, it began to crack, releasing ribbons of dark energy. But she couldn't break it because, like Rand, her eyes were rolled back, and she was completely frozen in place. Lucindur continued to play, and Torsten didn't dare move lest he disturb her harmony.

Whitney and Sora stumbled over, supporting each other while Whitney held his injured hand. "She's the sister Rand talked about when we were together, isn't she?" Whitney asked.

Torsten nodded.

"You yigging genius. I could kiss you!" Whitney exclaimed. He went to hug him, but Sora barred him.

"Don't," she said. "Don't disrupt anything."

"Aye, ye remember last time?" Tum Tum said. He leaned against a column, clutching his wounded leg with Aquira on his lap. The little wyvern seemed to have passed out from pain, wheezing with each unconscious breath.

"Aquira," Sora blurted, running toward them.

"She'll be fine, Lassie," Tum Tum said. "Focus on what needs be done."

"Now, there's a good question. What now?" Whitney asked.

"What are you talking about?" Torsten replied. "You both did this last time."

"The bar guai magically stabbed right into her!" With his good hand, Whitney reached for the Brike Stone nestled in Nesilia's hand, then stopped. She couldn't move, but the dozens of twisted bodies lying all around them had him justifiably cautious.

Whitney turned to Torsten. "This is just a stone."

"You useless—" Torsten's jaw clenched. "Do we kill the body then?"

"No," Sora said, circling around behind her. "She's trapped while Lucindur plays. But the moment we do that, she'll take over another of us."

Nesilia's eyes twitched. Her fingers shifted slightly.

"Well, we better hurry," Torsten said.

"Oh, thanks for the tip," Whitney said. He looked to Sora, opened his mouth to ask a question, but nothing came out. She too looked baffled.

Worse still, the roar of the wianu echoed. The sound was so close now, Torsten could do nothing but imagine them like they were in the streets of Latiapur, flouncing through the city, destroying everything, and wheezing for water. The clamor of stone crumbling and the shaking floor suggested just that.

He could also perceive the distant cries to "hold the walls" and "fight to the last breath." Sir Mulliner was a capable commander, but there was no holding back the tide of her horde. Eventually, it'd break through.

Torsten returned his focus to Whitney and said, "If Rand gets his sister to reject her, and we're not ready—"

"She'll kill us all and take back the body she treasured," Sora finished for him. She gazed sullenly down at her own hands as if picturing the blood that stained them while Nesilia was in control.

"I won't let that happen," Whitney said. "Never."

"That's not up to you," Torsten snapped.

"No, it isn't," said a voice from the door behind the Royal Council chairs.

All their eyes snapped up to see Dellbar, strolling across the dais. He tapped along with his cane, calm as ever. His head turned from side to side as though he could see the slaughter throughout the room.

"Dellbar, where have you been?" Torsten questioned.

"Waiting. Until the time was right," he said.

"What are you talking about?"

"Yeah, what he said," Whitney added, puffing out his chest.

Dellbar strode by Whitney like he wasn't even there. He stopped beside Nesilia, empty eye-sockets set upon her.

"The bar guai would have failed," he said. "There was no light in it. She would have broken free in moments, with the help of this upyr or not."

"Hey, you weren't there!" Whitney jabbed a finger, clearly forgetting his hand was injured. His face corkscrewed in pain, but he didn't back down. "If we'd stopped her then, all those people out there would still be alive. They'd all be alive!"

Dellbar rested his hand upon Whitney's shoulder. "No, there was nothing you could've done," he said softly. Then he moved around in front of Nesilia. "This is the moment it was always meant to be. Iam's great mistake, redeemed by the unbreakable love of those born into the darkness of this world."

"Dellbar, now isn't the time for your riddles," Torsten said, his arms growing weak from supporting Lucindur's. She wasn't heavy, far from it, but in her state, her entire body felt like dead weight.

"I often asked myself why Iam chose me when I cursed Him so," Dellbar said. "Now I know. That is His truth. The darkness cannot exist without the light, and so too, can it not die. So long as she remained buried, the feud endured. Now, it shall end, and this land of Pantego will finally be left in the hands of men."

A fiendish shout sounded above. Torsten looked up and saw a goblin skittering in through the broken spire. One, then two, then so many more. They hurled rocks and shot their poison darts as they crawled down the walls, many of them falling to their deaths as pieces broke away under their combined weight. More grimaurs joined them, squawking like vultures over corpses.

Sora quickly jumped forward and raised her arm. Fire arced from it, but not as a weapon. The very flames Torsten had watched destroy so much formed a protective shield over them, vaporizing all the projectiles before they could hit.

Her limbs all shook. Blood leaked from her nose.

A deafening roar was followed by a crash of stone. One giant tentacle broke through the ceiling, slithering down with the other beasts, followed by another—all Nesilia's enslaved monsters abandoning the war to protect her.

The barks and growls of hellhounds emanated from the back entrance leading to the castle undercroft and the destroyed crypts.

"Do something, you rambling fool!" Whitney shouted.

Dellbar dropped his cane, then closed his hands around Nesilia's, both sets covering the Brike Stone. He whispered under his breath, and with all the racket of creatures closing in around them, Torsten couldn't understand the words—only see the way his mouth formed Iam's name.

Nesilia twitched again, stronger this time. Dellbar held tight, and that same aura that formed around the brave priests outside formed around him. It swirled over their hands, mixing with the darkness of the Brike Stone. His empty eye-sockets turned to light like they had on the fields of White Bridge when Iam took over his body.

The air started to tingle. Everything shook. Sora screamed as she pushed her powers to the brink, her fiery shield pushing outward to repel falling goblins and diving grimaurs. The hounds scampered through the door and charged. Tum Tum hobbled forward on his injured leg and smashed one in the head with his hammer, then engaged another.

The wianu shattered the glass spire completely, and more tentacles thrashed in as its soulless eyes and terrifying maw appeared above.

Rand and Lucindur gasped at the same time. The latter's body fell limp in Torsten's arm, her hand slipping down, and she stopped playing for a moment. He feared the end had come. Then, a ghostly presence rose from the bosom of Sigrid's body. The shape of a women's face formed.

"You will not take this world from me, Iam!" Nesilia roared, now without any of Sigrid's voice in her own. It was all-encompassing, making even the roar of the wianu seem small and harmless.

"None of you will!" she went on. "Pantego is mine. You are all mine."

Sora was forced to her knees as more creatures, including the wianu, crashed upon her shield. It seared and burned, but slipped down to ground level. Some of its tentacles still gripped the ceiling, casting them all in shadow, closing in around them, one slowly wrapping Sigrid and Dellbar themselves.

"No," Dellbar replied. This time, it wasn't his voice. It was Iam again, Torsten was sure of it. "It's time for rest, my love. We've failed each other for far too long."

Light burst from the Brike Stone, forcing everyone but Torsten to shield their eyes. His blessed sight allowed him to see through it. Nesilia screamed in protest as her essence was drawn into the stone. Dellbar's eyeholes dimmed, and he collapsed to his knees.

Sigrid awoke, and in a matter of seconds, she sliced the wianu's tentacle off. The monster squealed and pulled back, not just to the hole above, but it fled like a frightened calf. The sea monster seemed intelligent, and now it was proven. It retreated before its own master could be fed to it and destroyed.

The other beasts didn't have the chance. Sigrid zipped around the room like a bolt of lightning, cutting them to ribbons until she stood in the center, panting like a wild animal with bodies falling around her. Her dark eyes darted around, confused, as if piecing together the world for the very first time.

"Siggy," Rand rasped. He scrambled to his feet and ran to her, holding her at arm's length. "You're here, sister. You're with me."

Torsten gently rolled Lucindur off him and laid her head down. The exertion had left her unconscious, but she was breathing. Whitney helped hold Sora upright, but Torsten raced past them to Dellbar. The High Priest held the Brike Stone with two hands, and the blood-red stone now glowed brightly enough to paint the entire room that way. Torsten couldn't perceive color well, but this could not be mistaken.

The stone churned violently. Dellbar could barely keep hold of it, but light funneled through his hands, sapping the color from his cheeks as it did. Killing him, Torsten realized. Nesilia's whispers filled the air around it, unclear, but laced with temptation. The thought of breaking her free even crossed Torsten's mind. He couldn't help it.

"Iam saved what little power in Pantego He had left for this," Dellbar groaned. "I can hold her, but not for long."

Torsten glanced up as the last of the wianu's tentacles receded. "The wianu. We have to get to one. They're fleeing to the water."

"Then we catch up to one," Whitney said, matter-of-factly.

"How?"

"Have some faith," Whitney said.

"He's right," Sora said. "Faith that Mahraveh was able to slow them down."

"We have to move fast," Torsten said. At that, an idea popped into his head. He helped Dellbar up, battling the swell of dark thoughts that came just by touching him. He led him toward Rand and his sister. "Sigrid, you're faster than any of us. Take him to the inlet. End this."

"No way," Sora protested. "We can't trust her. I saw in their minds... they both, wanted this."

"Do it for Kazimir," Whitney said. "Finish what he started."

Rand continued to hold her as her gaze passed across each of them. Her breathing started to slow.

"Sigrid, can you hear them?" Rand asked. "Can you hear me?"

"I can," she replied. "And I don't want any of their redemption."

"Siggy?"

"I'm done fightin." She seized Rand by the sides, looked straight into Torsten's face, and then, they were gone in a wisp of dust.

Whitney spun around, searching. "I hate when they do that."

"We'll take the priest ourselves," Sora said. "A horse. Torsten, we need a horse."

Torsten stared at Sigrid and Rand's bloody footprints.

"Torsten!"

He forced himself to focus. "The stables, there should still be some. Let's go." He placed his hand on the small of Dellbar's back and guided him along.

"I'll only slow ye down," Tum Tum said, still holding his wounded leg. "I'll stay with Lucy and the brave little wyvern." Aquira looked up at him with naught but her eyes.

"Scared of another fight?" Whitney asked as he retrieved one of his daggers and spun it on one finger.

"Whitney," Sora scolded, picking up her shortsword.

"Oh, he knows I'm kidding. That, right there, is the bravest dwarf I've ever known."

"And ye, the most dastardly thief," Tum Tum said, grinning.

They caught up to Torsten, and together, the same group that went traipsing through the Webbed Woods after Redstar and Bliss led Dellbar across the Throne Room. Soldiers at the castle gates were preparing to barricade it. Never a good sign.

Outside in the court, madness awaited. Uhlvark had his back against the gate, being rammed on the other side by something powerful. The simpleton looked terrified, no idea how strong he was. Archers on the walls fired off. Soldiers defended them against Drav Cra, remaining possessed, and monsters using rooftops in an attempt to leap over the walls. Some made it into the courtyard and rampaged around, but were quickly put down.

Beyond those castle walls, the entire city glowed from fire. Smoke commingled in the sky like a second set of low, dark clouds. To the south, the fortifications were ruptured. The hole looked like it had been caused by something the size of a wianu. Enemy Shesaitju warriors poured through, and Sir Mulliner was there with Sir Hystad leading a ground force in defense. Horses in the nearby stables whinnied and cried.

"There," Torsten said, pointing. "Go and get him on a horse."

"What about you?" Whitney asked.

"I'm going to clear us a path." He grasped Whitney's arm. "No matter what happens, you are worthy of your name, Whitney Godskiller." He turned to Sora. "And you, Sora. Whatever you were to Liam, he'd be proud of you today."

"I hate when you get mushy," Whitney said, fake-wiping his eyes.

"Go!" Torsten shoved Dellbar at them, and they ran across the chaotic courtyard. As they sprinted, Torsten heard a strange horn ringing, its tenor deep and cavernous like the depths of the earth.

He took off toward the gate first, and all the soldiers defending it.

"Uhlvark!" he shouted. "Uhlvark!"

The giant was too terrified to display his usual glee upon seeing a friend. His full weight held the gates closed, but every time it was rammed, spears stabbed through the opening and cut at him.

"Uhlvark, I need you to abandon the gate, and go with Dellbar again." Torsten pointed to Whitney and Sora, who were taking far too much time getting Dellbar onto a mount.

"But, protect gaaaaate," he said, then moaned as the gate lurched, and his thigh was stabbed before he and all the men pushing resealed it.

"You did such a great job," Torsten commended. "Now, they need you to be a hero."

"Herooo?"

"The very biggest. Go, Uhlvark. Your friend needs you now more than ever."

"I will help."

Soldiers protested as he pushed off and limped across the courtyard. More men flowed to take his place, but it wouldn't last long with the giant absent.

Torsten didn't wait to find out. He raced for the stairs, and a Drav Cra vaulted toward him, earning an elbow across his jaw. Stealing the man's axe to replace *Salvation*, Torsten kept going. Adrenaline helped him push his legs up the stairs. He ducked under another attack from a Glass soldier that was possessed, then bashed him in the face with the axe-handle.

The horn sounded again. Torsten pushed past an archer, reached the parapet, and leaned over. Nesilia's horde filled the city, rampaging through buildings, dragging out innocents, slaughtering anyone, and anything. But that's not where the horn came from.

A new army massed outside the walls of Yarrington. A blade of moonlight pierced the clouds, illuminating a part of them and allowing Torsten to see the sigil of the Three Kingdoms. Brouben was in their lead, his axe raised high as they began their charge.

Drav Cra horns sounded in response. A large portion of Nesilia's army rushed to the main gates to greet them, drawing soldiers away from the path leading to Dockside. The rest continued assaulting the keep.

"The dwarves stand with us!" Torsten bellowed. "Stand strong, warriors of Iam. The end does not come for us today. Archers, every one of you, focus on the east. Clear a path to the harbor."

Glassmen all around him cheered. The archers in towers and who weren't busy brawling all followed his command. Sir Mulliner called for a shield push, and Torsten gripped his new axe tight.

"For Yarrington!"

L

"C'mon, let's get him up," Whitney said frantically. It was bad enough that they were in a rush to catch a wianu before Dellbar lost his control over Nesilia, but the clamor of battle raged all around them... It was disorienting.

He and Sora cupped Dellbar's foot and helped him onto a horse that Sora was somehow able to calm despite the madness.

"Yigging Exile!" Whitney helped, grasping at his hand. He kept forgetting there was a hole through it. For whatever reason, it didn't hurt as much as it should have until he used it.

"Here, give me that," Sora said. She took his hand and lowered her head. She looked exhausted. Beautiful, but exhausted. Dark rings circled her eyes, and her own hands trembled as a bluish smoke snaked out from them, filling in Whitney's wound. The skin started to stitch itself over, and Sora would have fallen if Whitney hadn't supported her in return. She'd never used her power so much in so short a time.

"Sora," Whitney said. She didn't answer. His hand stopped healing, but she remained hunched over it, wheezing. "Sora," he repeated, this time rubbing her cheek with his thumb. "Are you okay?"

"I'm fine." She exhaled.

"You're not. Hey, look at me." He lifted her chin and tried to get her to make eye-contact, but her amber-hued beauties refused to focus. "Sora, I can handle this."

"Just get on the horse."

"Sora, please."

"We're ending this!" she yelled, throwing her arms down. A gust of wind that was in no way natural heaved Whitney up, leaving him no choice but to grasp for the mane of the—once again—terrified horse. Sora jumped up after him, sandwiching Dellbar between them.

Whitney felt the Brike Stone against his back, saw all the myriad ways they could fail and die. He even thought he heard Nesilia whispering promises like how she'd "give him everything he'd ever wanted." How she'd "make him a king." And the stone itself made him both hot and cold at the same time, confusing his body in ways that made no sense.

"Cut it free!" Sora shouted.

Whitney could hardly hear her over the sudden bellow of horns along with shouting from both armies. He fumbled for his dagger, then slashed the rope hitching the horse. It bucked hard, nearly throwing him off, but he clenched tight and leaned to its ear.

"You're okay, girl," he whispered. "You're okay." The horse neighed and thrashed, knocking over a bucket of feed as it rumbled out into the courtyard. A goblin charging them earned the wrong end of the horse's hooves.

"Shh," Whitney hushed, stroking its mane. "You get to help us save the world."

"When you are calm, so too will it be," Dellbar whispered. His voice was tinged with Nesilia's, and he groaned after speaking.

Whitney closed his eyes and focused on what he desired more than anything: an end to the fighting and adventuring. On that note, he understood why that devil, Sigrid, fled instead of helping them. Against all odds, he wished for the peaceful life of Troborough's farms and rolling hills, owning a little house with Sora, maybe a tavern. Perhaps they could raise a kid together and watch out for it like neither Whitney or Sora's parents had ever done.

Even the Brike Stone couldn't taint the vision. It had been Exile for Whitney in Elsewhere, and now it was the life he craved, that simple existence he'd fled for so long.

He exhaled and re-opened his eyes.

Now that the horse was steady, Sora shouted at him to get moving.

"Hold your horses!" he joked, then gave the thing a kick, and it bounded toward the break in the wall. He guided it to where Sir Mulliner was barking orders at the rear of a line of soldiers holding back invaders.

"Sir Mulligan, right?" he called.

The Shieldsman looked up through messy, bloody hair. "It's Mulli—doesn't matter. We can't hold them off without every sword. Get down here and start fighting, thief!"

Whitney ignored the insult. There wasn't time to put the rigid Shieldsman in his place. "The priest has Nesilia," he said. The Shieldsman gave him a questioning look that Whitney ignored. "We have to get to the wianu quickly."

"They fell back toward the harbor."

"We know that!" Sora snapped in a completely uncharacteristic moment that Whitney appreciated far too much. She was finally starting to realize his eternal struggle with dolts.

"We need to get to them."

"Then you'll have to fight through an army." Mulliner turned back to his men and hollered more orders about guarding flanks.

Another series of horns blasted. These a bit different.

"The dwarves stand with us!" Torsten screamed, now atop the walls, with an axe raised high. "Stand strong, warriors of Iam. The end does not come for us today."

"Where in Elsewhere did he get an axe?" Whitney asked.

"The dwarves fight with us!" a soldier yelled.

"Reinforcements!" cheered a few more.

Some of the Drav Cra pushing back Mulliner's troops peeled away, allowing their shield wall to hold steady.

Whitney glanced back at Sora. "Brouben?"

She nodded. "Has to be."

"Ha! Dwarves… Always late to the party."

"Sir Unger's letters must've gotten through to King Cragrock!" The Shieldsman exclaimed. "The dwarves stand with us."

"No, sir," Whitney said. "Those little buggers are here because of us. Now, if you don't mind, we need to reach the water, or all of this is a great big waste."

"I am helpiiiing friend!" Came the boisterous drawl of what could only be a giant. One rumbled toward them, not even giving a chance for the Glassmen to move. It simply knocked them aside and bowled through the Drav Cra on the other side. A dire wolf jumped and clamped onto his back, its claws drawing long, red lines. Torsten came sliding down the fallen portion of the wall and cleaved it, stem to stern.

"Are you coming or not?" he shouted.

Whitney didn't wait for Sir Mulliner to issue the order. He yelled, "Charge," and the entire company obeyed. Sir Mulliner echoed the same, as if his pride was wounded, but the effect was the same.

Bolstered by the giant's rampage and the arrival of reinforcements, the men rushed into battle. Whitney took another look back at Sora and Dellbar. The latter was hunched over, barely able to keep his eyes open, hands quaking over the stone.

Whitney gave the horse a kick and joined the push. The giant slammed a group of Drav Cra through a building. A possessed cultist hacked at his leg, knocking him to one knee. Turning, he roared and bit the man's head off.

"Blech," Whitney said.

Torsten bulled through a savage, then another. The giant flung the decapitated body down the street, and it hit a dire wolf with its terrifying gaze set upon Whitney and crew.

Whitney urged the horse faster. They bolted ahead of the charge, barreling through bodies, but there seemed to be an endless stream of enemies down the street.

"Whitney, duck!" Sora yelled.

He knew from experience that it was best to just listen to her. He lowered his head, pulling Dellbar with him, and Sora unleashed a wave of fire to clear their way.

It's Bridleton all over again, Whitney thought.

He kept the horse to the edges of the street as they pierced through like a fiery spear, Sora incinerating anyone and anything in their way.

They broke through a line of stalls in the South Corner market. Here, the battle was the same, but the players were different. Gray men scurried around like ants, stabbing and slashing at one another. It was nearly impossible to tell who belonged to which army. Zhulong tore through the streets, and Whitney did everything in his power to keep out of their way.

Finally, he decided to turn hard onto the main road leading to the harbor, the horse barely stayed on its hooves. Now, it was a full-out Shesaitju war waging all around them. Burning buildings. Barbed arrows zipping this way and that. A mounted zhulong charged at them from the side, and Whitney pulled mane to turn the other way.

Before it pummeled them, the giant's feet slammed down in the path. It grabbed the tusks and pushed, lifting the zhulong backward and causing the rider to topple off. Torsten buried an axe in his chest.

As the giant struggled with the beast, arrows stabbed into his chest. Another mounted zhulong rammed into his hip.

Sora grunted, and a spear of ice lanced from her hands, knocking the zhulong away. But it was too late. The giant lost balance and stumbled through one of Dockside's burning shanties, then kept falling, down the ridge, destroying everything in his path.

Whitney whipped the horse onto Port Street and peered through the debris. Massive, shadowy beings plunged into the inlet all the way across to lower Dockside.

"Whitney, I…"

He looked back and saw Sora slowly slipping off the horse from exhaustion. He did all he could. Holding Dellbar, so she didn't drag him off with her.

"Sora!" he shrieked.

"I've got her!" Torsten said. Before Sora hit the street, he caught her over the shoulder, spinning to cut down an attacker. Another charged at his back, but a sword jabbed through the man's head and killed him instantly.

"Sir Unger, we're barely holding them!" Lord Jolly said, wielding his weapon with his one hand and surrounded by a host of Shieldsmen guards.

"Keep it up!" Torsten said.

Whitney looked behind. Sir Mulliner's charge had been slowed. A demon spirit engulfed Mulliner, preparing to take control. He stabbed himself through the side instead, causing the being to chose another body, then ran at a cultist and head-butted through its mask. Around him, his men gave every ounce of life they had to keep pushing, to keep drawing enemies to themselves and away from Whitney and Dellbar.

Torsten hurried to the flailing zhulong the giant had flipped. He mounted it, Sora still over his shoulder, and somehow knew how to control the thing like he'd ridden one before. He slashed down with his axe, carving a path to the buildings Uhlvark crashed through.

"Go!" he yelled. "Go!"

So, Whitney did what he did best. He didn't think, and he took a shortcut. Sweeping his legs off the side of the horse, he grasped Dellbar by his pretty, white robes, looped his arm under his shoulder, and slid off the horse. Together, they ran. The priest could barely breathe.

They scaled the rubble with the help of Whitney's sure feet. Arrows raced by. Flame licked at his heels. He ignored it all, holding Dellbar tighter as they slid down a steep slope of broken wood. The giant was in a heap at the bottom level being hacked at by Shesaitju until his massive arms fell slack.

With his one free hand, Whitney clutched the grip of his dagger. He'd been in worse scraps. They scaled a caved-in roof, then slid down at the warriors, landing upon the giant. He ducked under a strike, yanking Dellbar back out of the way with him. His dagger shot up and hit flesh.

One down. Many more to go.

They circled around him, Nesilia whispering, "You can't win," from her prison in the stone.

"We can't win," Dellbar murmured as well, repeating it over and over. He was losing his control. The blood-red of the Brike Stone pulsed through his fingers, darkness draining the color from his skin.

"We will," Whitney said. He searched for the clearest opening when the giant gave him one last parting gift. He raised his arm and let it crash down like a fallen tree trunk, crushing Shesaitju and knocking the others down with the force of it.

Whitney pushed off and hit the cobbles. They were near a small square behind the local church dedicated to King Autla on the docks level. Dellbar resisted his pull now, like he didn't want Nesilia gone.

"No," he shrieked. "No, you can't take me."

"Come. On!" Whitney pulled him along with all his might, racing down the street, over bodies and rubble. They reached the planks of the dock, where more fighting raged. The city drowned in it.

Whitney spun to find an opening. Tentacles from surviving wianu dipped into the inlet all over, their dark figures vanishing below the surface. There had to be one left.

Dellbar yanked him down. "It's hopeless," he said. "It's always been hopeless."

"Whitney Fierstown!"

A blade stabbed toward Dellbar, but Whitney quickly shifted in front. "No!" he blurted. The razor-sharp edge of a spear stopped just at his chest, the shaft in the hands of Caleef Mahraveh.

She looked him in the eye, then down at the rambling priest. "Sorry, I thought he was possessed." Her eyes widened upon viewing the infernal orb in Dellbar's grip. "Is that… her?" she asked.

Whitney nodded. "But the wianu… they're all fleeing…"

"I trapped one on its own. There." She pointed with her spear, out into the water. The prow of a Shesaitju ship stuck up, and on it, he noticed the thrashing limbs of one of the beasts. Its roar was lost in the din of war, but it was moving. Alive.

"Finally, I've been itching for more Glassmen!" A deep voice said, then chortled.

Whitney looked left and saw a Shesaitju general so big he may have been a lesser giant. Black coloring oozed down his body, revealing spiky, white tattoos across his bulbous gut. He patted on a warhammer that made Tum Tum's seem like it was made for a child, and a host of nearly three dozen Shesaitju warriors laughed with him.

"And you, Mahraveh," he said. "Finally, we can have our first dance. Maybe I'll capture you instead of killing you. You'd make a fine wife yet."

Mahraveh brushed Whitney aside. "I've been waiting for this, Babrak," she growled. She stepped toward him and flourished her spear, ready to take him and his honor-guard on all by herself.

"My Caleef, get them to the beast!" someone shouted from behind.

"Oh, shog in a yigging barrel. Who is it now!" Whitney groaned. He looked back, still fighting against Dellbar's pulling, and saw Bit'rudam at the lead of a zhulong cavalry. Blood leaked down one side of his face from a gash across his left eye. Wounds covered his body, exposed by typical Shesaitju light armor, but he was still fighting.

And they weren't alone. Torsten charged with them, Sora seated behind him now, but resting her hands on the big man's shoulders to stay upright, though barely.

"Come here, you pis'truda!" Babrak barked. "Daddy can't protect you now."

Mahraveh clenched her jaw. Her knuckles went white as she squeezed her spear. Then she whipped around.

"Come on!" She clutched Whitney's arm and pulled, surprisingly strong, considering her stature. Together, they towed Dellbar across the street to the docks. Sections of planks were upheaved. Others collapsed into mud and water.

Shesaitju warriors were everywhere, and Mahraveh carved her way through them with speed and skill that was paled only by an upyr. She was a master with the spear. Whitney tried to get a few stabs in, but he was utterly useless—being helped by a Shesaitju. Shameful.

Behind them, Bit'rudam and Torsten led their zhulong against Babrak's men, protecting them from ambush.

They reached a branch of the docks, the slip sticking out into the inlet to receive galleon-sized vessels. The end of it was utterly devastated, but it would get them halfway to the trapped wianu. They would have to swim the rest.

Mahi stabbed her spear into the wood and used it to pole-vault herself ahead, bringing her leading foot down through a gray-skinned enemy to clear the way. She carved her route through attack after attack, and Whitney tried to keep pace, but Dellbar wasn't having it.

His heel caught a broken plank, and he fell. The Brike Stone didn't slip free, but he hit his knees hard. His body hunched over the stone, enfolding it against his chest. Tendrils of shadow and light slithered around his body. Nesilia's whispers grew louder, and he repeated them audibly. His eye-sockets were all black now. Lightless.

"Whitney!" Mahraveh called. She was all the way down the dock, a body collapsing in front of her.

"Buried, not dead. Buried, not dead," Dellbar said, squeezing the stone hard. "Liars, braggarts, thieves, drunks, and murderers!"

"Come on, you damn priest!" Whitney grasped the back of his robe and dragged him, but couldn't get far. It was as if the stone wasn't only absorbing all the light around them, but weighing them down now, too. His muscles burned.

"Iam, if you're with him, or anywhere. A hand here?"

A few planks snapped and collapsed. The wood all around them creaked. Whitney pulled as hard as it could, but it only made it worse. A long swim awaited, and he needed his strength.

Then, he felt a chill, heard a strange rasp, like wind through a canyon. He looked down, and a strip of the water turned to ice in a flash. He followed its path, to the edge of the docks where Torsten and Bit'rudam battled. Sora was on her knees at the coast, her hands upon the surface, using everything she had left.

The ice had collapsed the part of the dock he and Dellbar were on, making it impossible for Mahraveh to reach him. But it continued, freezing a path all the way to the trapped wianu. Sora forced a beleaguered smile. Whitney returned the same.

In the end, he knew it would be her and him saving the day. Not some Shesaitju princess. Not even Torsten. He rolled over to face Dellbar. The High Priest was on is back now, spine arched all the way up, writhing like he was in terrible pain.

"Buried, not dead. Buried, not dead," he continued to repeat, eyeholes blacker than the night sky.

"Priests," Whitney sighed.

Again, he didn't think twice. He reared back and kicked Dellbar across the face as hard as he could. Whitney pried the Brike Stone from unconscious fingers. The thing must have weighed a hundred pounds all on its own.

And the thoughts. They were exponentially stronger now, begging him to slit his own throat. To drown himself. It was like darkness made physical, seeping through his pores, taking control. Every temptation he'd ever received since leaving Elsewhere was nothing in comparison to this. Every time he blinked, he could see Nesilia's hateful eyes like they were his own. He could hear her cackling, telling him how hopeless it was to resist.

He pictured Sora's smile and fought back the tide. He could barely see straight, but he knew the way. All he had to do was run straight and not slip. What better job for the World's Greatest Thief?

"You should have never left Elsewhere," Nesilia said as he ran forward, her voice his entire world. Inside his head. Outside his head. Everywhere.

"First, I'll take you," she continued. "They, you'll watch through my eyes as I devour Sora. I'll peel Torsten's body open one layer at a time."

She laughed, and Whitney's heart palpitated. He sucked in air and kept pushing. He could see the wianu's dark eyes looking at him, its mouth stuck open and bleeding as it was pinned. Its roar became Nesilia's, and hers its.

"You will fail them all," she said. "Just as you've failed everyone you've ever met. You are a cancer to this world. You are what destroys it, and I am the purging fire that will make Pantego all it was meant to be."

The weight of the stone became unbearable, pulling him to his knees at the end of the ice, right before the wianu. He could feel her taking over, like her fingers were within his veins, clawing their way up his arms.

"No, all you're going to do is die!" Whitney cried, his throat stinging. He fought with everything he had to raise the Brike Stone with both hands. He tried in desperation to chuck it into the wianu's mouth, where Nesilia could forever join Kazimir in Nowhere, but he couldn't.

It was stuck, latched onto him like a parasite, its darkness threading his body.

"It is hopeless," Nesilia said. "The priest saw it. Your King saw it. So too, shall you. All you've done has been in vain. Why fight for this city? You hated its people all your life. Hero? You are far from it."

It took all his energy to turn his head and look back at the city she referred to. Yarrington, a place where nobles sit up high, and the rest are left to squabble for their scraps down below. Nowhere for a thief.

It burned and collapsed from war. Soldiers everywhere, killing each other. Even though there were possessed left and Nesilia's monsters, it was mostly men killing men, hatred, blinding them, and filling them with rage. Centuries of distrust and differing beliefs tearing them apart.

Yet on its edge, a Shieldsman fought beside a Shesaitju, riding a zhulong. A Panpingese mystic knelt on the shore, arms trembling, giving her life-energy to save people who would have hanged her if they knew who she truly was. Whitney focused on her, head hanging, hair draped over her eyes as she struggled to stay conscious.

"You'll never understand, Nesilia," he said, turning back to face the wianu. "And I'm sorry for that. I'm sorry Iam left you. But if there was ever really love between you, He would have fought through anything to reach you; battled demons and mystics on His way to Elsewhere, like my Sora did."

"Iam was a coward!" she screamed. Whitney's head felt like it was going to split open. "He'll always be a coward. And all those people you decided to care about will die because He isn't here. This is my world."

"You're right," Whitney said. "It is now. Iam's gone." He clutched the stone and pushed off to rise to his feet. The ice cracked beneath him. The stone's power pulled against him like he was finally being racked by the Yarrington guards for his many crimes.

He looked at Sora. Really looked at her. For her, he'd do anything.

"I always said I had a plan for how I was going to die," he said. In his mind's eye, he saw her face. His Sora. "The greatest heist there ever was—robbing a goddess of her world!"

Whitney pushed off, shattering the ice as he leaped at the wianu. It thrashed and tried to pull away, but Mahraveh had done her job well. Nesilia screamed as he soared through the air. His body twisted, and for the briefest moment, he got a glimpse back at Sora. He didn't look away.

The light of his world. His savior.

Then the teeth of the beast closed in around him. He felt nothing, nothing at all, as he was swallowed by darkness. Then, Nesilia's screaming stopped, the agonizing weight crushing his body disappeared, and his entire world went silent for once in his yigging life…

LI

THE KNIGHT

Torsten braced himself upon the walls surrounding the Glass Castle. The battle was over, but the sight before him, the city he'd grown up in… it was barely recognizable anymore. The fires had stopped burning at least, but every district was in shambles. The Northern Mason's District and the Central Markets were hit as severely as Dockside and were filled with so much rubble, they were still clearing it out.

It'd been a week since Whitney Fierstown gave his life to deliver the Brike Stone and Nesilia to Nowhere. Some said that maybe the fool messed up his throw and got himself eaten, that it wasn't a sacrifice. But those were whispers because the majority accepted him as the hero Torsten always wanted him to be. He knew in his heart it was true. Whitney wouldn't have let himself die, leaving Sora behind unless there was no other choice.

Or maybe he just wanted to steal the victory all for himself, Torsten thought, allowing himself a smile. That wouldn't be a surprise.

Regardless, the moment that Nesilia was defeated, the battle turned. The goblins and grimaurs wailed in terror and fled. The possessed did the same, running out through the walls and into greater Pantego, where they'd have to be hunted. It would be years before travel could be considered safe. The wianu, too, continued their retreat, and nothing had been heard about them since—not even from the fishing boats being used to clean Autla's Inlet.

The Drav Cra fought to their very last, but Brouben Cragrock's reinforcements helped defeat them. Babrak and his Shesaitju kept at it as well, but once he was captured, they were forced, by his cowardly hand, into surrender. Now, Torsten had every dungeon and holding hall in the city filled with enemy warriors, and no idea what to do with them. He supposed it would be up to Mahraveh. She earned that much, at least.

The dead were innumerable, from all sides, fighters and innocents alike. A constant flow of carts carried them beyond the city walls, piled by race or creed. Drav Cra were burned alongside monsters. Glassmen would be buried, if Torsten ever found enough land to dig thousands upon thousands of graves. The Shesaitju were brought to the coast. They were the easiest to get rid of. Luckily, the battle had left enough debris to drift them off on.

Torsten knew it would be simpler to burn everybody. Some of the Royal Council had even suggested it, Lord Jolly among them. Still, it seemed wrong to deny anybody their beliefs. That was how all the wars started, after all. Even those who followed Nesilia so blindly… it was time to turn the page.

Sighing, Torsten headed down from the wall. Two dwarves hauling a chunk of stone from the broken fortifications bumped him.

"Excuse us, me Lord," one said, more politely then Torsten usually got from dwarves.

Maybe things really are changing.

"No dawdling!" Brouben shouted over, standing atop a pile of boxes and ordering around his men. He offered Torsten a nod, and Torsten returned it before continuing on.

Their presence had been a blessing. Not only in helping end the battle after Nesilia was defeated, but in the cleanup. They didn't have to stay and help, but Brouben had insisted. And he didn't even demand a bit of gold for it like his father would have—not that the Glass Kingdom had much left to give anyway.

The dwarven Prince was King now, and the winged crown fit his head well. The way he told it, his father had abdicated the throne after three centuries, shamed after being tricked by the Buried Goddess. Brouben said that it was Whitney Fierstown who helped show him the way toward claiming the crown and joining the fight for their world. One more gift to Pantego from its greatest thief.

Torsten made it barely a few more steps across the courtyard before he was jarred by another worker. Then another. His days had gone from commanding men of war, to issue orders to the common folk, telling them where to put things, what to do next. Citizens from neighboring villages may have rushed back to their homes to make sure they still existed, but any who called Yarrington home extended their hand in service. Women, children, the elderly—it took everyone, and it would take so many more to make Yarrington a grand city once more.

Stepping into the castle's entry hall, Torsten spotted the Royal Physician rushing by.

"Master Pymer," Torsten called, hurrying to catch him.

"Yes, Master Unger?" Abijah Pymer asked. He turned, his entire face sagging from exhaustion. He looked ten years older than he had just days before. Now that the battle was over, he was at war. So many were injured all over the city, filing any shelter that could be found. His hands and clothing were stained with blood—not usually an appearance befitting a member of the Royal Council, but who would scold him for it?

"How is he?"

"Still asleep."

"Did you try—"

"Sir Unger, I have tried everything I was trained to try. Perhaps he will wake again, or perhaps it is not meant to be. Iam holds his fate now." Pymer rubbed his hands over his face. "Please, with all due respect, there must be somebody else who can keep watch over him. I barely have time to sleep, let alone attend today's Council meeting."

Torsten exhaled through his teeth. "You're right. You're doing a fine job, Master Pymer. Your predecessors would be very proud."

He forced a grin, then continued on his way. Torsten headed to climb the West Tower.

"Lord Unger," someone called up to him as he ascended the stairs. He stopped and looked down. Hovom climbed to greet him, face blackened by soot.

"Is everything all right, Hovom?" Torsten asked.

"I just got word from Taskmaster Lars. He says you want me to get a team of Shesaitju to retrieve the glaruium armor we disposed of?"

"Yes. Is that a problem?"

"No, it's…" he paused. "That doesn't seem crucial right now."

"Our Shesaitju allies won't be here forever. There is no metal more durable. We'll need it."

"My Lord, are you sure it's wise to—"

"Nesilia is gone. She can't control it any longer. The sooner we believe in that, the sooner we can go back to how things were."

"No lack of faith intended, but I don't think we can."

"Faith is not what's in question here," Torsten said. He let out a breath. "I'm tired of being afraid, aren't you? One day, there will be a King's Shield again, and a King to shield with it. And they must be as unbreakable as they ever were."

Hovom considered it for a moment, then struck his chest in salute. "Yes, my Lord."

Torsten returned the gesture. "And Hovom."

"Yes, my Lord?"

"Mahraveh told me your chains worked well."

His features darkened. "Not well enough."

"We wouldn't have survived if not for your work, Hovom," Torsten said. "You have my gratitude. Whatever comes next, I plan to ensure that you have a seat on the Royal Council."

"I… I…" Hovom struggled for words.

"No need to say anything, my friend. You've served in the shadows of the castle for long enough. The shield was nothing without its armorer."

Hovom's crooked lower lip started to tremble, then he bowed his head. "Thank you, Lord Unger."

"You've earned it." Torsten gave him a pat on the arm, then continued up the West Tower to the living floor. The halls were a mess. Doors had been bashed in by angry goblins. So many were dead— guards and hiding noblewomen, handmaidens, and Shesaitju women and children. Stolen jewelry and treasures. Still, the rest of the city had gotten it far worse.

Torsten made his way to a room at the far end. The door was open a hair, and Torsten quietly entered. Dellbar the Holy was on the bed where he'd been since Whitney ripped the Brike Stone out of his trembling hands. He still breathed but hadn't woken since.

"Still in the dark, my friend?" Torsten said, sitting down beside him. "I hope it's peaceful in there. She's gone, Dellbar. The goddess whose followers took everything from you, she's finally gone."

He rested his hand upon the man's chest, feeling his meager breaths. "Pantego needs you, Dellbar. We need—I need... to know if Iam is still watching over us."

"He is."

Torsten glanced up and saw Lord Jolly leaning against the doorway with his one arm. He'd suffered some bruises in the battle but had somehow survived the chaos in South Corner. Torsten had heard how the ambush failed, and the naval forces descended into a mad brawl beneath a smog of smoke. They'd held out long enough for Whitney to make it to the water, and that was all that mattered.

"How are you so sure?" Torsten asked.

"You can still see, can't you?" He gestured to Torsten's blindfold.

"I suppose."

Jolly entered the room and sat on an empty bed across from him. "He's here, Torsten, smiling down on all of us. After so long, it seems we finally ended the God Feud."

"And how many died in its name? How many died, because He couldn't love Nesilia?"

"Sometimes, love doesn't look like roses and sweets," Jolly said. "Perhaps, in these dark times, the best love Iam could have shown her was to let her go for good?" He sighed. "Either way, Torsten Unger, there's enough blame to go around."

"We couldn't have stopped this from happening. Nesilia was right about that. She was inevitable. Whether she arrived now, or a hundred years from now to torture Pi's great-grandchildren, she would have come. I think that's what Dellbar realized. The darkness was always coming, no matter how hard we fought to drive it back. Wiping away heathens and mystics in the name of Light... we always had to face the monster He made."

"There was once a monster you and I shared love for," Lord Jolly said. He scratched the stump of his lost arm. "Perhaps, our Lord, Iam, is more human than any of us ever cared to think."

"Like our great King."

Jolly grunted in agreement. "Still, that we've endured has to mean something. And all those people out there, burying dead loved ones, cleaning up a ravaged city that was the only world they knew… they need something to hold onto." His features darkened, and he looked to the floor. "My home is gone. I need something to hold onto. Some hope."

"I know. I haven't had the opportunity to say how sorry I am."

"Don't be. We won. That's what matters. And maybe, just maybe, Nesilia is the liar, and she and Iam were nothing. Maybe she made herself a monster all on her own."

Torsten nodded. "Maybe," he said out loud, but he knew deep down it wasn't true. He'd seen and heard enough by now. Witnessed enough to know that evil was created, not born, and it rarely happened on its own. Ever since the moment Whitney ended her, Torsten felt different. He couldn't quite explain it, almost like a weight was lifted from him.

He so desperately wanted Dellbar to wake so he could ask him. So he could find out the truth he felt in his soul—that Iam was gone—really gone—from this plane now, having given everything to right his wrong of a bygone age.

"If not, all we can look to do now is follow in his footsteps," he continued. "To right our wrongs. To fix Pantego, and make it a brighter place. That's all the faith I need."

Lord Jolly chuckled. "Righting wrongs? Where in Iam's name do we start?"

Torsten couldn't help but let out a small laugh as well. That was quite a question, one with too many possible answers to imagine. Closing the breach to Elsewhere and rebuilding Panping would be a good start. Training knights and priests to go out into the world and hunt down the demons still in possession of bodies. Finally restoring Winde Port, better than ever. And now Crowfall, too. Giving Mahraveh her Kingdom back. Finding a way to repay Brouben and the dwarves for arriving to help a people who had banished them to caves and mountains so long ago.

"Where to start, indeed," Torsten said.

"I think I have an idea," Lord Jolly replied. "Those people out there haven't only always placed their faith in Iam, but on this castle. On the

Crown. I know the battle has only just ended, but the throne can't remain empty."

"How do you name a King when all the Kings are dead?"

"How did Autla get his crown? Let me tell you. He declared that he was chosen and put it on his own damned head. Those who bowed first, fill Old Yarrington. Those who never did? Well, my ancestors got brought into the Glass another way."

"More war," Torsten lamented.

"Not if we make the right choice."

"And what choice is that?"

"The late King Pi selected his Royal Council. They may be young, inexperienced, hell one is a dwarf, but certainly, that means he entrusted us with the power to decide. The Nothhelms are gone, Torsten. There is nothing we can do about that besides move on."

"I'm guessing you don't want the crown?" Torsten asked.

"No," Lord Jolly muttered after a long pause.

"Why not, you? Your lineage traces back to the old Kings. Oleander trusted you. Pi trusted you. The men who laid down their lives along the waterfront, they trusted you."

"Alas, Crowfall is where I belong, Torsten. I'm needed there now, not here."

Torsten let out a low growl of frustration. "You couldn't just make it easy, could you?"

"Nothing about this is easy, but it's our duty." He leaned forward, placed a hand on Torsten's shoulder, and gazed straight into his blindfold. "I know who it would be if I had my choice."

"Don't start, Kaviel," Torsten scoffed. "I was born a Glintish street rat."

"Raised by Liam himself to knighthood to be the first of the Unger name. You led our armies when we needed you most and defended this city against things no other King ever even imagined possible."

"All I've ever done is fight. Fight to live. Fight for Liam, and Iam, I… that's not what Pantego needs anymore. If only Pi were still alive. He understood what it meant to bring peace."

"But he's not."

"That's all too clear."

"Torsten, what if the fight to rebuild our world is the greatest we've ever faced?" Lord Jolly asked.

"Then I will gladly face it, in the name of our Kingdom," Torsten said. "I serve, waiting for the day that there is no need for a Master of Warfare or a Wearer of White. War is all I know."

Lord Jolly exhaled, then stood. "Well, if not us, then who?"

Torsten couldn't deny that question had crossed his mind a few times since the battle ended. He knew it was impossible to leave the throne of the Glass Kingdom empty for long. Without a proper King, all the lords and cities who'd pledged fealty to the Nothhelms would break away after the dust settled. The empire Liam and his fathers had carved out would fall to pieces, to one day be put together by another conqueror in another series of wars.

Even if everyone got along and played nice in the wake of so much death, that was as inevitable as Nesilia had been. And as Torsten strolled through the halls of the castle that night, he hated that all he could think of were the wars to come, when the greatest he'd ever known had only just ended.

Wind howled as he stepped into the Throne Room, the ceiling broken apart. Fragments of glass still littered the grand carpet, which unfurled unto the throne's dais. It was torn and stained with blood that would never come clean. And the throne itself was ruptured—cracked down the middle with the left half in pieces.

Salvation lay upon what was left of the seat in three pieces. There was no crypt to return it to. It'd take years to dig out the caskets and the bodies buried by Nesilia and Sora's fight, if there was even anything left of them when they were found. Perhaps that was Nesilia's greatest revenge, to bury the most prominent followers of Iam as she'd been for so long. Liam's broken sword and a few other weapons reforged with silver were now all that remained of more than a thousand years of Glass Kings.

Torsten knelt before the throne and slowly reached for the sword's handle. He winced as he pictured the events leading to its breaking. Nesilia, slaughtering so many people until Rand Langley came and took up the blade himself. Now, he was gone too. Not a soul had heard of his or his upyr sister's whereabouts since the end of the battle, and Torsten supposed they never would.

Both deserved blame and punishment for what they'd done. Rand had betrayed and killed men of his own Order, his own King, Lucas... Torsten had yet to be able to find the young Shieldsmen's parents after the battle, but their shop had burned down with most of Dockside and South Corner. He had to hope they'd turn up somewhere. Sigrid, his sister, had murdered Queen Oleander and who knows how many more before Nesilia took control of her and killed thousands.

Nothing could ever redeem all the evil they'd been behind. Yet, Torsten couldn't help but wish that they found somewhere quiet—a shack by the water somewhere, fishing together... happy together. Finally, at peace. He knew he shouldn't—Lucas and Oleander deserved better—but he did.

A man and his upyr sister.

"Would you have sent an army after them to the ends of the earth?" Torsten asked of Liam as he raised the broken sword. "Or would you have let go, forgotten what was done, like you did with Sora?"

The wind whistled in the silence that followed, playing gentle melodies on the broken glass above. He wasn't expecting an answer, he never did, even all the times he visited the crypt to speak with his King. However, he usually felt something other than emptiness.

He closed his eyes, again picturing all the Shieldsmen who'd died right behind him. He saw Lucas, head chopped off by the very traitor who'd wielded *Salvation* and saved them. The world used to be so simple. There were Iam's faithful, and then everyone else. Now, there were too many shades between for Torsten to count.

Feeling a phantom tear upon his cheek, Torsten rubbed his face. "Why couldn't it have been me taken?" he asked, voice cracking. "Why them?" Not even out loud did he say, "Why him."

It was silly. In truth, he'd barely known the thief, but somehow, he'd become a trusted ally, if not a friend.

Torsten had been strong during the rebuild, firm with his orders, always standing proud. But here, alone, the weight of so many dead finally hit him. He leaned on the throne, the blindfold sliding off his seared eyes and up over his bald pate.

"Sir Unger, are you all right?" came Lucindur's soft, melodic voice. It startled him.

"I'm fine," he replied, mustering the most composed tone he could manage. He adjusted the blindfold and straightened his back. "Just thinking." It sounded like a question.

"About?" she asked, stepping forward.

"Everything. About Kings lost, and who should sit upon this throne now that they're all gone." He wasn't sure why he spoke so plainly with her. She wasn't a member of the court, not even from Yarrington, but she had a calming presence that made him feel she was worthy of his trust.

"Well, uh… I don't know anything about that," she said. Her hesitation told Torsten all it needed to. She was lying. She knew about Sora's true origin.

Torsten didn't press her further. Instead, he placed the broken sword down and pushed off the throne to rise to his feet.

Her features were bright, like she'd fully recovered from her exertion, though her eyes were puffy. No doubt from crying in a way Torsten's lack of eyes didn't allow. Whitney's death hit the whole group hard. Tum Tum worked through it by helping the other dwarves. Lucindur, by staying in the castle and repairing her instrument. And Sora… Torsten had barely seen her. She'd spent days down by the water, staring—probably wondering, as Torsten did, why not her? Maybe she hoped he'd swim to shore as if nothing in the world was wrong.

Torsten cleared his throat and said, "You look well."

"I'm feeling better," she said. "You have my thanks for allowing me to stay here. I know there are many out there who only wish to be so lucky."

"Without you, they'd all be dead. We'd all be dead."

The corners of her lips curled into a frail smile. "Like each of us, I did what I had to. I didn't choose my powers."

"Yet, you saved all of this with them. The Kingdom owes you a debt it can never repay, Lucindur of Glinthaven. You can stay as long as you like."

"I… thank you, Master Unger."

"Please, just Torsten."

"Thank you, Torsten."

They both looked to the floor for a few seconds, then Torsten regarded the salfio strapped to her back. "Is it working?" he asked.

"It is, yes. Thank the heavens a string didn't break this time. Though, I'd very much wish not to have to play again."

"That would be an injustice to this new world we are forging." Torsten swallowed back a suddenly dry throat. "The song you played when Nesilia was here. It was quite beautiful. I'd love to hear it again sometime, without all the…" He looked around, grimaced. "Well, you know."

"My mother taught it to me, who learned it from her mother, and so on. I'm not even sure what it's called. Passing down songs through generations is a right of passage amongst the Glintish."

"Is it? I've barely been there."

"You should visit sometime."

"If only I could."

This time, Lucindur looked around the devastated room, and her cheeks went a shade darker from embarrassment. She likely realized, as Torsten did, that it would be many years, maybe decades, before all Nesilia's damage was undone.

"Will you go back?" Torsten asked.

"Yes," she answered. "My daughter's there. And I don't think there's much use for Lightmancery any longer."

"Maybe not, but there are thousands of sad, homeless people outside these walls. Your music might ease their suffering, if you're willing to keep playing." He stepped up the dais, beside the throne, and pictured better days. "I used to hate when troupes and bards came through."

"Oh?"

"Oleander loved the distractions. Liam liked it when they were about him, until he couldn't care for anything at all. But I hated them. I never understood it. Why invest in make-believe, when a cathedral and Iam's grace were so near?"

"I suppose that's one way—"

"I do now, though," he said, interrupting. "I think you should stay for a little while. Bring your daughter. Play your music across the city and give Whitney the flamboyant funeral we know he would have wanted."

She chuckled. "Well, that's just it. Whitney wouldn't want anybody crying, but when I play this instrument, it brings out emotions and memories I can't control. There are so many dead. So many lost spirits. It would only make them more downcast."

"Maybe, that sadness is exactly what they need to feel."

Lucindur removed the instrument from her back and studied it. She ran her finger along the frets, plucking once as if to test it. The pitch was perfect, at least to Torsten's untrained ear. The sound echoed across the empty room. Torsten could feel it in his bones, and he staggered back into the throne, his hand stopping on top of *Salvation's* grip as he braced himself.

Clearly unaware of the effect it was having on him, Lucindur started to hum and play softly, that same song from earlier, and Torsten found it impossible to move. She wasn't lying. His heart grew heavy, and he longed more than ever that he could shed a tear, even just one. That he could let the pain out. With one hand, he pushed the enchanted blindfold up, the only way he could earn the sensation of closed eyes.

In a flash, he experienced it all—every moment in this room. From the good, like when he was a young ward to Sir Uriah, looking at the tall ceiling as if it were the most amazing thing he'd ever seen—which it had been—to stealing glances at Oleander during parties or meetings. Being knighted by Liam himself a few feet away from the throne.

And then, all the awful things. Sir Uriah, his mentor, going missing. King Liam's last breath upon this very seat. A possessed Pi causing war with the Shesaitju that killed so many. Cutting Valin Tehr's head from his shoulders.

Emotion crashed over him like a wave. His lips started to tremble; his chest constricted. He could barely breathe. The hand keeping him upright unconsciously clenched around *Salvation's* grip, and he squeezed tight as he could.

And as he did, he saw something he hadn't expected. No longer was he in the Throne Room, but far away, in a chamber with walls of red stone and thin windows. He saw Liam standing in front of a bed when a Panpingese woman dressed in the red robes of a mystic arrived at the door.

Torsten didn't need to ask himself who she was. When he saw her, he knew. She didn't only have Sora's ears, but her cheeks and her nose, her lips—this was the ancient one, Sora Sumati. She clutched her stomach, and Liam's eyes welled with tears.

"You're with child?" he asked as he slowly approached her. His voice cracked in a way unlike Torsten had ever heard from him.

Smiling, she said, "I am." Then, she took his shaking hand and pressed it against her belly.

"Our child?"

She nodded, and he threw his arms around her, and she, him. He squeezed her, letting his face be lost within her long, black hair. Torsten couldn't remember even seeing Liam hug Oleander, let alone hold her like that. Like there was nobody else in the entire world. Like how Whitney held Sora before they joined a war he wouldn't return from.

They were in love. Truly, and purely, in love.

"Torsten!" Lucindur yelped.

He heard her salfio drop, and then she ran to him. She pulled his enchanted blindfold down over his eyes, and he searched the room, totally confused about how he wound up on the floor. She grasped his hand, and it stung, and when he looked down, he saw that his palm was cut, *Salvation* just an arm's length away, a droplet of fresh blood on the broken edge.

"I told you I shouldn't play that song around so much pain and loss," she said, quickly tearing off a piece of her sleeve and wrapping his hand. She pressed, and the blood seeped through. All Torsten could picture was Sora the blood mage after she'd cut her hand to throw fire.

"I saw…" he stammered. "I saw… Liam?"

"King Liam, that's—" Lucindur glanced down at *Salvation*. "That was his sword, wasn't it? I'm so sorry, Torsten. Sometimes, if I play... unfocused, people around me feel the memories of those who've touched what they're wearing or holding. It's why I shouldn't—"

Torsten grasped her forearm, cutting her short. "She wasn't like the others," he said. "They were in love."

"What are you talking about?"

"Sora's parents. Liam. He loved her. A mystic, a foreigner, an enemy—he loved her."

Lucindur's eyes went wide. "Wait, you know?"

He nodded. "Sora isn't a bastard at all. She was his." He couldn't believe the words coming out of his mouth, but all became so clear. He was wrong. Iam had purposefully put Sora in his path all those moons ago. And all this time, he'd thought her powers a curse, even as they saved him and Pantego time and time again. This was precisely where he was meant to be.

Here, beside the throne, with a chance to right Liam's wrong, just as Iam had given everything to right His. Liam had fought countless wars against the evil mystics, only to fall for one and realize she was human after all. And he took that secret to his grave. That awful, horrible secret which would have undermined everything he'd ever done in the name of Iam—that there *could* be peace with those who weren't Iam's children.

It wasn't illness that killed Liam, or a lifetime of poison from the Queen he didn't love, like so many gossiped. It was that truth that broke him, that caused him to stop fighting until his body gave out. He'd lost the only person he'd ever loved and had hidden the miracle they'd created together. All because of his own pride.

Torsten scrambled to his feet, accidentally knocking Lucindur back. He stopped, frantically turning to steady her, then continued across the throne room.

"Torsten, what are you doing?" she asked, face wracked with concern.

"I..." He stopped over her salfio, picked it up. "Thank you, Lucindur, for showing me what I must do. Never... ever stop playing this." He returned the instrument to her before finally exiting the Throne Room, leaving her wearing a baffled expression and stumbling over words.

LII

THE MYSTIC

Sora sat at the edge of the docks, one of the few spots left intact. The whole of South Corner and Dockside looked like Winde Port all over again—far worse if she were honest. Ash blew on the air like snow, enough to make her throat sore. The Shesaitju were focused on cleaning out the inlet. Without many zhulong left to help, it was proving a grand undertaking.

However, this time, at least, the locals helped them. A bond forged by the heat of battle helped them work together without fighting. Sure, she overheard bickering and a derogatory term thrown here and there between races, but it never escalated beyond that. Maybe they were all just too tired.

Sora focused on the small fishing boats, finally dragging the wreckage of Babrak's ship ashore. It'd taken a week just for the cleaning efforts to reach the middle of the inlet. The rowers moved slowly, timidly, as if disturbing the body of the wianu chained to its prow might, somehow, invite Nesilia back.

It wouldn't. The moment Whitney gave his life to send her to Nowhere, Sora felt it in her blood—that ever-looming, dark connection to the Goddess was gone. The nightmares, gone. She should've been relieved, and yet, the absence of that feeling chilled her more than its presence ever had. Because she also knew that Whitney was gone with her. Not banished to Elsewhere where she could pluck him out—gone… really gone, forever.

She didn't even have a chance to say goodbye. Just a distant view of his patented smirk through her tangled hair before he carried the Brike Stone into the wianu's dreaded maw. If she'd only been stronger, maybe she could've reached him and helped him pry the stone loose to toss it in. Every moment she was awake, she replayed all the events of the battle in her mind, wondering where she could've slowed down and conserved her energy.

Killing Freydis could've been simple, but instead, she absolutely destroyed her. Like the mystics of old, she allowed vengeance to rule her.

Never again.

She could've let others die in the Throne Room instead of shielding them all. Instead, she drained herself until all she could offer was a bridge for Whitney that he'd take straight to his doom.

But she was no murderer, and to let those brave men die when she could have saved them…

Her fists squeezed as the wreckage, and the monster along with it, slid up onto the narrow beach near the western jetty. Before she knew it, she found herself storming toward it.

"Why!" she screamed, unleashing a fiery torrent upon all of it. People had to dive out of the way to escape her rage. The fire grew and grew, the heat stinging her cheeks. Parts of the ship were incinerated in an instant. She moved closer, every scream fueling the mystic blaze. The wianu's thick flesh flaked away to black dust, as if it were made of darkness. It didn't even have bones. It didn't even stink like burning, rotten flesh should, which only made her angrier.

"You promised to never leave me!"

The fire grew and swirled into a whirlwind, enveloping her, but unable to harm her because it was part of her now. Nearby water flash-evaporated. Men throughout the district shouted, fearful that battle had come for them again. Sora didn't relent.

Then, a hand fell upon her shoulder. A hand that should've been melted in an instant.

"A promise nobody could ever keep," Mahraveh whispered in her ear.

Hearing a familiar voice caused Sora to relent. The fire wisped away into embers, and she collapsed, exhausted from employing so much energy. Her knees banged on a hard surface where there used to be sand, and as the smoke settled, Sora realized that the entire coast had been turned to glass by the heat of her flames. A part of her still hoped that maybe Whitney's body might appear once the wianu was gone, but the monster was nothing but a scorch mark now.

"They want to keep the promise," Mahraveh went on, moving in front of her and crouching to look Sora in the eye. "With all their heart, they do. But men cannot control the world, and neither can we."

"I wish I could," Sora whimpered.

"No, you don't. Because then you would be exactly like Nesilia, and you are far from her."

"Am I?"

Mahraveh held Sora by the shoulders, unfazed by the heat radiating off her, protected by her Caleef skin. "You are still here, aren't you?"

Sora sniveled, then wiped her nose with her wrist. Mahraveh helped her stand, her feet cracking the newly formed glass down to a layer of untouched sand.

"I just don't know who to be angry at anymore," Sora said. "I didn't even get to say goodbye."

"I know," Mahraveh said, firmly. She had a way about her, not just consoling or desperate to make Sora feel better. She talked plainly, honestly. It was strangely comforting.

"My father died across a desert," she continued. "My oldest friend —a man I think I loved—died right in front of me by the hands of my own god. Saying goodbye would not have changed a thing. But the man you *know* you loved… the people here will call him a hero. They'll form statues of him, name things for him—buildings, children, cities even. All you need to know is that he did it for you."

Mahraveh's gaze swept across the battered harbor. She regarded the people helping, all of different types, her eyes freezing momentarily upon her second in command. Bit'rudam was busy herding zhulong to drag a bundle of rubble. He wore an eyepatch now, having lost his in the battle. The tiniest hint of a smile touched Mahraveh's lips. Sora had no idea she even had the capacity for such an emotion.

"Dying for each other, it's what separates us," Mahraveh said. "It was the strength of an afhem, and it will be the strength of all the Black Sands soon. I hold all the memories of the Caleef, and if just one of them were capable of what your Whitney was, we would have never lost our Kingdom to fear-mongers like Babrak."

"I hope you get it back," Sora said.

"From the mouth of a woman whose home village my father burned to the ground." She patted Sora's arm. "That is progress, no?"

"Progress…" Sora laughed quietly. Mahraveh apparently saw that as the end to their conversation and went to walk by, but Sora clutched her wrist.

"You were nearest to him at the end," she said. "Did you hear what he said?"

Mahraveh shook her head.

Sora bit her lip, then nodded. "I almost wish you would have lied." She'd tried to imagine it. How he'd said it was for her or something loving, but she knew Whitney. He probably looked Nesilia straight on and told her to go shog herself.

"No, you don't," Mahraveh said. "My apologies, Sora, but I must go. There is much to be done before we return home, and there are many hundreds of Shesaitju prisoners we must decide what to do with, including their leader."

Mahi glanced down, and Sora followed her gaze before realizing she was still squeezing the Caleef's wrist. Embers floated around her hand as her emotions fueled her power, but again, Mahraveh couldn't feel the heat.

"Oh, I'm so sorry." Sora quickly let go.

"Don't be. But if you'd like to unleash some more anger, there is plenty of rubble that'd take up less room as glass or ash." She tapped the glossy, flat surface beneath them with her toe, then hopped up to the docks.

"Lady Mahraveh!" Sora called up to her. The Caleef looked back. "Enough people died here today. Show them mercy… if you can."

Mahi pursed her lips, then offered only a soft grunt before she continued. As she went, Sora couldn't help but wonder what that beautiful young lady had been like before becoming Caleef. Would she be as unrecognizable as Sora would have been before the things Nesilia made her do?

Sora sighed and turned, looking down at the glass she'd made incidentally. In the reflection, she looked the same as she always had, though she knew she wasn't. Without Whitney now, she had no idea who the woman staring back up at her was.

Talons poked along her back, then dug into her shoulder. Aquira looked at the charred mark where the wianu had been, then made a few soft chirps.

"I know, Girl," Sora said, scratching the wyvern under the chin. "I miss him, too."

That feeling was multiplied as she looked into her reptilian friend's golden eyes. It hadn't been long after her reunion with Whitney that she'd met Aquira. They'd been through so much, the three of them…

Aquira purred and rubbed against the side of Sora's head.

"How is your wing feeling?" Sora extended the wyvern's left wing, sewn together with stitches. She'd attempted to fix it but still couldn't manage to summon forth the power of healing, like her anger bottled up that part of her.

Aquira stretched out and flapped both wings twice, then squealed in pain, curling the injured one in.

"I'm sorry, Girl," Sora said. "But it'll get better."

She thought, at that moment, she might be talking to herself. But would it? Would things ever truly get better?

She looked up and across Dockside. She didn't know the place. In fact, this had been her first time there. However, she knew it'd never look the same. The stacks and rows of wood shanties huddled between grand churches, it reminded her of the Panpingese District in Winde Port. Maybe it was better it would all change, just as her life would.

"C'mon, Girl," she said. "I can't be here anymore.

<hr>

Every corner of Yarrington reminded her of Whitney, even though it was in shambles, and she'd only been there with him once. She stopped on the Royal Avenue, outside of a place that used to be a bar. She and Whitney had shared a drink there shortly after returning from the Webbed Woods. Now, she couldn't even remember its name.

If only she'd been stronger that day. She'd put the idea in his head of them going to Yaolin and learning who Sora really was. If they hadn't, maybe she wouldn't know the truth of her parentage, but she might still have him. They'd probably be in Westvale or somewhere Whitney loved, living like kings and queens, figuratively.

She was so young and foolish then, with no idea that the only home she'd ever need was with him. Getting into trouble. Following his ridiculous, often contradictory code of conduct. Whitney was an enigma to himself and everyone around him, but she loved him for it.

Stopping outside the tavern, she ran her hand along a charred railing. The place was unrecognizable but lucky enough to still have a ceiling. The Glass army now used it as a place to house wounded, with surgeons, monks, and sisters of Iam flowing in and out with water and medical equipment. There was barely enough to spare.

All throughout Yarrington, she'd passed places like this. It couldn't be hidden in the back of a war camp, or in a ghetto. Everyone, every survivor, had to bear witness to the horrors of war. And as the memories of Whitney drew her inside, so did she.

That bar, the one where Sora and Whitney once shared that drink, was now lined with injured soldiers. Some groaned. Others were fast asleep. They were bandaged, missing limbs, everything.

Aquira made a sad-sounding whistle.

"I know," she whispered as she continued in deeper. The floor was wet from blood, and the water used to wash it off. She kept going until she found a man she recognized. Sir Austun Mulliner, lay alone on a bedroll, shaking in his sleep. He had a deep gash through his gut, which was filled with herbs. The skin around it was angry red, irritated, and covered in pus. Sweat poured down his forehead and drenched his blood-stained clothing.

"Sir Mulliner," Sora whispered, kneeling beside him. She took his clammy hand. He groaned and turned the other way as if he had no idea she was there.

"Infection set in a few days ago," a sister passing by, carrying a bucket of water, said. "I'm afraid it's only a matter of time before he's with Iam."

The sister continued on her way before Sora could turn and ask any more. From behind, she thought it looked like Bartholomew Darkings' daughter, hard at work being a better person than her father could've ever dreamed of being.

Sora looked back down, ran her hand across Sir Mulliner's forehead. He was on fire. She moved her palm down to cover his wound, then closed her eyes and looked within. Her powers ignored her, and she knew why. The ability to heal couldn't fight through rage, and that was all she felt.

She opened her eyes. Aquira crawled down from her shoulder and stood across from Sir Mulliner's broken body. The wyvern nuzzled against his neck.

Drawing a deep breath, Sora tried again. She remembered how, just like Whitney… just like all of them, this man had given all he had to spare the realm from Nesilia. She recalled Whitney purposely forgetting the Shieldsman's name, like he always used to.

A small but genuine chuckle slipped through her lips, and with it, she felt a surge. Her fingertips crackled with energy as bluish smoke expanded over Sir Mulliner's wound. First, the irritation became healthy skin, then the wound itself stitched over, layers of sinew and skin reforming one over the other.

Sora held her breath as she drew on the power in her blood, and only when the wound closed did she breathe. She staggered back, her legs weak. Tears streamed down her cheeks. Of all her powers, healing had always taken the most out of her. It was as if she were bestowing her life-force into another.

In an instant, Sir Mulliner returned from the precipice of death. He coughed a few times. All the color slowly returned to his face as he looked around, confused before his gaze stopped on Sora.

"You?" he rasped.

"I… yes…" she panted, barely able to form words. Clearly, she hadn't recovered yet from all her exertion against Nesilia and then on the beach.

"By Iam, how did you?" Nauriyal rushed over, patting Sir Mulliner, then lifting him to check the exit wound. "It's a miracle." She leaned his head back and offered him water.

In Winde Port, Whitney had once told her not to give a homeless boy gold because it wouldn't help. It'd feed him for a day, he'd said, and all the rest of the ghetto would remain starving. She loved Whitney, loved his eccentricities, but she finally knew how wrong he was.

Sora wished she could tell him so. Rub his face in it. Watch him squirm.

It was true, she couldn't help everybody. She'd pass out long before, but she was tired of using her powers for destruction. Wasn't that what undid the mystics in the first place? So, before Nauriyal and Sir Mulliner could offer their profuse thanks, she moved on to the next body.

There were limits. She wasn't sure of all of them, but she knew she couldn't regrow limbs or bring anybody back from the dead. She healed who she could, stunning the entire tavern into silence. After a handful, her legs were so weak Nauriyal had to help her walk, but she kept going. And even more, drawing on her own innate connection to Elsewhere like a proper mystic was no longer possible.

So, she snagged a surgeon's knife and cut her hand like she used to. And as the sacrifice flowed, she healed with blood magic. Whatever it took. Over and over, it was like she couldn't control it. Her vision went dark, and all she witnessed was the next body in front of her. She mended fractured bones, broken ribs, mortal wounds. She didn't hold back until she was done and took a step, then collapsed over a stool.

Aquira dug into her shoulder and flapped with all her might to keep her standing until her injured wing caused her to flop onto the bar. She squealed in pain, and the last thing Sora remembered was slashing her own left hand and healing Aquira's broken wing before she fell hard to the wood floor.

"Sora, you're all right."

Her eyes blinked open, and an unexpected face appeared above her.

"Here," Torsten said, offering a cup of water. "You need to replenish your fluids. You lost a lot of blood."

Sora absentmindedly grasped at the cup. Her hands stung so much, she nearly dropped it, but Torsten helped her hold on. Her throat burned with dryness, and her muscles shook. She struggled to raise her arm without his help.

She gulped down every ounce, forgetting to breathe. Torsten took the cup and placed it on a bedside table. Only then did she finally look around. She was within an opulent room that was obviously in the Glass Castle. Well, somewhat opulent, at least once upon a time. The blinds had been torn by goblins or grimaurs, and much of the furniture tipped and broken.

"What happened?" she asked.

She placed her hands on the bed to try and sit up, but again, her palms stung. Turning them over, she noticed the slashes on each, as well as smaller cuts up the length of her arms. Then, she recalled healing Sir Mulliner and so many others, until the memory became a fog.

"The way Nauriyal tells it, you healed dozens of people until you, yourself, collapsed," Torsten said. "Even Sir Mulliner spoke in praise, and he's much harder to please than me. Thank you, Sora. You did a great service to the Kingdom."

Sora grimaced. She looked inward, hoping the power to heal her own wounds might emerge, but she was too weak. "I'm surprised you see it that way," she muttered. "Didn't I taint them with my cursed magic?"

Torsten frowned. "It was much simpler when that was the answer, wasn't it?"

She wasn't sure how to respond, and he just kept looking at her—or, rather, his magical blindfold remained fixed upon her. Either way, it was unsettling.

"For you, perhaps," she said, a slight smile forcing itself onto her face.

"You really are his, aren't you?" he asked softly, like the very question might send the castle into ruin.

"I'm not—huh?" He'd caught her completely off guard.

"I can see it. Not the eyes, thanks to this." He tugged on his blindfold. "But something... you're not fully Panpingese."

"You can say 'knife-ear,'" she grumbled.

He stumbled over a response, jaw hanging in shock.

"Sorry," she said. "My head is pounding."

"No, I deserve it. I was cruel to you when we first met, and all you'd tried to do was heal me and fight my enemies. I should have seen it then."

"Seen what?"

"The miracle right in front of me."

Sora fought the pain in her hands to sit up and build as much distance across the bed as she could. "Torsten, have you slept at all? You sound insane."

"No, Sora, listen to me. Everything you were then stood against Iam and against my very being, but so many times, when hope was gone, it was you who saved us. Not your powers, not your blood magic —you. Iam was—"

"Oh, stop it with Iam," Sora groaned. "He didn't place me in those places."

"Maybe. Maybe not. But I should've had you hanged the moment we returned from the Webbed Woods instead of pardoning you. Something inside of me told me I shouldn't, and now, here we are."

"It's because you're a good man, Torsten. You wear your hate well, but deep down, you know that so many of the things your church of Iam stood for were perversions of men. They weren't Iam. Who knows what He truly thinks—thought? Was He the benevolent hero who ended the God Feud and saved us all, or did His stubbornness cause it?"

The holy knight bit his lower lip but said nothing.

Sora continued. "I've been with all the peoples in this land. Shesaitju, dwarves, mystics… they all tell a different story. But what I know now is all the old names we fall prostrate before, they're all gone. A memory. We have to move on."

"Sora, you're not listening to me," Torsten said. He scooted closer. "I followed Liam against all those same peoples. We crushed them, forced them to bend the knee and see the world our way. We made Pantego one giant mirror of our world. A glass kingdom…" He drew a deep breath. "All the conquests, and beauties, and faith in Iam couldn't fill the void in Liam's heart."

Sora's throat went tight. She couldn't respond even if she wanted to.

"I've witnessed miracles," Torsten went on. "Saw Pi reborn from death. Received sight when I'd lost my own. Saw a dastardly thief give his life to save everyone. But the true miracle was right in front of me all along. In all that hate, in all that war and death, Liam found something he truly cared for amongst the ranks of his most bitter enemies. He found love."

Torsten leaned over Sora and ran his fingers through her hair.

She recoiled, but only slightly, and only out of surprise.

"You are a miracle, Sora," he whispered. "Liam gave his very soul to hide you from his worst enemy—himself. And now, here you lay, and all the war-torn streets outside these castle walls speak of the 'knife-eared' mystic healing the injured, of the blood mage giving her own blood for others."

Sora cleared her throat. "I don't know what you want me to say, Torsten."

"I'm so tired of asking for miracles, and Dellbar told me to open my eyes to receiving them. You don't have to believe it's Iam that set us in each other's path, but I still have faith in the world He *wanted*, despite all His errors and those made in His name."

"Torsten, please don't say what I know you're about to."

"I had the honor of getting to know the real King Pi after Nesilia's influence left him," Torsten said, ignoring her. "He was all the best parts of his parents. I know who Pi would've wanted to take the throne."

She choked back tears and looked out the window, squinting through wet eyes. "No, Torsten."

"It's you, Sora," he implored.

"No…"

"It has to be. You can bring us together in a way that we never truly were. The daughter of our greatest King and his greatest enemy. The healer, whose ferocity mirrored her father's when she helped us save this city. If Pantego truly belongs to the Kingdom, then you are born in the Glass, raised by it. A blood mage like those favored in the north. A mystic who could garner the support of the broken East as we repair it. You are strong enough to stand before Mahraveh and the Black Sands and know her deepest pains. You are the bastard child of Pantego and all its many gods, not just the one."

"Torsten, I already told Whitney I don't want it. I never will."

"That is why it must be you."

"Then why not you?" She sat up further. "You're offering the Crown to me, but you could walk into that Throne Room, and there isn't a man or woman who wouldn't bow. You know that."

He shook his head. "It can't be me."

"It can."

"No!" he shouted, causing Sora to flinch. His hands squeezed the sheets, trembling. He took a few measured breaths to calm himself. "I can't," he said.

Sora took his hands to try and steady them from shaking. "You say it should be me because I don't want it, but neither do you. Otherwise, you wouldn't be here."

"I don't want it, that's true," he said. "But that's not it, Sora. You've seen what I'm capable of. I don't—I don't deserve it. You do. Everything you've fought through, all the scorn, the bad looks, the distrust. We have a chance to start over and end all of it. To change."

Sora opened her mouth to respond, but couldn't find the words. She sank back.

"You know," she said finally. "Whitney mentioned you all the time. Like you were actually best friends even though you hardly knew each other."

Torsten chuckled softly. "He really was a lunatic."

"He was. But that's the thing about Whitney. Despite all the bad things he ever did, the only people he ever cared about were good, deep down. Like Lucindur and Tum Tum. By Elsewhere, he found the soft heart of a monstrous upyr. You aren't the man you were, Torsten."

"Maybe not, but I know my place," he said. "My life is to serve this Kingdom. I made that vow when Liam knighted me, and I will never break it. And right now, against all odds, I believe that you are what is best for it."

"All because I have Nothhelm blood in me?" she scoffed.

"And so much more." He backed away from the bed, fell to one knee, and lowered his head. "The Royal Council will hear your story, and they will agree. Dellbar will wake, and a new crown shall find a new head. Sora Nothhelm, from this day, until the end of my days, you have my sword and shield. Or Iam, strike me down."

Sora's heart skipped a beat. She'd never been bowed to before—at least not when Nesilia wasn't inhabiting her body—let alone by a member of the Royal Council. She supposed that's why he did it. Those were the types of people he'd always served. Those who'd get bowed to once and realize they were exactly where they were ordained to be.

"And what if I reject their decision?" she asked.

"Then that crown will find a lesser head," Torsten replied. "And the Glass Kingdom, whatever it is to become, will be a lesser place."

His head remained bowed, and Sora couldn't help but stare. He actually believed what he was saying about her. If her birth were really a miracle, it had nothing on that. Only a year ago, he'd been disgusted by blood magic and her appearance.

She didn't answer right away. What she did know is that she didn't want to be Queen. There was nothing he could say or do that would ever change that. And she shouldn't be Queen. In charge of everyone simply because of a bloodline?

Without that, Torsten wouldn't even be considering it.

But she knew him. Torsten was bullheaded, even if he'd opened his mind beyond the strict dogma of his faith. He wouldn't back down unless she left him no other choice, and then council members and lords and ladies across Pantego would squabble over the Crown. There'd be more wars, more death—the very things that led Sora to grow up in a small village hidden away from everyone.

Yet, it was in that town she'd met Whitney. What would he do here? She recalled one of the lessons he'd imparted to her, unable to hide a small smirk. "The best way to get someone to do what you want is to make them think you're doing what they want," he'd said.

That was it. Her grift was in place. She'd take the crown, like all the treasures Whitney had stolen just for the fun of it, and then she'd do what Whitney often wound up doing without him ever realizing. She'd do the right thing. She'd place the crown upon the head of someone who'd proven he deserved it.

EPILOGUE

Tum Tum and Lucindur stood at the edge of Port Street—what was left of it. No longer were the shanties and decrepit buildings looming over the waters, those had all been cleared away to make room for new things, better things, stronger things. If anything were true and agreed upon by all, it was that Pantego would indeed become stronger through this trial.

They would learn. All of them.

The undertaking was unlike anything Tum Tum had ever been a part of. Sure, he'd run the Winder's Dwarf in Winde Port, and even built Gold Grin's Grotto in Yaolin City, but this… this was something else altogether.

The Shesaitju and dwarves had stuck around to clean up the city before returning to their own lands to deal with their own messes. New alliances forged between King Brouben and Caleef Mahraveh and the Glass Kingdom would ensure mutual aid between the powers of Pantego—at least until the next war came. Though Tum Tum hoped that maybe this one time, this last war might actually be the last one. Still, he wasn't naïve.

More important than all of that, however, was that for now, his would be the one and only tavern on the newly erected Dockside strip.

"It really is a gorgeous sight," Lucindur said, eyes set on the new building. Construction had been completed the day before, and now the finishing touches were being laid. White plaster was crossed by thick, oak beams. Several windows were spaced out, large enough to see those bustling within, preparing for the night's grand opening.

"Somethin no one ever said about Dockside," Tum Tum jested. "No better place for him, neither."

"He'd love it," Lucindur said.

"He does love it," Tum Tum said. "Wherever he is."

"I can imagine him, spinning tall tales of grand adventures."

"Mother!" Talwyn called from a window on the third floor of the adjacent building. "I can't find my light purple dress!"

"Well, then wear another," Lucindur said.

"I can't. The purple was Whitney's favorite."

Lucindur looked down at Tum Tum and rolled her eyes.

Whitney's old Troupe had arrived in Yarrington and were now permanent residents. The building, as beautiful as anything in Old Yarrington, would house them all, free of charge. They were to perform daily for all of the patrons in Dockside and beyond. For no longer was the district to be a stain upon the city, forgotten about and ignored, a place only for shipments to pass through. It would now be a haven for cultures brought together by the Glass Kingdom.

It was the least the former Pompare Troupe could do, Lucindur had told Tum Tum. Even she would play her now-infamous salfio, whose songs filled Yarrington in the days after battle, when all hope seemed lost, inspiring the workers to push through.

This wasn't just any tavern. *Godkiller's Tavern* sat directly before the landing where Whitney Fierstown had given his life to save the world by killing the Goddess Nesilia and earning the same title without contest.

"Whitney Godkiller," Tum Tum said aloud, chuckling lightly.

"Beats Blisslayer."

"Got that right," Tum Tum added.

A group of dwarves was hard at work erecting a new statue situated in the inlet, right where Whitney had died. Every ship arriving at Yarrington would have to pass it, which Whitney would have loved. A plinth with torches encircled it, ensuring every guest upon the deck would have their eyes drawn to the sea and recall the legend. It captured him in the very moment. As Whitney ran across the water, the entire world had held its breath. Now, he would be immortalized that way forever.

"The nose still ain't right," Tum Tum complained. "It's a bit flatter on the end."

"Don't you think you're being a little picky?" Lucy asked. She laughed. "Whitney would have made a joke about being picky over a nose."

"Aye," Tum Tum agreed. "But no. I ain't bein picky enough. Nothin's too good for that damned thief. Nothin."

"I suppose you're right."

Talwyn came out from the front door of the building wearing her purple dress. Gentry followed close behind, Aquira cradled in his arms. Sora had been gracious enough to give the boy guardianship over the wyvern, telling him that she'd come calling for her again someday. Tum Tum, however, knew why she left the wyvern behind. There were too many memories shared between Sora, Whitney, and Aquira, even from the first day Tum Tum had met her.

Tum Tum scratched her neck frills. "Good, bird," he said.

"Found it," Talwyn said, grabbing her skirt with both hands and giving it a playful twirl. "How do I look?"

"Gorgeous as ever," Lucindur assured her.

Gentry gripped Aqiura tight against his chest, his gaze frozen upon the statue. The boy barely stopped crying since their caravan had arrived, and he'd heard the news about Whitney. There had to be guilt over their last days together. Gentry kept wishing he'd been there. But Whitney had made the right decision in leaving him behind, and no one was going to fault him for it.

Tum Tum rustled the boy's hair and said, "He's in a better place now, lad."

Tum Tum knew it was a lie. He knew that anyone unlucky enough to be devoured by the wianu would be damned to live in Nowhere for all eternity, but Gentry didn't need to know that. No one needed the reminder, not even Tum Tum.

Lucindur smiled.

Talwyn wrapped her arms around her mother and let out a gentle sigh. "I didn't even get to say good-bye," she said.

"None of us did," Tum Tum said. "But we can say it now."

They all stood there, staring at the statue for as long as it took for them each to make peace in their own way. Gentry sobbed into Aquira's scaly neck. Talwyn absentmindedly toyed with the laces of her corset while muttering under her breath.

If nature was to be sad along with them, no one had mentioned it. The gallers had finally stopped feasting, and the gentle sounds of gulls filled the air, along with the clatter of hammers and other tools.

Bees buzzed merrily in a vast garden of flowers and greens spread across the front of Godkiller's tavern. Never before had Dockside smelled so good. The reek of death wasn't so bad anymore. Sora healing so many wounded and infected before setting off for the East didn't hurt with that. Someday, that stench would be gone for good. Tum Tum liked it, though. It reminded him of his friend somehow.

"The statue will be done just in time," said Brouben as he approached from behind them."

He startled Tum Tum, who whipped around, then bowed. Brouben had lent some of the Three Kingdom's finest masons to building the memorial to their mutual friend. Cost wasn't an issue. With his brother still serving as the Glass Kingdom's Master of Coin, it was considered a gift. An apology for being late to the battle.

"Relax, old friend," Brouben laughed. "If yer here, I ain't yer King."

"I still be a dwarf."

Brouben patted his back. "Aye, a dwarf welcome home whenever he pleases. There'll always be a seat in me court for the one who helped save the world."

Tum Tum raised his head and fought back tears. "Thank you, brother. But I have some unfinished business out here. For now, a night of free drink will have to do."

"Did ye think I was payin?" Brouben laughed again.

"Never would have dreamt it." They tapped their foreheads together, then Brouben returned to his entourage. His brother, Al, was giving him a tour of the new buildings and the harbor. A Shieldsman, wearing freshly forged glaruium armor, snuck away from their group and made his way toward Tum Tum's gathering. The stuff shined like it was made of pearls. Enough to make even a simple dwarf like Tum Tum envious.

"I hope you don't mind if I send in another unit to inspect?" Sir Mulliner said. He was one of the last remaining Shieldsmen in all of Yarrington. Now, he served as the Wearer of White, leader of all the new King's army.

Torsten had disbanded the King's Shield before the Battle of Yarrington, but now, they'd been reinstated. Though, Tum Tum rarely saw many outside of Sir Mulliner until today. The Shield's new purpose was the hunting down of demons still haunting Pantego and possessing good people. But with two kings to be present at Godkiller's Tavern, they'd been summoned back to serve as their namesake demanded.

Tum Tum was just relieved that Caleef Mahraveh was too busy cleaning up the mess in the Kingdom of the Black Sands to attend. Her terrifying Serpent Guards would have put a damper on the entire affair.

"By all means," Tum Tum said.

"Security is paramount. The new King and all the Royal Council will be attending. Everything must be perfect for him."

"This ain't about him, and he knows it better than anyone," Tum Tum argued.

"Even so," Mulliner said. Then he glanced at Whitney's statue and sighed. "Things will never be as they once were, will they?"

"I reckon not."

Sir Mulliner grunted, then huffed along to keep up with King Brouben. The Shieldsman didn't move as fast as he once might have after injuries sustained in the battle, even with the miraculous work of Sora's hand. But Tum Tum knew nobody would be more dedicated to ensuring that this evening went off without a hitch. He'd been establishing the protection plans for a month now, before Godkiller's Tavern was even close to done.

The squeak of the tavern door drew Tum Tum's attention to a middle-aged man and woman walking through the garden to stand before Tum Tum.

"That'll have to be addressed," Tum Tum grumbled.

The woman wore an apron, stained and covered in flour. The man had his arm around her waist. They both wore expressions that were the perfect representation of how everyone in Yarrington felt. It was a restrained joy. So many had lost so much, but as horrible as things had been, there was an excitement and hope that came with the restoration efforts.

"Horace, Vanelope, is tonight's menu ready?" Tum Tum asked.

"I can promise you that Yarrington has never tasted anything so delicious," Mr. Danvels said, eyeing his wife. "Mrs. Danvels really outdid herself this time."

"In memory of my boy," Vanelope Danvels said. She stared off across the water, not at Whitney's statue, but just in that direction. Tum Tum went to speak but wasn't sure what to say.

"We're in need of more sugar," she said, without averting her gaze.

"I'll get right on it," Tum Tum replied, but she was already heading back to the tavern without awaiting a response.

"Oi, Hamm!" Tum Tum called over to the man helping unload a cart of supplies. They needed all the help they could get in handling the crowds, and it seemed only right to invite the people who ran the Twilight Manor back where Whitney was from. "Send a runner for more sugar!"

"How much more could you possibly need?" he groaned.

"Ye flower-pickers love things sweet."

Hamm rolled his eyes. Tum Tum thought he saw him mutter "dwarves" under his breath in that same way Whitney used to. Letting it slide, Tum Tum returned his focus beyond the docks.

"Ye sure are quiet," he said to Lucindur, who now sat on a bench, tuning her salfio.

"I'm saving my voice for later."

"I just thought ye'd be more excited to hear that *King* Torsten was comin."

"Stop it," Lucindur said, color filling her face.

"No, really. I think he's got his... uh... blinded eye on ye, too."

Talwyn glanced back at her mother, eyes wide. She now sat with Gentry at the edge of the rebuilt docks, their feet swinging over the water.

"Don't look at me like that," Lucindur said.

"Mother, he's the King!" Talwyn said.

"And a damn good one at that." Tum Tum said. "So far, at least."

"I suppose he is rather handsome," Talwyn admitted, smiling widely.

"And brave," Gentry added.

"Okay, that's enough," Lucindur said. "Don't you and Gentry have some practicing to do?"

"Oh, you're never any fun," Talwyn said. "Come on, Gentry. Let's go. We need to get our second transition right, anyway." She pulled the boy and his wyvern along, complaining that his timing was off while hers was perfect.

Tum Tum watched as they left, wondering what they had planned for opening night. In addition to the Pompare Troupe, he'd hired Fabian "Feel Good" Saravia to come and be a part of the week's festivities. Rumor had it, the bard had even written a song in Whitney's honor—a duet which Lucindur would play with him. It was sure to be an evening to remember.

The finishing touches were being done upon Whitney's nose. Tum Tum ducked to view it from a low angle. He clapped his hands. "Pretty shog-shuckin close," he said. "Even Sora may not be able to tell the difference."

"It's too bad she can't be here," Lucindur remarked.

"Aye. But that lass is destined to do great things. She's got her own ways of honorin his memory. We'll be sure to toast to her tonight."

"Why not now?" Lucindur said, stowing her instrument and pulling a flask from her belt.

"Ye devil," Tum Tum said.

"Breklian brandy," she said, lifting the flask toward the statue. "To Whitney Fierstown, the Godkiller, and the Queen who ruled for a day."

She took a sip.

"Here, here," Tum Tum said, stealing it from her hand and throwing back a swig of his own. "To the best friends this dwarf has ever had the pleasure of knowin."

Torsten felt robbed, though he knew he shouldn't. Sora hadn't taken anything from him, in fact, quite the opposite, yet still, he did.

Is that what all of Whitney's victims felt like? he wondered.

He circled the Glass Throne like a wolf, its prey. He wasn't sure if anybody had realized yet that he hadn't even sat in it. Even after the coronation atop Mount Lister, when a glass and glaruium crown, forged by Hovom Nitebrittle from the melted armor of former Shieldsmen, had been placed upon his head by the High Priest—he hadn't sat.

It felt wrong. Sure, the throne had undergone a transformation after substantial repairs. However, it was still the same seat filled by Liam Nothhelm and dozens of Kings going back to Autla the First. Now, Torsten was supposed to share it. A man whose ancestors were not from Yarrington. The son of nobody. Sole member of the noble house of Unger.

"Whitney trained you all too well, you clever witch," he said to himself, referring to Sora. He'd hinged the entire fate of the Kingdom on her. Even if all of them didn't believe Sora was who they claimed, Hovom's word went a long way. He was nothing if not loyal and honorable.

They barely had a priest left alive or healthy enough, but after reluctantly agreeing to become Queen, Sora insisted they rush the coronation, under Iam, atop Mount Lister, as well as the legal paperwork. And the moment she attained the Nothhelm seal, she made her first decree.

Sora Nothhelm, Queen of the Glass Kingdom, renounced the throne and named Torsten her successor. He recalled the way his jaw dropped as she spoke the words in front of the entire court. The world seemed to stop. Everyone was in complete shock, except Sora. She simply smiled a thin, placid smile.

That was when Torsten knew she'd planned it from the moment they'd first talked. He'd studied her in their time together, learned how she ticked, what affected her and what made her worthy despite her upbringing—she'd done the same. Sora knew that Torsten's vows to serve the Nothhelm family with honor until his end would mean he couldn't refuse a royal decree.

And so, here he was, fresh off his own coronation, tricked into being named King.

A King who couldn't manage to sit in his own throne.

"You'll grow into it, Your Grace," a soft voice spoke.

He turned and saw Dellbar the Holy shuffling into the Throne Room, tapping along with his cane. Healing him was Sora's final gift before departing to the East, where she would fix what Nesilia had corrupted in the Red Tower. He'd never recovered completely. His voice was gruff and grating now, and he walked like an old man. Every day, he seemed more and more like Wren the Holy than the carefree drunkard he was when Torsten first met him.

"Like you did?" Torsten asked. He itched the top of his bald head, digging a finger under the glass band of his crown. It still irritated his skin, and the material was unexpectedly cold.

Dellbar shrugged. "I never asked for this. Never wanted it. All I did was hand a suffering man my blindfold, and here I am."

"And all I did was try and make things right."

Dellbar chuckled. "What a couple of old fools we are."

Torsten grunted and nodded. He moved back around the throne and returned to staring at it. "How am I supposed to do this?"

"With your eyes open."

"Very funny."

Dellbar arrived beside him and touched his shoulder. "Whether or not you believe this is where Iam always intended for you to be, here you are, Torsten Unger. No Liam to lead you. No Uriah to guide you. Only you."

"I liked you better when you spoke in riddles."

"And I miss drinking. Who would've thought the two men sitting in Valin's dungeon would wind up here?"

"That almost seems preferable," Torsten said.

Dellbar hooked Torsten's hip with his cane and turned him around. "Oh, stop it, Your Highness."

"That's enough of that," Torsten grumbled.

"Only you could find a way to wallow about being King. You were a street rat, and now, you're the most powerful man in Pantego."

"Yeah. A King whose first act was granting the Black Sands their independence."

Tucking his cane under his arm, Dellbar clapped his hands once, as if to stir Torsten's attention. "Maybe if you left these walls, you'd see that the people celebrate their new King. They know it was you and Caleef Mahraveh who helped save their Kingdom."

"It's not our statues being built in Autla's Inlet, Your *Holiness*," Torsten stated.

"No, but it was your armies," Dellbar countered. "Your leadership.

You give the people too little credit. You were one of them, after all. They're tired of wars and rebellions. Who better to protect them than the Wearer of White from South Corner?"

"You're relentless."

"I've been told."

Torsten laughed nervously, his hand sliding along the arm of the throne. "It's not like I can relinquish the crown. Two monarchs doing that back-to-back? The noble houses would all turn their hides on their pledges."

"They would, wouldn't they? She really is—what did you say—a clever witch?"

"I should've seen it coming."

"Maybe, however, she still has her part to play. Elsewhere can't remain open, and her support will help return the East to its former glory. A true union between Glassmen and the Panpingese will do wonders in restorations."

"Are you a strategist or a priest?" Torsten asked in jest.

Dellbar tapped his cane. "Enough of this, Your Grace. You spend any more time lurking here, and you'll be late."

"I'm not sure why I even agreed to this."

"A coronation is one thing, but the people need to see their King. You know that better than most. Tonight is about looking forward as we remember all those who were lost in the Battle of Yarrington—the Pantego War. And Whitney the Godkiller is a hero amongst the people."

"I think it's just Whitney Godskiller... like a name," Torsten said.

"Ah, yes. Well, that's silly. However, it wouldn't hurt your standing with them to see you celebrating his legend."

Torsten sighed. "Even from the grave, he tortures me."

"Just smile and drink," Dellbar said. "I'll show you how."

"I'm sure you will."

"Maybe you'll even meet a Queen. It'd be a shame for the House of Unger to die with you."

"Watch it, Your Holiness," Torsten scolded.

"Iam works in mysterious ways."

Torsten imagined a wink if the priest had any eyes left to do it with.

Dellbar snickered to himself as he stepped down from the dais, clacking along the marble. "Are you coming, Your Grace?"

"In a second," Torsten replied.

He faced the throne and took a few long breaths, then turned around. His legs went wobbly as he stood there. The crown continued to irritate.

He could almost feel the spirits of all the old Nothhelm Kings watching him as he bent to sit, Oleander behind them, wearing her permanent scowl. It'd be easier if he could know all their memories like Mahraveh was blessed with, but he didn't have that.

He could only start from the beginning…

It had been many months since Mahi had been in the Black Sands—the longest time away in her entire life. And yet, it was only then, as Latiapur appeared on the horizon through a thick layer of fog, that it felt like home.

As a woman, going there had always been a battle, a fight to impress her father's warlords, to convince afhems to join Muskigo's cause after their minds had been already poisoned by Babrak, to become a Caleef worthy of the title.

Like seemingly everywhere in Pantego, the buildings dotting the bluffs along the coasts were in ruins. From the Tal'du Dromesh, cracked open like a clamshell and flooded to the great rocks carved in the likeness of the Sirens supporting the Boiling Keep, pieces broken off by the tentacles of invading Current Eaters.

Now, she had one last fight, to take back a home that finally felt like a home to her after so much time away.

Ships flying the standard of Babrak's afhemate marked the sea. Banners, branded likewise, unfurled down the pointed-arch windows of the palace—her palace. He'd made himself comfortable in the short time he ruled the city he helped destroy.

"It breaks my heart, seeing Latiapur like this, my Caleef," Bit'rudam said, climbing up behind her on the prow.

Mahi turned back, using her spear to keep balance against the waves and the whipping winds. She eyed him. A light beard covered his chin now, his body finally learning to grow one. An eyepatch over the eye he'd lost fighting for Yarrington made him look like one of the ruthless pirates in the stories fathers told to scare their children. The rest of Bit'rudam's body wasn't yet covered with as many scars as Muskigo's had been, but he was on his way.

"Really?" Mahi said. "I find it quite beautiful. A reflection of its people."

"Not for long. The men are ready, my Caleef. The imposters will surrender and serve you, or they will die."

"You think I should have executed everyone who stood against us in Yarrington, don't you?"

He sighed. "It would have been the safest move."

"Since when have you ever known me to be safe?" She spun around and grinned impishly, then hopped down to the main deck. Her gaze swept across the sea. The Battle of Yarrington didn't leave them with much of a fleet—a single warship, a few fishing boats, and supply vessels Babrak had anchored off-coast before invading. But King Torsten had been generous with his provisions after upholding a promise he'd made to her at White Bridge.

He'd set her people free. No tribute required. No strings attached. It was everything Muskigo had ever wanted, given freely and without further bloodshed. They were the independent Kingdom of the Black Sands once more. And it was then, when a Glassman proved to be truly honorable, that she'd decided to spare her enemies. To show 'mercy,' as Sora had called it.

"We should at least send the traitors to the front lines," Bit'rudam said. "Let them lead the assault."

"And set the wheel of old rivalries that undid our people turning again? No." She closed her eyes and breathed in the salty air. "See, all the mistakes, all the errors—the Caleefs kept allowing them to be repeated, but I won't. We will stand together from this day, or we don't deserve to stand at all."

Bit'rudam took her hand. "And I trust your wisdom, with all that I am. I only worry one of them might stab you in the back."

"Let them try."

Mahi strolled along the deck, every warrior and sailor she passed taking a moment to show their respect. She swung around the center mast, then moved toward a portion of grated wood covered by a tarp.

She stepped over and ripped the tarp aside. There were no supplies inside the storage compartment, only a man. Because that's all Babrak was—a man, and barely one at that. The black paint he wore flaked off his body along with dried blood. His beard was unkempt and messy. Even his belly had shrunk after he'd been left to starve in the Glass Castle dungeons for months while Mahi's people helped clean up Yarrington.

She hadn't intended to stay so long before taking back Latiapur, but Torsten had earned the aid. He could have held onto Babrak as a rebel against the Kingdom but turned him over without complaint. What a day when she could trust a Glass King over a legendary afhem.

"We're here, pis'truda," she said, crouching over the grate.

He peered up, squinting against the brightness. Mahi wanted to kill him so badly, both now and in the battle, but she was glad she'd showed restraint then and would continue to do so. Now he looked just like he deserved to—like a stray dog.

"Mahraveh, please, listen to me," he stammered, voice hoarse from hollering as they stuffed him into storage and left him there for the long journey. "You don't have to do this."

"You have no idea what I'm going to do," she replied, seething.

"You spared my men. They are loyal to me—I can help you. Let me atone. I will serve you as I always should have. I see now that the Current flowed at your back, not mine."

"Shut your mouth, filth!" Bit'rudam barked, stomping on his fingers, which clenched the grate and sending Babrak cowering like a rat.

Mahi held up a fist to stop him, then leaned over the supply compartment.

"Our people deserve mercy," she said. "They followed only what they knew, but not you. You are infinitely more greedy than the Glassmen you so revile."

"You're making a mistake!" he rasped, clutching the grate again. "You entitled, skinny, wench. You won't hold this Kingdom longer than a day. They'll tie you up by your feet over the Sea Door if the treacherous Glassmen don't invade first. That is your fate, puny girl, and you know it."

Now it was Mahi's turn. She seized his hands and pulled. His face hit the grate. "No, Babrak. You see, all those people you left behind in Latiapur, who you believe are loyal to you… they will lay down their weapons. And then, they will watch as you are dragged through the city. They will witness your dishonor as you honor the old ways, take up the Dagger of Damikmagrin, and end your own life in shame."

"I would never," he grunted.

She pulled tighter. "And as the Current stops flowing in your veins, a new age will rise to greet us. The Black Sands will never be owned by greed again. That is your fate, pis'truda." She let him go, and he collapsed back into the shadow. "There will be no battle today; no more Shesaitju death."

He released a soft, pathetic chortle. "A hypocrite to the end, just like your father. You show my men mercy and not me. You will be the end of the Black Sands."

"No, Babrak," she said, calm as a Caleef should be. "You are not Shesaitju. You are not even worthy of the air you breathe."

Bit'rudam cursed him, spat at him.

Mahi grabbed the end of the tarp and pulled it back into place until all she could hear were the muffled sounds of him cursing and pounding the wood. Then, she stood and turned to face Latiapur like she'd never seen it.

Free. Home.

The mystics had been responsible for many horrible things. However, as Sora stood upon the shore, looking up at the Red Tower, she realized how vibrant their history was. An entire city was built around this place, and the carvings on each tier spoke of untold wonder.

It also spoke of greed, vengeance, corruption.

These things, and more, were the foundations for the fall of the Mystic Order, just like every other foul government of man.

Now, with Torsten Unger tricked into being named King of the Glass Kingdom, there was hope for reform, she hoped. Perhaps with the fall of the Nothhelm line, peace amongst races, creeds, religions, and cultures would be a reality not based upon bending the knee in the name of a single god.

She'd traveled to Yaolin City—which lay in ruin behind and around her, inhabited only by refugees and hideaways. She'd come to fulfill a promise to Torsten, and close the Well of Wisdom, cutting off the breach from Elsewhere. But on her way there, she'd realized her true purpose for the journey.

A different kind of closure.

This was the place she and Whitney were meant to go together after the Webbed Woods. This was the intended trip that started everything.

The iron gate around the tower squeaked as she passed statues of Glass soldiers placed as metaphorical guards. It wasn't locked anymore. There was no reason to keep anyone out. She was the last mystic in the known world.

As Sora walked, grass sprouted up from the dry ground, filling in her footprints and spreading along like the earth itself rejoiced over the return of the new Ancient One. For that was what Sora indeed was now. Although she didn't realize it, she'd felt it from the moment Aihara Na's body was destroyed, and power surged through her on the battlefield.

Little did Nesilia know that her actions, destroying Bliss in the former Ancient One's form, was also her ultimate downfall. It was what allowed for such raw energy to take down Freydis, to collapse the crypt, to build the ice bridge that led Whitney to end it all…

To end himself…

Sora shook those thoughts from her head. She would not let his sacrifice be in vain.

Stagnant pools of water surrounding the tower came to life in her presence. The vines scaling the walls, which were dead upon her arrival, now teemed. It may have been her imagination, but even the red stone seemed somehow brighter. She'd never thought about it before, but it felt as if the blood of Pantego flowed through its walls.

She moved slowly, the first time in weeks she could rest. These past months, as she pressed across the ravaged continent, it was this moment for which she longed. Her spirit begged for it.

Another long stride took Sora to the tower's gem-encrusted front doors. They opened of their own accord, as if the tower itself were beckoning her inside. She realized, it was.

This was far different than the last time Sora had been there, blindfolded like a prisoner, led through countless tests and trials to prove her worth. She recalled Madam Jaya and Kai—sweet Kai—and all those mystics who'd been slaughtered by Nesilia using her own powers. She remembered it like yesterday, yet it also felt like a million years ago—a distant memory in light of her new calling.

Presently, there was no need to prove her worth. She was all that was left of the once-grand Order. She would have to remedy that.

Crossing the entry hall, she stepped over bloodstains and passed upturned furniture before descending the circular stairs. Rooms cycled by, and with them, memories, each one belonging to one of those mystics. Though the rooms were now empty, Sora imagined filling them once more with those more worthy of carrying the gift of mystics, those who would care for and protect the virtue of Pantego, not exploit it as her predecessors had.

She would show King Torsten, who still ruled these lands, that magic wasn't something that needed to be feared, that it could help people. More than that, she would prove it to herself.

Sora stopped at one open door and stared inside. Beyond its threshold was a white room far larger than should have been able to fit within the tower. She still wasn't sure if it was magic or if they were just far enough below the waters that it extended beneath them, but it was in that room where she fought Madam Jaya in the form of Muskigo. How she hated that man, feared him, yet from his loins came one of Sora's greatest allies. Though she may not be Queen, Sora would strengthen the bonds between her people and those beyond the boundaries of Panping.

If not her, then who?

She continued downward until she reached the bottom. Large stone doors that she and Aquira had once blasted with flames loomed before her. She hoped she'd made the right decision in leaving the wyvern with Gentry. They'd forged quite a bond while Sora was trapped in Nowhere, and Sora knew that what she was meant to do had to be done alone, unhindered by emotion or distraction. Aquira brought too many memories that might cloud her judgement.

When she last stood before the stone doors of the Well of Wisdom, Whitney had been dead to her. This time, however, there was no hope of his return. After months, traveling by foot under the light of Celeste and Loutis, Sora had finally come to peace with that fact. She vowed that Whitney would live on through her valiant and just actions.

It was true, Whitney sacrificed himself for Sora, but he also did for others what they couldn't do for themselves. He had become the savior no one ever expected he was capable of being.

Sora knew that to be eaten by an otherworldly wianu meant eternity in Nowhere, but she had to hope and pray there was redemption for one who did it so selflessly.

She laughed to herself at the thought of Whitney Fierstown being a savior, at the self-proclaimed World's Greatest Thief doing *anything* selflessly.

Oh, the way things change, she thought.

Beyond the heavy stone doors, the Well of Wisdom called to her… begged her to complete the task she'd started so long ago. Within that pool was not just the entrance to Elsewhere, but the combined memories of every mystic who'd ever lived. It would contain everything she would need to lead Panping back into the powerful and prosperous Kingdom it once had been.

She believed that, under her guidance and friendship with Torsten and Mahraveh, there would be no fear of the Well and its powers becoming tainted. Not this time. She would not dishonor Whitney or her mother by turning his sacrifice into yet another war.

She stepped toward the doors, expecting to need to use all her strength to coerce them open, but this time they burst wide on their own. Cold greeted her. No longer were the waters blue with life, but they were black and rancid. The smell of death crinkled her nose. Spirits and demons whispered foul things in the darkness.

Sora would find a way to undo Nesilia's corruption. Somehow, she knew she had the ability to do it—a gift passed down from the spirits of her ancestors… from her mother.

This war with Nesilia had begun at the hands of her father and mother, both, when their decisions awakened her. It would end with Sora, here, now.

The Pantego Whitney Fierstown had died to save would be rid of Nesilia's darkness, once and for all.

"Where am I?" Nesilia asked, spinning. All she could see was blackness in every direction, spanning infinitely. It was like she was back buried beneath the mountain.

"Iam!" she screeched. "Is this another of Your tricks? I won't be stopped. Pantego is mine!"

Her voice echoed like the darkness, in every direction, spanning infinitely. But the sound only vanished into the nothingness. Nobody answered.

She started forward, legs quaking as nerves set in. "No, this can't be," she said. "I won't be buried again. I won't be stopped."

She screamed her throat raw and spun again, searching for a light, anything that might lead her out. She roared until she couldn't any longer, and she fell to her knees. Only, she had no knees. She could feel and touch nothing—was nothing—just darkness.

Suddenly, a force wrenched her back. Heavy, ravenous breathing reached her ears.

"Who are you!" she yelled. The moment she turned, the presence was gone. But when she turned again, a figure stood before her. He was barely visible but for a gleam of silver hair.

"I've been waiting for you, Nesilia," he spoke in thick Breklian accent.

"You?" she spat.

"Me," Kazimir said. "I so look forward to our eternity together."

Nesilia growled in frustration. "If you're here, then that damn thief is—"

"Gone," Kazimir said. Then he snickered. "You will appreciate this. With His last bit of power in this plane, Iam plucked the thief away and brought him to the Gate of Light. No, Nesilia. Here, it is only we who are to be damned forever."

"Iam… took… him?" she stammered. "Over me!"

"Of course, he did. You are damned."

"No! I will find a way out, and Pantego will fall, I swear it. I'll kill every last one of them, and then I'll climb to the Gate of Light itself and stab Iam through His rotten heart!"

Kazimir circled her. "Then I have to ask you, Nesilia. Do you not wish for more?" He lifted her chin with his finger, showing a glimmer of his fangs.

"Yes, yes, upyr. I do. I will give you everything if we get out of here. A world of your own."

He removed his finger, and her head sank.

Then he whispered, a hint of laughter in his tone. "Too bad. It's you and me here, alone. For all eternity. Dead... but not buried."

ABOUT THE AUTHORS

Jaime is the Audible #1 bestselling author of THE BURIED GODDESS SAGA. He lives in Texas with his wife and two kids. He enjoys anything creative, from graphic arts to painting. His office looks like the Avengers threw up on the walls.

Jaime has been writing since elementary school and is a bit of a grammar officer—here to correct and serve.

Rhett is a Sci-fi/Fantasy author currently living in Stamford, Connecticut. His published works include books in the USA Today Bestselling CIRCUIT SERIES (Published by Diversion Books and Podium Audio), THE BURIED GODDESS SAGA and the THE CHILDREN OF TITAN SERIES (Aethon Books, Audible Studios). He is also one of the founders of the popular science fiction platform, Sci-Fi Bridge.

If you enjoyed The Buried Goddess Saga, check out our newest collaboration The Luna Missile Crisis.

Audible number one best sellers Rhett C. Bruno and Jaime Castle return with a relentless sci-fi adventure that asks: What if?

The year is 1961. The Cold War is in full swing and the space race is on. Russia aims to send humanity to space. But what if space comes to humanity instead? Yuri Gagarin's epic flight into space is disrupted when an alien Mothership jumps into orbit, causing a cosmic car crash that defies all odds.

Everything changes. The US and USSR must quickly put aside their differences. In exchange for the Earth's help in the rebuilding of their Mothership, the mysterious aliens, the Vulbathi, offer promises of technology beyond humanity's wildest dreams. All the while, the world asks whether the Vulbathi are saviors or conquerors.

When an alien tech counterfeiter's mistake sets off a chain reaction, the fragile peace is threatened. Connor McCoy didn't mean to upset Earth's new intergalactic neighbors. He only wanted to make some cash.

Now, Connor is the only person who can stop the doomsday clock from striking midnight. That is if his estranged brother, an agent in the new Department of Alien Relations, doesn't stop him first.